Catrin COLLIER

Hearts of Gold
One Blue Moon

Catrin Collier was born and brought up in Pontypridd. She lives in Swansea with her husband, three cats and whichever of her children choose to visit. Her latest novel in Orion paperback is *Finders & Keepers*, and her latest novel in hardback, *Tiger Bay Blues*, is also available from Orion. Visit her website at www.catrincollier.co.uk.

By Catrin Collier

HISTORICAL

Hearts of Gold
One Blue Moon
A Silver Lining
All That Glitters
Such Sweet Sorrow
Past Remembering
Broken Rainbows
Spoils of War
Swansea Girls
Swansea Summer
Homecoming
Beggars & Choosers
Winners & Losers
Sinners & Shadows
Finders & Keepers
Tiger Bay Blues

CRIME (*as Katherine John*)

Without Trace
Midnight Murders
Murder of a Dead Man
By Any Other Name

MODERN FICTION (*as Caro French*)

The Farcreek Trilogy

Catrin COLLIER

Hearts of Gold
One Blue Moon

Hearts of Gold
First published in Great Britain by Century in 1992

One Blue Moon
First published in Great Britain by Century in 1993

This omnibus edition published in 2010
by Orion Books Ltd
Orion House, 5 Upper St Martin's Lane
London WC2H 9EA

An Hachette UK company

A CIP catalogue record for this book is available
from the British Library.

ISBN 9781407230177

Printed in Great Britain by CPI Mackays, Chatham ME5 8TD

www.orionbooks.co.uk

Hearts of Gold

For the people who lived in Pontypridd
and on the Graig during the depression.
Especially my grandmother Nurse Katherine
(Kitty) Jones, née Johns, who worked in the
Graig Hospital during those difficult years,
and my father Glyn Jones, who did so much
to guide me back into her world.

Acknowledgements

I apologise in advance for the length of this acknowledgement, but I owe a great debt to those survivors of the depression in Pontypridd who gave me their time, and generously shared with me their most personal and precious possessions – their memories.

My father Glyn Jones, who spent a year talking to everyone he knew in Pontypridd (and a few he didn't) in an effort to track down those who lived and worked there during the thirties. Not to mention the days and weeks he drove around with me, noting and explaining all the changes that have taken place since the depression. (And not only in the pubs.)

My mother Gerda Jones, for providing bed and board, and for listening patiently while my father and I tried to recreate a world that disappeared long before she came to Wales.

My aunt and uncle, Grace and Evan Williams, who still live on the Graig, in the house where I grew up.

My father's oldest friends, Cyril and Nellie Mahoney, who helped me from the outset, when this book was no more than a single scribbled idea in a notebook. It was their rich fund of stories that inspired me to take the project further.

All the staff of Pontypridd Library, especially Mrs Penny Pughe, who came in on her days off to help me with my research. They were working under incredible pressure and appalling conditions during the reorganisation of the library which took place when I was in the throes of trying to do my research. Without their heroic endeavours I would not have amassed anything like the material I now have to draw on.

Mrs Pat Evans, the librarian at East Glamorgan Hospital, for her time, help and unfailing sense of humour, and for putting me in touch with so many people.

Councillor Des Wood, a former Administrator of the Central Homes on the Graig, who drew up a detailed map and notes of the Homes as they were before they were rebuilt in the sixties (practically a book in its own right) and without whose assistance

I would never have finally tracked down the records of the old Graig Hospital.

Mr Colin Davies, who used to work in the Homes and who was kind enough to send me a booklet on the closing of the old Homes and the opening of the new Dewi Sant Hospital that stands in its place.

My family, old friends and neighbours from the Graig. Principally my cousin Marion who married into the fine Graig family of the Goodwins, and others whom I have not seen for many years. I always was an inveterate listener, even when they didn't know I was eavesdropping.

Marge Davies, the cousin my father rediscovered after more than half a lifetime, and who had so many stories to tell.

Jennifer Price for her unstinting, unselfish friendship and incredible generosity of spirit, and Margaret Bloomfield for her help in so many practical ways.

The best boss I've ever had, Jack Priestland, who doesn't mind me writing at work during the *quiet*? times.

My husband John and my children Ralph, Sophie and Ross, for their love, support and the time they gave me to write this book, and for not moaning, even when we drove around the Graig 'Again'.

And above all my editor Rosie Cheetham, who suggested that I write a book on my home town and steered it on course from the very beginning, and my agent Michael Thomas for his encouragement and many kindnesses.

Thank you.

I have taken the liberty of mixing real 'characters' such as 'Cast Iron Dean' who was well known in Pontypridd in the thirties with my fictional ones. The actual events involving the 'Forty Thieves' happened, and some women were sentenced to terms of hard labour for their involvement with the gang. However I would like to *stress* that all the main characters in this book, including those involved with the thieves, are fictitious, and creations of my imagination. If any reader mistakenly believes that they recognise themselves or a member of their family in any person depicted in this book, I can only say that I have tried to make my people representative of both the times and the place they lived in.

And while I wish to fully acknowledge the help I have received, I would also like to state that any errors in *Hearts of Gold* are entirely mine. I have tried to get at the truth wherever possible, but unfortunately many records have disappeared from the face of the earth, and the gaps have been filled in as far as possible by using newspaper accounts, and people's memories.

My hope is that the readers of this book enjoy this small glimpse of Pontypridd's past, as much as I enjoyed writing and researching it.

Catrin Collier, September 1991

Chapter One

'Bethan! Bethan!' Elizabeth rapped hard on the door of the bedroom that her daughters shared.

'Coming, Mam,' Bethan murmured sleepily. She listened as her mother retreated back to her own bedroom then, keeping her eyes firmly closed, she reluctantly forced her hand out of the warm cocoon of sheets and blankets to test the air. It was icy after the warm snugness of the bed, and she quickly pulled her arm back beneath the bedclothes for a few seconds more of blissful warmth.

'Bethan.' Once again Elizabeth's voice cut stridently through the frosty air.

'I'm up, Mam,' Bethan lied.

'I hardly think so.' Elizabeth opened the door and pushed the switch down on the round black box. Bethan screwed her eyes against the sudden glare of yellow light. It wasn't enough. Eyelids burning, she burrowed into the bed and pulled the blanket over her head.

'Breakfast in ten minutes, Bethan,' her mother's voice intruded into the warm darkness.

'Yes, Mam.'

She waited until she heard the fierce click of the iron latch falling on the bar. The third stair from the top creaked, then the seventh as her mother descended to the ground floor. Keeping her nose hidden beneath the blankets, she opened her eyes and peered sleepily at the room around her. Apart from a change of wallpaper, it hadn't altered since her grandmother had left it fourteen years before. The thick red plush curtains that had been hers hung, faded but well brushed and straight, at the windows. The old-fashioned Victorian mahogany bedroom furniture Caterina had inherited as a bride gleamed darkly against the heavily patterned red and gold walls. Her favourite Rossetti prints hung on the wall next to the wardrobe, and the pink glass ring holder, candlesticks and hair tidy that had been a present from her sons stood on the dressing table. The room might now belong to Bethan and her sister Maud, but it was also an encapsulation of Bethan's earliest childhood memories.

She had toddled in here when she was barely high enough to reach the washstand. Crouching behind the bed, she had watched her grandmother wash and dress, and afterwards sit on the stool in front of the dressing-table mirror to brush out her hair. Rich, black, it was scarcely touched with grey on the day she'd died. Once Caterina had finished, she'd turn and smile. A warm, welcoming, special smile that Bethan knew she kept just for her. And then came the excitement of *the tin*. The old Huntley and Palmer biscuit tin in which Caterina kept her prized collection of foreign coins. Bethan had spent hours as a child, sitting on the cold, oilcloth-covered floor at Caterina's feet; playing with them, grouping them into armies, fighting strange and wondrous battles that she'd heard the grown-ups talking about – Mons, Amiens, the Somme . . .

Not only Bethan's, but also her sister's and brothers' happiest childhood memories stemmed from the time when Mam Powell had lived with them.

Evan Powell's mother, Caterina, had been a large, warm-hearted, old-fashioned Welsh widow who'd spent her life working, caring and cuddling (or *cwtching*, as they say in Wales) her family. True happiness for her had ended along with her husband's life; contentment vanished the day Evan brought his bride into the family home. She'd tried valiantly to conceal her dislike of Elizabeth, but everyone who knew Caterina also knew that she'd never taken to her eldest son's choice of wife.

In her shrewd, common-sense way Caterina had summed Elizabeth Powell *née* Bull up as a cold, arrogant, snobbish woman but, concerned only for Evan's happiness, she would have forgiven Evan's love any failing other than hard-heartedness. Fearing for the emotional well-being of her unborn grandchildren, it was she who persuaded Evan to set up home with Elizabeth in the parlour and front bedroom of the house that her collier husband had bought for under two hundred pounds in the 'good times' before strikes and the depression hit Pontypridd and the Rhondda mining valleys. And she did it in full knowledge that Elizabeth would destroy the peace and harmony that reigned in the household.

Elizabeth fought hard against Evan's suggestion of setting up home with her mother- and brother-in-law, but Evan remained firm. Quite aside from his mother's wishes, finances dictated compromise. Not a man to shirk his responsibilities, he accepted that it was his duty as eldest son to support his mother and his wife, and the easiest way he could think of fulfilling both obligations was by installing them under the same roof. Besides, in his acknowledgedly biased opinion, his mother's house was amongst the best on the Graig.

Certainly the bay-windowed, double-fronted house in Graig Avenue had more than enough room for all the Powells – three good-sized bedrooms, a box room, two front parlours and a comfortable back kitchen complete with a range that held bread and baking ovens as well as a hinge-topped water boiler with a brass tap from which hot water could be drawn. Doors from the kitchen led into a walk-in, stone-slabbed pantry and a lean-to washhouse. The washhouse opened into the yard that housed the coalhouse and outside WC (all its own, not shared). It was a palace compared to the back-to-back, two-up one-downs at the foot of the Graig hill.

What Evan didn't discuss with Elizabeth, or his mother, was the full extent of the mortgage on the house. He had been fourteen, and his brother William twelve, when their father had collapsed and fallen in front of a tram at the Maritime pit. Jim Owen, the pit manager, sent Caterina Powell ten pounds to cover the funeral expenses. It was good of him. She knew full well that as the accident was her husband's fault, she was entitled to nothing. The Maritime's colliers organised a whip-round amongst themselves and raised another fifteen pounds. It was the largest sum ever collected after a pit death, and a fine testimonial to Evan Powell senior's popularity, but it wasn't enough to buy his widow, or his sons, security.

Evan and William left school the day of the funeral, and Jim Owen took them on as boy colliers out of respect for their father. So they began their working lives where Evan Powell senior had finished his, and without giving the matter a thought they also assumed his obligations, paying his bills, his mortgage, and providing their mother with housekeeping, the only money she ever handled. And she, too grief-stricken to realise what was happening, allowed her eldest son to assume the responsibilities of the man of the house – responsibilities he shouldered with a maturity far beyond his years. Time passed, Caterina's grief healed after a fashion – and then came Elizabeth.

The major alterations to the domestic life of the Graig Avenue household after Evan and Elizabeth's marriage came in the shape of the additions they were blessed with. Bethan was born seven months after their wedding day, Haydn less than a year later, Eddie on their fourth anniversary, and Maud on Bethan's sixth birthday. Caterina and Elizabeth were soon too busy to quarrel, and the initial resentment Elizabeth felt at her mother-in-law's insistence on holding on to the domestic reins of the household faded with the birth of Haydn. The babies generated enough work to keep a dozen pairs of hands occupied, let alone two. And although neither woman learned to like, let alone love the other, seven years under the same roof did teach them a wary kind of tolerance.

The thunder of Haydn and Eddie's feet hammering down the stairs shook Bethan out of her reverie. It would be wonderful to lie here for another two or three hours, staring at the walls, thinking of nothing in particular, but duty and her mother called.

Maud stirred next to her in the bed. Pulling the blankets close about her ears, her sister burrowed deeper into the feather mattress, making small, self-satisfied grunting noises as she curled complacently back into her dreams. Bethan looked enviously at the mop of blonde curls, all that could be seen of Maud above the blankets. What it was to be thirteen years old and still at school. If Maud got up two hours from now she'd still make it to her classroom in Maesycoed Seniors by nine – but there was little point in wishing herself any younger.

Grabbing the ugly grey woollen dressing gown that her mother had cut and sewn from a surplus army blanket three Christmases ago, Bethan sat up and swung her legs out of the tangle of flannelette sheets and blankets. Five o'clock on any morning was a disgusting hour to leave a warm, comfortable bed. On a cold,

4

dismal January morning it was worse than disgusting. It was brutal!

For all of her five feet eight inches, her feet dangled several inches above the floor. Mam Powell's bed was higher than any hospital bed. Easy to make, but painful to climb out of when there was ice in the air. Sliding forward she perched precariously on the edge of the mattress and ran the tips of her toes over the freezing floor in search of her pressed felt slippers. She found one, then, standing on her left leg, the other. As she shuffled across the room she thought wistfully of the last film she'd seen in the White Palace.

Claudette Colbert had floated elegantly around a vast, dazzlingly pale carpeted, beautifully furnished bedroom in a creamy lace and satin gown that she'd casually referred to as a 'négligé.' The actress would probably sooner have died than don a grey woollen dressing gown and flat tartan slippers with red pompoms. But then, Claudette Colbert looked as though she'd never had to trek out to a back yard first thing in the morning in her life. If the newsreels and Hollywood stories in the Sunday papers were to be believed, film stars had luxurious bathrooms with bubble-filled baths the size of the paddling pool in Ponty Park. And they could afford to keep fires burning in their bedrooms all night without giving a thought to the twenty-two shillings a load of coal cost a miner on short time and rations.

She twitched aside the curtains and tried to peer through the coating of frost on the window pane. Breathing on the glass, she rubbed hard with the edge of her hand and made a peephole. The street lamps burned alongside the houses in the Avenue in a straight line. Golden beacons radiating a glow that dispelled the navy-blue darkness, and lit up the high garden wall of Danygraig House opposite. Dawn was still hours away. She studied the unmade ground of the street beneath her. It was covered with a fine layer of white, but there were dark shadows alongside the stones. Too thin to be snow. Frost, and that meant a cold slippery walk down the Graig hill to the hospital.

She left the window and heaved on the bottom drawer of the dressing table. It jerked out sluggishly, with the stickiness of furniture kept too long in a cold, damp house. Rummaging impatiently through the tangle of clothes, she searched for an

5

extra pair of black woollen stockings. Nurses, especially trainee nurses, were only supposed to wear one pair, but her legs had been almost blue with cold when she'd left her ward at the end of yesterday's shift, and there hadn't been frost on the ground then. She found the stockings and tossed them on to the pile of underclothes and uniform that she'd laid out on the stool the night before. Warm legs were worth the risk of an official reprimand, even from Sister Church.

Heaving the drawer shut with her foot as well as her hands, she went to the washstand. She picked up the unwieldy old-fashioned yellow jug decorated with transfers of sepia country scenes, and tried to pour its contents into the washbowl. Nothing happened. Shivering as the chill atmosphere permeated her dressing gown, she brushed her dark hair away from her face and looked down into the jug. Pushing her fingers into the neck, she confirmed her suspicions. A thick frozen crust capped the water. Even if she succeeded in breaking through it without cracking the jug, the thought of washing in chunks of ice didn't appeal to her. Pulling the collar of her dressing gown as high as it would go, she tightened the belt and left the bedroom, stepping down on to the top stair.

Unlike the bedroom, the stairs were carpeted with jute, held in place with three-cornered oak rods. She trod lightly on the third and fourth stair from the top. Their rods were fragile – broken when her brothers, Haydn and Eddie, had purloined them to use as swords after watching a Douglas Fairbanks film. The rods had survived the fencing match, but neither had survived the beating her mother had inflicted on the boys with them when she'd found out what they'd done.

The light was burning in the downstairs passage as she made her way to the back kitchen. Her father, mother and eldest brother were up and dressed, breakfasting at the massive dark oak table that, together with the open-shelved dresser, dominated the room.

'Good morning, Bethan,' her mother offered frigidly with a scarcely perceptible nod towards the corner where their lodger Alun Jones was lacing up his collier's boots. Alun looked up and for all of his thirty-five years turned a bright shade of beetroot.

6

Irritated, Bethan pulled her dressing gown even closer around her shivering body.

'Good morning,' she mumbled in reply to her mother's greeting. 'The water in the jug is frozen, so I came down for some warm,' she added, trying to excuse her state of undress.

In middle age, Elizabeth Powell was a tall, thin, spare woman. Spare in flesh and spare in spirit. Bethan, like her brothers and Maud, was afraid not so much of her mother but of the atmosphere she exuded, which was guaranteed to dampen the most lively spirit. Elizabeth certainly had an outstanding ability to make herself and everyone around her feel miserable and uncomfortable. But she hadn't always possessed that talent. She'd acquired and honed the trait to perfection during twenty-one years of silent, suffering marriage to Evan Powell. Her silence. His suffering.

At the time none of the Powells' friends or acquaintances could fathom exactly why Evan Powell, a strapping, tall, dark (and curly-haired with it) handsome young miner of twenty-three had suddenly decided to pay court to a thin, dour schoolmistress ten years older than himself. But court her he had; and the courtship had culminated a few weeks later in a full chapel wedding attended by both families.

Elizabeth's relatives had been both bemused and upset by the match. In their opinion Elizabeth hadn't so much stepped down in the world, as slid. True, she had little to recommend her as a wife. Thirty-three years old, like most women of her generation she was terrified of being left on the shelf. She certainly had no pretensions to beauty. Even then, her hair would have been more accurately described as colourless than fair. Her eyes were of a blue more faded than vibrant, and her face, thin-nosed, thin-lipped, thin-browed, tended to look disapprovingly down on the world in general, and Pontypridd and the working-class area of the Graig where Evan Powell lived in particular.

She was tall for a woman. Five feet nine inches, and William, Evan's younger brother, rather unkindly commented that the one good thing that could be said about her was she looked well on his brother's arm . . . from the rear.

Before her marriage Elizabeth had possessed a good figure, and she'd known how to dress. But when marriage put an end to her career as assistant schoolmistress in Maesycoed junior school it also put an end to the generous dress allowance that had been her one extravagance. Not that she came to Evan empty-handed. She'd saved a little money of her own to add to the small nest egg her mother had left her, and Evan, generous and self-sacrificing to the last, had urged her to spend that money, or at least the interest it accumulated, on herself. However, her Baptist minister father had fostered a spirit of sanctity towards savings within the confines of her flat breast that was matched only by the feeling of absolute superiority to the mining classes that he had engendered in her narrow mind. She would have as soon pawned the family bible as used her deposit account to buy smart or fashionable clothes.

Their marriage, begun as an anomaly, continued in silence. Evan never discussed his feelings with anyone, least of all his wife, and Elizabeth, disgusted with herself for falling prey to what she privately came to consider a sad lapse into 'bestial passion', never divulged what had attracted her to Evan. Evan was extremely good-looking, even by Pontypridd standards, where well-set-up strongly built colliers were the rule rather than the exception. Six feet three inches in his stockinged feet, with an exotic, swarthy complexion that he'd inherited from his maternal Spanish grandfather, he was just the type to excite John Joseph Bull's suspicions.

John Joseph was Elizabeth's uncle, the brother of her dead father. A Baptist minister too, he knew, or thought he knew, everything there was to know about lust, as those who heard his sermons soon found out: 'A devil-sent demon to lead the weak and ungodly astray into a foul world of naked, hairy limbs, lewdness and lechery.' Small children sat bemused as he railed against both sexes for their fragile, miserable morals. Unlike some of his colleagues he realised that women could fall prey to the temptations of that particular cardinal sin as well as men. As an active revivalist, evangelist and minister of God, his knowledge was not based on personal experience, but on years of watching and noting the depths to which the people who lived within the boundaries of his chapel's sphere could sink. He ascribed his interest in the human condition to charitable motives. Evan, who was considered remarkably well read even for a miner, called it by another name. Voyeurism.

John Joseph's wife Hetty, a small, quiet, mousy woman some twenty years younger than he, had a sense of duty that extended into every aspect of their joyless married life, from the kitchen to the bedroom and the Sunday night ritual during which, after lengthy and suitable prayer, John Joseph lifted her nightdress — the only night of the week he allowed himself to do so.

Hetty was a paragon, but John Joseph saw enough miners' daughters and wives to know that other kinds existed. Some were even brazen enough to eye men while they sat in his chapel pews. He'd caught sight of them after the service, walking off shamelessly, arm in arm with their paramours into the secluded areas of Ynysangharad War Memorial Park, or up Pit Road where they disappeared into the woods around Shoni's pond.

The thought of his niece and Evan Powell following either route incensed and disgusted him. But Elizabeth Bull was way past the age when she needed a guardian's blessing to marry. He could do nothing except voice his disapproval. Which he did, long, loud and vociferously, both before and after the ceremony.

He'd refused to give Elizabeth away on the grounds that he wouldn't be an active party to her social demise. But his contempt for Evan and the mining classes didn't prevent him from officiating as minister over the proceedings. It also gave him the opportunity to speak at the small reception that his wife Hetty had dutifully arranged in the vestry. He saw himself as a plain-speaking man, but even Hetty, who was used to his harsh, God-fearing ways, cringed when he pointed a long thin finger at Elizabeth, glowered at her darkly and bellowed that he was glad, really glad, that his dead brother and sister-in-law were not alive to see their daughter sink so low.

Elizabeth recalled his words every day of her married life. They came to her even now as she looked around her kitchen and saw her daughter in a state of undress; the unhealthy colour rising in the lodger's cheeks as he surreptitiously ogled the curves outlined beneath the thin cloth of Bethan's dressing gown; her son and husband sitting at the table, boots off, not even wearing collars with their shirts. She felt that not only herself but her children had sunk to the lowest level of the working-class life she'd been

9

forced to live, and had learned to despise with every fibre of her being.

'I'll draw the water for you, Beth.' Haydn smiled cheerfully at his sister as he pushed the last piece of bread and jam from his plate into his mouth.

'Thank you.' Bethan walked past the pantry and unlatched the planked door that led into the washhouse. Switching on the light she sidestepped between the huge, round gas wash boiler and massive stone sink that served the only tap in the house. Opening the outside door, she caught her breath in the face of the cold wind that greeted her, placed her foot in the yard and slid precariously across the four feet of iced paving stones that separated the house and garden walls, grazing her hands painfully in the process.

She gripped the wall, desperately trying to maintain her balance while she regained her breath. The drains had obviously overflowed before the frost had struck, and the whole of the back yard was covered in a lethal sheet of black ice.

'Sorry, Sis, I would have warned you, but you came out a bit fast.' She squinted into the darkness, and saw her youngest brother Eddie brushing his boots on the steps that led to the shed and to the square of fenced-in dirt where her father kept his lurcher.

'I bet you would have,' she replied caustically. Rubbing the sting out of her hands she inched her way along the wall until she reached the narrow alley in the back right-hand corner of the yard that led to the *ty bach* or 'little house' that held the WC. Protected from the weather on three sides by the house, high garden wall, and the communal outhouse wall they shared with next door, it wasn't quite as cold as the yard, and, thanks to the rags that her father had wrapped around the pipes and high cistern, the plumbing worked in spite of the frost.

The heat blasted welcomingly into her stiff and frozen face when she returned to the kitchen. Haydn was sitting on the kerb of the hearth filling her mother's enamel kitchen jug from the brass tap of the boiler set into the range.

'Mind you top that water level up before you go,' Elizabeth

10

carped at Haydn. 'I've no time to do it, and if the level falls low the boiler will blow.'

'I'll do it now.' Haydn winked at Bethan as he handed the steaming jug across the table. Six feet tall, with blond hair, and deep blue eyes that could melt the most granite-like heart, Haydn was the family charmer. His looks contributed only in part to that charm. His regular features were set attractively in his long face, and his full mouth was frequently curved into a beguiling smile, but it was his manner that won him most friends. At nineteen, he possessed a tact, diplomacy and apparent sincerity that was the envy of every clergyman, Baptist as well as Anglican, on the Graig.

'You won't be topping up anything unless you hurry,' Elizabeth complained sourly. 'It's a quarter-past five now.'

'The wagons won't be leaving the brewer's yard until seven. I've plenty of time to get there, persuade the foreman to give me a morning's work, and load up before they roll,' Haydn said evenly, carrying his plate into the washhouse.

'It'll take you a good half an hour to get down the hill in this weather.'

'Don't look for trouble where there is none, Mam.' Haydn returned with a full jug of cold water, and pinched Elizabeth's wrinkled cheek gently as he passed. He was the only one of her children who would have dared take the liberty. 'I'll be in Leyshon's yard before I know it, with all that ice to slide down.'

'Taking the backside out of your trousers like you did when you were a boy. Well I've no money to give you for new ones.'

'I don't expect you to keep me, Mam.' Haydn dodged past and walked over to the hearth.

Not content with the sight of Haydn doing what she'd asked, Elizabeth turned on Bethan.

'And you, miss,' she said sharply. 'You'll have to get a move on if you're to be on your ward at half-past six.'

'I'm going upstairs now, Mam.' Despite what she'd said, Bethan still hovered uneasily next to Haydn. 'I'll just get a dry towel.' She unhooked the rope that hoisted the airer to the ceiling.

'And you can leave that alone when you like. I put a clean towel upstairs for you and Maud yesterday.'

'Thank you, Mam. I didn't notice,' Bethan said meekly. She

11

had achieved what she wanted. Her father and Alun Jones had pulled on their coal-encrusted coats and caps, picked up their knapsacks, and were heading out through the door. If she succeeded in lingering in the kitchen for another minute or two she wouldn't have to embarrass Alun, or herself, again by walking past him in her dressing gown.

'Good luck, snookems,' her father said with a tenderness that her mother never voiced. 'Not that you need it.' Snookems – it had been a long time since he had called her that. On impulse she replaced the jug on the tiled hearth, reached out and hugged him. His working clothes reeked of the acrid odours of coal and male sweat, but neither that nor the coal dust that rubbed off on her face stopped her from planting a hearty kiss on his bristly cheek.

'Thanks for remembering, Dad,' she murmured. 'I need all the luck I can get today.'

'Not you,' Haydn commented firmly, picking up the rag-filled lisle stocking that served as a potholder. 'You've done enough studying in the last three years to carry you to doctor level, let alone nurse.'

Bethan moved out of the way as he lifted the lid on the boiler. Clouds of steam filled the kitchen accompanied by a hissing, sizzling sound as water splashed over the hotplates as well as into the boiler.

'That's right, make a mess of it,' Elizabeth moaned. 'Just after I've blackleaded the top.'

'Looks like I have. Sorry, Mam,' Haydn apologised cheerfully. 'If you leave it, I'll clean it off this afternoon.'

'As if I'd leave it . . . '

'We're off then, Elizabeth,' Evan said softly, pushing the tin box that held his food and the bottle that held his cold tea into his blackened knapsack.

'About time,' she said harshly, angry at being interrupted.

'See you tonight, Bethan,' Evan murmured as he and Alun left the kitchen.

As soon as Bethan heard the front door slamming behind them she grabbed the jug and ran down the passage and up the stairs before her mother could find anything else to complain about. When she reached her bedroom she found the door closed and

12

the room in darkness. She switched on the light and carried the steaming jug over to the washstand.

'I thought you'd gone,' Maud mumbled sleepily from the depths of the bed. 'I had to get up to turn off the light.'

'Sorry. Go back to sleep.' She tipped the hot water into the bowl and took the soap and flannel from the dish. The marble surface of the washstand was cold, the flannel encrusted with ice. Shivering, she stooped to look in the mirror while she washed, wishing herself shorter and more graceful, like Maud or her best friend and fellow trainee nurse, Laura Ronconi.

She was huge. Big and clumsy, she decided disparagingly, as she sponged the goose pimples on her exposed skin. Life was completely unfair. She was the eldest, why hadn't she been blessed with Maud's looks? Her younger sister was a fragile five feet four inches, with the same angelic blue eyes and blonde hair as Haydn. Not yet fourteen, she had the quiet grace of a girl on the brink of attractive, elegant womanhood. While she had a dark, drab complexion, and the height of a maypole.

She finished washing, tipped the water into the slop jar beneath the stand, and began to dress. Her hair wasn't *too* bad, she decided critically, studying the cropped black glossy waves, which Maud had coaxed into a style that wouldn't have disgraced an aspiring Hollywood starlet. And her eyes, large, brown and thickly fringed with lashes, were passable. Her mouth and nose were *all right*, taken in isolation; the problem came when the whole was put together. Particularly her enormous shoulders. Wide shoulders looked good on her father, Eddie and Haydn, but they looked dreadful on a woman. Life would be so different if she'd been born pretty. If not small, fragile and blonde like Maud, then at least petite, vivacious and dark like Laura.

The chill damp of the bedroom penetrated to her bones. Turning her back on the wardrobe mirror she pulled on her clothes as fast as she could. Chemise, liberty bodice, vest, long petticoat, fleecy-lined drawers, two more petticoats, one pair of stockings. She picked up the second pair and noticed a hole. Unrolling one of the stockings from her leg she reversed them, donning the one with the hole first, trying valiantly but vainly to manipulate the hole to the sole of her foot.

Uniform dress, belt with plain buckle; she tried – and failed –

13

to suppress an image of herself wearing the coveted silver buckle of the qualified nurse – apron, cuffs, collar and finally the veil that covered her one good feature, her hair. Marginally warmer, she stood in front of the oval mirror on the wardrobe and tried to see the back of her heels. There was a noticeable and definite light patch on her right heel. She debated whether to remove the extra pair of stockings, but the cold decided for her. If she was lucky Sister Church would be too busy, or too cold herself, to spend time checking the uniform of her final-year trainees.

'Could be your last day as a student nurse.'

Bethan looked from her reflection towards the bed. Maud's eyes were open.

'You're tempting fate,' she retorted.

'You're more superstitious than Mam Powell ever was. I'm tempting nothing,' Maud said grumpily. 'If you don't pass, no one will.'

'Well I'll find out soon enough.' Bethan hung her dressing gown in the wardrobe, and folded her nightdress before stuffing it under the pillow on her side of the bed. 'See you tonight?'

'If Mam will let me, I'll bake a celebration cake.'

'Don't you dare.'

Bethan switched off the light and left the room. Running down the stairs, she lifted her cloak from the peg behind the front door and returned to the kitchen.

'You're not leaving yourself much time to eat your breakfast,' Elizabeth complained as she walked through the door.

'I'm not that hungry.' She pulled a chair out from under the table. The kitchen was hot and steamy after the bedroom. Oppressively so. She cut a piece of bread from the half-loaf that stood, cut side down, on the scarred and chipped wooden breadboard that had been a part of the table furniture for as long as she could remember. The farmer's butter that had been bought on Pontypridd market was warm and greasy in its nest on the range, and the blackberry jam she had helped her mother make last autumn was freezing cold from the pantry.

'I suppose you'll get your results today,' her mother observed as she poured out two cups of tea.

'I hope to.' Bethan pushed her chair closer to the range so she could make the most of its warmth while she ate. The boiler and fires in the hospital were banked low with second-grade coal that smouldered rather than burned, barely warming the radiators and covering the yards with smut-laden black smog. She cut her bread and jam into small squares and began to eat. Elizabeth sat opposite her, sipping her tea with no apparent enjoyment. Bethan didn't attempt to talk. She'd never been close to her mother and didn't miss intimate conversations with her, because they'd never had one. Her father had always tried to help with her problems. He'd given her all the childhood hugs, kisses and treats that she'd received at home, and if she needed a woman to talk to now, she went to Laura or her Aunt Megan.

A month after Evan and Elizabeth's marriage, Evan's younger brother William began courting Megan Davies. Megan was the antithesis of Elizabeth. To use Caterina Powell's terms, she was 'a nice, warm-hearted Welsh girl, who knew where she came from' (a reference to Elizabeth's refusal to acknowledge her own mother's working-class roots). The daughter and sister of policemen, Megan Davies was smaller, prettier and stronger-willed than Elizabeth, and she point-blank refused to move into the Graig Avenue household. She wouldn't have minded sharing a home with Caterina, in fact she probably would have welcomed the opportunity, as her own mother had died when she was twelve, leaving her with a father and six brothers to look after, but as she put it baldly to William, 'I would as soon move into the workhouse as into the same house as Elizabeth.'

It was left to Evan to solve the problem. Unbeknown to Elizabeth, he took a morning off work, saw the bank manager, and extended the mortgage on the house so he could buy out his brother's share. Elizabeth was furious when she discovered what he'd done and, martyr to the last, took every penny of her hitherto untouched savings and paid off as much of the debt as she could. A lot more than Evan's pride was damaged by her gesture, but tight-lipped he said nothing and complained to no one.

Blissfully ignorant of Evan's pain, Megan and William were ecstatic. They put down a payment on a small, flat-fronted, terraced house in Leyshon Street. Its front door opened directly on to the pavement. A long thin passage (when she saw it Megan cried, 'God help if you're fat!') led past the tiny, square front

15

parlour to the back kitchen. A lean-to washhouse, two skimpy bedrooms, a box room, and a back garden big enough to accommodate the coalhouse, outside WC, washing line, and precious little else comprised the rest of the house. But Megan and William were over the moon. Three streets down the hill from Graig Avenue, they were close enough to visit William's mother and brother whenever they wished, and far enough away to avoid Elizabeth – for most of the time.

Elizabeth disliked Megan from the first, not least because she had rich brown hair and eyes, a clear, glowing complexion and a slim petite figure that looked well in the discounted clothes that she bought from the shop where she worked. Pregnancy took a heavy toll on Elizabeth's health and looks, and by the time William and Megan fixed a date for their wedding she was on her second. Stubbornly refusing Evan's offer of a Provident cheque to buy a new outfit on the grounds that they couldn't afford the shilling in the pound a week repayment, she went to the wedding in a baggy old maternity dress that she knew full well he hated.

Her Uncle John Joseph, who did the honours for William and Megan as he'd done for her and Evan, publicly pitied her, telling her how ill she looked in a booming voice that carried to every corner of the chapel. Satisfied with her sacrificial gesture, she refused to enter the Graig Hotel where the reception was being held, and returned to the house with her baby, secure in the knowledge that she had ruined the day for Evan and upset Caterina. But the wedding was only the first of many irritants that Megan introduced into her life.

Although Megan had come from Bonvilston Road, which was across town and as alien to the people of the Graig as distant places like Cardiff, she was instantly accepted into the community. Elizabeth felt the slight keenly. Despite the fact that she'd lived most of her life in and around Pontypridd, everyone on the Graig referred to her as 'the young Mrs Powell' to differentiate between her and Caterina. In a village where first-name terms were the rule rather than the exception the title was an insult, particularly when Megan was Megan from the outset. As popular, well liked and accepted as Caterina, Evan and William.

Elizabeth burned at the injustice of it all. In the early days of her marriage she'd desperately tried to please her neighbours.

16

She'd joined several of the committees of her uncle's chapel. She'd visited the sick, cleaned the vestry, organised Sunday-school outings, and even offered to coach backward children with their school-work. But in doing all of that she'd failed to realise the potency of her neighbours' pride. Rough, untutored, self-educated, they earned their weekly wages the hard way, and held their heads high. Taught from birth to scorn 'charity', they mistrusted the motives that lay behind her overtures. And she, schooled by her father and uncle in 'charitable deeds', was incapable of helping people from a sense of fellowship or kindness simply because she'd never possessed either of those qualities.

It never crossed her mind to blame her own shortcomings for her isolation from the community. Uncultured and uneducated as her neighbours were, they could sniff out those who condescended and patronised a mile off, and she continued to condescend and patronise without even realising she was doing so. Outwardly she and Evan were no different from anyone else. They had no money to spare or to 'swank' with. In fact between the demands of her children, the mortgage, and what Evan gave his mother, most weeks she was hard put to stretch Evan's wages until his next pay-day. But close acquaintance with poverty did nothing to diminish her sense of superiority. If anything it entrenched it, along with her longsuffering air of martyrdom.

A year or two passed and she gave up trying to make friends of her neighbours. She decided she didn't need them. After all, they were hardly the type of person she'd associated with in training college, or during her teaching days. Instead she concentrated on domestic chores, filling her days with the drudgery of washing, cooking, cleaning, mending and scrubbing. Making herself a slave to the physical needs of her family, and keeping herself and them strictly within the bounds of what she termed 'decency'. But in the daily struggle whatever warmth had once existed between herself and Evan was irretrievably lost.

When war broke out and flamed across Europe in 1914 it affected even Pontypridd. In the early days before conscription some men, including miners, volunteered, sincerely believing they were marching to glorious battle and an heroic personal future that would return them to their locals by Christmas (with luck, covered with enough medals to earn them a few free pints). Evan knew better. So did William – when he was sober.

William and Megan celebrated their fourth wedding anniversary in 1915. Caterina looked after baby William, and William, excited by his and Megan's first night out together in a long time, went to town. They started the evening at six o'clock in the Graig Hotel then gradually worked their way down the Graig hill, via every pub, until they reached the Half Moon opposite Pontypridd Junction station, and just the other side of the railway bridge that marked the border between the Graig hill and town.

Concerned about the state William was getting himself into, Megan stuck to shandy; and even then she sat out a couple of rounds. There were over a dozen pubs either on or just off the Graig hill, and William had a pint in every one. Before he'd married Megan he'd been capable of drinking almost any man in Pontypridd under the table and walking a straight line home afterwards. What he hadn't taken into account was his lack of practice at sinking pints since his marriage. When money was tight, the man's beer was generally the first thing to go, and Evan had warned him, 'The price of getting a woman into your bed is every coin in your pocket.'

William was an inch or two shorter than Evan, but he was still a big man, and she worried about getting him home. Megan suggested that they catch the second house in the New Theatre. As it turned out, William didn't need much persuading. He was having difficulty in standing upright, let alone walking, and he loved the music hall. In his genial, euphoric state he treated himself and Megan to one shilling and threepenny seats in the stalls. It was an unprecedented extravagance that changed his life. If he'd bought his usual sixpenny gallery seats he wouldn't have been able to reach the stage as easily as he did.

The musical acts were good, very good. There was a ventriloquist, an American jazz band, and an extremely attractive blonde soprano who burst into rousing choruses of patriotic songs. Unfortunately for William, and a good ten per cent of the men in the audience, she was joined on stage by a recruiting sergeant, who beckoned them forward. Mesmerised by the blonde, and singing at the top of his voice, William took up the invitation. Happy, drunk and on stage for the first time in his life, he signed

18

the paper that the sergeant thrust under his nose – and found himself an unwilling conscript in Kitchener's New Army.

Megan cried, but her tears softened nothing but her cheeks. William was shipped out that same night. She received a couple of abject, apologetic letters, then a postcard emblazoned with a beautifully embroidered bluebird, holding an improbably coloured flower in its beak and a banner proclaiming 'A Kiss from France'. A week later an official War Office telegram was delivered to her door in Leyshon Street:

'Regret to inform you Pte William Powell killed in action.'

His commanding officer wrote to her, a nice enough note that told her little about William's life in the army or the manner of his death. Six lonely, miserable months later she gave birth to William's daughter. She named her Diana after a character in one of the Marie Corelli novels that she'd borrowed from Pontypridd lending library.

Megan wasn't one to break under grief. She had two children, and a war widow's pension that wouldn't even cover the cost of the mortgage. Ever practical, she asked for, and got, a job scrubbing out the local pub in the early morning. But even that wasn't enough, so she put two beds in the front parlour, and took in lodgers. It wasn't easy to work even part-time with little ones to care for, and Caterina used Megan's plight as an excuse to leave Graig Avenue and move into Leyshon Street.

Evan paid another visit to the bank manager. He took out a third mortgage on the house, this time for the maximum that the manager would allow, and insisted on giving his mother every pound that he'd raised. Elizabeth was devastated, and not only financially. Not realising how much she'd come to rely on her mother-in-law's assistance with her children, she'd barely tolerated Caterina's presence whilst they'd lived together, but after Caterina left, she felt her loss keenly. That, coupled with the crippling increase in the mortgage repayments, gave her yet another reason to feel rejected and ill used by Evan's family.

Bethan was six, Haydn five, Eddie two and Maud a baby when their grandmother moved into their Aunt Megan's house. They missed her warmth, her love and her cuddles, but fortunately Megan's was within easy walking distance even for small legs, and for once in his life Evan stood up to Elizabeth, overrode all her objections and actively encouraged his children to visit his mother and sister-in-law.

Much to Elizabeth's chagrin Evan also developed the habit of dropping into Megan's whenever he walked the Graig hill. The neighbours began to fall silent when she passed. She sensed fingers pointing at her behind her back; whispers following her when she left the local shops. She didn't need her Uncle John Joseph to tell her that, in Graig terms, 'Evan had pushed his feet under Megan's table'.

As jealousy took its insidious hold, Elizabeth reacted in typical martyred fashion. She became colder, and at the same time a more efficient housewife. Whatever else was being said, she made certain no one could cast a critical eye at her house or her children. Everything and everyone within the confines of her terraced walls shone and sparkled as only daily rubbing and scrubbing could make them.

In time the inevitable happened, the gossip-mongers tired of talking about Megan and Evan, and turned their attention to other things. But Megan, young, attractive, footloose and fancy free, was never out of the limelight for long. Interest in Evan was superseded by interest in Megan's lodgers, particularly one Sam Brown, an American sailor turned collier who'd made his way to Pontypridd via Bute Street, Cardiff, and the first negro to live on the Graig. Caterina's presence in Leyshon Street kept Megan just the right side of respectability – just – because other gentlemen callers besides Evan and Megan's brother Huw found their way to her door.

The most frequent visitor was Harry Griffiths, a corner shop-keeper. By Pontypridd standards Harry was comfortably off, by Graig standards he was a millionaire. Popular, and well loved by his customers because he and his father had almost bankrupted themselves by financing the grocery credit accounts of the miners during the crippling, hungry strikes of the twenties, he could do no wrong in the eyes of his neighbours. Megan couldn't have picked a better 'gentleman friend' if she'd tried. He was married, but the gossips had long since discovered that it was a marriage in name only as his wife refused to give him 'his rights'. They lived above his shop, which was housed in a large square building that dominated the corner of the Graig hill and Factory Lane.

20

Old Mrs Evans, who lived in rooms above the fish and chip shop opposite, saw him pulling the curtains of the box room less than a week after his wedding, and it wasn't long before everyone on the Graig became acquainted with the Griffithses' sleeping habits, as Mrs Evans continued her reports at regular intervals. The old iron *single* bedstead in the box room acquired a fresh coat of paint and a blue spread. Harry's clothes were hung on hooks behind the door, and a rag rug laid over the bare floorboards.

Mrs Evans was obliged to adjust her hours, and change to a later bedtime when Harry took to eating supper every evening with Megan in Leyshon Street, but then, as she whispered to Annie Jones who worked in the fish shop, 'A man's entitled to a bit of comfort, and if he can't get it at home, who can blame him for straying.' Certainly not the women whose credit was stretched by Harry when their husbands fell sick or were put on 'short time' by the pit owners. Megan had steeled herself to face worse. Fingers were pointed, but not unkindly. Only Elizabeth gave her the cold shoulder, but the relationship between her and Elizabeth was so strained already, she barely noticed the difference.

The war widows on the Graig generally fell into one of two categories. There were those who became embittered, afraid to love anyone, man, woman or child, lest they suffer loss again, and there were those like Megan who were prepared to reach out to anyone who needed them, hoping that in doing so they would, in some small way, assuage their grief. Megan found enough love and understanding for everyone she came into contact with. Her children, her mother- and brother-in-law, her nieces and nephews, her lodgers, her friends, her neighbours – her generosity became a byword on the Graig and an object of Elizabeth's scorn.

When Caterina died after a short bout of pneumonia Elizabeth expected her children to stop visiting Leyshon Street, but if anything their visits became more frequent. It was as if Caterina's death drew the children, Evan and Megan closer together, and shut out Elizabeth all the more. Caterina had always been the one to contact Elizabeth, and invite her to all the family births, deaths, marriages and celebrations. After she died Megan never climbed the hill as far as Elizabeth's house again, although she cleaned the Graig Hotel, which was practically on the corner of

Graig Avenue, six mornings a week; including, much to Elizabeth's disgust, Sunday mornings.

Bethan, like her brothers and sister, learned early in life that if she wanted, really wanted, anything other than plain food and carbolic soap and water she would get it in Leyshon Street, not at home. After Caterina's death Megan assumed the role of family confidante that had been Caterina's. And it was Megan who presented Bethan with her first lipstick and pair of real silk stockings, on her all-important fourteenth birthday. Thrilled, Bethan had rushed home to show them off. Tight-lipped, Elizabeth took the items from Bethan's trembling hands and threw them into the kitchen stove. Bethan retreated sobbing to the bedroom she shared with Maud, and later, when Evan came home from work, he wormed what had happened out of her.

He said nothing to either his wife or his daughter, but on payday Elizabeth's housekeeping was short by the amount he'd taken to replace Megan's gifts. Elizabeth learned her lesson. From that day forward she confined her disapproval of Megan and her presents to verbal lashings, nothing more.

Whenever Bethan, Maud or the boys returned from Megan's with something in their hands, Elizabeth would enquire coldly if it had been bought with Harry Griffiths' money. The children too learned their lesson. They hid the presents Megan gave them and ceased speaking about their aunt, their cousins or the visits they made to Leyshon Street in their mother's presence. So Bethan and her brothers grew up: unwilling participants in a conspiracy of silence.

Bethan learned about subterfuge before she even went to school. Whenever she did anything she knew her mother would disapprove of she ran to Caterina and later to Megan who would make it come right. She knew she could count on her aunt and grandmother to mend her dresses, or replace the pennies she lost on the way to the shops. They wiped her tears, and slipped her a few coins for treats and school outings when Elizabeth wouldn't, and until Bethan left home at fourteen years and three months old to work as a skivvy in Llwynypia Hospital she never questioned how her Aunt Megan, a widow with two children of her own, could afford to be so generous to her nieces and nephews.

And even when she was old enough to look at Harry Griffiths and see the answer in his frequent visits, she couldn't find it in her heart to condemn her aunt.

She loved Megan far too much to do that.

Chapter Two

'It's ten minutes to six,' Elizabeth said loudly, looking at the grease-stained face of the black kitchen clock that had been a wedding present from her Uncle John Joseph.

'I know, Mam. I'm not meeting Laura until six.' Bethan finished her tea and opened the cupboard set into the alcove between the range and tiny square of window that looked out on to the walled-in back yard. She took her toothbrush from the cracked coronation mug that held all the family brushes, and went into the washhouse. Rubbing the brush in the thick damp grains of salt that were spread out on an old saucer, she cleaned her teeth thoroughly under the running tap.

'Five to six, Bethan.'

'Yes, Mam.' She returned to the kitchen, replaced the brush and put on her cloak.

'I suppose you'll be late tonight.' Elizabeth's pronouncement was more of a condemnation than a question.

'I don't think so.'

'There's no celebration arranged then?'

'Not straight after work, Mam, no. If ... ' She crossed her fingers behind her back, not to irritate Elizabeth, who abhorred all things superstitious. 'If I pass, we'll celebrate at the hospital ball tonight.'

'You're going then?'

'I said I was, Mam,' Bethan replied patiently.

'Fine state of affairs,' her mother railed bitterly. 'In my day a young girl would sooner die than be seen entering a public hall where drink was sold.'

'It's a ball, Mam. Doctor John and his wife are going, and Matron, and Sister Church.'

Elizabeth sniffed loudly to emphasise her disapproval.

'I'll be home about seven then,' Bethan said quietly with a touch of her father's resignation in her voice.

She laced on the boots she'd cleaned the night before, and

24

exchanged the warmth of the kitchen for the cold of the passage. The wind seared, needle sharp, into her face as she opened the front door. Drawing her cloak close, she stepped cautiously on to the doorstep and slammed the front door.

A frost haze haloed the street lamps, and her breath clouded foggily in her face as she pulled on a pair of knitted gloves. Placing one foot warily in front of the other she descended the sloping path and half-dozen steps that led down to the Avenue. Setting her head against the wind she walked in the shelter of the high wall that fronted the terrace. Large iron keys protruded from the doors, as they had done ever since she could remember. No one locked themselves into their home in Graig Avenue; the neighbours would have labelled anyone who tried 'strange'. A knock, followed by the turning of the key, was all that was needed to gain admittance to any house – although the neighbouring housewives seldom exercised their prerogative at Elizabeth's door.

Thin layers of ice cracked and crunched beneath her boots as she picked her way along. The one good thing about unmade roads was that they were easy to walk on in cold weather. The frost dried the mud so it didn't dirty boots, and the rough stones broke up any dangerously large expanses of ice.

Laura Ronconi was waiting on the corner, half hidden in the shadow of the high wall that fronted the six more forbidding grey houses at the beginning of the terrace.

'Today's the day,' Laura smiled brightly, her dark eyes gleaming in the light of the lamp above her.

'I've been trying to forget that ever since I got up.'

'You've nothing to worry about.' Laura led the way down the hill towards the main road. A shire horse, its nose and flanks steaming in the cold morning air, stood placidly, blinkered and harnessed, in front of the dairy as Alwyn Harries, a slightly deaf hunchback with a gammy leg, manhandled the milk churns on to the back of the cart.

'Good morning, Mr Harries,' Bethan shouted loudly, the clouds of her breath mingling with that of the horse.

'Morning, Nurse Powell, Nurse Ronconi.' He tipped his flat cap to both of them. 'Colder than yesterday.'

They nodded agreement as they went on their way.

The Graig hill was steepest at its foot, where it left town. That's not to say that it wasn't steep elsewhere. The incline from Graig Avenue to Danycoedcae Road, the last road built across the mountain side, and the street where Laura lived with her enormous family, was also lung-burstingly steep. Even the fittest men who took the short cut up through Iltyd Street, and the rough sheep track, were winded before they reached their goal. But the road below Graig Avenue flattened out, and the incline remained gentle until you reached Griffiths' shop on the corner of Factory Lane. So the two girls had no difficulty in crossing the Avenue below the dairy, rounding Vicarage Corner and out on to Llantrisant Road.

The frost on the main road had dissipated in the heavy morning traffic. Work began early for the fortunate few – those miners who'd been lucky enough to hold on to at least some of their six-thirty shifts in the depression-affected pits – even on cold January mornings. And besides the miners, who left their beds confident that there was work to be done and a wage packet at the end of the week, there was a small army of men like Haydn, and Eddie, who left their houses before six every day, in the hope of finding a few hours' paid work loading brewery wagons, or helping out on the carts that left the rag pickers' yard on Factory Lane.

The hill was nowhere near as slippery as Bethan had expected. Ice still lay in patches, but where it had been thickest it had already turned to a damp slush that clung to her boots. Her only fear was that they'd be filthy before she reached the hospital and that would gain her yet another lecture and black mark from Sister Church.

'Good morning, Bethan.'

She looked up to see her Aunt Megan, pouring buckets of warm water over the doorstep of the Graig Hotel.

'Aunt Megan, it's lovely to see you,' she smiled.

'Good luck, bach. It is today isn't it? Your results I mean.'

'Do you know, you're only the second person to wish me luck.' Bethan ignored the bucket, mop and dirty water, and hugged her aunt.

'Don't do that, you silly girl, you'll dirty your uniform.' Megan pushed Bethan away with her red, work-roughened hands.

'I don't care,' Bethan laughed.

'Had a super dress in yesterday, your size too,' Megan whispered, holding her mop in front of her like a weapon. 'Red silk, just right for the ball tonight.'

'I might not be going,' Bethan protested.

'You will,' Laura chipped in. 'She's being silly, Mrs Powell. She stands a better chance than any of us.'

'Even if I do go, I don't need a new dress,' Bethan protested. 'I've hardly worn my ringed black velvet.'

'You've worn it to every hospital ball for the past three years,' Laura said indignantly.

'I'll do the silk at a special price. You can pay me sixpence a week,' Megan offered persuasively.

'It seems such a waste to buy evening clothes that are only going to be worn once or twice.'

'It won't do any harm to look,' Laura suggested. 'And I have to call in on you on the way home from work anyway, Mrs Powell. If that's all right of course. I was hoping you'd have something to suit me. Have you?' she demanded eagerly.

'I've a lovely gold net, and a blue taffeta, both small sizes. I'll hold them for you until tonight.'

'Would you? Gold net sounds stunning. It would look good in the ball description in the *Observer*. After the hospital board ladies, and doctors' wives of course. Nurse Ronconi, in a stunning creation of gold net,' she murmured dreamily.

'Don't tempt fate,' Bethan warned. 'You haven't seen the dress, and you might not be able to call yourself Nurse tonight.'

'Job's comforter.' Laura stuck out her tongue.

'I'll see you both about seven.' Megan threw the last of her water into the gutter.

'Thank you, Auntie.' Bethan kissed Megan on the cheek. Avoiding the puddles, she and Laura hurried on.

'I really do have to call in on your aunt tonight,' Laura explained breathlessly, running to keep up with Bethan's long strides. 'I'm out of powder, perfume and lipstick.'

'After what you bought before Christmas?' Bethan asked incredulously.

'It doesn't go very far.' Laura shrugged her shoulders. 'Particularly in our house. Just be glad you've only got one sister pilfering your things. It's murder having five.'

Bethan dropped the subject. Laura was one of eleven, six girls and five boys. But they'd never gone as short as some of the other Graig children. Their parents were Italian immigrants, and their father had progressed from selling ice cream from a handcart in Market Square, to owning two cafés. One in the centre of Pontypridd, which Laura's eldest brother Alfredo 'Ronnie' Ronconi ran; and one in High Street, just below the hospital. All the Ronconi children were well fed and dressed, and whatever they earned, they kept. Unlike Bethan. Her father, along with the other miners in the Maritime, had been put on a three-day working week at the end of last year and, as her mother was so fond of pointing out, no one could keep a family on what he brought home. He did his best. Like every short-timer and unemployed man in Pontypridd, he tried to pick up casual work on the days he was free. There was fair amount of it – the rag and bone carts, the market traders, the brewery yards. The problem was that for every hour's work there were a hundred or more men prepared to undercut their fellows, and boys like Eddie were more often successful than their fathers, for the simple reason that they were prepared to work for less money.

Bethan earned twenty-five shillings a week. If (she couldn't even bring herself to think when) she qualified, it would go up to thirty-five. Good money by any standard. She already gave her mother fifteen shillings a week, and chipped in to help with expenses whenever she could. She knew her father found it difficult to live with the notion that she was contributing more than him to the family kitty, but neither of them had any choice. The mortgage had to be paid; and the expense of keeping the boys, not to mention Maud, grew heavier with their increasing sizes. On top of the cost of food, extra coal to supplement Evan's reduced collier's ration, gas and electricity, there was the question of the boys' clothes. Bethan had been saving for months to buy both of them decent suits and overcoats. She'd managed to kit Haydn out on Wilf Horton's second-hand stall on the market, but only because he was into a man's size, and men who were out of work were queuing up to sell their good clothes. Boys' clothes were different. Every family in Pontypridd was anxious to buy their sons good outfits in the hope that smart clothes would impress a prospective employer. Poor Eddie was walking

28

around in an overcoat that didn't cover his forearms, and trousers that had been twice turned. She had twenty-five shillings hidden in a wooden jewellery box that Haydn had made her in the school woodwork class, but decent overcoats Eddie's size started at two guineas in Leslie's stores, the cheapest shop in town. And that was without a suit.

'You're quiet,' Laura observed as they passed the yellow-lit window of Harry Griffiths' grocery shop.

'I was thinking about Eddie. He needs a good overcoat in this weather. The one he's wearing is miles too small for him.'

'Didn't you see the *Observer* on Saturday? There's a sale on in Wien's. All ladies' blouses and jumpers are down to a shilling from four and eleven, and youths' lined overcoats down from twenty-nine and six to four and eleven. Sale starts this morning. Our mam intends to be first in the queue.'

'Youths' sizes will probably be too small for our Eddie.'

'Our Joe wears youth sizes and he's bigger than your Eddie.'

'Oh if only I wasn't working,' Bethan complained in exasperation.

'You could slip out lunch time.'

'We're not supposed to leave the hospital.'

'Goody two-shoes. I'll go for you if you like.'

'So you can get caught instead of me? Do you think they'll have anything left tonight?' Bethan demanded anxiously.

'They might and they might not. Isn't that your Haydn?'

Bethan looked down the hill and saw her brother climbing, cap in hand, dejectedly back up it.

'No work today?' Bethan commiserated.

'There were fifty in Leyshon's yard this morning. Old Prosser said I'd had more than my fair share and it was the turn of the married men. Can't argue with that, I suppose.'

'Could be just as well,' Bethan said, trying to cheer him up. 'I need you to do me a favour.'

'What kind of favour?' Haydn asked suspiciously, his pride bristling at the thought of taking charity from his sister.

'There's a sale on in Wien's. Laura says they're selling youths' overcoats for four and eleven. You know where I keep my money?'

'Yes.'

29

'Take it and see what you can get for Eddie. If you like it, Eddie'll wear it.'

'Beth, you shouldn't have to do this . . . '

'If you see anything for yourself, get that too. If you and Eddie look smart I know, I just know, you'll get jobs,' she pleaded. 'You can pay me back then. Think what a difference it would make at home if you two were in regular work?'

'You'll let me and Eddie pay you back?'

'Of course I will. You'll go then? To the sale I mean.'

'I'll go,' he agreed dully.

'Thanks a lot,' she smiled.

'We'd best run, Bethan.' Laura grabbed her arm. 'If we don't, Sister will have us for breakfast. Bye, Haydn.' Laura flashed a look, half shy, half coquettish in Haydn's direction.

'Your Haydn?' Laura began as soon as they were out of earshot.

'Yes,' Bethan murmured absently, trying to walk carefully and quickly around the slush at the same time.

'Is he still sweet on Jenny Griffiths?'

'As far as I know.' Bethan looked at Laura, wondering if she knew more about Haydn's affairs than her.

'Shame,' Laura sighed wistfully.

'Laura!' Bethan exclaimed. 'He's a year younger than you.'

Laura halted at the huge wooden gates of the workhouse, and gazed after Haydn's retreating figure. 'When it comes to some things, age doesn't matter,' she said, grinning suggestively.

'Your father and Ronnie been chaperoning you everywhere again?' Bethan asked as she led the way around the corner to the main gates.

'Absolutely everywhere!' Laura complained. 'This morning Ronnie shouted at me for saying good morning to the paper boy. And he's only twelve, poor lamb.'

'Poor you, more like it,' Bethan laughed.

'It's all right for you,' Laura said testily. 'Your father's quite human. I told Ronnie straight last night that Italian men only lock up their wives and daughters because they know from personal experience that Italian men can't be trusted to keep their hands off any woman between fifteen and thirty that they're not related to.'

'That must have gone down like a lead zeppelin.' Bethan smiled at the porter on gate duty as he waved them through.

'Remember Cardiff Infirmary?' Laura murmured wistfully. 'There I could talk to anyone I wanted . . .'

'And generally did.'

'You can't blame me,' she retorted. 'Not after being wrapped up in cotton wool by Papa and Ronnie until the day I left home. And to think I was stupid enough to come back. I must have been insane to have even considered it.' They crossed the women's exercise yard and made their way towards the towering, grey stone maternity block. 'And now look at me,' she continued to grumble, 'working on a maternity ward of all things, when I really want to nurse on men's surgical.'

'Last time I looked in, I didn't see any tall dark handsome men waiting to fall in love,' Bethan teased.

'Were there any fair ones?' Laura mocked, still thinking of Haydn.

'None that would have interested you.' Bethan opened the heavy oak door of the ward block that housed the maternity unit.

'Oh well I can live in hope. And who knows, if Frederick March or Gerald du Maurier is brought in, they may mix maternity up with men's surgical. And even if they don't, by the end of the day we'll know whether we're qualified or not. And if we are,' she lifted her eyebrows suggestively, 'we can always request a transfer.'

'You're a hopeless case,' Bethan laughed as they climbed the steep flight of stone stairs. 'I really must remember to warn my brothers about you.'

'Both of them?' Laura asked indignantly.

'Both of them,' Bethan retorted firmly, as she unfastened her cape and prepared herself for duty.

As far back as she could remember Bethan had wanted to be a doctor. The proudest day of her life was when she passed the entrance examination to Pontypridd girls' grammar school, the saddest when she realised that a drastic cut in miners' wages had robbed her father of sufficient money to keep her there. Her mother's unemotional, realistic attitude had taught her to accept the inevitable. Enlisting the aid of a sympathetic teacher she

31

applied to every hospital in the area, and at fourteen left home to take up the position of a 'live-in' ward maid at Llwynypia Hospital in the Rhondda. When she was sixteen the sister on her ward recommended her for nursing training in the Royal Infirmary in Cardiff. And she'd loved it.

Laura arrived to train alongside her, and they'd shared a cubicle in the nurses' hostel. Both of them soon discovered that trainee nurses were treated worse than domestics. The work was hard, the split shift hours impossibly long, their superiors demanding, but Bethan found her patients and their ailments fascinating, and when things were really tough, Laura was always there with a joke to lighten the load.

During the three years she'd trained she and Laura had scarcely seen their families. Trainee nurses' holidays rarely coincided with Christmas or Easter, and summer visits to Barry Island on the train with the other girls, and winter window-shopping trips around Cardiff had taken up most of their fortnightly free afternoons. But just as they'd finished their third-year finals, Bethan had received a letter from her mother suggesting a move to the Graig Hospital so she could help out with family finances. Realising that Elizabeth would only have made the suggestion as a desperate last resort, she saw Matron, and applied for a transfer without giving a thought to what her own plans might have been. And Laura, always the supportive best friend, decided to make the move with her.

Times were hard for everyone, but when she returned home they managed. Her father had three days' work guaranteed in the Maritime every week. The boys had left school, although Haydn, like her, had dreamt of going to college, and both occasionally brought home the odd few shillings. However, it was her own and her father's much-reduced wages that kept the family going.

'Only sixty seconds of freedom left and then it'll be twelve hours before we can call our souls our own again,' Laura muttered as they shuffled into line behind the qualified nurses ready for the ward sister's inspection.

'Ssh,' Nurse Williams, one of the qualified nurses, admonished as the squeak of rubber-soled boots over linoleum heralded the approach of authority.

Both Laura and Bethan had found the Graig Hospital very different to Cardiff Infirmary. The first thing she and Laura had discovered was that the place was known by many names, any one of which was enough to strike fear into the hearts of the poor and elderly who were terrified of dying alone and abandoned in one of its wards. The name least used was the official one, 'The Graig Hospital and Infirmary'. In newspaper reports of its social and fundraising functions it was generally referred to as the Central Homes, because all the wards, although housed in separate blocks, occupied the same vast tract of land sandwiched between the railway lines at the bottom of the Graig hill.

Despite the efforts of the staff to educate patients, few people differentiated between the hospital wards and those of the homes, although they were run as separate units, the hospital dealing with the sick, and the homes with the destitute. The destitute and 'casuals' generally entered the site through massive, high wooden doors that fronted High Street, and the sick and maternity cases by the huge metal main gates situated around the corner in Court-house Street. To the locals, the whole complex was known by its Victorian name, 'The Workhouse'. And they, like their parents and grandparents before them, knew many who had entered its high-walled precincts only to leave for an unmarked grave in a derelict corner of Glyntaff cemetery.

Bethan and Laura had only ever worked on the maternity ward in the hospital. A VD ward, euphemistically described as the 'clinic' because one was held there two days a week, and wards for the terminally ill were housed in the same block as the maternity unit. On these wards were mainly miners, young girls, and children who'd contracted tuberculosis or one of the other severe, and often fatal, respiratory illnesses that haunted the mining valleys. A separate block behind the maternity unit held 'J' ward, a unit for children under three, sick, orphaned and those whose parents had been admitted as destitute.

J ward was the only ward in the hospital where the sick and 'parish' cases overlapped. The rest of the homes side was virtually a closed book to Bethan. She came across the inmates often; it was difficult not to. Squads of young, pregnant girls from the

33

'unmarried mothers' ward wearing the 'workhouse' uniform of grey flannel were often commandeered to scrub the miles of stairs, corridors and outside steps of the complex. If it wasn't the pregnant girls and women who were hard at work, then it was the orphans from Church Village homes who'd reached the age of sixteen without finding a foster parent, job or sponsor. The council had no other recourse but to send these 'adult orphans' to the homes, where they carried coal, laid fires, swept yards and washed bedlinen for their daily bread and marge until they found either a sponsor or a job. And with the town strangled in the grip of a depression that was vacating shops and bankrupting longstanding, respectable traders at an alarming rate, most of the inmates could be forgiven for believing that they were in the workhouse for life.

Those who could no longer pay their rent, the elderly who couldn't look after themselves, girls who disgraced their families – they all ended up in the Graig. Occasionally Bethan heard cries from the yards as families were split up. Men to the male, and women to the female casual wards, their children under three to J ward, those over three and under eleven to Maesycoed Homes, a couple of miles away, and those between eleven and sixteen to Church Village homes several miles away. The elderly went to the geriatric wards. In addition to these semi-permanent inmates, every evening Bethan and Laura passed lengthy, verminous queues of 'occasionals' waiting to sign into a casual ward for the night. Three hours of coal shovelling or stick chopping earned them a delousing, bath, evening meal, breakfast and bed. There were always more casuals in winter than summer, but if they were capable of walking, they signed themselves out the next morning. Even in a snowstorm.

The nurses on the casual wards had a more difficult job in many ways than the nurses in the hospital, but Bethan sensed a 'looking down' by the medical staff on those who worked with the destitute. It wasn't simply that they spent their days delousing patients, and supervising menial tasks; it was the lack of any 'real' medical work. Bethan knew one or two of them, widows or women with unemployed husbands, who'd been forced to take on the role of family breadwinner. She felt sorry for them and, when she wasn't too busy to think, wondered why they didn't apply for a transfer to the hospital. One of the reasons could have been Lena Church.

Sister Lena Church was the martinet who ran the maternity ward. She'd been christened 'Squeers' by a nurse when a stage production of *Nicholas Nickleby* had played at the Town Hall. The name had stuck, and not only because she had a squint. If she had any saving graces, neither her nurses nor her patients had seen any sign of them.

'Homes side has rung through. Unmarried has gone into labour.' Sister Church paused in the doorway of the sluice room where Bethan was scouring bedpans. 'I only hope they're not sending her over too early. The last thing we need is workhouse clutter on this ward. When you've finished that, get the delivery room ready and the bath run. But mind you don't skimp on those bedpans to do it. There's enough cases of cross-infection without you adding to them.'

'Yes, Sister.' Bethan fought the temptation to bite back. Sister's commands were like sergeant-majors' orders, never a please or a thank you. But three years on the wards of Cardiff Infirmary had accustomed her to routine brusqueness. What she found difficult to accept was the underlying hint that any job entrusted to her would not be carried out properly.

Head down, she continued to scrub until she heard the squeak of Sister's rubber-soled boots walking past the door and down the ward that housed the mothers. Then she turned on the cold tap, rinsed and disinfected the pans, and stacked them on the shelf above the sink. She washed and dried her hands, mournfully examining their cracked and sore state before removing her rubber apron. Straightening her veil, she left the sluice room and turned left, out of the main ward into a corridor. She walked into the principal delivery room and reflected, not for the first time, that it was a miserable place in which to make an entry into the world.

Its one small-paned window overlooked an inner courtyard hedged in by high, grey stone walls which darkened the atmosphere even further. The room itself was half tiled with brick-shaped tiles. Time and countless trolley knocks had cracked and stained their surface, transforming them from white into a patchwork of grubby beiges and greys. A mahogany dado separated

35

the tiles from the upper wall, which was glossed the same sickly shade of green as the rest of the hospital. A grey metal bedstead covered by a pink rubber sheet was the only furniture. No table, no chair, no pictures on the wall to relieve the monotony, only a cumbersome radiator built on a gigantic scale, that ironically did little to warm the room. Bethan laid her hand on it. It was warmer than the air. Marginally. Rubbing warmth into her hands, she left the room to fetch bedlinen and a birth pack.

'Patient's on the stairs, and Sister's screaming because the bath isn't run.' Laura poked her head around the door. 'Here, I'll finish that, you sort out the bathroom.'

Bethan ran.

There was only one bathroom on the ward, off the same corridor as the delivery rooms and linen cupboard. It contained two baths. Bethan sat on the edge of the one nearest the door and pushed the wrinkled rubber plug into the hole. She turned on the hot tap. A thin stream of lukewarm, brownish water trickled into the tub, covering a bottom long since denuded of porcelain covering by the friction of countless bodies and scourings with Vim. As soon as she sat down, she realised how tired she was. She'd been on her feet all morning, and her nerves were stretched. A porter had mentioned that Matron was calling the final-year students into her office one at a time to give them their examination results. Bethan hadn't worked in the hospital long enough to know whether this was normal practice. If it wasn't, did it mean that the results were dreadful? If she failed would she lose her job, or would the hospital authorities give her a chance to repeat the year and try the examinations again? So much depended on Matron's recommendations in cases of failure, and Matron based her decisions on Sister's reports. She really should have made more of an effort to get on with Squeers.

Reaching out she fingered a thin wedge of foul-smelling yellow soap in the dish at the side of the bath. It fell to pieces in her hand, melted and watery.

'Powell!'

She jumped as though she'd been scalded.

'Yes Sister.'

'What do you think you're doing?'

'Testing the bathwater, Sister,' Bethan lied promptly, standing

36

stiffly to attention. Three months' training on Sister Church's ward had given her an aptitude to tell untruths she wouldn't have believed herself capable of acquiring a year ago.

'I see,' the Sister echoed sharply. 'Well, while you're "testing the water", the patient is waiting at the door of the ward. Bring her here and supervise her bath. I'll turn off the tap,' she said coldly, as though she couldn't even trust Bethan to complete that simple task.

The wards in the maternity section led into one another, and Bethan walked quickly out of the side corridor into the room that housed the mothers. Pushing open the double doors at the end, she went into the nursery. She loved this ward, with its aroma of talcum powder and fragile new life, and normally took time to linger among the rows of placid pink babies tucked up in their cots. Even now, rushed as she was, her steps slowed as she glanced into the cot of baby Davies; a sweet little girl with a mop of dark curly hair who'd rapidly become the staff favourite, although none of them would have willingly admitted such favouritism.

'Nurse! Nurse!' The cry was accompanied by a furious knocking on the far door that led into the main corridor. She broke into a run.

'She's in a lot of pain, Nurse.'

'All right, Jimmy.' Bethan smiled reassuringly at the tall, thin gangly porter who'd been sent from Church Village homes to the Graig Hospital on his sixteenth birthday, and worked his way up from the status of inmate to porter, a position he'd held for over thirty years.

'Breathe deeply . . . ' Bethan looked from the pale, strained face of the young girl to Jimmy.

'Maisie. Maisie Crockett, Nurse,' Jimmy supplied anxiously.

'Maisie?' Bethan looked for a resemblance between the young girl who stood, hunched and trembling before her, and her old schoolfriend from Danygraig Street.

'You remember me then?' Maisie clutched her abdomen as another pain gripped her.

'Of course I remember you.'

'I've seen you around the hospital. I didn't think you wanted to know me,' Maisie gasped.

'Now why should you think that?' Bethan wrapped her arm around Maisie's thin shoulders.

'You know . . . this . . . ' Head down, humiliated by her condition and weakened by pain, Maisie cried. Harsh, rasping sobs that tore violently through her throat.

'Don't worry, Maisie,' Jimmy was almost in tears himself. 'Nurse will see you all right.'

The girl clung to his arm, reluctant to release her hold.

'Sorry, Maisie, but Jimmy can't come in here.' Bethan looked meaningfully at the porter and he prised Maisie's fingers away.

'Sister on the homes side said to tell you she went into labour four hours ago. Shouldn't be long now,' Jimmy whispered. Bethan nodded.

'You're going to have to be quiet now, Maisie. We have to walk through the nursery.' She turned and pushed backwards through the double doors. Maisie stifled her sobs as Bethan led her, head bowed, through the nursery and mothers' ward into the side ward. Sister Church was waiting impatiently in the bathroom. Wearing her most intimidating expression she looked Maisie up and down before turning to Bethan.

'Bathed, shaved and in the delivery room in ten minutes, Powell,' she barked.

'Yes, Sister.'

Used to life in the homes section, Maisie began to undress without being told. Sister Church left. Bethan followed her as far as the linen cupboard. Unlocking the door from a bunch of keys that hung at her belt she removed a coarse grey towel, white cotton shift, grey striped flannel dressing gown and a new cake of carbolic soap. When she returned Maisie was sitting, shivering, in the water.

'They shaved me before I came over,' Maisie said plaintively.

'In that case, shout as soon as you've finished washing, and I'll help you out of the bath. I'll be outside the door.'

'Thank you.' Maisie smiled for the first time, grateful for the unaccustomed privacy.

Bethan returned to the linen cupboard. A pile of sealed cardboard boxes were stacked close to the fire door. She took the top one and ripped it open; the stench of carbolic sent her reeling. Struggling, she dragged the heavy box to the cupboard and began to stack the tablets of soap, the old ones to the front, the new ones at the back. Squeers could return at any moment and she was a stickler for order, and what she called 'stock cycling'. It was understandable in the drug cupboard, but there seemed little point in doing it with soaps and linens.

'Matron wants to see you.'

Bethan started at the sound of Laura's voice.

'You gave me a fright!'

'Did you hear what I said? Matron wants to see you.'

'Matron . . . ' The implication of Laura's words sank in and she dropped the soap.

'Now look what you've done,' Laura complained. 'You've dented the soap, and smeared it all over Squeers' nice clean floor.' She bent down and scooped up the cakes that were scattered from one end of the corridor to the other.

'Have you been up?' Bethan demanded.

'P comes before R. Remember your alphabet.'

Bethan straightened her veil, and her skirt. 'How do I look?'

'Like you're scared to death. Go quickly, before Squeers comes and finds some excuse to keep you here.'

Bethan scurried out of the door. Fortunately Sister was occupied with a patient at the far end of the ward. She left the maternity section and ran through the female exercise yard to the administration block as fast as she decently could, straightening her veil and apron again when she reached Matron's door. She hesitated for a moment to catch her breath. The lights still burned in the corridor although the sun had risen hours ago. Not that she could see any of it, only dismal grey rain clouds that shone wanly through the high corridor windows.

Breathing easier, she stared at the top half of the office door. Her heart was pounding so fast she could hear the rush of blood drumming in her ears. She waited, counting slowly to ten. One . . . two . . . three . . . The door opened.

'I thought I heard someone. Come in, Powell, come in.'

Straightening her back, Bethan walked in. The office was warm and cramped, its painted walls running with condensation between the book-lined shelves.

'Sit down.'

Two upright chairs were set in front of the desk. Bethan took the one nearest the fire. A few moments later she regretted her choice. This fire, unlike every other in the hospital, burned with a resolute, radiant cheerfulness that scorched her legs.

'Right, Powell, let's see what we have here.' Matron eased her bulk into the comfortable, padded chair behind her desk and thumbed methodically through the pile of papers before her, leaving Bethan free to study the room and fall prey to every spectre of failure that rose from the depths of her imagination.

Alice George was far too intimidating a figure to acquire a nickname. No one in the hospital from the ward maids and porters to the senior doctors referred to her as anything other than 'Matron'. She ran the wards and supervised her sisters with a rod of iron that was as even-handed and fair as it was inflexible. Rules were her lifeblood. It was rumoured that she'd been seen reciting hospital regulations during a service in St John's church instead of the Lord's Prayer, and no one, least of all Bethan, had thought to question the story's veracity.

The unkind described Matron as fat; the kind, plump. She was a short, dark woman, with beady black eyes that overlooked nothing. Every speck of dust in awkward corners and every trivial misdemeanour committed by probationers and domestics came under her scrutiny. Laura had been called up before her more times than she cared to remember. Bethan, with her more careful ways and healthier respect for authority, had never been in her office before now.

'You know why I sent for you, Powell?'

Bethan slid nervously forward to the edge of her chair.

'The results of my final nursing examination?' she enquired hopefully.

Matron smiled in an attempt to lighten the atmosphere, but the gesture was wasted on Bethan.

'You've passed, Powell. With distinction. Your name came top of your year.'

Bethan slumped in her chair. She'd passed. She'd really passed!

'I've recommended you for midwifery training.'

'Pardon, Matron?'

'I've recommended you for midwifery training. It means another full year's study, and I warn you now, the examination for the midwifery certificate is not an easy one. But there's a shortage of good midwives, and I believe you have the makings of a very good one indeed. Afterwards, may I suggest, you complete the six months' public health course. That will qualify you to work as a health visitor. God only knows,' Matron added irreverently, 'there's an even greater shortage of those, particularly in this area.'

'The midwifery certificate.' As the words sank in so did their significance. Another full year on Squeers' ward.

'I know another year of study is an unappealing prospect, Nurse Powell' – 'Nurse Powell.' Someone in authority, someone other than the patients had actually said it – 'But you will be on full pay while you train. Thirty-five shillings a week and a further five shillings when you qualify. You don't have to make your decision now.' Matron rose majestically and walked out from behind her desk. 'Think it over, and when you come to a decision make an appointment to see me. But remember,' she cautioned, 'you haven't much time. The list of candidates has to be in by the end of the month. Should your decision be a positive one, the board would want to offer you a contract. One year initially.'

'Yes, Matron. Thank you very much, Matron.' Bethan struggled to regain her composure.

'Is there anything you want to ask me?' Matron enquired.

'I can't think of anything. Thank you.' Bethan fumbled her way to the door. If she trained as a midwife, the board would offer her a contract. On Squeers' ward! But if she passed, it would mean two pounds a week. Two pounds!

She turned back as she reached the door.

'I don't need to think it over, Matron,' she said quietly. 'I'd like to put my name down for the course.'

'Good,' Matron beamed in approbation. 'It will be hard. Studying as well as working full time. But I think you'll find it rewarding, and you've already proved that you have the aptitude. When you return to your ward ask Ronconi to come here.'

Dismissed, Bethan returned to the ward at a much slower pace than she'd left it. She walked round a squad of young men sweeping the outside paths, without really seeing them. Stepping over two unmarrieds who were scrubbing the corridor, she pushed open the double doors and entered the nursery where the babies were beginning to whimper. The twelve o'clock feeding

41

time was still three-quarters of an hour away. It was just as well that the ward was virtually soundproof; another half an hour and the din would be unbearable.

'Sister said would you please go to the delivery room the moment you get in,' one of the ward maids ventured shyly as Bethan passed the table where the babies were changed. Bethan tickled the squalling baby in the maid's hands, before moving on. Laura was taking the mothers' temperatures.

'I'll finish that,' Bethan offered, washing her hands at one of the sinks. 'Matron wants to see you.'

'I'll have to finish it,' Laura moaned, 'you're wanted in the delivery room. Well?' she demanded.

'I've passed.'

'Knew you would,' Laura crowed. 'Go on, you'd better get into the delivery room before Sister has your guts for garters.'

'I'll take over, Ronconi,' Staff Nurse Evans offered as she came into the ward from her tea break. 'Congratulations, Nurse Powell, I heard about your distinction. Top of the year isn't bad,' she winked.

'Typical,' Laura griped with a grin on her face. 'Leaving nothing for the rest of us to do.'

'Going to study for your midwifery?' Nurse Evans asked.

'Yes,' Bethan stammered. 'Yes I think so.'

'You won't catch me doing any more studying,' Laura said emphatically.

'You haven't been offered the chance yet,' Nurse Evans laughed. 'Go on off with you, Ronconi, you too, Nurse Powell.'

Laura suddenly realised that she was on the brink of moving up from the ranks of the unqualified. She was leaving the ward as Ronconi, but she could return as Nurse. It felt good, very good indeed.

'You'd best gown and mask up before you go into the delivery room,' Nurse Evans warned Bethan. 'Looks like a difficult one.'

When Bethan finally entered, she found Sister Church, Nurse Williams, the other staff nurse on the ward, and a doctor huddled around the bed.

'Powell, at last.' Sister glared at Bethan above her mask.

'Sorry, Sister, I was with Matron.'

'So I've been given to understand. Well, if you'd be kind enough to assist Doctor John and Nurse Williams here, I can get on with my other duties.'

Bethan took Sister's place alongside the bed. Maisie was lying on her back, her eyes rolling in agony, and even Bethan's comparatively inexperienced eye could see that something was seriously wrong.

'Chloroform, Nurse Williams,' Dr John ordered.

His voice didn't sound right to Bethan. She looked at his eyes, all that could be seen above the mask, and he nodded to her. 'Nice to be working with you, Nurse Powell.'

Flustered, she looked away. One of the first lessons she'd learnt was that doctors *never* talked to nurses. They were incomparably above and beyond the nursing staff in every hospital hierarchy. Besides, this Dr John was most definitely not the Dr John she knew. This Dr John was taller, broader and, judging by his voice, a good deal younger than the tall, thin, grey-haired man who visited the ward three mornings a week and sent Dr Lewis out on his emergencies.

Uncertain whether to reply or not she looked down at the bed, where Maisie had caught hold of her hand.

'Bethan, is that you?' Maisie squeezed her hand forcefully.

'You know the patient, Nurse?' The doctor's voice was soft, carefully modulated for a sickroom.

'We were at school together,' Maisie gasped.

'Old friends are the best, Maisie. That was quick, Nurse Williams,' he said pleasantly as she returned with the chloroform mask and bottle. 'Right, Maisie, we're going to put you to sleep for a little while, and when you wake up the pain will have gone. Keep hold of Nurse Powell's hand . . . '

'Bethan,' Maisie pleaded plaintively.

'Right, Bethan's hand.' His eyes wrinkled in amusement.

'Congratulations, Nurse Powell.' Nurse Williams clamped the mask over Maisie's face. 'Top of the year and a distinction, I hear.'

Bethan mumbled a reply as the doctor prepared the chloroform drops. It would take her a while to get used to this camaraderie from the senior staff, particularly if compliments were going to be offered over patients' heads.

'Well done, Nurse Powell,' Dr John congratulated enthusiastically.

'I had no idea I was working with such nursing talent. Now, if you could take over from Nurse Williams and steady the mask with your free hand?'

'Yes, Doctor.' Bethan took the mask and pressed it gently over Maisie's nose. The girl's eyes rounded in fear.

'Don't worry, Maisie,' she murmured, 'you'll be fine. A few moments and it will all be over.'

Maisie clawed at the mask with her free hand. To Bethan's embarrassment the doctor placed his hand firmly over hers, then slowly, drop by drop, he poured the chloroform. Maisie's eyes clouded, and her hands fell limply on to the bed. Nurse Williams moved quickly. She hauled back the sheet and strapped Maisie's legs into the stirrups while the doctor scrubbed his hands and picked up the forceps.

'This is going to be tricky. I'd be grateful if you could try to hold the patient still.'

Bethan clamped her hands on Maisie's shoulders. She looked down and watched as the doctor extracted one tiny wrinkled leg, then another. An interminable wait followed, during which she found it difficult to breathe. The cap covering the doctor's forehead moistened with sweat despite the chill in the room. Maisie moaned, a low bestial cry, as he worked frantically to free the tiny body imprisoned within her. Then suddenly, without any further drama, he lifted his hands. In them was the small, waxy, silent white form of a baby.

'Nurse?' he demanded urgently.

Nurse Williams took the child, leaving him free to cut the cord. The moment he severed it, she forced her fingers into the baby's mouth, and held it upside down. Nothing! The doctor tore the gloves from his hands and held the child by the heels, hitting it lightly on the back with his free hand.

A thin, weak wail filled the room. Bethan breathed again. She'd assisted at too many stillbirths to take life for granted.

'It's a girl.' The doctor wrapped her gently in the coarse towel that Nurse Williams handed him. 'A little small, but all there,' he announced cheerfully.

'I'll take her to the nursery,' the staff nurse volunteered.

'And when you've deposited her there, have a well-earned rest. Nurse Powell and I can wrap up here.'

'Can you?' the staff nurse asked eagerly. She hadn't had a break since she'd entered the ward at six-thirty, and the thought of putting her feet up, even for ten minutes, seemed like heaven.

'Of course we can, and Nurse?'

'Yes, Doctor?' She hesitated in the doorway.

'Thank you for your help.'

The staff nurse positively purred at the unaccustomed praise. Slightly embarrassed, Bethan turned her attention to Maisie.

Dr John pulled down his mask. When Bethan glanced up, he was leaning against the wall, his head in his hands. He saw her looking at him and shook his head.

'I hate the touch-and-go ones,' he said drily. 'Six years as a medical student and I'm still not used to death.'

'Then you've only just qualified?' Bethan asked, without stopping to think that she was talking to a doctor.

'Last summer. This is my first job. I'm assisting my father.'

'Doctor John?' she blurted out.

'You've worked out the family connection?'

She tried, and failed, to think of a witty retort. She'd never been one for spontaneous repartee, not like Laura. Maisie moaned again, he moved over to the bed and checked her pulse.

'The lady's waking up. Let's hope there'll be no more complications.'

The next hour was a busy one, and Bethan learned that young Dr John was nothing if not thorough. He didn't leave the ward until Maisie regained consciousness, and she still had to wash, change and make Maisie as comfortable as a patient who has just given birth can be made. Even awake, the girl seemed to be in a stupor. Bethan chatted as she worked, telling her that she had a lovely little girl, and that she'd be seeing her soon, but she failed to elicit a response. Undeterred, she persisted in talking about the child.

'She's small but all right, and with care, she won't be small for long.'

'Am I going back to the unmarrieds ward?' Maisie whispered finally.

'Not just yet,' Bethan replied calmly. 'You'll be with us for at least ten days. I'll be passing your house tonight. Do you want me to call in —'

'No!'

That single word said everything. Bethan finished doing what she had to in silence. As soon as Maisie was ready for the ward, she called one of the maids and told her to summon a porter. By the time Maisie was safely bedded down in a side ward away from the 'respectable' married patients, it was three-thirty in the afternoon and Bethan was free to take her lunch break. She went to the ward kitchen, hoping to find fresh pies and pasties cadged from the Hopkin Morgan van that delivered to the main kitchen. She was disappointed. There was a quarter-full tray of stale iced buns and a pot of stewed tea. Nothing more. She couldn't do much about the buns but she drained the tea down the sink, tipped the leaves in the waste bucket and started again.

'Laura did well then?'

'She did?' Bethan looked up from the gas that she was trying to light, and saw Glan Richards, the ward porter, who also happened to be her next-door neighbour.

'She got a distinction. Of course she couldn't make it to top of the year like you . . . '

Bethan switched off the gas that was refusing to light, tore a piece off a bun and threw it at him. It hit his nose, fell into the open kettle and blossomed over the surface of the water.

'Now look what you've made me do,' she complained, emptying and rinsing out the kettle.

'What *I* made you do? You just wait until tonight.' He tried to grab her by the waist but, too quick for him, she ducked and moved away. 'You are going to the hospital ball aren't you?' he asked anxiously.

'Yes, but that doesn't mean I want to see you there,' she said tartly, sticking her tongue out at him.

Glan smiled, a winning smile that he practised in front of the mirror every night.

'Why fight me, Beth?' He put his hand on her shoulder. 'You know you can't resist me.'

She tried the gas again. This time it caught and she dropped the taper she was holding into the sink, but not before it singed the tips of her fingers.

'Resist you! Times like this I could quite cheerfully brain you,' she exclaimed feelingly, brushing his hand off her.

Glan's smile never wavered. He took her outburst in good humour. He was used to being put down by the nurses, especially Bethan whom he'd known since their mutual school days in Maesycoed Infants. Above medium height with well-developed muscles, brown curly hair and pleasant open features, he was fairly good-looking and proudly aware of the fact. He lived at home with his mother and his father, a bullying collier who tried to dominate every single aspect of his timid wife's and children's life, which was why Glan was the only one left at home. But even Mr Richards senior had failed to prevent Glan from growing a moustache and fancying himself as a second John Gilbert; a fantasy founded in a surfeit of Hollywood films viewed from the bug run in the White Palace.

'Come on, Beth,' Glan crooned in what he imagined to be a seductive manner. 'Walk home from the ball with me tonight and I'll show you the moon as you've never seen it before.'

'I'd rather give the ball a miss.'

'You can't miss the ball. Rumour has it you're going to be the guest of honour.'

'Laura!' Bethan reached past Glan and hugged her friend. 'Congratulations.'

'Of course I couldn't do as well as you . . . '

'No one could,' Glan echoed.

'Is that tea you're making, because if it is, I'll have a cup.' Laura pushed Glan aside and sat on one of the hard wooden chairs that were ranged opposite the sink. 'Qualified nurses can demand to be put on early tea,' she winked at Glan.

'I'm on late lunch,' Bethan griped.

'Poor you. Have you seen the new doctor?'

'I have,' Bethan concurred, her mouth full of stale bun.

'Isn't he wonderful?'

'If you like the smarmy kind.'

'Smarmy!' Laura exclaimed indignantly. 'Smarmy! Bethan, you're the limit. He looks like Ronald Colman and has the manners of the Prince of Wales.' The kettle boiled, and she tipped hot water into the teapot to warm it. 'He can carry me off any time he likes.'

'Who? Glan?' Nurse Williams asked innocently, walking into the kitchen.

47

'Nurse Ronconi is smitten by Doctor John,' Glan glowered indignantly, sticking rigidly to his position in the doorway in the hope of getting a fresh cup of tea.

'Young Doctor John?' Nurse Williams proceeded to lay out cups and saucers. 'Forget it, ladies. Remember hospital rules, no fraternisation between doctors and nurses. Besides, rumour has it he's spoken for. Anthea Llewellyn-Jones,' she divulged archly.

'Good. That leaves all the more for us porters,' Glan leered, lifting his eyebrows.

'All the more what?' Laura demanded testily.

'Good times,' he suggested mildly, retreating from the belligerent tone.

'Haven't you got work to do?' Nurse Williams enquired.

'I have.' He ducked out of the doorway.

'Exiled to tea in the boiler room,' Laura laughed.

'You're not serious about Doctor John are you?' Bethan asked Laura after Nurse Williams had made two cups of tea and taken them to Sister's office.

'Depends on what you mean by "serious". I love a challenge. Not that Anthea Llewellyn-Jones would be that. And then again I wouldn't mind going to the New Theatre with him, or a dance. Not the hospital dance of course, that's a bit public. But a Saturday hop in Porth or Treorchy out of sight of the gossips, not to mention my brothers, with an opportunity to cuddle up on the train on the way home, now that's a different proposition.' Her dark eyes sparkled with mischief. She loved winding Bethan up.

Bethan poured out their tea.

'If you're angling for Prince Charming, you'd better sort out a better golden coach than your brother's Trojan van for tonight.'

'That's the fairy godmother department.'

'If you ask me, Pontypridd's a little short on those.'

'Then I'll improvise. If that gold net that your aunt has fits, it'll do for a start. Just remember, Miss Top of the Year, I laid claim to him first.'

'You can have him.'

'Such generosity. In return I give you Glan.'

'You can't, you'll need him yourself.'

Laura looked quizzically at Bethan.

48

'According to the fairy story, Cinderella needs a rat to turn into a coachman.'

'And mice to turn into horses. Fancy coming to the boiler room with me?' Glan interrupted from the corridor.

'People who eavesdrop deserve to hear nasty things.' Bethan tipped the remainder of her tea down the sink.

'Two waltzes and you'll change your mind about that moonlight walk,' Glan whispered into her ear as she passed him.

'One outing with you will last me a lifetime, Glan Richards,' Bethan muttered over her shoulder, referring to a visit she'd made to the Park cinema in his company.

'We'll see,' Glan muttered darkly. 'We'll see.'

Chapter Three

Darkness falls early on the Graig hill in winter. By the time Laura and Bethan left the hospital at seven, the street lamps had been lit for hours, throwing yellow smudges of light into an atmosphere filled with needle-sharp darts of rain, and on to roads spattered with glistening pools of black water.

'It's freezing,' Laura complained, pulling her cloak tightly around her shoulders.

'No it isn't,' Bethan contradicted. 'If it was this would be hail not rain.'

'Always have to be so literal, don't you?'

'Now that's a big word.'

'It comes from having a brother who's taking his matriculation next year.'

'Tony?'

'Who else?' Heads down, they ran out of the gates and walked up High Street as fast as they could. 'Papa thinks he's going to be a priest, but Papa's going to be disappointed. Tony follows Ronnie. He likes the ladies too much.'

'At sixteen?'

'You're never too young.'

'Our Eddie's sixteen, and all he can think about is boxing.'

'That's what he tells you. Evening, Mr Smart, off to buy sweets then?' Laura asked cheerily.

'Terrible craving to have, and by the way, congratulations, Nurse Ronconi, Nurse Powell.' He tipped his hat to them as he entered Davies' shop, the busiest sweet shop on the Graig. There were large cracks between the floorboards in front of the counter, filed wide enough to drop betting slips down to the bookie's runner who waited in the basement to catch them. Bethan knew that both her brothers worked there whenever they could. Haydn told her they couldn't afford not to, it was too well paid. Five shillings for a day's easy work. But ever since she'd found out what they'd been doing to boost their contribution to the family kitty, she'd lived in terror of a knock on the door. The police picked up the bookie's runners in turn, and she'd read in the Pontypridd *Observer* only last week that one had been fined ten pounds with an alternative of six weeks inside. If it had been Haydn or Eddie, it would have had to be prison. There was no way they could raise that kind of money without getting into debt, and Elizabeth wouldn't stand for that.

'Congratulations, Bethan, Laura.' A young girl dressed in a thin cotton frock totally unsuitable for the time of year spoke shyly to them as she lugged a basket of potatoes out of the greengrocer's.

'Here, Judith, let me help with that.' Bethan hooked her fingers around the handle.

'And what do you mean by "congratulations"?' Laura asked.

'Glan told Mam that you both passed your examinations and that you,' she pointed a grubby finger at Bethan, 'passed as high as you can go.'

'He did, did he?' Bethan murmured.

'Thank you, Glan,' Laura said warmly. 'What's the betting that we've nothing to tell our families when we get home.'

'Everyone's ever so proud of you.' Judith tried to pull the shrunken cardigan she was wearing higher round her neck. 'Mam said if I work hard in school, I could be a nurse.'

'I bet you'd make a good one too.' Bethan released her hold on the basket as they approached the junction of High and Graig Street. 'Mind how you go now.'

'Thanks, Bethan, I will.'

Cold and wet, they left the gleaming shop windows of High Street behind them and began the long climb up the hill. The street was busy with shoppers. Women or errand-running children, spending the pennies or, if they were lucky, shillings, that their menfolk had scavenged during the day. The less fortunate among them putting a small piece of boiling bacon or a slice of brawn 'on the slate' until dole or pay-day. Every shopkeeper on the Graig had a book that in theory was worth at least twice his weekly takings.

A few men, caps pulled low, collars high, sidled out of the pubs. As they passed the Morning Star Bethan glanced in and saw their lodger Alun Jones sitting in the corner with a red-haired, blowzy-looking woman.

'That will be one less mouth for your mam to feed tonight,' Laura commented. They crossed the road, chilled to the bone, scarcely able to breathe through the cutting, driving rain as they turned up the narrow gully that led into the middle of Leyshon Street. Bethan tapped Megan's door and turned the key, shouting as she walked through. William, Megan's eighteen-year-old son, poked his head out of the kitchen door.

'Nice line in drowned rats you've brought with you, Beth.'

'Less of your cheek,' Bethan warned. She was as fond of William as she was of her own brothers. Tall, dark and handsome like Evan, the similarity between him and his uncle had often caused comment, but only among those who couldn't remember his father.

'Look out, Mam,' he called to Megan. 'Mermaids coming.'

'Get on with you, Will.' Megan pushed him aside as she bustled to the door. 'You poor creatures, come in, sit yourselves down next to the fire, and have a good warm.' She moved a pile of clothes off one chair and the cat off the other. Bethan and Laura felt as though a furnace door had opened in front of them. Hot and humid, the damp cooking and washing smells of the kitchen closed around them like a scalding wet blanket. A pan of stew was bubbling on the range, and an appetising aroma of lamb and vegetables wafted above the other odours. Bethan sniffed the air appreciatively; she hadn't realised how hungry she was.

'Here, take off those wet things and have some tea with us,' Megan ordered.

'We'd love to, Auntie Megan,' Bethan said quickly, 'but we daren't. They'll be waiting for us at home.'

'You had your results then.' Megan crossed her arms over her overall breast pocket and beamed. 'Two distinctions, I hear.' She was too tactful to mention she'd also heard that Bethan had come top of the year, but her pride in her niece's achievements shone in her eyes.

'Congratulations, Bethan, Laura.' They both turned around and saw Hetty Bull sitting perched in the corner on a kitchen chair.

'Aunt Hetty, I'm sorry I didn't see you there,' Bethan apologised. 'How are you?'

'Fine,' Hetty said automatically with a small, shy smile. 'Your uncle will be so pleased for you.'

'She came out best in the year,' Laura said, pointing a wet thumb at Bethan.

'I knew you'd pass. I just knew it.' Megan brushed a tear from her eyes and hugged her niece. 'I only wish Mam Powell was here to see it.'

'Knowing didn't stop her from paying a fortune teller to make sure,' William interrupted. 'Congratulations, girl. I always knew you'd come for something.'

'And me?' Laura flirted provocatively.

'I'll try to stay well, and out of the Graig Hospital.'

'Can I hit him, Mrs Powell?'

'Be my guest, but it doesn't do any good.' Megan released Bethan, dried her tears, and opened a suitcase half hidden behind one of the chairs. 'Here, as you're pushed for time you can pick what you want out of these.' She lifted a couple of large flat cardboard boxes on to the table. 'And while you're looking I'll get your skirt, Hetty, and the dresses I promised the girls from upstairs.'

'How much are these?' Laura held up a box of powder.

'Large boxes ninepence, small sixpence, all the lipsticks are fourpence. The small bottles of Evening in Paris are sixpence, the large ninepence. The bottles of essence of violets are ninepence, but they're really big.'

'I don't know how you do it, Mrs Powell,' Laura commented as she opened the lid of the largest box.

'Special prices?' Bethan raised her eyebrows.

'I won't deny that I don't make as much profit out of you two as I do out of some of my customers, but I do well enough,' Megan said as she left the room.

'First time I've heard customers complain that the goods are too cheap.' William took a wide-rimmed, thick white china bowl out of the cupboard and helped himself to a generous portion of stew from the pan. 'Sure you won't have some?' He offered the bowl to Hetty, who retreated even further into her shell.

'That's very generous William, thank you. But I must go and

53

make the minister's tea. I have it here.' She patted a bag that contained half a pound of best sliced ham for him and a small portion of salted dripping for her.

'Have you seen Haydn?' Bethan asked, remembering the overcoat she'd asked him to buy for Eddie.

'Yes,' William said mysteriously. He set the bowl on the table, took a spoon from the drawer and sat down. Dipping the spoon into the stew, he lifted it slowly to his lips and blew on it.

'And?' Bethan demanded.

'He looked very well.'

'William!'

'Is he teasing you again?' Megan burst through the door, her arms full of dresses.

'Need you ask?' Bethan retorted.

'Not when you call him William. He's just like his father was. Infuriating.' A momentary fondness flickered in her eyes. 'Here, Hetty, this is yours. Mrs Morris took it in a good four inches at the waist. She said it's the smallest waist she's ever sewed for, and it's about time you put on a few pounds.'

'I've always been the same size, Megan,' Hetty said mildly. 'And thank you for arranging this. How much do I owe you?'

'Nothing, love, Mrs Morris said it only took her a few minutes to do.'

'Oh I couldn't . . . '

'Course you could.'

'Well thank her very much. And tell her if there's anything I can do for her she only has to ask. Well I must be on my way, the minister will be wanting his tea straight after the deacons' meeting and I mustn't keep him waiting.'

'See you soon, love. William, see Mrs Bull out.'

'Here we go.' William took Hetty's parcels and carried them to the front door for her. They looked slightly ridiculous, the small mousy woman trailing behind the tall strapping young man.

'I'll never understand why Hetty always refers to John Joseph as "the minister",' Megan said when she heard the door close. 'Do you think she calls him that when they're alone together?'

'Even in bed I should think,' Laura said wickedly.

'Poor woman probably sleeps at his feet,' William added as he returned to his stew.

54

'That's quite enough, William. Laura, this is the gold net.'

Laura dropped the lipstick she was holding back into the box. 'Oh Mrs Powell, it's lovely. Really lovely.' She fingered the layers of net, pulling them back to inspect the underskirt of cream satin. 'I've never seen anything like this on the ten-bob rail in Leslie's.'

'And you won't.' Megan dumped the rest of her load on one of the armchairs. 'It's from my special stock, and it's only seven and six.'

'Really! It's absolutely gorgeous. It simply *has* to fit. Can I try it on?'

'William,' Megan turned to her son, who was sitting engrossed in his meal, 'out.'

'Mam, it's freezing in the passage,' he complained.

'And these poor girls have just walked up the hill in the pouring rain. They need a warm more than you. Out.'

'Mam!' Even as he protested, William picked up his plate and spoon and left his chair.

'The stew will keep you warm,' Megan consoled soothingly.

'It'll freeze out there.'

'I don't mind changing in the washhouse, Mrs Powell,' Laura offered.

'You'll do no such thing, my girl.'

Laura had her cloak and dress off the moment William closed the door.

'This is for you, bach.' Megan opened a thin, flattish box. A mass of flame-coloured silk burst out. 'A present,' she said proudly. 'From all of us to a clever girl.'

'Auntie, I couldn't possibly . . . '

'Yes you could. Come on now, let's see it on you.'

It fitted Bethan to perfection. A long, low waistline skimmed her narrow waist and slim hips, flaring out into a flowing, floor-length skirt that swirled elegantly around her legs. The sleeves were short and full, cut on the same bias as the skirt. She walked up to the sideboard and stooped to peer at herself in the oval mirror that hung above it. The neckline was low, lower than anything she'd ever worn before judging by the three inches of woollen vest that protruded above it.

'Oh Beth, it looks perfect on you,' Laura cried. 'You can wear it with your black crocheted shawl. You know, the one your grandmother left you.'

'Here, you can't see yourself like that. Look at yourself properly.' Megan lifted the mirror from the wall, and held it sideways, tilting it, so Bethan had a full-length view. The dress was truly stunning. Even the soaking wet veil that covered her hair and the heavily ribbed lines of her bulky underwear couldn't destroy its impact.

'Please Auntie Megan, let me buy it off you?' she pleaded.

'You won't take a present from me, now?'

'Of course I will. But not this. It must have cost a fortune.'

'I'll get William to put in an extra shift,' Megan winked.

'Auntie . . . '

'It's from all of us, for passing.' There was a tone in Megan's voice that Bethan knew from past experience wouldn't brook further argument.

'Thank you. Very much,' she said quietly.

'And don't go hugging me.' Megan pushed her away, 'At least, not until you put the dress back in its box. Don't you know silk creases, you silly girl?'

'When you've finished admiring yourself, perhaps you'd care to pass judgement on me.' Laura stood in the only clear space in the room, behind the table and in front of the tiny window that overlooked the back yard.

'You sparkle like one of those glittering angels you get in Woolworth's to go on the Christmas tree,' Megan smiled.

'You look beautiful,' Bethan complimented sincerely.

'Only beautiful?' Laura complained. 'I was hoping for sensational.'

'You won't get that wearing those shoes and stockings,' Megan laughed, 'but it does fit well. The colour suits you. Brings out your complexion nicely.'

'I'll take it, Mrs Powell, and these two lipsticks, the large powder and the Evening in Paris scent.' She pulled a ten-shilling note out of her purse and put it on the table. Megan took down a tin emblazoned with Lord Kitchener's portrait from the mantelpiece, pushed in the note and counted out four pennies.

'Thank you, Mrs Powell.'

'Don't mention it, love.' Megan turned to Bethan. 'You've got the silk underwear I gave you for Christmas?'

'Yes, I've been saving it for tonight.'

'Good girl, and here's two pairs of silk stockings, one for each of you. My present and no argument.'

'Can I come back in?' William pleaded pathetically from the other side of the door.

'In a minute,' Laura shouted, as she and Bethan shed their finery and struggled back into their damp uniforms.

'If you want to dress here tonight, you can,' Megan whispered to Bethan as she opened the kitchen door.

'Nurse Powell, Nurse Ronconi.' Charlie, Megan's latest lodger, was standing in the passageway hanging up his working coat. William, soup bowl in hand, retreated up the stairs to make room for the women to walk out of the kitchen.

'They really are nurses now, Charlie,' he called out. 'They qualified. With distinctions,' he added emphatically in a singsong tone.

'My very good wishes,' Charlie said solemnly in his thickly accented voice as he shook the rain from his white-blond hair.

'Thank you,' Bethan replied stiffly.

'Your tea's all ready in the kitchen, Charlie.'

'Thank you, Mrs Powell. I'll wash before I eat.'

Bethan and Laura followed William's example and stepped up on to the stairs to allow Charlie to pass.

Light-footed and athletic, Charlie gave the impression of being much larger than he actually was. William, at six feet three inches, was a good five inches taller, but Charlie was much broader, his square-shaped body thickly roped with well-developed muscles. He had lodged with Megan for only two months, sharing the front parlour with Sam the negro miner who'd boarded with her for over thirteen years. Unusually for the Graig where everyone knew all there was to know about everyone else, no one knew anything other than what was obvious about Charlie; not even Sam who'd introduced him into the house after meeting him at a party in Bute Street, Cardiff docks.

Charlie had sailed into Cardiff on board an Argentinian meat ship. On the strength of that experience he'd talked himself into a job with a wholesale butcher who supplied the traders on

Cardiff market. Deciding to expand his business into retail and anxious not to offend his existing customers, the butcher rented a stall on Pontypridd market and offered Charlie the chance to run it on a commission basis. If Charlie was pleased at the trust his employer was placing in him, he didn't show it. He accepted the job in the same flat, unemotional way that he accepted everything life threw at him. First he found his stall, then he set about looking for lodgings in Pontypridd.

Those who worked alongside him on the market said he was as strong as an ox and could just about carry a dead one on his back. He helped anyone who wanted a hand with lifting heavy weights or setting up a stall, but beyond those bare facts, his life remained a mystery. No one even knew his first name. Megan and Sam had heard it and said that it was Russian and unpronounceable; after a few futile attempts they simply gave up trying, and when Wilf Horton on the second-hand clothes stall christened him Charlie, the name stuck. Despite his size, pale complexion and white hair, which was unusual in the Valleys, he had an uncanny ability to melt into the crowd.

Rarely speaking unless spoken to, and then never beyond the usual pleasantries, he lived on the fringe of Pontypridd life. The best that could be said about him was that no one had a word to say against him, the worst, that no one had a word to say about him at all. Megan, William and Diana, used to strangers living in their home, took to him at once, simply because he was quiet, clean and helped around the house without being asked. Bethan, for no reason that she could put into words, was afraid of him. Whether it was the nature of his job, or what she saw as an unnaturally cold expression in his pale blue eyes, prickles of fear crawled down her back every time she found herself in the same room as him.

She'd voiced her misgivings about Charlie to Megan and William but they'd laughed at her, especially William who, much to her embarrassment, had taken great delight in telling Charlie what she'd said. She drew little consolation from the Russian's continued distant politeness. It was enough that he knew what she thought. And that knowledge brought a blush to her cheeks whenever she found herself in his company.

*

Kissing Megan goodbye and shielding their new acquisitions under their cloaks, Bethan and Laura left Leyshon Street and cut up Walter's Road, past Danygraig Street, to Phillips Street. Although the backs of the houses in Phillips Street faced Graig Avenue there was no thoroughfare between the two roads. But there was Rhiannon Pugh.

Bethan and Laura climbed the steps of the first house in Phillips Street, knocked on the door, turned the key and walked into the passage.

'It's all right, Mrs Pugh, don't disturb yourself, it's only us,' Bethan called out.

Mrs Pugh hobbled to her kitchen door and opened it.

'Come in, come in.' Her broad smile of welcome was like winter sunshine touching a withered landscape. 'Nice to see you, girls. I've got the kettle on, all ready.'

'Sorry, Mrs Pugh, no time for tea today, we've got to get dressed for the hospital ball, but we'll have two cups tomorrow to make up for it,' Laura apologised.

'Heard that you both passed your examinations with flying colours,' the old lady smiled. 'Good for you.'

'They're so short of nurses they couldn't do anything but give us our certificates,' Laura joked as she led the way into the kitchen. 'Mm, fresh Welsh cakes, they smell delicious.'

'I baked them specially for you two. Our Albert used to love Welsh cakes.'

'In that case we'll make time to eat one,' Bethan said.

Rhiannon Pugh was a widow. Her only son Albert had been killed in the same pit accident that took her husband. Alone in the world, she was happy to allow her friends and neighbours to use her house as a thoroughfare between the three terraces of Leyshon Street, Danygraig Street, Phillips Street and Graig Avenue. Universal concern for the old lady's welfare meant that the short cut was put to frequent use.

Mrs Pugh took two garish blue and yellow plates from the dresser, and laid a couple of Welsh cakes on each.

'Here you are, girls, pull the chairs close to the range, it's cold outside.'

'And wet,' Laura complained, watching the steam rise from her damp cloak. She took the plate from Rhiannon's shaking

59

hand and bit into one of the thick flat cakes. 'These are good,' she mumbled, her mouth full. 'You really must give our Ronnie the recipe for them.'

'The secret's in the kneading,' Rhiannon winked. 'I keep telling him that. The kneading. But mind, you need a good griddle iron. And then you've got to watch them.'

'You certainly do that, they're a lovely colour,' Bethan agreed.

'When you see your brother, Laura, thank him for the meat pie he sent up with Mrs Morris from the Avenue. I had it for my tea. Don't forget now.'

'I won't forget.' Laura popped the last piece of cake into her mouth.

'And you, thank your Haydn for the potatoes he brought me this afternoon, Bethan. He said Mr Ashgrove gave him more than your mother could use when he delivered for him this morning.'

'I'll do that.' Bethan followed Laura's example and swallowed the last of her cake. 'Thank you for the Welsh cakes, Mrs Pugh. See you tomorrow. Don't come out now, we'll close the door.'

'I will stay here if you don't mind, love. This damp doesn't help my rheumatism one little bit. See you tomorrow?'

'Same time. Bye.'

Laura and Bethan carried their dishes out to the washhouse and put them in the enamel bowl in the sink. They left, latching the door securely behind them. They weren't worried about the washing-up they'd created. Mrs Pugh had a lodger, Phyllis Harry, who worked as an usherette in the White Palace. She'd been engaged to Albert, Mrs Pugh's son and, more like a daughter than a lodger, she moved in after Albert's death and took care of whatever Mrs Pugh couldn't. And for Rhiannon Pugh's sake, she welcomed the neighbours who treated the house as a thoroughfare.

It was very dark in the garden, and Bethan and Laura fumbled their way up the steps. Graig Avenue seemed positively floodlit when they finally emerged opposite Bethan's house.

'Our Ronnie will take us down at half-past eight. We'll pick you up here to save you dirtying your shoes.'

'That gives me barely half an hour to have tea, wash, dress and do my hair,' Bethan complained.

'You don't need to do a great deal to yourself besides wear that dress. Sixpence says that Glan asks you for first dance.'

'He can ask all he likes,' Bethan laughed.

She ran across the road and up the steps. Opening the door, she shook out her cape and hung it up. She was depositing the box containing her precious dress and stockings on the floor of the front parlour when her father called out.

'That you, Beth love?'

'It is.' She made her way to the kitchen. It was warm and humid just like Megan's and Mrs Pugh's. The table was laid, and a pile of the same type of thick earthenware soup bowls that William had used were warming next to a simmering pan of faggots and mushy peas on the range.

'Heard you passed.' Her father waylaid her and gave her a hug. 'Clever girl.'

'Aren't I just?' She kissed his cheek.

'Knew you'd do it.' Her brother Eddie came up from behind and tapped her across the bottom.

'Taa . . . raaa . . . ' Maud walked in from the pantry, bearing a rather lopsided sponge cake bedecked with a thick coating of icing sugar and blazing candles.

'Stuff and nonsense,' Elizabeth said tersely, irritated by the fuss the family was making of Bethan's results. She recalled the time when she'd gained a teaching certificate with distinction and received no more than a passing 'You did what was expected of you, Elizabeth' from her parents. 'And who told you that you could waste candles, Maud Powell, when it's no one's birthday? Do you think money grows on trees?'

'It's my birthday next and I'll do without them on my cake,' Maud said, almost in tears.

'It's not every day our daughter passes her examinations, with distinction,' Evan interposed.

'And comes top of her year,' Maud added proudly.

'There's plenty of others that have done as well,' Elizabeth commented coldly. 'And I'm sure their families aren't losing their heads over it.'

Without looking at one another, or Elizabeth, everyone tacitly ignored her contribution to the conversation. Time and constant exposure had made the entire family, with the exception of Maud,

61

immune to all but her bitterest pronouncements. And Maud was learning.

'Glan has a lot to answer for,' Bethan said after she ceremoniously blew out the candles.

'Next door's Glan?' her father asked.

'He sneaked out lunch time to buy cigarettes and gave Mrs Lewis in the newsagent's our results. By the time we left the hospital it was over the whole of the Graig. Even Mrs Pugh knew. We've been congratulated all the way up the hill.'

'You deserve it, love,' her father smiled proudly. 'Hospital ball tonight?'

'Yes, Ronnie's taking us down in his van.'

'When will he be here?' Maud asked.

'Half-past eight.'

'It's five-past now. You'd better get your skates on.'

'Not before she's eaten a proper meal,' Elizabeth said sharply, spooning two faggots and a ladleful of peas on to the top plate.

It wasn't until they sat at the table that Bethan realised that not only the lodger but also Haydn was missing. Her father saw her glance at her brother's empty chair.

'Haydn was mad when he realised he'd miss you tonight, but he brought good news home before we heard yours today.'

'What?' Bethan asked hopefully, thinking of the coat she'd asked him to buy.

'He's got a job. Full time. Twelve and six a week,' Eddie said a little wistfully.

'Where?' Bethan asked excitedly.

'Town Hall,' Elizabeth snapped. 'Low wages, and unchristian hours. The Lord only knows what kind of people he'll come up against there. Working every evening except Sunday if you please. Four until midnight.'

'It's permanent, Elizabeth, and a start for the boy,' Evan interposed.

'A start in what, that's what I'd like to know?' She slapped a plate on the table in front of Evan, splashing mushy peas over his shirt front.

'He's stagehand and callboy, and helps out at the box office,' Eddie whispered to Bethan.

'Twelve and six a week is no wage for a nineteen-year-old boy,' Elizabeth railed bitterly.

'It's a wage that plenty round here would like to have.' There was a note in Evan's voice that quietened Elizabeth. She continued to dish out faggots and peas in a tight-lipped martyred silence. She'd had her say, made everyone uncomfortable, but that was as far as it would go. She'd always balked at out-and-out argument, because she thought scenes 'vulgar'; the kind of thing only the uneducated, unrefined working classes indulged in.

Her reticence infuriated Evan. He'd grown up with parents who'd made a point of frequently 'clearing the air'. They'd also periodically cleared the dresser of plates, and broken the odd window pane or two, but they'd never failed to kiss and make up before bedtime, and Evan was conscious that his own marriage lacked the passion that had characterised his parents' relationship. Loving or hating, at least they'd felt something for one another. The only things left between him and Elizabeth were the children they had made, and mutual irritation. But twenty-one years of marriage had taught him how to handle his wife, including how to utilise her fear of open discord to gain silence when he could no longer bear the sound of her carping.

Rhiannon's Welsh cakes had taken the edge off Bethan's appetite, but she forced herself to eat, finishing the faggots and peas in less than five minutes.

'I have to get ready,' she said, rising from her chair.

'Can I help you?' Maud pleaded.

'You sit down and eat your meal, young lady,' Elizabeth commanded.

Bethan filled a jug with hot water from the boiler as Maud spooned up the last of the mess from her plate.

'Now can I go?' she pleaded.

'You may, though I don't know why I bother to cook a decent meal when all you do is wolf your food and run. When I was a girl, my family made a point of conversing with one another at the table.'

Elizabeth almost smiled at the memory of her childhood. When she wasn't consoling herself with thoughts of her teaching days, which time and nostalgia had endowed with a rosy hue that had little basis in reality, she sought comfort in inaccurate memories

63

of her upbringing in the parsimonious home of her minister father.

Haydn Bull had, unfortunately for the emotional well-being of his daughter, disregarded the actual situation of his house, flock and purse, and elevated himself to the ranks of the middle classes. Apart from the Leyshons who owned the brewery and lived in Danygraig House, the bleak, grey stone villa set in its own grounds below Graig Avenue, there had been no middle-class families on the Graig. And there was only a handful in Pontypridd to challenge his belief in his change of station. The only tangible result of his adopted airs and graces was the further isolation of his family from the community, and a dwindling congregation in his chapel, which had pleased the Methodists if not the chapel elders.

Evan glanced despairingly at Elizabeth before leaving the table for his chair, which was to the right of the range facing the window. He delved under the cushion at his back and produced a copy of Gogol's *Dead Souls* which he'd borrowed from the Central Library. Eddie finished his meal and carried the dishes through to the washhouse. Maud refilled the boiler, and Bethan left the room, stopping to pick up the box from the front parlour as she went upstairs.

She switched the bedroom light on with her nose, set the jug down on the washstand and threw the box on to the bed, before walking over to the window to close the curtains. The rings grated uneasily over the rusting rod as she shut out the darkness. Facing the wardrobe mirror she tore the veil from her head and looked in dismay at her hair. It clung, limp and lifeless, to her head, as straight as a drowned cat's tail. Grabbing the towel she rubbed it mercilessly between the rough ends of cloth until it frizzed out in an unbecoming halo.

'Here, let me do that.' Maud closed the door behind her and took the towel from Bethan's hands.

'I haven't got time to set it.'

'Yes you have.' Maud leaned over and opened one of the small drawers built around the dressing-table mirror. She took out a dozen viciously clipped metal wavers. Combing Bethan's hair, she marked a parting and fingered a series of waves, crimping them firmly into the metal teeth.

'That's the two sides done –' she surveyed her handiwork critically – 'and there's six left for the back. You could tie a scarf over your head and leave them in until you get to the Coro,' she suggested, referring to the Coronation ballroom, where the hospital ball was being held.

'I could,' Bethan agreed doubtfully. 'But where would I put them? I can hardly cram them into my evening bag.'

'Leave them in Ronnie's van and pick them up on the way back. Mind you do. I need them for Saturday.'

'Going to Ronconis' café with the girls?' Bethan raised her eyebrows.

'And the boys,' Maud replied disarmingly. 'Right, that's your hair finished.'

Bethan leapt up from the dressing-table stool, and tried to unbutton her uniform dress and tip water into the bowl at the same time.

'Shall I get your ringed velvet out of the wardrobe for you?'

'No.' Bethan nodded towards the bed.

'Someone's been to Auntie Megan's,' Maud sang out, lifting the top off the box. She stared at the dress. 'Bethan, it's tremendous. Oooh, it's real silk . . . '

'Be an angel and get the underwear Auntie Megan gave me for Christmas. It's the top drawer of the dressing table. And the essence of violets Eddie gave me, the powder and lipstick you gave me.'

'What did this cost?' Maud probed tactlessly, holding the dress up in front of her and swaying before the wardrobe mirror.

'It was a present. For passing my exams.'

'You lucky duck. I'll never be clever enough to try, let alone pass anything. What are you going to wear on top? Surely not your old black coat?'

'Mam Powell's shawl, and the only coat I possess.'

'It would look better with furs.'

'Anything would look better with furs. I must ask Haydn to borrow Glan's gun and go up the mountain and shoot something. Mind you, it will take an awful lot of rats to make a coat.'

'When I'm old enough to go to balls I'm going to have furs,' Maud pronounced decisively, laying Bethan's dress on the bed.

'The underclothes?' Bethan reminded.

She finished washing, picked up a bowl of talcum powder from the dressing table and puffed it liberally over herself, then looked down. She was standing in a puddle of white dust.

'Don't worry. I'll wipe it up before Mam sees it,' Maud offered.

'You won't forget?'

'Promise.' Maud extricated the underwear and scent. Picking up Bethan's jewellery box she lay down on the bed next to the dress and rummaged through the trinkets. Bethan slipped on the silk underwear. Checking the seams in the mirror, she rolled and clipped on the stockings Megan had given her, then sat in front of the dressing table. She dabbed a little rouge high on her cheekbones, face powder on her nose, combed Vaseline on to her eyelashes, pencilled over her heavily plucked eyebrows and liberally coated her lips with 'flame-red' Hollywood stick, 'as worn by the stars'.

'Scent,' Maud prompted.

Bethan dabbed scent behind her ears, on her throat, hair and in the crooks of her elbows and knees. Then, on hands and knees, she scrabbled in the bottom of the wardrobe she shared with Maud. After throwing out two worn pairs of plimsolls and a pair of rubber boots, she finally came up with the black patent strapped sandals she wanted. As soon as she buckled them on she picked up the dress. Holding it carefully she slid it over her head and Maud buttoned up the back.

'What jewellery?' Maud asked.

'The black glass necklace and earrings Haydn gave me for my birthday. They'll match the shawl.'

'You don't want to wear the Bakelite piggy I gave you?'

Bethan looked hard at her sister. Maud had a peculiar sense of humour, but she could also be over-sensitive at times.

'Got you going, didn't I?'

Bethan threw her powder puff at her.

'Great, now I get to clean up the bed as well as the floor.'

'Serve you right.'

At twenty-five minutes to nine Bethan stood in front of the mirror. She turned on her heel and tried to view herself from the back. The dress was incredible. Beautifully cut, it clung tightly, if a little too revealingly, to her bust, waist and hips and swirled fashionably around her long slim legs. For the first time in her life she felt very nearly pretty.

'Will you lend me that frock when I go to my first ball?'

'If you grow another six inches. I'm not lopping that much off the bottom.'

'I wish I was tall and dark like you.'

'And I wish I was small and blonde like you.' Bethan leaned over and kissed Maud's cheek carefully so as not to smudge her lipstick. 'Thanks for the help. I couldn't have done without you.'

'Your bag,' Maud reminded. Another two minutes were spent frantically searching the back of the wardrobe for the black sequinned bag that Bethan had bought in a mad moment of extravagance from Wilf Horton's second-hand stall on the market. Bethan draped the shawl around herself while Maud filled the bag. She managed to stuff a lace handkerchief, a small bottle of essence of violets scent, a comb and Bethan's lipstick into the cramped interior.

'All I need is some change and I'm set to go.'

'What happens if your nose gets shiny? You've no powder.'

'I'll borrow Laura's compact.'

'You'd better pull that shawl higher or Mam won't let you out of the house.'

'It's not too low is it?' Bethan asked anxiously, checking her reflection one more time.

'Depends on what you mean by low. It'll be too low for Mam but I dare say the men who dance with you will find it interesting. There goes the door.'

'It'll be Ronnie.'

'Don't panic, I'll stall him.'

'Who's panicking?' Bethan demanded hotly.

Maud reached the foot of the stairs just as Bethan left the bedroom.

'My word!' Ronnie, all slicked-back hair, dark eyes and flashing white teeth, grinned up at Bethan. 'We are beautiful tonight. Iron curlers must be all the rage. Laura's wearing hers too.'

Bethan stuck her tongue out at him, hitched her shawl higher around her throat and descended the stairs. 'I'm off then,' she called to the back of the house. Evan and Eddie came out of the kitchen, followed by her mother.

'That's some dress,' Evan commented.

'Scarlet woman,' Eddie grinned.

'I needn't ask where you got that!' her mother exclaimed sourly. 'All I can say is that you must have more money than sense.'

'Auntie Megan gave it to me,' Bethan muttered, pulling on her shabby black coat and buttoning it to the neck.

'As I said, more money than sense,' her mother retorted.

'When will you be home?' Evan asked.

'Don't worry, Mr Powell, I'm picking the girls up,' Ronnie said in a tone more paternal than fraternal. 'The ball finishes at twelve, so even allowing for their gossiping I should have them home before one.'

'That's good to know,' Evan nodded.

'Don't forget you have work tomorrow morning,' Elizabeth reminded.

'She's not likely to do that.' Evan leaned over and kissed Bethan on the cheek, scratching himself on one of the iron wavers. 'Have a good time, love,' he murmured, rubbing his chin.

'I will.' Bethan pulled a coarse woollen headscarf from the peg above her head, folded it cornerwise and tied it over the metal curlers. 'Bye.' She squeezed Maud's hand, waved her fingers at Eddie, picked up the hem of her dress and took a deep breath before stepping out of the house.

Chapter Four

The Coronation ballroom was built on the second floor of the arcade of the Co-operative stores. The Co-op occupied two whole blocks between Gelliwastad Road and Market Square, with the intersecting road of Church Street terminating in the Co-op arcade. The windows of the ballroom overlooked both the arcade and Gelliwastad Road, and there was a fine view of the solid grey stone police station. Through the wired-off grilles that shielded the station's basement windows, shadowy figures could sometimes be seen pacing the cells, and the town wags insisted that the Coro had been sited so that potential drunks could view their overnight accommodation.

As ballrooms go, the Coro was not wonderful. It couldn't hold a candle to the beautifully moulded elegance of the blue and cream ballroom in the New Inn, or the white and gold function room of the Park Hotel. Viewed in harsh daylight, it was no more than a bleak assembly hall, proportioned too long for its narrow width, the floor covered with thick brown rubberised linoleum, the walls painted an unprepossessing dingy cream. But that night, by dint of imagination and a great deal of hard work, the ball committee had transformed it into a glittering fairyland.

Silver tinsel and fetching blue and red crêpe paper decorations, tortured into fabulous shapes by pressganged nurses and idle ladies of the crache (those rich enough to employ servants to do their dirty work), hung in clusters from the ceiling and walls. Even Bethan and Laura had done their bit by 'donating' an evening to help pin up the home-made ornaments.

The manager of the Co-op had entered into the spirit of the evening. The windows in the arcade shone with electric lights as though it were Christmas, not January, and there were no shoddy sales goods on offer. He was astute enough to realise that more customers with money in their pockets would pass his windows that night than on the last Saturday before Christmas, and so had arranged lavish displays of his most luxurious and expensive clothes and trinkets.

The hospital ball was the charity event of the year. Everyone who considered themselves anyone wanted to be seen to be supporting the cottage hospital. Entirely funded by voluntary contributions, money from the depression-depleted miners' union, and as many five-guinea-a-year subscriptions as the Hospital Board could muster, the hospital was in dire need of cash. Particularly as the board had taken it upon themselves to build a new wing to house a four-bedded children's ward and an up-to-date X-ray room: additions that had been completed and were now operational, but not yet paid for.

The ball was organised by, and mainly patronised by, the crache. The doctors belonged to that social group; the nurses did not, but they along with anyone else who could afford the ten and sixpence that the tickets cost were invited, and generally only those nurses who were on duty on the night turned down the invitation.

Ronnie slowed the cumbersome van to a crawl as he entered the top end of Taff Street. He steered carefully through its narrow precincts until he reached Market Square. Swinging the wheel abruptly to the left, he bumped over the cobbles of the square and ground the van to a halt in front of the entrance to the arcade. Laura and Bethan were still frantically unclipping the metal wavers from their heads when Ronnie stopped the engine.

'My hair's damp,' Laura said mournfully.

'It'll be even damper when you go out there,' Ronnie observed happily.

'It's not raining is it?' Bethan asked, dreading the prospect of water splashes staining her silk dress.

'Just miserable and misty. I'll come in at twelve.' He looked at his sister. 'Buy you a night-cap.'

'Must you?' Laura wailed.

'Oho, now you're the great qualified nurse you're ashamed of your brother?'

'No, only the way you interrogate whoever I'm with.'

'If you spent your time with decent boys I wouldn't need to interrogate them,' Ronnie retorted warmly.

'And you wouldn't know decent if you saw it,' Laura dismissed him contemptuously. 'I've seen some of the girls you go out with.'

'Who I go out with is none of your concern.' Ronnie rammed his index finger close to Laura's nose. 'But I know spiv when I see it. That porter Glan you primp and wiggle —'

'Wiggle! *Wiggle!*' Laura's face reddened in fury.

'If Papa knew the half of what you do . . .'

'That's right, bring Papa into it. We all know you can't breathe without Papa's say-so.'

Laura threw the remainder of her wavers into the front pocket of the van and wrenched open the door. Bunching up the skirt of her gold net she teetered on the side of the bench seat, poised to jump down.

'Here, you haven't even got the sense to wait for me to help you.' Ronnie leapt out of his side, walked around the front of the van and lifted Laura down, dumping her unceremoniously on the pavement. 'Your turn.' He looked up at Bethan.

'I'm quite capable of climbing down myself,' she said primly. The last thing she wanted was any man, even one she'd grown up with like Ronnie Ronconi, comparing her weight to Laura's.

'Nursing's softened your brains,' he groused angrily. 'You're as stupid as Laura.' He grabbed hold of her by the waist, lifted her out of the cab and deposited her next to the seething Laura. 'See you at twelve,' he said stiffly. He climbed back into the driving seat of the Trojan and revved the engine.

'Men!' Laura snarled furiously. 'They're all stupid, but Italian men are stupider than most.'

'Ronnie's more Welsh than Italian.'

'That's as may be, but he thinks like an Italian,' Laura said illogically, walking into the arcade and flouncing up the stairs.

A wave of warm scented air greeted Bethan as she followed Laura. People were milling in every available inch of space. Men in dark dinner suits, boiled shirts, stiff collars and white or black ties. Ladies in frocks of every hue and fabric known to the fashion trade. Laura made a bee-line for the cloakroom only to find it as crowded as the foyer. Bethan queued to deposit their coats while Laura fought for a space in front of the single mirror. The ante-room was packed with nurses not only from the Central Homes,

71

but also from Llwynypia and the Cottage Hospitals, as well as the ladies of the town's prominent citizens.

Bethan found Laura, and they spent five minutes squashed together, reapplying their lipstick and teasing their damp hair into waves.

'That dress makes you look entirely different,' Laura commented, as, much to the relief of the other ladies, they finally walked away.

Bethan glanced at the subdued gold and cream shades in Laura's dress and contrasted them with the crimson swirls of silk that flowed around her own ankles.

'You don't think it's too much do you? The neck . . .'

'Is perfect. Where's your confidence, Nurse? Good evening, Doctor Lewis,' she called out to Trevor Lewis, Dr John senior's assistant.

Trevor Lewis, a thin, diffident man whose clothes always hung on him as if they'd been handed down by a much larger older brother, walked over to them. 'Nurse Ronconi, Nurse Powell. Can I book a waltz with each of you?'

'For you, Doctor Lewis, anything,' Laura flirted outrageously. Giggling like a pair of schoolgirls they heaved and pushed themselves into the room.

'So much for the grand entrance,' Bethan muttered between clenched teeth.

'Ladies, I have your drinks.' Glan waylaid them with three glasses of orange juice balanced precariously.

'I'm not thirsty.' Laura waved her fingers dismissively as Bethan breathed in and slipped sideways between an elderly plump dowager and her equally plump, cigar-smoking husband.

'But . . . but . . .'

Bethan could still hear Glan's spluttering 'buts' as Laura caught up with her. Tables had been placed around two sides of the room, and most were already taken. At the far end, opposite the door, a raised dais had been erected, and Mander's Excelda dance band was in full flow, playing a jazzed-up, foxtrot version of 'They Didn't Believe Me'.

'Bethan, Laura, over here.'

'See what passing exams has done for us? First-name terms, no less,' Laura said in a loud voice.

'Ssh.'

'That's a fabulous dress,' Nurse Williams enthused, pulling out the chair next to her own for Bethan to sit on. 'I saw it in Howell's window in Cardiff. It was an absolute fortune . . . '

'Twelve guineas,' Nurse Fry interrupted.

'This was never in Howell's window,' Bethan said quickly. 'My aunt gave it to me.'

'Rich aunt, lucky you,' Nurse Fry said maliciously.

'She's not rich, she's an agent for Leslie's stores.'

'She never got that from Leslie's.'

'She also sells "specials",' Bethan explained impatiently. 'Clothes that local dressmakers pass on to her to sell. It's one of those. It hasn't even got a label.'

'Clever dressmaker,' Freda Williams mused. 'It wasn't made by Mrs Jenkins was it? Lewis Street?'

'I'm sorry, I don't know. I didn't think to ask.'

'The bodice would look better without the shawl wrapped around your throat,' Laura whispered in her ear.

'Nurse Ronconi, Nurse Powell, your drinks.' Glan plonked the orange juices in front of them, slopping the liquid.

'Thank you,' Laura said heavily. 'But I prefer my drink in the glass.'

Uncertain how to take the comment, Glan hovered uneasily next to their table.

'Doctor John's in fine form,' Freda said conversationally, in an attempt to lighten the atmosphere.

Bethan looked towards the front of the hall where Dr John senior was holding forth at a round table set in prime position to the left of the band. He had a large party gathered around him. His wife, his assistant Trevor Lewis, the matron Alice George, the Reverend Mark Price, the vicar of St John's church on the Graig, and his wife Angela were all sharing his table and, judging by the way they were laughing, a joke.

'There he is,' sighed Nurse Fry, 'over by the bar. Isn't he heavenly?'

'Young Doctor John?' Laura looked to her for confirmation. 'Who else?'

'That's young Doctor John?' Bethan cried.

'You should know, you worked with him all afternoon.'

73

'He was gowned up and had a hat on.'

'Hat or no hat, you gave me first claim,' Laura muttered into her ear.

Bethan had noticed that Andrew John was tall, broad-shouldered and well built, but she'd failed to realise how concealing a surgeon's hat and mask could be. He was easily the most handsome man she'd seen off a cinema screen. The dark brown hair that had been hidden under the theatre cap held a rich tint of auburn, and his face, oval, smooth-skinned and with a dark Ronald Colman moustache, attracted the attention of every female under forty, married as well as single, in the room. He smiled and nodded to her and she blushed crimson with the knowledge that she'd been staring at him. She turned abruptly and knocked one of the orange juices Glan had placed on the table. None of the juice touched her own or Laura's dress, but Glan's trousers were soaked.

'I'm dreadfully sorry,' she apologised, jumping up and delving into her handbag for her handkerchief.

'I bet you are,' Glan said viciously, all too aware of who she'd been staring at.

'You can borrow my handkerchief, Glan.' Laura added insult to injury by tendering a purely decorative scrap of silk and lace.

'Keep it.' Glan's temper boiled dangerously close to eruption.

The band chose that moment to stop playing, and Bethan sensed the attention of the dancers focusing on their table. Glan threw Laura's handkerchief to the floor and glowered at Bethan. She stepped back, and promptly trod on a foot behind her. She turned to find Andrew John's face inches away from her own.

'I was going to ask you for the next dance, but now you've broken my foot I'm not sure I'm capable of a limp, much less a foxtrot.'

'I'm terribly sorry, I didn't mean to . . . '

'I don't think there's any serious damage, but it might be just as well to make sure,' he said gravely. 'As you're a qualified nurse now, would you help me into the cloakroom so you can make a thorough examination?'

Bethan stood dumbfounded for a few seconds, then saw a peculiar glint in his eyes. 'You're not serious?'

'No,' he said slowly. 'I'm not serious.'

The MC's voice crackled over the microphone and the strains of 'If I Should Fall in Love Again' filled the room. Andrew took her by the hand, nodded to the fuming Glan, and led her on to the floor.

'That porter has blood pressure,' he commented blandly. 'Just look at his colour.'

Bethan was too mortified to do anything other than stare at the left shoulder of his tailored dinner suit.

'Are you always this quiet, or is it something I've said?' he asked on the second circuit of the room.

'It's what I've done,' she murmured miserably.

'Tipping orange juice over that porter? I assumed it was a clever ploy calculated to cool his ardour.'

'I didn't do it deliberately,' she protested.

'I know you didn't,' he said gently. 'It's been quite a day for you hasn't it? Qualifying. Helping to deliver your friend's baby, and now this?'

'I'm beginning to think I should have had an early night.'

'And lost an opportunity to air this frock.' He held her at arm's length for a moment. 'Now that would have been a crying shame.'

Bethan managed a nervous smile as they resumed dancing. She would have been happier if he'd chosen Laura. Laura was more his type. They could have laughed and been witty together, and she could have sat in the corner and watched enviously with all the other nurses. Unlike her, Laura took good-looking, well-heeled men in her stride. But she, for all of her training, or perhaps because of it, was always intimidated by the likes of Andrew John. The first lesson she'd learned in hospital was that doctors were second only to God. And everything about Andrew John – his conversation, his clothes, his accent – confirmed his superiority. She was used to men like her father who spent their lives grubbing for pennies to buy the bare essentials. What little free time they had was spent earnestly reading and discussing communism as a possible solution to the problems of the working, or unemployed, classes.

Even youngsters like Haydn, Eddie and William were too busy trying to scratch a living to have much time or money for fun. In contrast Andrew looked and behaved as though he hadn't a care in the world. But then, she reflected, his father was not only

75

a doctor who didn't have to fear the spectre of rising unemployment, but also the landlord of several houses, and that, at a time when most families in Pontypridd were hard pressed to keep a roof over their heads, put him firmly in the crache.

The band droned softly on. Perspiration trickled down her back. She became more nervous with every step she took. Yet, much as she wanted to, she couldn't blame Andrew for making her feel awkward; she couldn't fault the way he held her. A dance with Glan, or any of the other porters for that matter, would have turned into a wrestling match by now.

'I don't suppose I could interest you in an orange juice when this dance is over?' he asked, breaking the silence.

'Nurses aren't supposed to fraternise with doctors,' she retorted primly.

'They have to at hospital balls,' he protested. 'If they don't who are we supposed to dance with?'

'The town's socialites.'

He laughed. 'You have a tongue in your head after all. Now tell me, just who in Pontypridd do you call a socialite?'

'Well,' she looked around the room, 'there are the Misses Rees-Davies, the solicitor's daughters.'

'They're a trifle elderly for me.'

'That's unkind.'

'Unkind maybe, but true.'

'Miss Henrietta Evans? Now you can't say she's too old.'

'No, but she hasn't had an original thought since the day she was born, and I'm not sure she had one then.'

'You don't need original thoughts to dance.'

'No, but dancing is such a repetitive exercise it helps to have a partner capable of some conversation.'

'Anthea Llewellyn-Jones?' Bearing the gossip in mind, she watched his reaction carefully. 'You can't accuse her of not having any thoughts?'

'No, she has too many and all of them boring. I danced with her at the tennis club ball and as a result I can now recite the entire catalogue of recent flood and mine disasters and the names of all the committees that have been set up to assist the afflicted. Please,' his dark eyes gleamed as he looked at her, 'don't suggest I repeat the experience.'

'I think people can make all the suggestions they like, but I don't believe for one minute that you'd be affected enough by anyone's opinion to do anything you didn't want to,' she smiled.

'Good Lord, you can smile as well as talk. This must be my lucky night.'

'Are you always like this?'

'Like what?'

'Like turning everything into a joke.'

'Joking is an extremely serious business.'

'Really?'

'You must allow me to teach you just how serious, some time.'

The band ceased playing and she broke away from him and applauded.

'I think, Doctor John, it's time that you danced with someone else; nurse or socialite, it really doesn't matter.'

'And if I don't want to?'

'If you want to continue dancing you're going to have to. If I remain with you, people will notice. And I don't intend to attract any gossip, especially with Matron sitting in the room.'

He shook his head dolefully. 'So beautiful, and so hard-hearted.'

She turned her back on him and returned to the table, which had been washed down and dried by the barman. A crowd of porters had gathered around Laura and the two senior nurses. Glan, she noted gratefully, was not among them. There was no shortage of partners for the next dance, or the one after that. But no matter which porter she danced with, her attention wandered, and she found herself looking at her fellow dancers hoping to catch another glimpse of Andrew John. Flippant and frivolous as he undoubtedly was, he'd breathed colour and life into an existence she'd never considered drab or dull until that moment.

The hours blurred by in a haze of scented heat and soft romantic music. Just before the bar closed at eleven she and Laura treated themselves to a sherry, and bought a conciliatory pint of beer for Glan. They'd only just returned to their table when Laura glimpsed Ronnie entering the room.

'Oh blast, here comes trouble,' she complained, hiding her sherry glass in her hands.

'Haydn's with him.' Bethan waved to her brother and he joined

77

them. She pushed out Nurse Fry's chair. 'I heard about the job. Congratulations.'

'The wages aren't wonderful, it's only twelve and six for a six-day week, but it's steady, and Wilf said I can still help out on his market stall two mornings a week, so that'll make it fifteen shillings. Not up to your standard,' he grinned, 'but there's prospects.'

'Here you are, mate, get that down you.' Ronnie dumped two overflowing pint pots on the table.

'I thought stop tap had been called,' Laura complained, edging away from the glasses.

'It has, but Dai Owen's behind the bar and he owes me a favour.'

'When you get to hell you'll try to tell the devil that he owes you a favour,' Laura snapped acidly.

'Been eating razor blades?' Ronnie enquired mildly.

'How would you like to dance with me?' Haydn left his chair and offered his hand to Laura.

'I would love to.' Laura glared furiously at her brother as she walked away.

'I hope that wasn't one of dear sister's hints that I should ask you to dance.' Ronnie sank laconically into the seat Laura had vacated. 'Because if it was, I'm simply not up to it. I've had a swine of a night in the café, if you'll pardon the expression. Nothing but cups of tea, packets of PK and people warming themselves at my expense.'

'Look on the bright side, at least you weren't rushed off your feet.'

'I'd rather be rushed off my feet than lose money on heating and lighting and listen to the moans of my underworked cook. Take my advice,' he swallowed a large mouthful of beer in between words, 'never employ an Italian cook. They're all raving mad.'

'As I'm never likely to be in a position to employ anyone I'll take your word for it.'

Ronnie swung his feet on to a vacant chair, took another mouthful of beer and let out a large satisfied burp as the MC called the last waltz.

'May I borrow your lady?' Andrew asked, climbing over Ronnie's legs to get to Bethan.

'Be my guest, take her,' Ronnie offered expansively.

'That's uncommonly generous of you.'

'Not at all, old boy,' Ronnie accurately mimicked Andrew's public school accent. 'It's not as if you're asking me to do anything that requires effort.'

'Nice boyfriend you have there,' Andrew observed as he led Bethan away from the tables.

'Ronnie is Laura's brother and nobody's boyfriend.'

'I'm not surprised.'

'Ronnie's all right,' she laughed. 'He just takes a bit of getting used to.'

'I'd rather not try if it's all the same to you. But talking about getting used to people, how about you getting used to me? There's a Claudette Colbert film showing in the Palladium the second half of this week.'

'I know. Laura and I are going on Saturday.'

'Laura?'

'She's dancing with my brother over there.'

Andrew peered in the direction Bethan had indicated.

'I've seen her somewhere before.'

'She works on the ward with me.'

'Ah, a fellow nurse. In that case she won't mind if I tag along with you?'

'Nurses aren't supposed to . . . '

'I know, I know . . . aren't supposed to fraternise with doctors. But have a heart. I've just returned to Pontypridd after six years in London. Apart from my parents and their friends I don't know a soul here. Now tell me, what possible harm can a trip to the cinema with both of you do?'

'That depends on who sees us.'

'I thought people went to the cinema to watch films, not the audience.'

The band stopped playing and streamers of finely cut crêpe paper cascaded down from nets strung close to the ceiling.

'I'm saying please nicely, just as my mother taught me.' He brushed a clump of red and blue streamers out of his hair. There was such a pitiful expression on his face she burst out laughing.

'We pay our own way,' she said firmly.

'In this day and age of the emancipated woman, I wouldn't dream of treating you.'

'All right.'

'What did you say?' he shouted above the strains of 'Auld Lang Syne'.

She stood on tiptoe and whispered into his ear, 'I said all right.'

Glan, who'd spent the whole of the last dance standing on the sidelines watching Bethan and Andrew John, chose that moment to step forward. Catching her unawares, he gripped her right elbow painfully and propelled her forwards, away from Andrew into the thick of the crowd who were linking arms and singing in the middle of the room.

'Should auld acquaintance be forgot . . . '

The music resounded in her ears, closing out all other sounds. Dr John senior was standing opposite her, his face flushed with heat and whisky. She turned and saw the top of Andrew's head, but he seemed very far away, separated from her by a mass of chanting, swaying bodies.

'Happy New Year, Beth, a little late, but better late than never.' Glan bent his head to kiss her, she ducked and he kissed thin air.

'Don't you dare take liberties with me, Glan Richards,' she hissed vehemently. She broke away and pushed backwards.

Laura was waving to her from the doorway, her arm full of coats. She pointed down and mouthed, 'I've got yours as well as mine.'

'Come on, Sis, follow me.' Haydn appeared at her side. Pushing ahead, he cleared a path through the crowd. 'Here.' He took her coat from Laura and helped her on with it.

'Thank you.' Bethan looked around as she slid her arms into the sleeves. Dr John senior was shaking hands with everyone who'd sat at his table, but she could see no sign of Andrew.

'Come on then, before the rush,' Ronnie shouted impatiently, from the foyer.

Dragging her feet, Bethan reluctantly followed the others down the stairs and into the arcade. The Co-op windows were still lit. No expense spared on hospital ball night. They walked towards

Market Square, their footsteps resounding over the tiled floor, echoing upwards to the high vaulted ceiling.

'Holy Mother but it's cold,' Ronnie complained, buttoning his coat to the neck.

'That's blasphemy,' Laura crowed victoriously.

'I was merely making an observation to the Blessed Virgin,' Ronnie contradicted.

Ignoring their bickering Bethan looked out from the shelter of the arcade into the deserted square. Gwilym Evans' windows were in darkness. No lights burned to celebrate the ball there. The fine misty rain had turned to a cold, penetrating icy sleet that burnished the cobblestones to pewter. She turned up her coat collar and pulled her gloves out of her pocket.

The heavy footsteps of someone running thundered up close behind them.

'Goodnight, Nurse Powell, Nurse Ronconi.'

'Starting a marathon, Doctor John?' Laura asked.

'No. Getting my father's car out of the New Inn car park before the rush starts.'

'You could have gone the back way, mate,' Ronnie said helpfully. 'Quicker.'

'It would be if the shutters weren't down and locked at the Gelliwastad Road end.' He stepped close to Bethan. 'Ronconis' café on the Tumble. Six o'clock Saturday night,' he muttered under his breath.

He was gone before she could reply. She looked back. The arcade stretched out behind her, full of laughing, chattering people. She watched as they swarmed towards Gelliwastad Road. The shutters were clamped back, exposing a square of dark sky, cut midway by the dour grey outline of the police station. A gentle smile played at the corners of her mouth. He'd lied – he'd run to catch up with her! That had to mean something. Bracing herself, she followed the others into the freezing cold of Market Square.

She was still smiling when she and Haydn let themselves into the house. They paused on the doorstep to wave goodbye to Ronnie and Laura who, judging by the erratic way in which the van turned in the narrow street, were still at it hammer and tongs.

'Italians!' Haydn said, stepping inside as the van finally drove off down the street.

'Lovely, warm people.'

'Like that doctor you were dancing with?'

'Doctor John?'

Haydn reached past her to hang up his coat and she saw that he was watching her closely.

'I hardly know him,' she protested. 'I only worked with him for the first time today. We delivered Maisie Crockett's baby. It was touch and go. The baby nearly died.'

'Maisie from Phillips Street?'

She nodded.

'I didn't even know she was married.'

'She's not.' Bethan brushed the surface rain from her coat as she hung it up. 'She's living in the homes.'

'Poor bugger,' Haydn said with feeling.

'Haydn! Bethan! Is that you?'

'Yes Mam.' Haydn frowned as he walked down the passage. 'I thought you'd all be in bed.'

'It's just as well we're not,' Elizabeth complained. 'No one could possibly sleep through the racket you and Bethan are making.'

He opened the door and they walked into the kitchen. 'What in hell . . . '

'And I'll have none of that language in this house.'

'Sorry, Mam,' Haydn apologised automatically, as he rushed across the room to where Eddie sat slumped in Evan's chair. 'What happened to you, mate?' he asked, pushing aside the damp cloth Evan was holding over Eddie's swollen right eye.

'I would have thought that was obvious.' With a look of pure venom Elizabeth wrung out a second cloth that was soaking in an enamel bowl on the table.

'You had a fight?' Bethan asked, pushing Eddie's hair back and peering into his eye.

'They were looking for sparring partners for the boxers down at the gym,' Eddie mumbled from between split and swollen lips. 'Look, I got two bob.' He put his hand in his pocket and pulled out a coin. 'I wanted to give something towards the silver nurse's buckle Dad and Haydn have been saving for. Here, Dad. Take it.'

Tears blinding his eyes, Evan fumbled at Eddie's hand and palmed the coin. Bethan held her father's hand for a moment, then she took the cloth and dabbed at the swellings on her brother's face.

'Being a sparring partner is a mug's game,' Haydn said angrily as he checked over the rest of his brother's body.

'I know.' Eddie's left eye shone with excitement in the firelight. 'That's why I asked Joey Rees to train me. You can win as much as five pounds in a good fight. Think of it, five pounds for one night's work. I won't get it yet, of course. But Joey says that I could be a first-class lightweight. Haydn –' he reached out and grabbed his brother's arm – 'I could make more money than I ever would working down the pit or in the brewery yard. I just know I could. A few months of that and we'll all be rich.'

'Over my dead body,' Elizabeth proclaimed.

Evan slumped back on the kitchen chair and looked at the two shillings he was holding. 'There's not many rich boxers, son,' he warned.

'But there are an awful lot of punch-drunk ones,' Haydn said acidly. 'You only have to look as far as Cast Iron Dean in Phillips Street.'

'He made his money.'

'And spent it. What's he got to show for it now?' Haydn demanded.

'What about Jimmy Wilde?' Eddie bit back. 'He's been everywhere. London, America . . . stayed at the best hotels, eaten the best food. He bought his own farm –'

'There's a lot more to life than money, son,' Evan interrupted softly.

Eddie opened his left eye and looked around the shabby kitchen, the white strained faces of his family.

'If there is I haven't found it,' he said stubbornly. 'All I know is there's got to be more than getting up in the morning and queuing for the dole, or half a day's work. And if boxing puts money in my pocket and the best food on my plate instead of bread and scrape here, then I'm going to box. And no one in this family is going to stop me. Now or ever,' he added defiantly.

The silence after Eddie finished speaking was total and crushing. Bethan continued wiping and cleaning the mess on his face. But after a while she couldn't see the cuts and bruises. Her tears obliterated everything. Even the look of impotent misery on her father's face.

Chapter Five

'Look, are you going out with Andrew John tonight or aren't you?' Laura demanded of Bethan as she carried two cups of tea over to the corner table of Ronconis' café that they'd commandeered. 'Because if you are, I'm leaving now. I'm not in the habit of playing gooseberry . . . '

'I've told you,' Bethan repeated impatiently. 'He's only just returned to Pontypridd after six years away. He knows no one and he's lonely.'

'Lonely my eye!' Laura exclaimed scornfully. 'Men who look like him are never lonely, they . . . '

'For goodness' sake keep your voice down,' Bethan hissed. She looked up and smiled at Ronnie, who was leaning sideways on the counter within easy listening distance. 'For the last time, he wanted me to go to the Palladium with him and when I told him that I was going with you he asked if he could tag along, and I said yes,' she continued in a whisper.

'Do you, or do you not, want me to scarper?'

'Of course not.'

'I would if I was in your shoes,' Laura said philosophically, as she tipped sugar into her tea.

'You're the one who fancies him, not me.'

'All's fair in love and war.'

'This is not love,' Bethan protested vehemently.

'But it could be. Just look at who's coming through the door.'

Bethan glanced up and choked on her tea. 'Honestly, Laura, isn't there anything in trousers that you don't fancy?'

'Not much between the ages of eighteen and thirty. Cold enough for you, William?' she shouted to Bethan's cousin.

'It's real brass monkey weather out there!' William replied as he breezed into the café along with a draught of freezing air. Charlie walked in behind him, and closed the door with a resounding clang of the bell.

'Two hot teas to thaw out two icemen, please, Ronnie.' William stood in front of the chipped and scarred wooden counter, and rubbed his hands vigorously together. 'Charlie and I are blue already and there's three hours to go before the bell for the bargain rush.'

'I thought they'd drop the prices early on a night like tonight.' Laura eyed William coyly. He gave her the full benefit of his most beguiling smile, but it was the blazing coal fire alongside her table that had really taken his eye.

'No such luck.' William left the counter and squeezed a chair in between Laura and the fire. 'Nine o'clock bell, not before.'

'Be kinder to the poor people waiting to buy their Sunday meat to ring the bell now.' Bethan looked out through the steamed-up window at the women and children huddled in layers of shabby clothes, who were walking up and down, shivering and waiting for the moment to come.

'Be kinder to the poor devils behind the stalls.' William pulled off his fingerless gloves and blew vigorously on his frozen white hands. 'Thanks, mate.' He took the tea Charlie brought over from the counter. Bethan shifted her chair, making room for Charlie to sit alongside her, in front of the fire. The Russian moved a chair into the vacant space, and nodded his thanks.

'Is a man allowed to ask where you two are going all tarted up like that?' William studied them over the rim of his thick earthenware mug.

'No,' Ronnie shouted above the noise of the steamer from behind the counter, 'they'll bite your head off.'

'We're not "tarted up",' Bethan protested indignantly. 'I've had this coat for five years.'

'It's not the coat,' William smiled snidely. 'It's the perfume, the silk blouse you bought off my mother yesterday, when a jumper would be more serviceable, not to mention the smile and the whiff of excitement in the air.' He winked at Ronnie. 'I think you'd better warn every man who walks in here that these two are out on the razzle and looking for husbands.'

'The men are safe enough,' Ronnie drawled as he polished the water urn with a damp rag. 'Five minutes of Laura's company should be more than enough to make any man run a mile. If he doesn't, he's either a fool or a madman.'

'Why, you –' Laura looked around for something to throw, but Bethan had already put the salt and pepper pots out of reach.

'Oh . . . Oh . . . Oh . . . '

'Doing impressions of Father Christmas?' Bethan asked William caustically. 'Little late aren't you?'

'Or early,' he said absently, staring at the door.

She looked up and saw Andrew standing in the centre of the café. 'Time we went, Laura.' She jumped to her feet and promptly knocked over her chair.

'Can't wait to get at him, can you?' William leant over and picked up the chair. 'And by the way, Beth,' he muttered in a stage whisper, 'you need more powder on your cheeks. They're *very* red.'

She lifted the spoon out of William's hot tea as she passed and laid it on the back of his hand. He yelped, but she ignored his cry and carried on walking.

Andrew smiled when he saw her.

'I hope you don't mind, Trevor was at a loose end so I invited him to join us. He's waiting outside.'

'Trevor?'

'Doctor Lewis. Trevor Lewis,' he explained.

'Of course we don't mind.' Bethan gave William a sharp kick on the ankle for pulling on her coat. 'I don't think you've met my cousin William?'

'Your cousin?' Andrew raised an eyebrow. 'How do you do, Mr . . . '

'Powell.' William extended his hand.

'Ah yes, it would be wouldn't it?' Andrew's smile broadened.

'If you don't mind I won't get up, I haven't thawed out yet.'

'It is cold,' Andrew agreed.

'Not so you'd notice.' William reached out and fingered the cloth of Andrew's coat. 'Cashmere,' he nodded approvingly. 'Nice stuff. If you ever want to sell it, I'll get you a good price.'

'William!' Bethan admonished indignantly.

'I appreciate the offer, Mr Powell, but as I've only just bought it I think I'll hang on to it for a year or two,' Andrew said evenly.

'The offer'll hold until then. This is a mate of mine, Charlie Raschenko.'

'Mr Raschenko.' Andrew winced as Charlie took his hand in a bone-crushing grip.

'You've met my brother,' Laura said over-sweetly, smiling at Ronnie who was leaning on the counter.

'I've had the pleasure.' Andrew extricated his bruised hand, and walked towards the counter, happy to be heading towards the door and the outside. He shook hands gingerly with Ronnie, then turned to Bethan. 'I don't want to rush you, but if we're to get there on time, we'll have to make a move.'

'Town Hall pantomime for the kiddies?' Ronnie enquired condescendingly.

'That's your taste, dear brother, not ours,' Laura replied, gathering her things together. 'Bye, everyone.' She waved as she followed Bethan and Andrew out of the door.

'Don't be late or Papa will shout,' Ronnie called after her.

'That depends on what we're doing,' Laura countered cheekily as she closed the door. 'Some things are worth a shout or two from Papa.'

'The car's in the station car park.' Andrew held up his hand, halting a dray-cart so they could cross Taff Street.

'Wouldn't it be easier to walk to the Palladium?' Bethan asked suspiciously.

'It would be if we were going there, but Trevor has tickets for the Moss Empire Circus.'

'At the Empire Theatre in Cardiff?' Laura demanded eagerly.

'Where else?' Andrew answered for Trevor, who left a circle of young men to join them.

'Boys from my YMCA drama class,' he apologised briefly. 'Hope you don't mind me coming with you?'

'Of course we don't,' Laura said generously, thinking about the tickets. 'Well, what are we waiting for? Let's go.'

Bethan trailed behind Andrew and Laura as they wove through the crowds who were pouring up the alleyway steps alongside Gwilym Evans and into Market Square. She'd been looking forward to a night out with Andrew and Laura. But a foursome with Trevor Lewis and a trip to Cardiff put quite a different complexion on the evening that lay ahead. A threesome could be put down to innocent friendship, a foursome could be construed as men chasing women. And quite apart from the doctor/nurse fraternisation embargo, there was the question of where Andrew lived.

The Graig and the Common were situated at opposite ends of Pontypridd for very good reasons. Their residents didn't mix. They had very different life-styles and lived in entirely different worlds, and although the depression had affected both, on the Graig it had cut essentials such as food down to two scrap meals, or in extreme cases one a day. On the Common it had merely cut the servants' wages.

She knew that her father would disapprove if he could see her now, and that thought upset her. Too many girls on the Graig had been dazzled by middle-class boys dangling middle-class riches, only to end up as inmates on the 'unmarrieds' ward in the Central Homes.

'Andrew can be a bit overpowering, but he means well,' Trevor ventured, stepping alongside her.

'Yes I know,' she agreed noncommittally. 'Have you really got tickets?'

'Yes. A friend of mine offered them to me when I was having a drink with Andrew after work last night.'

'And Andrew bought them?'

'He did,' Trevor confirmed sheepishly. 'He said you wouldn't mind making tonight a foursome.'

'Of course we don't mind,' Bethan said warmly. Even under the uncertain light of the street lamps she could see the shiny patches on the cuffs and elbows of Trevor's overcoat. She and Laura had noticed soon after going to the Graig that, for a doctor, Trevor's shoes and clothes were distinctly shabby. But Bethan liked him all the more for his down-at-heel appearance. It gave him a kinship with her own background. Perhaps his wages, like hers, were needed by his family for more important things like rent and food. And she had elaborated on the few bare facts that she knew, imagining either an unemployed father, or one on 'short time' like hers.

Trevor couldn't have been more unlike Andrew. Quiet, rather shy, even with patients, he exuded diffidence rather than confidence. He was a favourite with the nurses because his 'in need of care and attention' appearance coupled with his gentle manner appealed to their maternal instinct.

'Congratulations, by the way, I haven't had a chance to compliment you or Laura on your results,' he said suddenly.

'Thank you.'

'Quite a boost for the Graig, getting the nurse with the top marks in the examination. How do you like nursing with us?'

'It's different from the Royal Infirmary.' She stepped into the road to avoid a young woman carrying a baby in a shawl wrapped around her coat, Welsh fashion. She was pushing a battered pram loaded with another two children, who were half buried under a mound of newspaper-wrapped potatoes and swedes.

'The patients can't be all that different. I grew up in the dock area of Cardiff. There's a lot of similarities between the back streets there and the Graig.'

'There's always similarities between one poor area and another.'

'Cockles, love, halfpenny a pint. Cockles, sweet cockles. Go on, sir, buy the lady a bag of cockles.'

Bethan shook her head at old Will Cockles who stood on the corner of Market Square. 'Have you any family left in Cardiff?' she asked curiously.

'My mother, two sisters and a brother.'

'Four children,' she smiled. 'Just like us.'

'My father was killed ten years ago. He was a docker, in Cardiff. The rigging broke as they were unloading a ship. Two days before it happened I won a scholarship to County School. I didn't want to take it, but my mother insisted I went. She said she could keep the family until I began work. I don't think she bargained on my getting a second scholarship to medical college. I was twenty-three before I earned a penny.'

'You were lucky your family could hold out that long.'

'Very,' he agreed drily. 'My brother and sisters could have done with some of my luck. They're all out of work now.'

'My father's on half-time and my youngest brother can't find work,' Bethan commiserated.

'Come on, Trevor,' Andrew called from the bridge opposite Rivelin's. 'We don't want to be late.'

Conscious that they'd been dawdling, Bethan and Trevor quickened their pace, but they didn't catch up with Andrew and Laura until they reached the station yard.

Andrew's car was pale grey with chrome trimmings, very shiny and, judging by the strong leathery smell of the interior, very new. He unlocked the door, and the interior light showed rich, gleaming walnut facias and pale grey upholstery. Bethan caught a strong whiff of expensive men's cologne as Andrew held the door open for her and Laura to climb into the back. When he closed the door behind them she glanced out of the window, to see if anyone was watching. The usual ladies of the town were standing in front of the old stone and red-brick wall that enclosed the yard. One of them sidled up to a passing man, her garishly painted face shining like a clown's under the artificial light.

'Nice car,' Laura commented, settling her skirt around her knees.

'Glad you like it,' Andrew called over his shoulder. He grinned at Trevor. 'Crank's under your seat.'

Trevor fumbled beneath his seat, lifted out the crank and went to the front of the car. Three turns and the engine purred into life. Once Trevor had climbed in again, Andrew slid the car in gear and manoeuvred out of the station yard.

Bethan and Laura sat back and tried to look as though they drove out to take the air every night of their lives. Apart from a few odd trips in Ronnie's Trojan baker's van, it was the first time either of them had ever travelled by private transport. But whereas Laura revelled in the experience, allowing the sense of luxury to wash over her like a warm, perfumed bath, Bethan was beset by guilt. It was more than just the fact that Andrew and Trevor were doctors. It had something to do with her own sense of self-value – as though Andrew, the trip, the car were too good for her, and any moment he'd find out the truth. That she, Bethan Powell, simply wasn't worth the time and attention he was expending on her. Or, worse still, was the outing simply a ploy on his part to get her alone and defenceless in an isolated spot where he could 'take advantage' of her?

Laura, bubbling over with excitement, began to talk about the last circus she'd seen. Trevor was infected by her mood and joined in, with Andrew, who was concentrating on driving, chipping in with the odd remark. They reached the outskirts of the city just after seven o'clock, and Andrew dropped them outside the Empire Theatre while he went to find a parking space. As they waited for him in the foyer, Bethan used the time to study the clothes of the women around her; she wished she'd taken the trouble to dress up a little more, although as she was wearing the new grey crêpe de Chine blouse she'd only just bought from her aunt, and her best navy-blue serge skirt, it was difficult to know what, besides the red dress or her black figured velvet, she could have put on.

Trevor dug into the pockets of his overcoat and produced the tickets. Laura shrieked in excitement.

'You've got a box!'

'Purely by default. A friend of mine bought it for his family, but they've gone down with influenza. He sold it cheap. He said he owed me a favour,' he added as an afterthought.

'You must belong to the same tribe as my brother.'

'Tribe?' He looked at her blankly.

'Someone always owes my brother a favour.'

'Then he's luckier than me.'

'The favours Ronnie's owed never extend to theatre boxes.'

'This was a one-off.' Trevor looked around the crowded foyer searching for a glimpse of Andrew.

'I hoped you'd wait.' Andrew suddenly appeared behind them, his hat pushed to the back of his head, his face glowing pink from the cold. 'Shall we go up?'

Neither Laura nor Bethan had been to the Empire Theatre before. Their acquaintance with the glamorous world of live show-business had been restricted to the dog-eared, slightly grubby New Theatre and the Town Hall in Pontypridd. Shortage of money in both theatres had meant that the tarnished gilding remained tarnished, the marked paintwork stayed marked, and the once plush seats in the auditoriums stood as shiny, bald pink monuments to the depression.

Here everything gleamed, newly restored, painted and sparkling in royal, opulent colours of red, gold and cream. There wasn't a speck of dust or dirt anywhere, and as they mounted the stairs to the circle Bethan noticed that even the people crowding into the doors that led to the stalls seemed better groomed than those in Pontypridd.

They were shown to their seats by an usherette who fluttered her eyelashes and pouted seductively at Andrew. Trevor relieved them of their coats while Andrew went to the confectionery kiosk.

'Do you know the cheapest seat in the stalls is two shillings?' Laura whispered while Trevor was hanging their coats on the back of the box door. Bethan shook her head and peered over the edge of the balcony. The theatre, like Laura, was buzzing with suppressed excitement, and she wished that she could relax enough to be swept up in the tide of gaiety.

Andrew returned with two programmes and an enormous box of chocolates. Handing them to Bethan he pulled a chair up alongside hers, leaving Trevor no other option but to sit next to Laura. Discordant notes filled the air as the orchestra began to tune up. The curtain twitched intriguingly, the lights dimmed and a hush fell over the auditorium.

Bethan passed the chocolates and a programme on to Trevor. Leaning forward she stole a sideways glance at Andrew under cover of the darkness. He smiled at her. Embarrassed, she looked away quickly, upsetting herself with the thought that he'd probably visited hundreds of theatres before, no doubt in the company of dozens of different girls. Perhaps she was reading too much into the evening. It could be just as he'd said, he wanted friendship and companionship, nothing more. They'd enjoy themselves, and afterwards, when the show was over, he'd shake her hand, drop her off at the corner of Graig Avenue and that would be that. A memorable night for her, just another amusing evening for him.

Once the orchestra struck up the opening number, and the curtain rose, she forgot her preoccupation with Andrew. Multi-coloured images whirled around the stage as acrobats dressed in red and blue silk jumped on and off circling horses. The music raced, quickening to a foot-tapping, pulse-racing speed.

The horses circled for the last time, left as the curtain fell and a troop of performing dogs yapped in front of the footlights, accompanied by their trainer. To 'Oohs' and 'Aahs' they went through their paces until the last black and white mongrel jumped through the final hoop and the curtain rose on a tightrope act. Bethan leaned forward on the balcony, resting her chin on her hand, completely enthralled. Her father had taken all of them to the circus once, when a touring company had pitched a tent in Pontypridd park. But it had been nothing like this.

Human act followed animal act in bewildering variety. Monkeys, trapeze artists, camels, clowns, elephants, jugglers, a knife thrower, flame eater . . . they took their bows, the curtain fell, the music stopped and light flooded the auditorium.

'It's not over is it?' she asked, blinking at the brightness.

'No,' Andrew laughed. 'Half time.' He rose from his seat. 'Can I get you a drink? Ice cream?'

'Ice cream if you let us pay,' Laura said pertly.

Trevor coloured, but Andrew held out his hand. Laura delved into her bag and produced half a crown.

'Ice cream for everyone?'

'Yes please,' Bethan answered.

'I'll help you carry them,' Trevor offered, following him out.

'This is the life.' Laura rifled the box of chocolates and popped one into her mouth.

'You'd better not get too used to it. Work tomorrow.'

'Don't be a grumble-grumps and remind me.' Laura took another chocolate. 'Tell me, how come you get the rich handsome one when I laid claim to him first? Not that I'm complaining, Trevor is rather sweet in a little-boy-lost way, and he does have prospects.'

'Laura, we're out with them for the evening, not heading up the aisle.'

'Speak for yourself. I could do a lot worse than marry a doctor, even a poor one.'

'If you want to swap seats . . . '

'If I want to?' Laura dug her elbow into Bethan's ribs. 'Where've you been looking. The eminently eligible Doctor John is smitten, and alas not with me. But don't worry, I know how to retire gracefully from the fray. And I'm suitably grateful for my consolation prize.'

'Now you're being ridiculous,' Bethan said irritably.

'Here you are, ladies.' Andrew pushed his way into the box, his hands full of ice-cream wafers.

'I feel like Orphan Annie on a Christmas treat,' Laura said, wrapping her hanky around her wafer.

'You're that hard done by?' Andrew asked drily.

'You're a doctor, you should know. "Nurse get me this, nurse get me that, nurse bow your head the doctors are passing. Run water into the sink for him, make sure it's not too hot, not too cold, no, not that soap, a new piece. Hold out a clean towel so he can dry his hands, and pick it up when he's done and dropped it to the floor."'

'It can't be that bad,' Andrew protested.

'Believe me it is. You should try standing in our shoes some time,' Laura replied.

'Sorry I took so long, there was a massive queue.' Trevor pushed his way awkwardly into the box, carrying a tray of glasses filled with orange juice.

'I didn't give you enough for orange juice,' Laura protested. 'Not at these prices.'

'My treat,' Trevor insisted.

'In that case, thank you,' she smiled and took a glass.

Andrew took the tray from Trevor and handed a glass to Bethan as he resumed his seat.

'I take it you're enjoying the show.'

'It's wonderful . . . ' She hesitated, seeing a mocking glint in his eye.

'Chocolate, before Trevor and Laura eat them all?' he asked, taking the box and putting it on the balcony next to her.

'No thank you.'

'You don't like chocolates?' he asked incredulously.

'Not very much,' she admitted.

'What do you like?'

'Oranges. I love oranges.'

'In that case you must marry me, I have this horror of middle-aged fat ladies who eat too many chocolates.'

'Ssh!'

The hissing came from the neighbouring box as the lights dimmed and the band started playing. The curtain rose on a fenced-in stage. Laura grabbed Trevor's arm as an immense tiger prowled towards the footlights. The creature lunged forward and rattled the bars and a couple of women in the front stalls screamed.

'You can hold my hand if you're afraid,' Andrew teased.

Bethan ignored his offer, but noticed that Laura was still pressing her cheek against Trevor's shoulder.

The second half passed even more quickly than the first. A

95

whirl of tigers, more clowns when the cage was being dismantled, Cossack dancers, more ponies – this time accompanied by cowboys and Indians, a snake-charmer, a balancing act, and eventually the grand finale. But no matter how vigorously she and the rest of the audience clapped, cheered and called for encores, all they got was another bow from the performers.

'Supper?' Andrew enquired, helping her on with her coat.

'I should get back,' she said doubtfully. 'My parents think I'm at the Palladium.'

'It's only ten o'clock, I'll have you back by twelve I promise.'

She looked to Laura, hoping for moral support, but Laura and Trevor were already discussing the merits of one café as opposed to another.

'As long as we go straight to Pontypridd afterwards,' she relented.

Supper was a bottle of wine and an omelette in a small café close to the dock area, and by the welcome they received, it was obvious that Andrew and Trevor had both been there before. True to his word, as soon as their plates were cleared and the wine bottle emptied Andrew drove to Pontypridd; this time Laura sat in the back with Trevor, leaving the front seat free for Bethan.

Bethan saw only two houses with the lamps lit as they travelled up the Graig hill, and even those lamps were in the bedrooms. She gripped the front of her seat nervously, hoping that her mother hadn't taken it into her head to wait up for her, or worse still, come out on to the doorstep to greet her. Andrew steered up High Street into Llantrisant Road, and bypassing the turning to Graig Avenue he stopped the car at the end of Danycoedcae Road. Trevor stepped out and opened the door on Laura's side.

'If you don't mind, I'll get out here too,' Bethan said as she struggled with the door handle.

'I thought you lived in Graig Avenue?' Andrew waved goodnight to Laura.

'I do.'

'Then I'll drive you down. I can always come back for Trevor.'

'The road isn't made up on Graig Avenue. It would play havoc with your car.'

'I'm a doctor. I make house calls on all kinds of roads, so one more rough surface won't make any difference.'

'You'd wake the neighbours.'

He looked at her, trying to decipher her features under the indistinct light of the street lamps. 'You're ashamed to be seen with me?' he asked.

'Not ordinarily,' she tried to make light of her reluctance, 'but it is nearly twelve o'clock.'

'Oh dear, don't tell me, you're about to turn into a pumpkin.'

'No.' Bethan struggled to keep her rising irritation in check. 'I have a family and neighbours who may resent being woken up by a car engine at this time of night.'

'In that case I'll walk you home.'

'No really, please. I don't want you to go to any trouble.'

'No trouble I assure you, and as you won't let me drive you it's the least I can do. Besides, your family really would have cause for complaint if I allowed you to walk home alone at this hour.'

He turned off the engine and dimmed the lights. She got out of the car. The air was bracing on this part of the mountain, even in summer. Now it sliced through their overcoats like the cutting edge of an icicle. He called out softly to Trevor.

'I won't be long.'

Bethan turned up her collar and walked across to the footpath that led down to Iltyd Street.

'Wouldn't it be better to go by the main road?' he suggested as he joined her.

'It's much quicker this way.'

'I don't doubt that it is, but I'd rather not break my neck.'

'The path is quite straightforward. Here —' without thinking she held out her hand — 'just be careful when you step over this rock, it's the only one the boys couldn't move.'

He intertwined his gloved fingers with hers, and hung on to them as they walked down the dark hillside. He didn't let go, even when the lights of Iltyd Street burned overhead. Hands locked, huddled into their coats, they walked quickly, crossing into Graig Avenue and the shadow of the wall of Danygraig House.

'That's it, there,' she whispered. All the houses were in darkness. The cost of heating and lighting ensured that most of Graig people went to bed early. Even on Saturday nights.

He looked up at the twin bays, the square of etched glass above the door, and the upstairs sash windows. All were in darkness.

'Everyone in bed?' he whispered.

'I hope so,' she said fervently, not wanting to explain that they lived in the back kitchen.

He held her hand briefly. 'Thank you, Bethan, for a lovely evening.' For once she could detect no hint of mockery in his voice.

'No, it's I who should be thanking you.' She hesitated, expecting a kiss, a fumbling, demanding hand beneath her coat after all the money he'd spent on her.

'I'm glad you enjoyed it. I hope you and Laura will join us again some time.'

'I'd like to.'

'Good.' He glanced up at the star-studded, clear night sky. 'I must come up here more often. I never knew the stars shone so brightly over the Graig mountain.'

'There's no smoke to cloud the sky because we can't afford to keep our fires in all night.'

'That's what I like about you, Bethan, you're so prosaic.'

Unsure of what he meant, she didn't answer. He bent his head and brushed his lips lightly across her forehead, so lightly that afterwards she wondered if he'd kissed her at all.

'Goodnight.'

He turned to face the wind and walked away. She watched his tall dark figure merge into the shadows around the corner. Then, crossing the road she mounted the steps to her front door. The evening had ended as she'd hoped: with him leaving without making a pass, groping beneath her coat or creating a scene. All the things that Glan would have done as a matter of course. He hadn't even tried to set a date for another outing, just a vague, 'I hope you and Laura will join us again some time.' But then, it didn't matter. Did it? She'd had a good time. Seen the circus from a box she could never have afforded. Ridden in a car. Eaten supper in a café late at night. Drunk her first glass of wine with a meal.

Andrew John had treated her to an absolutely perfect evening. Given her a taste of a glittering, sparkling world she thought she'd never experience. She should be feeling on top of the world.

Instead she felt unaccountably depressed, restless – and angry. Angry with him for introducing her to something she could never have – for ending their relationship before it had even begun.

Chapter Six

'And just where do you think you've been until this hour young lady?'

'Sorry, I know it's late, Mam. Laura and I . . . '

'That was Laura who walked you home was it?' Elizabeth sneered. 'Taken to wearing men's clothes, has she?'

'Mam, if you'll let me explain . . . '

'There's nothing to explain. I know exactly what you've been doing, my girl. I can smell the drink on you from here.' Elizabeth's face darkened with a contemptuous, naked anger that Bethan had witnessed only a few times in her life.

'I had a glass of wine with my supper,' she retorted defensively.

'Wine is it? I suppose you think wine is one step up from beer?' Elizabeth's voice rose precariously close to hysteria as she followed Bethan down the hall into the back kitchen. 'Do you think it's any better to be a rich man's whore than a poor man's?'

'Mam!' Bethan whirled around and faced her mother only to see her father standing in the passageway behind them. They'd been so wrapped up in their quarrelling they hadn't even heard him come down the stairs.

'That's enough, Elizabeth.' Evan advanced towards them bare-chested, his trouser belt hanging at his waist, his shirt flapping loosely on his arms.

'Look at her! Just look at her!' Elizabeth screeched. 'Your darling daughter. The whore!'

'I said that's enough, Elizabeth,' he repeated sternly. He turned to Bethan. 'Go to bed, girl. Now,' he commanded.

'That's right. Send your little darling to bed,' Elizabeth mocked. 'We all know she can do no wrong in your eyes. Your little darling . . . the whore,' she hissed, repeating the word, conscious of the effect it was having on Evan. 'My father always said that colliers, not the devil, invented whores. Well, collier or not, Evan Powell, I'll not have a whore under my roof. I'm telling you now . . . ' she ranted, pointing at Bethan. 'Get her out, or I'll put her out. She's no daughter of mine.'

'You don't know what you're saying, woman.' Evan pushed himself between her and Bethan.

'Oh yes I do, and she goes . . . '

'That suits me fine,' Bethan shouted, goaded to breaking point. 'I'll pack my bags now.'

'Don't be silly, love. Where would you go at this hour?' her father said testily.

'She can go back to wherever she's been until now.'

'For Christ's sake, woman, shut up.' Evan turned fiercely on Elizabeth.

'Don't worry, Dad. I'm going.'

Bethan saw her parents through a red haze of anger that had been slow in coming, but smouldered all the fiercer for its tardiness. 'Just remember one thing,' she flung the worst thing she could think of in her mother's face, 'I didn't ask to come back here. You begged me because you couldn't make ends meet. I can have a place in a nurses' hostel any time for the asking. And I'll be a damned sight better off —'

'Bethan!' The cry came not from her mother, but her father. Her hand flew to her mouth. 'Dad,' she whispered. 'Dad, I'm sorry, I never meant . . . '

'See,' Elizabeth crowed. 'See what an ungrateful wretch you've spawned.'

'Go to bed, Bethan.' Evan leaned wearily against the door frame so she could pass him in the narrow doorway.

'I didn't mean . . . '

The words died on Bethan's lips. Her father wasn't looking at her. He was staring at her mother, a strange expression in his eyes. Head down, she ran along the passage and up the stairs.

Haydn and Eddie were sitting side by side on the top step, hunched and shivering in the nightgowns Elizabeth had patched together from Evan's old shirts.

'What's happening, Beth?' Haydn whispered.

'Nothing.' She brushed past him tearfully.

'Noisy nothing,' Eddie said tactlessly.

She slammed the bedroom door on them.

101

'Beth?' Maud's voice echoed sleepily from the dark lumpy shadow that was the bed.

'Go to sleep,' Bethan ordered, banging her ankle painfully in the blinding darkness.

She almost fell on to her side of the bed and began to undress, allowing her clothes to fall any shape on to the floor. Fumbling beneath her pillow she finally found her nightdress and pulled it over her head before she stole between the sheets. Tensing her body she strained to listen to what was happening downstairs.

At first Maud's heavy breathing seemed to drown out all the other noises of the house. But then she heard the boys blunder their way back to their bedroom. Still listening intently she lay awake until the first cold fingers of dawn crept through the thick curtains to lighten the shadows from black to grey. No other sound reached her during those hours. No voice was raised in the kitchen, and no foot stepped on to the stairs.

Elizabeth sat up in the parlour all night. She was conscious of one thing and one thing only. Of the depth to which her children had sunk. Haydn working night after night in the Town Hall rubbing shoulders, and heaven only knew what else, with chorus girls, drunken spivs, played-out musicians – the dregs of the theatrical world. Eddie practically living in the gym at the back of the Ruperra Hotel, fighting, smashing men's faces in and having his own beaten in for a pittance, and – even more sickening – because he enjoyed the feel and smell of violence. Bethan spending her evenings in public halls where drink was sold. Going out with men, drinking – and no doubt allowing herself to be pawed like an animal.

She recalled the time when she'd been able to control almost all of their waking moments. Almost all – because she'd never been able to prevent them from visiting Leyshon Street. They'd been such plump, pretty children. She'd taken pleasure in bathing them, dressing them in warm flannel nightgowns and tucking them up in cosy beds.

Most of the time they'd paid heed to her and done what she'd wanted them to. Now . . . now she felt as though her world was breaking up, her values shattering, and the children she'd struggled to keep clean and fed had gone the way of all the worthless working-class children around them.

She finally had to accept that none of them would now aspire to climb out of the back streets of the Graig, let alone to greatness. Neither Haydn nor Eddie would become a minister of God like her father and uncle. The girls wouldn't teach as she had done. Instead, Bethan, the most intelligent of all of them, had become a nurse. She wrinkled her nose at the thought of what Bethan did every day of her life. Messing with people's naked bodies. Women in childbirth . . . she shuddered in disgust, wishing she'd never borne any of them. All motherhood was pain. The pain of conception, of birth, and this – the ultimate and worst pain of all. The pain of losing them.

At a quarter to six in the morning Bethan lifted down the cardboard suitcase she'd carried her clothes home in from Cardiff. Then she remembered the look on her father's face when she'd threatened to move out. Swallowing her pride she put it back on top of the wardrobe, and washed and dressed ready for work.

She had to walk through the kitchen to go out the back. Her mother was alone, engrossed in blackleading the stove. If she heard her entering she made no sign of it; nor did Bethan acknowledge her.

For the next few days a mixture of mortification and smouldering anger kept Bethan away from the house as much as possible. She went there only to sleep. She ate her breakfast, dinner and tea, such as they were, on the ward, and had supper at Megan's, buying bloaters, meat pies, pasties and slices of brawn in the grocer's opposite the hospital to offset the cost to her aunt. Megan, used to the vagaries of her brother-in-law's household, was quietly supportive. Her father and her brothers tried to smooth things over, and Maud complained that she hardly saw her, but she excused her absences with brief references to pressures of work.

She wasn't exaggerating about that. Her shifts began at six-thirty in the morning and finished at seven at night. Afterwards she stayed behind in Sister's office, studying until ten or eleven o'clock. The midwifery certificate covered a vast amount of both text and practical knowledge; following Matron's suggestion, she made full use of the small library kept locked in the cupboard of Squeers' office.

She soon found out that Matron had told her the truth. It was difficult to do a full day's work and study at the same time. When she'd been a probationer in Cardiff Infirmary, concessions to studying time, scant though they'd often been, had at least been made. Squeers didn't even pay lip service to the idea. And now she and Laura were qualified the sister took care to see that every minute of their ward time was spent on their feet and working. But although the job was demanding she enjoyed it, and she was grateful that it left her very little time to think of what was happening at home – or of Andrew.

She looked for him constantly and even saw him occasionally, but never alone. He was either on ward rounds with his father and Trevor, or they were both gowned and masked with a patient lying between them. It didn't help when Laura returned from a day off in the middle of the week with bright, shining eyes, a definite lilt to her voice and tales of an outing with Trevor, whose free time had miraculously coincided with hers. Flushed with, if not love, at least the beginnings of fond affection, she renounced all her claims to Andrew in favour of Bethan. Bethan scoffed at Laura's teasing, but it didn't stop her from manoeuvring to get close to Andrew whenever he visited the ward.

Envy hadn't been part of Bethan's nature until she watched Trevor and Laura during the week that followed. She grew taciturn and silent, particularly in Laura's presence. Totally preoccupied with thoughts of Andrew, she regretted what she saw as her dark, amazonian figure, contrasting it with Laura's pert, petite appearance. Would Andrew have asked her out again if she'd been prettier? More talkative, like Laura?

She grew pale, lost weight, and close to the end of her unbroken stint of duty, she felt both physically and emotionally drained. She had a two-day break coming to her, but she was dreading it. She'd toyed with the idea of spending most of it in the reading room in Pontypridd's lending library, resolving to get up early and study in the morning; after buying a few dainties in town, she would invite herself to Megan's for tea and supper. But she took no pleasure in the prospect. In fact she took pleasure in very little except Haydn's good fortune in finding work, and the rapid progression of her studies.

Two days before she was due to take her leave, Squeers came down with influenza. The night sister was shifted to day duty, and Matron sent for Bethan and asked if she'd work two nights, to cover for the sister's absence. Pleased to be singled out for the responsibility, she agreed, leaving late in the afternoon to catch a few hours' sleep before returning for the night shift.

She tossed restlessly on the bed from three o'clock until five, then finally rose to wash and dress. Downstairs she walked in on the entire family, who were sitting around the table in the kitchen eating tea. Her father, Maud, Haydn and Eddie greeted her warmly, and for the first time in over a week she was persuaded to join them. Her mother had made an enormous bread pudding, heavy on the stale bread and light on the fruit, like all the others she'd baked since Evan had been put on short time, but it was topped by a thin layer of delicious sugary pastry. Cooking, like the other domestic skills, had been studied by Elizabeth until she had passed from mere proficiency to mastery. The only factor that blighted her recipes was the quality of food she could afford to buy.

Evan, airing paternal pride, asked Bethan how she was progressing with her studies, but the rest of the family were even more silent than usual. Maud had caught a cold, and coughed violently between mouthfuls of warm pudding and tea. Bethan laid her hand on her sister's forehead and, discovering that she had a temperature, suggested that her sister go to bed after the meal. Before Elizabeth could complain about walking up and down stairs with trays, Evan offered to make a batch of the home-made, vinegar-based remedy that Caterina used to brew whenever one of the family went down with a cold.

Eddie had been withdrawn and sullen since the night he had been used as a punchbag in the gym, and he ate quickly. Without a word he carried his plate to the washhouse and disappeared out of the back door and up the garden, ignoring Haydn's shouts.

'I was going to walk down the hill with him,' Haydn complained, finishing his pudding.

'I'll walk down with you,' Bethan offered, picking up his plate as well as her own.

'I've got to go in five minutes.'

'So have I.'

Bethan left the plates in the enamel bowl on the wooden board next to the sink in the washhouse, and looked for the stone foot-warmer that only came out when one of them was ill. She found it behind a sack of carrots on the floor of the pantry.

'Who's that for?' Elizabeth demanded when she saw her filling it with hot water from the boiler.

'Maud, she has a fever,' Bethan replied when she'd recovered from the shock of hearing her mother speak directly to her.

Elizabeth sniffed loudly, but said nothing more. Bethan followed Maud upstairs, and tucked her into bed with a scarf around her throat, a handkerchief under her pillow and the foot-warmer at her feet.

'Dad will be up in a minute with some of Mam Powell's tonic. See you in the morning.' She smoothed Maud's hair back, away from her face.

'Thank you,' Maud croaked, snuggling under the bedclothes.

'What are big sisters for?'

'To pay for little sisters to go to the pictures?' Maud suggested hopefully.

'You're not going anywhere,' Bethan pronounced authoritatively, lifting the blankets up to Maud's chin.

'Not now, but I might be on Saturday.'

'We'll see. Sleep well, see you in the morning.'

Although the sky was heavy with the promise of rain, it was still dry when Haydn slammed the door behind them.

'Long time no talk, Beth,' he said cheerfully.

'Sometimes I think all there is to life is work, work and then more work.'

'I know what you mean,' he sympathised. 'It's the same in the Town Hall. Haydn get me this, Haydn get me that, Haydn clean this floor. Haydn sweep up between the seats. Haydn . . . '

'Last in always gets the dirty work to do. I thought you knew that.'

'I do. I just didn't realise there were so many bloody awful jobs that needed doing.'

'Haydn!'

'Sorry, Beth.'

'You didn't think it would be all glamour did you? Delivering flowers to the chorus girls, and wild parties backstage after the show.'

'No . . . oo . . . o,' he said slowly. 'I've hung around the Town Hall too long for that. But then again a man can live in hope.'

'Hanging around isn't the same as working in a place.'

'I've found that out. Take no notice, Beth. You've caught me at a bad time. Other people get early morning willies, with me it's evening. Besides, I know I'm damned lucky to have any kind of a job. And this one –' he grinned slyly – 'well it does have its compensations. Some of those chorus girls you mentioned aren't half bad.'

'I see.' She gave him a telling look. 'Does Jenny Griffiths know how you feel about them?'

'That's the other thing,' he said mournfully. 'Working these hours, I only get to see her on Sundays.'

'You could give her a ticket for the show and walk her home afterwards.'

'Now that's an idea.'

'If you do, don't forget to check with her father that it will be all right for her to be out so late.'

His mouth fell into a downward curve. 'Harry's all right, but her mother thinks Jenny could do a lot better than me.'

'Then she's a fool!' Bethan protested indignantly.

'Thanks, Sis, I could always rely on you to stick up for me. By the way,' he said casually, 'while we're on the subject, who's this doctor?'

'What doctor?'

'Don't give me that. The one that brought you home early Sunday morning.'

'It wasn't Sunday morning. It wasn't even midnight.'

'Whatever.' Haydn refused to be sidetracked. 'Who is he?'

'He works in the hospital. I hardly know him. He just happened to have a couple of spare tickets for the circus . . . '

'In the Empire Theatre Cardiff?'

'I haven't noticed a circus in Pontypridd this week,' she said sarcastically.

'Beth, you don't just happen to have a couple of spare tickets for something like that. Bill Twoomey's been trying to get hold of some for his family for weeks, and working in the Town Hall he's in the know. They're like gold.'

'People always feel they owe their doctor a favour,' she said carelessly. 'Which reminds me, I've a bone to pick with you. Thank you for putting my money back in my box, but where's the overcoat I asked you to get our Eddie?' she asked, deliberately steering the conversation away from her personal life.

'I wouldn't have made a dog's bed out of the ones in Wien's.'

'I was afraid of that when Laura told me the price. You're still working for Wilf aren't you?'

'Yes, and I'm always on the lookout, you know that.'

'Have you been paid yet?' she asked shrewdly.

'By Wilf? Every shift I do. On the nose.'

'Not by Wilf, by the Town Hall?'

'Got to work a week in hand,' he grumbled.

'I thought so.' She unzipped her shopping bag and reached down for her purse.

'Here.' She tried to slip him half a crown.

'No, Beth. We can't keep relying on you to bail us out.'

'Did Dad say that to you?' she asked suspiciously, remembering her outburst.

'No.'

'Go on, take it,' she insisted. 'Pay me back next week. You'll be moneybags then.'

'I don't need it.'

'I know you don't, but I don't like the thought of you walking around without any money in your pocket. And if you see something that will suit our Eddie you can always put a bob down so they'll hold it. Quick, take it, or I'll be late.'

'All right then,' he agreed finally. 'Thanks, Beth.'

'See you in the morning.'

'It's funny to have a sister working nights.'

'It's funny to have a brother working,' she smiled.

'It'll be funnier still to have two working.'

'Is there any chance of our Eddie finding anything?' she asked hopefully.

'Not that I've heard.'

'Then he's still going down the gym?'

'Did you really think he'd stop because of what we said?'

'No. Just wishful thinking.'

'He's got to make his own life, Beth. We all have.'

'Said with the wisdom of old age?' she laughed.

'You don't do any near enough of that, Sis.'

'What?'

'Laugh,' he said seriously as he walked away down High Street.

She had little time to think about what Haydn had said as the tail end of the evening dragged on into night. The maternity ward was never peaceful. As soon as one babies' feeding time was over, there was the next to superintend. In between there were restless mothers to soothe, and an unexpected admission who'd gone into labour three weeks before time.

With only one second-year trainee and two ward maids to help her, she did the best she could, detailing the maids to the routine tasks of feeding and changing the babies, and entrusting the care of the patient to the trainee when she had to leave the labour ward. At a quarter-past midnight the baby was born with the minimum of fuss, but before the trainee could take him to the nursery the mother began to haemorrhage.

Bethan's first instinct was to shout for help, then with a sinking heart she realised she was it. The senior nurse on duty wasn't even a qualified midwife. Taking a deep breath, she subdued the tide of panic.

'Take the baby to the nursery, then bring a sterile pack and the drugs trolley straight here. Then telephone for the duty doctor. *Hurry!*' she shouted as the trainee stared, mesmerised by the rapidly deepening puddle of blood on the rubber-lined bed sheet. The girl looked from the bed to Bethan, wrapped a towel tightly around the baby, and ran.

At that moment the responsibility she had so proudly assumed crushed Bethan with the devastating effect of a collapsing pit shaft. The woman on the bed was slipping away, already in the semi-comatose state that precedes death from massive blood loss. Bethan lifted the thin, calloused hand, took the barely perceptible pulse and studied the patient. Her face was prematurely aged, lined by years of worry, childbearing and trying to make ends meet. The admission card had detailed this as her eleventh pregnancy, but Bethan had no way of knowing how many of her other children had survived, or how many orphans there'd be if she died.

The trainee returned with the trolley, and Bethan set to work. Praying that her fumbling efforts would be enough, she spent the following hour and a half pounding and kneading the patient's uterus, desperately trying to recall everything that had been done in similar cases when she'd sat by as an interested pupil. Long before the hour and a half was up she had good cause to regret her lack of foresight in not realising then just how swift and sudden the transition from onlooker to nurse in charge would be.

'Trouble, Nurse Powell?'

She turned her head. Andrew was standing in the doorway of the delivery room, cool, unflustered and incredibly handsome in a black evening suit, boiled shirt, black tie and white collar.

'The patient's haemorrhaging,' she said harshly, turning back to the bed. 'I'm doing what I can, but it's not enough.'

He stepped closer, taking off his coat.

'What do you think?' he asked briefly. 'Operate?'

'You're the doctor.'

'And you're the nurse,' he said evenly. 'You must have seen a dozen cases like this.'

'Operate,' Bethan agreed.

He used the small theatre in the outside corridor, and as Bethan couldn't leave the ward in charge of a trainee, he asked the sister from the men's ward who had a qualified staff nurse in attendance to help him. As soon as the duty porters wheeled the patient out, Bethan checked her ward. The maids had just finished the two o'clock feed and, for once, all the mothers were either sleeping or resting peacefully. She told the trainee to clean the labour room and change the bed, and asked one of the maids to make tea and bring her a cup in the sister's office. Emergency or not, she still had to update the patients' record cards, and she felt as though someone, or something, had pulled her plug. It would be difficult to keep her eyes open until her shift finished at seven.

She closed the office door behind her. The fire was smoking miserably behind its tarnished mesh guard. She unhooked the metal screen from the iron grate and tried to poke some life into the coals. The crust of small coal broke, revealing glowing embers beneath. She replaced the guard and kicked off her shoes, resting and warming her feet on the hearth kerb. The ward maid knocked and carried in her tea. For once it was fresh, not stewed.

Revelling in the luxury of being able to put her feet up she leaned back on her chair and glanced up at the uncurtained windows. White streaks of rain were lashing down on the black glass. She felt warm, cosseted and comfortable, ensconced in an overworked nurse's idea of heaven.

After half an hour of writing, she left the office to check the ward. Everything had remained quiet, so she returned to the record cards. She was still sitting, pen in hand, cards on lap, in front of the fire when Andrew returned.

'She's very weak.' He shook the flat of his hand from side to side. 'We'll know one way or the other tomorrow.'

'The birth was straightforward. No problems,' she explained defensively. 'When it happened it was so sudden. . . . '

'Believe me, she wouldn't have lasted until I got here if you hadn't done what you did.' He untied the green gown he was wearing and pulled down the mask. 'I'll get rid of these. Want some tea?'

'I ought to see to the patient.' She rose stiffly from her chair, putting the record cards on to the desk.

'There's nothing for you to do.' He pushed her back into her seat. 'Sister Jenkins from upstairs is staying in the theatre with the patient. I thought it best not to move her for an hour or two. She'll call if we're needed. Tea?' he repeated.

'Yes please.' She sank back down and checked her watch. Half-past three. Another three and a half hours before the night shift ended.

Andrew returned. He was in shirt-sleeves, his black tie hanging loose around his neck, his coat slung over one shoulder.

'Obliging ward maids you have there. They said they'd bring in fresh cups as soon as it's made.' He sat in the chair behind the desk and swung his feet on to the wall. Crossing his hands behind his head he closed his eyes and leaned back. The clean, sharp smell of male perspiration tinged with the heady scent of his

111

cologne filled the warm office. Shy and a little embarrassed by the unaccustomed intimacy, Bethan returned to the record cards.

The maid brought the tea with a quick curtsy and a shy glance at Andrew. He sat up. Leaning over the desk he lit a cigarette with a heavily engraved gold lighter.

'Cigarette?' He pushed his case and lighter towards Bethan.

'I don't smoke.'

'I should have remembered. Sorry I took so long to get here.' He inhaled deeply and blew long thin streams of smoke from his nostrils. 'I was at the tennis club ball in the Park Hotel. The message bounced from home to the Park Hotel twice before the porter found me.'

Bethan knew from his dress that he'd been at a formal 'do'. There was no reason for her to be upset, but the thought of him laughing, dancing and talking to other girls hurt her with a pain that was almost physical.

'I would have asked you to come with me, but you were on duty,' he murmured as though reading her thoughts.

'How did you know I was on duty?' she broke in quickly. Too quickly. She could have kicked herself when she saw his wry smile of amusement.

'I read the duty roster for this ward.'

'You read the rosters?'

'Among other things. You're off on Wednesday and Thursday this week.'

'Off the ward, but I still have to work for my certificate.'

'All work and no play makes Jill a dull girl.'

'Possibly, but I'm not Jill.' She paused, as it hit home that the sour note in her voice sounded exactly like the one that dogged her mother's speech.

'Laura and Trevor spent their free day in Cardiff. I had hoped we could follow their example.'

'And do what?'

'Window-shop, see a film, eat. The things that normal people do outside of hospitals and infirmaries. I'll pick you up in Station Square at ten on Wednesday morning.'

'I can't afford the time.'

'Of course you can,' he said in exasperation. 'That's why you're given days off. To do nothing in particular. Even the hospital board recognises that you can't work people like machines. Ten, Station Square?'

She stared into the fire, refusing to look at him. She was honest enough to admit to herself that she would rather go out with Andrew than any man she'd ever met. One evening in his company had been enough for her to fall for him, to use Laura's language. But the sheer intensity of her feelings terrified her. He was a doctor. He was rich. He could have any girl he wanted – and probably had, she thought cynically.

She realised already that she wanted him to regard her as something more than just a diversion from boredom, and she doubted that he'd see a nurse from the wrong side of the tracks as anything else. She also had a shrewd suspicion that one date with Andrew John could, if she wasn't careful, make her reject out of hand anything less that other men had to offer.

'I assure you, that although I'm a doctor and you're a nurse, my intentions are strictly honourable.'

'I don't doubt it.'

'It's more than just this doctor/nurse thing isn't it?' he asked. 'Is it Laura's brother, or that porter? Because if it is I'll bow out now.'

'No, nothing like that,' she replied swiftly.

'Then what?'

'Nothing,' she said decisively, sweeping her doubts to the back of her mind. 'I'll meet you in Station Square, only at twelve, not ten. I'm on nights again tomorrow, and I'll need a couple of hours' sleep.'

'Good,' he smiled. 'Now that's settled I can go and check on my patient, with luck on my way home.'

The money Bethan had saved for an overcoat for Eddie went on a green wool dress and a down payment on a new navy-blue coat at her Aunt Megan's. She tried to justify the extravagance with the thought that there'd be extra money in her pay packet at the end of the week, but she still hid her new clothes from everyone except Maud.

Her sister's cold had worsened, settling into a hacking, feverish chest infection that Elizabeth had been forced to acknowledge, but even Maud's illness couldn't dampen Bethan's excitement at the prospect of a day out with Andrew. On Wednesday morning the routine update of patients' notes and ward handover to the sister who was standing in for Squeers seemed to take for ever.

It was a quarter-past eight before she reached Graig Avenue, tired and breathless from running all the way up the hill. Haydn had gone to work on Wilf's stall in the market and her father and Eddie had walked down with him, hoping to pick up some work themselves. Her mother had cleared away the breakfast things and changed out of the overalls she wore in the house, ready to go shopping. After a stern injunction to Bethan to clear up any mess she made, Elizabeth left.

Bethan checked on Maud, who was still coughing despite Evan's remedy. She returned to the kitchen to make a fresh pot of tea. While it was brewing she looked at the kitchen clock. Half-past eight. No one would be in before ten at the earliest. She ran outside and unhooked the tin bath from the nail hammered into the garden wall. Her father and their lodger Alun bathed after every shift, out the back in summer, and in the washhouse in winter. Eddie and Haydn bathed in the washhouse before bed on a Friday night, but she and Maud weren't so lucky. Her mother frowned on them bathing, preferring them to wash in the privacy of their room where there was no risk of their father, the lodger or their brothers walking in on them.

She carried the bath into the washhouse, and wiped it over with the floorcloth before taking it into the kitchen. She stood it on the rag rug in front of the range. Lifting down the enamel jug from the shelf where Elizabeth kept her pots and pans she drew off hot water from the boiler, careful not to allow the level to get too low before topping it up. After she'd filled the bath with as much hot water as she dared, she tipped in a couple of jugfuls of cold.

She took Maud's tea upstairs. Shivering in the freezing bedroom she tucked Maud in before returning to the kitchen with her scent, dressing gown and the flannel, towel and soap from their washstand. Closing the curtains in case any of the Richards should happen to walk into their yard, she stripped off and poured a little of the essence of violets into the water. Two minutes later she was sitting in the tub, sponging her back, revelling in the feel of the warm scented water trickling over her bare skin.

Forgetting that she only had a limited amount of time she decided to wash her hair. Ducking her head between her knees she soaked it before rubbing the bar of soap into a lather that covered her hands, and then her head. Luckily she'd left the enamel jug on the hearth, so all she had to do was refill it with the now cool water from the boiler to rinse off the suds. When it was squeaky clean, she wrapped it in the towel, closed her eyes, and wriggled down as low as she could. When she opened her eyes again the water was cold, the hands on the clock pointed to twenty past nine, and her fingers were as wrinkled as her mother's scrubbing board.

Jumping up she pulled the towel from her hair and hastily rubbed herself as dry as she could in the soaking cloth. Moving quickly she stepped out on to the rug and tied on her dressing gown. Her mother never lingered any longer in town than she had to, and if she came back and found out that the bath had been carried into the kitchen there'd be hell to pay.

Bethan emptied the bath with the jug. It was long slow work, particularly as she had to watch that she didn't spill a drop of telltale water on the kitchen rugs. It was a quarter to ten before the bathwater was low enough for her to grab hold of both handles and carry it out through the door.

'What do you think you're doing?'

She jumped, slopping a good pint of water on to the floor.

'Sorry, didn't mean to scare you.' Eddie walked into the kitchen. 'Here, let me take the other handle. Haven't you got enough sense to realise that you could do yourself a permanent injury trying to carry that out by yourself?'

'I was trying to be quick before Mam comes back.'

'I saw her going into Uncle Joe's house as I crossed the Graig mountain.'

'Thank God for that.'

Eddie's eyes were shining, his face filthy, blackened by a thick layer of coal dust.

'What have you been doing?' She didn't need to ask. She already knew.

'Getting coal.'

115

'Off the wagons in the colliery sidings?' she accused him heatedly.

'Maud needs a fire in that bedroom. It's freezing.'

'You could cop a two-pound fine for that. Jail, because we couldn't pay.'

'They'll have to catch me first. And before you ask, the coal's already safe and sound in the shed along with what's left of Dad's ration. There's no telling it apart, and as soon as I've given you a hand with this, I'll lay a fire in your bedroom.'

Bethan gripped hold of the bath handle. She was too ashamed to say any more. As the only one earning any real money she should have done something about the temperature in the bedroom before this. Spent the money she'd wasted on a new dress on coal. She'd been so wrapped up in Andrew and the row with her mother that she'd managed to forget Maud's illness for hours at a time.

'One two three, lift,' Eddie ordered. Shuffling along, they carried the bath through the washhouse towards the back door.

'You can't step out here without slippers on.' Eddie heaved her out of the way, stumbled and tipped the water all over the yard, soaking the flagstones.

'That will never dry before Mam comes,' she wailed.

'I'll tell her I washed it down.'

'She won't believe that,' Bethan rejoined crossly.

'She will if I tell her next door's cat dragged a dead rabbit across it. Right, you go and dress and I'll wash here,' he ordered, embarrassed by the amount of cleavage she was showing.

She saw what he was looking at and pulled the edges of her dressing gown closer together. 'I won't be long.' Grabbing the towel, her discarded clothes and her scent from the kitchen floor, she raced through the passage and up the stairs.

Maud was sleeping fitfully, her cheeks bright red, burning. If the fever didn't break soon Bethan resolved to ask Andrew to call in and take a look at her. Dressing as quietly as she could, she started with the silk camiknickers and petticoat that she hadn't worn since she'd washed and aired them in her bedroom. (Elizabeth had taken one look at the flimsy garments and refused to hang them on the airing rack in the kitchen.) She finished with the new green wool dress and plain black low-heeled shoes. She looked herself over in the mirror, her thoughts an uneasy mixture of guilt over the new dress and regret for her decidedly worn shoes, handbag and dated hat. All things considered, she didn't look *too* awful. She screwed her eyes in an attempt to view her profile in the wardrobe mirror, and gave up when Maud tossed restlessly from her back on to her side.

Stealing out, she closed the bedroom door softly and shivered her way down the stairs and along the passage to the kitchen.

'Want some tea, Beth?' Eddie asked.

'Not if I've got to make it.'

'It's all done.' There was a hurt tone in his voice.

She pulled one of the kitchen chairs close to the range, unwrapped her hair and began to towel it dry.

'Mam'll go berserk when she finds out that you've gone to bed with wet hair.'

'I'm not going to bed,' she said, blessing Eddie's lack of observation. Haydn would have spotted the new dress and smelt the scent by now.

'Then where are you going?'

'To Cardiff.'

'Cardiff's even worse. Going out with wet hair, just after a bath? You out to catch pneumonia?'

'You sound just like Mam.'

'Does she know what you're up to?'

'No. And you're not going to tell her. Are you?' she asked anxiously.

'What's it worth?'

'Sixpence.'

'Make it another seven bob and you're on.'

'You little. . . . '

'I need the money.'

'What for?'

He picked up the teapot from the range, took off the cosy and filled the cups he'd taken down from the dresser.

'What for?' she repeated, forgetting her hair for a moment.

'Gloves,' he answered reluctantly.

'Boxing gloves?'

'I'm good, Beth. I really am.'

'I saw how good you were the other night.'

117

'No you didn't,' he broke in angrily. 'That was the first time I'd ever climbed into a ring. I really am good, everyone in the gym says so. Once I get gloves I'll go round the fairground booths. A few weeks of that and I'll make enough to pay you back and chip in my corner here. Come on, Beth, a month at the most and I'll give you a quid. I'd ask Dad but he's never got any money, Haydn hasn't been paid yet and Mam won't give me a penny. You know what she is,' he added acidly.

'I haven't got it to give to you.'

'It's like that, is it,' he said sourly.

She opened her handbag. 'I can give you half a crown now, and five bob on Friday when I've been paid.'

His face lit up. 'If I put half a crown down today, George will hold them until Friday.'

'George?'

'It's his gloves I'm buying. Beth, you're a darling.' He hugged her out of sheer excitement, then, realising what he was doing, he dropped his arms.

'Fool, more like it.' Her face fell, serious at the sight of one or two cuts and bruises that hadn't quite healed. 'Just don't go getting yourself into a real mess, or I'll never forgive myself.'

He grinned. 'Me? I'm immortal, Beth, I thought you would have realised that by now.'

She tried to quell her misgivings. Eddie was entitled to his dreams. She'd found out long ago that they were the only thing that made the harsh reality of life on the Graig bearable. Since she'd qualified, her fantasies of Florence Nightingale nursing had been replaced by hazy, formless desires that somehow encompassed Andrew John. Haydn had hopes of a theatrical career that would sweep him from dogsbody in the Town Hall to success on the London stage. Her father dreamt of a workers' uprising that would revolutionise the face of the Valleys. Maud had mapped out a future rags-to-riches plan for herself roughly based on the plot of *Jane Eyre*. The only problem with Eddie's dream was that it was easier to put into practice and far more dangerous than any of the others. But fear for Eddie's health and life gave her no right to stop him from trying. For all she knew he might be the lucky one: the next Jimmy Wilde to come out of the Valleys with enough talent to earn himself a slice of the good life he craved for.

And even if he was on a hiding to nothing, who was she to stop him? Better for him to hold on to his dream, no matter how hopeless, than lose all hope for something beyond the grim reality of the present — like their mother.

Chapter Seven

Andrew had parked his car and was sitting waiting for Bethan in the station yard car park. She saw him as soon as she emerged from under the railway bridge, her face flushed with the walk down the hill, her hat and new coat damp from the fine misty rain. She quickened her pace and ran towards him. He stepped out and opened the passenger door.

'I'll start the engine.'

'I'm sorry, am I late?' she asked breathlessly.

'Not at all.' He turned up the collar on his burberry and closed the door for her. Taking the crank from under his seat, he paused for a moment to admire her long slim legs clad in shining, flesh-coloured silk. A few minutes later they were dodging brewery carts and grocers' wagons on Broadway heading towards Treforest on the Cardiff Road.

'Well,' he looked across and smiled, 'you have a whole day free, Cinderella, what would you like to do with it?'

'Window-shopping, the cinema, tea?'

'Those were my suggestions.'

'I haven't any better ones.'

'Lunch first? Or have you eaten?'

'I haven't eaten,' she admitted.

'Then lunch it is.'

He drove off the road in Taffs Well. Turning right he steered the car up a small country lane that meandered through the woods surrounding the romantic, fairytale Castell Coch.

'Where are we going?' Bethan demanded, a sharp edge of concern in her voice.

'To have lunch.'

'Up here?' A chill prickled down her spine. Her mother's frequent and disturbingly graphic warnings sprang to mind as she realised she was on her own, miles from anywhere with a man she scarcely knew.

'Look on the back seat.'

120

She did, and saw the corner of a wickerwork hamper poking out from under a rug.

'That – is lunch. I asked Cook to pack it for us. Now all we need is the right spot.'

He found it almost at the summit of the mountain. A small dirt-track, its far end barred by a rotting wooden gate that looked as though it hadn't been opened in years. He pulled to a halt and turned off the engine. Evergreens and conifers hedged them on both sides, so closely that if they hadn't travelled along the lane Bethan would have doubted its presence. The only open view was over the gate in front of them.

Andrew turned round and knelt on his seat. He handed her the blanket while he unbuckled the strap that secured the lid of the hamper.

'It will soon be cold without the warmth of the engine so wrap the rug around yourself,' he ordered briskly. 'Now what have we here?' He lifted out two steep-sided glass bowls topped with squares of gingham tied with string. He handed them to her, and took out two forks and a plate wrapped into a parcel of grease-proof paper. 'Brown bread, and lemon.' He balanced the plate on the dashboard and gave her a fork. 'And prawns in aspic – ' he took one of the bowls from her – 'try it.' He removed the gingham and squeezed a slice of lemon liberally over the food. 'It's good. I know picnics should be held in summer, but I couldn't resist the temptation to have one now. I love picnicking, brings back memories of childhood and all that.'

She took a wedge of lemon. Conscious of her vulnerability, she contrasted Andrew's childhood memories with her own. The present fare couldn't be further removed from the jam sandwiches wrapped in newspaper, a bowl of whatever wild berries were in season, and the bottle of water that she and her brothers had devoured on the side of the Graig mountain when they were small.

Thrusting his fork into the aspic, Andrew began to eat. 'Don't you like prawns?' he asked as she picked one out of the jelly and examined it closely.

'This is the first time I've tried them.' She put it into her mouth and began to chew. Her mouth was dry, and she almost choked when she tried to swallow it.

121

'They're not unlike cockles. Fishy and salty, with the taste of the sea.'

'They don't look like cockles.' She extricated another from its bed of aspic. 'They look . . . they look naked,' she blurted out, without thinking what she was saying.

'Naked?' He lifted his left eyebrow.

She blushed. 'It's just that they're so pink.'

He burst out laughing. 'What it is to have the mind of a child.'

'I haven't. . . . '

'I'm sorry.' He held up his hand in front of her. 'I didn't mean that the way it sounded. Glass of wine?'

'Wine?'

'It's probably not as cold as it should be. . . . ' He leant close to her and she backed away, hitting her spine painfully on the door handle. Sliding his hand under her seat he pulled out a green bottle wrapped in wet towels. 'There's a couple of glasses and a corkscrew in the glove compartment.'

'Do you always think of everything?' She handed him the corkscrew and held on to the glasses.

'Only where picnics are concerned.' He finished forking the prawns into his mouth, tossed the bowl into the back seat, and jammed the bottle between his knees. It was open in a minute: the wine was clear, sparkling. Unlike anything she'd drunk before.

'If you finish the prawns, we can move on to the next course.' He pulled open the door of the glove compartment, and placed both glasses on it. Then he produced two large plates individually wrapped in damp muslin and thick folds of greaseproof paper. Uncovering hers, she discovered slices of cold chicken breast, lean ham and neatly turned-out moulds of potato salad, grated carrot and rice. She tried her best to eat, but could barely manage a quarter of what was on her plate. Even his food emphasised the difference between them. When she organised a picnic the best she could manage was bread and dripping, brawn, sliced cold heart and dry bread. For the first time she found herself wondering what his home was like. He'd casually mentioned Cook. There would undoubtedly be other servants – kitchen and parlour maids, the sorts of position Maud would apply for when she left school, and count herself lucky to get. A daily 'skivvy' for the heavy work, someone like her Aunt Megan – an odd-job man cum gardener, young like Eddie – or an unemployed miner like her father.

'And here we have the *pièce de résistance*.' Andrew held a glass preserving bottle in front of her. 'It looks disgusting I grant you,' he said, struggling with the top, 'but looks can deceive.'

'Preserved fruit salad,' Bethan ventured, staring at the mishmash of pale fleshy bits floating in murky liquor.

'My father's idea of a winter fruit salad.' He wrenched open the lid and decanted the contents into two china bowls decorated with red and burgundy-coloured cherries.

Bethan tentatively dipped her spoon into the mess, extracted a piece of soggy, colour-bled strawberry and put it into her mouth.

'What is it?' she gasped.

'Summer fruits in Jamaican rum.' He spooned a generous portion into his own mouth. 'My father's favourite dessert. And the only thing in the house made entirely by him. As the season progresses he puts a couple of pounds of every fruit that ripens in the garden into a huge earthenware pot that he inherited from his father, covering it with rum as he goes along. By the time winter sets in, the pot is full enough to keep his after-dinner conversations genial until the next lot is ready.'

Bethan felt as though her mouth was on fire, but for politeness' sake she dipped her spoon into the mess again. This time she found a cherry.

'There's oranges in here,' she said in surprise. 'Surely you don't grow those in your garden.'

'Only in my father's imagination. Here.' He refilled her wine glass.

'Are you trying to get me drunk?' She wouldn't have asked the question if the mixture of rum and wine hadn't already gone to her head.

'No,' he replied quietly. 'Just trying to get you to relax a little. I don't think I've ever met anyone who's been quite as nervous or suspicious of me before.'

She took the glass and stared into it.

'Don't you like it?' he asked.

'It's better than the fruit salad.'

He picked up the bowl from her lap, and winding down his window tipped the contents outside. She sat back in her seat and looked over the gate down into the valley below. She followed the course of the river Taff as it wound between patchwork fields, wooded copses and narrow threads of stone houses.

'I hope the rain stops when we get to Cardiff,' she said for the sake of saying something.

'It won't make any difference to us if it does. The arcades are best for window-shopping, and I'll try and find a film with plenty of sun in it. It'll be black and white sun of course,' he said earnestly.

She smiled.

'That's better. Here, let's finish this.' As he emptied the last of the wine into their glasses, his hand accidentally brushed against her arm. She jumped as though she'd been scalded.

'I didn't bring you here to have my evil way with you,' he said quietly, gazing into her eyes.

'I'm sorry.' She was close to tears.

'You really are in a state, aren't you? Here – ' He wedged the bottle of wine in the hamper and handed her his handkerchief. She dabbed at her eyes with it. It smelt of fresh air and new starch.

'Would you like anything else?'

She shook her head.

'In that case I'll pack up and we'll go.'

He folded the dirty plates and crockery into a cloth, then drained his wine glass and laid it on top before closing the lid.

'I won't be a minute.' He picked up the starting handle.

'Andrew, I'm sorry. Really sorry,' she said with difficulty.

'For what?' he smiled. 'Being a nice girl?'

He glanced at her frequently as they continued their journey. She sat perched on the edge of her seat, smiling tautly with her mouth but not her eyes, very obviously what his mother called 'sitting on pins'. He recalled the first time he'd seen her tall, slim figure striding briskly along the hospital corridors. Even the convent veil that covered her hair, and her pale complexion drained by overwork and the drab surroundings, had failed to detract from her exotic Mediterranean beauty. Then she'd turned, and a single glimpse of her magnificent dark eyes had been enough to make him forget his current girlfriend and offer to cover for his father on all maternity ward emergencies.

At the hospital ball he'd seen the humour and intelligence that lurked beneath the surface of basic insecurity, and the evening at the circus had shown him how very different she was from the self-assured, middle-class, somewhat selfish and often mindless girls he'd known in London. When he'd moved to Pontypridd to join his father he'd assumed that he would follow the carefree path of many and varied girlfriends and happy off-duty hours spent in search of the good times that he'd had in London. But he'd reckoned without the effects of the economic slump. The dour grey stone buildings and air of grim poverty that clung to the streets in the town soon came to epitomise the word 'depression' for him.

'Good times' in Pontypridd were few and far between, even for the young. Survival, not fun, was the major concern and preoccupation. He knew from something Laura had said that Bethan's father was on short time and her brother out of work. That made Bethan with her regular job the family breadwinner. So he put her serious outlook down to too much responsibility too soon. And that made him want to introduce some harmless frivolity into her life. If anyone needed it, she did. Every time he looked at the patients in the maternity ward he saw her as she might be ten years from now. Married to an unemployed miner. Her slim, lithe figure bloated from bad food and constant child-bearing; her pale, delicate skin chapped, roughened and reddened by cold weather, even colder water and a life lived out in a smoky back kitchen. The prospect saddened him. He liked her, felt sorry for her, and at the same time longed to protect her from the miserable effects of the soul-destroying poverty that ultimately crushed most women of her class.

Part of her attraction lay in her vulnerability. As an incurable romantic, her plight brought out the Sir Galahad in him that his mother had nurtured with frequent readings of Arthurian stories. But he recognised that his romantic feelings for Bethan were just that – romantic. And he knew from previous liaisons just how transient romanticism could be. As his father light-heartedly but frequently pointed out, it was one thing to court a girl, quite another to marry her, and he was astute enough to realise that

125

whatever happened between him and Bethan probably wouldn't last very long, simply because she didn't fit into his world any more than he fitted into hers.

He'd never known anyone like her. Unlike all the other girls he'd gone out with, she was working class and, despite her diffidence, possessed a mind of her own. The differences between them were far greater than the common threads that bound their complementary professions, but if anything the disparities made him more interested in her as a person. Or at least that was what he tried to tell himself. He'd never been quite so confused about what he felt for a girl before. Wary of the stage and film stereotype of the caddish middle-class male who deliberately sets out to seduce the poor working-class girl, he decided that for once he would be the perfect gentleman, opting for platonic friendship in the true tradition of Sir Galahad. So with a sharp pang of regret he pushed from his mind all thoughts of enjoying the kind of sensual and easy physical relationship with her that his looks, carefree manner and open purse had brought him with the London ladies.

Not for one minute did he consider that he wouldn't have thought her friendship worth cultivating if she'd been fat, frumpish or looked other than she did. His paternalistic desire to give her and, incidentally, himself the elusive good time closed his mind to everything except the kindness he sincerely believed he was bestowing on her.

He parked the car close to Queen Street station, and from there they walked to the shopping centre. Bethan had often spent afternoons in Cardiff with Laura when they'd been at the Royal Infirmary, but Andrew stopped to browse in small out-of-the-way shops she never knew existed: second-hand bookshops, crammed to the ceilings with musty, leather-bound volumes and framed prints; galleries that displayed black-framed oils and watercolours on crooked walls above rickety staircases. And antique shops – real antique shops, as different from Arthur Faller's pawnbroker's shop in Pontypridd as chalk from cheese.

These shops didn't even hold goods against future payment. The merchandise on display was uniformly old, in good condition, and not an item of clothing amongst the stock. Fine French

126

china and porcelain. Elegantly turned, mahogany Regency furniture. Scenic oils of rural landscapes no longer recognisable as part of modern industrial Wales. Ornate, highly wrought late Victorian jewellery, heavily encrusted with precious and semi-precious gems, and lighter, more tasteful early ornaments that Andrew examined with interest.

They were in a small booth in the arcade when he appealed to her for assistance.

'It's my mother's birthday next week,' he explained. 'Would you help me choose a piece for her?'

'But I don't know her taste,' Bethan protested.

'Good.' He smiled at the perplexed look. 'Good taste,' he qualified patiently. 'Which is what I suspect yours to be.'

Flattered, Bethan bent over the glass display table and studied the pieces.

'I like that,' she said slowly, a little uncertain of herself.

'The blue enamelled and gold locket?'

She nodded.

'My suspicions are correct. You do have good taste.' He called the proprietor.

'Very nice, sir, very nice,' the man repeated, sensing a sale in the air. 'The lady has an eye for excellence if you don't mind my saying so.' He unlocked the cabinet with a key that hung on his watch chain and delicately removed the locket, laying it out, face uppermost in the palm of his hand. 'Late Regency and in superb condition, which isn't surprising considering where it came from. Can't say any more than that, sir. Confidentiality you know,' he whispered close to Andrew's ear. 'The maker's mark is on the back,' he continued in a louder voice. 'French, authenticated early nineteenth century, and I can offer it to you for a very good price.'

The very good price sent Bethan reeling. Twenty pounds! She thought of what her family could do with twenty pounds.

Andrew carried the locket over to the window, and while he examined it more closely she wandered round the rest of the shop. Judging by the mound of black leather jewel cases on display, there was no shortage of women prepared to part with their rings and necklaces, and there was an abundance of other valuables: silver and gold cigarette cases, watches, hairbrushes and ladies' toilette sets. She couldn't even begin to imagine having enough money to buy such luxuries and envied the people who had them to sell. One gold cigarette case would buy new outfits for Haydn, Eddie and her father. And put Sunday dinners on their table for a month or two.

'Ready? Ready to go?' Andrew repeated in reply to her quizzical look.

The shopkeeper opened the door for them with much bowing and scraping. The heavens had opened while they'd been in the shop, and Andrew turned up the collar of his coat and opened his umbrella as they reached the mouth of the arcade, placing it more over her head than his own.

'Here, take my arm,' he said as he looked up and down the street. 'Is there anywhere special you'd like to visit?'

'Nowhere.'

He pulled his pocket watch out of his waistcoat and flicked it open.

'It's too early for the cinema. We could have tea? Are you hungry?'

'Not really.'

'We could visit my favourite place in Cardiff. Game for a mystery tour?'

'I'd be interested to see your favourite place.'

'Favourite place in Cardiff,' he qualified. 'Let's go.'

He walked past a large department store and into another arcade that opened out next to a churchyard.

'It's so quiet here,' she murmured. The only sound was the rain pounding on the gravestones and the thick leaves of the yew trees. 'You'd never think you were in the middle of a city.'

'Or next to the market,' he agreed. 'Sometimes when I come to Cardiff in the summer I just sit here for a while, watching the world go by.'

'You watch the world go by?'

'Occasionally,' he replied unconvincingly.

He clenched her arm tightly in the crook of his elbow as they left the shelter of the arcade for the open street. Turning left he led her up a step into a building. He shook the umbrella and folded it while she wiped the raindrops from her eyes and hat, then she looked around in amazement.

'I've never seen anything like it.'

'I have, but not in Wales. Isn't it magnificent?' He was as pleased with her reaction as if he'd been personally responsible for the décor.

They were in a long corridor, the ceiling plastered, arched and moulded after the Norman style. The walls were tiled – but with tiles that would have done justice to an Oriental mosque, brilliantly patterned and coloured in a multitude of blending and contrasting styles. The narrow tile borders were moulded, thrown into sharp relief above and below the bands of squares that bore designs in every conceivable colour and flow of lines.

She walked slowly, running her fingers along the walls, allowing the textures and colours to assail her senses. The corridor finally ended in a sharp left turn and she looked back to see Andrew smiling.

'Watching your reaction is almost as good as seeing it again for the first time.'

'What is this place?' she asked.

'Public library.'

'I wish I'd joined when I was in the Royal Infirmary.'

A pointed, rather forced coughing echoed towards them.

'Reading room around the corner,' he whispered. 'If we creep along quietly, we can take a look at it on the way out.'

Embarrassed, she hung back, but Andrew forged ahead oblivious to her discomfort. She followed shyly and found herself in a large, pillared and niched room, as beautifully decorated as the corridor but far lighter and altogether airier.

'It takes very little to imagine a stunning harem girl sitting at one of those windows,' he whispered in her ear as they left.

'Is that why you like it?'

He laughed out loud, throwing his head back as he opened his umbrella.

'No. I'll like it even when I'm too old to appreciate beautiful girls.' A sudden violent downpour drowned out his words. Taking her arm he quickened his pace, steering her into a Lyon's tea shop. He helped her off with her coat, and they sat at a table resplendent with white linen tablecloth and napkins. An impeccably turned-out waitress came to take their order, and without

129

consulting Bethan he ordered a plate of mixed cakes and a pot of tea for two.

'I think we've exhausted the arcades, and we can't really walk around the streets in this.'

'No we can't,' she smiled, beginning to relax. The unease she'd felt when she'd been alone in the car with him had vanished during their walk around the city. She glanced at the occupants of the other tables then looked back at him, managing to sustain eye contact even when he winked at her.

'We have an hour to kill before the film. We may as well wait here in comfort.'

'Yes,' she agreed.

'I thought we'd go to the Pavilion in St Mary Street. It has talkies.'

'All singing, all dancing, all talking ... ' she began in the manner of the promotional trailers in the cinema. Suddenly she felt happy. Very happy indeed.

'I don't know about all singing or all dancing. There's a court-room drama showing this week. With Pauline Frederick and Bert Lybell.'

'I love Pauline Frederick.'

'Who doesn't?' he asked drily, leaning to one side so the wait-ress could lay out the cakes and teapot. The girl dropped a curtsy, straightened her cap and with a backward glance at Andrew left. Bethan poured out the tea, feeling very grand and privileged. It felt good to know that other women in the room were admiring Andrew and probably envying her.

'Tomorrow?' he asked. 'Would you like to do anything special?'

'You're off duty tomorrow as well?'

'I told you. I read rosters.'

'I don't know. I really should work.'

'Nonsense. You must be way ahead with your studies.' He helped himself to a large cream bun, dividing it into two with his fork and spoon. 'Pity it's not high summer. I could think of lots of things to do in fine weather.'

'Such as?'

'Motor to the coast.'

'I love the sea.'

'Really? Most girls don't like the beach because the wind and the sand mess up their hair.'

'I'm not most girls.'

'I noticed that the first time I met you, which is why you're sitting where you are.' He put three lumps of sugar into his tea, hesitated and added a fourth. 'The beach in winter is very impressive, and if the weather's like this I know a very good tea shop in Porthcawl.'

'No picnic?'

'You'd like another picnic?'

'Yes please.' She lifted a chocolate éclair on to her plate. He stared at her for a moment.

'Then a picnic it is,' he mumbled through a mouthful of cream and choux pastry.

'I wish you'd let me drive up your street.'

'So you can bring all the neighbours out on their doorsteps. No fear,' she said firmly.

'You had a good day?'

'A very good day. Thank you.'

'You enjoyed the film?'

'Very much.'

'And you'll still come out with me tomorrow? Even after this?' He leaned towards her and brushed his lips over hers.

'Even after that,' she whispered. Her lips tingled, tantalised by the light touch of his. For the first time in her life she felt as though she actually wanted a man to kiss her, and kiss her hard.

'I parked outside the vicarage so you could call for help if I became too ardent,' he joked, seeking her hands with his.

She looked up at him, glad of the darkness that concealed the colour flooding into her cheeks, embarrassed by his veiled reference to her earlier behaviour. Shyly, tentatively she lifted her face to his. He needed no other invitation. His lips bore down on hers. She raised her arms, and running her fingers through his thick, curling hair she pressed her head against his. Weak, breathless, she was conscious only of the crushing of the heavy layers of woollen clothing that separated their bodies – his breath, warm, moist as it mingled with hers – the smell of his cologne

131

as it filled her nostrils – the sensation of slow-burning, heavily restrained passion.

'I think I'd better walk you up the Avenue before you're the talk of the neighbourhood,' he said huskily as a light flicked on in one of the cottages opposite the car.

They walked in silence. When they reached her house he whispered, 'Ten o'clock tomorrow.'

'Station car park?'

He nodded and walked away quickly. Taking a deep breath she climbed the steps and opened the front door. The kitchen clock was chiming the hour. Eleven. Heart pounding, she switched on the light and walked down the passage, bracing herself for another ordeal with her mother.

The room was in darkness, but not deserted.

'Hello, love.' Her father's voice floated from his chair. 'I've been enjoying a quiet time. Want to sit with me a while? There's a fresh pot of tea on the range.'

'Thanks, Dad.' She unbuttoned her coat, and asked the question uppermost in her mind. 'Where's everyone?'

'Your mother's gone to bed with a headache. Eddie's walked down the hill to meet Haydn, and Alun's out. Want to tell me what you've been up to?'

'I've been picnicking.' She kicked off her shoes and sat in the chair opposite his, waiting for her eyes to become accustomed to the gloom.

'In this weather?'

'In this weather,' she laughed. 'And then I window-shopped in Cardiff. Had tea in Lyon's café. Saw a talkie, a really good one, and ate fish and chips on the way home.'

'This boy of yours. Is he a good one, Beth?' he asked gravely.

'I think so, Dad.' She leaned forward and hugged her knees. 'I think so,' she repeated slowly.

'That's all right then.' He reached for the cups and put them slowly and deliberately on the table. 'We all want to see you enjoy yourself, love. But none of us wants to see you get hurt.'

'Don't worry, Dad.' She picked up the teapot and began to pour. 'I won't.'

Bethan's relationship with Andrew, and Laura's with Trevor,

soon became the worst-kept secrets in the Graig Hospital. And within a very short time Bethan discovered that despite the embargo she no longer cared what anyone, even Squeers and Matron, thought about her or her liaison with Andrew.

Some of Andrew's self-confident, happy-go-lucky attitude rubbed off on her. Haydn no longer complained that she rarely smiled. Now she not only smiled but frequently laughed, even in her mother's presence. She only had to catch a glimpse of Andrew across one of the yards in the Central Homes or in the corridor of the hospital to get a surge of happiness that would lighten her step and last her the whole day.

Eligible, charming and incredibly handsome – and out of all the girls he could have chosen, he'd chosen her. Everything he said to her, every place he took her to, every moment they spent together, became precious memories to be mulled over, and dwelt upon.

Hidden beneath her underclothes in her drawer lay the chocolate box Andrew had bought at the circus. She'd distributed the last of the chocolates to Maud and her brothers, and as winter faded she filled it with mementoes of her outings with Andrew.

There was the streamer that she had found caught in the neckline of her dress after the hospital ball. One of the programmes he'd bought at the circus; a sugar cube from the Lyon's café, and the ticket stubs from the film he'd taken her to in Cardiff (stubs that she'd retrieved from under his seat when he thought she was picking up her handbag). A perfect round pebble he'd pulled out of a rock pool at Rest Bay, Porthcawl. More cinema ticket stubs – from Pontypridd this time. A programme from a variety show they'd seen in the New Theatre, another from the Town Hall, a wrapper from a bar of chocolate they'd shared . . . every day off brought a new addition.

Two or three nights a week Andrew and Trevor would sit in his car around the corner from the hospital in Courthouse Street, and wait for her and Laura to finish their shifts. Then he'd drive up the Graig hill and drop them off at Leyshon Street, where they changed clothes in Megan's bedroom. With their uniforms folded into bags, they'd spend what remained of the evening in one of the villages on the outskirts of Pontypridd. They visited cinemas in Aberdare, Abercynon, Llantrisant and the Rhondda, and after-

133

wards they ate fish and chips out of paper bags and newspaper in Andrew's car. And when Trevor finally saw Laura to her house in Danycoedcae Road, Andrew walked Bethan the long way home, over the Graig mountain.

When she was with Andrew, Bethan was happy – happier than she'd ever been before. When she was alone, particularly in the early hours of the morning, she fell prey to ugly fears and insecurities. What she feared most was that he'd desert her for a prettier girl from his own class. But even that fear receded as days of unbroken courtship turned into weeks. Then one day as she and Laura walked through the female exercise yard on their way to the maternity unit they saw the green spikes of daffodil shoots pushing their way up in the narrow strip of soil beneath A and B ward windows, and she realised that her relationship with Andrew had survived a whole half-season.

'The first signs of spring,' Bethan observed triumphantly.

'You know what that means,' Laura commented significantly.

'Warm weather, light clothes, outings to the park and the seaside. Trips into the country, lots of fresh air, and if Andrew's right, the disappearance of Maud's cough.'

'Lazy afternoons spent lying next to Trevor on the beach. Warm evening walks up the mountain. . . . '

'Have you mentioned these thoughts to Ronnie?' Bethan teased.

'Don't have to, his mind runs like a sewer.'

'If he suspects that you're still going out with Trevor he won't let you out without a chaperon.'

'Ah, but he thinks I finished with Trevor weeks ago. And he can't say anything to wholesome outings with my girlfriends, now can he?'

Laura leaned back against the wall of the main dining room and breathed in deeply, but all she could smell was the strong odour of cabbage water wafting out of the kitchens. Bethan stood next to her, still smiling at the thought of all she had to look forward to. The Easter Rattle Fair would be held soon, closing the streets of the town to traffic and opening them to stalls and crowds. Andrew had promised to teach her tennis on the courts in Pontypridd Park and put her up for membership of the tennis club. He'd offered to take her to the beaches at Barry Island and Porthcawl, and even mentioned Swansea.

And there was always the hope that things would improve at home. Haydn's job had worked out well; perhaps it was Eddie's turn next. There had been a lot of talk about changes coming to the Maritime. The pit might open five days a week and revert to full-time working, in which case Maud could stay in school. . . .

The hysterical screams of a woman shattered the peace in the yard and with it went all the castles that Bethan had built in the air.

'If that's someone in labour, tough,' Laura said emphatically. 'I've got another ten minutes of this tea break to go.'

Glan and Jimmy appeared in the doorway of K ward dragging a girl between them. She was shouting obscenities at the top of her voice, kicking, spitting and scratching at everyone unfortunate enough to be within her reach.

'Isn't that Maisie Crockett?' Laura asked.

Bethan ran across the yard.

'Stay clear, Nurse Powell,' Sister Thomas, the nurse in charge of K ward ordered loudly. 'You could get hurt.'

'Went berserk when they took her baby from her,' Glan explained as he struggled to pin Maisie's arms behind her back. 'Come on, girl,' he addressed Maisie irritably, 'you're on to a loser. You can't fight me and win.'

'Maisie, listen to me. Rules are rules.' The sister stood in front of Maisie, trying to force the girl to look at her. 'You've done nothing but sit around and look after your baby for six weeks. You can't expect that to go on. You have to work to support you both. And if you work hard, you'll see her for an hour on Sunday. It's not as if they've taken her to the ends of the earth,' she explained gently. 'J ward's behind the maternity unit, not in Africa. Now come along, be a good girl, say you're sorry and we'll forget about this outburst.'

'I want my baby,' Maisie hissed, spitting like a cornered cat.

'You're not doing your baby or yourself any good with all this nonsense,' the sister said in a firmer tone.

'Bastards!' Maisie screamed venomously, going wild. 'Bastards, you've no right to take my baby. She's mine!' She pulled away and kicked Glan in the shin. He relaxed his hold for an instant and she lashed out at Jimmy, broke free and ran back towards J ward, where the babies and toddlers under three were kept.

'Sister Thomas, what is the meaning of this?'

'Oh Christ, the Master, that's all we need.' Glan stopped rubbing his leg, and grabbed Jimmy's arm. Together they ran past the dispensary after Maisie. Sister Thomas was in the middle of her explanations to the Master when Glan and Jimmy returned, frogmarching the still defiant Maisie between them.

'I've heard enough, Sister Thomas.' The Master glared at Maisie. 'There's only one way to deal with recalcitrant paupers, my girl, and you're going to find out what that is.' He turned to Glan and Jimmy. 'C ward,' he commanded.

'The men's ward?' Glan countered in amazement.

'Padded cell, and don't release your hold on her until she's safely inside. Sister Thomas, don't expect her back, I'm telephoning the police. Maisie'll be spending the night in the cells down the station. Where she goes after that will be up to the magistrate.'

Bethan went to Sister Thomas and picked up her hand, which was bleeding badly.

'Maisie bit it,' the sister explained.

'I'll clean it up if you like,' Bethan offered.

'That would be good of you.'

Maisie screamed just one more time before Glan and Jimmy, with the assistance of the Master, heaved her round the corner and out of sight. Feeling faint, the sister sank down on the steps of K ward. Bethan rubbed her temples.

'Sometimes,' Sister Thomas said weakly, 'just sometimes I hate this job.'

'I'm not surprised,' Laura said mildly. 'I'd better be getting back. Don't worry, Beth, I'll tell Squeers where you are.'

'Thanks.'

Bethan sat alongside Sister Thomas and looked up at the square of clear blue sky framed by the rooftops of the workhouse buildings. It seemed paler, more washed out than a moment earlier. The air held an uncomfortable damp chill. She glanced down the yard towards the daffodil shoots. They were very small, no more than buds. Spring was as far away as ever. She'd been a fool to think otherwise.

Chapter Eight

On Easter Sunday the sun beamed down on Graig Avenue, softening the harsh grey outlines of the buildings and the drab brown and black tones of the pressed dirt streets. It directed brilliant spotlights on to the few daffodil buds brave enough to poke their heads out of the dry, barren mountain soil that filled the handkerchief-sized gardens, and it shone warmly on Bethan as she stepped out on to her well-scrubbed doorstep.

'You going to chapel, Beth? Or high church now you're keeping company with a doctor?' Glan enquired snidely.

She looked over the low wall that separated the front of her house from next door, and saw Glan togged out in his best navy-blue rayon suit, sitting cap in hand in front of the bay window closest to her. 'None of your damned business where I go, Glan Richards,' she replied briskly, pulling on the white gloves she'd taken out of mothballs to wear with the long-sleeved blue and mauve floral cotton frock she'd bought from Megan the day before.

'Swearing. On Easter day too. Well I'm a forgiving sort of a chap, and seeing as how we're both dolled up in our Sunday best, how about some company to walk down the hill with?' He took a comb out of the top pocket of his jacket and ran it through his heavily creamed hair.

'I have enough company,' Bethan answered sharply.

'I wish you didn't,' Eddie observed glumly as he, Maud and Haydn came out of the house.

'Didn't the Easter bunny bring you any chocolate eggs to sweeten your temper?' Glan jumped down his steps and followed them on to the Avenue.

'Maud made us some beauties,' Haydn gloated, hooking his arm around his sister's shoulders. 'Little chocolate ones in sponge cake nests.'

'Lucky you,' Glan grumbled. 'Mam thinks chocolate eggs are a lot of nonsense. All I managed to scrounge was one of the hardboiled eggs left over from those our Pat and Jean painted for their kids. And being Pat and Jean they used red paint that went through the shell and dyed the whites pink.'

'Different,' Haydn said pleasantly. 'Talking about your mam, where is she?'

'Went down early to help lay out in the hall ready for the chapel tea.'

'Some people are gluttons for punishment,' Eddie grumbled mutinously, straightening an old crumpled tie of Evan's that he wore at the neck of his only collar.

'You'll eat the tea this afternoon, same as everyone else,' Maud rebuked. 'And if we don't step on it, we'll be late for the service.'

'Mustn't upset Uncle John Joseph,' Eddie cautioned.

'Sooner we get there, sooner we'll be back.' Haydn pulled his cap over his face, and offered Bethan his other arm.

'That doesn't apply to chapel. Sooner we get there, longer we'll sit on hard benches, and the number our bums will be,' Eddie said crudely, trying to wind Maud up. Maud refused to be wound up.

'Isn't it a beautiful day,' she said as they walked, glancing coquettishly at Glan from under her eyelids.

'And you're too young to be doing what you're doing,' Haydn admonished, pulling her away from Glan.

'How am I ever going to learn how to flirt if you get in the way every time I try to practise?' Maud protested.

'Practise all you like,' Glan offered with a sly look at Bethan. 'I don't mind little kids.'

'I'm not a little kid,' Maud complained furiously.

'Boxing tomorrow?' Glan asked Eddie, looking at Maud in a new light.

'Thought I might visit the booth in the Rattle Fair,' Eddie murmured.

'That's a mug's game if ever there was one,' said Haydn, very much the big brother.

'Uncle Joe's going to collapse when he sees us all walking in together.' Maud changed the subject, trying to smile at Glan behind Haydn's back.

'He'd only do that if Dad walked into chapel,' Eddie said.

'Communists don't go to chapel,' Maud commented primly.

'I think Dad would, if anyone other than Uncle Joe was the minister,' Eddie contradicted.

'What about your father, Glan?' Haydn asked. 'He's not a communist and he doesn't go to chapel.'

'He's not much of anything except a drinker.' Glan glanced over his shoulder in case someone was eavesdropping. 'He says time's too precious to waste sitting about in chapel listening to preachers who've never got off their arses to do a day's work in their lives.'

'Bethan, Maud!' Diana shouted to them as they rounded the corner by the Graig Hotel. She was wearing a light green and white flower-sprigged dress and a white straw hat. William had on a new three-piece suit.

'I wish I had a mother who was an agent for Leslie's,' Glan said enviously, thinking, but not daring to speak his mother's opinion that Megan and her children made more out of her relationship with Harry Griffiths than she did from her agency.

'Bad case of jealousy, Glan?' Bethan asked.

'Nice suit,' Glan conceded to William, staring at the grey and blue wool cloth pin-stripe.

'I'd sell it to you if I thought that taking it in a yard or two at the shoulders and a foot or two on the trouser bottoms wouldn't spoil the cut.'

'You're barely an inch taller than me,' Glan protested.

'But what an inch.'

'You. . . . '

'Easter. Good will to all men,' Bethan interrupted, sensing a fight brewing.

'That's Christmas.' Eddie halted in front of the chapel. The reedy strains of the organ floated out into the street along with a heady mixture of Evening in Paris, camphor and mothballs. 'As this was your idea, Beth, after you.'

Aunt Hetty was playing the organ as usual, the music resounding to the arched roof of the fifty-year-old building. Bethan led the way into the back pew, pushing Maud next to the wall so she could keep an eye on her. Haydn followed, with Eddie next to him and Glan on the end of the bench. The pew in front of the pulpit was packed with sober-suited deacons. Her mother had taken her place in the second row, alongside the deacons' wives, an honorary position granted to her in accordance with her status as John Joseph's niece, and only living relative after his wife.

A thud followed by a chorus of subdued titters came from the gallery overhead, traditionally the province of the children. Bethan had happy memories of sitting up there, chewing ends of 'sweet tobacco' and the 'sweepings' that Haydn used to bring back from the stalls on the market. Even as small boys he and Eddie had haunted the place, begging for odd jobs, carrying parcels for heavily loaded customers, laying out gimcracks on the displays, clearing up the rubbish that accumulated around the traders' feet. Once the stallholders realised that they could trust the boys, they paid them in halfpennies, sweepings (whatever they could glean from the rubbish) and spoiled and leftover goods. The halfpennies had been hoarded, the hard goods traded or swapped and the edibles devoured in chapel on Sunday mornings, out of sight and reach of Elizabeth.

The music became vibrant, the vestry door to the right of the pulpit opened and John Joseph Bull, resplendent in white wing collar, dark suit and black bow tie, entered the chapel and climbed on the rostrum to the pulpit. He pointed to the board that carried the hymn numbers and the congregation rose to the opening bars of 'There Is a Green Hill Far Away'.

The only part of chapel that Bethan really enjoyed was the singing, particularly when it was bolstered, as it was now, by the full choir. Clear waves of pure music echoed down from the rafters, breaking into crescendos that carried with them the swell of absolute emotion. And croaking along with the tide of sweet voices were the discordant, hoarse, gravelly chants of the old men, John Joseph's foremost amongst them.

As a child Bethan had never understood the see-saw arrangement of chapel services. The up side of the singing which lightened people's spirits was invariably followed by a depressing down side, when her uncle began his own particular brand of hellfire sermonising. Today, after the prayers and a second hymn, he laid his handwritten notes on the pulpit and stared down at the assembled men, women and children. Each curled into their seat, desperately trying to appear small and inconspicuous as his powerful voice began to recite a catalogue of dire, red-hot torments that the devil kept in readiness for those who transgressed from the straight and narrow.

His bony index finger sought and pointed, and even tough, hardened miners shuddered, closing their eyes and knotting their hands into fists, as guilt coursed swiftly through their veins.

'You. Yes you there, Robert Jones!' The full force of his wrath descended on a hapless miner sitting in the pew opposite Bethan's. 'You know what you've done! So does God. And I know.' He appealed to the deacons' wives in the second pew. 'He took his pay. His three-day pay. Money which his wife needed to keep his children's bodies and souls together. And what did he do with it?' He whirled, a dervish in a flapping black coat. 'He drank it. Every penny! And while he lay retching in the gutter his wife was forced to beg shopkeepers for food for her crying babies. He drank the devil's brew, and let his family starve.'

In the shocked and absolute silence Robert stared down at his feet, too mortified to move or attempt to reply. A child tittered out of sheer nervousness, and John Joseph's hawk-like eyes scanned the hushed crowd searching out the culprit.

'Well might you laugh, Freddy Martin,' he shouted. 'I know and God knows what you stole from the market last Saturday. He sees into the black and sinful hearts of boys who slide sugar crumbs from the edge of sweet stalls into their pockets. Crumbs that aren't theirs to take. And you – ' He turned on two unemployed boys who'd been fined for playing cards in the street, moved on to a wife who'd quarrelled publicly with her neighbours – no one in the congregation was safe from his prying, self-righteous condemnation.

Anniversary of the Resurrection it might be, but for all that John Joseph's anger remained harsh and unabated. He'd never made any allowances for the weakness of his fellow man, and he wasn't about to begin now. His voice rose to a fever pitch of indignation as he shouted out the names of those who had sinned, followed by details of their transgressions. Bethan stared down at her gloved hands. She found it difficult to meet her uncle's eyes over the tea table in the back kitchen of Graig Avenue, let alone when he was preaching.

She glanced surreptitiously around the pews, lowering her lashes whenever anyone caught her eye. The deacons' wives had decorated the chapel with vases of daffodils and catkins, but the clothes of the congregation alone would have testified to the season. Everyone had made an effort, no matter how little they had. Even old Mrs George, who'd worn the same rusty black cotton dress to chapel for as long as Bethan could remember, had taken the trouble to wash, press and trim it with a twopenny lace collar. All the men's collars were stiff with starch and gleaming white, in some cases whiter than the shirts they topped. Best shirts generally lay wrapped in tissue paper in drawers between one Sunday and another. Even the hats that the women wore, and the men held in their hands, had been brushed until the felt had piled into balls.

Studying her neighbours' clothes was infinitely more diverting than listening to her uncle. Shutting her ears to the sound of his voice Bethan picked out the women from Leyshon Street. She'd met most of them in Megan's house. Betty Morgan who had six children, and whose husband was on short time like her father, was dressed in a smart, white-trimmed navy crêpe de Chine. Her next-door neighbour Judith Jones was dressed either in green silk or the best imitation of it that Bethan had seen, and all six Morgan children were wearing new white socks and sandals. Little wonder that William and Diana could afford new clothes. Megan's business must be booming, though heaven only knew how her customers were affording it.

A crash rocked the pulpit and jolted her sharply back to awareness. Her uncle appeared to be staring straight at her although it was difficult to be sure, as his eyes were deep set, half hidden beneath bushy grey brows. The blood rushed to her face, burning her skin. The tension in the atmosphere grew bitter, almost tangible, unbearable in its intensity. Slowly, ever so slowly, John Joseph uncurled his fingers from the edge of the wooden lectern. He lifted his hand, pointed and spoke the one word dreaded above all others by the women in his flock.

'Harlot!'

Every eye in the chapel focused on the hapless victim. Phyllis Harry, shoulders hunched, head lowered beneath the brim of her cheap straw hat, cowered in the corner of her pew.

'Scarlet woman! Follower of the devil's ways. She carries the child of sin within her. God knows, and it is by His will that we are no longer deceived by a wolf in sheep's clothing.' John Joseph's eyes remained focused on Phyllis as he stepped backwards out of the pulpit on to the rostrum. 'We must, all of us,' his eyes scanned the silent, expectant congregation, 'follow God's Law.' His voice deepened, booming with a strength that matched that of the organ. 'If thy right eye offends thee, pluck it out.' His hand moved up to his eye and a collective gasp rippled through the assembly. 'If thy right arm offends thee, cut it off,' he decreed, slashing the flat of his hand towards his shoulder. 'If thy son or daughter walks hand in hand with the devil, shun them. If thy brother or sister ceases to follow in the steps of the Master then. . . . ' He paused and waited expectantly for his sentence to be finished. He was not disappointed.

'Cast them out!' The cry was taken up by those sitting in the front pew, and people further back who wished for a place on the privileged benches.

'Cast them out.' John Joseph echoed the words softly, thoughtfully, as he gazed into the mesmerised faces. 'It is not a step we take lightly. But didn't the Lord Himself overturn the tables of the Pharisees in the temple? Pharisee!' He homed in on Phyllis. 'Neglected, her sin will spread like a cancer.' He stepped down from the rostrum and moved into the central aisle. 'We dare not be complacent,' he thundered. 'Its seed lies within us all.' He bore down on the rows of silent people. 'You – ' he pointed to Jimmy, the porter from the Central Homes. 'And you – ' this time it was a deacon's wife. 'But you, good people, fight to suppress your baser instincts. As does every decent man and woman. We must be ever vigilant. We must strive every day, every hour of our lives. We must fight with every inch of strength we possess. Fight though it costs us our last breath. And even as we fight – the devil lies in wait. He sits there – ' he stretched out his arm to Phyllis – 'fat, complacent, licking his lips as he leads the weak into hell. He sits in God's House, masquerading as the meek. Shun him. Root him out. Destroy him and all his works. As he knows no pity, neither shall we.'

He lowered his voice to a whisper that carried to every dusty corner. 'Should we fail, should we show mercy, the rot that lies within will contaminate us all. It will contaminate you.' He turned to Mrs Richards, Glan's mother who sat in the centre of the middle pew, the layers of her well-covered body quivering. 'And you – ' He clamped his hand on Mrs Evans who lived above the fish and chip shop. 'Should we turn our backs and ignore the cancer, it will grow. Feed upon our fragile hearts of godliness. We *must* be strong.' He paused for breath, allowing the full effect of his words to sink in. 'The Lord taught that there are times when to be merciful is to be weak. There is only one path open to us. We must cast out the devil that is among us. Cast out . . . Cast out. . . . '

The deacons and their wives took up the chant. Soft at first, it built into a deafening crescendo.

'Out! Out! Out! Out! Out! Out!'

Maud gripped Bethan's arm, pinching her flesh until it burned. Casting fallen women out of chapel was a rare feature of John Joseph's ministry. As far as Bethan knew it had only happened twice before, for the simple reason that John Joseph, flanked by a full complement of deacons, visited the miserable girls in their homes as soon as the news broke, before they had time to set foot in chapel. But infrequency didn't make these occasions any the less dreaded by most of the women in the congregation. Even now the only ones who seemed to be enjoying the proceedings were John Joseph, his deacons and the privileged women in the second pew.

Bethan gritted her teeth and held Maud's hand. The object of her uncle's scorn was trapped in the centre of a pew four rows in front of them. Her heart went out to the pathetic creature. Phyllis Harry? The Phyllis who lived with Rhiannon Pugh? Bethan turned to Haydn, and saw shock register on his face. The same thought was in both their minds. Phyllis was in her late thirties, plain . . . she'd never done any harm. In fact there probably wasn't a child on the Graig she hadn't been kind to at some time or another. Turning a blind eye when they'd smuggled baby brothers and sisters into the White Palace under coats, or in through toilet windows. Handing out boiled sweets in the intermission to those who didn't have the halfpennies to buy ice-cream cornets. . . .

A buzz hummed around those who weren't chanting. Only one word was intelligible above the noise. A word that voiced the question uppermost in Bethan and Haydn's minds. 'Who?' Who could the father possibly be?

Coat billowing, John Joseph sailed down the aisle with the deacons following, a tide of grim-faced lieutenants in his wake. He halted alongside the pew in front of the one where Phyllis sat, white-faced and immobilised by terror. It emptied as if by magic, the occupants melting into the aisles on either side as they tried to lose themselves amongst their fellows. John Joseph walked into the wooden pen and halted in front of Phyllis. Only the back of the pew stood between them. He leaned over and jabbed his forefinger into her chest. She shrank from him, hitting her back on the pew. Wincing, her eyes fogged by tears, she edged sideways in a futile attempt to escape.

'Only the devil would have the gall to sit here, in His house. You . . . ' He lunged after her, stepping out of his pew before she could reach the end of hers. 'You are not fit to walk the same earth that our Lord trod.'

Eddie rose to his feet. Haydn, realising what was in his brother's mind, grabbed hold of Eddie's coat. Crouching on hands and knees Phyllis slid out of the pew backwards, trying to edge around John Joseph. Then, as the chanting increased in intensity, the first stone was thrown, hitting Phyllis high on her left cheek-bone, drawing blood.

Neither Bethan nor Haydn saw where it came from. Afterwards Bethan realised that her uncle must have primed the deacons for them to have carried stones into the chapel. Phyllis screamed, more from fear than pain. The congregation, whipped into a frenzy, surged towards the back of the chapel . . . and Phyllis.

She struggled upright but the crowd hemmed her in on every side. One of the deacons' wives spat on her, the spittle trickling down the sleeve of her yellow and green print dress. Another threw her hat to the floor and pulled her hair. Sickened, Bethan turned away, pulling Maud close to her.

'Eddie!'

She heard Haydn's cry and saw her younger brother, fists flying, fight his way towards Phyllis. But before he could reach her John Joseph fell silent. He held up his hand and the crowd parted, allowing the choking, sobbing woman to stumble towards the closed doors at the back of the chapel. Eddie clambered over

145

their pew, forced his way through and reached the doors before Phyllis. He wrenched them open and in the only gesture of sympathy he was able to make smiled at her. She didn't even see him. Tripping over the worn doormat she fell, grazing her knees on the pavement outside. Eddie tried to go after her, but a bellow from John Joseph froze him in his tracks.

'Only the devil's paramour would run after the devil.'

Colour flooding into his cheeks, Eddie slammed the door shut, thumping his fist impotently on the jamb.

'The hymn.'

Flustered, Hetty began to play, mixed up the notes, and began again. It took another curt command from John Joseph for her to realise that she was still playing 'There Is a Green Hill Far Away'.

People shuffled back to their seats. John Joseph returned to the rostrum, singing every step of the way. He'd stage-managed the affair brilliantly. The words that resounded into the air, thrilling the congregation were 'Fight the good fight with all thy might.'

Eddie didn't return to his seat. When Bethan looked back she saw that he'd remained standing in front of the closed door, staring at John Joseph.

'Christ is thy strength and Christ thy right,' John Joseph bellowed. 'Lay hold on life and it shall be. . . . '

The deacons picked up the collecting plates. Another musical note joined in with the singing — the quiet clinking of coins. Bethan reached for the white straw bag she'd bought to go with her new dress and fumbled for her purse. She clicked it open and felt the coins inside. Taking out two joeys — silver threepenny bits — she slipped one to Maud and held the other in her gloved hand. The collecting plate was full by the time it reached her. It always was at Easter. People who couldn't afford to put food on their tables more than once a day always seemed to find pennies for the collecting plate. They were too afraid of John Joseph not to.

She waited for Maud to lay her offering on the plate, then turned to pass it to the pew behind her. As she did so she glimpsed one of the deacons handing Eddie a server. Eddie took it, and passed his hand over the plate before returning it to the deacon with a wry smile. She couldn't be sure, but she thought she'd

146

seen Eddie remove, not add, coins. The notion troubled her, and she glanced back when the hymn had finished. Eddie slipped his hands into his pockets as he returned to his seat alongside Haydn. Then she knew for certain. She looked nervously at John Joseph. He'd closed his hymnal and was beginning the prayers. If he'd noticed anything he would have announced it to the assembly. Of that much she was certain. Two castings out in one day would have been too good an opportunity to miss.

Eddie was the first to leave the chapel. William and Haydn weren't far behind him. Bethan followed as soon as she mustered Maud and Diana.

'Straight home?' Haydn asked, looking to Bethan.

'I'm calling in on Rhiannon Pugh.'

'There's nothing you can do, Beth,' Haydn said.

'What you're trying to say is I've my reputation to think of,' she retorted hotly.

'Our mam'll already be there,' William chipped in, trying to defuse the situation.

'Your mam hasn't got a reputation to care about,' Glan smirked as he joined them.

'You take that back right now.'

'Or?' Glan taunted.

'Or I'll punch you on the mush.'

'Not here, later on the mountain if you have to,' Haydn whispered, looking to the chapel doorway as he stepped between them.

'Name the time and place,' Glan retorted.

'The old quarry, three o'clock this afternoon.'

'I'll be there.'

John Joseph, with a deacon and three middle-aged women walked into a puddle of sunshine on the pavement and remained there talking. Diana forced a smile, took hold of her brother's arm and pulled him round the corner, the others following at a slower pace.

'Push off, Glan,' Diana ordered vehemently once they were out of earshot.

'It's a free country.'

147

'You're not wanted.' Eddie crossed his arms over his chest and blocked Glan's passage. 'Get the message.'

Glan took the hint. As the others climbed the flight of stone steps that led from Graig Street to Leyshon Street, he retreated round the corner.

'Beats me why she came to chapel in the first place.' William brought up the topic uppermost in everyone's mind.

'Beats me how John Joseph knew.' Haydn leaned against the railings and waited for Bethan and Diana to walk up the steps. 'I didn't even realise she was knocking around with anyone.'

'Whoever he is, he's a right bastard to leave her to go through that on her own.'

'Eddie. Language,' Haydn reprimanded.

'Well he is,' Eddie protested.

'I agree with Eddie,' Diana said warmly. 'From a woman's point of view . . . '

'Woman.' William choked on the square of chewing gum he'd put into his mouth.

'We are women too,' Maud insisted. 'Everyone knows that girls mature long before boys.'

'And who told you that, rat's tails?' Eddie pulled the plait that stuck out beneath her straw hat.

'Never you mind.' She linked arms with Diana and they walked on up the street, their noses in the air.

'Look out!' William shouted to the neighbours who'd moved their kitchen chairs into the street to enjoy the spring sunshine. 'Their ladyships are airing their maturity.'

'Don't you three ever let up?' Bethan said irritably.

'Sorry, Beth,' Haydn apologised.

'You could at least *sound* sorry!'

'I am. I really am.' He held out his hands, palm up.

'You're going to have to do better than that if you want to tread the boards in the Town Hall instead of scrubbing them.'

'Ouch, Beth, that hurt. Come on, I've said I'm sorry. What more do you want me to do?' He dropped the pose and slipped his arm round her shoulders. 'Don't let it get to you.'

'Don't let what get to me?' she asked, removing his arm.

He shrugged and grinned at her. 'The weather?' he suggested mildly.

'Now you're being ridiculous.'

'I see that uncle of yours has been at it again.' Mrs Plumett, who lived two doors down from Megan, nodded to Bethan and Haydn.

'He's no uncle of ours,' Eddie said warmly.

'Shame on him,' Mrs Plumett continued as if he hadn't spoken. 'Nice girl like Phyllis too. She deserves better than that. Caring for Rhiannon the way she has all these years. Your mam's up there doing what she can,' she said to William. 'And Rhiannon's already said that Phyllis will go to the workhouse over her dead body. As long as she has a roof over her head, she'll see that Phyllis has one too. Mind you,' she whispered, dropping her voice, 'if you ask me Rhiannon hasn't been looking too well lately, and then . . . well . . . ' she pulled the edges of her cardigan together, trying to make the sides meet across her vast bosom, 'there's no saying what'll happen then. Phyllis could end up on the street yet. You know what Fred the dead is like?' she prattled on, referring to the local undertaker cum builder who owned a fair number of the houses in both Phillip and Leyshon Street. 'He won't let a woman like Phyllis take on the rent book. You can be sure of *that*,' she finished, triumphant in the knowledge that she'd been the first to think that far ahead.

'I'm sure that whatever needs doing to help Phyllis or Rhiannon will be done,' Bethan replied noncommittally.

'Oh, I wouldn't be too sure of that if I were you. You know John Joseph and his brigade. Holier than thou and a moth-eaten blanket. Still, you being a nurse and working on the labour ward, you could do a lot if your uncle lets you.'

'You can count on me to do whatever I can.'

'And I'm sure Phyllis will be grateful. I must go or my old man's dinner will be burnt.' With that she ran through her open front door, down the passage and into her back kitchen. Bethan heard the washhouse door slamming and Mrs Plumett calling to her neighbour over the garden wall.

'In five minutes it'll be all over the Graig that you approve of Phyllis. And that, dear sister, as far as the gossips go, makes you no better than her.'

'Seems to me Maud's right.' Bethan glared at him. 'It's always the women who are left to clear up the mess.'

149

Before going to chapel Elizabeth had prepared the Sunday dinner of rolled breast of lamb, stuffing, mint sauce, roast potatoes, cabbage and gravy to celebrate Easter. She'd also given her children strict instructions to hurry home after the service to help put the finishing touches to the meal. But angry and restless, Bethan stuck by her decision to visit Phyllis. She went to Rhiannon's house alone, making Maud and the boys walk the long way home past the Graig Hotel, but she saw neither Rhiannon nor Phyllis. Megan had taken charge of the house, and she was keeping most of the neighbours, particularly the gossips, firmly at bay.

Rhiannon and Phyllis were sitting in the front parlour, in itself an event, for no one had entered the room except to clean it since the funeral of Rhiannon's husband and son. The door was firmly closed and Megan was ferrying cups of tea through from the kitchen when Bethan knocked and walked in.

'Oh it's you, love,' Megan said, dropping the aggressive stance she'd adopted.

'I came to see if I could help,' Bethan murmured rather inanely. Now she was actually in the house she felt quite useless. And nosy. Just like Mrs Plumett.

'If I thought you could do anything to help I'd take you in, love, but they're best left on their own for a bit. Rhiannon needs to get used to the idea of Phyllis being in the family way. Look, I'll be back in a minute.' Megan pushed open the door with her hip and took in the tea. When she came out she carried two empty cups and saucers stacked in one hand. She closed the door and took Bethan into the back kitchen.

'I'm staying for a bit,' Megan continued. 'Just to see to the callers.'

'It was awful. . . . ' The tears she'd kept buried beneath a surface of anger welled into her eyes.

'You don't have to tell me, love,' Megan said bitterly. 'I've seen John Joseph's casting outs for myself.'

'I should have done something.'

'What?' Megan demanded.

'I don't know. Something. I could at least have helped her to get out of the chapel quicker.'

'If you'd tried to help Phyllis you'd only have given them an excuse to throw stones at you as well. No, love, it's my guess that you did the same thing I did when your uncle cast out Minnie Jones the year our William was born.'

'Sit tight and watch,' Bethan said disparagingly. 'That doesn't make me feel any better.'

'I never said it would. But I made my protest afterwards,' Megan said proudly. 'I swore I wouldn't set foot in the chapel again while John Joseph preached there, and I haven't.'

'Are you telling me to do the same thing?'

'No one can tell you to do anything like that, love.' Megan filled the kettle in the washhouse and walked back into the kitchen to set it on the range. 'That has to be between you and your conscience. But I do know this much. If you decide to boycott chapel you'll have your mother as well as John Joseph to contend with. And that's without bringing God into it.'

Chapter Nine

'Cat got your tongue?' Andrew asked Bethan as he changed down into second gear in preparation for the long slow drive up Penycoedcae hill.

'No,' she said abruptly. Too abruptly.

'Come on, something's the matter,' he pronounced with an irritating superiority. 'I know it is, so you may as well tell me first as last.'

'Are you church or chapel?' she demanded.

'Now that's a strange question. Why do you ask?'

'I just wondered.'

'Church. St Catherine's.' He named the largest church in town that stood, resplendent in its Victorian glory, in the centre of Pontypridd, next to the police station on Gelliwastad Road. A church that catered unashamedly for the crache of the town.

'You would be,' she said bitterly.

'What's that supposed to mean?'

'Nothing. Take no notice. It's just me.' She stared blindly out of the car window, oblivious to the fresh spring beauty of budding trees and green fields.

'Look, baa lambs.'

'Second childhood?' she enquired frostily.

'I always think the mothers look so old and grubby compared with the young,' he continued, unabashed.

'Bit like the difference between young girls and old women.'

'You sound like one of the old women.'

'I feel like one.'

'I don't know, you get Easter Sunday and Monday off, the two days any one of the staff nurses would give their souls, if not their virtue, for. Presumably you've had nothing more taxing to do this morning than go to church and eat lunch with your family. And now you have a highly desirable and amusing bachelor like myself at your disposal, and what do you do? You growl in a mood more fitted to a night of thunderstorms than a heavenly spring day.'

Lunch, she thought bitterly. Just one more word to remind her of the gulf between his family and hers. The crache consumed lunch on the Common, the working class downed dinner on the Graig.

'I don't go to church, I go to chapel,' she snapped.

'I beg your pardon,' he apologised heavily. 'I didn't mean to upset your ladyship.'

'I know you didn't.' Her anger deflated into shame. 'I told you, it's me.'

'Would it help to talk about whatever it is?'

She closed her eyes against the glare of the sunshine and remembered the events of the morning. Each and every shameful detail was recalled in appalling clarity. John Joseph, his dark eyes shining, elated as he stood triumphant and secure in the midst of his deacons. Phyllis pathetic and cowed, spittle running down her spring dress, blood on her cheek where the stone had hit her. . . .

'No,' she said decisively.

'In that case do you mind telling me where we're going?'

'Anywhere.'

'Mumbles Pier so I can throw you off?'

She looked at him. He stuck his tongue out. She laughed in spite of herself.

'That's better.' He narrowed his eyes against the strong sunlight. 'Pass my sunglasses please, they're in the glove compartment. Now can we discuss where we're going?'

'Anywhere you want to.'

'Anywhere?' He raised his eyebrows, and adopted an excruciating foreign accent. 'Right, young woman, how about I carry you off somewhere warm and exotic. Like – ' he leaned across and whispered close to her ear – ' 'a silk-draped harem in the wilds of the Sahara.'

'Saw too many Rudolf Valentino films when you were young did you?' she enquired sarcastically.

'Of course, didn't every child? My mother used to drag me along every chance she got. Life with Father was so very, very humdrum.'

'That I don't believe.'

153

'You've only ever seen my father directing patients' treatments and hospital policy. At home my mother won't allow him to be important.'

'Just how many other women would you like in this harem of yours?'

'That depends on how quickly you wilt in a hot climate.'

'Why, you. . . . '

'Don't hit me when I'm driving or we'll end up in a ditch.'

He swung the car around the corner past the Queen's Hotel, carried on for a couple of miles until the few cottages that were Penycoedcae were well and truly behind them, then pulled into the side of the road. Leaving the engine running he reached across, wrapped his arms around her and kissed her full on the mouth. She relaxed against him, warm and secure in his embrace. They'd come a long way since the awkward beginnings of their first outing to Cardiff.

'Right, for the last time where do you want to go?' He released his hold on her and turned to face the wheel.

'The sea?' she suggested.

'Don't you have to be back early?'

'No. I told my father to expect me when he sees me.' She could have added 'and now my mother knows better than to interfere' but her strained relationship with her mother was something she'd kept from Andrew.

'Good.' He pulled his watch out of the top pocket of his silk shirt and flicked it open. 'Two o'clock.' He did some quick calculating. 'If we get a move on we can have at least four hours there, and still be back before midnight.'

'Four hours where?'

'You'll see when we get there.'

He put the car into gear and pulled out into the lane; with his arm round her shoulders he steered skilfully along the winding road. She snuggled up to him, conscious of the warmth of his body beneath the blue blazer and thin shirt, the smell of his cologne as it clashed with and finally overpowered the essence of violets she was wearing.

'Share a cigarette?' he asked.

'Do I ever?'

'It sounds more polite than asking you to light one for me.'

She slid her hand into the blazer pocket closest to her and removed his gold lighter and cigarette case. Lighting one, she placed it between his lips.

'Thanks.' He wound down the window and rested his elbow on the open ledge. 'Settle down, we've a long way to go.'

'How long?'

'The Sahara side of Porthcawl.'

Knowing she wouldn't get any sense out of him while he remained in this mood, she did as he suggested. Resting her head on his shoulder she closed her eyes, pushing the images of the morning's service to the back of her mind. She wondered at the miracle that had enabled her to build a happy, relaxed relationship with Andrew despite the strain of their first outing together.

Although they went out in a foursome with Trevor and Laura as often as staff rosters allowed, she preferred and treasured the times, like now, when she and Andrew were alone. He was less of a public entertainer, more sensitive and aware of her feelings without an audience. And although she still occasionally woke up in the small hours, cold at the thought of where their relationship might end, afraid because she knew she had come to rely on him far too much, she continued to be free of such worries while they were together. She felt incredibly alive when she was with him, a kind of elation that blocked out every other aspect of her life. It was as if she only really lived in his presence.

Those who were closest to her – Megan, her father, Laura, her brothers and Maud – suspected that she was in love, but she continued to stop short of analysing her feelings. If anyone had tried to present her with the evidence she would have laughed. For quite apart from the social gulf, underlying the strong emotions she felt for him was an inherent fear. She had seen at first hand the damage that love could cause. Her mother wielded the power it gave her like a lash, using it to strip her father of everything he valued and held dear – dignity, independence, even the small pleasures he tried to take in the simple everyday facets of life.

She was aware that there were other kinds of relationship: those in which gentleness and consideration prevailed over the desire to subjugate. Some marriages were undoubtedly based on mutual understanding and affection. She only had to look as far as her father and contrast the air of patient, resigned sadness he wore like the proverbial hair shirt whenever he was in her mother's company with the jolly exuberance of Laura's father, who was always hugging and kissing his plump, happy wife.

But until now she'd never considered such a partnership relevant to her. When she'd taken up nursing she'd mapped out her future in terms of a career where hard work and celibacy came before any thought of a personal life.

There'd never been much time for boys. An occasional, unmemorable trip to the cinema in Cardiff with Laura and one or two of the porters from the Royal Infirmary. And before that, outings with her brothers, William, and Laura's brothers. They'd gone out as a crowd, visiting the cinema when they had a few pennies to spare, and Pontypridd park, Shoni's pond or the Graig mountain when they didn't.

Once, soon after she'd returned home from the Infirmary, she'd visited the White Palace with Glan. Neither had forgotten the episode, but for different reasons. He, because he was continually nagging her to repeat the experience; she because the evening had ended with her slapping his face soundly when he'd tried to kiss her. Now . . . she wrapped her arm round Andrew's and snuggled closer to him; now, she actually liked being kissed.

'We're here.'

Disorientated, she opened her eyes and looked around. She hadn't known the world could be so green. Even the air seemed green, filled with a clear jade light that danced off the thick, curling new leaves of trees and bushes.

'Come on, I'll introduce you.' He turned off the car engine, opened his door and walked around to hers. She stretched her cramped limbs and stepped out of the car, shivering in the cool spring air.

'Over there, look.'

A breathtaking view over a thickly wooded hillside swept down towards a wide, flat, grassed valley floor branded with a meandering snake of silver river. And beyond the river, towering green-capped cliffs sheltered pale golden sands fringed by crashing breakers.

'You wanted the sea?'

156

'It's beautiful. It's like it's never been touched.'

'Oh but it has.' He opened a low barred gate that she hadn't noticed and beckoned her forward. She followed him up a narrow gravel path bordered by hedges of white-blossomed may, or 'bread and butter' trees as the children on the Graig called them, eating the leaves when they had nothing more tasty to put into their mouths. Encroaching on the path were clumps of poppies. Andrew halted in front of a wooden door, bleached dry by the sun.

'It's not much,' he smiled. 'Just a wooden summer chalet, but we used to have great fun here when we were kids.' He produced a large key from the top pocket of his blazer and unlocked the door. Pushing hard he scraped it over a flagstoned floor. 'Faugh.' He wrinkled his nose in disgust. 'I hate being the first one in after the winter.'

She followed him into a small, pine-boarded kitchen.

'Welcome to the John summer residence.' He opened a case-ment window set over the sink. 'It may look dirty, damp and musty now, but there's nothing amiss that a good scrub and a summer's warmth won't cure. Do you like it?'

'Like it? I love it.' She looked around. A square pine table, four pine wheelback chairs round it, stood in the centre of the room. A pine dresser, its shelves bare, its cupboard doors closed, stood against the wall opposite the door. Brightly coloured rag rugs lay on the floor next to the door and in front of an old stone sink with a brass tap.

'All the comforts of home.' He turned on the tap. Nothing happened. 'Well almost, water's still turned off.' He crouched beneath the sink and twisted the stopcock. 'My mother bought the rugs at a church sale of work. She used to enjoy shopping for this place when we were small.'

'The "we" being you and your sister?' He nodded. She knew from hospital gossip that he had a married sister a couple of years older than himself. But this was the first time he'd mentioned her.

'Come on, I'll show you the rest. Not that it's much.'

He walked out of the kitchen into the gloom of an inner hallway. There was no window; from the light that filtered in from the kitchen she could see that the wood planking walls were painted cream. There were four doors. Three led into good-sized double bedrooms with large windows overlooking the woods. Two of these contained sets of twin beds, the third a double. The bedsteads were plain unvarnished pine, with mattresses wrapped in rubber sheeting to protect them from the damp. The walls and floors were of stripped pine planking, the furniture pine chests of drawers and ottomans, no wardrobes. And like the kitchen all the rooms had a pervasive, thick musty atmosphere of neglect and disuse.

'My father got a local chap to cover this area in when he bought the place. Must be over twenty years ago.' He opened the fourth door. An overpowering dry warmth wafted out to greet them. 'It used to be a veranda, but he planked the walls and put in windows. The door from here to the garden stuck three or four years ago, and I never bothered to plane it. If you want to get out in a hurry you have to use the windows.'

'Sitting here must be like sitting in a goldfish bowl in the woods.'

He laughed. 'I suppose it is. The best view is down this end.' He walked past the two large picture windows that framed the woods, turned left around what had been the corner of the house, and paused before a massive window that looked out over the headland towards the bay.

'Three Cliffs,' he said as proudly as if he were showing her a painting. 'The finest view on Gower.'

'It's wonderful.'

'Isn't it just? Here, help me pull off these dust sheets. I don't know why I bothered to lay them out last autumn, there's so much glass here the damp disappears as soon as the sun shines.' They uncovered a rattan three-piece suite with cushions upholstered in thick, faded but serviceable green linen. She pressed down on one with her hand. It was quite dry.

He sank down on a chair, and pulled her on to his lap.

'I'd forgotten how much I love this place. Strange, I used to spend more weekends here when I was living in London than I do now. Get the train from Paddington to Pontypridd on a Friday night. Borrow one of my father's cars, motor down, eat supper here, and stay until Sunday afternoon.'

'You used to come down here a lot?' She left his lap and stood in front of the window, a maggot of jealousy worming away inside her at the thought of all the girls he must have brought here. Girls like Anthea Llewellyn-Jones who would have been only too happy to go away with him for a weekend.

'Every time my tutors threatened to kick me out for not doing enough studying. This became my work base. The family gave up on it years ago. I don't think my parents have been here more than once or twice in the last five years. Sometimes they lend it out to friends. Fanny. . . . '

'Fanny?' she turned to face him.

'My sister,' he explained. 'Her name's Fiona but I call her Fanny, mainly because she hates it. She loathes this place. No hot and cold running water, no bathroom. Only an old thunder-box out back.'

She remained silent, angry with herself for falling prey to jealousy. He hadn't made her any promises. She had no right to question him about the women in his past.

He left the chair and joined her at the window. 'Would you like a walk? It's too late to go to the beach, it's a lot further than it looks. But we could walk across there.' He pointed to some grey stonework barely visible through the trees on the hillside. 'Those are the ruins of an old Norman castle. If you won't let me play at harems with you, then perhaps I can persuade you to play at knights and ladies.'

'Are you sure the beach is too far?'

'We'll come here early on your next day off.'

'Tomorrow?' she asked hopefully.

'I thought you wanted to go to the Rattle Fair?'

'I do.'

'Then it'll have to wait until the next one.'

'Promise?'

'Promise.' He unlatched the windows and threw them wide. 'Come on, if we leave everything open this place will air out by the time we get back, then I'll make you tea. Totally from tins,' he said gleefully as if it would be a great treat.

They took it in turns to visit the outhouse before they left. He apologised for the primitive facilities. She said nothing, wondering if he realised that the only house that could boast a bathroom on the Graig was that of the Leyshons.

She enjoyed the walk. It blew away cobwebs accumulated

159

during a winter spent working in the hospital, and she even managed to forget the events of chapel that morning in the novelty of the clifftop scenery. Until that moment the sea had meant either Barry Island or Porthcawl. Built-up resorts with rows of stiff wooden chalets, bathing huts, funfairs and railway stations large enough to accommodate the thousands of day trippers that swarmed down on them from the coal-mining valleys. This charming, unspoilt bay set in a wilderness of green pastures and trees entranced her, and although Andrew assured her that there were other chalets close by, she refused to look at the red and grey roofs, preferring to cling to her first impression of total and absolute solitude.

When they returned after an hour's hard walking her feet were blistered from her new shoes, but the air in the chalet was definitely fresher. She sat at the table while Andrew ran the water, first washing out then filling a kettle he produced from the walk-in pantry.

'Last one to leave before winter sets in makes sure there's a fire laid for spring. Not that it always burns, mind you.' Using his cigarette lighter he lit a ball of newspaper and pushed it beneath a pile of logs in the grate, which was built beneath a chimney, the only stone-built part of the chalet.

The paper smouldered reluctantly, then just when Andrew decided to pull the fire out and relay it, it burst into flames. He hung the kettle on a chain over the fire.

'Now, like the three men in a boat we have to pretend that we really don't want tea. Then the kettle will boil, which is more than it will do if we watch it. Let's see, what have we here?' He left the fireplace and walked into the pantry. 'Tinned fruit, tinned sardines, and,' he frowned as he held up a jar filled with dark greenish liquid and some very dubious-looking solids, 'what do you think? Pickled gherkins or eggs?'

'Medical specimen?'

'You could be right. The last time I came here I was studying for my finals.'

'All of a sudden I don't feel very hungry.'

'Coward. How about we settle for tea and I buy you fish and chips on the way home?'

'It's Sunday.'

'So it is. Oh well, we'll have to make do with what's in the car.'

'You brought a hamper? I thought you only decided to come here when we were in Penycoedcae.'

'You know me and picnics. I like them even on slag heaps. If you use the water to wash a couple of plates and glasses I'll bring it in.'

'What about tea?'

'Why drink tea when we can have wine?'

He went to the car while she rummaged through the dresser. She came across a set of thick blue and white clay pottery plates, cups and saucers, and a tray of bone-handled knives and forks. The glasses she found on a high shelf in the pantry, along with a stack of tea towels, tablecloths and enamel bowls. By the time she'd washed some dishes he'd rifled the hamper, laid the cloth and set out a plate of rolls filled with ham and cheese, a bowl of fresh fruit and opened the bottle of wine.

'If we fill our plates we could take this through to the veranda,' he suggested.

They ate and drank sitting side by side on the rattan couch, watching the flaming ball of the dying sun sink slowly over the horizon.

'How would you like to retire here with me? We could grow old together, watching sunsets, drinking wine. . . . '

'Without work there wouldn't be any money to pay for wine.'

'Always the practical one.' He took the wine glass gently from her hand and set it on the floor next to her chair. Then he leaned over and kissed her. She responded, slipping her hands beneath his jacket, running her fingers over the smooth silk of his shirt.

'If we're going to do this we may as well do it in comfort.'

He undid his tie, took off his jacket, unbuttoned his braces and flung them on to one of the chairs. Then he kicked off his shoes without undoing the laces. 'Come here, woman,' he commanded, pulling her down alongside him, until they both lay full length on the couch.

His body, hard, unyielding, pushed her into the soft cushions at her back. He kissed and caressed her, embracing her body with his own, arousing the slow-burning passion that he had carefully

161

nurtured in her since the night she had first trusted him enough to return his kiss.

His hand sought her breast, stroking its contours through the thin material of her dress, awakening sensations that were new and wholly strange to her. Face burning, she clung tightly to him, wrapping her arms around his neck, hoping that he'd stop. Kissing she enjoyed, but she wasn't ready for anything more. Not yet. Not now. And when she felt his fingers fumble at the buttons on her bodice she clamped her hands firmly over his.

'Bethan.' His eyes, dark, serious, stared intently into hers. 'Darling,' he pleaded. 'Just this. I promise you, it will go no further.'

He kissed her again, but she froze, tensing her muscles until her entire body was rigid. Too embarrassed and ashamed to look at him she kept her eyes tightly closed, furious with herself for failing to control the tears that welled beneath her eyelids.

'Bethan, what's wrong?' he demanded.

When she didn't reply he swung his legs on to the floor and reached for his jacket. Searching through the pockets he extracted his cigarettes and lighter. 'I knew there was something on your mind when I picked you up. Is it something I've done?' he asked, cursing himself for losing control. He didn't want their relationship to end. Not this way. Besides, he should have known better. The first thing he'd discovered as a probing adolescent was that there were no girls so moral as those brought up in the ways of the Welsh chapels.

'It's not you, it's me.' Clinging to him she buried her head in his shoulder.

He lit his cigarette, pulled a table with an ashtray closer to the sofa and inhaled deeply. 'Are you fed up with me?' he asked simply.

'No.'

'Well that's a relief.' He leaned back against the cushions. 'Look,' he waved the cigarette he was holding towards the window, 'the sun's shining, spring's here, you have me. Now what can be dreadful enough to spoil all that?' he joked nervously.

'If you'd been there this morning you'd know,' she retorted vehemently, frightened by his questions. (That the thought she didn't care about him should even cross his mind!) 'But as you're not chapel you can't even begin to imagine it.'

'Imagine what?'

'The stoning.'

'Stoning.' A frown appeared between his eyebrows. 'Stoning out of unmarried pregnant women?'

She nodded.

'I've heard of it happening in chapels in the Rhondda. But surely to God it doesn't go on today. And on the Graig of all places?'

She blurted out everything. John Joseph's triumph in condemning Phyllis from the pulpit. The way he and the deacons had rounded on Phyllis as she'd fought to get out of the building. The women spitting, the stone being thrown. He listened in silence, holding her, stroking her hair away from her face, and when she finally ceased talking, he kissed away the tears that fell despite her efforts to contain them. Tears of sympathy for Phyllis, and rage against her uncle.

'You poor, poor darling.' He pulled her head on to his shoulder. Wrapping her arms around his chest, she was acutely aware of his heart beating beneath her hand.

'This minister, he's your uncle?' he murmured, breaking the silence when he had to move to stub out his cigarette.

'Yes.'

'Good God, no wonder you're mixed up. But you're a nurse, sweetheart, and half a midwife to boot. Surely I don't need to tell you what causes pregnancy?' He smiled, shaking his head as she blushed. 'Darling, I respect you, and I love you.' He was as surprised by his spontaneous declaration as her, but he continued, not wanting to think too hard about the implications of what he'd said. Not yet. 'If I didn't I wouldn't be spending as much time with you as I am, and the last thing I'm going to do is leave you alone and pregnant to face a chapel full of monsters. Bethan,' he lifted her chin, forcing her to look into his eyes, 'I care about you. I'll never do anything to hurt you. You must believe that. The problem is you're beautiful, extremely desirable and I'm weak. But I promise you now. I'll never be weak enough to forget myself. Never.'

She tightened her arms, holding him close with every ounce of strength she possessed. The only sound in the room was their soft, rhythmic breathing. The peace was absolute, the air warm from the sun's rays beating on the windows throughout the day. She could smell the dust, the odour of his perspiration mingled with the perfume of cologne, the aroma of wine wafting from the open bottle standing on the floor next to the sofa.

He ground his cigarette to dust in the ashtray before kissing her again.

'Do you think you could trust me enough to pick up where we left off?' he asked softly.

Her eyes were huge, liquid, almost luminous pools in the gathering dusk. She lifted her hands to the back of his neck and pressed her lips to his. Without his braces his shirt worked loose from the waistband of his trousers. Shyly, hesitantly she pushed it aside, running the palms of her hands over his naked back. He gripped his collar and pulled his shirt off over his head. His skin was unbelievably white and smooth, smoother than the silk of the shirt he had thrown to the floor.

Moving his hand he slipped the buttons of her bodice from their loops. Excited, and more than a little afraid, she dug her nails into his back, but this time didn't try to stop him undressing her. Gently, very gently, he pulled her dress and chemise down over her shoulders, exposing her breasts. Her cheeks burnt crimson as his fingers gently teased her nipples.

'You're beautiful, Bethan,' he murmured thickly, staring at her.

'I love you, Andrew.' She lay back and closed her eyes, trying to forget her mother's warnings, the events of the morning, everything except his declaration of love, and the feel of his fingers on her skin as he caressed her.

Slowly, gradually she warmed to his touch, relaxing enough to allow his sensuous stroking to hold sway over both her body and her mind. And even when his hands were supplanted by his lips she made no effort to stop him. He loved her. Really loved her, and she him. What could possibly be sinful about that?

'Bethan, it's Easter Monday,' William complained as she walked through Megan's front door at eight o'clock in the morning. He turned his back and hitched the cord of his pyjama trousers higher, concealing a bruise he'd got, courtesy of Glan. His only consolation was that Glan had more, and blacker ones. 'Don't they sleep in your house?' he moaned.

164

'Not during the day.' Ignoring his state of undress, she pushed past into the kitchen. Megan was outside, unpegging the salt fish that she'd soaked and hung out the night before.

'Just in time for breakfast, love.' She bustled in with an enamel bowl full.

'I've had mine, thanks, Auntie.'

'But you'll have a cup of tea.'

'Love one. I called in to see if you've anything new.'

'Had some smart two-pieces in on Saturday night. Specials. One's your size, lovely dark green, linen. And there's a nice cream silk blouse that will match it to a T. Are you in a hurry, or have you got time for that cuppa?'

'I could murder a cuppa.' Bethan pulled one of the kitchen chairs from under the table and sat down.

'Not meeting him early then today?' Megan said archly.

Bethan coloured. 'Not till eleven o'clock.'

'When are we going to get a chance to see this young man of yours then?'

'Some time.'

'Soon I hope. I want to give him the once-over. Make sure he's the right one for you.'

'He's the right one for her,' William called out as he walked through the kitchen on his way to the outside privy. 'Doctor who's not short of a few bob to put a nice bit of stuff on his back, or on his arm, eh Beth.' He winked at her as he ducked out of the washhouse door, still bare to the waist, his pyjama trousers flapping in the breeze.

'Take no notice of him, love, he can't bear the thought of anyone having money when he's got none.' Megan took two cups and saucers from the dresser and set them on the table. Removing the teacosy, she felt the side of the pot before pouring it out. 'I'll make some fresh in a minute but this will do to be getting on with.' She spooned a generous helping of fat from her dripping bowl into the cast-iron frying pan on the range. 'By the way, I've something else in that might interest you.'

'I think I'll settle for the suit. I've got to start saving. . . . '

'Why bother, love? If there's one thing I've learned over the years it's that the rainy days are always here and now. Besides – '

Megan swirled the melting fat in the pan – 'you're only young once. Look as pretty as you can while you can, that's my motto.'

'I've nothing to show for my pay rise.'

'You've a wardrobe full of clothes, and God knows you needed them.' Megan tipped the fish into the pan. 'And the something's not intended for you. I've two men's suits upstairs. One your Eddie's size and one your Haydn's. They're brand spanking new. Six bob each.'

'Six bob! Wilf Horton's are ten, and they're second-hand.'

'Specials,' Megan said airily.

'Specials out the back door of a tailor's warehouse?' Bethan asked suspiciously.

'Nothing like that.'

'We don't need handouts.'

'Even if you did I haven't any to give. Six bob includes my profit. When you've finished your tea take a look at them.' Megan turned the fish over carefully. 'They're in a brown paper sack in my bedroom behind the dressing table. The women's suits are on top of the wardrobe.'

Bethan carried her empty cup into the washhouse, bumping into William, who was washing under the cold tap.

'Comes to something when a man can't strip off in his own house,' William complained.

'Man! It's not that long ago I helped your mam bath you in that sink,' Bethan retorted.

'I can vouch for that,' Megan joined in from the kitchen. 'Will, when you've finished messing out there, take Bethan upstairs and show her where I keep the men's suits.'

'No peace for the wicked.'

'Breakfast!' Megan yelled in a voice loud enough to carry half-way down the street. Charlie came in from the garden where he'd been cleaning his shoes. He nodded in reply to Bethan's quiet hello as he waited patiently for William to finish at the sink. Bethan returned to the kitchen where Diana and Sam, washed and dressed, were already sitting at the table helping themselves to fish, and the bread that Megan was cutting and buttering at a rate of knots.

'No breakfast for you, young man, until you dress,' Megan said sharply as William walked in.

'Nag nag nag.' William planted a smacking kiss on Megan's cheek. 'She loves me really,' he grinned at Bethan.

'Do I now?' Megan asked.

William led the way upstairs, lifting out the sack of men's suits from behind Megan's dressing table before disappearing into his box room. Bethan looked around. She could barely move for piles of boxes and cardboard suitcases. Lifting the sack on to the home-made patchwork quilt that covered the bed, she opened it. It held two suits. A navy-blue, shot with a fine grey pin-stripe, and a plain mid-grey flannel. Both had waistcoats complete with watch pockets, but the grey flannel was shorter in the leg than the pin-stripe so she presumed that was the one Megan intended for Eddie. She felt the cloth between her fingers. It was a good lightweight wool mix. Although she didn't know much about men's clothes she could recognise quality when she saw it.

'Smart, eh?' William walked in behind her, his braces dangling down over his trousers, his fingers busy as they tried to push his collar through the studs in the neck of his shirt.

'Here, let me.' Bethan pushed his hands aside and took over.

'Ow! Your nails are long.' He rubbed his chin ruefully. 'Doctor into vicious women is he?'

'Lay off.'

'Lay off what?' he enquired innocently.

'You know what.'

'If I did I wouldn't ask.'

'What do you think of these?' she asked.

'The suits?'

'What else?' she snapped irritably. 'There are times when I could brain you, William Powell.'

'Promises, promises,' he sighed. 'But going back to these,' he picked up the grey suit, 'I liked them enough to buy two off Mam with the money I earned on the stalls last week.'

'Then they'll be all right for our Haydn and Eddie?'

'I should cocoa. Here – ' he lifted one of the largest cardboard suitcases on to the bed and opened it. 'Shirts, ties and socks. Everything a young man about town could want to go with his new suit, and,' he sidled up to her, 'for you, madam, very cheap.'

'When you've finished practising your sales patter, find me a shirt and tie to go with each of these. The socks I can manage myself.'

'What size is Eddie?'

'Sixteen.'

'I wouldn't have said he was a bull neck.'

'It's got worse since he started going down the gym.'

'Haydn?'

'Sixteen and a half.'

'Two white linen shirts, four collars to match, one set sixteen, the other sixteen and a half, half a crown the lot and studs thrown in for free. You can't do better than that.'

'You should be on the market full time instead of down the pit three days a week.'

'I'm working on it. Socks – ' He tossed her a bundle. 'Pure wool, and only fourpence a pair. How many would madam like?'

'Four pairs.' She pulled out two pairs of grey and two of navy.

'Ties – ' he looked thoughtfully at the suits laid out on the bed – 'what do you think? This red and blue stripe for the grey, the plain grey for the pin-stripe.' He held them up.

'Looks good to me.' She piled them on top of the shirts and socks.

'Then I take madam is satisfied.' He left the bedroom and picked up his waistcoat and jacket from the banisters.

'Now look at you,' she teased. 'All done up like a dog's dinner.'

'Easter Rattle Fair.' He raised his eyebrows. 'Never know what a fellow like me might find down there.'

'Stalls to put up?'

'You don't think I'd wear this,' he shrugged his waistcoat over his shoulders, 'to put up stalls do you? Besides, I did that last night. We didn't finish till four, that's why I slept in.'

'Haydn and Eddie with you?'

'And your father.'

'That's why none of them stirred this morning.'

'And what time did cashmere coat bring *you* home last night?' he asked pointedly. 'It must have been late seeing as we didn't walk down the Graig hill until eleven.'

'Late,' she replied succinctly.

'Be careful with that one, Beth,' he warned, dropping his bantering air. 'He's crache.'

'I hadn't noticed.'

'I'm serious. Wouldn't want to see you get hurt by the idle rich.'

'He's hardly idle, he's a doctor.'

'He seems to have all the time in the world to run around in that car of his.'

'You look after your concerns, I'll look after mine,' she snapped.

'Speaking of my concerns,' he slipped his arms through the sleeves of his jacket, 'you and Laura going to the fair?'

'Yes,' she answered warily, wondering what was coming next.

'Anyone going with you?'

'No one you'd be interested in.'

'I was wondering if any of Laura's sisters were going?'

'Like Tina for instance?' she asked shrewdly. Tina was six months younger than William. They'd gone to school together and become far too friendly for Laura's father and Ronnie's peace of mind. So much so that Signor Ronconi had expressly forbidden Tina to talk to William when her brothers weren't around.

'Maybe,' he murmured casually.

'And you say you're worried about me getting hurt. You're on a hiding to nothing there, William Powell.'

'You know something I don't?'

'I know that nice Catholic girls don't go out with chapel boys.'

'I can become a Catholic,' he said brightly.

'Uncle John Joseph would stone you down the Graig hill let alone out of chapel if he heard you say that.'

'He's not my uncle, thank the Lord,' William said irreverently. 'And after yesterday's uplifting experience I'm looking for a new place to spend Sundays. I might . . . just might take a walk down Broadway to see what Father O'Rourke has to offer.'

'Are you sure you know what you're doing?'

'Put a good word in for me with Tina, Beth, and I'll stop annoying cashmere coat.'

'You are serious aren't you?'

'You serious about cashmere coat?'

'That's different.'

'How?'

'I'm older. . . .'

169

'Oh ho ho. Age has nothing to do with it, Granny. Bet you a pound that I catch Tina before you catch cashmere coat.'

'Will you stop calling him that?'

'I will if you promise to talk to Tina.'

'Like marries like, Will,' she warned. 'The Ronconi girls are all earmarked for nice Italian boys.'

'I can be a nice Italian boy. Wanna hear me talk?' he asked, imitating Laura's father's accent.

'I'm being serious.'

'So am I.' He picked up the bundle of clothes from the bed. 'I know I can be a nice Italian boy, Beth. But be honest. Can you see yourself running a ladies' committee for the "Miners' Children's Boot Fund" in a house on the Common?'

Before she had a chance to answer he turned his back on her and carried the clothes downstairs. There was no need for her to mull over what he'd said. Andrew's declaration that he loved her had sent the same thoughts worming through her mind like maggots in a rotten apple. All William had succeeded in doing was stirring the whole mess up.

Chapter Ten

After William clattered downstairs Bethan picked up the box from the top of the wardrobe. Inside were two ladies' costumes, one a bottle-green coarse linen, the other a light blue wool. Both were styled along the same lines, with close-fitting jackets and long, narrow skirts. Closing the bedroom door she tried on the green linen. Beautifully cut, fully lined in silk, it might have been tailored for her. She turned around slowly in front of the dressing-table mirror whilst doing some rapid calculations in her head.

The boys' clothes came to fifteen shillings and tenpence. Even allowing for Megan's prices the costume would be at least another ten shillings. Twenty-five shillings and tenpence, and she barely had fifteen shillings in her purse to last her until pay-day . . . and she really needed a hat. . . .

'Mam sent me up to see if you needed help.' Diana walked in, still chewing a mouthful of bread and butter. 'Ooh that does look good on you. It's only seven and six too.'

'How does your mother manage to keep her prices down?'

'He who asks no questions gets told no lies.'

'I really need a hat to go with it,' Bethan murmured more to herself than Diana.

'They're over here.' Diana produced a hatbox from under the bed. Lifting out one hat after another she shook a plain black felt with a small brim from the pile. 'This looks good and it will go with practically anything.'

'It will, won't it,' Bethan agreed, perching it on the front of her head.

'And that's only two bob, making nine and six in total, and here's the silk blouse Mam was talking about.' She produced yet another package from under the bed, and handed Bethan a blouse. 'Pure silk, hand-embroidered collar and only ninepence.' Bethan fingered the silk. It felt cool, luxurious. The kind of blouse the crache would wear. If she didn't get it now, at this price, she never would. She was earning good money. If she didn't buy any more for a while . . . . The excuses whirled around her head as she wrestled with her conscience. Finally she decided. She took the hat from her head and unbuttoned the jacket.

'Keeping it then?' Diana asked.

'We'll see.' She folded the costume carefully and laid the hat and blouse on top of it before slipping her dress back on. When she turned round Diana had already replaced the hatbox under the bed. She helped tidy away the shirts, ties and socks, while Diana packed away the blue costume. Then both of them lifted the suitcase off the bed, smoothed over the counterpane and checked the room before going downstairs.

'All right, love?' Megan was clearing the table when Bethan and Diana returned to the kitchen. Charlie and Sam were sitting, like a pair of bookends, in the easy chairs either side of the fire, but William was still eating.

'I think so,' Bethan replied doubtfully, still trying to work out what her 'tab' stood at.

'You out to give your boys a good Easter treat?' Megan nodded at the clothes that William had heaped on the dresser.

'And myself if I can run to it,' Bethan said wryly, holding up the hat, blouse and costume.

'Nine shillings for the three. And with the discount on the boys' stuff we'll call it twenty-five bob.'

'I make it more than that,' Bethan insisted.

'I make my profit. Besides, customers like you save me a lot. You buying in bulk means that I've less stock sitting around gathering dust and losing money.' Megan pulled a black card-covered exercise book out of the drawer in her dresser.

'I owe you three pounds at the moment. . . . '

'Two pounds ten, love, you paid me ten bob last week, and with today's little lot it comes to . . . ' Megan scribbled a few figures in the margin of her book and bit her bottom lip in concentration.

'Three pounds five shillings,' Bethan interrupted.

'Spot on, love,' Megan agreed.

'I can give you ten bob now. . . . '

'Don't you go leaving yourself short. Not on Rattle Fair day.'

'She doesn't need money. She's got her fancy man to treat her,' William winked, as he finished his breakfast.

Bethan glared at him and he burped loudly.

'Piggylope,' Diana remonstrated from the scullery, where she was rinsing dishes in the stone sink.

'William picked up his plate and carried it out. 'Miss starched knickers,' he whispered into Diana's ear.

'Mam! William said a naughty word,' Diana protested.

'Here's the ten bob.' Bethan took advantage of the altercation between her cousins to push the note on to Megan.

'You sure you're not making yourself short now?'

'I'm sure.'

'William, wrap and carry those suits up to Graig Avenue for Bethan.'

'Aw, Mam, I promised to meet the boys. . . . '

'The boys can wait,' Megan said firmly.

'I'll carry them, Mrs Powell.' Charlie lifted his boots from the hearth and took off his slippers. 'I want to see Mr Powell about some business. That's if you don't mind walking with me, Nurse Powell?' He looked at Bethan.

'Of course not.' Bethan took the sheet of brown paper William handed her and laid the boys' clothes in the middle of it.

'Here, love, I've a carrier bag for your suit.' Megan produced a brown paper and string bag from behind one of the easy chairs. 'See you later at the fair?'

'I expect so.' Bethan finished tying the parcel and folded the costume and hat inside the bag.

Charlie left his chair and took the parcel from the dresser. He waited quietly for Bethan to precede him. She led the way out through the front door. The street was teeming with people: children playing with sticks, stones and empty jam jars in the gutter, their parents gossiping in doorways. One or two of the women had carried chairs and bowls on to the pavement and were peeling vegetables and keeping up with the gossip at the same time.

'Mrs Morgan – ' Charlie tipped his hat to Megan's immediate neighbour as he shut the door.

'That's a big parcel you have there, Charlie. Megan doing business even on Easter Monday?'

'Not really, Mrs Morgan,' he answered evasively. 'Mrs Jones – ' He removed his hat as they passed another neighbour.

To every other adult on the Graig, Mrs Morgan was Betty, Mrs Jones, Judy, but Bethan had noticed that Charlie addressed everyone, even Megan, formally. It was as if he wanted to maintain the barriers that he'd erected between himself and those he'd chosen to live amongst. Walking side by side, the parcel swinging heavily in Charlie's hand between them, they turned the corner of Leyshon Street and made their way towards the Graig Hotel. Bethan glanced up Walter's Row to Phillips Street. The curtains were still drawn in number one. Her heart went out to Phyllis.

Charlie stopped and looked at her. Flustered she moved on, and they covered the distance between Walter's Row and the vicarage on the corner of Graig Avenue in silence. If the lack of conversation bothered Charlie he showed no sign of it, but Bethan felt she had to say something. Finally she resorted to an inane 'The weather's quite nice today isn't it?'

'Yes,' he agreed flatly.

She made no further attempt to talk. Half-way up Graig Avenue they met the vicar of St John's, his young and extremely pretty wife clutching his arm as she teetered along the rough road on heels that were too high for safety.

'Wonderful Easter weather, Bethan, Charlie,' he greeted them as his wife smiled warmly.

'It makes a welcome change after the winter,' Bethan agreed.

'We've just called in on Mrs Pugh and Miss Phyllis Harry,' he said with a significant look at Charlie. 'They're very grateful for your efforts on their behalf, Charlie. And your support, Bethan,' he added as an afterthought.

Bethan looked at Charlie, wondering what his 'efforts' might be.

'It's Mrs Powell you should be thanking,' he mumbled.

'I'll call in later to thank her, never fear. But the assistance Mrs Powell has given Miss Harry in her hour of need in no way depreciates the value of what you've done for the unfortunate household. As a vicar of the Church I know how scarce real Christian charity is in cases like Miss Harry's. The ladies would like to see you so they can thank you in person. Will you promise me that you'll call on them?'

Charlie nodded but said nothing.

'And both Miss Harry and Mrs Pugh are grateful for your kind wishes, Bethan.'

'I didn't think they knew I'd called.'

'They knew,' the vicar said drily. 'In a week or two when things are quieter I'm sure they'll welcome another visit.'

'I'll make a point of calling in.'

'Good. See you both at the Rattle Fair.' He tipped his hat and he and his wife went on their way.

Charlie crossed the road and Bethan had difficulty keeping up with him, but he hung back when they reached her house. She ran up the steps to the front door, turned the key and shouted for her father. Evan opened the kitchen door and ushered Charlie through the passage, parcel and all. The front parlour door, usually kept firmly closed, was open. Bethan glanced into the room that Haydn and Eddie usually referred to as 'the holy of holies'. Her mother had taken the dust sheets off the Rexine-covered suite and was busy straightening and dusting the ornaments on the mantelpiece. A sure sign that Uncle John Joseph and Aunt Hetty were going to visit.

'Where are the boys?' Bethan asked.

'Out the back with Maud,' Elizabeth replied tersely. 'Are you here to help or just passing through?'

'I'm meeting Laura in half an hour.'

'I suppose you'll be out all day?'

'Probably.'

'You won't be back for dinner or high tea?'

'No.'

'I don't know what your uncle and aunt are going to say about that,' Elizabeth pronounced stiffly.

'I'll see them another time.'

'When, that's what I'd like to know?' Elizabeth called after her as she walked away. 'You haven't got a minute to spare for your family these days.'

'Sorry, Mam,' Bethan said automatically. She wasn't in the least bit sorry. As a child she'd loathed holiday tea times when her uncle and aunt came to visit. Her mother always forced her father to wear a collar, and the whole family to sit stiffly upright around the kitchen table taking small bites and chewing quietly. If anyone dared deviate from Elizabeth's idea of correct behaviour they received the full force of the cutting edge of her tongue in front of Uncle John Joseph, who could never resist putting his oar in and belittling the culprit further. And after tea the entire family 'retired' (John Joseph's expression) to the front parlour to listen to his diatribes on how the advent of the wireless set and the cinema had caused the downfall of morality and religion in Welsh society.

As a small child Bethan had confused her uncle with the devil, and Sundays spent in the front parlour with hell. Looking back, it was an understandable mistake for a small child to make. John Joseph's entire conversation had always revolved around sin and the threat of eternal damnation, and his tall, thin, sardonic figure presiding over the gloomy gatherings in the front parlour wasn't that far removed from the traditional warning posters of hell.

She was looking forward to her day out at the Rattle Fair with Laura, Andrew and Trevor, but if there'd been no Andrew and no Rattle Fair, a brisk walk through the fresh young nettles that grew in wild abandon on the north side of Shoni's pond would have been infinitely preferable to the afternoon's entertainment mapped out by her mother.

She tried to creep into the kitchen, pick up the parcel and tiptoe out through the washhouse door without disturbing her father and Charlie. But her father was watching for her. Interrupting his conversation with Charlie he looked up quizzically as she reached for the parcel.

'Aunt Megan found a suit for Eddie,' she explained.

'And you bought it for him?'

'It's on trial. To see if it fits.'

'And if it does?'

'Aunt Megan will put it on her book. It's very cheap.'

'When you say Megan's book, you mean the one you've opened with her?'

'Eddie's been promised three mornings' work in the brewery yard next week. He'll soon pay for it himself.'

A sharp frown creased Evan's forehead. He was sitting hunched forward, leaning towards the range, his shoulders rounded like those of an old man. There were faint touches of grey in the roots of the black hair at his temples, grey that Bethan hadn't noticed before. If Charlie hadn't been in the room she would have attempted to caress and kiss the frown away. She'd tried to help, and only succeeded in hurting his pride, even more than her mother did with her constant nagging.

'Do you really think the union strong enough to make these demands, Mr Powell?' Charlie asked, breaking the tense silence.

'The strength of the union is not the issue. The demands have to be made. If they're not, we'll none of us have jobs to go to.'

Bethan listened to them for a moment, and when she was certain that her father's attention was firmly fixed on what Charlie was saying she took the parcel and went through to the back yard. Sunshine blinded her after the gloom of the house. Narrowing her eyes she saw Maud and Haydn sitting on the top step talking to Glan over the wall that separated the two backs.

'Enjoy your morning walk?' Haydn asked.

'Yes. Here's something for you and Eddie.'

'Something for me?' Eddie shouted from the fenced-off upper yard where he was filling the lurcher's water bowl. 'What is it? Something nice, I hope.'

'Got something nice for me, Beth?' Glan leered.

'Eddie's cheerful today,' Bethan observed, deliberately ignoring Glan.

'For a change.' Maud looked slyly at Haydn.

Haydn took the parcel from Bethan and fought with the knot on the string. He unfolded the brown paper and lifted out the grey suit that was on top.

'We supposed to just take these off you, Beth?'

'Auntie Megan had them in last night. They were too good a bargain to miss so I took them on spec hoping they'd fit.'

'This for me?' Haydn asked, holding up the grey.

'No, the stripe is. And I got you a few other things while I was at it.'

'Lucky sods,' Glan muttered enviously, peering over the wall at the contents of the parcel.

'How much was this little lot, Beth?' Haydn demanded.

'Not a lot. Auntie Megan has the account.'

'What's not much?' he pressed.

'Hadn't you better try them on to see if they fit before asking how much they are? And before you say any more, I only brought what you both need. Have you thought what you're going to wear to work when your one and only suit needs cleaning? And Eddie hasn't even got a one and only.'

While Bethan was glaring at Haydn, Maud tried to ease the situation by holding up the grey suit to Eddie as he latched the gate on the dog pen.

'Fancy yourself in this then, boyo?' she asked.

'Mmm.' Eddie flicked the jacket over gingerly with the tip of his grubby forefinger. 'Waistcoat as well.'

'Of course,' Bethan said defensively. 'Nothing but the best.'

'How much do we owe you, Sis?' Eddie asked.

'Nothing yet. I've taken them on spec.'

'Well what do you say, Haydn, shall we try them on?'

'No harm in that.' Haydn folded the paper back over the suits and dusted off his trousers as he rose from the step. Bethan breathed easier. She hadn't expected them to give in so easily.

Maud moved so Eddie and Haydn could walk down the steps. Bethan rested her elbow on the wall and allowed herself a small smile of triumph as they passed.

'You'll either get the money or the suits back tonight, Beth.' Eddie dumped the can he'd used to fill the dog's bowl in the corner of the yard. Bethan looked up and saw a cut on his chin that she hadn't noticed when they'd eaten breakfast together the day before. His left cheekbone was also bruised, but there was a look of quiet determination in his eyes that made her blood run cold.

'The Rattle Fair! Of course. You're going to fight.' It wasn't a question.

'As soon as they open the boxing booth. Come and watch. If you've any money to spare you can place a bet. You won't lose,' he said cockily.

She shuddered.

'And I won't get hurt either,' he insisted. 'I've learned a lot in the last couple of months. Joey's been training me, and training me good. I'll be the breadwinner in this family soon, Beth. Not you. And I'll make enough to pay for half a dozen suits for each of us, Mam and Dad included. You'll see if I'm not right.'

The Rattle Fair was held every Easter in Pontypridd. Every other fair that visited the town pitched on the vacant lot, sometime

178

cattle market, known as the Fairfield opposite the Palladium cinema at the north end of town. But the Rattle Fair was held courtesy of a charter which enabled it to pitch in the centre of the town itself. The Dante family, who owned and ran most of the fairs that visited Pontypridd, erected their rides and booths along the main thoroughfares including Taff Street and Market Square. The police in compliance with the order closed the town to all traffic, diverting non-fair carts and vans around Gelliwastad Road.

Roundabouts and brightly painted garish stalls that sold every conceivable kind of useless object and edible delicacy cluttered the streets from one end to the other, and in prime position in Market Square stood the coughing, wheezing engine that drove the machinery and powered the organ that announced to everyone within a mile's listening distance that the fair had arrived. It was *the* place to visit after dinner on Easter Monday. But it was just after eleven o'clock in the morning when Laura, wearing a new and most becoming (from Megan's stock) lilac spring suit, and Bethan in her green costume and cream silk blouse emerged from under the railway bridge. The Ronconis always opened their café in town on Rattle Fair afternoons, but today they had decided to hold a family dinner in the place first, and Laura had invited not only Bethan but also Trevor and Andrew to join the family party.

More nervous than Bethan had ever seen her before, Laura tripped along the streets on heels twice as high as those she normally wore. Both of them were careful to avoid the grimy outstretched hands of the street urchins who'd camped among the stalls since before dawn in the hope of cadging scraps from the food vendors or winning free rides from the 'softer' fair folk.

'Ronnie's told the cook to make a chicken dinner. Roast potatoes, peas, stuffing, all the trimmings,' Laura said fussily. 'There'll be brown soup first, and apple pie and Papa's ice cream for afters. Do you think Andrew and Trevor'll be happy with that?'

'They'll be hard to please if they aren't.' Laura's edginess was beginning to irritate Bethan.

'It's just that I want everything to be absolutely perfect. You know what bears Papa and Ronnie can be.'

179

'It's serious between you and Trevor, isn't it?' Bethan asked suddenly.

'Yes,' Laura admitted, pulling nonexistent wrinkles out of her new cotton gloves. 'Promise you won't breathe a word of this to Andrew.'

'A word about you being serious?'

'About what I'm going to tell you, you clot. If you tell Andrew he'll only go blabbing everything to Trevor. Those two are like Tweedledum and Tweedledee.'

'I hadn't noticed.'

'You haven't noticed anything except Andrew's dark brown eyes since New Year's Eve.'

'Don't be ridiculous . . . ' Bethan began coldly.

'Oh come on, Beth, it's not a sin to be in love.' Laura paused, then giggled. 'And then of course it might be.'

'A sin?'

'In the eyes of the Church what Trevor and I do is classed as sinful. But I don't see anything wrong with it,' she lifted her chin defiantly, 'particularly as he's far too caring and careful to see me land in the same mess as poor Phyllis.'

'You mean you and Trevor. . . . ' Bethan paused, too embarrassed to continue.

'Of course. Are you saying that you and Andrew don't?' Laura exclaimed incredulously.

With her face burning, Bethan shook her head.

'To think of Andrew . . . ' Laura's eyes grew round in amazement. 'He's lived in London, and everything. He never struck me as backward about coming forward, not like Trevor. Now he needed a bit of pushing.'

'Pushing?'

'You know what I mean.'

Bethan crossed the road in advance of Laura. She had a fair idea what Laura meant by pushing, but she didn't feel like discussing the details in any great depth.

'Being a doctor has its advantages,' Laura continued when she caught up with Bethan. 'For one thing Trevor doesn't have to sidle up to old Dai Makey in the market to buy his French letters. You know our Tina is friendly with Dai's daughter Pru? Well when she called in on Pru one day she caught Dai and his wife rolling the . . . the letters,' she giggled, 'in talcum powder. Trevor told me Dai charges half a crown just for one. No wonder the unmarrieds ward is so full. If you ask me, the quickest way to empty it would be to hand out free French letters to everyone who wants them.'

'Ssh.' Bethan pulled her out of the path of a group of gaping, dumbstruck children.

'Anyway,' Laura continued lowering her voice, 'Trevor might not be as well heeled as Andrew, but he does have prospects. And although his car isn't quite in the luxury class, it gets us to where we want to go. You wouldn't believe the quiet lanes that he knows. . . . ' She gave Bethan a hard look. 'You're not having me on about you and Andrew are you?'

'No,' Bethan protested indignantly, leading the way round the back of the stalls to the canvas-walled alleyway that had been created on the pavement in front of the shops.

'I just find it hard to believe. You do know he's absolutely mad about you?'

'I'm not so sure.'

'Beth, you're *impossible*. He jumps through hoops, switches duties, and breaks all kinds of engagements with his family just to spend his days off with you.'

'Who told you that?' Bethan asked suspiciously.

'Who do you think?'

'Trevor?'

'They are best friends.'

'And Andrew told Trevor that we were. . . . '

'Good Lord, no. I don't think they talk about anything as personal as that.' Laura skipped over a pile of debris at the back of the candyfloss stall.

'Why not? We do.'

'I suppose we do. How did we get on to this subject in the first place?'

'You were telling me about the dinner Ronnie organised and your father. . . . '

'That's right, Papa,' she mused thoughtfully. Her expression changed completely. 'Beth, you wouldn't believe what he did when I told him about Trevor on Friday night! Doolaly Tap wasn't the word for it. And as soon as he started performing everyone ran and hid except Mama and Ronnie. Mama wanted to, but I stood in front of the kitchen door and wouldn't move, leaving her with the choice of either staying or sitting in the washhouse. Nothing would have budged our Ronnie of course. He loves Papa's tempers. When he's not on the receiving end of them, that is,' she added bitterly.

'Have you warned Trevor what he's walking into today?'

'I didn't dare. He'd never have agreed to come if I had. Besides, Papa did eventually calm down, a little,' she qualified. 'At least he went from raving lunacy to ordinary temper when I told him Trevor was a doctor. Ronnie was no help. The only comment he made in Trevor's favour was that an Irish Catholic doctor was better than a Protestant Welsh miner, but only just. Then Papa turned on Mama and blamed her for talking him out of sending me to my grandmother in Italy, as he wanted to when I was sixteen. When Mama pointed out that I was a qualified nurse, he said he'd rather have a decently married Italian housewife for a daughter.'

'Sounds fun,' Bethan said ironically.

'Oh it was. Papa finished off by screaming up the stairs at my sisters. He swore blind that he won't let any of them out of his sight until they reach sixteen and then he's packing each of them off to Italy in turn. That makes Tina overdue for the journey. I don't think she's recovered from the shock yet. Not that she's talked to me about it. I've been sent to Coventry for making Papa angry in the first place.'

'Does your father mean it?'

'You know Papa. At the moment he does.'

'Poor William,' Bethan said feelingly.

'He's still sweet on Tina?'

'Isn't Tina still sweet on him?'

'I've just told you, she's not talking to me. Oh Beth, I'm so worried. What if Papa hates Trevor on sight? It was as much as Mama could do to persuade him to let Trevor come to dinner in the café today.'

'I don't know whether I should thank or kick you for inviting Andrew and me.'

'Don't you see, I need you and Andrew there. Papa's always liked you, and Andrew can charm the birds off the trees when

182

he wants to. And with you two sitting at the table I don't think Papa'll dare make a scene. At least that's the plan. And as he can't very well ignore someone who's eating with us he's going to have to talk to Trevor, and when he does he's bound to see how wonderful he is.'

'And if he doesn't?' Bethan probed.

'I'll have to elope. I'm old enough.'

'Elope as in get married?'

'Of course. What do you think I've been talking about for the last half-hour. Trevor asked me to marry him on Friday evening after work. We've nothing to wait for except more money, and we can save as well when we're married as we can now.'

'You'll have to give up nursing.'

'That won't matter, I never really saw myself as the Florence Nightingale type. Besides I spend every penny I earn on clothes, and thanks to Megan my wardrobe should last me until Trevor gets a better-paid post. He earns four pounds a week now,' she said proudly. 'Another two years should make it six. And although we haven't enough money to buy a house straight off, we certainly have enough to rent one. Glan says there's one going in Maritime Street for ten bob a week, and we shouldn't spend more than a pound a week housekeeping, so with luck we'll manage to save the deposit for a decent place of our own within a year. Maybe even a house on the Common.'

'Sounds like you've got it all worked out,' Bethan murmured wistfully. While Laura had been talking, her mind had painted a picture of the terraced houses in Maritime Street, or rather one in particular. Newly decorated and papered, tastefully furnished, and her caring for it, cooking delicious meals in the kitchen while she waited for Andrew to return from the hospital in the evening. Suddenly it all seemed so very attractive, and Laura had it within her grasp.

'Neither Trevor nor I have saved a bean,' Laura prattled on, 'me because . . . well you know where my money goes, and Trevor's been supporting his mother and his brother and sisters. But I'm sure we'd be able to scavenge everything we need, and what we don't need we'll do without. Once his sisters and brother are settled his mother can move in with us. She's so sweet, Beth. And she really likes the idea of Trevor marrying me. . . . '

'You've met her?'

'On Saturday. I was dying to tell you all about it in work yesterday but you had to be off, didn't you. I know we won't quite have the start you and Andrew'll have. His father will probably buy you a mansion on the Common. . . . ' She stared at Bethan. 'Don't tell me you and Andrew haven't even talked marriage?'

'We're just good friends.' Bethan repeated the trite phrase without even thinking what she was saying.

'Just good friends my eye. The man's besotted. God, you're either a cold fish or a slow worker, Bethan Powell. I thought you'd have chosen the ring pattern by now.'

'Ring pattern?' Bethan asked blankly.

'Engagement ring,' Laura explained impatiently. 'Trevor and I are going to choose one in Cardiff on my next day off. . . . Oh God there he is!' Laura muttered, catching sight of Andrew and Trevor, cigarettes in hand, waiting outside the café door.

'Do you think they've already knocked and your father wouldn't let them in?'

'Don't tease, Beth, I'm in no mood for it. What's the time?'

Bethan opened her handbag and looked at her nurse's watch that she'd pinned inside the flap.

'Nearly half-past eleven.'

'Dinner won't be until twelve. Back me up if I suggest a stroll round the town.'

'Hello darling.' Andrew winked at Bethan, before turning to Laura. 'What have you done to this fellow?' he demanded mischievously. 'He's an absolute wreck.'

'I think we should go for a walk around the town. See what's going on,' Laura suggested loudly.

'Not on your life.' Andrew pushed a large cardboard box towards Trevor with his toe. 'For one thing your brother's already seen us, and for another, Trevor couldn't carry this another step.'

'What is it?' Laura asked.

'A case of decent wine to sweeten your father,' he grinned. 'If a quarter of what I've heard about Italian fathers is true, we're going to need every drop.'

The warm Italian welcome that the Ronconis extended to Bethan was as cordial as usual. It even embraced Andrew, but it stopped short of Trevor. A German spy captured during the Great War couldn't have been put through a more intense interrogation than the one Papa Ronconi subjected him to. Half a dozen of the largest tables had been pushed together in the centre of the room and covered over with Mrs Ronconi's biggest damask tablecloth. Gleaming like freshly cut coconut it was graced by the family's best silverware and china that had been specially brought down for the occasion in the back of Ronnie's Trojan van the night before.

Unwilling to sit alongside Trevor and Andrew and listen to what her father was saying, Laura donned an apron and busied herself, cleaning the tables and straightening the chairs that Ronnie had cleaned and straightened the night before. Bethan hid in the kitchen with Mrs Ronconi and Laura's sisters. But when the soup thickened and the chickens turned a dark brown at their extremities Laura's mother had no choice but to begin serving the meal. She laid the tureen proudly in the centre of the table, and Ronnie opened one of the bottles of wine that Trevor had presented to Laura's father. Bethan recognised the label: the bottles were from Andrew's father's cellar, the same vintage that Andrew took on their picnics.

The meal wasn't as bad as Laura had expected. Thanks to Andrew there were no embarrassing silences. He excelled himself. One amusing story followed another, and he took every opportunity to present Trevor in a good light. He deferred to Trevor's judgement on all things from politics to current medical advances – not forgetting to sketch in glowing colours the brilliant career that every doctor of note in the area confidently predicted for Trevor. And when he wasn't praising Trevor, or the cooking, or the Signor Ronconis' (father and son) business acumen, he was complimenting Laura's mother on her children, or smiling and joking with Laura's sisters until all of them, even Tina, fell madly in love with him.

After the apple pie and ice cream had been cleared away he even succeeded in winning Ronnie over by producing a bottle of Napoleon brandy to complement the cigars that Trevor handed round. Bethan studied them as Andrew clipped off the ends, noting that they too were the brand that Dr John senior smoked.

Following the example of the women of the family Bethan gulped her coffee and rose to help clear the table, but Andrew forestalled her.

'That was a wonderful meal,' he thanked Mrs Ronconi effusively, 'and we'd love to stay longer, but unfortunately I promised my parents that we'd pick up my sister and her husband from the station at one-thirty. They're coming in on the London train. Please forgive me for cutting such a pleasant time short, and having to take Bethan with me.'

'We understand the value of family promises,' Laura's father said ambiguously, as he struggled to his feet. His vast stomach shook in unison with his arm as he pumped Andrew's hand enthusiastically. 'Good of you to join us. You must come again.'

'I hope next time it will be our turn to play hosts,' Andrew said with a significant look at Trevor. 'Thank you so much for inviting us. Mrs Ronconi, Ronnie, nice to see you again. Tina . . .' he went around the table shaking hands, and kissing blushing cheeks. 'See you later, Trevor, Laura.'

If looks could have killed, Laura would have slain Bethan there and then. Andrew waited impatiently as Bethan untied her apron and fixed her hat on, securing it with the neat pearl-headed hat pin that had been part of her inheritance from her grandmother. Then he ushered her smartly out of the front door before she even had time to say her goodbyes properly.

'We're not really meeting your sister are we?' she asked as the door clanged shut behind them.

'Of course.'

'Andrew, not now. I look dreadful.'

'For pity's sake, she's my sister not the Queen. Come on, we've barely ten minutes before the train comes in.'

The two glasses of wine she'd drunk with the meal swam fuzzily in her head as she marched briskly alongside Andrew, or at least as briskly as the fair paraphernalia would allow, towards the station. Andrew bought platform tickets in the ground-floor office and raced up the wide stone staircase that led to the trains. Bethan tried to keep up and failed. He waited for her by the ticket collector's booth.

'Unfit, Nurse Powell?'

'After a meal like that, yes,' she panted.

'It was rather good wasn't it,' he agreed. He handed the tickets to the uniformed official. 'London train?' he enquired.

'Platform two. Due in three minutes, sir.'

'I love the certainty of railway staff,' he whispered as he took hold of her elbow and ushered her down the platform.

'I wish you'd given me some warning about this,' she pleaded. 'I must look dreadful.' She rummaged in her handbag for her powder puff.

'You look beautiful. Here – ' He took a clean handkerchief out of his top pocket and wiped a smut from her chin. She glanced down her nose trying to see if there were any grease stains on her costume from the café kitchen.

'You look absolutely perfect,' he grinned. 'Come here, woman.' He wrapped his arms around her. 'You know, the best thing about railway stations is that people turn a blind eye to things that they'd "tut" at in the park. I don't know why we haven't thought of coming here before.' Bending his head to hers, he gave her a long, lingering kiss.

'Now you'll have to reapply your lipstick,' he laughed as he released her.

'Thank you very much, Doctor John,' she said peevishly. Suddenly weak at the knees, she looked at the benches, saw the dirt on them and decided against sitting down.

'How was Laura this morning?' Andrew asked, staring up the line in the direction the train would come in. 'Frankly there were times when I wondered if Trevor would make it to the café in one piece.'

'I've never seen her so nervous,' she mumbled as she dabbed lipstick on her mouth. 'Did you know that Trevor had asked her to marry him?'

'He told me when he came round on Friday night, late. Or should I say early Saturday morning.'

'You didn't say anything to me yesterday.'

'Laura warned Trevor against saying anything, she wanted to tell you about it herself. So I could hardly pass on information that I wasn't supposed to know. Look, here's the train. Three minutes to the dot.' He checked his watch. 'I take my hat off to British Rail. For once they're spot on time.'

Chapter Eleven

Laura wasn't the only one in town who was nervous that day. At two o'clock Eddie entered Captain Dekker's boxing booth flanked by his trainer Joey, and Haydn. The bravado that had sustained him at home fled in the face of the large crowd pressed tightly around the roped-off makeshift ring.

'You'll be fine, boyo. Don't think about them, just pretend you're in the gym.' Joey, who knew exactly what Eddie was feeling, slapped him soundly on the back. Eddie looked coldly at the old man, and for the first time saw him as he really was. Teeth missing, nose broken and pushed sideways, eyes bloodshot, sunk into a prematurely aged and wrinkled face, jaw broken and badly set. He'd told everyone he was the one who'd make it. World champion? But Joey had once believed in his own ability every bit as much as Eddie believed in himself now. And you only had to look around the town or the gym to see those who were even worse off than Joey. Punch-drunk, with slurred speech that no one could understand, not that they said anything worth understanding. Men like Cast Iron Dean. Once hailed as the strongest man in the world, now a blind wreck that the kids ran from on sight, and jeered at behind his back.

'It's not too late to walk away, Eddie,' Haydn murmured, blanching at the sight of the dried bloodstains on the canvas floor and walls of the booth. It was the best, or perhaps the worst thing he could have said.

'I'm here to stay,' Eddie snapped. 'But if you want to go, feel free.'

'That's not what I meant and you know it.'

'Haydn, Haydn, over here!' Four of the chorus girls from the current show at the Town Hall were sitting on one of only two benches in the booth. Sandwiched between them was the show's comedian.

'Come on, I'll introduce you,' Haydn offered.

'To them?' Eddie stared at their faces, heavily painted to

announce to the world that they were on the stage. He'd never seen so much make-up on a woman close up before. Not a young one, and certainly not out of the station yard.

'Come on, they don't bite.' Haydn pushed Eddie ahead and Joey, reluctant to allow his protégé out of his sight, followed.

'Eddie, Joey, meet Polly, Daisy, Doris, Lou, and the best comedian in Wales, Sam Spatterson.'

'Best comedian in the British Empire, old boy,' Sam corrected.

'My apologies,' Haydn smiled. 'Best comedian in the Empire. Everyone, this is my kid brother Eddie and his trainer Joey.'

'Trainer. Oo . . . ooh you're a boxer,' Daisy squealed as she caught hold of Eddie's arm and pulled him down on to the bench next to her. 'I just love strong, powerful men,' she purred.

Too embarrassed to say anything, Eddie stared at his feet.

'He's a world champion in the making, miss,' Joey said proudly.

'He doesn't look much like you, Haydn,' Doris said pertly. 'Sure your mother didn't stray from the nest?'

The blood rushed to Eddie's face.

'I'm sure.' Haydn gave Eddie a warning frown. Even he occasionally found it hard to reconcile the risqué talk of showbusiness people with that of 'normal' life. He couldn't expect the same kind of latitude from Eddie, who'd never been backstage in the Town Hall in his life.

'Tell me, Eddie,' Daisy whispered in his ear as she fingered his biceps, 'are you doing anything later, after you've boxed?'

'I hadn't thought about it,' he mumbled.

'If you aren't you could come and see me in the show.' She puckered her bright red lips as though preparing to kiss him. 'I have a spare ticket here.' She pulled a warm crumpled ticket out of the front of her low-cut blouse and thrust it into the breast pocket of his new suit. 'Don't forget now,' she crooned seductively. 'Afterwards we could paint the town red. What about it, strong man?'

'Lay off, Daisy,' Haydn warned. 'That's my kid brother you're talking to.'

'Ooh, big brother can get masterful.' Doris opened her eyes wide. 'I never knew you had it in you, callboy.'

'I'll see you ladies tonight,' Haydn retorted suggestively.

'Promises, promises,' Daisy cooed as Eddie extricated himself from her grasp and rejoined Haydn and Joey.

'Will you really see those girls tonight?' Eddie asked as they walked back towards the ring.

'Of course, I'm working, remember.'

'I forgot.'

'Girls like that aren't worth a farthing,' Haydn said with all the assurance of his nineteen years. 'It's nice girls you should be making cow's eyes at.'

'Like Jenny Griffiths?' Eddie couldn't resist the taunt.

'Yes. If you must know, like Jenny Griffiths. But if on the other hand you're looking for a bit of skirt to take up Shoni's pond tomorrow you couldn't do better than Daisy. By all accounts she's made men of many boys.'

'Sure you don't mean mincemeat?' Joey interrupted. Eddie turned to the old man in surprise. He'd almost forgotten he was there. 'You want to win fights, boyo? You stay away from women. That's my advice. Women concentrate the blood where it's not needed or wanted in a fight. And they stop it from flowing to where it is.'

'Can you see Bethan anywhere?' Eddie asked, embarrassed again.

'She said she'll be here this afternoon, and that means she will,' Haydn reassured him.

A voice boomed from the centre of the ring: 'Here we have big bad brutal Billy . . . '

Joey pressed close to Eddie. 'This is where you start fighting, boy. Watch. Eyes and ears. Remember. Eyes and ears. Listen to the ref. Watch their boy's movements, think about his training. After you've seen two or three of the Captain's lads you'll be able to pick out their weaknesses. And there's always weaknesses. Knowing your opponent is half the battle, boy. And when you know enough to take him on, we'll make our move. And not on one of your venture five bob, win a quid challenges either.'

'Five bob. Only five bob a challenge. Any man who can go for more than five minutes in the ring with Bad Billy Bater and stay on his feet gets a crisp, crackling pound note. Now who's going to be the first taker to down this man. . . . '

The crowd gasped as Big Billy stepped over the ropes into the ring and stripped off his robe. He was an enormous hulk of a man. His face battered, his back and chest above his shorts black and blue from the punches he'd taken in the last town. He grinned vacantly at the crowd and held his hands high.

'Please, Joey. Let me have a go at this one?' Eddie pleaded, dreading the encounter but anxious to have it over and done with at the same time.

'Not yet, boy. Not yet.' Joey put his arm round Eddie's shoulders. 'See those bruises. No boxer worth his salt would let an opponent get close enough to leave marks like that. His brain's gone. No medals to be won flattening a has-been like Bad Billy. He's Jim Dekker's punchbag. The real talent comes out with the five-pound offer not the quid. Remember. Eyes and ears, boy. Eyes and ears.'

Eddie leaned uneasily against one of the posts that held the canvas ceiling over the booth. Haydn put his hand into his pocket and pulled out a packet of PK. He offered one to his brother. Waiting was definitely the worst part of this game.

'Andrew's kept your existence quiet enough. But then he always was tight-lipped about his girlfriends, even when he practically lived with us in London. Heaven knows why, because I've been dying to have a sister-in-law.' Fiona Campbell-White, *née* John, pressed her hand over Bethan's as they sat together in the back seat of Andrew's car. 'There's so many things I could tell a sister-in-law that I couldn't tell a brother,' she confided in a voice that carried to Andrew.

'Perhaps now Bethan can see why I've kept her away from you for so long.' Andrew changed gear, ready to take the hill to the Common.

'Why, dear brother?' Fiona purred sweetly. 'Were you afraid that I'd tell her what a rotter you really are?' She glanced slyly at Bethan.

Bethan was amazed at the similarities between brother and sister. Fiona was a beautiful feminine version of Andrew. They had the same dark eyes, smooth tanned skin, and glossy black hair. But Fiona's curls had been tamed into the classic, perfect bob that belonged to the world of advertising posters, not real life. Expensively dressed in a tan, fur-trimmed costume, set off by matching crocodile-skin shoes and handbag, she exuded wealth and confidence with every whiff of her exotic perfume. Even her husband seemed to be one of her accessories. Good-looking in a smooth, matinée-idol, middle-parting sort of way, he was beautifully dressed in an immaculately tailored pin-stripe suit. The whole image of well-heeled affluence that they projected contrived to make Bethan feel grubby, working class and more inadequate than ever.

'So what's new in the medical world down here, Andrew?' Alec Campbell-White asked heartily.

'Not a lot.'

'Have you decided to take up my father's offer of a post in the surgical department of Charing Cross?'

'No. Not yet.' Andrew glanced in his mirror at Bethan who was sitting very stiffly and quietly.

'Here we are, home!' Fiona exclaimed excitedly. 'And everything looks just the same.'

'It would, wouldn't it,' Andrew commented wryly.

'It was good of you to meet us, old boy, I know you and. . . .'

'Bethan,' Andrew supplied.

'Bethan must have had a million other things to do.'

'Nothing as important as meeting my favourite brother-in-law and unfavourite sister. Here, I'll give you a hand with the cases.' Leaving the engine running he stepped out of the car and opened the boot.

'But you are coming in, aren't you?' Fiona demanded of Bethan as Andrew and Alec swung the set of matching brown leather cases out of the car and into the front porch.

'Afraid not, Fanny,' Andrew answered for Bethan. 'We've promised to meet friends in town. But we'll be back for dinner.'

'Look forward to it, old boy,' Alec said cheerfully as Fiona rang the doorbell.

Andrew slammed the boot shut. Climbing back into the car he patted the vacant passenger seat.

'Join me?' he asked Bethan.

She did as he asked, waving shyly at Fiona in return to her enthusiastic goodbyes.

'I didn't know we were dining with your family tonight,' she said as he left the driveway for the road.

'I'm sure I told you.'

'And I'm sure you didn't.'

'It's no big deal, Beth.' Instead of turning down the road into town he steered the car along the rough road that skirted the Common and the bleak moor that surrounded the cenotaph.

'Where are you going?'

'Somewhere where we can talk.'

'I promised to go to the boxing booth this afternoon.'

'The boxing booth!' he exclaimed in horror. 'Bethan, have you ever been in one?'

'No, but my brother Eddie is fighting.'

'In that case I'll take you. But they don't even open until two and nothing much happens for the first couple of hours. If I promise to get you there in the next half-hour, can we talk for ten minutes now? I want to explain. . . . '

'There's no need to explain anything,' she said quickly. She had a sudden premonition that jarred uneasily with his decision to introduce her to his family. He was going to London to take up the post that Alec had mentioned. Laura and Trevor were getting married and Andrew was saying goodbye. She began to shake, terrified at the thought of a future without him.

'You just took me by surprise,' she gabbled hastily. 'You never said anything about meeting your family. . . . '

'You don't want to meet them?'

'No . . . yes. Of course I don't mind meeting them. It's just that. . . . ' She fell silent, conscious that she was talking simply so she wouldn't have to listen to what he had to say. He continued driving until the road ended in a narrow lane. After a mile of winding turnings and sharp corners he pulled into a lay-by beside a farm gate. He switched off the engine and turned to face her. She was staring at her handkerchief, knotting its corners into tortuous shapes with her tensed fingers.

'Don't you think it's time you met my family?' he pressed.

'It's good of you to ask me.'

'Do you or don't you want to meet them?' He lifted her chin with his finger, forcing her to look at him.

'If you want the truth, I'm scared to death of meeting them,' she admitted.

'Why, Beth? You already know my father, and my mother's

sweet and old-fashioned. Not in the least bit modern or strident like Fanny.'

'Sounds to me as if you don't like Fiona very much,' she observed neatly, attempting to divert his attention from his father. How on earth could he say that she knew his father? Nurses bowed their heads in the hospital when the senior doctor passed. He talked about him as if they were used to exchanging pleasantries.

'Take no notice of Fanny,' he said glibly. 'Sibling rivalry. We've hated each other since cradle days.'

'Why?'

'No reason. All reasons. Don't you hate your brothers and sister?'

'No.'

'Oh dear. I had no idea you belonged to a perfect family.'

'My family's anything but perfect.'

'At last. We have something in common.'

'Imperfect families?'

'Come to dinner? Please?' he smiled. 'I'd lose all credibility with Fanny if you didn't. And I told my mother to expect you.'

'When?'

'This morning.'

'I could have made other arrangements.'

'I told you to keep the whole day clear.'

'All right I'll have dinner with your family tonight.' She summoned up her courage. 'On one condition,' she blurted out quickly before she could change her mind.

'Name it.'

'After we've been to the Rattle Fair, you take me home to change, then you can meet my family first.' She wanted to add, 'so you can see who and what I really am' but pride held her back. If he really loved her, home, background and family would make no difference.

'I thought you were never going to invite me,' he smiled. 'Now that's settled how about picking up where we left off in the station.'

He cupped his hands round her face. Drawing her close he kissed her, effectively preventing her from voicing any of the mass of questions that slithered through her mind. But his lovemaking

194

failed to still her doubts. Was he leaving? Going to London? If so why did he want her to meet his family? Yesterday he'd said he loved her. Was that a trite, meaningless remark — a product of passion — of the moment — or the truth? Laura and Trevor were to marry and they. . . .

'I don't think we'd better go too far down this road,' he said huskily pulling away from her. 'Not here. Not in daylight.' He buttoned her blouse and jacket. 'Of course,' he murmured looking into her eyes, 'I could take you home this way tonight after dinner, or better still invite you to my rooms.'

She thought of what Laura had said — 'Are you sure you're not having me on about you and Andrew?' Was that the way to become an indispensable part of a man's life? Because if it was . . . 'I'd like that,' she agreed softly. He smiled as he reached for the starting handle. He'd always dwelt upon the differences between Bethan and the other girls he'd spent time with. But there were similarities too. And it was reassuring to know that once warmed up a Welsh chapel girl wasn't that far removed from her London counterpart after all.

The boxing booth was warm, humid and airless beneath the thick canvas walls and ceiling. The atmosphere within was gloomy in the half-light, heavy with unhealthy excitement and the fetid smell of stale male sweat. Andrew paid the shilling admission fees for himself, Trevor, Laura and Bethan to ensure they'd get a seat on the benches. Those who paid sixpence were fortunate if they got standing room that allowed them to see over the heads of the ex-professional and amateur boxers who'd laid claim to the prime area around the ring.

'Can you see Eddie anywhere?' Bethan asked Laura anxiously.

'Once we're on the benches we'll get a better view.' Trevor wrapped his arm protectively around Laura's shoulders. 'This really is no place for women.'

'And why not?' Laura demanded, spoiling for an argument after the stresses and strains of the afternoon.

'If you're serious about marrying this lady you'll have to learn that anything a man can do, a woman, particularly this woman,' Andrew pointed at Laura with his wallet as he pushed it back into his inside pocket, 'can do better.'

'Not boxing,' Trevor said firmly.

'Oh I don't know,' Andrew mused airily. 'Would you fancy going three rounds with Squeers?'

Bethan giggled as a sudden, very real image of Squeers in boxing shorts and vest sprang to mind.

'The moment we've all been waiting for; Gentlemen . . . and Ladies.' Jim Dekker himself stepped into the ring. He bowed towards Laura and Bethan and the bench where Doris and Daisy were still sitting. 'The supreme challenge, and the supreme purse. of the day. A single, crisp five-pound note for any man brave enough to step into the ring with Dekker's champion. Ladies and Gentlemen. Let's have a round of applause for Daring Dan Darcy.' He swung round and a tall, well-built man climbed into the ring behind him. Holding his gloved hands high to the shouts and applause of the crowd, Daring Dan took his bow.

'God, how the mighty have fallen,' Trevor mumured under his breath.

'Blasphemy.' Laura nudged him in the ribs.

'It's starting,' Andrew warned Trevor. 'Another month and you'll be wearing a ball and chain.'

'What did you mean about the mighty falling?' Bethan asked nervously, scanning the crowd for a glimpse of Eddie as she took her seat.

'Ever heard of Dan Farrell?' Tevor replied.

'No. Should I have?'

'Five years ago he was the best. Tipped for world champion. And that's him now.' Trevor nodded towards the ring, where Dan had stripped off his robe and was flexing his biceps.

'What happened?'

'Could be any one of a number of things. Drink, high living. . . .'

'Women?' Andrew suggested innocently.

'Are you going to hit him, Bethan, or shall I?' Laura enquired frostily.

'Vicious too,' Andrew continued to tease Trevor.

'Come on, lads, don't be shy,' Jim Dekker shouted. 'First man to stay on his feet for three rounds with Daring Dan takes the pot. Five pounds! Who'll be the first taker? Five pounds for ten-bob entry fee?'

'Oh no you don't, Jim Dekker,' Joey shouted. 'You don't pull that one. Not in this town. It's five not ten bob.'

'Trying to put an honest man out of business, Joey,' Jim bit back humorously.

'Fair's fair,' someone in the crowd heckled.

'It's always been five bob,' Joey retorted sharply.

'Fair's fair,' the same man chanted.

'Show me your challenger,' Jim answered. 'And I'll show you what's fair.'

'Here.' Joey pushed Eddie's hand up, and Bethan started, almost falling off the bench.

'That your brother?' Andrew asked, trying to size up Eddie's chances.

'That's my brother.' Bethan fought back the tears that welled into her eyes.

'Seeing as how's he's a nipper, Joey, I'll allow him a try at five bob,' Jim conceded. 'Over here, lad.' He pointed to the pegs where contenders could hang their clothes.

Bethan watched Haydn follow Eddie to the corner of the booth. Then she saw her father push his way through the crowd towards the boys. The bookie who fixed the odds on the fights and made the real money for Dekker eyed Eddie carefully as he stripped off his suit, shirt and tie. He was wearing his shorts under his trousers.

'I never realised Eddie was so skinny, Beth,' Laura whispered in a voice that carried above the hubbub of noise.

'Neither did I.' Bethan paled as she compared her brother's underdeveloped figure with that of the seasoned boxer who was preening and parading in the ring.

The bookie, hat pushed back on his head at a rakish angle, sidled up to Andrew. 'Enjoying yourself, sir?' he enquired.

'Yes thank you,' Andrew replied with an amused glance at Trevor.

'Men of substance like yourselves,' he touched his hat to Trevor, 'tend to enjoy the sport a little better if they've a small matter on the outcome. If you know what I mean?'

'We know what you mean,' Andrew muttered under his breath, putting the poor man out of his misery. 'What are the odds?'

'Ten to one against the youngster pulling it off, sir.'

Andrew took out his wallet. 'Tenner on the challenger, all right?' he asked, folding a note into the bookie's palm. The man glanced at Eddie to check his prognosis. He nodded and slipped his hand into his pocket.

'I want to put some money on too.' Bethan fumbled in her handbag. The bookie looked anxiously around the booth at all the heads tall enough to be policemen. Andrew put his hand into his wallet again. 'Fiver for the lady.'

'Andrew. . . . '

'Pay me later.' He pocketed the slips the bookie handed him.

The man moved on past Trevor, who handed him a pound, to the people sitting behind them. Bethan stared at Haydn and Eddie, willing them with all her might to look at her. But as her father reached them they went into a huddle with Joey, the crowd closed in and they were lost to view.

'We're in the wrong business,' Andrew observed as he watched the bookie circle the booth. 'He must have taken the best part of fifty pounds in the last five minutes.'

'He'll be in the wrong business if Bethan's brother wins,' Trevor replied. 'Is he good, Bethan?'

'I don't know.' Worried about the five pounds that Andrew had handed over so glibly, and that she had no hope of repaying if Eddie lost, she couldn't bring herself to think about his prospects. 'If the way he talks is anything to go by, he's brilliant.'

'Believing in yourself is half the battle with a boxer,' Trevor commented.

'You know a lot about boxing all of a sudden.' Laura eyed Trevor suspiciously.

'Used to box in medical college.'

'You're joking.'

'Now why should I joke about something like that?'

Ignoring the bickering Andrew closed his hand over Bethan's. 'They stop these things long before anyone gets really hurt,' he asserted quietly.

'I've seen just how careful *they* are,' she answered scathingly. 'Eddie's been beaten to pulp in the gym once. Perhaps it would be different if he could get a steady job. It's not as if he hasn't tried, but his efforts don't seem to get him anywhere, and now he sees this as a way out.'

'It might prove to be just that. That old boy with him looks as though he knows what he's doing. I'm sure he wouldn't put your brother in the ring if he didn't think he stood a chance.'

'But he's much smaller than the one he's going to fight.'

'That can be an advantage.' Trevor leant towards her. 'Think of Jimmy Wilde.'

'Ladies and Gentlemen, give a big warm Pontypridd welcome to Eddie Powell.' Dekker shoved Eddie into the centre of the ring. 'He's one of your own. From the Graig.' The crowd went crazy. Shouting, cheering, cat-calling and stamping as if it was the Saturday penny rush in the pictures.

Bethan looked past Eddie and saw the bookie who'd taken Andrew's money standing alongside her father and Haydn. Both had their hands in their trouser pockets. If Eddie went down they'd be in the pawn shop with the new suits, her costume, and the jewellery she'd inherited from her grandmother tomorrow.

A very tense Eddie returned to his corner. Haydn pushed on his gloves. Joey laced them. The final knot was tied. Jim Dekker waved him forward. Eddie gave one quick last conscious look at Joey who stood, towel slung over his shoulder, behind his corner.

Dekker spoke, but Bethan didn't understand a word he said. The atmosphere swirled, a hot black whirlpool pierced by flashing red arrows. At the centre was Eddie, alone, skeletally thin. Dekker moved backwards. A bell clanged and Dan and Eddie raised their gloves. She gripped the edge of her seat as they circled one another warily around the canvas-covered boards.

The champion was playing with Eddie. Even Bethan with her limited knowledge of boxing could see that. A sudden swift right – a left – another right – Eddie dodged them as fast as they came. Then came a resounding whack which cracked through the air like a whiplash. She closed her eyes tightly and bit her bottom lip until she could taste salt blood.

The crowd booed. She opened her eyes. Blood was streaming from a cut high on Eddie's right cheekbone. He stumbled. She cried out. He threw a wild punch. By sheer fluke it landed on Dan's unguarded left jaw. The tension in the booth grew to explosive dimensions as the champion closed in.

Fists pummelled into naked flesh; close punches jabbed into Eddie's ribcage. Dekker shouted. The clinch broke and the crazy dance began all over again – circling – shadow boxing – feinting – circling . . . .

Andrew prised Bethan's fingers from the bench. She gripped his hand fiercely, digging her nails into his wrist. Eddie threw a punch that again connected with Dan's jaw. Dan retaliated with a blow that landed high above Eddie's eye. Blood spurted, joining the flow from the cut on Eddie's cheek. Fresh stains were added to the rust-coloured splashes that spotted the canvas floor.

'Why won't someone stop it?' Bethan pleaded impotently; her fingers were knots of pain she was barely aware of.

Smiling triumphantly, Dan swayed drunkenly on his feet. Half blinded by his own blood Eddie threw all his strength into a left targeted at the same spot he'd attacked throughout the bout. The crowd roared as it hit home. There was a crack followed by a dull thud. Bethan couldn't bear to look. She clung to Andrew, burying her face in his tweed-covered shoulder. The sound of a child's number chant filled the air:

'One . . . two . . . three . . . four. . . . '

She blocked out the sound. Eddie was bleeding. From his head. She recalled all the punch-drunk boxers she'd seen. Harry Mander, Joey Rees. . . .

'It's safe to look if you want to. The first round's finished and your brother's still on his feet.'

She peered over Andrew's arm. White and trembling, Eddie was sitting on a three-legged stool in the corner of the ring. Joey held a wet towel over his eye. Haydn had handed him a water bottle and he was swilling his mouth out and spitting into a bucket that her father held in front of him.

'You shouldn't have bet so much money,' she breathed without looking at Andrew.

'The odds were too good to miss.'

'Your brother,' Trevor patted her hand. 'He's good.'

'He is?'

'You don't know?'

The bell rang and Andrew gripped her fingers. The insane dance began again, only this time the punches were flung wider, but not by Eddie. He kept himself taut, compact. Presenting a small, flitting target that darted around the ring – a flea teasing a floundering rat. Bethan cried out and crushed Andrew's hands

200

fiercely every time Dan aimed a punch. But time after time he hit thin air. The blood rushed to Dekker's face as he strove to contain his irritation.

Eddie's right shot out of nowhere, hitting Dan soundly on the jaw. The crack of the impact was followed by a crash as Dan's head hit the canvas. The bell rang. No one noticed it was half a minute early.

'I'm taking you outside,' Andrew whispered, rising from the bench.

'No,' she hissed.

'You can't stand much more of this. You're as white as a sheet.'

'I couldn't bear not being able to see.'

'I didn't know you could through closed eyelids.' The sarcasm was lost on her.

Dekker and two of his fighters were working vigorously in their corner trying to revive Dan with wet towels and vinegar. Joey crouched in front of Eddie, mouthing last-minute instructions. Her father looked up at the crowded benches, saw her and smiled. He bowed his head towards Eddie. Eddie nudged Haydn and they both waved.

'Who's that with your brother?' Andrew asked.

'The tall dark one is my father,' she said proudly, 'the fair one is my older brother.'

'Close-knit family. Where's your mother?'

'At home making tea for my uncle,' she answered automatically, not really registering what he'd asked.

'The minister?' he persisted, trying unsuccessfully to divert her attention.

The crowd, growing restless, heckled, booed and stamped their feet, drowning out any further chance of conversation. Sensing trouble in the air Dekker signalled to the timekeeper. The bell rang. Bethan clutched Andrew and screamed in horror as Dan flung himself forward and threw his whole weight into a blow aimed at Eddie's head. Her brother ducked, and the booth faded. She was aware only of a blackness tinged with red, a distant roar that pained her ears.

'He's won,' Andrew shouted. 'He's won. Your brother, Bethan. He's won!'

She struggled to focus her eyes. Dan was flat on his back on

201

the canvas. Eddie, blood streaming down his face, stood wild-eyed and panting in the centre of the ring. Joey clambered over the ropes and lifted his hand high into the air.

'Next world flyweight champion,' Joey shouted ecstatically above the noise of the crowd.

'Some brother you've got there, Bethan,' Trevor complimented.

'I always knew that.' She was crying. Tears streamed unchecked down her cheeks as she stared at Eddie. Shocked no longer, he was grinning at the crowd, confident and victorious. But all she could think of was that neither she nor Haydn nor her father would ever be able to stop him from boxing again – and again.

Chapter Twelve

'Table for — ' Andrew checked the size of his party — 'eight please, Mr Rogers.'

'Of course, Doctor John.' Dai Rogers, under-manager of the New Inn Hotel bowed, fawning not so much because of Andrew but Andrew's father, and his influence. 'This way please, Doctor.' He led them past the magnificent central staircase that dominated the entrance hall to the hotel, and into the comfortably furnished lounge. He beckoned brusquely to a waiter, who immediately finished scribbling down the order he was taking and rushed to his side.

'We have a nice table in the corner, Doctor John,' the waiter ventured, pointing to a low round table surrounded by comfortably padded red plush chairs.

'It will do fine,' Andrew agreed briskly. 'And as it's thirsty work watching boxing I'll have a beer. Trevor?'

'Pint as well, thank you.'

'Haydn, Eddie, William?'

'I think pints will be fine for all of us,' Haydn said quickly, forestalling William, who was on the point of asking for whisky, and looking out for Eddie who was was still a little shell-shocked as well as overawed by the surroundings.

'Five pints please,' Andrew said to the waiter. Dai Rogers continued to hover at the waiter's elbow, making sure that he wrote the order down correctly.

'Ladies?' Andrew looked to Bethan, Laura and Jenny Griffiths who sat nervously on the edge of the chair next to Haydn's.

'Sherry,' Laura said decisively. 'A large one. I need it.'

'Anyone would think you'd just gone three rounds with Desperate Dan, not Eddie. Bethan?'

'I'll have a sherry as well please.'

'Miss Griffiths?'

'Jenny,' she said shyly. 'Could I have a lemonade please?'

'Most certainly. Two large sherries, one lemonade and sandwiches for eight. Ham and pickle, and cheese and cucumber all right with everyone?'

'Cakes?' Laura enquired hopefully.

'And a plate of cakes. Cream and plain.'

Rogers nodded to the waiter, who disappeared in the direction of the kitchens.

'Pleasure to serve you, Doctor John. As always.'

'Thank you, Mr Rogers, it's a pleasure to be here.'

Left to the peace of the secluded corner, Andrew sat back and pulled out his cigarette case. He offered it around. William, Haydn and Trevor helped themselves, Eddie declined.

'What does it feel like to have won your first important bout?' Andrew asked, wanting to break the ice.

'All right,' Eddie answered briefly, resting his battered face on his hand.

'It's good of you to come with us. I suspect you would rather have stayed in the booth with your friend.'

'I think it's just as well Eddie left when he did,' Haydn said. 'Jim Dekker was about to make him an offer and Joey has other things in mind for his protégé.'

'That's not to say I won't try my hand in a boxing booth again,' Eddie contradicted truculently.

'You'll never make odds again like the ones you made today,' Andrew commented. 'I hope you put the maximum you could afford on yourself?'

'We all did.' William smiled, cheering up at the sight of the beer arriving. 'If he'd lost there would have been a queue of Powells a mile long outside the workhouse in the morning.'

Bethan set her mouth into a thin hard line at William's bad joke. She loved William as much as she loved her brothers, but she knew their faults and failings. It wasn't difficult to read the small signs of resentment against Andrew and the privileged world he represented. And she was furious with Haydn and William for playing down to Andrew, deliberately setting themselves out to be coarser, less educated and less intelligent than they really were.

The way they were acting made her ashamed. She hated them for forcing her to face up to the changes Andrew had wrought in her in such a short space of time. A few months with him had been enough for her to adopt his ways – to deliberately refine the roughened edges of her Welsh accent, to watch what she said, and the way she said it, in his company. To take good food, drink, and things like tea out in hotels for granted. For the first time she realised that the boys had noticed the changes and despised her for it. Almost as much as they despised Andrew for being, crache.

There was a flurry of activity; the waiter laid the sandwiches, cakes, plates, knives and forks on the table. As soon as he left, Andrew, still very much the host, handed around the sandwiches. They all began eating with the exception of Eddie who sat supping his pint slowly.

'I wish you'd let me look at your face.' Bethan moved her chair closer to his.

'It's fine,' he insisted irritably.

'It doesn't look fine.' She touched his bloodied cheekbone with the tips of her fingers.

'The cuts are superficial,' Trevor said authoritatively. 'It's the bruising you're going to have to watch.'

'I bet they don't feel superficial.' Andrew smiled amicably at Eddie in an attempt to win him over.

Eddie didn't return the smile. Instead he sat sullenly staring down into his beer. He didn't feel like talking. In fact he didn't feel much like anything. He'd been looking forward to winning his first real, meaningful fight for so long that now it had actually happened he felt flat. He'd wanted to stay in the booth and discuss the possibility of a job with Dekker, but Dekker had been put in a foul mood by his champion's failure, and Joey had pushed him out with a sharp 'Play the booths, boy. Don't work in them. That's a sure road to nowhere.'

He drained his beerglass and put it down. Sliding his fingers inside his starched collar he tried to loosen it. He felt on edge, out of place, ridiculous. Like when he was seven years old and his mother had forced him into an angel's costume for the chapel pageant. He glanced across at Bethan's boyfriend, and put the man into the smarmy, not to be trusted category. The doctor probably meant well, he allowed grudgingly, but everything Andrew John did and said smacked of condescension. It was as if he wanted the whole world to know he had money and could afford to spend it. He'd bought Bethan and now he wanted to buy them all. Well he for one wasn't impressed. If Dr high-and-mighty John had wanted to treat them to tea he should have met them half-way and taken them all to Ronconis' café. There at least they would have been on familiar territory, not this . . . this stuffed-shirt place.

He decided he'd had enough. He'd just won a fight. He had a fiver in his pocket and he didn't have to put up with anything he didn't want to. He left his chair awkwardly, kicking the table and slopping the beer and sherry on to the cloth.

'Where you off to?' Haydn asked.

'See Joey.' He fumbled in his pocket. All he had was the five-pound note he'd won, and a penny-farthing, and that wouldn't cover the cost of a pint, not in the New Inn.

'This one is on me, Eddie,' Andrew said quietly, seeing Eddie's hand slide into his pocket.

'Buy you one next time I see you. Bye everyone.'

Bethan's voice floated after him as he left the room. 'Haydn, is he all right? Shouldn't one of us go after him?' Then came Haydn's voice uncharacteristically cutting and impatient. 'For pity's sake, Beth, he's seventeen. It's time you broke the apron strings.'

Eddie paused to straighten his tie in front of the large gilt-framed mirror that filled the end wall of the lounge. He took a moment to study their reflections. Haydn, his hand on Jenny's knee under the table where he thought it couldn't be seen, still arguing with Bethan. William oblivious to everything except his beer and the food, helping himself to another sandwich. Laura grinning like a miner who'd just been put on double rate drooling over the skinny fellow she was with, and that dark, smarmy sod eyeing Bethan as though she were on offer in the cattle market. He just hoped Bethan wasn't too dazzled to keep her wits about her.

He left the hotel and walked out into the sunshine. The street was packed with people, the music from the organ blasting at full tempo. He pulled his flat cap down low, covering his damaged eye, and walked up towards Market Square.

'Cockles, sir? Sweet cockles?'

'Candyfloss, sir. Candyfloss for your lady?'

'I've got no lady,' he replied gruffly.

'You have now, Eddie. Bye, Doris.' Daisy waved goodbye to her friend as she hooked her arm into his. 'I was hoping I'd see you again.' She smiled at him, displaying two rows of pearly white teeth set into very pink gums between even pinker lips.

'Come on, sir. Buy the lady a ride on the wooden horse.'

'Swinging boats, sir. Be amazed what you can do with a lady in a swinging boat.'

'Cheeky beggar,' Daisy retorted, pulling Eddie along with her as she struggled against the tide of people towards the top end of Market Square.

'Shooting, sir. Nothing like a gun to impress the lady. Win her a prize?'

'I'd love that little monkey, he's cute.' Daisy's eyes sparkled with reflected sunshine as she gazed adoringly at Eddie.

'The monkey's not up for a prize, miss.' The stallholder stroked the small creature clinging to his shoulder. 'But you can have a nice ornament for your bedroom?' He held up a grotesque chalk figure of a shepherdess.

'The monkey or nothing.' Daisy made a sulky mouth.

'Goldfish, miss.' He held up a large sweet bottle in which fish were circling one another in a stew that was more fish than water.

'How about a toy monkey?' Eddie pointed to one pinned to the side of the booth.

'Twelve hits of the target, sir, and he's yours.'

'I'll take twelve shots.'

'Penny a shot. Four for threepence.'

Eddie handed over his precious fiver.

'Four pounds nineteen and threepence change, sir.' The stallholder shovelled four pound notes into Eddie's hand and topped them with a pile of change. Eddie counted the whole amount carefully from one hand into the other, calling the stallholder back sharply when he realised he'd been short-changed by half a crown.

'Can't blame a chap for trying, sir,' the man said cheerily, handing over the missing coin together with the rifle and pellets. Eddie loaded a pellet and looked down the barrel. 'North,' he murmured to himself.

'Did you say something?' Daisy asked.

'They bend the barrels to lengthen the odds in their favour. Whenever my father took us to the fairs when we were little he always used to make for the shooting galleries so he could point out the defects in the guns. If they were bent upwards it was north, downwards south. This one's north.'

'No bent gun barrels here, mate,' the stallholder shouted angrily.

Eddie didn't bother to answer. Instead he lifted the rifle, took aim and fired. It was difficult to know who was the more surprised when he made bull's-eye, Daisy or the stallholder. He fired his remaining shots in quick succession. Each one hit the centre of the target, and the man grudgingly unpinned the toy from the canvas.

'Here you are, miss.' He leaned over and handed it to Daisy, brushing her hand with his own as he did so.

'Sure you won't change your mind about giving away the real thing?' Daisy smiled.

'Depends on what you've got to offer,' the man said, eyeing her appreciatively.

'The lady's with me,' Eddie snarled.

'Looks like she'd prefer a monkey.'

'I'd be careful what I say if I were you,' Daisy wrapped her arm around Eddie's. 'He's just knocked out Dekker's champion.' Eddie pushed his cap to the back of his head, and glared furiously, unwittingly exposing his cut and bruised eye.

'Sorry, mate. Didn't mean nothing,' the stallholder apologised.

Eddie turned away and Daisy, still clinging to his arm, tottered alongside him.

'Well you've got your monkey,' Eddie said. 'Where to now?'

'Ride on the horses?'

They waited for the largest roundabout in the fair to stop. Painted gold, with beautifully carved red and gold wooden horses and cockerels riding three abreast, it was the oldest ride in Dante's fair and his pride and joy. Caught up in the rush of people clambering off and on, Eddie pulled Daisy up the steep wooden steps. He sat on one of the inside horses and she climbed up in front of him, sitting demurely in a side-saddle position, her right arm low around his waist. It was the first time Eddie had been physically close to a woman outside of the family and a peculiar mixture of pride, shyness and embarrassment beset him as he delved into his trouser pocket for two pennies to pay the boy who was collecting the fares.

The organ music rose to a crescendo as the roundabout began to turn. Slow at first, it gradually rotated faster and faster. The horses moved up and down with a speed that seemed geared to the music, and Daisy squealed and wriggled closer to Eddie on each downward movement. The warmth of her hand burned his back even through the thick layers of his suit jacket and trousers. Then, without warning, she wrapped both her arms around his waist. Bending her head to avoid the pole that stood between them she brushed her lips over his. A peculiar excitement coursed through his veins, leaving an odd deflated, tinny taste in his mouth when the ride finally ended. Buffeted by the crowds they left the roundabout and stood in the middle of Market Square.

'Where to now?' Eddie asked.

Daisy pulled up the sleeve of her long white cotton glove and squinted at her rolled gold watch. 'I have to be in the theatre soon. Two shows tonight.' She made a face.

'Oh.' He didn't know what he'd hoped for, but it certainly hadn't been that. He should have known. After all, Haydn had introduced them, and he'd moaned enough about having to work tonight. He waited foolishly, feeling clumsy and ham-fisted next to her small, perfumed, feminine figure.

'I do have time for a quick drink.' She smiled at the crestfallen expression on his face. 'And if you want to watch the show I could leave a ticket at the box office for you. Second house finishes at half-nine. I'm free then if you want to take me somewhere.'

'I'd like that.' His spirits soared at the prospect.

'Where's a good place to drink?' she asked.

It may have been his imagination but he thought he saw her glance towards the New Inn. 'Two foot nine,' he said boldly, giving the town's pet name for the back bar of the Victoria at the top end of Taff Street. From what Haydn had said some of the theatrical crowd from the New Theatre went there, and perhaps Daisy might feel at home in the surroundings.

'Two foot nine?' She looked at him and giggled. 'Where *did* it get its name from?'

'The length of the bar.'

'Ooh. I didn't think of that.'

She took his arm and they walked past the New Inn. Eddie saw a few boys from the Graig and a couple of men from the gym. He spoke to all of them, taking care they saw that Daisy was with him, but when the coins in his pocket began to disappear over the bar of the two foot nine on gin and tonics for her, beer for him and a couple of pies he began to regret picking her up. The five pounds meant a great deal to him. He'd never had so much money in his life, and he'd intended to take care of it. He stared at the clock on the white-tiled wall and tried to focus his eyes. The room blurred around him and his hand shook as he replaced his empty glass on the table.

'Time I left.' Daisy made a face as she downed the last of her gin. 'Tell you what,' she ran her fingers along the lapel of his coat, 'why don't you walk me to the theatre via the park?'

'The park isn't on the way to the theatre,' he protested dully.

'But it could be, sweetie. It could be.' She picked up her handbag. They walked out of the pub and retraced their steps towards the centre of town, turning right by the Park cinema and crossing the bridge that led from Taff Street into Ynysangharad Park. The revue that Daisy was in had only been in town for a week, but she'd obviously taken time to find her way around and Eddie allowed her to lead the way. She turned right again after the bridge and they walked past the tennis courts along the bank of the river. Not many people walked that way, especially when the fair was in town, and Eddie in his drink-fuddled state wondered where she was taking him.

'This will do nicely.' She sat down in a patch of high grass behind a bank of bushes and trees, and patted the ground beside her. 'Join me?'

He bent his knees and landed heavily next to her. The greenery appeared to be swimming and the sky was revolving above his head. She pressed him back against the tree and slid her hands inside his coat, running her nails over the buttons on his waistcoat.

'I do love fighters.' She unfastened his waistcoat and moved on to the buttons on his shirt.

'What are you doing?' he asked thickly.

'What do you think?'

She kissed him, thrusting her tongue inside his mouth. He tried to kiss her back but he was impotent, helpless, overwhelmed by the soft feel and exotic smell of her body. Her face powder cloyed in his nostrils, mixing with the warm, musky scent of her perfume, so different from the light flowery toilet waters that Bethan and Maud used. Pulling her skirt high she straddled him, her hands busy with the buttons at the waistband of his trousers. He held her, lightly at first then as her kisses grew more intense he found courage enough to hold her tight.

She pulled back from him and he felt her fingers unfasten the buttons on his fly.

'Relax,' she whispered into his ear. 'No one can see us.' She took his right hand and laid it above the stocking top on her naked thigh. He left it there, stiff and immobile.

'I think you need a little more help, sweetie.' She leaned back and unbuttoned her blouse. She wasn't wearing underclothes, and he found himself staring at the small pink nipples on her naked breasts. He watched mesmerised as she shrugged off the blouse and tossed it on to the grass behind them.

'Are all Welsh boys as backward about coming forward as you?' she laughed. She laid her hand on top of his and pushed it up until he could feel the lace that trimmed the edge of her silk French knickers. 'How about we get this out of the way as well?' She unbuttoned her skirt, pulled it over her head and threw it on to the blouse.

'You're . . . you're beautiful,' he choked.

'I know.' She tossed her head back confidently. 'But thank you for saying so. Come on, sweetheart,' she wheedled impatiently, 'this body isn't just for looking at. It won't break if you touch.'

Steeling himself he ran his hands over her naked back, inadvertently pulling down her knickers as his hand slipped on her smooth skin.

'That's it, sweetie, *now* you're getting the hang of it. Try sliding your hand down a bit more.' She opened his trousers wide, and moved her fingers expertly, teasing him to a throbbing erection that made his face burn.

'You really are slow,' she complained playfully, rearranging his clothes. 'Most men would have tossed my knickers in the river by now. Here, do you want me to do it for you?' She arched backwards, wriggling out of the scrap of silk and lace, and lay down on the grass.

'What you waiting for? I'm here ready, willing and able.'

Eddie stared at her for a moment, studying the exposed curves and contours of the female form that had remained a mystery to him for so long. Then slowly, tentatively he reached out and laid a hand on her naked breast.

She smiled. 'Do you want me to undress you, sweetie? Or can you do it yourself?'

The suit jacket he had been so proud of that morning was flung, a heap of crumpled cloth, on the ground. She scratched his chest with her long, sharp, red-varnished nails as she undid the buttons on his shirt and wrenched it off his back.

'Steady now,' she warned as he lunged towards her. 'Oh my God, you haven't done much of this before, have you?' she gasped as he fell clumsily on top of her. 'Here,' she opened his trousers wide and pulled them down over his buttocks, 'can't get far with these on either, that's for sure.' She yanked down his underpants. 'Take your time now, ducks. Aim true and get it right, for my sake. That's it, slow and steady,' she sighed, helping him inside her. 'Not too quick, no sense in hurrying, it'll be over before we start the way you're going at it. Don't look down. Just put your hands here, and here – ' She planted his hands firmly, one on each breast. 'And if you can manage three things at once you could try kissing me as well.'

'Easy isn't it?' she giggled as he came up for air. 'Just like riding a bike.'

'It's a damned sight better than any bike I've ever ridden,' he cried feelingly as she wrapped her legs around his back. 'It's bloody marvellous,' he crowed as she thrust herself hard against him.

'If you're going to do this sort of thing regular, love,' she offered kindly, wincing and digging her nails into his back, 'you need to organise yourself a bit of practice. It'll do wonders for you. May even rub the rough edges off this caveman technique of yours.'

Eddie was too far gone to hear what she was saying. He was

212

off, sailing on a wondrous sea of sensual pleasure that had opened into a whole new world. One he never wanted to leave.

The sun was low on the horizon when Andrew drove Bethan out of the station car park and up the Graig hill.

'Sunshine can brighten anything, even the homes,' he observed, noticing how the last rays of the dying day played on the grey stonework of the eight-foot wall around the infirmary and workhouse.

'It's been a lovely day,' Bethan answered mechanically. She was fighting a headache that came from wine and sherry drunk too early in the day, followed by too many roundabout rides.

'For some,' he answered. 'Trevor's like a dog with two tails.'

'Laura said it went well between her father and Trevor after we left. It must have. They're getting engaged officially next weekend.' She screwed the handkerchief she was holding into a tight, damp knot.

'Are we invited?'

'Yes. Ronnie's organising a party in the café on Saturday night.'

He stopped the car in front of the Graig Hotel.

'I'm not going for a drink in there,' she said quickly. 'Someone would be knocking the door to tell my mother before you even got to the bar.'

'And your mother doesn't know that you have the odd glass of wine or sherry?'

'No.'

'Your secret is safe with me.' He removed the keys from the ignition. 'And I wasn't suggesting that we should drink in the Graig Hotel.' He pointed across the road to a small lane that opened out between two rows of terraces. 'Does that lead to the famous, or should I say infamous, Shoni's pond?'

'Yes,' she answered shortly. Apart from being a lovers' haunt, Shoni's was inextricably bound up with her childhood memories. It was the place where her father had taught them all to swim, and to fish with bent pins tied to string, and empty jam jars. They'd picnicked there on bread and dripping inexpertly put together by either herself or her father, for Elizabeth would never go to Shoni's, referring to the small lake and surrounding greenery as a filthy place, fit only for animals and beggars.

213

'Would you like to show it to me?' Andrew asked.

'I have to dress for dinner, remember?'

'We dine at eight. It's only six now.'

'You promised to meet my family.'

'Not for two hours, I didn't.' When she didn't answer, he opened his door. 'I'm not suggesting a quick roll in the hay,' he said lightly. 'Only a short walk. I need some peace and tranquillity after the noise of that fair.'

'It'll take us about three-quarters of an hour to walk there and back,' she warned.

'The sooner we start, the sooner we'll be back.'

'This will cause a stir,' she said as she stepped out of the car.

'What?'

'Your car parked here.'

'No one will notice it.'

'Oh yes they will, and as everyone knows exactly who it belongs to, tongues will wag about us and Shoni's tonight.'

'All the tongues are at the fair.' He crossed the road and began walking up the lane.

'Not all,' she said, glancing back at the hotel. A group of women were congregating outside the jug and bottle bar of the pub.

'I can put up with a bit of gossip if you can,' he said glibly.

'Doesn't anything ever bother you?' she asked in exasperation.

'Bethan my sweet,' he put his arm around her waist, 'you're a lovely girl, but you'd be even lovelier if you didn't take life so seriously.'

'Round here life is serious,' she said with an edge of resentment.

'All the more reason for me to introduce you to other places.'

They continued to walk along the path in silence. The track was well trodden, black with coal dust, the worst of the potholes filled in with stones and dirt by the children who rode their home-made go-carts and old pram wheels to Shoni's every chance they got. The further they went from the houses, the greater the profusion of wild flowers. Bethan saw the first of the season's bluebells peeking out amongst the celandine, buttercups and harebells. Then came the infinitely sweet, sad song of a solitary lark. She'd felt angry and bitter, for reasons she hadn't examined too closely because of an ugly suspicion that they stemmed from

214

jealousy of Laura and Trevor's happiness, but all of that dissipated as the countryside closed in around her. For the first time that day she felt quiet and at peace with herself.

'Who would have thought there could be so much beauty so close to such ugliness?' Andrew said spontaneously as they stood before the dark expanse of water surrounded by trees that was Shoni's pond.

'Ugliness?' she questioned, picking up a stone from the shore and skimming it across the surface of the pond. 'Are you saying that the Graig is ugly?'

'No uglier than a few other places,' he said in an attempt to soften his declaration. 'In fact it's not half as bad as some areas of London.'

'It's strange,' she said thoughtfully. 'I've never really thought about whether it's ugly or beautiful. It's simply home.'

'If depressing. All those miserable grey stone buildings. Narrow dark streets, scruffy kids. . . . '

'I was one of those scruffy kids once.'

'No you weren't. You've always been beautiful.' He took her in his arms and kissed her, an oddly chaste and sober kiss after the passion earlier that afternoon. 'I suppose we should be going back,' he said as he released her.

'We should.' She picked up another stone and sent it flying across the water. He reached for his own stone, but when he threw it it landed in the centre of the pond, creating waves that travelled outwards in ever-increasing circles until they broke on the shore. They stood and watched for a moment, lost in their own thoughts.

She expected him to say something on the walk back. She wanted to ask him about his plans for the future. A hundred times over she framed the question that was uppermost in her mind — 'Are you going to London?' She even pictured the look on his face as he responded. But try as she might, she couldn't answer the question for him.

The car was enough to create a stir amongst those residents of Graig Avenue who either hadn't gone to the fair or had returned early. A dozen ragged urchins and half a dozen young men clustered around the bonnet before Andrew even had time to open his door.

'Is it safe to leave it here?' he asked Bethan, not entirely humorously, as he looked at the crowd around them.

'Perfectly,' she assured him touchily, deeply regretting the crazy impulse that had caused her to invite him to her home.

'Here, mister, want your car cleaned? I'll do a first-class job. Only a tanner.'

'I'll do it for a joey, mister.'

'Twopence, mister.'

'Clear off, the lot of you,' Bethan said sharply. 'Quick, before I put my hand behind you.'

To Andrew's amazement they all scarpered, reconvening in a tight knot in front of the wall opposite, out of Bethan's reach.

She turned her back on them and climbed the steps to her house, Andrew following, confident and smiling.

'It's only me,' she called out as she opened the door. She walked through to the kitchen without a backward glance. The room was still warm from the stove that had been stoked high earlier that day to cook the main meal, but no washing hung, airing on the rack. It never did on days when Elizabeth expected her uncle to visit.

'Bethan, I wasn't expecting you back early.' Her mother halted on her way from the pantry to the table. Bethan noticed that Elizabeth was wearing her best black frock, and the tray she was carrying was piled high with china that was usually kept in the sideboard in the front parlour. Obviously John Joseph hadn't yet arrived, and Bethan fervently hoped that he wouldn't appear in the next half-hour.

'I've not come back for tea. I've brought someone I'd like you to meet.' She smiled tentatively at her father, who was also wearing his Sunday-best suit and collar. He was sitting bolt upright in his chair in front of the window, reading a book from the lending library. Evan returned her smile, then saw the tall figure of Andrew standing behind her.

'Doctor John, isn't it?' He rose from his chair and extended his rough, calloused hand.

'Please call me Andrew.' For once Andrew bypassed etiquette and shook hands with Bethan's father before her mother.

'Pleasure to meet you, Mr Powell, Mrs Powell.' He touched Elizabeth's cold fingers with his own.

'Pleased to meet you,' Elizabeth said stiffly. 'Will you take a cup of tea with us?'

'Only if you're having one,' Andrew said pleasantly.

'I was just about to make one.' She picked up the kettle and went into the washhouse to fill it.

'Don't make one for me, Mam,' Bethan called, 'I'm going up to change.'

'Change?' Her mother appeared at the washhouse door and looked her up and down.

'I'm going to Andrew's for dinner, and there's a stain on this suit,' she answered defiantly, as she left the room.

'Do sit down, Andrew, please,' Evan offered, hovering in front of his chair.

'Thank you, I will.' Andrew sat on one of the wooden kitchen chairs grouped around the table.

'How long has this been going on then?' Evan enquired, as he resumed his seat. The contrast between Evan's politeness and the bluntness of the question took Andrew aback.

'Do you mean my seeing Bethan?' he asked warily.

'Aye, that's what I mean.'

'We've been spending the odd afternoon together since I came to Pontypridd in January.'

'The odd afternoon?' Evan put down his book and peered at Andrew through narrowed eyes.

'We're friends,' Andrew asserted with more confidence than he felt. There was something in Evan's cool, appraising gaze that made him feel uncomfortable.

'I see,' Evan commented in a tone that clearly said he didn't.

Elizabeth returned with the kettle. She took a pair of tongs, lifted the hotplate cover on the stove and set the kettle to boil and the teapot to warm on the rack above.

'You work in the Central Homes, Doctor John?'

'Please call me Andrew,' he repeated. He found Evan disconcerting, but there was something in Elizabeth's cold eyes that sent a chill down his back. 'Yes, I work in the Central Homes.'

Elizabeth lifted down a tin caddy decorated with scratched and faded pictures of roses and spooned tea into the pot, then she

217

took four of the best cups from the tray on the table, and set them out in front of Andrew. 'Would you like a rock cake or a scone, Doctor John? They're quite fresh. I baked them this afternoon.'

'Thank you,' he replied. He wasn't hungry, but he thought that sampling Elizabeth's cooking might give him the opportunity to compliment her.

While Elizabeth was in the pantry buttering the scones, Maud opened the door and bounced in.

'Have you met my younger daughter, Andrew?' Elizabeth enquired coolly from the pantry door.

'No I haven't had the pleasure, but of course Bethan has told me about all of you,' Andrew said as he rose from his seat.

'She would!' Maud exclaimed pertly. 'I'm Maud.' She looked down at the table. 'Best cups, you are honoured.'

'Fill the milk jug, Maud,' Elizabeth ordered abruptly.

Andrew sat on the edge of his chair, and fervently wished that Bethan would finish whatever it was that she was doing. He looked across the room and saw the book that Evan had laid face down on the hearth and decided to make another attempt at conversation.

'*Crime and Punishment*, Mr Powell, you enjoy Russian literature?'

'I do.' Evan pulled out his pipe and a tin of tobacco, and began to pack the bowl. 'And like most miners I appreciate the socialist ideals of the Soviets.'

'Anyone who lived here would.'

'Do you mean the Graig or Pontypridd?'

'Both. This area has created a great deal of wealth for the nation, but precious little of it has been ploughed back into the Valleys. I don't mean now, in the depression, but earlier,' he said, mindlessly repeating one of his father's favourite observations. As the town's medical officer Dr John senior constantly railed against the housing and living conditions in the town.

'I doubt that the lack of amenities in the town has affected you personally, Andrew,' Evan said pointedly.

'No, not personally, at least not until recently,' Andrew agreed. 'But I grew up watching my father trying to combat illnesses caused by poor living conditions. And now I'm faced with patients who have the same problems. Nothing seems to have changed here in the last thirty years.'

Evan looked at him, a shrewd light in his eyes. 'Let's hope something changes in the next thirty.'

'Your tea, Doctor John.' Maud, a sickly smile on her face, gave him a cup. 'Milk? Sugar?'

'Scones, Andrew?' Elizabeth handed him an empty small plate and a large one laden with buttered scones. 'Jam and cream's on the table.'

'Thank you, a plain one will be fine, and milk and three sugars in my tea please, Maud.' He took a scone and laid it on his plate.

'Is that why you came back to Pontypridd?' Evan pressed. 'To try to do something about the living conditions of the working classes?'

'I don't know about the living conditions,' Andrew mused honestly, 'but I certainly hope to improve the standard of health care.'

'You won't do that until you eradicate poverty,' Evan observed realistically.

'At least we can try,' Andrew replied, manfully struggling with a mouthful of dry scone and blatantly flirtatious looks from Maud at the same time.

'Sorry I took so long.' Bethan bustled into the room wearing a calf-length green silk frock that buttoned modestly to a small collar at the neck. She was carrying a matching blue and green silk jacket, and a blue leather handbag dyed the same colour as her shoes.

'Another new outfit?' her mother commented disapprovingly.

'I bought it from Aunt Megan some time ago,' Bethan lied defensively.

'Seems to me a lot of your wages end up in Megan's pocket. More tea, Andrew?' Elizabeth enquired as Andrew left his seat.

'I'm afraid we haven't time, Mrs Powell. The scone was delicious, but we have to leave. My mother is expecting us.'

'What a shame. My uncle, the minister John Joseph Bull, is coming to take high tea with us. He's bringing his wife. It would have been nice if you could have stayed.'

'Thank you for the invitation, Mrs Powell. Perhaps another time.'

'It's been a pleasure meeting you, Andrew. Hope we see you again soon.' Evan left his chair as Bethan opened the door.

'The pleasure was all mine. Mr Powell, Mrs Powell, Maud.' Andrew smiled at all of them as he left the room.

'Don't be late, Bethan,' her mother admonished, returning to her pantry as they walked out through the door.

'Don't worry, Mrs Powell, she'll be safe enough in my parents' house. And I promise to bring her home before midnight.'

'Your father keeps later hours than us,' Evan remarked loudly.

'I'll be fine, Dad,' Bethan shouted as she ran down the steps.

'That's quite a family you have there,' Andrew said once they were closed into the privacy of his car.

'What's that supposed to mean?' Bethan asked, on the alert for anything that sounded remotely like a sneer.

'What it said. Your sister's going to be a stunner, your father's incredibly astute and intelligent. . . .'

'For a miner?' she broke in nastily.

'For a man,' he replied firmly. 'And your mother . . .' his voice trailed as he tried to think of a flattering adjective to describe Elizabeth, 'is imposing?' he suggested cautiously, pushing the gearstick into reverse and driving backwards towards Iltyd Street.

'Imposing?'

Glad of an excuse to turn away from her he twisted his head to negotiate the corner. 'She's also a very good cook,' he added blandly.

'Imposing and a very good cook,' she repeated slowly.

He stopped the car to change into first gear.

'Tell me, is your mother imposing and a very good cook as well?' she asked.

Not quite knowing what to expect he looked at her, then he saw mischief in her eyes. Unable to contain himself a moment longer he burst out laughing. She put her hand on his knee.

'I love you, Doctor Andrew John, even if you are an insincere idiot.'

'Quick, someone's looking.' He bent his head to hers without taking his hands off the steering wheel. 'One kiss now and we'll set the whole town talking.'

She leaned across and kissed his lips. He lowered the handbrake and the car began to roll down the hill.

'Release me, woman,' he shouted, hoping that the shocked and startled Mrs Richards would hear him. 'Can't you wait until we get to Shoni's?

'There goes your reputation, Nurse Powell,' he laughed as they turned the corner on to Llantrisant Road.

'And yours, Doctor John.'

'A man doesn't need a reputation. Too much baggage.'

'Is that so?'

'That's so.'

They were both still laughing when he drove under the railway bridge and into the town.

Chapter Thirteen

Andrew's parents lived in a large comfortable villa set in fair-sized private walled gardens, but to Bethan it seemed like a mansion. In fact every aspect of the suburbs on the Common amazed her. The mature trees that shaded the pavements on the wide, well-planned roads and avenues. The nurtured front gardens with their flowering bushes, banks of daffodils and narcissus, and green manicured lawns. The clean, clear aspect over the entire town that sprawled, dirty and untidy, along the valley floor. Distance and sunlight even lent a fairytale enchantment to the bleak slag heaps and grimy colliery on the hillside to the right.

Bethan had only ever walked up to the Common a few times in her life, and then it had been on Armistice days, following her father and the other miners as they trailed behind the Great War veterans who marched to the cenotaph, built high on the hill above Ynysangharad Memorial Park. If she'd seen the neat streets of semi-detached and the walled gardens of the larger villas then, she'd paid no attention. She'd certainly given no more thought to visiting one of them than to the concept of flying to the moon.

Andrew steered the car through the impressive wrought-iron gates that his father had erected to replace those melted down in the war, and into the old coach-house that was now used as a garage.

'Before we go remind me to show you my rooms,' he said as he opened the door for her.

'Your rooms?' She looked quizzically at him.

He pointed to the ceiling. 'We've done up the old stableboy's quarters. Dual purpose – keeps me out of Mother's hair, and gives me privacy.'

She smiled woodenly.

'You'll be just fine,' he whispered, pinching her cheek. 'They'll love you.'

A maid wearing the standard black dress and white starched and frilled cap and apron opened the front door.

'Thank you, Mair,' Andrew handed her his hat.

'Máir?' Bethan looked at the girl's face.

'Wondered if you'd recognise me in this get-up, Beth,' the girl screeched. 'How's Haydn?' she asked, forgetting herself and earning a frown from Andrew.

'Where is everyone?' Andrew asked heavily.

'In the drawing room, sir,' Mair bobbed a curtsy.

Bethan stood bewildered and more than a little lost in the hall. A massive curved staircase swept upwards to the first floor with all the grace and elegance of those she'd seen in the pictures. A few pieces of heavily carved, dark oak Victorian hall furniture stood against the walls between the panelled doors. Stained-glass windows puddled the black-and-white-tiled floor with pools of brilliant crimson and sapphire light. Andrew put his arm protectively around her shoulders and propelled her gently forwards. He passed what seemed like a dozen doors before he finally opened one that led into a room that could have swallowed the front parlour in Graig Avenue four times over and still had space to spare.

'Mother, Father, this is Bethan.' He gave her a small push.

'I'm very pleased to meet you, Mrs John.' Bethan shook Andrew's mother's hand. Small, and surprisingly fair given the dark colouring of her children, Andrew's mother had the figure and disarmingly naive demeanour of a young girl.

'We've been so looking forward to meeting you, Bethan. You've met Doctor John of course?'

Bethan automatically dropped a curtsy to Andrew's father.

'We're not in the hospital now, Bethan,' he laughed. 'You met my daughter and son-in-law earlier, I believe?'

'Hi, Bethan,' Fiona smiled at her from the depths of the sofa where she sat, feet curled beneath her like a kitten.

'I'm so glad you didn't dress,' Andrew's mother observed in a tactless, futile attempt to put Bethan at ease. 'We rarely dress for dinner in the spring or summer, it seems wrong somehow on light evenings.'

Bethan immediately compared her light silk dress with Mrs John's pale blue organza and Fiona's black lace. Hers was undoubtedly cut along simpler lines, but it was passable. Thanks to Megan, her clothes didn't let her down, even in this company.

'Jolly nice to see you again,' Alec said enthusiastically before returning to the paper he was reading.

'Shall we all sit down?' Andrew's mother said brightly.

Andrew stood in front of the leather chesterfield alongside Alec, and as his parents had obviously been sitting on the only two single chairs in the room Bethan had no choice but to sit next to Fiona.

'Drink, everyone?' Andrew's father rubbed his hands together as he walked over to a wooden bar in the corner of the room.

'That would be nice,' said Andrew's mother.

'Usual, dear?'

'No, darlings,' Fiona said firmly, uncurling her long legs from beneath her. 'No one drinks sherry in London any more. Only cocktails.'

'Cocktails!' Mrs John demurred. 'I really would prefer a nice sweet sherry.'

'Mother, you're *so* archaic,' Fiona complained petulantly. She joined her father at the bar. 'Now let me see,' she peered short-sightedly at the array of bottles, 'is there any ice?'

'In the ice bucket,' Dr John senior said drily.

'Very witty. Right, I'm going to make a Harvard cocktail.'

'She's been making those since we crossed the pond last year to visit my cousin in New York,' Alec said loudly for Bethan's benefit.

'Would you believe there's no cocktail shaker here?' Fiona looked disapprovingly at her father.

'There's one in the kitchen.' Her mother rang a bell pull that hung close to her chair. Mair appeared a few moments later.

'Mrs Campbell-White needs the cocktail shaker, Mair.'

'Yes ma'am.'

'Right!' Fiona looked along the shelves behind the bar. 'I'll need this.' She lifted a bottle of brandy on to the bar counter.

'Not my Napoleon,' her father groaned.

'Daddy, you're impossible! If cocktails aren't made with first-class ingredients they're practically undrinkable. Now what else . . .' she mused, biting her bottom lip. 'Oh I know. Angostura bitters and Italian vermouth. . . .'

'Under the bar,' Andrew interrupted, watching the proceedings with an amused grin.

'I was going to add crushed ice.' She took a silver-plated cocktail shaker from Mair, and dismissed her.

'It should be mushy enough by now,' Andrew commented. 'That ice bucket leaves a lot to be desired.'

'Mushy is not the same as crushed. Is it, darling?' she appealed to her husband.

'Don't ask me, I'm no expert on cocktails.'

'Coward.' She made a face at him. 'Right, here we go.'

'Aren't you supposed to measure the quantities carefully?' Andrew asked as she poured a liberal stream of brandy into the shaker.

'Not Fe, old boy,' Alec said cheerfully. 'Measuring jugs interfere with her creativity. The beauty of her cocktails lies in their element of surprise.'

'That I can believe.' Andrew watched as Fiona tipped in a generous amount of vermouth and filled the shaker with ice.

'Now for the good bit.' She rammed the lid on, held the shaker between her hands and twirled it vigorously from side to side.

'Do you think we're going to survive this experience?' Andrew's mother looked playfully at Dr John senior.

'Oh I think so, dear. Remember she only visits us once or twice a year.'

'Cocktails are served.' Fiona placed half a dozen glasses on the bar, and decanted the mixture evenly between them. Andrew handed them round before sipping his gingerly.

'Well?' his father demanded.

'Not bad, not bad at all. I take my hat off to you, Fanny, you have hidden talents.' He held his glass high. 'Here's to all of us.'

'To us.'

Bethan held her glass up with the others before drinking, but she felt like an interloper not a participant in the scene. Conversations bounced around the room like tennis balls across a court but, too shy to make a contribution, she remained silent. She looked frequently to Andrew hoping to catch his eye, but he always seemed to be engrossed in something his father or Alec was saying. In the end the sound of the doorbell came as a relief, if only because it heralded change. Andrew looked at his mother.

'Someone expected?' he asked.

225

'Only the Llewellyn-Joneses,' his mother answered. 'We owe them, and it seemed a good night for them to come.'

'Speak of the devil,' his father said cheerfully as Mair opened the drawing-room door. 'Come in, come in.' He shook hands with all three guests, and made the necessary introductions, referring to Bethan as Andrew's friend and prevailing on Fiona to make more cocktails.

Mr Llewellyn-Jones was the manager of Barclays Bank. His wife, a large florid woman, was a well-known charity worker in the town. Bethan had seen her serving dinner to the paupers in the workhouse dining hall on Christmas Day. Their daughter Anthea was an attractive, pleasant girl in a petite, dark-eyed, dark-haired Welsh sort of way, but Bethan couldn't suppress the spiteful thought that her attractions had been bolstered since birth by every advantage that money could buy.

Anthea's hair was expertly waved, back as well as sides. Her white silk dress was styled and tailored to emphasise the good features of her figure, and conceal those that were not so good. She smiled constantly, had a kind or flattering remark, albeit insincere, for everyone in the room, including Bethan. But no amount of kindness could make Bethan like her. From the moment Anthea Llewellyn-Jones walked into the drawing room she couldn't help but compare the warmth of the welcome Anthea received with her own lukewarm reception. But more than that, she knew that someone like Anthea, with all the advantages of money, social position and background, would, in Dr and Mrs Johns' eyes, make a far more suitable wife for Andrew than a mere nobody like herself.

A gong resounded outside the door.

'Dinner, at last,' Dr John beamed at the gathered assembly. They left the drawing room for the gloom of the oak-panelled dining room, furnished with the same type of heavy Victorian furniture as the hall. The enormous rectangular table was covered with a gleaming white damask cloth, on which nine covers of silverware and porcelain had been laid.

'Mrs Llewellyn-Jones, there on the doctor's right.' Andrew's mother began to arrange her guests with the same care she'd devoted to the table decorations. 'Mr Llewellyn-Jones, here, next to me.' She patted the place setting with a coy flirtatious glance at her male guest of honour. 'Fiona darling, I suppose you'd better sit opposite your husband or you'll mope. Bethan, perhaps you'd like to sit next to Alec, Andrew next to Miss Llewellyn-Jones.' She surveyed her handiwork as they took their places. 'Now isn't this cosy?' she beamed.

Bethan sat rigidly on her high-backed chair. Every time she tried to relax the carvings bit painfully into her spine. Dr John said a short grace, hock was poured into one of the four glasses at each place, and a maid Bethan hadn't seen before, handed the hors-d'oeuvres. Bethan looked for Mair and saw her hovering next to the sideboard; evidently she'd been regulated to a second-ary serving position. Bethan turned her attention to the array of cutlery before her, and suffered a moment of blind panic before remembering the etiquette books that Laura had devoured during their first months of training in the hope that she'd be swept off her feet by a millionaire patient. 'Start from the outside and work your way in' was sound advice, but 'Watch others and do as they do' was sounder.

She slowly unfolded and settled her linen napkin on her lap, using the time to study everyone's behaviour before copying them, terrified lest she make a mistake, disgrace herself and embarrass Andrew.

'These canapés are delicious, don't you think?' Alec said, as he helped himself to more from a glass plate that had been placed in front of them.

'Yes, delicious,' she echoed inanely, picking at one. She glanced at Andrew, seated further down the other side of the table and deeply engrossed in conversation with Miss Llewellyn-Jones. A moment later Anthea's silvery laughter was joined by Andrew's deeper, more robust tones.

'What do you think, darling,' Mrs John called down the table to her husband, 'Andrew's agreed to escort Anthea to the golf club garden party next week.'

The doctor smiled and carried on talking to Mrs Llewellyn-Jones. A suffocating wave of jealousy rose in Bethan's throat. She choked on a sliver of pastry, turned aside and spat it into her napkin, hoping no one would notice. She needn't have concerned herself. They noticed, but were also too well bred to comment.

The hors-d'oeuvres plates were cleared away by Mair and thick slices of broiled salmon were handed around with a boat of tartare sauce, by the upper maid.

'You always find such good fish, Mrs John,' Mr Llewellyn-Jones complimented. 'This is a truly magnificent specimen.'

'I chose it myself, and the recipe is one of Mother's.'

'My wife always superintends the preparation of the fish herself. Won't trust the cook,' Dr John laughed.

'Most wise,' Mrs Llewellyn-Jones agreed. 'You can't get a good cook these days for love or money. They're simply not bred to it like they used to be. When I was a girl Mother never had any servant problems and now. . . . '

The conversation ebbed and flowed while Bethan played with the salmon on her plate, skinning it, picking out the bones, occasionally ferrying a small forkful of the bland, glutinous flesh to her lips.

'I haven't seen you in town, Miss Powell. Are you from this area?' Miss Llewellyn-Jones enquired politely in a sweet, clear voice.

'Yes,' Bethan replied shortly, colouring at the attention.

'It's strange I haven't seen you before. But then you really *should* join the Ladies' Guild. Absolutely *everyone* belongs to it,' she gushed. 'We meet every Tuesday and Thursday afternoon in one another's homes, and we do such super things. Don't we, Andy?' she appealed familiarly.

'Bethan hasn't time to join you frivolous lot,' Andrew said, gallantly coming to her rescue. 'She works.'

'How marvellous,' Anthea beamed. 'Tell me, what do you *do*, Miss Powell?'

'I'm a nurse.' Bethan laid her knife and fork down on her plate, finally giving up on her fish.

'How *fascinating*. I wish I'd done something as noble as that.'

'You, my darling daughter, would never have stayed the course,' Mr Llewellyn-Jones said dismissively, as he helped himself to a fistful of salted almonds from a bon-bon side dish. 'You haven't the patience to read a cookery book let alone tend to a patient.'

'Mrs John, I appeal to you,' Anthea pleaded. 'I'm an excellent worker aren't I?'

'You most certainly are, my dear,' Mrs John agreed decisively.

'Anthea was a pillar of strength when we organised this year's hospital ball. The committee simply couldn't have managed without her.'

Bethan thought of the tedious hours that she and the other nurses had been forced to put in, either before or after their long shifts, making decorations and garlanding the Coronation ballroom. But she said nothing.

'Fiddling with frills and folderols is very different to nursing, even I know that much,' Mr Llewellyn-Jones said boldly, overriding his wife and Mrs John's objections.

'Daddy!' Anthea protested strongly. 'Decorating the hall was anything but fiddling with frills and folderols. We used a lot of skills absolutely *vital* to nursing. Flower arranging for a start.'

Bethan thought of the bare rooms and corridors of the Graig Hospital and wondered if Anthea had ever been there and taken a good look around. Mair stepped forward and cleared away the remains of the fish course. The first maid replaced the empty hock bottles with bottles of sparkling wine. Bethan hadn't been slow in drinking the hock, but she managed to finish her first glass of wine before the entrée was handed. Chaudfroid of pigeon. She'd never eaten pigeon before and felt sick when she realised what the plump, golden carcass on her plate was.

'Have you ever thought of going to London to nurse?' Alec asked kindly, realising that no one else was making an effort to talk to her.

'No . . . no I haven't,' she stammered, trying to hide most of the pigeon under her knife and fork.

'Pay is extremely good, much better than here,' he said heartily. 'And the nursing is more interesting. If you decide on one of the larger hospitals like Charing Cross, where I happen to practise, you'll work with all kinds of specialists. Learn to cope with diseases you never even knew existed.'

'Now that's an offer you can't possibly refuse,' Andrew called down the table, cheering her with the thought that he was paying her some attention after all. 'Bearing in mind that London's a filthy place to live.'

'It is not . . . ' his sister began warmly.

'It's cleaner than this valley, old boy,' Alec interrupted. 'And although I haven't worked with this little lady I bet she's a first-class nurse. And we're jolly short of those. She'd really be appreciated on my wards. You wouldn't believe some of the dross we've had to make up to sister level lately.'

'Oh I would. I've only just left the Cross, remember.'

'Stop encouraging him, Andrew, all he ever talks about these days is the lack of trained nurses, and it's *so* boring,' Fiona complained.

Once again the conversation slipped past Bethan without giving her a real opportunity to join in. Mair cleared away the remains of the pigeons and the upper maid set a roast leg of lamb and carving knives before Dr John senior. Dishes containing boiled new potatoes, mint sauce and asparagus *au gratin* were placed in the centre of the table, and a pile of warm clean plates stacked next to the lamb.

Bethan had never seen so much food laid before so few people. There were families of twelve and more on the Graig who didn't consume this quantity, let alone quality, in a week. Dr John cut a choice slice of the lamb for her and she quietly stopped him from cutting more. The maid handed down her plate as Andrew made a joke that she didn't understand, but she joined in the laughter anyway. She helped herself to small portions of asparagus and potatoes from the tureens that the maid handed, and tried to smile at everyone like Anthea Llewellyn-Jones.

After her awkward beginnings it seemed scarcely possible that things could deteriorate, but as the meal progressed she felt increasingly isolated. Perhaps her father was right? The gulf between the Common and the Graig – Andrew and her – was too wide to bridge.

She retreated deeper and deeper into her shell of silence, watching Andrew and Anthea, trying desperately to follow every word of their conversation. Studying the expressions on their faces, she suffered agonies every time Anthea laughed and looked up at him with her adoring, deep brown eyes. On the few occasions when someone troubled to speak to her she said only what was necessary, as succinctly as manners would allow. She ate little and drank a great deal, as the repartee sparkled around the table. There was talk of the theatre. Plays that Alec and Fiona had seen in the West End. Magazines that she had never seen in the shops, let alone read. People she knew only as names in the columns of the Pontypridd *Observer*.

By the time all vestiges of the lamb together with the hock and wine glasses had been cleared away and replaced by champagne and the final sweet and savoury courses of gooseberry fool, fresh cream and cheese ramekins, her head was swimming. Realising that she was rapidly becoming what Haydn called 'sozzled' she made an effort, and managed to eat most of the gooseberry fool that the maid had heaped into her dessert bowl in the hope that it would sober her up. But before she finished the course her champagne glass had been refilled twice, minimising any effects that the food might have had.

'I do so lo-ove champagne, don't you?' Alec whispered in slurred tones that told her his head was in no better condition than hers.

'Right, brandy time I think, my dear, don't you?' Andrew's father stood up and walked a little unsteadily to the sideboard. 'Any ladies care to join the gentlemen in a spot of Napoleon?'

'I think the ladies would prefer a liqueur with their coffee in the drawing room, darling,' his wife said as she left the table. Bethan looked helplessly at Andrew, who merely smiled at her before taking a fat cigar from the silver box that his brother-in-law handed him. She had no option but to follow the back of Anthea Llewellyn-Jones out through the door.

A steaming silver coffee pot and an array of delicate porcelain cups were laid out on a small table in front of the sofa in the drawing room. Andrew's mother began to dispense coffee and sickly sweet cherry brandy liqueurs.

'Nursing must be a fascinating profession,' Anthea Llewellyn-Jones said to Bethan, making a studied, gracious effort to bring her into the conversation.

'It is,' Bethan agreed. 'Particularly the nursing I'm doing now.'

'The new ward and X-ray machine must be an absolute boon to everyone at the Cottage.'

'The Cottage?' Bethan looked at her, confused, before registering what she was talking about. 'I don't work in the Cottage Hospital.'

'Really? Then where?' Anthea asked blankly as if the Cottage was the only hospital in Pontypridd.

'The Graig.'

'The Graig?' Anthea's mother looked vaguely shocked. 'I had no idea. There are so many wards there, and some dreadfully pathetic cases . . . ' She turned crimson. 'Particularly in the work-house section,' she added as a hasty afterthought.

'I work on the maternity ward.' Bethan suppressed a smile. She knew why Mrs Llewellyn-Jones had blushed. According to the nurses who worked on the venereal disease wards, a good two-thirds of their patients belonged to the crache of the town. 'I'm training to be a midwife.'

'How fascinating,' Fiona drawled. 'Then you'll actually deliver babies.'

'I do that now.'

'How wonderful. Do tell all about it.' Anthea sipped delicately at her cherry brandy and sat, waiting expectantly.

To be entertained by tales of the coarse working classes, Bethan thought contemptuously. She recalled the cold, bare rooms she worked in; the mothers worn down by inadequate food and poverty. The maternity ward in the Graig was as far removed from this overfurnished, gilt-edged drawing room as a shanty was from Buckingham Palace. She could no more discuss the blood, sweat and toil of labour in these surroundings than her father could have expounded his Marxist theories.

'There's not much to it,' she answered evasively. 'We're so short-staffed I not only deliver babies with only a student nurse to call on, I also fill in for the night sister whenever she's sick.'

'Andrew does speak very highly of your ability,' Mrs John said gently.

'I do no more than any of the other qualified nurses who work in the infirmary,' Bethan said quickly, bristling at the patronising tone.

'Well, things have certainly altered since my day,' Mrs Llewellyn-Jones commented. 'Women had no thought of a career then. Outside of a husband and marriage, that is.'

'Oh I don't know.' Mrs John rose unexpectedly to Bethan's defence. 'My sisters worked as VADs during the war, and I myself would probably have done the same if I hadn't had the children to look after.'

'Ah but war times were very different from now.'

'Perhaps not so much for women of my class.' Bethan finally reached a breaking point that wouldn't have come without the cocktail, hock, wine, champagne and liqueur.

A deathly silence fell over the room for a moment.

'It is good of Andrew to agree to escort me to the golf club garden party, Mrs John,' Anthea purred, setting her back to Bethan.

'Nonsense. You've had such wonderful times together since you were children. It should be such fun. . . . '

Bethan felt as though someone were twisting a knife in her gut. She looked up at the open doorway. Andrew was standing framed in it. He winked at her.

'Coffee, darling?' his mother offered.

'No thank you, Mother. I'm going to whisk Bethan away if I may. Trevor and Laura are calling into my rooms to discuss their engagement plans. In fact,' he glanced at his watch, 'they should have been there as of ten minutes ago.'

'Engaged. How wonderful,' his mother said despondently with a sideways look at Bethan.

'If you'll excuse us, Mrs Llewellyn-Jones, Anthea, Fanny.'

'You'll pick me up half an hour before the party, Andy?' Anthea asked.

'We may both pick you up if I can persuade Bethan to come.'

'Lovely to meet all of you.' Heart soaring at Andrew's reply, Bethan showed the first signs of animation since she'd entered the house. Smiling at everyone she gathered her handbag and jacket from the arm of her chair. 'And thank you very much for a lovely dinner, Mrs John. You'll say goodbye to Doctor John for me?'

'Of course, dear.'

'We'll go out through the french doors so as not to disturb anyone. Bye, ladies.' Andrew put his hand under Bethan's elbow and pushed her into the garden.

'You see,' he said blithely as they crossed the lawn. 'Not ogres at all.'

'That,' she replied, 'depends entirely on your point of view.'

A path led round the side of the black and white Tudor-styled coach-house to a door in the side wall. Andrew pulled a bunch of keys out of his pocket, and selecting one he fitted it into the lock.

'Are Trevor and Laura really coming?' she asked as he swung open the door.

'His car's already here.' He pointed to a rather battered, shabby vehicle parked close to the gates. 'He brings Laura here most nights when he's not on call. They borrow my spare bedroom.' He grinned at her blushes. 'You're not shocked are you? I assumed you knew all about it.'

'Laura did mention something today,' she admitted reluctantly.

'Today!' He stepped into a small, white-painted brick hallway, switched on a light, pulled her in and closed the door behind them. 'It's been going on for months,' he called back as he ran up the stone stairs two at a time.

'It can't have been,' she protested. 'They only started going out with one another four months ago.'

'Going out?' He raised his eyebrows. 'Is that what you call it?' He opened a door at the top of the stairs. 'Come on, slowcoach. The hall and stairs are not the best place to linger. They're basic to say the least, but there didn't seem much point in doing anything to bare brick. The interesting bit begins here.' He held open the door for her and she walked straight into a living room: a beautiful room with a polished wood floor that was almost covered by a deep blue and cream Persian carpet.

'Welcome to my lair,' he said proudly.

The room was filled with the golden rays of the evening sun. Light and airy, it was dominated by a large mullioned window that overlooked the garden. In front of the window, set sideways to make the most of the view, were two comfortable sofas covered in deep blue tapestry with between them an ultra-modern low table, skilfully crafted in blond wood. A bookcase of the same light wood, crammed to capacity with books and ceramics, filled the back wall. In an alcove behind the door was a sideboard, dining table and four chairs, in the same design as the rest of the furniture. Even the paintings were modernistic – lines and shapes of colour that Bethan couldn't even pretend to understand . . . or like.

'Small, but it has everything I need. Come and see the rest.' He crossed the room and opened a door in the far wall. Bethan found herself in a tiny hallway with four doors opening out from it. 'Bathroom.' He pushed one of the doors and revealed a bath, basin and toilet. The walls were fully tiled in white and trimmed with mahogany. 'Kitchen, at least that's what I call it. It's roughly half the size of my mother's pantry.' He showed her a tiny cupboard-sized room. One wall was filled by a sink set below a window, another held a cupboard topped by an electric hotplate, the third a few shelves on which was stacked an elegant set of plain white china.

He pointed to a door and held his finger to his lips.

'Trevor's universe,' he whispered, 'so I daren't open it, but it's just as well you can't see inside. The suite's dreadful. I inherited it from my grandmother. One of those hybrid things that's too good to throw out and not nearly good enough to put anywhere where it can be seen. So despite the fact that I hate Victorian furniture, Mother decided I should be the one to inherit it. But then I was in no position to argue because I spent every spare penny I had on this.'

He opened the final door in the small hallway. His bedroom was huge: the same size and shape as the living room, with the same mullioned windows that overlooked not only the gardens but the whole of the town spread out like a diorama below. He walked over to the window and knelt on the cushioned ledge. 'I often sit here in the night before I go to bed. When the lamps are lit it's like looking at an illuminated map. And as you can see I have all home comforts to hand.'

'A radio.' She fingered the Bakelite casing on the set that stood on one of the bedside tables. What they would have given at home for a radio, she thought wistfully.

'It's not as powerful as the radiogram in the living room.'

'You have a radiogram as well? I didn't see it.'

'You're not supposed to. I don't like things like that on display. I've hidden it behind one of the couches. But here's different. This room is just for me, and my very special guests. Which is why I had a small bar built into this.' He pulled a box trolley towards him, and opened the lid. 'Gin, brandy, whisky, iced wine?'

'You have ice too?'

'I confess I asked Mair to fill an ice bucket earlier and bring it over.' He took off his jacket and flung it over a chair. His wallet fell to the floor. 'Which reminds me, madam,' he picked it up and opened it, 'I haven't given you your winnings.'

'I didn't give you any betting money.'

'Here,' he handed her nine five-pound notes, 'five pounds at ten to one. Fifty pounds less the five you owe me.'

'I can't take it.'

'Why? I took a lot more than that off the bookie. If you feel at all guilty give it to Eddie. He earned it.'

'I suppose he did.' She took it and pushed it into her handbag.

'Right, now that's done. Drink?'

'I think I had enough earlier.'

'So did I, but that's no reason to stop. It doesn't hurt to let your hair down once in a while.'

'Doctor's diagnosis?'

'Of course.' He opened the wine and poured out two glasses.

She walked around the room looking at everything, trying to commit every detail to memory so she could imagine him here, alone, when they were apart. She rested her cheek against the plain navy-blue silk drapes, touched the bronze figures that held the stained-glass shades of the lamps, rested the palms of her hands on the smooth sweep of the heavy navy and red silk bedspread.

'This is a beautiful room,' she whispered, suddenly aware of how alone they were. Of why he'd brought her here.

'I'm glad you like it. I have a penchant for beautiful things.' He stood up and ran his fingers through her hair. 'All beauty,' he said quietly. 'The exotic, the modern and the artistic.' He pointed to an enormous copy of Manet's *Olympia* that hung, framed by silk drapes above his bed. She stared at the nude, fascinated, yet shocked by its blatant eroticism.

'I don't know how any woman could do that,' she said when she realised he was waiting for her to react.

'Do what?'

'Pose in front of a man without any clothes on.'

'Perhaps she was in love with Manet. From the way he's portrayed her he was obviously in love with her. And you have to admit she is very beautiful.'

Taught from childhood by Elizabeth that nudity was disgusting, she found it difficult to equate beauty with a woman's naked body.

'But my darling,' he bent his head and kissed her, 'she can't hold a candle to you.'

He kicked the door shut with the heel of his shoe.

'Trevor and Laura?' she protested.

'Will lock the door behind them.'

'Your parents?'

'Have no key, and visitors to take care of. Besides they know better than to barge in here without an invitation. I told you. This is my lair.'

He gently removed her hat and handbag from her trembling hands and threw them on to the window-seat. She turned her back on him and looked out of the window.

'Beth, I love you,' he murmured. Standing behind her he wrapped his arms around her, cupping her breasts with his hands. 'Don't you think I've been patient long enough?' he asked softly. 'I could have brought you here instead of taking you to Cardiff that first time we went out alone together.'

'Like Trevor did Laura?'

'We're not Trevor and Laura.'

She turned to face him. Sliding her hands up to his neck she pulled him close and returned his kiss. Still kissing, he drew her down on to the bed. She lay next to him, the wine she'd drunk making the ceiling spin. She tried to think clearly, evaluate the choices open to her. But she couldn't. His presence overwhelmed her senses. The smell of brandy and tobacco on his breath – his cologne – the touch of his fingers burning into the skin on her arm. . . .

He rolled close to her, pinning her down. His hand slid high beneath her jacket, unfastening the buttons on her dress. His tongue darted into her mouth. She lifted her arms to his face, and stroked his cheeks.

'I love you, Bethan Powell,' he mumbled hoarsely. 'More than you can ever begin to know.'

'I love you too, Andrew.' Evading his hands she struggled to sit up on the bed.

'Beth . . . ' he begged.

She removed her jacket and tossed it on to a chair. Then she

237

slid her arms out of the sleeves of her dress and pulled it down to her waist.

Struck dumb, he stared at her, and in that precise moment she felt as though she could see her future mirrored in the depths of his dark eyes.

'Are you sure?' he asked huskily.

She thought of Laura, her friend's amazement at the revelation that she and Andrew had never made love. Of Anthea Llewellyn-Jones waiting in the wings. She loved Andrew, and she knew now that she would do anything . . . anything to keep him.

'I'm sure,' she said decisively, with a tremor in her voice that belied her words.

He reached out and, very slowly, very deliberately pulled her dress down over her legs. She shuddered, afraid that he'd be repelled by her naked body, terrified of what he was about to do to her. Sensing her fear and sensitive to her natural modesty he curbed his mounting passion, left the bed and hung her dress and jacket in his wardrobe.

'I'll be back in a moment,' he murmured, lifting down a thick towelling bathrobe from the back of the bedroom door. 'You're shivering, get into bed before you catch your death of cold.'

She undressed in record time, slipping between the clean, cool linen sheets, so different from the tired, furred, flannelette ones her mother used. She lay, rigid with fear, wondering whether or not to remove her bloomers. He returned before she'd made a decision. Closing the door behind him he locked it and slid between the sheets, still wearing his robe.

She started at the feel of his bare legs touching hers. He rubbed his hands vigorously down her arms.

'You're freezing, woman,' he complained. 'Come closer and I'll warm you.' She inched towards him. 'That wasn't an order,' he murmured. 'Relax. I'm not going to hurt you, darling. Not now. Not ever.'

His mouth closed over hers. He kissed her deeply, thoroughly. His hands moved to her breasts, his fingers teasing, stroking, arousing her nipples just as they'd done the day before. She wrapped her arms around him, running her hand down beneath his robe at the back.

Gently, unhurriedly he caressed her bare skin with the tips of

238

his fingers, sliding his hand down to her waist where it encountered the elastic of her bloomers. He pushed them aside and moved his hand into the valley between her thighs.

She clung to him, burying her head in his robe. It took all the self-control he could muster, but he managed to restrain himself until he succeeded in rousing her passion to the same pitch as his own. Only then did he open his robe and remove the one remaining garment. At that point she no longer cared about anything except Andrew and what he was doing to her.

He eased himself on top of her. She gasped as a sharp, intense pain shot through her.

'Darling,' he smoothed her hair away from her tear-filled eyes, 'I'm sorry,' he murmured, 'so sorry.'

She locked her arms and legs around his body, imprisoning him in a shell of her own making. 'Don't stop,' she pleaded breathlessly. 'Please, Andrew, don't ever stop.'

'You bloody fool,' Haydn shouted as he tripped over a body in the shadows on the steps of the stage entrance to the Town Hall. 'You trying to kill someone or what?'

'Or what,' Eddie mumbled between thick and swollen lips.

'Eddie?' Haydn peered into the battered face of his brother. 'What the hell are you doing here at this hour?'

'Waiting.'

'For what? Not for me, I'll be bound.'

'No.'

'Oh God don't tell me! You got mixed up with one of those girls. Which one was it. Daisy? Doris?'

'Have you seen Daisy?' Eddie asked eagerly. 'She was supposed to meet me here after the show. . . . ' His voice faded as he realised what he was saying, and worse still, who he was saying it to.

'She went off hours ago with the conductor,' Haydn snapped.

'Conductor?'

'Band, not tram, you clot.'

'That's just what I am,' Eddie mourned miserably. 'A bloody clot. No good to anyone. . . . '

'You get drunk earlier?'

'No,' Eddie protested indignantly. 'Why?'

239

'A hangover would explain the self-pity. Look, stay here, I'll finish checking around, give Fred a shout and walk home with you.'

Ten minutes later the two brothers were kicking their way through the litter and debris that the Rattle Fair revellers had left behind in Market Square.

'Pity, it all looks so grubby after the event,' Haydn complained as he peeled a soggy ice-cream wafer from the sole of his shoe.

'What does?' Eddie asked despondently.

'Nothing you'd know about.' Haydn touched his cap to a woman who was pulling down the shutters on a boiled-sweet stall.

The square was quiet. A few fair people and a couple of conscripts from the town were packing away the rides. They moved swiftly, unbolting, unbuckling and folding the metal structures into smaller units that could be easily stacked on the wagons that waited to transport them to the next town.

'Want a pint?' Haydn asked, overcome by a sudden wave of compassion for Eddie.

'It's after stop tap.'

'Not if you're in the know,' Haydn boasted as they walked under the railway bridge and up High Street. When they came to the side door of the Horse and Groom he knocked just once above the latch. The door opened a crack and a woman peeped out.

'Haydn!' she shouted. 'Everyone, it's Haydn! Come in with you. Come in.' She flung the door wide. 'Who's this you've brought?' She eyed Eddie warily.

'My brother, the boxer. Can't you tell from his face?'

'If you're Haydn's brother, you're more than welcome.' She closed the door behind them. 'What's it to be, boys? Pints?'

'He's buying.' Eddie pointed to Haydn.

'After what you won today?'

'I didn't place a bet on myself and get money for nothing like you.'

'Pints will be fine, Bess.' Haydn thrust his hand into his trouser pocket.

'You look smart, Haydn. New suit?' A girl with the most improbable red hair that Eddie had ever seen sidled up to them.

'This old thing—' Haydn fingered his lapel— 'only had it today.'

'You're a scream.' She hung on to his arm as they walked through to the back bar. Eddie looked around in amazement. The room was smokier, stuffier and packed with more people than he'd ever seen it during regular hours.

'Haydn, give us a song, boyo?' a man Eddie didn't know shouted as they entered the room. 'Here, quiet everyone, Haydn's here.'

'Come on, Haydn, give us a song and I'll put up pints for you and your friend,' Wilf Horton, rather the worse for drink, shouted from across the room.

'Friend?' Haydn winked at Eddie. 'Pint?'

'Suits me.' Eddie leaned against the wall.

Haydn stood in front of the bar and a hush fell over the crowd. A short fat man pushed his way through to a beer-scarred piano that stood in the corner.

' "Rose of Tralee"?' he asked, supping his pint before setting it down on the top.

Haydn nodded. The man began to play and Haydn came in after the introduction. Eddie had heard his brother sing many times before, in church, in the choir, and around the house, but never a song like 'The Rose of Tralee.' And never in a pub crowded with people none the better for drink. The rapt, expectant silence continued as Haydn carried his voice into a full crescendo, and even when he reached the chorus he attracted no more than a faint humming accompaniment from the more experienced singers amongst the customers.

When the pianist finally played the last soft note the hush continued for a few more seconds, then uproar broke out. Glasses were hammered on tables, feet drummed the floor, someone cried 'again' and the plea was taken up around the bar. For the first time Eddie realised that his brother had talent. Real talent. While he'd sung, he'd held the audience in his hand. He could have done anything he'd wanted with them.

'Hey, less din!' the landlady shouted sharply. The noise ceased and everyone heard a hammering on the outside door.

'I'll deal with this, Bess,' the landlord ordered; he walked down the passageway himself.

'Oh God, it's a copper,' someone shouted as he opened the

241

door. Eddie pulled his cap down low over his eyes as Megan's brother Huw entered the pub.

'Pint, constable?' Bess asked.

'Pint? I should be booking everyone here.'

'Not on fair night,' Wilf Horton pleaded. 'Give a man a break.'

'Only if that lad sings "I'll Take You Home Again, Kathleen".' Huw Davies' face split into a huge grin at the joke he and the landlord had shared at the customers' expense.

'Well if it's going to keep everyone here out of clink – ' Haydn finished his pint in one draught. Before he had time to dump the empty glass on the bar another three were set before him. He pushed one over to Eddie and resumed his place in front of the crowd.

'I'll Take You Home Again, Kathleen' was followed by 'If I Should Fall in Love Again'. More pints appeared, and after a drinking interval Haydn began the Al Jolson favourite, 'Mammy'.

'Your Haydn's learned a lot about phrasing and timing since he's worked in the Town Hall.' Huw nudged Eddie.

'I didn't know he was this good.'

'Oh he's good all right, lad. But then talent runs in the family. Drink up. I owe you a pint after the way you boxed today. You turned my bob into ten.'

'Cheers.' Eddie'd never had so many free pints in his life. 'Tell me, is it always like this?' He jabbed his finger at the crowd while the landlord pulled two more pints.

'Only on Christmas Eve and Rattle Fair day when the lads have had a chance to earn an extra bob or two helping to put up the stalls and rides. First time here after hours?'

'Yes.'

'Well here's hoping it won't be your last.'

Two songs later Haydn joined them. The perspiration ran down his face as he gulped the first of the line of six pints that were waiting for him.

'At least we've got nothing to get up early for tomorrow,' Haydn said as he took a deep breath. 'No fair, no market, and I've just about given up on the brewery.'

'And no money,' Eddie said glumly.

'You won a fiver.' He took a hard look at Eddie as Huw

turned to talk to the landlord. 'You haven't lost it have you?' he challenged.

'Not exactly.'

'What do you mean "not exactly"?' Haydn demanded. 'Damn it all . . . ' An ugly suspicion crossed his mind. 'You bloody fool! You gave it to Daisy didn't you?'

'She'd had her rent money stolen – I snagged her stockings and lost her knick . . . ' Eddie turned the colour of strawberry jam and stared gloomily into his glass.

'She gave you a hard luck story and you gave her a fiver?' Haydn snarled contemptuously.

'Not all of it.' Eddie put his hand in his pocket and pulled out a two-shilling piece.

'That all you got left? Two bob?'

Eddie nodded pathetically.

'Well I hope she bloody well earned every penny?'

'Earned. . . . '

'Don't be thick! You know what I mean. Did she earn it?'

Eddie recalled the afternoon. Daisy lying naked in the long grass. The flies crawling over his naked back as he thrust himself inside her. . . . A large, self-satisfied smirk crossed his face at the memory.

Mollified, Haydn calmed down.

'What can I say except that thanks to you I won enough today to pay for both our suits. Good luck to you, boy.' He pulled another two pints from the stock on the bar towards them. 'Five pounds is steep but Daisy comes expensive. Others have paid more. And when it comes to the things that matter, quality matters more than price. At least that's what Dad always told me.'

Eddie pushed his cap to the back of his head, looked Haydn squarely in the eye and laughed for the first time that day. Haydn was right. When he came to think about it Daisy was quality. What she'd given him was priceless.

Chapter Fourteen

'Has he taken her home yet?' Dr John asked his wife as she switched off the light and drew back the curtains.

'The garage doors are open and his car's gone,' she answered abruptly.

'It's easy to see what you think of that one,' he commented, kicking off his slippers and climbing into bed.

'I never said. . . . '

'That's just it, Isabel,' he observed evenly. 'You never said. You don't have to. After thirty-two years I know you better than to need words.' He patted her arm as she sat beside him on the bed.

'Oh she's a nice enough girl, I suppose,' Isabel added in a tone that said she didn't think so. 'It's just that. . . . '

'She isn't good enough for Andrew?' he interrupted.

'You sound as though you're making fun of me.'

'Don't be so sensitive, darling. I'm agreeing with you.'

He laid his head back on the pillow. The brandy, wine and champagne he'd drunk earlier blurred the fringes of his vision, so he closed his eyes. An image of Bethan came to mind. Dark, slim yet curvaceous – voluptuous . . . yes, that was the word he was looking for . . . voluptuous, with deep smouldering eyes, and a wide, welcoming mouth. He rubbed his hands over his temples. He'd better watch himself, he was beginning to think like the gossip columnist in the *Sunday People*.

'She is a pretty girl,' he chose his words carefully, 'and I'm sure that's all Andrew sees, a pretty girl to help him while away his idle hours. He'll soon tire of her, dear, and then he'll go looking for someone more like himself. Someone he can really talk to. Take my word for it. It will pass.'

'Do you think so?' It was a plea for reassurance.

'I don't know of a doctor who didn't have a fling with a pretty nurse in his youth.'

'Yourself included, I suppose.'

'Present company excepted.' He kissed her hand.

'Liar,' she said fondly.

'Well if it's any consolation I realised early on that despite her medical training she wouldn't make a suitable wife, not for me, or any doctor thinking of career advancement. And given time, and Andrew's ambition to become a fully-fledged surgeon, he'll come to the same conclusion. That's if he hasn't already. Smart move of yours to invite the Llewellyn-Jones girl. They seemed to get on well together.'

'Didn't they?' Isabel gloated. 'But you'll still talk to him?'

'If I have to. But really, dear,' he held back the bedclothes for her to climb into bed, 'I don't think it will come to that. He's a sensible boy. Believe me, he'll soon see the situation for himself.'

The following morning Maud was up early and in Megan's house before eight.

'You told your mother that you're going rag picking with Diana?' Megan asked as she slapped plates down on the table.

'Not exactly,' Maud admitted reluctantly.

'I thought so. Then the pair of you,' Megan looked from Maud to Diana, 'mind that you come straight back here as soon as you've finished to have a bath in the washhouse. You're going to need it after you've been in the rag picker's yard all day,' she warned Maud. 'And remind me to go through your clothes before you go home. Your mother will go spare if she finds a single louse or flea on you. And God knows there's enough of both down Factory Lane.'

'I'll do that. Thanks, Auntie Megan.' Maud took the slice of bread Megan handed her and smeared butter over it.

'We'd best get going,' Diana said impatiently, walking past the table and grabbing a Welsh cake. 'There's always a huge queue on school holidays, and latecomers get sent away.'

'Mind you get Jim Rags to pay you twopence,' Megan called after them, as they went out through the front door. 'He tried to fob Jinny Makey off with only a penny for a full day.'

'We won't take less than twopence, Mam. Promise. See you tonight.'

'It doesn't seem right, lying to everyone,' Maud protested as they ran past the turning to Factory Lane and straight down Llantris-ant Road towards town.

'I told you. Mam wouldn't let us go if we said where we were off to,' Diana snapped impatiently. 'And Mrs Jones will give us a free trip to Cardiff and half a crown each for helping her. That's got to be better than twopence for a whole day sorting rags in the smelly sheds.'

'Why doesn't she take her own kids and save five bob?' Maud asked suspiciously.

'Too young to flutter their eyelashes at floorwalkers and dis-tract them,' Diana informed her as she gave a laudable Mary Pickford impression.

'You girls are late,' Judy Jones complained as they ran breath-less into the ticket office.

'I know. I'm sorry. She. . . . ' Diana pointed to Maud, 'wanted a second breakfast.'

'I've got the tickets,' Betty Morgan called from the front of the queue at the ticket booth.

With the two women humping three large Gladstone bags between them, the four of them ran as fast as they could up the wide flight of steep stone steps, reaching the platform just as the guard was putting the whistle to his mouth.

'Quick.' Betty wrenched open the door to a third-class carriage and they all tumbled in, slamming it just as the whistle blew.

'We'll sort you out in Cardiff.' Judy studied Maud from between narrowed eyes. 'Has Diana told you what we'll be doing?'

'Not really,' Maud answered, a little bewildered by the air of importance and urgency.

'Perhaps it's just as well,' Betty smiled. 'You can't beat true innocence.'

Maud had only ever been on a train to Cardiff twice in her life, both times when her father had been working a five-day week. Lucky enough to have a window seat she made the most of the special trip, sat back and watched the scenery glide past. The smoky, soot-blackened yellow bricks of the backs of terraced houses, the overgrown embankments, wildernesses of scrap iron in the merchants' yards, the stations and the villages rolled past.

Treforest, Taffs Well, Radyr and eventually Cardiff Queen's Street then General.

'Straight to the ladies' waiting room,' Betty barked, gathering her bags together the minute the train stopped. Diana and Maud traipsed behind the women feeling a bit like chicks following two overblown hens.

'Right, you know what to do, Diana. Take Maud into the cubicle with you.' Betty thrust her Gladstone bag into Diana's hand as soon as they entered the toilets. Diana took it, pushed Maud into a cubicle, followed her, locked the door and opened the bag.

'What's in there?' Maud asked.

'Clothes. We can't go like we are. Quick, get your dress off.'

While Maud was undressing Diana pulled out two plain grey cloche hats, two matching grey woollen dresses, cableknit lisle stockings and two pairs of practical lace-up black shoes.

'Daughters of the crache,' she explained in a posh accent.

'I didn't know you could talk like that,' Maud gasped.

'Practice makes perfect,' Diana said airily, very much the experienced tutor to Maud's apprentice. 'And if you can't talk the same you'd best keep your mouth closed. Here, put this coat on, follow me and do whatever I do.'

Betty and Judy were in the ladies' waiting room when they finally emerged. Maud scarcely recognised them. Judy was wearing a thick layer of make-up, flared slacks and a white blouse ornamented by a royal blue and white name tag that sported the name 'Miss Barker'. Underneath the name in smaller letters was the title 'Windowdresser'.

'Howell's,' Diana explained briefly. Judy pulled on a calf-length blue coat that buttoned to the neck, fastened it, and rolled her trouser legs up to her knees exposing flesh-coloured stockings.

'Here, Diana, take this to Left Luggage.' Betty crammed her own, Judy's and the girls' clothes into one of the bags. Then she picked up one of the Gladstones, Judy the other. 'Here we go. Maud, watch Diana, do everything she does, and don't say a word unless you're spoken to, and then only yes or no. I don't have to tell you that you're not to tell a soul about this?'

'Diana warned me.'

'Good. Here's Diana. Hold her hand and walk behind us.'

Diana and Maud entered Howell's behind Betty. They'd lost sight of Judy somewhere along the way. Betty made a direct bee-line for the ladies' wear department.

'Three floorwalkers, six assistants. The two either side of the shoe department will be going on eleven-fifteen tea break with the tallest of the floorwalkers,' Betty whispered *sotto voce* to Diana.

'Can I help you, madam?' a black-skirted, white-bloused assistant enquired.

'Yes, I want matching dresses for my daughters.' Betty's accent had also undergone a miraculous transformation. 'Something in royal blue?' she said loudly for the benefit of the assistants in the shoe department. 'With matching hats, gloves and shoes of course. It's for a wedding. In London,' she added proudly, if superfluously.

'If madam would care to come this way.' Betty followed her, and the girls followed Betty. By explaining fictitious, trivial details in a loud voice, and by demanding that the dresses be matched exactly to shoes and hats, Betty succeeded in commanding the attention of three of the six assistants. Spot on eleven-fifteen, two of the remaining three and the tallest of the floorwalkers went to tea. One minute after that the last assistant's attention was taken up by another customer.

'This won't do. Won't do at all,' Betty said abrasively. Diana picked up the prearranged cue. Turning abruptly she caught her elbow on the outstretched arm of a plaster tailor's dummy that was modelling an outrageously expensive example of the latest sequinned evening fashions on a central display. The dummy rocked precariously on its perch. Diana screamed, so Maud screamed too. The two floorwalkers rushed to catch it, while Betty apologised to all and sundry. And during those few seconds Judy appeared, coatless, scarf covering her hair, brush and feather duster in one hand, bag in other. She walked behind the counter, opened the panel that led out to the windows and closed it behind her.

The first thing she did was kick off her shoes. Then, trousers flapping around her ankles, she commenced stripping all of the dummies in the window of their clothes, accessories and jewellery, taking the time to fold everything carefully and neatly into her

248

enormous bag. By the time Betty had moved on to looking at cerise gowns as an alternative to blue for her daughters, she'd finished.

It was twenty-nine minutes past eleven. One minute before the end of tea break for those off the floor.

'Hey you!' the senior floorwalker shouted as Judy closed the panel behind her.

'Me?' she asked calmly, valiantly suppressing her initial reaction to run.

'Yes. Can you do something about this model?' he asked, with a backward glance at Diana. 'Customer knocked it over and damaged the sequins on the dress.'

Judy dropped her bag, walked over to the dummy and examined the cloth. Four of the sequins were bent; she succeeded in straightening them with her fingernail.

'If you give me a hand to strip it I'll take it up to repairs,' she said abruptly.

'Can you have it back by this afternoon?'

'Yes. I should think so.'

He lifted down the dummy and between them they peeled off the gown and wrapped the naked plaster body in a sheet, lest it offend the delicate sensibilities of shoppers. Laying the evening gown on top of the clothes bulging out of her bag, Judy walked on into the men's department. Removing a stack of pullovers, shirts and ties from the edge of the counter she tucked them under her arm and proceeded to the lift. The lift attendant helpfully assisted her to stack her load behind the metal safety grille. She got out at the third floor and went into the ladies' cloakroom. Betty and the girls walked in a few minutes later.

While Judy was busy rerolling her trouser legs, untying her scarf and donning her coat in one cubicle, the three of them crammed into another and split Judy's haul between the two bags. Diana took one, pushed the other into Maud's hand and led the way out of the cloakroom, and out of the store.

Maud had never been so frightened in her life. Her mouth was dry, her hands wet and clammy where they gripped the bag. Every murmur of conversation, every glance that came her way from a floorwalker or assistant sent her heart into palpitations.

Smiling at the doorman Diana walked confidently out on to the street. Two minutes later Maud joined her.

'Tea in Lyon's, I think. Shopping is so tiring,' Diana said loudly for the benefit of the doorman in her 'posh' accent.

'Sweets from a baby,' Betty laughed later over a cup of tea in the station buffet. 'Here's your half-crowns, girls.'

'And here's these.' Diana put her hand into her pocket and pulled out a dozen costume rings. Maud stared at them in disbelief. 'Where did you get those?'

'I tried one on,' Diana said indignantly.

'Just one,' Maud repeated dully, 'I know, I saw you.'

'Sweets from a baby.' Diana's laugh joined Betty's.

'And crache clothes for us.' Judy touched her cup to Maud's. 'Congratulations on joining the forties. You're just the type of new blood we need.'

'The forties?' Maud echoed in bewilderment.

'Forty thieves, clot.' Diana put her arm around Maud's shoulders. 'Or should I say forty-one.'

The weeks that followed her first visit to Andrew's rooms were idyllic ones for Bethan. She used some of the money Andrew'd given her to clear her debts with her aunt and loan Eddie a small float to tide him over. Even after a wild spending spree in Megan's she still had thirty-two pounds to hide in the bottom of her jewellery box. Her father seemed happier than he'd been for weeks. And when he took to wearing his best suit, polishing his shoes and stepping out in the evenings via Rhiannon's house, she assumed that he was putting his winnings to good use in the Graig Hotel. She was glad for him. He deserved a few pints after the gloom of a winter spent on short-time work.

Eddie bought himself a new and better pair of gloves and practically moved into the gym at the back of the Ruperra Hotel on Berw Road. No one was more delighted than her when Joey Rees fixed it so Eddie got a job as dogsbody and late-night general cleaner for a bob a night and his gym fees. Elizabeth was quick to point out that six bob a week wasn't enough to keep a baby, let alone a grown man, but Eddie, flush with new-found confidence after winning his fight and laying Daisy, wasn't to be easily put down. Not even by his mother.

He threw his first week's money on the table and told her to keep it. He still had his days free to put up market stalls, work in the brewery and, best of all, run for the bookies who were only too keen to employ him now they knew he could take care of himself, and their cash.

Haydn began leaving for work early in the afternoon. Bethan found out why when she saw him serving in Harry Griffiths' shop beside a proud and blushing Jenny one afternoon. Maud's cough disappeared, just as Andrew had promised it would, and, happy and healthy, she took to spending all her free time with Diana. At weekends they became inseparable, and Maud slept over at Megan's most Friday and Saturday nights with her cousin, chiefly because she enjoyed the relaxed atmosphere but also because the distance made it impossible for her mother to monitor her movements.

Elizabeth continued to moan, but her moans were always easier to bear in the warmer weather when everyone found it simpler to get out of the house.

With her family as happy as they could be, and spring gliding peacefully into a full-blown, warm, beautiful summer, Bethan and Andrew found the time and the passion to create wonderful, exquisite moments that would last both of them a lifetime. They spent every minute when they weren't actually sleeping, or working, together. And occasionally they even managed to contrive to spend some of their working time in one another's arms.

They touched fingers as they passed in the corridor. They stole moments from meal breaks and met in deserted side wards and corridors. Whenever Squeers set Bethan menial duties in the linen cupboards or sluice rooms she ran along quickly with a light step, a delicious sense of expectancy buoying her spirits in the hope that *he'd* be there, waiting to drag her into a secluded corner and steal a kiss. She only had to catch sight of him across the yard or in a corridor for her limbs to grow liquid with longing. And throughout each and every long, hard-working hour there was the prospect of the evening and weekly day off that lay ahead. Glittering golden times that more than compensated for the slights and indignities she suffered at Squeers' hands.

Sometimes Trevor and Laura joined them on their outings but more often than not they were alone, not simply because Laura and Bethan's days off rarely coincided. Each of them valued the moments they spent with their partner too much to share them even with close friends.

Neither Andrew nor Bethan were anxious to repeat the experiment with their respective families. Once or twice a week they went to his rooms, but always late in the evening when he knew his parents would be out, or occupied with visitors. If they had a whole day free they generally drove down to the summer chalet on the Gower; if they had only a few hours or an evening they contented themselves with a walk in the country. Not up Pit Road to Shoni's pond, but further afield. Andrew drove her to the primrose-strewn fields around Creigau, or the picturesque woods above Taffs Well in which nestled the Marquess of Bute's fairytale Castell Coch with its red turrets and grey stone walls. They were magic times. Bethan was too much in love to question anything Andrew did, said or thought. To her, he was always kind, gentle, funny and loving. Very, very loving.

There were moments when she had doubts, particularly when Laura talked about engagement rings, weddings and household linen, but when she was actually with Andrew all uncertainty melted away. He didn't even have to provide excuses for his tardiness. She thought them up for herself — he was considering her nursing ambitions — allowing her time to complete her midwifery certificate. They were happy as they were — what was the point of hurrying? He'd told her he had very little money of his own — he probably wanted to save a deposit large enough to buy a house like his father's . . . she could find a million and one reasons why they shouldn't rush headlong into marriage like Laura and Trevor. And in the mean time she wrung every moment she spent with him dry.

For his part Andrew loved Bethan and told her so — often. If his love was more selfish, less intense than hers, neither of them was sufficiently aware of the difference for it to matter. Once he succeeded in crossing the bounds of courtship and became her lover, sexual obsession took over from romance. He lived for the moments he was alone with her. They made love in his flat, the chalet, secluded areas in the country and — on one glorious, insane

252

occasion – in Squeers' office at three in the morning when Bethan was on night duty and he'd been called into the maternity ward on an emergency.

His parents never said a word in favour of, or against, Bethan. They didn't have to. His father was politeness personified whenever he came across Bethan in the hospital, even going so far as to acknowledge her presence with a nod: an unheard-of courtesy from the senior medical officer to a junior staff nurse. But for all of their forbearance Andrew knew that neither of his parents considered Bethan suitable material for a daughter-in-law. To begin with there was her acquaintance with their under-housemaid. Then there was her strong Welsh accent, her upbringing on the Graig, her chapel connections – the John family had been Anglican for three generations – her miner father and his links with the Communist Party. Dr John senior had taken the trouble to find out what he could about Bethan's family, and he'd lost no time in passing on the information he'd gleaned to his son.

And quite aside from all these things, which were mentioned indirectly and often, whenever he took his meals with his parents there was the memory of the time he'd brought her to dinner. Again it wasn't what his mother said, it was what she left unsaid.

Anthea Llewellyn-Jones had such sparkling wit. She had a word for everyone no matter who they were. She was never tongue-tied or overwhelmed in company. The praise – and the sniping – went on and on, and he was left in no doubt that if it had been Anthea Llewellyn-Jones he was 'stepping out with' his parents wouldn't be pressing him so hard to take up the offer of a short-term placement on the surgical team at Charing Cross. Nor would he have received quite so many offers of late-night whiskies from his father during which the talk inevitably turned to cautionary tales on the dangers of becoming entangled with the wrong kind of girl.

But he was young, he was in love, and it was easy to shrug off his parents' obtuse and not so obtuse hints and advice. Marriage couldn't really come into the equation, not yet, and not for some time. Ambitious and financially dependent on his parents, he had two more years of study in Charing Cross, which he'd have to complete soon if he was going to gain his Fellowship of the Royal

College of Surgeons before his thirtieth birthday, as his father had done before him.

Meanwhile he loved Bethan enough to tarry in Pontypridd and delay his return to London. He'd even toyed vaguely with the idea of asking her to accompany him when he did go. But not as a wife. As a nurse.

As Alec had said, there were plenty of openings for nurses in London. She'd easily get a room in a hostel, and they could live very much as they did here. He loved her, but not enough to lower his standard of living to what she was used to, or Trevor was prepared to accept. Married life in a squalid little house without a bathroom, garden or rooms of the size he was accustomed to wasn't his idea of bliss. So he put the idea of marriage out of his head almost as soon as it entered it. And then again, why even consider it? Bethan hadn't mentioned it. They were both of them extremely happy the way things were. Why change them?

'So you'll come?'

'Andrew, I've never been to a garden party.'

'All the more reason to go to one now.'

'With you and Anthea Llewellyn-Jones?'

'Forget Anthea Llewellyn-Jones.' He crossed over to the desk where she was writing reports and took the pen from her hand. 'Enough, woman, I want you and I want you now.'

'Andrew, the day shift. . . . '

'Won't be on for another hour and a half. It's babies' feeding time, and – ' he kissed the back of her neck – 'I've taken the precaution of locking the door.'

'The reports have to be finished.'

'How much more do you have to do?'

She picked up another pen, inserted a nib and dipped it into the inkwell.

'I have to sign the last one,' she teased.

'Sometimes I think God put women on earth just to torment man,' he sighed in mock exasperation.

'And now that I've signed it I have to check the ward.'

Skilfully avoiding his moves to intercept her, she slipped under his arm and unlocked the door, opening it wide, so if he spoke he'd risk waking the ward. She paused for a few moments for her eyes to become accustomed to the subdued nightlights that burned at either end of the long room, then she trod lightly down the centre aisle checking the occupant of each bed. She stopped to place her hand lightly on the forehead of Mrs Roberts in the end cubicle who was recovering from fever. Her skin was still cool, as it had been since midday when the fever had broken. She left the ward and checked the delivery rooms. Clean, bare, they stank of chloroform and antiseptic. Closing the door she walked back through the ward to the nursery. The trainee was supervising the two ward maids who were feeding the babies bottles of water in the hope that they would eventually stop waking for non-nutritious liquid and sleep through. Not that the ploy worked. It generally meant that the tiny scraps of humanity screamed until six o'clock when they were finally handed to their mothers.

'All quiet, Mills?' she asked the trainee.

'All quiet, Nurse Powell.'

Bethan closed the door and returned to the office. It was empty. Assuming that Andrew had gone to check on his patient who was still in the operating theatre, she sat in the easy chair, rested her feet on the hearth and read through her reports. Satisfied that she'd done all she could, she piled the papers on to the corner of her desk, curled her feet beneath her and closed her eyes.

'Asleep on duty, Nurse Powell?'

She opened her eyes, Andrew was standing in front of her, his face flushed.

'Been outside?' she asked.

'Left something in the car.'

She knew what the 'something' was. He, like Trevor, had begun to raid the stocks of contraceptives in the family planning clinic in Ynysangharad Park.

'Drink?' he asked, producing a hip flask from his back pocket.

'Not before I come off duty. Squeers will have my guts for garters if she smells brandy on my breath during the change-over.'

'What I like most about you, Nurse Powell,' he sat on the edge of the desk close to her, 'is your delicate turn of phrase.' He took a long pull from the flask and rubbed his hand lightly along her neck and shoulders. 'You back for good? Or are you likely to disappear again?' he asked.

'For good unless there's an emergency.'

'Reports finished?'

'Quite finished.' She left her chair, locked the door and leaned against it.

'In that case, let's begin.' He sat on the chair she'd vacated and pulled her down on to his lap. Kissing her, he slid his hand up her skirt. 'Nurse Powell! I'm shocked.'

'Why?' she enquired innocently. 'Wasn't it what you wanted?' She pulled her bloomers out of her pocket and dropped them to the floor.

'Suppose there'd been another doctor on duty.'

'I don't take them off for any other doctor.'

'That's reassuring to know.'

'We haven't much time,' she whispered, tugging at his trouser belt. 'I'll have to check on the ward again in a quarter of an hour.'

'I'll try to make it last that long,' he murmured. She laughed softly as she thrust her hand down inside his underpants, teasing an erection.

'You're a great one for promises, Doctor John.'

'You'll see just how great in a moment.' He wrapped his arms around her. 'What would I do without you, Beth?'

'Install a cold shower in your rooms?' she suggested lightly.

A moment later only the sounds of their breathing and her quiet moans disturbed the night silence of the peaceful office.

Andrew was waiting for her outside the gates when her shift finished.

'We never did decide about the garden party,' he said as they climbed into his car.

'I told you I've never been to one.'

'There's a first time for everything.'

'I've nothing to wear.'

'You can start with this.' He pulled a small leather-covered box out of his pocket.

'What is it?' Her heart was racing. It looked like a jeweller's box. Could it be. . . .

256

'Why don't you open it and see?'

With fingers that had suddenly grown stiff and clumsy she wrenched it open. Nestling on a bed of satin was the locket she'd helped him choose in Cardiff.

'This is your mother's.'

'No. It was never intended for her. I was going to give it to you on your birthday. But I thought, What the hell, that's not until December. You do like it?' he asked anxiously, studying the strange expression on her face.

'I love it,' she whispered, hugging him, hiding her head in his neck so he wouldn't read the disappointment in her eyes. She'd hoped for a ring that carried the same message of commitment as the one Laura wore on her left hand.

'Here, let me.' He took the locket from her hand and fastened it round her neck.

'No one's ever given me anything as beautiful as this,' she said bravely, fingering it lightly as it hung at her throat.

'Then you'll wear it to the garden party?'

'I still have nothing to go with it.'

'Then go to this famous aunt of yours that you've never allowed me to meet and buy something.'

'Drop me off now and you can meet her.'

'At – ' he flicked open his pocket watch – 'eight on a Sunday morning?'

'You'll never find a better time. She'll have finished work, and be cooking breakfast.'

'Work?'

'She cleans the Graig Hotel.'

'I've never paid a social call at eight on a Sunday morning before.'

'Didn't you just say there's a first time for everything?'

Chapter Fifteen

As Andrew drove into Leyshon Street Bethan directed him to Megan's house and he pulled up outside. The only other vehicle in the street was the milkman's cart. Eddie whistled as he walked towards it, carrying a handful of milk jugs.

'Working?' Bethan asked excitedly.

'Only for a few days.' He interrupted his whistling to answer as he laid the jugs on the back of the cart and pulled the top off a churn. 'Alwyn's sick, so Dai the milk asked me to take over for a week or two. Doctor John,' he acknowledged Andrew reluctantly, as he dipped a ladle into the churn and began to fill the jugs.

'Won any fights lately?' Andrew asked amiably, trying to make conversation.

'Only sparring in the gym, Doctor John.'

'Please call me Andrew.'

'Yes, well, I'd like to stop and chat but I have to get on. I'm late as it is and church people want their milk early on a Sunday. See you later, Bethan.'

Bethan waved goodbye to him and rapped on Megan's door as she walked in. 'Come on,' she said impatiently to Andrew.

'God, I might have known it would be you,' William complained as he walked down the stairs dressed only in a pair of trousers.

'The morning after the night before?' Bethan enquired cheerfully.

'What else?' He opened the kitchen door for her. 'Come in, Doctor John, please.'

Wishing he'd never suggested meeting her aunt, Andrew reluctantly followed Bethan into the kitchen.

'Bethan love.' Megan was frying salt fish on the stove, just as Bethan said she would be. She turned her head, saw Andrew and immediately wiped her hands on her apron. 'And this is your young man?'

'Andrew, Auntie Megan. Doctor Andrew John.'

'Please, call me Andrew.' Andrew was beginning to feel as though that was the only thing he said to members of Bethan's family.

'Well, I asked Bethan to bring you here so we could take a look at you, but I didn't expect her to bring you first thing on a Sunday morning. You'll stay to breakfast of course?'

'I'm afraid I can't, Mrs Powell, I have to call in on a patient on the way home.'

'Both of you been up all night I suppose?' She looked sharply at Bethan.

'Yes, but unlike William we've been working,' Bethan said loudly for William's benefit.

'How do you know I haven't?' he answered as he banged the washhouse door on the way out to the toilet.

'I'm sure your patient isn't going to die in the next half-hour, Andrew, so I'll not take no for an answer. I've more than enough fish and bread and butter for everyone. Pull up a chair and sit yourself down.'

'Auntie, we couldn't. You weren't expecting us.'

'There's plenty of room if that's what you're worried about. Diana and Maud came in so late last night they won't be up for hours. And mind, not a word of that to your mother. I doubt that she was ever young. Not in the same sense as those two, any road.' Megan shook the fish briskly in the pan. 'And the tea's already brewed, so the best thing you can do is keep quiet and pour us all a cup, Beth.'

Deciding that further protest was useless, Andrew sat on one of the kitchen chairs, and watched Bethan as she removed her cloak and moved around the kitchen, laying bread, sugar and milk on the table.

'Well, from what Bethan tells me this has been going on a good while between you two,' Megan said as she took the tea Bethan handed her. 'Serious is it?'

'Auntie . . . ' Bethan protested vigorously.

'I suppose you could say that,' Andrew grinned.

'I hope you're treating her well? That's my favourite niece you've got there you know.'

'My favourite girlfriend too.'

'Mam ... Mam ... where the hell are you?' William burst through the washhouse door, his fly unbuttoned, his hair standing on end.

'Language, William,' Megan said sternly. 'We've company and if I've told you once I've told you a hundred times I won't have you tearing around. ... '

'Mam, there's coppers driving up the Graig hill. Four vans and a car packed with them. Mrs Evans sent young Phillip over the backs to tell us.'

'God help us!' The colour drained from Megan's face as she struggled to think coherently. 'Go next door, Will, and warn Betty and Judy. Now quick. Not that way,' she shouted as William went towards the front door. 'Over the wall at the back. Tell them to dump whatever they've got in the house. Pass it down the street ... get the kids to carry it up the mountain or over to Shoni's. ... '

William didn't hang about. He was back out through the door, and leaping one-handed over the wall before Bethan had time to wonder what was happening.

'Oh God, Huw warned me this was coming,' Megan moaned. 'Only yesterday he told me to get rid of everything. I should have listened to him.' She dropped the fish she was frying on to the range to burn. Running to the door she shouted up the stairs. 'Diana, Maud, quick, bring down all my stock. All the specials. Coppers coming.'

Andrew continued to sit in his chair, totally bemused by the bedlam that had broken out around him. Megan dashed back through the kitchen and into the washhouse. She thrust a tin bucket under the tap and began to fill it. Black smoke billowed out from the pan she'd left on the range, and Bethan jumped towards it, picking it up, only to immediately drop it again.

'You've burned your hand.' Andrew leaped out of his chair.

'It's nothing.' She stooped to gather up the fish that were scattered all over the hearth. 'Damn, I've cracked a tile,' she swore as she lifted the pan from where it had fallen, face down. A sound of tin scraping over stone came from the washhouse as Megan heaved the copper boiler close to the sink. Bethan left the pan and the fish on the hearth and went to help. She took the lid off the boiler as Megan emptied the contents of the bucket — floorcloth, scrubbing brush and all — into the boiler.

Diana, wearing a red flannel nightdress, raced through the kitchen into the washhouse and dumped an armful of clothes into the water. 'Maud's throwing them down the stairs, Charlie and I are carrying them through.'

'You know where everything is upstairs. Go back up and I'll help Charlie,' Bethan ordered, bumping into him as she ran out of the washhouse into the kitchen.

A jumble-sale-sized pile of clothes, shoes and hats lay at the foot of the stairs.

'The shoes?' she asked.

'Dump everything in,' Megan shouted as Charlie picked up a second, indiscriminate bundle.

'We all knew it would come to this.' Sam, still buttoning his shirt, bounded out of the front room and scooped up a pile of hats.

'Take the hats over the back,' Megan shouted at him as soon as he walked into the washhouse. 'Dump them somewhere. Get Will to give you a hand.'

'They're all knocked off, aren't they?' Bethan asked Charlie, looking to him to confirm her suspicions.

'Of course they're bloody well knocked off.' It was the first time Bethan had heard him swear. 'How else do you think she manages to sell clothes like these at the prices she's been charging?'

Bethan collected an armful, and following Charlie's example she scrambled into the washhouse and threw them into the tub. Andrew was still standing in front of the range totally mystified by the proceedings. A hammering on the door was followed by a shout.

'Open up. Police!'

'I'll deal with it.' Charlie walked slowly towards the front door; Maud and Diana, clutching their nightdresses, raced along the landing back into Diana's bedroom.

'That's the last of it.' Diana scooped up a tie from the banisters and threw it at Bethan as she disappeared into her room. Bethan opened the stove and tossed the incriminating article on top of the coals. She heard Charlie talking to the police at the door. Red-faced, William appeared in the washhouse.

'Coppers got there same time I did,' he panted. 'They're pulling Betty's house apart. Judy's not faring much better.'

A stranger's voice, loud, official, spoke in the passage.

'We have a warrant, Mr Raschenko. So if you'll kindly step aside?' The sound of hobnailed boots echoed into the kitchen from the passage.

'Mrs Powell, police to see you.' Charlie entered the kitchen and stood aside. A sergeant and two constables pushed past him into the room; two more hovered just outside the door.

'Mrs Powell?'

'Sergeant?' White-faced, Megan looked up, but she continued to stir the soup of cold water and clothes in the boiler with a wooden spoon.

'You recognise the rank, Mrs Powell?'

'I should. I've enough family in the force.'

'Then you know what this is?' He pulled a warrant out of his pocket.

She stepped as far as the washhouse door and glanced at it. 'It appears to be in order.'

'You've no objection to us searching the house then?'

'It would be pretty pointless objecting when you've brought one of those with you,' she retorted tartly.

'Right.' The sergeant turned to his men. He pointed to the two outside the door. 'Upstairs. Search everywhere, and I mean everywhere. Under the beds, in the pillows, bolsters and eiderdowns. Pick up any loose floorboards, go into the attic. Open all the drawers, the wardrobes, pull the furniture away from the wall. You know what we're looking for?'

They nodded acknowledgement before thundering up the stairs.

'May I ask what's going on?' Andrew interrupted.

'That's what we're here to find out. . . . ' The sergeant looked at Andrew for the first time since he'd entered the room, and instantly changed his tone from hectoring to polite. 'Aren't you young Doctor John?' he asked.

'Yes,' Andrew replied shortly, suddenly realising the implications if it became known that he'd been in a house that the police had seen fit to raid.

'May I ask what you're doing here, sir?'

Andrew hesitated, uncertain how to answer.

'I asked him to come and take a look at my sister,' Bethan lied promptly. 'She's recovering from pleurisy, and I'm worried about her.'

'Is that right?' the sergeant asked.

'It is,' Andrew agreed.

'Strange time to make a house call isn't it, sir?' the sergeant pressed.

'Not really,' Andrew replied brusquely, angered by the man's officious tone. 'Nurse Powell here is the duty night nurse on the maternity ward in the Graig Hospital. I was called there early this morning to deal with an emergency, and when she told me of her concern for her sister I offered to examine the girl. I've never heard a doctor's dedication to his patients labelled as strange before, Sergeant. And as for the time, when you've been up most of the night another half-hour is neither here nor there.'

Maud chose that moment to creep down the stairs. She appeared in the doorway of the kitchen, her face flushed from her recent exertions. She began to cough, a rough hacking cough that shook her whole body. Bethan couldn't be sure whether the outburst was real, or skilful acting.

'Maud, what are you thinking of? You've only got a thin nightdress on, and you've no shoes on your feet.' Bethan went to her and put her arm around her shoulders. 'Come on, back up to bed.'

'There's men in our bedroom.' Maud began to cry weakly.

'I'll come with you.' Glad of an excuse to leave the kitchen Bethan steered her gently up the stairs.

'Hadn't you better examine your patient, Doctor John?' the sergeant asked.

'He already has,' Bethan answered for Andrew from the stairs. 'Thank you very much for coming, Doctor John, especially after a night of emergencies. It was very good of you. I'll see that she gets plenty of rest, and I'll get the prescription made up in the hospital pharmacy tomorrow.'

'Don't forget to do that. And it was no trouble to come here, Nurse Powell. Now if you'll excuse me, Sergeant, I have other calls to make.'

'Just a minute, sir, if you don't mind. I won't keep you much longer. You,' he pointed to one of the two constables standing in the room, 'search the front room.'

'That's my lodgers' room,' Megan protested.

'This warrant covers the whole house.'

'There's nothing there.'

'Nothing, Mrs Powell?' The sergeant lifted his eyebrows. 'What kind of nothing?'

'The same kind of nothing that's in this whole house,' she snapped angrily.

'Then you won't mind if we take a look.'

'It's all right, Mrs Powell,' Charlie walked to the door. 'I'll go with him.'

'Same thing,' the sergeant said briskly to the constable. 'Leave nothing unopened, no piece of furniture unmoved.'

'And you—' the sergeant turned to the one remaining constable – 'you start here. Beginning with that dresser.'

The policeman went to the dresser and pulled out the drawers. He tipped them upside down on the floor, checking the backs before rummaging through the contents.

'There's a book here, Sarge.' He held up Megan's exercise book. Megan gripped the wooden spoon so hard her knuckles turned white as the sergeant flicked through the pages.

'Lot of transactions in here, Mrs Powell. Lot of money changing hands. Business good?' The sergeant raised his eyes slowly and stared at Megan.

'I can't grumble. I'm an agent for Leslie's stores.'

'Some of your customers have been seen in model frocks. The kind of clothes you can't buy in Leslie's.'

'My aunt sells clothes that the local dressmakers make up on spec,' Bethan said defensively as she returned from upstairs.

'That so?' The sergeant closed the book and laid it on the table in front of him. 'Now that's not what I heard. But then I hear a lot of funny things. Know what the "forties" are, Nurse?'

'I've no idea,' Bethan said coldly.

'You surprise me. Never heard of Ali Baba and his forty thieves? I thought every kiddy'd either read the book or seen the pantomime. And then again—' He paused for a moment as he opened a box that the constable had lifted out of the dresser. It was Megan's cosmetics box. Crammed full of lipsticks, perfumes and powder. 'You have your very own "forties" here on the Graig. Thieves one and all, and we're well on our way to rounding them up. It's just Ali Baba's cave of goodies that we're looking for.' He picked up a handful of lipsticks and allowed them to run through his fingers back into the box.

'There's nothing stolen in there . . . ' Megan began hotly.

'Did I say there was?' the sergeant continued conversationally. 'Now what was I talking about? Oh yes, these forty thieves. They're good, you know. If not the best.' He walked over to the small window and peered out the back. 'Shop detectives tell us they can get a frock off a display stand in the window of Howell's in Cardiff. Even a twelve-guinea red silk frock. Isn't that right, Mrs Powell?'

Andrew blanched as he recalled the dress that Bethan had worn to the hospital ball.

'They can go into a shop, act pleasantly, even innocently, and walk out with a dozen shirts or blouses tucked into their bags or under their skirts. Coats, costumes, make-up, lipsticks, face powder, perfume. . . . ' He took the box from the table, rattled it, and carried it over to the window. 'All child's play to them. They even manage the odd man's suit, or rug. Nothing's sacred, too hot or too heavy. Isn't that right, Mrs Powell?'

'I don't know what you're talking about.' She picked up a thick bar of green soap from the windowsill above the sink and began to grate it over the water.

The washhouse door banged and William walked in, still barefoot, his hair ruffled.

'And who might you be, young man?' the sergeant asked, stepping over the constable who was still rummaging in the dresser cupboards.

'William Powell. Mr Powell to you,' William asserted full of bravado.

'He's my son,' Megan said defensively.

'Where've you been, lad?'

'Out back. Is it a crime now for a man to visit his own outhouse?' He looked to the ceiling as a loud crash resounded from upstairs.

'That depends on what a man keeps in his outhouse.' The

sergeant nodded to the constable. 'Out there quick. Check the coal shed, the outhouse and anything else in the garden.'

'What right do you have. . . . '

'They've a warrant, William,' Megan warned.

'They've no bloody right to wreck our things.' He picked up the dresser drawers from the kitchen floor.

'Less of that language, young man,' the sergeant warned heavily. 'Or we'll be arresting you for profanity. And for your information we've every right to search any household where we've reason to believe stolen goods are being concealed.'

'You'll find nothing stolen here.'

'That's not what we heard.'

'If you wanted to turn our house over why didn't you ask one of my uncles,' William asked angrily. 'They're all po-faced coppers just like you. . . . '

'William,' Megan admonished.

'Not just like me, lad. They're related to you. That's why we had to draft the Cardiff boys in to do this little job.'

Boots thundered down the stairs. The two constables came in with the entire contents of Megan's wardrobe in their arms. They threw the clothes on top of the box of cosmetics on the table.

'Good-quality clothes, Sarge, just like they showed us.'

'So they are. You have anything to say, Mrs Powell?'

'Those are the only clothes I possess.'

'And?'

'And nothing. Do you expect me to walk around naked?'

'Not naked,' he fingered a silk blouse, 'but not dolled up to the nines either. Where did you buy these?'

'Local dressmakers, mostly. Women on the Graig may not have the money of the crache, but we've eyes in our head. We buy material on Ponty market and copy what's in the shops.'

'Copy?' He took a closer look at the stitching on the blouse.

'Cheap sewing machines can sew as well as expensive ones,' Megan pronounced bitterly.

'Let's get this straight.' He held up the blouse. 'You're saying this was made here, on the Graig?'

'I'm not sure.'

'What do you mean, you're not sure?'

'I don't keep books on where I get all my clothes. Some of them are presents. From friends,' she snapped.

'Gentlemen friends?'

'You mind what you're saying to my mother,' William broke in hotly.

The constable barged into the washhouse from the garden.

'Nothing, Sarge. Back's clean,' he announced.

'Sure nothing's been flushed down the toilet?' the sergeant demanded.

'Nothing I can see, Sergeant.'

'Put your hand down, did you?' William enquired snidely.

'No patches of loose earth, no signs of recent burial? Nothing under the coal in the coalhouse?' the sergeant continued, ignoring William's question.

'Nothing, Sarge,' the constable insisted. 'I looked. And there's precious little of anything in the coalhouse. Even coal.'

'Price it is are you surprised?' Megan prodded as many of the clothes under water as she could.

'You two, back upstairs,' the sergeant ordered the two constables who'd carried Megan's clothes into the kitchen. 'And you, back to the dresser.' He pointed to the policeman in the washhouse.

The constable pushed past Megan's washtub. As he did so he looked down.

'My mam never does that,' he criticised abstractedly.

'What, lad?' the sergeant asked.

'Puts dark clothes in with light. She says they run.'

The next thirty minutes crawled past at a snail's pace. Bethan stood, frozen to the wall that separated kitchen and passage, too shocked and too shamed to look Andrew in the eye, as the policemen pulled garment after garment from the boiler. All were dripping wet. Some had shrunk. On some the colours were running, but most were still recognisable as quality clothes. And each and every one matched a description on a long list that the sergeant constantly referred to and checked them off against.

Megan stood still and silent, a pale effigy as they dragged the clothes from the tub. She didn't even object when they heaved the sopping, soaking mess of cloth over the rug and table in the kitchen through the passage and out of the front door. Only when the tub contained nothing but water did the sergeant ask if she had anything to say. She lifted her head, looked at him once before turning to William and Bethan.

'Only that I, and I alone, am responsible for this. No one in this house except myself knew where my stock came from.'

'Your suppliers?'

'I'm not prepared to say any more,' she said sternly, lifting her chin defiantly.

'You won't tell us who did your thieving for you, yet you expect us to believe that your family are innocent? That they lived here, saw you sell these clothes to your cronies day after day, without knowing where they came from?'

'It's the truth,' Megan insisted fervently.

The sergeant studied her. Cool, calm, unflustered, she showed no signs of emotion and he knew he would get no further with her while they remained in the house. He shouted for the constables to finish whatever they were doing in the front room and upstairs. Charlie left the position he'd taken up in the hall while they'd carried out the clothes, and returned to the kitchen. William put his hand on his mother's shoulder.

'Go to Diana, Will,' she said abruptly. 'You'll have to look after her now.'

'Mam. . . . '

'Just do it,' she said harshly. 'Go on, Will,' she added in a softer tone. 'For me.'

He pushed his way past the policemen on to the stairs where Diana and Maud, still wearing their nightdresses, were huddled together. He stepped over them. Sitting one step behind he put his arms around their shoulders.

'Doctor John,' the sergeant addressed Andrew, 'I'm sorry to have kept you here, sir, but it's against regulations for anyone to enter or leave a house during a search. Excepting police officers of course. I hope you understand.'

'I understand,' Andrew said hollowly, looking anywhere but at Bethan.

'You're free to go.'

Andrew walked over the soaking wet linoleum and rug towards the door.

'Aren't you forgetting something, sir?' the sergeant asked as Andrew reached the door.

'Like what, Sergeant?'

'Don't all doctors carry a bag?'

'Only sometimes, Sergeant.'

He turned on his heel, walked out of the house, and straight into a tightly packed crowd of people. The pavement was jammed for a good twenty yards either side, with women, children and men craning their necks, desperate to catch a glimpse of what was going on inside the house. A sudden loud screaming to the left caught everyone's attention. The sea of heads turned as though pivoted on an extension of a single neck. Three large, red-faced, burly policemen were dragging a plump, dishevelled woman from the house next door. She was completely hysterical. A man stood behind her, hemmed in the doorway by another policeman. He was holding a baby in his arms and a toddler by the hand. He shouted something to the woman, but the sound of her cries drowned out his words. Three other children of various ages and sizes tried to keep a grip on the woman's skirt, all of them bawling at the top of their voices. Two of the policemen uncurled their fingers as the third bundled the woman into the van. The door slammed, the engine started and the van careered off up the street. Someone threw a stone. It hit the side of the van and rebounded into the crowd.

'Next one to pull a trick like that gets arrested,' an authoritative voice shouted. 'Man, woman or child, it makes no difference.'

Andrew recognised the imposing figure of Superintendent George Hunt who ran Pontypridd police station with military precision.

'Doctor,' he greeted Andrew. 'I wouldn't stay here if I was you,' he cautioned seriously. 'There might be trouble.'

'I came here on a call,' Andrew explained, perpetuating the fiction Bethan had concocted.

'If we need medical assistance we'll send for the police surgeon,' the superintendent said shortly.

'I was just on my way.' Trying to ignore the angry faces, and angrier talk of the crowd, Andrew fought his way to his car. One or two men blocked his passage, but once they saw who he was they stepped aside, allowing him to open the door and climb in.

All he could think of as he drove down the Graig hill was just how narrow an escape he'd had. Not only his own, but his father's hard-earned reputation would have been on the line if the police had decided to take him down to the station for questioning along with Megan. And Bethan – he was grateful to her for her quick wits – he could never have lied as promptly, or manufactured an excuse as good as the one she had, which enabled him to leave straight after the search. It had been clever of her. But at the same time he was absolutely bloody furious that she'd risked his good name and character by taking him to Megan's in the first place.

It wasn't until later, after he'd shaved, bathed and retired to bed for a couple of hours' sleep, that he thought about the full implications of Megan's arrest from a viewpoint other than his own. If – and from what little he knew, the 'if' was likely to be accomplished fact – if Megan had been charged with selling stolen goods, that made Bethan, Laura and half the women on the Graig guilty of receiving them. A scandal on that scale would rock Pontypridd. He could hear his mother's voice, scathing in its condemnation –

'Did you really expect anything else, dear, from a girl born and brought up on the Graig?'

Chapter Sixteen

Megan's house fell unnaturally silent after she was taken away. Charlie alone seemed capable of logical thought or action. First he saw to the two girls sitting on the stairs with William.

'Hadn't you better get upstairs and dress?' he suggested gruffly in his guttural accent. The sound of his voice roused Bethan. She stared despairingly at the chaos around her. Then she thought of Megan, alone in the police station, no, not alone, they had taken Judy Jones and Betty Morgan, she'd heard their screams. Her tired brain groped with what needed to be done, trying to sort out tasks into order of priority. The house had to be put back together again. But Megan needed help.

'William,' she said urgently. 'Run home and get Daddy.'

'But your mother. . . . '

'Don't speak to my mother. Just tell Daddy we need him. Now, quickly. And while you're there find Haydn. Ask him to run down to Griffiths' shop and tell Jenny – ' she hesitated for a moment, then threw caution and euphemism to the wind. Megan had been arrested. If that wasn't an emergency, she didn't know what was – 'and Harry what's happened. Perhaps if Harry Griffiths comes here he can talk to Daddy. Between them they might know what to do.'

William still sat, shell-shocked, on the stairs.

'Go on, Will, what are you waiting for?' she demanded angrily.

'I think I'd better put a pair of shoes and a shirt on first,' he said wearily.

She looked at him and saw that he was still dressed only in his trousers. 'Sorry. Of course you'd better dress.'

'Diana, Maud,' she called out, after William had left the house. 'As soon as you're dressed see what you can do to tidy the mess upstairs.'

'Bethan, it's awful,' Maud wailed. 'They've torn the pillows and bolsters open. There's feathers everywhere. . . . '

'Find Auntie Megan's sewing kit. Diana will know where it is.

Stuff the feathers back in and sew them up,' Bethan ordered sharply. She bent to the floor and began to gather the contents of the dresser from the floor. 'I'll start in the washhouse.'

She jumped at the sound of Charlie's voice; she'd forgotten he was there. A few minutes later she heard the sound of the boiler being dragged over the flagstones towards the back door, closely followed by the gush of running water as he turned the tap set in the bottom of the boiler on, over the outside drain.

She put the things she'd picked up on to a chair. Then she looked at the floor. It was soaking wet and filthy, heavily marked by the dirt carried in on the hobnailed boots of the constables. She gathered the rag rugs and carried them out the back, then she went to get the scrubbing brush and bucket from under the sink. She found the bucket along with the soap Megan had been grating, but there was no sign of the brush or floorcloth. She looked around, before walking across to the boiler and lifting the lid, but there were only the dregs of dirty water in the bottom.

'Have you seen the scrubbing brush?' she asked Charlie.

'If it was in here they probably took it with the clothes,' he said, heaving the boiler back into position.

Bethan's self-control finally snapped. 'The swines. The absolute swines!' she shouted, wanting to scream something far worse, but unsure what. 'How in hell can we clean up when they haven't even left us a cloth or a brush to do it with!' Venting her anger she kicked the boiler viciously. Then, as abruptly as it had erupted, her fury subsided. She sank weakly against the drum and began to cry.

'Nurse Powell? Bethan?' Charlie's fingers banded around her forearms like metal vices. 'Come on, pull yourself together. You have to be strong,' he hissed quietly. He was close, so close she could see the frown lines etched in his pale forehead. 'William and Diana are good children. But they are just that. Children. They need you.'

'They have you and Sam,' she muttered mutinously.

'No they don't,' he asserted forcefully. 'Sam and I are lodgers. Drifters. Here today, gone tomorrow. No one can rely on us. Do you understand? No one. You have to pull yourself together for their sakes. You and your family are all they've got.'

She looked at him, made a supreme effort and stiffened her

resolve along with her back. 'I'm sorry,' she apologised bleakly. 'That was unforgivable. It won't happen again.'

He released his hold on her, but she could still feel the force of his fingers compressing her flesh. Lifting her arm she wiped the tears from her eyes on her sleeve. Charlie looked at her and nodded briefly, as though he approved of her self-control. 'I'll go up the road and borrow what we need. Then we can start cleaning this mess up.'

A procession of neighbours came to Megan's house that morning. They brought dinner plates piled high with thick wedges of bread pudding and Welsh cakes, pop bottles filled with home-made elderberry, blackberry and nettle wine – and sympathy. They sat on the chairs in Megan's kitchen and spoke in reverential, hushed tones. The only way they knew how to express their feelings for what had happened was by following the pattern that had been set down to cope with a different kind of loss. But it took Diana to voice what was uppermost in everyone's mind.

'Anyone'd think someone had died here,' she said loudly as one group of visitors trooped out and another in.

Haydn came with orders from Evan that Maud should go home at once, and stay there. He told Bethan that their father had decided to walk across town to Bonvilston Road to see if he could find Megan's brother Huw, the one person Bethan hadn't thought of contacting. William was walking down the hill with him as far as Harry Griffiths' shop.

Old Mrs Evans and Annie Jones knocked on the door and followed Haydn into the house. They took one look at the feathers floating down the stairs and set to work with Megan's mending kit. While they repaired the damage Haydn gave Charlie a hand to move the heavier pieces of furniture back into position. With Annie's help Diana and Bethan soon managed to restore order to the bedrooms, and once the repairs were finished and there was only cleaning to be done, Bethan left Diana to it and went to see to the downstairs.

She was scrubbing the constables' dirty footprints from the washhouse floor when William returned with the news that Harry Griffiths had thrown all caution to the wind and was going to the police station in person.

'Are you sure that's what he intends to do?' she asked.

'I'm upset, not stupid, Beth,' he said angrily.

'Does his wife know?' she questioned anxiously.

'She was in church. And as Jenny wasn't too keen on the idea of staying at home to face her mother's return on her own, I brought her back with me.'

'I don't think that was a good idea, William.'

'If you won't make Jenny welcome I know someone who will,' William said irritably, watching Haydn sneak a kiss from Jenny when they thought no one was watching.

Bethan decided Harry Griffiths was a fool to flaunt a relationship that he and Megan had struggled to keep discreet, if not secret, for so long. But not wanting to add to Diana and William's problems she kept her opinion to herself and carried on scrubbing. When the floor was clean enough for her, she washed out the scrubbing brush Charlie had borrowed, tipped the dirty water down the outside drain and rinsed the bucket. Then she took a short breather. Leaning against the outside wall of the house she watched the sunshine as it played over the square of tilled earth where Megan grew a few vegetables. Then she noticed her uniform. Her dress, apron and stockings were filthy. It was just as well that the sun was shining, she thought wearily, because at the risk of offending Mrs Richards and the other chapel-going neighbours, who checked back gardens for evidence with which to confront those who broke the 'no work on the Sabbath' rule, she'd have to wash them before the stains had time to set. Mud was a devil to shift, even when it was fresh.

She picked up the bucket, stowed it under Megan's sink and checked the meat safe that hung high on the pantry ceiling. There were two breasts of lamb in it. While Haydn stoked up the oven with a bucket of coal, she boned and rolled the breasts, leaving Jenny and Diana to prepare the potatoes and cauliflower that she found on the pantry floor. Someone – she wasn't sure if it was Haydn, William or Charlie – opened one of the bottles of home-made wine while the dinner was cooking. Forgetting her sleepless night and the fact that she hadn't eaten since midnight she downed the glassful Haydn handed her in one gulp. It went straight to her head and her limbs. They felt strange, heavy and leaden, but the feeling didn't stop her from drinking a second glass. Or a third. And by the time Evan returned with the news that Huw was going to the police station to see if he could find out anything, the second bottle had been opened.

It seemed ridiculous to stick rigidly to tradition in a household that had been turned upside down during the course of one short morning, but she dished up dinner at one-thirty, as Megan would have done. No one was very hungry, but all the bottles of wine that the neighbours had brought round were drunk. The brews weren't quite up to the standard of the hock or sparkling wine in Dr John senior's cellar, she decided critically when she was well into her third glass of blackberry wine, but they certainly had the desired effect.

'This is good wine, Dad,' Haydn commented as he refilled the tumblers. 'Why don't we ever have home-made wine at home?'

'You know why,' Evan replied tersely.

Bethan kicked Haydn under the table. She was old enough to remember the arguments between Caterina, who'd been an expert wine brewer, and her mother, who wouldn't have a bottle of anything alcoholic kept, let alone drunk or brewed in the house.

'You working tonight, love?' Evan asked her.

'Yes,' she answered, surprised that someone should want to talk about the normal world. In all the trauma of Megan being carted off to jail she'd forgotten about mundane things like hospital and work.

'In that case you'd better go home and get some sleep.'

'I'll clear the dishes first.'

'Diana and I'll wash them,' Jenny offered, 'and Haydn will dry.'

'If you get him to do that, you'll get him to do more than he's ever done at home,' Evan joked.

'I do plenty at home,' Haydn protested.

'I could sleep on one of the beds upstairs,' Bethan interrupted.

'No point, love,' Evan said. 'I'm staying. Tell your mother I'll stop here for as long as I'm needed.'

'I'm nineteen, Uncle Evan,' William said angrily, spoiling for a fight. 'Old enough to look after the house and my sister.'

'No one doubts that, Will, but when your Uncle Huw gets here there'll be decisions to be made on things like solicitors. Three heads will be better than one. And tomorrow morning you may need an extra pair of legs to run errands to the bank, or police station.'

'I suppose you're right,' William conceded grudgingly.

'Go on, girl, off you go,' Evan said to Bethan.

She left the table and took her cloak from the peg behind the door.

'Thanks for staying and doing everything, Beth.' Diana gave her a bear hug and a kiss.

'Yes, thank you, Beth,' William said gratefully. 'See you later?'

'I'll call in on my way to work.' Bethan walked unsteadily to the door. The crowds had dispersed, but there were still puddles on the pavements where the policeman had heaped the wet clothes. Without thinking she turned left at the end of the road and walked up to Rhiannon Pugh's house. Opening the door she went in and bumped into Phyllis in the passage.

'I'm dreadfully sorry.' She hesitated, ashamed and embarrassed at breaking in on Phyllis's privacy unannounced.

'It's all right,' Phyllis said. 'You've come from your aunt's?'

'Yes.'

'We're very sorry, Bethan. It's a terrible thing to have happened.'

'Thank you.' Bethan was amazed that Rhiannon and Phyllis, incarcerated as they were by Phyllis's shame, should have heard the news so soon.

'If there's anything we can do?' Phyllis offered hesitantly.

Bethan struggled to suppress the tide of hysteria that rose in her throat. The thought of the outcast helping the criminal seemed very peculiar. 'There's nothing anyone can do,' she said finally. 'That's why I left.'

'I shouldn't keep you.' Phyllis glanced self-consciously at her stomach.

'Phyllis,' the wine had loosened Bethan's tongue, and she spoke where she normally would have stayed silent, 'if you ever need a nurse who's half a trained midwife I'm only across the road. I'll come over day or night, you do know that.'

'Thank you.' Phyllis flushed crimson. 'I might be grateful for help some time.'

'I'd better get going. I'm whacked. I worked all last night and I'm on again tonight.'

'You must be exhausted,' Phyllis agreed. She opened the back door. 'It's been nice talking to you, Bethan. You'll be coming through tonight?'

'If you don't mind.'

'We'll be glad to see you.'

Bethan walked up the steps, opened the door in the back wall and stepped out into Graig Avenue. A crowd of children were playing in the dirt in front of her house. They fell silent when they saw her, a sure sign that the news had already travelled from one end of the Graig to the other. She passed them, climbed up to her front door and opened it. A foul smell of burning cloth greeted her. Panicking at the thought that hot coals had dropped out of the stove on to the hearthrug, she dropped her cloak on the passage floor and ran into the kitchen. Her mother was standing in front of the stove, a knee-deep pile of clothes heaped on the rag rug at her feet. The stove door was open and she was picking up the garments one by one with wooden tongs and stuffing them on top of the coals.

'Stop!' Bethan screamed. She ran across the room and tried to pick up as many of the clothes as she could in an attempt to save them.

'Dad told her to do it, Beth.'

She turned and saw Eddie sitting in the dark corner of the room behind the dresser.

'Chances are they're all nicked, and we can't take the risk of the police coming round and finding them. Not after what's happened to Aunt Megan,' he said despondently. 'Dad said they could have us all up for receiving.'

'I told him,' Elizabeth crowed triumphantly. 'I told your father the first time I clapped eyes on Megan. I said she was trouble, but he wouldn't have it. Oh no. Not him.'

Bethan released her hold on the clothes bundled in her arms. They fell limply to the floor. She stared at them. They were so fine – so beautiful. She could never hope to replace them. Not only the things she'd bought for herself, but the suits and shirts she'd bought for the boys. She looked at her hands. She was still holding one frock – the red silk she'd worn to the hospital ball. She lifted it up, resting it against her cheek for a moment. Then she remembered what the sergeant had said:

277

'They can even take a twelve-guinea red silk frock out of the display case in Howell's window.'

She allowed it to slide through her fingers. 'I need to wash my uniform,' she said flatly. 'As soon as I've done that I'm going to bed.'

'I washed and ironed your spare dress and apron yesterday. They're hanging in your wardrobe,' Elizabeth replied in a tone that, for her, was gentle.

'Thank you, Mam.'

Bethan dragged her feet as she climbed the stairs. She couldn't remember when she'd last felt so tired. Her bedroom window was wide open, the lace curtains blowing in the breeze. She tipped water from the jug into the bowl on the washstand and washed her hands and face. Afterwards she steeled herself to open her wardrobe door. Pushing Maud's clothes aside she saw her uniform. Behind it hung her grey dressing gown, a plain blue serge skirt, two white cotton blouses, and her ringed black velvet. All the clothes she now possessed. She pulled open her dressing-table drawer. Her everyday plain, serviceable underclothes were stacked neatly in a row. The delicate, frothy lace and silk concoctions Megan had given her had gone. Stripping off her uniform, she emptied the pockets and folded it, ready for the wash. Stretching out on the bed in her underclothes she closed her eyes.

She felt as though she'd only been asleep for a few minutes when a loud hammering on the front door woke her. Pulling the pillow over her head she turned over, hoping that whoever it was would get what they'd come for, and go away. Moments later Eddie clumped noisily up the stairs.

'Bethan,' he shouted. 'Bethan, are you awake?'

'I am now,' she answered crossly.

'Uncle John's sent for you. He says he needs you. It's urgent.'

'He doesn't need anyone,' she answered sleepily.

'Your Auntie Hetty's been taken ill,' her mother said as she walked into the room. 'How soon can you get ready?'

Bethan reluctantly dragged herself out of her bed. She felt hot, sticky and dirty, but she made do with tipping more water on to what was already in the bowl. Sponging as much of herself as she could reach with a wet flannel wrung out in the cold soapy water, she rubbed herself dry and dressed quickly in her clean uniform. She only just remembered to run a comb through her hair before tying on her veil. Her mother and Eddie, hat and cap on, waited in the passage for her. Maud was standing beside them.

'Eddie's coming with us,' Elizabeth said briskly, stumbling over her words from nervousness at the summons. 'We may need him to run errands. Maud's staying behind to mind the house.'

Maud smiled at Bethan. She didn't seem to be disappointed at being left out. But then none of them had ever considered a visit to Uncle John's as a great treat.

'Did Uncle John say what was the matter?' Bethan asked, picking up her cloak which was still on the floor where she'd left it.

'No. He sent Tommy Bridges' boy. There wasn't a note, just a message for you to get there as quick as you could because Auntie Hetty'd been taken ill.'

There wasn't time for any more talking. Elizabeth hurried down the hill looking neither left nor right, leaving Bethan to keep up as best she could. Sensing that his sister was exhausted, Eddie lagged behind so he could walk with her. Every muscle in Bethan's body was aching. She forced herself to go on, though every inch of her was crying out for rest.

'Have you any idea what time it is?' she asked Eddie as they passed the chapel.

'It was five o'clock when we left the house.'

Five o'clock! Only another two and a half hours before she had to go back on duty.

'What I can't understand is why Uncle John sent for you. If Aunt Hetty's that ill he would have been better off sending for the doctor,' Eddie said thoughtfully.

'Pure miserliness,' Bethan whispered in a voice too low to carry to her mother. 'He would have to pay a doctor, and he doesn't have to pay me.'

Elizabeth halted outside the door of a large stone house built a few doors downhill from the chapel. She rapped the door hard and John Joseph Bull opened it himself. His tie was askew, his collar crumpled. Unheard-of, previously unseen phenomena.

'Quick,' he cried out in anguish. Stepping on to the doorstep he heaved Bethan into the house. 'In the scullery. Quick.' 'The

279

scullery?' Strange name for a washhouse Bethan thought in one of those peculiar moments of logical clarity that often accompanies severe shock.

Hetty Bull was lying on the floor in front of the gas stove that John Joseph had bought to save the expense of feeding the kitchen range with coal throughout the summer months. Her feet were curled around the leg of the wash boiler, and the rubber tube that connected the boiler to the gas supply had been removed from the boiler end of the connection and was firmly clamped between Hetty's teeth.

'I sent for you as soon as I found her – you will do something?' It was a plea from the heart.

Elizabeth moaned. Eddie stumbled to the back door and heaved his Sunday dinner up in the yard. Bethan looked around. The windows and doors in the washhouse were wide open but she could still smell gas.

'You have to do something,' John Joseph begged frantically. 'You have to do. . . . ' He wove his fingers together ready for prayer, fell to his knees and sobbed.

One look at Hetty was enough. There was nothing Bethan or anyone else could do to save her. Her face was blue, her lips black. Her eyes, wide open, stared vacantly at the ceiling. Bethan knelt by Hetty's side and gently removed the tube from her mouth. Someone, presumably her uncle, had already turned off the gas. She closed Hetty's eyes and straightened her bent limbs.

'I'm sorry, Uncle John, she's dead. Been dead for some time by the look of her. You'd better send for the undertaker and the doctor.' For the first time in her life she wasn't afraid of him. 'You'll need the doctor to sign the death certificate,' she explained.

'Bethan,' he begged. 'Please, Bethan, send for someone you know. I can't have this – ' he looked down at the gas tubing – 'this . . . on the death certificate. Think of what people will say. The scandal. . . . '

Then she understood why her uncle had sent for her. His wife was dead and he was worried about gossip. He couldn't bear the thought of fingers being pointed, of the ruin a scandal like this would make of his life.

'Eddie?' she called out to her brother. 'Run and get Fred the

·dead. Tell him what's happened and ask him to come here as quickly as he can. Then go to the hospital and tell them you have to get hold of Doctor Lewis. Remember the name. Doctor Trevor Lewis. Tell them it's an emergency.'

'Wouldn't it be easier if I had a note or something?' Eddie asked. She picked up a pad and pencil that was half lying under her aunt. There was writing on the top page. Without thinking she tore off the first sheet and scribbled a note for Eddie. 'Go on now, quickly,' she ordered brusquely.

Sickened yet fascinated by the sight of the dead body, Eddie couldn't resist taking one last look before rushing out of the door.

'Did Hetty write that note?' her mother asked.

Bethan picked up the piece of paper she'd discarded earlier. She read it before passing it on to Elizabeth.

So sorry. I bought clothes from Megan. I can't live with the sin on my conscience. Forgive me. Hetty.

Bethan watched as her mother read it and passed it on to John Bull. Typical of Hetty, Bethan thought despondently. To apologise and ask for forgiveness. Even for dying.

Chapter Seventeen

The undertaker arrived before Trevor. Bethan made him wait in the front parlour while she stayed in the washhouse with the body. Her mother busied herself making cups of tea for everyone and fussing over John Joseph, who sat slumped in his study, his head in his hands.

'Doctor's here,' her mother announced at last, opening the door and showing Trevor in. She closed the door on them.

'You look done in, Beth,' Trevor said tactlessly as he crouched next to the body.

'I feel done in,' she agreed wearily. 'But as we're into handing out compliments, you don't look much better.'

'I've had a rough afternoon down the police station.' He opened Hetty's eyes, checking her reflexes in the perfunctory manner doctors employ when examining corpses. 'A couple of women went completely hysterical after being arrested for shoplifting. Two constables were injured, not to mention what they did to the cells.'

'The women?' Bethan asked anxiously. 'Are they all right?'

'One of them cracked her knuckles punching a policeman in the eye, apart from that they're fine.'

'You didn't come across a Megan Powell by any chance did you?'

'Your aunt?'

'Yes, my aunt,' she agreed miserably, loath to share her family's disgrace with anyone, even Trevor.

'No, I didn't see her. But then there were a lot of them there, and I only saw the ones who needed calming down.' He took his thumb from Hetty's eyelid and looked at Bethan. 'Your aunt's been arrested?' he asked.

'This morning.'

'Bethan, I'm sorry,' he apologised. 'I wouldn't have said anything if I'd realised. . . . '

'It's all right. Really.' She picked up Hetty's cold, dead hand.

'And this is your aunt too?'

'On my mother's side.'

'And I thought *I* was having a day of it.' He shook his head, opened his case and removed a death certificate.

'You said there was a lot of them. How many?' she demanded.

'I'm not sure. About twenty I think, but the sergeant said they were bringing in more. He was jubilant. Said they'd cracked a well-organised gang that they'd been after for years.'

'The forties,' she murmured.

'Sorry?' Trevor asked, bewildered.

'That's what the sergeant called them. "The forty thieves".'

Trevor straightened Hetty's head as he finished his examination.

'Bethan, I hate having to do this, but I'm going to have to put gas poisoning on the certificate.'

'I know.' She lifted up her aunt's hands and crossed them over her chest.

'That means the coroner will have no choice but to bring in a verdict of suicide.'

'You don't have to explain the situation to me. But my uncle is waiting in his study. I think he'd appreciate a word.'

'How has he taken this – ' Trevor pointed at Hetty with his fountain pen.

'Badly. He's very . . . very upset at the thought of what a verdict of suicide could do to his reputation,' she said hesitantly.

'Eddie was telling me he's a minister.'

'That's right.'

'Then this is going to hit him doubly hard.' He finished writing, and stuffed his pen into the top pocket of his suit. 'You on duty tonight?'

'Yes.'

'I'll take you down to the hospital after I've talked to your uncle.'

'You don't have to,' she said wretchedly.

'I know. But I have to go there anyway.'

'Before you see my uncle, go into the front parlour and ask the undertaker to come in please.'

'I'll do that.'

Bethan helped Fred to wash her aunt and lay her out. While

283

they cleaned the body, Elizabeth went upstairs and sorted through Hetty's things. She returned with a white shroud, socks and cap that Hetty had stitched in preparation for the eventuality of death. Bethan dressed her aunt with Fred's help. When she'd finished, her mother fastened a plain gold cross around Hetty's neck, and eventually, after a great deal of difficulty, managed to force back on the wedding ring that Hetty had removed before gassing herself.

Fred scooped the body into his arms and carried it into the front parlour, where the coffin stood open and waiting.

'Do you want me to screw the lid down, Mrs Powell?' he asked Elizabeth.

'No . . . yes . . . I don't know.' Elizabeth hesitated. 'Bethan, what do you think we should do?'

Bethan stared at her mother in amazement. She'd never consulted her about anything before.

'Better close it,' she answered decisively. 'But don't screw the lid down. Then if anyone wants to look at her they can.'

'Righto, Nurse. Now, about the arrangements?'

'You're going to have to talk to my uncle about those.' Bethan glanced at the parlour clock. It was a quarter-past seven. 'I have to go to work.'

'I'll see him as soon as he's finished with the doctor.'

He left the room and hovered discreetly in the hall.

'I'd like to stay, Mam, I really would,' she apologised. 'But there's no one else to take over the ward.'

'I understand perfectly, Beth,' her mother said sincerely, without a trace of her usual sarcasm. 'Thank you for what you've already done. I'm not sure I could have coped without you.'

'You would have done fine, Mam. You always do.' Realising how badly shaken her mother'd been by Hetty's death, she hugged her for the first time since childhood. 'See you in the morning.'

She met Trevor in the passage.

'Ready?' he asked.

'Quite ready.'

They walked out into the street, passing a few people who were on their way to evensong.

'I hope my uncle's made other arrangements.'

'If he hasn't one of the deacons will come down and find out what's happened.'

'I suppose you're right.' She climbed into his battered car, so different from Andrew's.

'I thought I'd had a rotten day. But you've had a worse one,' he observed as he sat beside her.

'That's life.' She tried to smile at him, but tears started in her eyes.

'Sunday nights are generally quiet. If you're lucky you might get some sleep.'

'Don't tempt fate.'

He drove in through the main gates and parked the car.

'Thanks for the lift, thanks for coming when I needed you, and thank you for talking to my uncle. I know it couldn't have been easy.' She kissed his cheek.

'Beth?' The doctor in him registered the signs of shock – the pale, strained look on her face; the dark smudges beneath her eyes; the way her hand trembled as she reached for the door handle. 'Your uncle told me about the suicide note. I'm most dreadfully sorry. If there's anything else I can do . . . ' His voice trailed helplessly.

'That's all I seem to be hearing from people. Be different, Trevor. Offer to take me out and get me drunk.'

'Would it help?'

'Probably not. But it would be fun. See you.'

He followed the progress of her tall slim figure as she walked across the women's exercise yard. When she disappeared around the corner of the main kitchen, he looked at his wristwatch. He stared thoughtfully at the grey buildings for a moment, then drove around in a wide circle before manoeuvring back out through the main gates.

When Andrew woke, the muted light that percolated through the thick lace at his bedroom windows was a deep gold. He blinked at his surroundings, then his thoughts turned to the events of the morning. He felt sick as he contemplated facing his parents, but he knew he ought to see them as soon as he was dressed. Better they hear what had happened in Leyshon Street from him first. In a town the size of Pontypridd there'd be no shortage of people

285

wanting to tell them that he'd been caught sitting in a house the police had raided. Enough of their acquaintances had frowned on his relationship with Bethan to want to indulge in that delight.

He threw back the sheets and blankets, stepped naked from his bed and wandered into the bathroom. He put the plug in the bath and turned on the taps. While the water was running he returned to the bedroom to check the time on his pocket watch. Nearly seven o'clock. He'd slept practically the whole day away. Leaving the bedroom he went to check the food situation in his kitchen. Despite the assertions of independence he'd made to Bethan, he still ate most of his meals in his parents' house. The only things in his cupboard were a tea caddy half full of tea, a jar of sugar, a tin of coffee and a tin of shortbread biscuits. Crunching a biscuit he lit the gas and put the kettle on.

Half an hour later, bathed, shaved and dressed casually in white flannels, open-necked shirt and a cream cashmere sweater he walked across the garden to his father's house. The french doors to the drawing room were open. His mother was sitting in a chair in front of them reading the latest copy of *The Lady*.

'Andrew,' his father greeted him from behind the bar. 'Joining us for dinner?'

'If it's all right with you.'

'Of course it's all right, darling. It's only fruit, cheese, cold meat and salads. But there's plenty,' his mother said as she laid the magazine down on a side table.

'That sounds fine,' he murmured absently. 'I've been sleeping all day, so I couldn't face anything heavy. Thank you.' He took the whisky his father poured him and sat on the sofa. Leaning back he stretched out his legs.

'You look tired, Andrew,' his mother observed solicitously.

He tossed off a good half of the whisky and cleared his throat, dreading their reaction to what he was about to say. 'There's something I have to discuss with you,' he said, broaching the subject with difficulty.

'Would it have anything to do with a police raid on a certain house in Leyshon Street early this morning?' his father asked.

'It would.' He sat forward cradling the whisky glass between his hands. 'I take it you already know all about it.'

286

'Did you expect us not to?' his mother said in a brittle voice. His father flashed her a warning look.

'Superintendent Hunt telephoned this morning.' His father carried the whisky bottle over from the bar and topped up Andrew's glass. 'He said he was very concerned to see you there. He didn't say so in actual words, but I got the distinct impression that he didn't entirely believe your story.'

'I sensed that much,' Andrew replied honestly.

'You told him you were there to check on a patient?'

'Bethan did,' Andrew answered sheepishly.

'Whatever,' his father remarked dismissively. 'The long and the short of it is, he's suspicious. He also went out of his way to make sure your presence in the house went unnoticed by the press, which I must say in the circumstances was uncommonly kind of him. He couldn't do anything about the people who were there, of course. But with luck they should have plenty of other gossip to occupy themselves with.'

'You have to admit, Andrew, that you've hardly been discreet about your relationship with that woman,' Mrs John broke in feelingly. 'From what Superintendent Hunt told your father it's common knowledge. A topic of conversation to be discussed in every household on the Graig.'

'What happened in Leyshon Street today is hardly Bethan's fault,' Andrew insisted defensively.

'Do you really expect us to believe that her aunt was one of the ringleaders in a gang of shoplifters, directly involved with selling stolen goods, and Bethan didn't know a thing about it?'

'I'm certain she didn't.'

'What about her clothes?' Mrs John asked pointedly. 'The few times I've seen her she's always been extremely well dressed. Where did she get them from?'

'Her aunt,' he admitted.

'I see.'

'It's not what you think. . . . '

'What we think is of little importance, Andrew,' Dr John said firmly, breaking up the impending argument between mother and son. 'It's what the whole town thinks that concerns me. I've been a physician here all my working life. I have a certain standing in the county of Glamorgan. I, and my family, are expected to

287

behave in the accepted manner. Like Caesar's wife all of us have to be above reproach and suspicion. And if I, and you after me, am to continue to work and live here I don't see how it can be otherwise.'

'I'm sorry to have brought this whole sorry mess to your door,' Andrew apologised contritely.

'Well now you've brought it, the question is what do you intend to do about it?' His mother left her seat and paced to the cold, empty fireplace, screened off by tapestry for the summer.

'I don't know.' Andrew left the sofa, walked over to the bar and poured himself another whisky.

'It's plain enough to me.' A note of hysteria crept into Isabel John's voice. 'You have to break off whatever's going on between you two,' she shouted. 'Immediately. . . . '

'Didn't you say earlier that you had something to check in the kitchen with Cook, dear?' Dr John prompted gently.

'No . . . I. . . . '

'You wanted to tell her which of the cold meats to cut,' he prompted.

'Yes I did.' She squared her shoulders and took a deep breath. 'Thank you.' She looked at her son as she left the room. 'I'm only thinking of you, darling,' she said softly.

Andrew took his glass and walked over to the open window. He preferred his mother's hysteria to her understanding.

'I think the best thing you can do, son, is go away for a while. You obviously need time to think things out for yourself. Why don't you take Alec's father up on his offer? Go up to London for a few months. Work on his surgical team. It will be good experience for you. Stand you in good stead, no matter whether you finally opt for general or hospital practice.'

'I'll think about it,' Andrew said dully, promising nothing as he stared blindly at the garden.

'A short spell in London will enable you to put things in perspective. I'll be able to find a locum to fill your place easily enough, and until I do, Trevor'll double up. He's only too keen to earn extra cash these days. You could go up tomorrow. Stay with Fe and Alec. You know they'd love to have you.'

Andrew continued to gaze blankly at the magnificent display of summer roses that formed the centrepiece of his parents' garden.

'Just how much does this girl mean to you?' his father asked bluntly.

'I don't know.' He wasn't lying. After the events of that morning he genuinely didn't know what he felt for Bethan. His feelings were in turmoil. When he was with her all he wanted to do was undress her and himself and make love. But then again, the sensation wasn't a new one. He'd experienced it before, with other girls. It was just that in London there'd been many other girls. Here in Pontypridd there was only one.

Elated at Andrew's honest revelation Dr John picked up the whisky bottle and joined his son in front of the window.

'I got entangled with a working-class girl once,' he confided as he refilled both their glasses. 'Now your mother's not around I don't mind telling you she was magnificent. Especially between the sheets, if you get my meaning.'

'I get your meaning.' Andrew stared at his father in amazement. Having never considered his father's youth, or the women he'd known before his mother, he was slightly shocked by the revelation.

'You can want to make love to a woman without being in love,' Dr John persisted. 'All sorts of men have found that out. My father told me once that there were two kinds of women. The ones you dally with, and the ones you marry with.'

'Isn't that a little old-fashioned?'

'The war changed many things. But it didn't change people's quality. Take your Bethan for instance. She's certainly pretty enough,' he conceded. 'Curves in all the right places, nice smile, nice enough manners, but a bit quiet, wouldn't you agree?'

'She was when she was here,' Andrew concurred ambiguously.

'What I'm trying to say is that she's probably been careful to show you only her best side. Think about it, Andrew. Can you honestly tell me that you really know her? Hasn't the thought crossed your mind that she's reticent when she's here because she knows that she doesn't fit into our style of life?'

'But she isn't quiet when we're alone together.'

'How many deep, meaningful discussions have you had with her?' Dr John pressed.

'A few,' Andrew retorted sullenly.

'When you both had your clothes on?'

Andrew reddened.

'I'm sorry, that was below the belt, but look at her family, son. What do you know about them? Her father's a miner on short-time working,' he answered for him. 'Her eldest brother earns a pittance in the Town Hall. The other one can't even find a job. And there's a daughter still in school so she can't contribute anything. I've seen enough families like that to know what the temptations are. They see people like ourselves, living well, in a reasonable house with a car; eating the right food, with enough money in our pockets to visit the right places, and they grow envious. They don't see the work we do, only the rewards, and they go out to get what we have the only way they know how. They turn to crime.'

Andrew wanted to tell his father that he was wrong. Very, very wrong. But then he remembered Megan Powell.

'Have they charged Bethan's aunt?' he asked, hoping against hope to find another way out.

'Oh yes. Her and eighteen other women. And from what the superintendent said to me this morning, they're the tip of the iceberg. There's a lot more to come.' He drank some of his whisky and rocked slightly on his heels. 'Bethan's aunt is as guilty as Cain,' he affirmed strongly. 'You know that, don't you?'

Andrew recalled the clothes that Bethan and Charlie had carried through the kitchen and thrown into the wash boiler. Bethan's complicity was something he could hardly bring himself to think about, let alone divulge to his father. But much as he might want to, he couldn't wipe his memory clean. Just how many Powells were as guilty as Cain? 'What will they do to Mrs Powell?' he asked.

'They'll go easier on her than on some of the others because she's already decided to plead guilty. Saves the court a lot of bother, but then – ' his father refilled both their glasses – 'unfortunately she's refusing to talk. The sergeant said her sentence would be a lot lighter if she fully co-operated. Needless to say she won't.' He shook his head and shrugged his shoulders. 'That's these people all over for you. Misguided sense of loyalty. In the end she'll probably get a heavy fine. An order to make some kind of restitution to the injured shopkeepers will be made, that's if she has any assets to speak of. Plus a long sentence and hard labour of course, to deter anyone from picking up where she left off.'

'How long is long?'

'Ten years. Possibly more. Andrew, do try to see this from your mother's and my point of view. Superintendent Hunt warned us that this is just the beginning. There's more to come. Now just suppose for a minute that Bethan's involved. . . . '

'Dad. . . . '

'Hear me out, Andrew,' he barked. 'What if she's arrested for receiving? You can't even begin to imagine what that would do to you. You've been seen with her around the town. You've taken her to decent places, introduced her to decent people. I'm not decrying your motives in doing that. You were going out with the girl, and because you're the kind of person your mother and I have brought you up to be – honest, uncomplicated and straightforward – you went out with her openly. But everywhere you went together she was seen, smart, well dressed and wearing the kind of clothes that a nurse couldn't possibly afford to buy on a hospital board's wages. Particularly when she's practically been supporting her entire family. Let's look on the bright side. Even if she isn't charged, she'll be seen as a thief's accomplice.'

'But. . . . '

'And if you continue to see her – ' his father didn't quite manage to conceal the edge of anger that was lying just beneath the surface of his outwardly reasonable attitude – 'you'll be tainted by the same gossip.'

Andrew sank on to the sofa, his head in his hands.

'Look, I know your mother better than anyone. I know she frequently worries about things that never happen, but in this instance she's right. Go to London, boy. Alec's father will see that you're worked hard, but not so hard that you won't have time for a social life. Meet a few other girls. A month from now you'll be a different man. Take my word for it.'

Mair knocked on the door.

'Dinner?' Dr John asked sharply.

'No sir. It's Doctor Lewis. He says he has to see young Doctor John urgently.'

'Then show him in, Mair.'

Trevor walked in. 'I'm sorry to intrude on you like this, sir,' he apologised.

'No intrusion.' Dr John senior was glad of an excuse to break off his talk with Andrew. He had nothing constructive to add. The rest was up to Andrew, and the common sense he fervently hoped would prevail. 'If you haven't a prior engagement, stay to dinner,' he offered hospitably.

'I couldn't possibly.' The slum boy that was never far from the surface invariably made Trevor uneasy in the middle-class atmosphere of Dr John senior's house.

'Nonsense, if you've no other engagement we'd love to have you, wouldn't we, Andrew?'

'What? Oh yes of course, do stay,' Andrew reiterated unconvincingly.

'I need to speak to you, Andrew.'

'And I need to take a trip to the wine cellar. See what I can come up with that will go with cold meat and salad,' said Dr John senior.

'Is this about Bethan?' Andrew asked.

'Yes,' Trevor answered with an embarrassed look at Andrew's father, who was still hovering by the door.

'You may as well say whatever you've got to say in front of my father,' Andrew said with a touch of bitterness. 'If he doesn't already know about it, you can be sure that the superintendent will be on the phone to inform him in the next five minutes.'

'That's unfair, Andrew.'

'At the moment I don't feel very fair.'

'I've just come from Bethan's aunt's house,' Trevor burst out, trying to say what he'd come to say as quickly as possible so he could leave the heavy atmosphere and go to visit Laura. After the events of the day he needed to see her even more than usual.

'Is one of them ill?' Andrew asked anxiously.

'She's dead.'

'Who's dead?' Dr John pressed.

'Bethan's aunt,' Trevor repeated in exasperation.

'But she's in the police station,' Andrew insisted.

'Not Megan Powell. Hetty Bull.'

'The minister's wife!' Andrew exclaimed.

'Yes. She gassed herself. Her husband sent for Bethan as soon

292

as he found her, but there was nothing either of us could do by the time we got there. I saw a note she'd written. Apparently she'd bought some clothes from Megan Powell. Said she couldn't live with herself. I suppose it was impossible for someone as religious as her to come to terms with the idea that she'd worn stolen clothes,' Trevor finished awkwardly.

'The chickens are really coming home to roost on this one,' Dr John murmured, unable to suppress a hint of 'I told you so'.

This second blow, coming so soon after the first, devastated Andrew. He slumped forward on his seat, head in his hands again. The telephone rang and his father went to answer it.

'Bethan looks dreadful,' Trevor ventured. 'She seems to be shouldering a lot of the burden. But she still insisted on going to work tonight.'

'She would,' Andrew said without emotion, inviting no further comment.

'That was the superintendent on the telephone.' Andrew's father stood in the doorway. 'They've arrested two girls. Maud and Diana Powell. Are they related to Bethan?'

'Maud's her younger sister. Diana's her cousin. But they're children. They're only fourteen,' Andrew protested.

'Evidently they're both old enough to steal,' his father pronounced dismissively. 'They wouldn't have been arrested if the police had any doubts about their guilt. And you'd better brace yourself, boy. There's worse.' Dr John took a cigar from the silver box on the bar. A bad sign: Andrew had never seen him smoke before dinner until now. 'Unfortunately for you, and for us as a family, the police suspect there's a connection between you and the nurse they saw in the house this morning.'

'Bethan?' Trevor asked.

Andrew nodded miserably. 'But they haven't arrested her?' It was more a plea than a request for information.

'Not yet they haven't. But in Superintendent Hunt's opinion it's only a matter of time,' his father said firmly, straying well beyond the narrow bounds of the information that Hunt had been prepared to impart. 'Andrew, really, you have no choice. The sooner you're in London the better for everyone concerned. If they arrest her, there's no knowing what she'll say once they get her in the police station. Knowing of our influence with people

who matter, she may even send for you. Think of the disgrace.'
When Andrew remained silent he lost his temper.

'Damn it all, boy, if you won't think of yourself, think of me, of what I've worked for. Of your mother, and Fe. Don't fool yourself, news of this mess will reach even London, and neither of them will be able to hold up their heads again. All because their son and brother got involved with a family of common thieves. . . . '

Trevor stood up and walked towards the door. 'I have to go. I'm on duty.'

'You still have to eat, boy, and it's ready. I'll telephone the hospital to let them know where you are.' Dr John rejected his excuse out of hand. 'Andrew?' He stood in the doorway, his hand poised on the doorknob.

Defeated, Andrew looked up at his father. 'You can send a telegram to Fe and Alec. Tell them I'll be up on the morning train,' he agreed wretchedly.

'I'll try telephoning them first.' His father left them; a few moments later they heard him speaking on the telephone in the hall.

Andrew sat on the sofa staring down into his empty glass. He wanted to speak to Trevor – to look at him – but he gagged on the unspoken words. Afraid to say anything in case he saw something akin to the contempt he felt for himself mirrored in Trevor's eyes.

The quiet night Trevor had wished for Bethan hadn't materialised. A mother went into labour. A ward maid, one of only two on duty, vomited and had to be sent home, making it impossible for the trainee and the other maid to cope with the normal workload, let alone the additional strain of looking after a patient in labour. By two o'clock Bethan felt tired enough to sit on the floor and cry. But she forced herself to go on. Checking feeding times, delivering the baby, cutting the cord, washing both mother and infant, writing reports. There wasn't even time to take a break until four o'clock in the morning.

When she was finally free she went into the sister's office and shut the door. The room held so many memories. She only had to close her eyes to see Andrew standing next to the fireplace, arms outstretched, ready to embrace her. . . . She opened them again. There was no Andrew. Only two piles of paperwork. And the one that had been completed was by far and away the smaller. Sweeping them both aside she sat down and rested her arms on the desk. For the first time that day she indulged in the luxury of a waking moment to herself. She went over the events of the morning. Saw again the look of horror on Andrew's face as the policemen clumped their way into Megan's house; the shock registering in his eyes when he realised why she and Charlie were running through the house with bundles of clothes in their arms.

Suddenly she remembered that he'd promised to call for her that afternoon. He'd wanted to take her to a garden party. Garden party! They'd discussed it only that morning. It felt like a lifetime ago. So much had happened in the space of a day. She consoled herself with the reflection that even if he'd driven to Graig Avenue she might not have been there. Hetty. . . .

She was tormented by a ghastly, very real image of her aunt the way she'd found her. Lying on the floor of the washhouse, her feet curled around the boiler, dead . . . Dead! As a nurse she'd seen death many times, in many different guises, but apart from her grandmother who'd died peacefully in her sleep, it was the first time she'd witnessed the final tragedy in her own family.

Hot stinging tears of grief and remorse for missed opportunities burned at the corners of her eyes. She hadn't known Aunt Hetty well enough to care about her. Not in the way she cared for Megan. But she'd pitied her. Hetty'd been so small, so fragile – so totally subservient to her overbearing, self-righteous husband. She hadn't had much of a married life – hadn't had much of a life at all. If only she'd made the effort to get to know Hetty better. She might have been able to do something, at least given her a few happy times – hours they could have shared, the way she'd shared part of her life with Megan.

Overwhelmed by grief, misery and sheer loneliness she laid her head on her arms on the desk and allowed her tears to flow, unchecked.

Andrew drove through the town at breakneck speed. On the seat of the car next to him was a letter he'd written to Bethan. He'd penned it after dinner in his father's study while his father and a

295

reluctant, pressganged Trevor had lingered over their coffee and brandy. As soon as he'd finished it he'd returned to the dining room and asked Trevor to deliver it to Bethan after the London train had left. But Trevor had refused. And to his amazement his father had agreed with Trevor.

'You'll have to see her, Andrew,' he declared as he passed the cigars and the brandy bottle round the table a second time. 'Take my word for it. Letters are never final. Not like telling her to her face. A letter will only give her an excuse to see you again and drag the whole thing out. Write to her and you could be enmeshed in the trauma of this for months. Best to see her before you go, even if it means catching a later train. Tell her straight off that it's over. A clean break's what's needed here.'

Neither he nor Trevor had said anything. When they left the table he'd tried to persuade Trevor to join him in his rooms, but Trevor had refused, and left soon afterwards. Trying not to think about the reasons that lay behind Trevor's uncharacteristic reticence, he'd said goodnight to his parents, walked across the garden and packed his bags for London. But all the time he'd been clearing his rooms, shutting away the things he wouldn't need into cupboards, the letter he'd written had lain, like some evil talisman, on the table.

He'd taken a bottle of whisky into the bathroom with him when he bathed, but neither the warm water nor the alcohol soothed him. He'd picked up a new book, one he'd looked forward to reading, from his shelves and carried it to bed, but both sleep and the ability to concentrate on the printed word eluded him. Bethan's image intruded persistently into his mind, colouring whatever he looked at with her presence. He saw her dressed in her uniform, working through the night on the ward. When the half-bottle of whisky was empty and he couldn't stand the screaming silence a moment longer, he left his bed, dressed and went to his car.

He drove into Courthouse Street and parked on the road before walking through the gates into the hospital. The porter called out suspiciously as he passed, then he recognised him and smiled sheepishly.

'Sorry, Doctor John, didn't know there'd been an emergency call.'

'It's all right, Ernie,' Andrew shouted, not wanting to get involved in a discussion about a nonexistent emergency. 'I won't be long.'

'Go ahead, Doctor.'

He walked on through the quiet, deserted yards. The shadows of the tall buildings loomed out to meet him, huge, almost tangible in the indistinct light of the early-morning low moon. He looked up. Lights were burning in the maternity ward, the only lights that burned at full strength in the block. Another birth?

He opened the door slowly, holding it carefully lest it swing back on its hinges and make a noise. Then he climbed the steps, treading lightly, taking them two at a time. A maid and a trainee were settling the last of the babies down after their boiled water feed. He acknowledged them with a brief nod as he walked through to the ward. The glass in the office door shone bright yellow. A light was burning at full strength. That probably meant Bethan was doing her reports. He glanced at his watch. Five o'clock. Not much time before she had to prepare for the morning's change-over. Perhaps it was just as well.

He opened the door without knocking and walked in. She was slumped over the desk. His throat went dry. He thought of Trevor's revelation about her aunt. Had she . . . his heart in his mouth he crept up behind her. Her breath was falling, light, evenly from her parted lips. She was asleep. He leaned against the wall, dizzy with relief. Then he saw her cheeks. They were wet with tears.

He crept to the easy chair next to the fireplace and waited, silently rehearsing what he would say when she woke.

Bethan fell from sleep, landing into consciousness with a start. Her head ached and her limbs were stiff. She opened her eyes, totally disorientated as her mind strove to recognise her surroundings. Then she panicked. She wasn't alone. There was someone in the room with her. She looked around and saw Andrew sitting in one of the chairs next to the gaping black hole in the fireplace. She stared at him, wondering if he were real or a figment of her sleep-numbed imagination.

'You looked so tired I didn't want to wake you,' he said at last.

'I shouldn't have been asleep. If anyone but you had found me

I'd be hauled up before Matron. . . . ' Her hands went to her veil, automatically securing and straightening it. Then she looked at her watch. 'Is that the time? I must check the ward.'

'I'll wait for you.'

She smiled at him as she left, a smile he was unable to return. She walked up and down the aisle between the beds, pausing as she reached the side of the mother who'd just given birth. Then she checked the nursery. She tried not to think of what Andrew wanted. Or why he'd come. She had her suspicions, but until he actually voiced the words they remained just that, suspicions. Eventually she had no reason to tarry longer. She went into the small ward kitchen, washed her hands and face, and made two cups of tea. Then she carried them into the office.

'Tea.' She set the cups on the desk.

'Thank you.' He might have been a stranger she'd just met. She looked at the chair on the other side of the empty fireplace, thought better of it and returned to her seat behind the desk.

'Look, Andrew, about this morning. . . . '

'Beth!' It was as much as he could do to stay where he was. He had to keep reminding himself of what his father had said about two kinds of women. Physical attraction. That's all that lay between them. Nothing more. 'Please don't say anything.' He held up his hand. 'At least not until I've finished. This is going to be hard enough for me as it is.'

She looked down at the pile of reports suspecting, and dreading, what he was about to say.

'I've decided to go to London. At least for a while. Until the scandal . . . until what . . . what happened this morning dies down,' he stammered clumsily. 'I'm taking up Alec's father's offer of a surgical post in Charing Cross,' he explained superfluously.

'Must you?' She spoke so quietly he couldn't be sure afterwards whether he'd heard her or his own conscience.

'I've talked everything over with Father. It's for the best, Beth. I'm sorry about what happened today. Both your aunts. . . . '

'Thank you,' she interposed hollowly.

'But it's not just your family, Beth. You have to realise what the gossip generated by this sort of thing could do to me . . . to my family,' he said, unconsciously reiterating his father's arguments.

She nodded, suffocating on her tears, unable to speak.

'A doctor can't risk any scandal, you of all people should know that.'

'Yes,' she whispered.

'I don't think you quite understand. I'm leaving now, in an hour or so. I don't know when I'll be back. I'm sorry it has to end like this between us, Bethan.' He rose from his chair.

'Andrew, please, take me with you,' she begged, blocking his path. 'Please don't leave me here,' she implored, forgetting all pride and dignity as the spectre of a life without him rose terrifyingly from the depths of her nightmares.

He'd prepared himself for a dignified parting scene. A little cold, unemotional and theatrical perhaps, but he'd pictured himself walking away while she stared silently after him. This was one eventuality he hadn't mentally rehearsed for. She flung her arms around him, entwining her fingers tightly around his neck.

'Please, Andrew, take me with you,' she sobbed. 'I swear I won't be any trouble. You don't even have to live with me. I'll find a job, a room. Just come and visit me when you can – please, Andrew. . . . '

'You don't understand.' He gripped her wrists, forcing her arms away from his body. 'I'll be working, living with Fe and Alec. I won't have time to see anyone.'

'Andrew, I love you,' her voice rose precariously high, 'I couldn't bear to live without you.'

'For pity's sake, Bethan, stop being so melodramatic,' he said harshly, concerned about the noise she was making. 'Of course you can live without me. And it's not as if I'm going to the outer reaches of the Antarctic. I'm only going to London. It's a few hours away on the train. And although we can't . . . can't be what we were to one another, we can still be friends.' He threw her the sop in the hope that it would calm her.

'If you go I know I'll never see you again. Please, Andrew –' Her voice dropped, until it was barely audible. 'Please.'

He looked at her calmly and dispassionately. Weeping, dishevelled, verging on hysteria. He recalled his mother and Fe's restraint in everything they did. Then he remembered how long it had taken him to rouse Bethan's passions. How she'd behaved in the privacy of his bed. A wave of nausea rose in his throat. He couldn't take any more. Not from her. Not like this.

'I have to go,' he said abruptly, disentangling himself from her arms.

'Andrew!' The cry was agonising in its intensity.

He tried to concentrate on what his father had said. It had all made sense in the drawing room at home. Now, none of it made any sense. He only wanted to hold her close. Smother her face with kisses. Console her. Tell her he loved her, that it would all come right. Instead he balled his hands into tight fists. His father had told him to finish it before he left. He remembered her aunts, her sister. The scandal, the gossip. . . . it was her fault. The fault of her family. He didn't want to end their affair. Her family — what she was — had forced his hand. And he was hurting every bit as much as her. He lashed out, said the worst thing that came to mind.

'It's over. I daren't risk demeaning myself or my family any more than I already have by continuing to see you. You've dragged me down as far as I'm prepared to go.'

He heard her cry out his name. The sound echoed at his footsteps every inch of the way as he walked across the yard and into the street where he'd parked his car.

The cry followed him home, and back to the station. He wasn't free of it even when his train pulled into Paddington and he called a taxi to take him to Fe's house.

Chapter Eighteen

The following days passed in a nightmarish haze for Bethan. She rose from her bed after sleepless nights, washed, dressed, walked to the hospital, worked, came home, sat on a chair in the kitchen, played with whatever food her mother put in front of her, stared into space until it was time to return to her room, when she lay down on the bed next to Maud, before beginning the process all over again.

Everywhere she looked, everything she did, brought back memories of the time she and Andrew had shared. And when she found the happiness of the past easier to live with than the cold, comfortless reality of the present she closed her mind to the events of the last night Andrew had visited the ward. She was aware of very little besides Andrew and what she'd felt, and still felt, for him. She walked across the exercise yards in the hospital recalling the times she'd done so with him at her side. She climbed the hill towards home, looking at the streets not as they were, but as they'd appeared from the windows of his car. She went into town, only to see him in shops, in doorways, stepping out of the New Inn – wearing his evening suit – one of his lounge suits – his flannels. She saw his hat on the head of every man she passed. She thought she saw him playing tennis on the courts in the park, caught sight of his even, regular features in the face of every man she met.

She began to live for the times when she was alone and could conjure up images that were far more substantial than anything around her. Hour after hour she lay next to him on her bed. The walls of her room changed, transporting her back to the opulent luxury of his bedroom, or the bohemian comfort of the glassed-in veranda of his parents' chalet.

She was only vaguely aware of events that didn't concern Andrew happening around her, and she had no real recollection of any actual conversations. She was too busy remembering her discussions with Andrew and recreating new exchanges that they might have had if they'd still been together.

Someone, probably Evan, told her that Megan had been sentenced to ten years' hard labour. Maud wandered in and out of their shared bedroom, quiet and subdued after her few hours of hard questioning in the police cells. She hadn't been charged with anything, and was careful not to tell anyone, not even Bethan, of the true extent of her involvement with the gang. She became quieter, more withdrawn as she continued to live in fear of being found out. But Bethan was oblivious to Maud, let alone the changes in her. Unfortunately for everyone Elizabeth wasn't. Lacking any real evidence she ranted and raved at Maud whenever they were in the same room, and Evan had to exert all the authority he could muster to quieten her. There was also a bustle and a fuss about Megan's house that took up a great deal of Evan's time, but Bethan couldn't have said precisely what it was all about.

She knew that her Aunt Hetty's funeral was going to be a private one because that was what she told Matron when asked. She lost all track of time. She no longer cared what she looked like. The only time she glanced in a mirror was to check whether her face was clean and her veil was straight. Days and nights came and went, merging into one. She no longer had the acumen nor the desire to differentiate between the two. She was too busy weaving not Andrew, but his ghost into her life.

On the day of Hetty's funeral she went straight from the night shift to the chapel. Standing between her mother and Maud her thoughts left Andrew for the first time since he'd gone, and centred on the small dark wood coffin that lay on the floor in front of the pulpit. Apart from four deacons and a visiting minister who'd been called in to read the burial service, only John Joseph and her immediate family were present. The shame of Hetty's suicide coming so close after Megan's disgrace was too acute for her uncle to allow outsiders to witness it. Her brothers, her father and John Joseph himself had carried the coffin from the house into the chapel between seven and eight in the morning. The timing was carefully arranged to minimise the risk of curious pedestrians gawping at the cortège. All the colliery shifts began

302

at six-thirty, and the shop assistants, clerks and schoolchildren didn't leave their houses much before eight.

The service lasted a scant five minutes. There were no hymns. Bethan glanced at the empty seat in front of the organ and wondered who would play it now. There wasn't even a sermon, only a short prayer mercifully free of the kind of rhetoric her uncle usually employed, which the visiting minister spoke in soft, soothing tones. As soon as he finished speaking, the deacons picked up the coffin and stowed it in the hearse. Her uncle sat alongside the driver in front of the coffin, leaving her entire family to pile into the second and only other car that he had hired.

They drove slowly down the hill, past the hospital where the paupers leaving after their night's lodging stripped off their caps as a sign of respect, skirted the edge of town, and out along Broadway to the forlorn corner of Glyntaff cemetery reserved for those who were outcasts, even in death. The paupers and the suicides.

They stood silently on the muddy earth alongside the grave as the coffin was lowered in by two workmen in dirty boots and grimy trousers. Her uncle mumbled a few words that made little impression on Bethan. The only thought that entered her head was that they seemed to bear no relation to Hetty or her life.

Afterwards she went home to bed. She was glad she was back on night shift because it meant she could sleep during the day in a bed she didn't have to share with Maud. Those days were the best because she was free from grinding chores – free to think of Andrew. To allow her imagination to run riot, to once again lie alongside him – feel the brush of his skin against hers, the hardness of his muscular back beneath her hands, his lips as they met hers. And so the pattern became established. Work, home, dream – wash, dress, work, home. . . .

Trevor and Laura tried to help. She listened patiently to their plans to include her in their outings, then she fobbed them off with the excuse that she was on night shift for at least another two weeks and they were both on days. She was grateful she was able to do so. She couldn't bear to watch them, to witness their happiness. All she wanted was to be left alone with her routine, her memories and her imaginings.

The days grew shorter and colder. The edges between reality

303

and fantasy blurred to the point when she actually began looking for Andrew. Sometimes she sought him for minutes at a time before she remembered – and with remembrance came the first of the pains. Real, acute physical pains that made her sick in the pit of her stomach, gave her blinding headaches and dizzy spells. She tried to cope with them, and when she couldn't she looked at the painkillers in the drug cabinet on the ward. It would have been simple enough. She was in sole charge in the night. She could have written up doses on record cards for patients who didn't need sleeping draughts. But something, probably fear of Squeers, held her back. Instead she reached for the brandy bottle that was always kept locked in Squeers' desk. It was easier to take a drink from that. She checked the level before she started and was careful to refill it to the same mark with water. But after only two nights she realised she was drinking water. That was when she opened her jewellery box and took out one of the pound notes Andrew'd given her from the bets he'd placed on Eddie. That morning on her way back from work she knocked on the back door of the Horse and Groom and asked for a bottle of brandy. The landlord didn't even question her motives. A nurse asking for brandy was common enough. When that bottle ran out she went to the Morning Star, comforting herself with the thought that there were enough pubs on the Graig to keep her going for months before anyone became in the least suspicious.

Her father and her brothers watched her grow daily thinner, paler and more remote. They noticed that she rarely went out. When Evan plucked up courage to ask after Andrew she simply said he'd gone away. There was no outburst, no tears, only the same blank, dead look in her eyes that had worried him for weeks.

'Eddie, what are you doing here?' Laura asked as she walked out of the hospital gates at the end of her day shift. 'Bethan's on nights you know.'

'I know,' he said awkwardly. 'It's you that I'm waiting to see, not her. Buy you a cup of tea?'

She lifted her cape and pulled out her nurse's watch. Trevor was on duty, but he'd said he'd try to call up her house. On duty days that could mean any time. But just in case he managed it, she wanted to go home and change out of her uniform. 'I'm sorry, Eddie, not tonight. I have to. . . . ' She saw the dejected look on his face and changed her mind. 'All right, one quick cuppa in our café, but I warn you now if it's my love you're after I'm spoken for.'

Eddie blushed at her poor joke and followed her to the café.

Too early for the evening idlers, and too late for most of those finishing work for the day, the place was quiet. There was no sign of Laura's father, only Tina who was serving behind the counter. Eddie bought two teas and carried them over to the table in the corner by the front window.

'Miserable weather,' Laura said, staring at the rain patterning the glass.

'Summer's over.'

'Not entirely I hope. I'm getting married in October and I want the sun shining down on us. You are coming, aren't you? We sent your whole family invitations.'

'If you have I'm sure we'll all be there,' Eddie said.

'Hasn't Bethan said anything?'

'No. Not really,' Eddie admitted reluctantly.

'Typical,' Laura snorted. 'She seems to be in a dream these days.'

'That's what I wanted to see you about,' Eddie said quickly as he spooned four sugars into his tea. 'Haydn and I got talking . . .' he hesitated, not quite sure how to go on. He hadn't wanted to do this but Haydn had insisted that one of them talk to Laura for Bethan's sake. 'He wanted to see you himself, but it's not easy for him with the hours he works. . . . '

'Is there a point to all this?' Laura asked impatiently.

'We're worried sick about Bethan,' Eddie blurted out. 'Have you see her lately?'

'Not really. Not to talk to,' she evaded neatly, as she stirred her tea. It was the truth. Trevor had told her what little he knew about Andrew's break-up from Bethan, but even that little had been tempered by Trevor's sense of delicacy, and she hadn't wanted to press him. She was too happy to want to dwell on other people's misery. Especially that of her best friend. 'Bethan's on nights, I'm on days – ' She shrugged her shoulders. 'We work

305

on the same ward, but not at the same times. I've hardly seen her in weeks.'

'She's not herself,' Eddie continued, repeating Haydn's words. 'She's not eating properly – not sleeping – Laura, do you know what happened between her and that man? He's not around any more, and if he hurt her. . . . ' He curled his hands into fists.

'You mean Andrew I suppose.' She shook her head as she lifted her teacup to her lips. 'I told you, I haven't seen Bethan to talk about anything.'

'But he's gone?' Eddie persisted like a dog worrying a rat.

'He went to London to take up a surgical post,' Laura murmured.

Eddie looked at her blankly.

'He's gone to be a doctor in a London hospital,' she explained irritably.

'And left our Beth high and dry?'

'It might not quite be the way it looks,' Laura said diplomatically. 'They could have wanted to take a break from one another.'

'I don't think so, and neither does our Haydn. She's not herself. Something must have happened. . . . '

'It could have been your aunt getting arrested,' Laura said thoughtlessly.

'What do you mean?' Eddie demanded churlishly.

'He's a doctor, Eddie. He has a position to keep up, and he might feel . . . might feel . . . ' She faltered as she understood the implications of what she was about to say.

'Disgraced?' Eddie suggested bitterly. 'Like my mother. She says she can hardly hold her head up when she walks down the street. Between what Auntie Megan's done and Aunt Hetty. . . . Bloody hell!' he said slowly. 'You're trying to tell me that he thinks our Beth isn't good enough for him!'

'I could be wrong, Eddie.' She stared at him helplessly, frightened by the force of anger she'd unleashed. She wanted to say something that would calm him, but she didn't know what. Eddie wasn't like her brothers or Haydn. He was a much simpler boy who tended to see things in black and white. Perhaps it was the best way for someone who intended to earn his living from his fists.

'That smarmy bastard. . . . '

'Language, Eddie!' she warned. 'You don't know the truth of the matter any more than I do. A lot of things can happen between a man and a woman.'

The blood rushed to Eddie's face. Unable to meet Laura's eyes he looked down at his bootlaces, wondering if Laura had heard something about him and Daisy.

'If you want to find out what's really wrong, you're going to have to ask Bethan,' Laura said firmly. 'But if I were you I'd be careful. She might not want to talk about it.'

'Because he dumped her?'

'Or because she dumped him,' Laura said quietly. 'Have you thought of that?'

Evan, Alun and William dragged their feet as they walked up the Graig hill. It was a glorious autumn evening. A huge glowing orange sun sank slowly over the slate-tiled rooftops of the stone houses, bathing the streets in a soft glow that washed the harsh grey, brown and pewter tones of the dirty streets to lighter, kinder shades. If the men had looked to the heavens rather than their feet they might have appreciated just how beautiful the sunset was, but neither its beauty nor the warmth of the evening air on their faces, blackened by a day spent working underground, could lift their spirits. And all of the colliers who walked in front, beside or behind them were the same. Dour, grim and silent.

Evan paused as they reached the entrance to the gully that cut between Llantrisant Road and Leyshon Street. William pushed his knapsack further over his shoulder and looked apprehensively at his uncle. Only the whites of his teeth and eyes showed through the thick layer of coal dust that covered his face.

'What's going to happen, Uncle Evan?' he asked anxiously.

'You heard the man speak, same as me,' Evan replied with unintentional gruffness.

'But I've Diana to consider. Uncle Huw says we may have to sell the house to pay Mam's restitution costs as it is.'

Evan relented. 'We'll sort out something, boy. Don't worry. They can't let us all starve to death. Look, I've got to go home, wash and have tea. I'll come down and see you later. We'll have a talk then.' He would have liked to ask his nephew and niece to come up to his house for tea. But aside from Elizabeth's upset over Megan's disgrace and her vow that she wouldn't let either of Megan's children cross her doorstep again, there was the news he had to tell her. News that could stretch her strained nerves to breaking point. Afterwards he might well have good reason to want to leave the house for Leyshon Street.

He turned his back on William and carried on up the Graig hill with Alun walking close on his heels. As they rounded the vicarage corner they caught up with Viv Richards, Glan's father.

'Fine mess we're in now, Evan,' he commented acidly.

'Aye.'

'Well I'll see myself and my whole family out on the road before I'll go begging for help from anyone. That's all I can say about it.'

'Let's hope it won't come to that, Viv.' Evan watched Viv's short stocky figure as he mounted the steps next door, then found himself measuring the distance between the pavement and the house. Imagining how the front would look covered with furniture when the bailiffs came. Shaking his head in an attempt to free himself from the image, he turned the key in his door and walked through to the kitchen.

Elizabeth was spooning drops of batter on to the hotplate of the stove. A small stack of pikelets piled on a plate on the warming shelf above her testified to her industry.

'I've set up the bath out back,' she greeted him brusquely.

'Thank you, Elizabeth.' Evan sat on the stoop between the washhouse and the kitchen and unlaced his boots. Alun stepped over him and walked out to the sink.

'All the children out?' he asked, wanting to make sure they wouldn't be interrupted for a while.

'Haydn's in that shop again, working for nothing as usual. Bethan's upstairs. Anyone'd think the girl's going into a decline. She's got work in another hour and a half, and if I've called her once I've called her a dozen times. Well, I'll not call her again. It's up to her to get herself to the hospital on time. And Maud and Eddie have gone over the mountain to look for blackberries. I told them there was no point in going. The season's over. There's only the small wormy ones left that the birds don't want.'

She scooped up a pikelet and flicked it over. While it was cooking she stirred a pan of tripe and onions that was simmering in the oven. Evan decided to take the bull by the horns. There wasn't going to be a good time to tell Elizabeth the news he was carrying, and the sooner he began the sooner it would be over with. He kicked off his boots, stood up, and closed the door behind him, shutting Alun into the washhouse.

'You're not going to give the lodger first bath are you?' Elizabeth said in disgust. 'And just look at those socks. You're covering the floor with coal dust. You're undoing all the work I've done today by just standing there. . . . '

'I'm on my way. It's just that there's something you should know, Elizabeth, and it can't wait.'

'What is it now?' She flicked a cooked pikelet on to the pile and spooned another ladleful of batter on the hotplate. 'More bad news about that sister-in-law of yours? Because if it is. . . . '

'It's not about Megan. Manager made an announcement today. The pit's closing at the end of next week.'

Naked fear and panic flashed over her face as she dropped the spoon she was holding on the hearthrug. 'You'll just have to find work in another colliery. You'll have to go up the Albion or down Trehafod. . . . '

'There's no point in going to any colliery. They're all closing. The Maritime, the Albion. . . . '

'Fine! Just fine!' she shouted furiously. 'It's no good talking like that. There has to be work somewhere. All you have to do is go and look for it. If you don't – ' her hand flew to her mouth and she closed her teeth around her fingers in an effort to stop herself from crying – 'we're for the workhouse. Oh God – ' She sank to her knees and picked up the spoon. 'My uncle always said it would come to this if I married you. The means test and the workhouse, and all you can say is there's no point in looking for work. . . . ' She began to sob. Bone weary, sick and terrified what the future might hold, Evan turned his back on her.

'At least if it comes to the workhouse our Beth will be able to look after us.' With that parting shot he unlatched the kitchen door and walked into the washhouse. Alun Jones had stripped down to his trousers and was waiting patiently to use the tub. Evan tore off his shirt, knelt beside the bath and thrust his head under the warm water. He took the soap from its cracked saucer and rubbed it into a lather. Then he realised he'd left his towel and clean clothes on the airing rack above the range where Elizabeth kept them warming.

'Do me a favour, Alun,' he called out, his eyes closed against the soap. 'Fetch me my towel and clothes from the kitchen.'

'Aye.'

He heard Alun walk back and was half tempted to dress outside and go down to Leyshon Street through the back garden. He couldn't face Elizabeth again. Not yet. He needed time to think things out first.

Bethan rose late, washed, dressed and walked downstairs into the doom-laden atmosphere of the kitchen. She scarcely had time to sit down before her mother regaled her with the full story of her father's redundancy. Evan himself didn't say a word. He simply sat in his chair, pushing threads of tripe and onions around his plate. Bethan smiled at him, but he kept his head down and her smile was wasted. She would have liked to reach out and hug him, but her head was swimming and she wasn't sure she'd be able to move without falling over. Her senses were invariably numbed these days. Drinking all day, working all night, and general antipathy had taken a toll, and not only on her looks. She was constantly dizzy and nauseous. She had no appetite and even on occasions like now, when she sat at the table with her family and forced herself to eat, she rarely kept her food down for long.

Life had become one long, grinding chore. The studying that she'd made an effort to keep up with, even when she'd been going out with Andrew, had been abandoned. She'd become obsessed with finding strength enough to get her through her nights of work, so she could spend her days in the comfort and seclusion of her bed with a bottle tucked beneath the pillow. She carried one bottle in the bag she took to work in case she couldn't quite make it through the night, but she was careful to hide a second behind her drawer in the dressing table. Brandy had become a lifeline she could no longer live without. She bought plenty of cheap cologne in Woolworth's and had taken to sprinkling it liberally over her clothes and into her washing water; even going so far as to rinse her mouth out in it when she left her bed at the end of the day, lest any of her family recognised the smell on her breath. And being in charge of the ward during the night had its compensations. If her behaviour seemed a little odd or erratic there was no superior to question it. And by directing others to complete tasks she was wary of doing herself in case she botched them, she managed – by the skin of her teeth sometimes – but she managed, to keep her secret.

But there were times, like now, when she was sitting with her family, when she felt she wasn't actually living life. Merely watching it; like a patient in a tuberculosis ward, forced to stand behind a glass window.

She tried to follow her father's example and concentrated on eating the tripe and onions. She had only swallowed three mouthfuls when she began to retch. She left her chair clumsily and ran out, only just making it to the *ty bach* in time. She lay on the flagstoned floor next to the bench seat in a cold sweat, shaking from head to foot, hoping and praying that her mother wouldn't allow any of the others to go after her. The last thing she wanted was to try to explain the state she was in to Maud.

Her luck held. After five minutes she could sit up. She leaned back against the wooden door, careful to avoid the whitewash on the walls that came off on any surface that brushed against it. A few moments later she was able to struggle to her feet. Holding on to the wall she made it as far as the sink in the washhouse, where she washed her face in cold water and rubbed her teeth with her finger and salt from a block her mother kept next to the washing blue on a high shelf.

'Are you all right?' Elizabeth shouted irritably from the kitchen.

'Fine, Mam,' Bethan called back tremulously.

'We can't have you coming down with anything. Not now when your father's lost his job.'

'For Christ's sake, Elizabeth!' Evan growled with uncharacteristic savagery. 'I've another one and a half weeks to go.'

'And afterwards?' Elizabeth demanded, cold fury glittering in her eyes.

'If you go on like this there won't be an afterwards,' he threatened. Pushing his chair back from the table he picked up his boots from the hearth and lurched towards the front door.

'That's right,' Elizabeth taunted. 'Run away from the problem

311

just as you always do. Well this time you haven't got your precious mother or sister-in-law to rush to. . . . '

Bethan crept upstairs and reached for the bottle in her bag. She put the whole of the neck in her mouth and drank deeply, pausing only when she heard the creak of the top stair. She pushed the bottle back into her bag, only just managing to stopper it as Maud entered the room.

'Beth, what's going to happen to us?' she asked tearfully.

'I don't know.' Bethan heard her voice slurring and realised she was drunker than she'd ever been in the house before. She sat down abruptly on the dressing-table stool and fiddled with her veil. Fortunately Maud was too upset to pay much attention.

'I went to see Mrs Evans today with Diana,' she began tentatively.

'Mrs who?' Bethan tried and failed to focus on her sister.

'Mrs Evans. The deputy headmistress in Maesycoed Seniors.'

'Don't know her.'

'Of course, I forgot you went to the grammar school. Anyway in spite of all . . . all that police business she agreed to write out a reference for Diana. She's applying for a job as a ward maid in Cardiff Infirmary. They need girls to start in September. I'm sure if I asked her she'd write one out for me too. Do you think I should apply?'

'It'll be hard work in Cardiff Infirmary. And not all of it pleasant,' Bethan warned, upset even in her drink-fuddled state at the thought of her sister working as a skivvy in that environment. Maud wasn't strong. She still coughed occasionally, and winter was coming. There had to be something better for her to do, if only they could think of it.

'I don't mind hard work, Beth. You know that. I've been looking around and jobs aren't that easy to come by. I'd rather be a maid in a hospital than in a house, and that's all that seems to be on offer. Besides Dad will be hard put to keep Mam and himself now he's out of work and we can't –'

'Can't what?' Bethan interrupted.

'Haydn says we can't expect you to keep us for ever.'

'Haydn should keep his mouth shut.'

'I was thinking about doing this even before Mam told us about the Maritime closing, honest. You know what it's been like between Mam and me since Diana and I were taken down the police station. I'd rather live away like you did. Of course I'd miss you, and Dad and the boys, but it's not as if I'd be on my own. I'd have Diana,' she said bravely.

Bethan looked hard at her sister. Even with the edges of her slight figure fuzzy, blurred by drink, she looked small, very young and very vulnerable. Bethan grew angry, not with Maud, but with the unfairness of a life where Maud's only way out into the world was through skivvying in a hospital where they'd wring every last ounce of work from her. She wanted to kick someone and there was no one to kick. If she'd been alone she would have picked up the bottle again. Maud reached out, and Bethan opened her arms.

'I miss you already, Beth. It's strange not having you here in the nights to talk to.' Maud gave her a hug that took Bethan's breath away.

'If you're going to be a ward maid you'll have to get used to being by yourself.'

'I suppose I will. You are all right aren't you?' Maud looked keenly at her sister.

'Just tired, that's all.' Bethan extricated herself from Maud's arms, lifted the bottle of cologne from the dressing table and splashed it liberally over herself, soaking the front of her uniform.

'You've drenched yourself,' Maud complained.

'Bottle slipped in my hand,' Bethan lied. She dragged herself to her feet, forced herself to put one foot in front of the other and stood up. Then she knew that she shouldn't have drunk that last mouthful of brandy. 'I've got to go,' she mumbled thickly.

'Can I walk down the hill with you?' Maud pleaded. 'I don't want to stay in the house. Please?'

'Come on then. As long as you're quick.' Bethan wanted to be alone, but she was in no state to argue with Maud. She staggered unsteadily down the stairs. Eddie was sitting on the bottom step lacing up his boots.

'Off out?' Maud asked.

'Down to see Will and Diana. Anywhere's got to be better than here.' He jerked his head towards the kitchen door where Elizabeth was crashing the pots and pans as she cleared away the remains of the meal.

313

Bethan lifted her cape from the hook at the back of the door and they set off together. She was glad when Maud decided to join Eddie in visiting their cousins. The fresh air was making her feel extremely peculiar, and Eddie gave her some very odd looks before he and Maud left her at the foot of the lane that cut between Leyshon Street and Llantrisant Road. By the time she'd walked down the hill and was crossing the yard of the hospital she felt as though she were walking on rubber sheeting that had been stretched to its utmost. Her feet sank further and further down with every step she took. She had great difficulty in picking her legs up in order to place one foot in front of the other. No matter how much effort she put into it, she seemed to make very slow progress.

The staircase that led up to her ward was the worst. The steps were like wedges of sponge. Thick, jelly-like, they soaked up her footfalls and gave her no purchase from which to take the next tread. She kept her eyes fixed on the top and made a superhuman effort. The final step grew in size. It swallowed not only her boot but all of her, and she felt herself falling down and ever downwards into the depths of a huge dune like the ones Andrew had taken her to in Porthcawl. The sand closed over her, soft, warm, comfortingly, blotting the need for effort from her mind.

'I think she's coming round.' Laura's voice echoed towards her from a great distance. She couldn't see Laura. Only hear the sound of her voice as it rolled over a landscape of peaked sand dunes like the ones in the Foreign Legion films.

'I hope you're right.' This time it was a man speaking. 'She gave her head one hell of a mighty crack.' A man? Could it be Andrew? She struggled over the dunes, her feet still slipping, as she searched the horizon frantically for a glimpse of him.

'Bethan? Bethan? Can you hear us?' She ceased to struggle. There was no point. The voice was too coarse, too heavily accented to be Andrew's. It was Trevor's. 'What's Squeers decided to do?'

'She's with Matron now. They've sent a message to one of the sisters who's taking her day off. Matron says that if the sister can't take over she'll cover the ward herself. Trevor, what do you think happened? Did she just trip on the stairs like you told Squeers?'

Trevor knew precisely why Bethan had fallen, but he didn't intend to tell anyone. Even Laura. He could see the reason for Bethan's downfall in her flushed cheeks, her cold, clammy hands, her abnormal heartbeat and the odour of eau de cologne on her breath and on her uniform that didn't quite mask the smell of brandy. He could have kicked himself for allowing it to happen. He should have seen it coming.

'I feel sick,' Bethan moaned pathetically, reluctantly leaving her desert landscape for the antiseptic reality of the hospital bed that Trevor had dumped her in.

'I'm not surprised.' Laura rushed to her side with a kidney bowl. She held Bethan's head between her cool hands, steadying her mouth over the bowl. Bethan went through the motions, but very little came up. She felt absolutely wretched and ashamed. Hating herself for having to rely on Laura to take care of her. But she had enough common sense left to realise that she was too ill to take care of herself.

'Didn't you eat before you came out?' Trevor asked her sharply, as Laura went to empty the bowl.

'Yes,' she mumbled weakly.

'I don't believe you,' he said furiously. 'If you had, you would have brought up something more than bile.'

'I haven't been able to keep any food down for weeks,' she excused herself miserably.

'But you've been able to keep brandy down all right?'

She opened her eyes. He was looking straight at her. She began to deny his accusation, but there was something in his dark eyes that dared her to continue.

'For God's sake, Bethan. You're a nurse. You of all people can't plead ignorance. If you won't think of yourself, think of what you might do to a patient when you're floating around in this condition.'

'I'm sorry, Trevor. It won't happen again,' she apologised abjectly.

'Too bloody royal it won't. The first chance I get I'm going to tell Matron that the strain of night duty is too much for you. And when you switch back to day shifts Squeers will be at your elbow all day long. That should put paid to any secret drinking sessions, at least while you're on the ward. And before you go looking for the bottle in your handbag, I've tipped it away.'

Sudden agonising cramps cut across her abdomen and she curled up on the bed, her face muscles contorting with the effort it cost her to fight the pain.

'I'm not surprised you're in this state,' Trevor lectured heavily. 'Have you been trying to live on a diet of pure brandy for long?' He leaned over her, straightened out her legs and laid his hand on her stomach. His face grew serious as he poked and prodded her.

'Oh God, Beth. I'm sorry, I had no idea. Does Andrew know?'

'Know what?' she gasped as another pain crippled her.

He looked at her closely. 'I know you've been in a stupor since Andrew left, but you must know you're pregnant. Four or five months by my reckoning.'

She closed her eyes and tried to recall when she'd last bled. She couldn't even remember. It had been some time before Andrew left. And that had been a lifetime ago. She went cold with fear. She couldn't have a baby. She simply couldn't. Not now. It wasn't possible.

'Look, I'll go and bring the car round to the entrance,' Trevor said, embarrassed by his earlier anger. 'Then I'll take you home.'

After he left she broke out into a cold sweat as fear beset her. She felt sick again, and there was no sign of Laura. She looked around and saw the depressingly familiar walls of the delivery room. Crawling off the bed she made her way into the corridor, passed the bathrooms and went into the toilet. All she could think of was Trevor's damning diagnosis. She remembered Maisie and the other girls she'd delivered from the 'workhouse' side of the homes.

She collapsed on the floor. That was now her. She'd been a fool. A complete and utter fool. This was one disgrace that no one in her family would be able to take.

Desperate for a solution she cast her mind back to the women who'd been admitted after they'd paid visits to backstreet 'cure-alls'. Old women who operated in their kitchens and washhouses with knitting needles and phials of mercury. She shouldn't have to resort to them. She was a nurse. If only Megan was within reach. She'd know what to do. Then she recalled something one of the women who'd got rid of a child had said when she'd been brought into the ward. All she had to do was go home. Trevor might have poured one bottle of brandy away but there was another full bottle wedged behind her drawer in the dressing table. Her mother had used the stove that day, so that meant there had to be hot water. If she waited until everyone went to bed, ran a hot bath and drank the brandy while she was sitting in it she wouldn't have any more problems.

It would soon be over. And she promised herself that the bottle at the back of her drawer would be the last bottle of brandy she would ever drink. A few more hours – that's all it would take to straighten everything out, and put her life back on course. If it worked, if everything came right, she vowed to God that she'd devote her life to nursing, and never, *never* commit a sin again.

Chapter Nineteen

Bethan lay awake in her bed and listened to the sounds of the house closing down for the night. Maud was the first to walk out into the yard. She heard the distant murmur of voices as her sister returned to the kitchen and spoke to her mother. The kitchen door opened and closed. The stairs creaked and Maud stole into the bedroom and switched the light on.

She strained to keep her eyes closed and her breathing soft, regular. Feigning sleep she heard a splash as Maud tipped water into the bowl and washed. That was followed by the thud of flannel petticoats hitting the lino. The light went off. Moments later the bedsprings dipped and creaked as her sister climbed in beside her.

'Beth, you awake?' Maud whispered anxiously.

She remained still, loglike. Maud turned over. She stayed silent, locked into her own misery, reliving the awful moment when Trevor had brought her home. Seeing again the look of shock and fear on Maud's face as Trevor and Laura had carried her up the steps and through the front door with the news that she'd had a bad fall. There'd been such a fuss – her mother scolding her and everyone else within earshot; Eddie asking questions which Trevor and Laura pretended not to hear; her father mouthing platitudes that soothed no one, least of all himself. And none of them had even guessed at the extent of her true disgrace. That knowledge still remained her and Trevor's secret. But for how long?

How could she have done it? Allowed herself to be taken in by Andrew, to fall in love with him and bring dishonour on her entire family. She tried to hate him, to blame him for her drinking – for the shameful state she was in – but a cold logical voice of reason rose unbidden from the back of her mind, telling her that if he was guilty of anything, then so was she. He might have made the first move, but he'd never forced himself on her, and it hadn't taken her long to become every bit as willing and ardent

318

as him. The truth was that Laura had excited her curiosity, and she'd wanted to wear Andrew's ring, as Laura did Trevor's. If she'd been trapped, it was by her own desire to become Andrew's wife.

Her biggest mistake had been in believing that the easiest route to marriage was via the bedroom. Andrew'd never lied to her. Never promised her anything other than outings and picnics. She'd simply set her sights too high. When he told her he loved her she'd been the one to equate love with marriage, not him. And now, after what had happened to Megan, it was totally ridiculous of her to imagine that an educated, respectable doctor would involve himself with a family of criminals.

Wallowing in the luxury of self-pity, tears fell thick and fast from her eyes on to the pillow. A cramping pain shot through her foot. She moved it involuntarily and Maud stirred sleepily beside her. She had to remain still. She had to! At least until everyone was asleep. She tried to concentrate on the sounds downstairs.

She heard her mother raking the ashes out from underneath the fire in the oven. There was the dull slam of iron on iron as she damped down the flames with small coal, and closed the flue door. Just as well it wasn't the one night in the week when her mother allowed the fire to burn out so she could give the stove a good cleaning. Six nights a week her mother banked the fire, on the seventh she raked the coals and doused the embers. If tonight had been that night it wouldn't have suited her purpose at all.

Elizabeth went out the back before climbing the stairs. Bethan sensed her mother pausing for a moment outside their bedroom. She breathed in deeply, exhaling loudly in a parody of sleep. Moments later Elizabeth opened her own bedroom door and closed it. The sound of curtain rings grating over the pole echoed through the dividing wall closely followed by the screech of china sliding over the marble surface of the washstand. The floorboards protested as Elizabeth moved around the room while she undressed. Bethan waited patiently until she heard the final moan of the bedsprings on her parents' bed. All she had to do now was wait for her father, the lodger and her brothers.

Footsteps resounded in the street outside. She heard Haydn,

Alun and Eddie shout goodnight to Glan. Eddie must have left Leyshon Street and walked down to the Town Hall to pick Haydn up. From there they must have gone to the pub, because that was where Glan and Alun spent most of their evenings. Eddie laughed, a wild, high-pitched giggle as the front door opened. He only ever laughed like that after he'd been out with Haydn. She didn't need to see them, or smell the beer on their breath. They'd had a few. She wondered where they'd got the money from.

She continued to listen, tense and nervous, waiting for the familiar sequence of events. The latch went on the kitchen door as they took it in turns to go out the back. She picked up her nurse's watch from the bedside table and tried to read its hands but the plush curtains were firmly drawn and it was too dark. She tried to guess the time. Her mother always went to bed at ten. It could have been half an hour, or an hour since.

The latch went on the downstairs room directly below. Alun was going to bed. Soon afterwards the boys with much 'hushing and shushing' climbed the stairs and went into their own bedroom. A loud crash rocked the house. Eddie began to laugh again, and Elizabeth's voice cut, harsh and reprimanding, from her bedroom. Silence reigned once more. There was only her father to come.

The boys were both snoring when the key turned in the lock of the front door again. The heavy tread of her father's boots clumped down the passage and out the back. He must have lingered over a pipe in the back kitchen, because it was a long while before he came upstairs. The bed sighed as he climbed in beside her mother. She listened for the sound of their voices. Neither spoke. But that didn't mean that they slept. Her mother had been so angry earlier in the evening she could be playing doggo, just as Bethan was.

There was a steady tramp of feet as a late-night reveller, or worker, walked beneath her window up the Avenue. Then more silence. Later a dog barked in Phillips Street below them. Someone shouted at it. A cat screeched. And still she waited. Holding her breath, rehearsing a hundred times the moment when she'd finally put a foot out of bed. She just had to be sure that no one would be awake.

When she could stand the suspense no longer she rolled over

to the very edge of the bed. Slipping her feet out first she slid on to the floor. She crouched on the lino and eased open her dressing-table drawer. It gave a few inches. Then it stuck. She pushed her arm into the small gap, bruising the inside of her elbow as she fumbled around. She couldn't reach the bottle. The drawer wasn't pulled out far enough. She tugged at it again. This time it came out with a jerk that sent her reeling backwards, but even as she fell her hand closed over the bottle she'd secreted behind it. Not daring to feel beneath the bed for her slippers or rummage in her wardrobe for her dressing gown, she crawled towards the door, lifted the latch and, keeping her fingers on the metal bar, slowly drew it open. Resting her hands on the banisters and the wall she hopped over the stairs that creaked. She dared not put on the light when she reached the bottom step. Instead she fumbled along the narrow passageway. No longer familiar it took on terrifying twists and turns. Walls stood where there were none in daylight. The edges of the rag rugs curled, waiting to trip her up. Her heart felt as though it was pounding in her mouth when she finally made it into the back kitchen. She closed the door, leaned back against it and switched on the light, very conscious that she was directly below her parents' bedroom.

She had intended to carry the bath in from the back yard, fill it with boiling water from the oven, and sit in it to drink her bottle of brandy. Now she'd actually made it as far as the kitchen she realised how impossible that would be. The sound of the washhouse door opening would, in all probability, be enough to wake her mother, who was a light sleeper at the best of times. There was no way she could lift the bath from the garden wall, which was very close to her parents' open window, without making a noise. And then she would have to refill the boiler once she'd drained it, a noisy operation even in daytime. And aside from her parents above her, there was the lodger sleeping in the next room.

She sank down on one of the kitchen chairs and tried to collect her thoughts. She had to get rid of her problem. Of that much she was certain. She regarded her pregnancy as a problem, not a child. No images of babies crossed her mind. The likes of Baby Davies tucked up in her cot in the nursery of the Graig Hospital, all curly hair, sweet mouth and peaceful closed eyes above a small

321

round lump of nappy, was as far divorced from the predicament she was in as the Graig mountain from the Common.

All she could think of was destitution She only had two pounds left of the forty-five Andrew had given her. It was barely enough to rent a room for herself for a month, and that was without taking food into consideration. With Megan in prison there was no saviour on her horizon to support her in the same way Rhiannon Pugh was supporting Phyllis. Once Elizabeth became aware of the baby's existence, daughter or not she'd throw her out on the street. Left to his own devices her father might have taken a more charitable view, but it was her mother not her father who laid down the rules of the house.

Her Uncle John Bull would see that she was never accepted in his or any other chapel again. She'd be shunned, perhaps even stoned like Phyllis. Her only recourse would be the unmarrieds ward in the workhouse, where she'd have to wear the grey flannel workhouse dress. She wouldn't even be allowed to keep or wear her own underwear. She'd be forced to scrub floors and yards for her keep until her child was born – and afterwards she'd have to live in the homes until someone either adopted it or took pity on her and gave her a job as a live-in maid. Even then she'd have to hand over whatever she earned for her own and her baby's keep. That would be her life. She'd have no opportunity to save anything for a better one. There wouldn't even be any hope. She'd be like Maisie Crockett. . . .

She shook herself free from the bleak picture she'd painted of her future and looked at the clock. The hands pointed to three. Her mother always rose at five. Two hours. That was all the time she had. Tomorrow Trevor would return. He could slip up, say something untoward. Her mother might guess. She daren't risk putting off what had to be done for another day. Cradling the bottle of brandy on her lap, she considered the alternatives to a hot bath. Epsom salts . . . placing her feet in a bowl of scalding water . . . knitting needles – she caught sight of her mother's steel pins crammed into an empty jam jar on the windowsill, and shuddered. The hands on the clock pointed to ten minutes past three. Steam rose gently from the water boiler in the stove. If she was going to do something she'd have to do it now. But not here. Anyone passing through on their way to the back yard would see

322

her and if Alun and her brothers had been drinking that could be in the next few moments.

There was only one room in the house that was shut off, the front parlour. She tiptoed back down the passage. A full moon shone in through the lace curtains that hung at the bay window, creating a beautiful pattern of shadows on the floor. She rolled the rug back lest she soil it, and stood the bottle of brandy on the linoleum next to the couch. Returning to the kitchen she fetched one of the old sheets from the back of the washhouse that her mother kept to use as dust sheets when she was spring-cleaning. She had to risk the sound of running water, but not a bathful. A bucketful would have to be enough. She rinsed out the enamel bucket from under the sink and filled it with boiling water from the stove. It came out bubbling. It took two trips to refill the boiler with her mother's enamel jug. Switching off the light and closing all the doors she carried the steaming bucket into the parlour and set it, and herself, down on the dust sheet. She skimmed her fingers across the surface of the water and only just stopped herself from screaming. It was scalding hot. She touched everything she'd gathered around her. The dust sheet, hot water, brandy – what if she passed out with the pain, or was sick? Deciding she couldn't risk either, she sat on the Rexine-covered sofa and pulled the dust sheet up beneath her nightgown. Then closing her mouth around the brandy bottle she began to drink. She didn't find the courage to lower her feet into the water until the bottle was half empty.

Elizabeth rose before five as she did every day. She liked to blacklead and clean the oven and boil the water for tea before Evan and Alun rose at half-past. She dressed in her bedroom, putting on a grubby house overall, only stopping to wash her hands and face and brush her hair. She would have a good wash later, when all the dirty household chores had been completed and she had the house to herself.

The first thing she did on entering the kitchen was check the stove. She poked up the fire, breaking the crust of small coal she'd laid the night before. Then she raked the ashes out on to the hearth. Fetching the ash bucket from the washhouse she shovelled the residue on top of yesterday's, picking out any bits

323

that weren't burnt to dust to put back on the fire. When the grey dirt had been swept up and deposited in the bucket, she built up the fire with fresh coal and sticks from the scuttle that Evan had refilled before going to bed. Recollecting the events of yesterday evening she was even more parsimonious than usual, resolutely replacing five lumps of coal and a handful of sticks from her normal morning's allowance. Soon even Evan's reduced coal allowance would be gone. And she couldn't begin to think how they would afford twenty-five shillings for a load of coal with no man's wages coming into the house.

She went to the washhouse to fetch the bucket. She spent five minutes hunting high and low for it before eventually making do with the bowl she kept for soaking Evan's pit clothes. By five-thirty she'd washed the hearth and cleaned and blackleaded the top of the stove. While the kettle boiled she scrubbed her hands and arms under the cold tap in the washhouse. When she'd finished the water had boiled, and steam was just beginning to rise from the porridge oats she'd mixed with water in her mother's old fish kettle and set on the range. She laid the table, cut bread and carried the butter and jam in from the pantry.

Punctually, at five-thirty, Evan and the boys came down the stairs, and Alun walked in from his room. They fought over the tap in the washhouse, ate the breakfast laid out on the table and left, Alun and Evan to the pit, the boys to the market. It was Haydn's day to work for Wilf Horton, and Eddie had decided to go down to Market Square with him in the hope of picking up some casual work.

Left once more in sole possession of her domain, Elizabeth cleared the dishes, stacked them in the washhouse and relaid the table for Maud. She wondered what to do about Bethan. Perhaps she should take her breakfast up to her bedroom? It was probably best to wait until Maud had left. Bethan had certainly looked ghastly last night when young Dr Lewis had brought her home. But she hadn't entirely believed his and Laura's story that Bethan had slipped on the stairs in the homes and fallen. However, Bethan herself hadn't said much. Refusing even Maud's offer of help, she'd put herself to bed. But young Dr Lewis must be worried about her to say he'd call again today. She hoped the stupid girl hadn't done herself a serious injury. Without Bethan's contribution to the household budget she'd be hard put to buy food, let alone pay the mortgage next week.

She poured herself a cup of tea from the cold dregs in the pot and looked at the clock. It was past seven, time to call Maud. She left the kitchen and shouted from the foot of the stairs. Then, and only then, did she lift the hotplate cover and put the kettle back on to boil. She only ever brewed fresh tea if someone else in the house wanted a cup, considering it a selfish extravagance to do so just for herself.

Ten minutes later, washed, dressed, hair neatly combed back and tied at the nape of her neck, Maud appeared. She sat at the table and ate the porridge Elizabeth put in front of her in silence. When she finished she carried the plate through to the washhouse, returning to drink the tea that her mother had poured for her.

'Bethan was well enough to go to work then?' she asked innocently.

'Not likely, young lady,' Elizabeth said sharply. 'Not after that fall she took last night.'

'Then where is she?' Maud asked, looking around the kitchen.

'Where you'd expect her to be. In bed.'

'She wasn't there when I got up,' Maud asserted.

'Did you disturb her in the night?'

'Not that I know of, Mam. She was sleeping when I went to bed.'

Elizabeth left the kitchen and ran upstairs. She crashed open Maud and Bethan's bedroom door. The bed was neatly turned back, the curtains pulled, the sash window left open six inches at the top, just as she liked Maud to leave it. She darted into the boys' bedroom. She couldn't imagine why, but she thought it might just be possible that Bethan had gone in there. The bed was rumpled untidily, the wardrobe door left ajar, the window and curtains still closed. It was messy, but empty. In her own room the blankets were turned back and the window open, just as Evan had left it. She stepped across the landing to the box room and pushed open the door. It shuddered protestingly across the bare floorboards. The cardboard boxes in which she'd stored the wooden bricks, fort and doll's house that Evan had made for the children when they were small were piled neatly along the wall on the left-hand side of the room. She looked behind the

325

door. Her college textbooks were stacked where she'd left them, under a thick layer of dust. No one had been in here.

Fear slimed, sick and leprous from the base of her spine. If Bethan had left her bed to go to the toilet she would have seen her pass through the kitchen. She remembered Andrew. His sudden departure from Pontypridd. It was as if Bethan's disappearance had turned over a stone in her mind, uncovering a seething nest of fears she'd been terrified of for years. All she could think of was Hetty.

She almost fell down the stairs in her haste to return to the kitchen. On the way she opened the door to Alun's room. The air was stale, musty. The single bed was made, the sash in the centre of the bay open a scant half inch at the top. But it was tidy, his clothes hung away on the rail Evan had hammered across the alcove. She called out Bethan's name. Quietly at first, then louder, not really knowing why she did so when it was plain to see that Bethan wasn't in the room.

She closed the door and entered the back kitchen, checking the pantry, the washhouse and the back yard while a bewildered Maud looked on. She climbed the garden steps, looked in the coalhouse – the dog run – the shed where Evan kept his tools –

'Beth is all right, isn't she, Mam?' Maud demanded pathetically, seeking reassurance.

'I don't know,' Elizabeth replied tersely. She closed all the outside doors and ran back down the passage. Perhaps Bethan was in the street – she wrenched open the front door, looked up and down. . . .

'Nice morning, Mrs Powell,' Glan's mother called from next door where she was scrubbing her doorstep. 'How's your Bethan? Heard she took a bad fall last night.'

'She's going to be fine, thank you, Mrs Richards.' Elizabeth shut the door on the street. The parlour . . . she tried to open the door and failed to move it more than a few inches. Something was behind it. She pushed with all the strength she could muster and stumbled over the body of her daughter.

Bethan, wearing only a nightdress, lay on the floor, an empty bottle of brandy in her hand. Her feet were in the bucket, which had fallen on its side. The water it had held had flooded the linoleum, damming up against her rolled-up, best handstitched tapestry rug. Elizabeth knelt down and placed her hand on Bethan's forehead. It was burning. She moved the bucket and Bethan's feet fell out into the puddle of water. She thrust her hand into her mouth to prevent herself from crying out. The skin hung in long white threads from the red, raw mass of Bethan's feet. Someone screamed. It wasn't until Maud called to her from the passage that she realised she was making the noise herself.

'Mam. Mam!'

'Stay there, Maud,' Elizabeth commanded. Years of discipline paid off. Maud remained exactly where she was. Elizabeth thought rapidly. The bucket – the brandy bottle – she knew exactly what Bethan had done. She'd tried the same trick herself years ago. It hadn't worked then, and judging by the spotless state of Bethan's nightdress it hadn't worked now. If it had worked for her . . . if . . . She heaved the thought from her mind. 'Bethan's ill,' she said quickly. She studied her daughter's mutilated feet. She didn't want to send for help, but this was way beyond her nursing capabilities. 'Run down the hill as fast as you can to Uncle John's. Tell him . . . tell him that we need Doctor Lewis quick. Tell him to send messages to the hospital and anywhere else he might be.' She stared at Maud's face, white, strained. 'Do it!' she shouted. 'Now!'

Maud sprang to life. Not waiting to exchange her slippers for her boots, she wrenched open the front door and fled down the steps.

Elizabeth put her arms around Bethan's shoulders and lifted her out of the pool of water. She had dreaded something like this since the day Bethan was born. Now that it had actually happened she didn't feel any of the emotions she thought she would. She wasn't angry. She didn't want to punish Bethan – in fact one glance at Bethan's feet told her that there'd been punishment enough, and to excess. Instead of wanting to cast Bethan out, she held her close. Her heart reached for Bethan's as it had never done before. This was one problem they would face together, as mother and daughter.

Bethan's eyes flickered open, as Elizabeth stroked the hair away from her face. 'It's all right,' she murmured softly, laying Bethan's head down on her lap. 'I've sent for Doctor Lewis. He'll know what to do. It's going to be all right.'

Bethan looked down, plucked at her nightdress, checking the damp patches. Seeing only clean water she began to cry. She pressed her hand against her stomach. 'Mam. I'm sorry,' she whispered. 'I . . . ' She faltered. She had no apology. No defence to offer.

'It's all right. Try not to talk. You need to conserve your strength.'

'Mam, please, don't throw me out,' she pleaded feverishly. 'I have nowhere to go, I. . . . '

'Bethan, it's going to be all right,' Elizabeth said in the strong voice Bethan hadn't dared disobey from childhood. 'I know you're going to have a baby.'

Bethan stared at her mother, wide-eyed, disbelieving. Her mother knew what she'd done, and she was caressing and petting her? She had no memory of her mother ever doing that before.

'Don't worry, Bethan, I won't let you go on the streets or into the workhouse.' Elizabeth voiced her own fears of twenty-one years before. 'First we nurse you back to health, then we'll sort out your problems.' She looked hard at her daughter. 'Just promise me one thing?'

'Yes, Mam,' Bethan murmured. At that moment she would have promised her mother anything.

'No more tricks like this.' Elizabeth threw the bottle into the bucket with a crash. 'They don't work. All you'll succeed in doing is killing yourself. Now here, put your arms round my neck, let's see if we can lift you out of this puddle on to the couch.'

In one single blinding, screaming moment Bethan's feet came to life. She couldn't have moved them to save herself from death. If anyone had offered to amputate, she would have allowed them to do so, and gladly. Clinging tightly to her mother she sobbed as she hadn't done since childhood. Elizabeth's tears mingled with her own as they fell into the puddles on the floor. For the first time in her life Bethan actually felt close to the woman who had borne her.

'Andy, Anthea, is that you?' Fiona called out as she heard the maid open the front door.

'It is.' Andrew dropped his doctor's bag on to the hall floor, divested Anthea of her coat and hat, and handed them to the maid.

'Dwinkie?' Fe waved a cocktail glass in front of their noses as she peeped around the drawing-room door.

'I'd love one,' Anthea cooed.

'What is it?' Andrew demanded suspiciously, eyeing the peculiar colour of the liquid in her glass.

'Champagne cocktail, with some of my added, my-ster-ious ingredients,' Fiona purred.

'I think I'd prefer a small whisky, thank you.'

'You're worse than Father.' She made a face at him. 'Be adventurous for once in your life.'

'I value my stomach too much to take a chance.' He followed Anthea into the drawing room, and slumped down into a chair next to the drinks tray. 'Alec home yet?' he asked.

'Hours ago,' she drawled. 'He's speaking to Daddy on the telephone.'

'Daddy – ' He left his chair, 'I'd like to talk to him.'

'Daddy England, not Daddy Wales,' Fiona said irritably. 'There's some men-only thing on tonight, and they're both going. I don't suppose you two would like to take me out, would you? I hate staying in when Alec's out having fun. We could go to the cinema, or a show?'

'Fine,' Andrew agreed enthusiastically, ignoring the tight-lipped expression of annoyance on Anthea's face.

Anthea had written to Fe soon after his arrival in London. Pleading boredom, an empty wardrobe and a desperate need for an urgent London shopping trip she'd ask Fe if she could visit. Ever accommodating, and only too glad to have someone to stay to help amuse and lighten her lonely days, Fe had welcomed her with open arms, but Andrew had seen the heavy hand of his mother's interference in the scheme. And five days and nights spent under the same roof as Anthea had done nothing to dispel the unpleasant notion.

Anthea rose early so she could breakfast with him and, worse still, chatter about trivial nothings when all he wanted to do was eat, drink and read the paper in silence. She rooted out the small café where he and the doctors lunched when they could get away from the hospital, and turned up there with Fe in tow, feigning

329

amazement at his presence. She 'happened to be making her way back to Fe's', or 'passing' in the evenings when he was returning to Fe's after finishing work in the hospital for the day, a stroll he'd always regarded as a pleasant one until she joined him. And whenever they were alone together she prattled on about how wonderful life in London was; what a marvellous doctor's wife his mother made; and how well she got on with his entire family. Rather obvious topics that did nothing to endear her presence to him.

'Right, where shall we go?' Fiona asked as she handed Anthea a cocktail and Andrew a whisky.

'Cinema,' he suggested, thinking that at least he wouldn't have to talk to either of them while the film was on.

'I'll have a look at what's showing,' Anthea volunteered, cheering herself with the thought that Fe might go to bed early when they got back, leaving her alone with Andrew.

'Thank you,' Fiona smiled as she handed Anthea the paper. 'You've no idea how much I was dreading this evening.'

Andrew sipped his whisky slowly. He could understand his sister's reluctance to spend an evening by herself. He hadn't been comfortable in his own company since he'd left Pontypridd. The problem was, he often felt lonelier, more solitary and miserable when he was with someone else. Particularly Anthea. Outings with her had, if anything, sharpened his longing for Bethan. He missed her with a pain that became more acute with each passing day.

'Dinner won't be long.' Fiona freshened up his and Anthea's glasses. 'Oh, I almost forgot, there's a letter for you, Andy.' She picked up an envelope off the tray and waved it in front of his nose with a sly glance at Anthea. 'It's from Pontypridd,' she said, lifting her eyebrows suggestively. 'And it's not from Daddy or Mummy.' She sniffed the paper. 'There's no perfume. Your little nurse may belong to a den of thieves, but I'm afraid she isn't in the least bit romantic, dear brother,' she teased.

'Give me that, Fanny,' Andrew said irritably.

'My my, we are a crosspatch aren't we? What's the matter, Andy? Finding it difficult to get rid of her? Won't she take no for an answer?'

'Some women just don't know when to let go,' Anthea said,

allowing her acid thoughts to reach her tongue for the first time in Andrew's presence.

Andrew wasn't proud of the way he'd left Pontypridd and sought refuge in London, and every time he recalled how he'd taken leave of Bethan his blood ran cold. But Fiona's constant carping about her was driving him to distraction. He grasped hold of her wrist, making her cry out, then he tore the letter from her hand.

'That hurt,' she complained petulantly, rubbing her wrist.

'It was meant to.'

'Is it a love letter?' She tried to sit on the arm of his chair and look over his shoulder at the same time.

'It's from Trevor Lewis,' he snapped, flicking through the pages.

'Oh how disappointing.' Her face fell as she checked the signature. 'I suppose I should go into the kitchen and chase Cook up about dinner.'

'That might be an idea. I'm starving.'

'Do you want to come, Anthea?' she asked. 'If we leave grumpy to himself he might change his mood.'

Rebuffed, glasses in hand Fiona and Anthea wandered off. Andrew read and reread his letter. There wasn't a word about Bethan from beginning to end. Most of it concerned the wedding that was scheduled for the end of October, and there was a reminder in the final paragraph that he'd promised to act as best man, but if he couldn't make it for any reason they would understand and ask Trevor's brother to take his place.

The sheet of paper fell from his hand as he refilled his glass. Bethan would undoubtedly be there. Laura had always said that she'd wanted her to be bridesmaid. A vivid image of Bethan came to mind, reminding him just how much he loved and wanted – no, needed – her.

He swallowed the whisky and poured another. His father wasn't always right. Perhaps there was a way for him and Bethan after all. London was a cosmopolitan place. Cosmopolitan enough even to swallow a disgraced Welsh nurse and her husband. The idea appealed to him. He could go home, see her at the wedding, and ask her to return with him. Accommodation wasn't a problem. Half of London was up for rent, and if they started off modestly like Trevor and Laura – what the hell. They'd make it through. Thousands of other couples did. He didn't stop to consider that his thinking was a complete turnaround from that of only a few short weeks ago.

He'd been a fool not to have asked her to marry him when he'd had the chance. And if his parents kicked up a fuss, so what? He was qualified. So was Bethan. They could both get work. They'd survive without any help. His parents would have to come to terms with his choice of wife. Bethan was the only one who mattered. They didn't even have to marry in Pontypridd, they could marry here. He would carry on working at the Cross – go home to her every night instead of to Fe and Alec. Her aunts' transgressions were of no interest to anyone in London. No one would give a toss about anything that had occurred in Pontypridd. Most people didn't even know where it was. And in time she wouldn't be known by the name of Powell any more. Not even in Wales.

He finished his whisky and reached for the bottle again. He checked the date of Trevor's wedding on the letter. It wasn't that far away, another five weeks. He frowned as he lifted his glass. He couldn't wait that long; not after the way he'd treated her. He had to write. Tell her he was sorry. That he loved her. That he hadn't been thinking straight the last time he'd seen her.

A smile crossed his face for the first time since he'd been in London. His future stretched out before him, cosy with domesticity, glittering with the rewards of career achievement. A future that included love, Bethan, surgical duties in the Cross and a small but comfortable apartment to return to in the evenings. It didn't once enter his mind that perhaps he'd damaged his relationship with Bethan beyond repair.

Chapter Twenty

'You sure you'll be all right?'

'I've been fine every day so far, Mam.' Bethan sat in her father's easy chair in the kitchen with her feet propped up on a stool Haydn had made. There was a cup of tea at her elbow and a book from Pontypridd lending library that Maud had got for her on her lap. Two walking sticks leaned against the frame of the kitchen stove next to her. Her feet had healed enough to allow her to hobble out to the yard and back. She was grateful for small mercies; the pain of the walk was infinitely preferable to using the chamber pot her father had brought down from upstairs.

Elizabeth fixed her hat on firmly with the jet-headed pin that had been her mother's and checked her image in the mirror that hung above the stove. Her grey coat was close on twenty years old and it showed in the threadbare lines around the collar. The black felt hat was even older. Her dress was newer; bought at the market it was a cheap one that had shrunk in the wash. Its narrow lines skimmed even her thin figure too closely.

The woman who glared back at her from the glass was wrinkled, lined, old before her time, the result of trying to subsist for too long on air that was heavier on coal dust than oxygen, and on food bought with an eye to cost rather than nourishment. Cheap food, cheap housing, cheap clothes, she thought disparagingly, thinking not for the first time since Bethan's 'accident' of the clothes she'd be wearing if she'd managed to succeed where Bethan had failed.

But even then, unlike Bethan she'd had to struggle through all the physical and mental agonies of a failed abortion attempt with no one to help her, no woman to confide in. No one brought her cups of tea to soothe away her hurt. She'd been left to work through throbbing, pain-filled days. Her only comfort, if it could be called by that name, had been Evan's reluctant, martyred,

333

declaration: 'I'm responsible for your condition, and I'll do what's right by you, never fear.'

She'd felt that she had no choice but to accept his sacrifice. She held him to his promise, married him knowing that he loved Phyllis Harry. That if he and Phyllis hadn't had a stupid row that fateful night, he'd have been with her still. He never would have got drunk, made a pass at her after choir practice. A pass that had flattered her into forgetting herself for the first and hopefully last time in her life. If she hadn't given in, been stronger, if . . . if . . . Bethan would never have been conceived. . . .

'You all right, Mam?' Bethan asked concerned.

'Fine.' She picked up her handbag from the chair next to the range. She really had to stop thinking in terms of 'what if twenty years ago'. She wasn't doing anyone, least of all herself, any favours. 'I won't be long.'

'Give Uncle Bull my regards,' Bethan muttered from behind her book.

'I will.' Elizabeth pulled on her shabby cotton gloves and left.

As she walked down the hill she considered the immediate problems that faced her. Bethan! There was only one way out of that situation. She hadn't discussed it with anyone, and didn't want to. Gossip spread like wildfire on the Graig. One whisper to a neighbour could spread scandal over the entire hill, but sooner or later she'd have to trust one other person. And it wouldn't be her uncle. He was too wrapped up in the traumas of his own problems to spare time for the troubles of others. John Joseph Bull wasn't the same minister who'd ruled his wife and his parish with a rod of iron a few weeks before. He was a broken man, totally reliant on the daily trips she made down the hill to clean his house and prepare his food. Without her, he would have been sitting in squalor in front of an empty table.

She knocked on his door. John Joseph's door, along with the doors of the Leyshons' large house and that of the vicarage, were the only ones on the Graig that didn't have keys protruding from the locks. He opened it himself, and preceded her into the kitchen without a greeting. She noticed that his shoulders were rounded. Hetty's passing had pitched him from the prime of life into stumbling old age, a transformation she wouldn't have believed possible in such a short space of time if she hadn't witnessed it herself.

She'd never seen him stoop before, and when he turned to face her, running his fingers through his uncombed hair in an attempt to make himself more presentable, she noticed that the grey hairs at his temples had multiplied. Even his face had altered. It was thinner, more haggard.

'Elizabeth, you don't have to watch me as though I'm a child,' he said irritably. 'The cawl you made yesterday is still good.'

'You haven't eaten much of it,' she commented, lifting the lid on the pot and stirring it. She replaced the lid, lifted the pot off the shelf above the stove and put it on the hotplate. Only then did she put down her bag, take off her gloves and hat and hang her coat on a peg at the back of the kitchen door. 'I may as well check on your stove as I'm here.' She pulled open the door. 'Look at that,' she complained, opening it wide so he could see the dying embers. 'It's almost out.'

The coal scuttle hadn't been touched since she'd filled it the day before. She picked up the tongs, and fed the fire with large lumps of coal and a smattering of small coal from the bucket kept next to the scuttle. John Joseph sat in a chair by the table and watched her as she worked.

'Would you like some tea?' she asked, suspecting from the absence of dirty dishes that he hadn't eaten since she'd left the house the day before.

'I'll have a cup if you're making one.'

She allowed the remark to pass without comment. She filled the kettle and set it on the range. 'You promised to watch the fire,' she reprimanded. 'Did you put a match to the one I laid in your study?'

'No. The weather's not cold enough for fires yet. Besides I went out yesterday.'

'Where?'

'The chapel. Just for a look around,' he qualified.

Elizabeth saw the admission as progress. He'd avoided entering the chapel or seeing any of his deacons or parishioners since the day of the funeral. A lay preacher had taken the service every Sunday since Hetty had died.

'I talked to the chapel committee yesterday,' he volunteered. 'I think it might be a good idea for me to move. There's a chapel in Ton Pentre in the Rhondda, or rather two that have no minister. Too poor to afford one. But I won't need much money now that Hetty's gone.'

'What did they say to the idea of you leaving?'

'It was decided that I should discuss the matter more fully with the deacons.'

She took down the old cracked blue and white cups and saucers from Hetty's dresser and made the tea, bringing in sugar and milk from the pantry.

'Uncle, it won't be as easy for me to visit you in Ton Pentre,' she warned.

'I know that. And I thank you for what you've done out of charity for me, Elizabeth, but it's time I moved on,' he said harshly, his voice cracking with strain. 'You've enough troubles in your own house without coming here to take on mine. Has Evan finished in the pit yet?'

'Tomorrow's his last day,' she answered curtly.

'How are you going to manage?'

'I don't know.' She poured the tea, rammed a handknitted cosy on the pot, and sat stiffly across the table from him.

'How's Bethan?'

'Still unable to work. Doctor says she could be off as long as two months.' She couldn't look him in the eye when she spoke about Bethan.

'Stupid thing to do,' he commented. 'Knock a bucket of boiling water over when you're drawing it from the boiler. I don't understand. . . .'

'I told you, it was easily done. I was there,' she lied.

'Yes . . . yes of course, you said,' he continued impatiently. 'But if the bucket was balancing on a piece of coal you'd think the girl would have noticed.'

'She didn't, and there's no point in talking about it.'

'At least you've got Haydn in work.'

'He doesn't bring in enough to keep himself.'

'Then that husband of yours will have to do something.'

'Easier said than done with all the pits closing.' She lifted the cosy from the pot, and poured out two more cups of tea, pushing the sugar and milk towards him.

'I've something here that may help. It's not a solution, but you may find it useful.' He rose unsteadily to his feet and walked over to the cupboard set in the alcove to the right of the stove. He lifted down an old chipped jug. Pushing his fingers inside he pulled out a roll of notes held together with an elastic band. 'I found a bank book amongst the things in Hetty's drawer when I was clearing it out. Didn't even know she had money of her own. Probably her father gave it to her when she married. She certainly hadn't put any into the account for years.' He thrust the bundle at Elizabeth. 'I couldn't use it. Not Hetty's money. You were always kind to her, Elizabeth. She would have wanted you to have it. Particularly now with Evan unemployed.'

'I couldn't . . . ' Elizabeth began half-heartedly. Money would solve so many problems. Especially now.

'Take it.' He pushed the roll into her hand as he sat down. 'I feel it's tainted,' he declared, negating any notions she might have had about his generosity. 'It brought no happiness to Hetty. And it's not enough to bring you happiness either. I think you'll need a great deal more than the seventy pounds in that roll for that. But it's enough to pay something off your mortgage.'

Elizabeth stared at the bundle of five-pound notes in her hands. She hadn't touched a five-pound note since she'd given up teaching.

'I suppose I could use it to pay some bills.' She walked over to the chair where she'd left her handbag, opened the clasp and secreted the roll in the bottom.

'Of course if you'd prefer to open a post office account for each of the children and put something in it for them to remember their aunt by, that will be all right by me too. Only don't tell them it's there. Otherwise they'll spend it before they really need it. Especially Bethan and Haydn. Those two dress far too smart for my taste.'

'I won't tell them, Uncle.' She looked at the notes one last time before closing her handbag. Her mind worked feverishly. Hetty's money could be used to buy Bethan respectability. She could think of no better use for it than that.

'Mam, no!' Bethan protested tearfully.

'You have no real choice in the matter, girl,' Elizabeth pronounced firmly. 'As I see it there's only three roads open to you. Either you go into the homes like Maisie Crockett, become a pariah and outcast like Phyllis, or marry. And I can think of no other man who'll take you with the doctor's bastard growing bigger inside you every day.' Elizabeth painted the options as bluntly and as crudely as she was capable of, hoping to shock Bethan into submission.

'But I hardly know him. I don't even like him. He's old . . . he has bad teeth . . . he drinks. . . . '

'He's only thirty-five, and he's a good, God-fearing, Christian, chapel-going man. And if he does take a drink I'm sure it's not more than your father does from time to time,' Elizabeth added acidly.

Bethan remembered something her Aunt Megan had said one morning after she'd finished working in the Graig Hotel.

'Damned North Walian. Swept him and that widow of his out with the slops again this morning. There's more than a touch of your uncle's hellfire and damnation about that one, only he isn't even honest about it. All chapel on Sunday, and boozing when he thinks no one is looking. This is not the first morning I've put him out of the Graig Hotel when your mother thought he was staying with friends. Give me my heathen lodgers any day of the week.'

She shuddered.

'Have you anyone else in mind?' Elizabeth asked nastily.

'No,' Bethan admitted.

'Then we have no choice. Just for once in your selfish life think of someone other than yourself. This would kill your father if he got to know about it. Eddie and Haydn would feel duty bound to tackle the man, and to what end? To one of them getting hurt. Killed even, knowing what Eddie's like when he's roused to a temper. And what about Maud? Have you considered what her reputation would be when this little lot becomes the property of every rumour-monger and gossip on the Graig? She'd be known as the sister of a whore.' Elizabeth spat out the final word.

The speech had the desired effect. Bethan's raw nerve had always been her brothers and Maud. She'd spent her life playing the role of the protective older sister; she couldn't abandon it now. She stared down at her bandaged feet, resting on the stool.

'Do what you think best, Mam. You always do in the end,' she added bitterly. But the bitterness was lost on Elizabeth.

Elizabeth picked her time. After the evening meal Evan helped Bethan upstairs to her bedroom then left for a union meeting. Maud went to jazz band practice with the Dan-y-Lan Coons, and Eddie walked down the hill to the gym. She hadn't seen Haydn since midday when he'd gone to Griffiths' shop. By now he'd be working.

She cleared away the dishes quickly, and glanced at the kitchen clock. It was nearly seven. Maud was expected home first and she wouldn't be in the house until half-past eight at the earliest. Drying her hands on her overalls, she took them off and hung them on the back of the door. Straightening her blouse, she walked to Alun's door.

'Mr Jones, may I have a word with you?'

He opened the door. 'If it's about the rent, Mrs Powell, it's not due until Saturday and I am good for it.'

'I don't doubt that you are, Mr Jones. It's not about the rent.'

'Please come in. Sit down.' He pointed to the only chair in his room. An old upright kitchen chair. She sat on it.

'I wanted to ask you what you intend doing now?'

'Now that the pit's closed you mean?'

She nodded.

'I'll be honest with you, Mrs Powell. I don't know.'

'When you first came here you said that you were trying to save enough money to open a lodging house?'

'That's right.' It was a sore point with Alun. After a childhood and adolescence spent working fourteen-hour days on the hill farms and in the slate quarries of North Wales he'd promised himself an easier life. The rumours that reached North Wales from the south said there was good money to be earned in the Rhondda pits: five years' hard graft was all that was needed for a man to earn enough to set himself up for life. But here he was ten years later with only twenty pounds to his name, no job and still no sight of that good life ahead.

'Have you managed to save enough money towards that lodging house of yours?' Elizabeth prompted, breaking into his reverie.

'No. I haven't managed to save a penny since we were put on short time, and now . . . ' he shrugged his shoulders, 'I have twenty pounds put away. That's not enough to secure a house, and furnish it.'

'How much more do you need?'

His eyes gleamed hopefully. Could Mrs Powell be looking for an investment? He knew about her uncle the minister. And by all accounts her father had been a minister too. Chapel people were notorious misers. If she had her own money she could be looking to hide it from the parish relief investigating officers before Evan went on the dole.

'I could probably go ahead if I had another fifty,' he said carefully, watching her face for signs that he'd gone either too high, or too low. 'If I had that much I'd be able to buy all the furniture I wanted and put a deposit down on one of the four-storeyed houses on Broadway. There's one that I've had my eye on for months. The bank evicted the owners and foreclosed on the mortgage. They're asking two hundred pounds, but now that the pits are closed they might drop to a hundred and eighty, perhaps even lower. But whatever the final figure they'll still be looking for a deposit of fifty. It's in a bit of a state, been empty for a while, but there's nothing wrong there that I couldn't put right.'

'The mortgage would be a good ten to fifteen shillings a week,' Elizabeth warned.

'I'd have the rents to pay it with. There's a three-roomed basement that could be let out as a separate flat. Two rooms and a kitchen above the basement, and six bedrooms and a box room above that on two floors. I intend to let out the flat for seven and six a week . . .' He looked at her. 'You don't think that's too much do you?' he asked seriously. 'It's half a crown less than the houses in Leyshon Street.'

'It would be worth about that if it's got its own entrance,' Elizabeth observed practically.

'It's got that all right, back and front. I thought I'd live in the two rooms on the same floor as the kitchen and let out the rest. Seven shillings and sixpence a week for a single, and six and six each for those sharing a double. For that I'd have to give them breakfast and tea of course, but given enough beds – that's why I need the extra money,' he explained, 'to buy the beds. I could get at least ten men into those six rooms. With the rent from the basement that would make over three pounds ten shillings a week coming into the house. Even allowing for food and a woman to come in and do the cooking and cleaning, I reckon on clearing at least one pound ten shillings a week. If I paid that off the mortgage the house would be mine in no time.' He smiled, happy that he'd found someone prepared to listen to his scheme.

'I can see that you've got it all worked out, Mr Jones.'

'I've had nothing else to think about. It's been pretty obvious which way the pits have been going for a long time. Things would be a lot different if I had that fifty pounds, I can tell you, Mrs Powell,' he added craftily. 'First one house, then who knows, another maybe. Perhaps even a third if I could find the right people to run them for me,' he said unsubtly. 'Lack of money has never stopped me from dreaming.'

'If I gave you fifty pounds. Gave . . . ' Elizabeth repeated. She saw the greed in his eyes and knew she'd marked the North Walian right.

'What could I do for you that's worth that much, Mrs Powell?' he asked cautiously.

'A favour,' she said carefully. 'And before I tell you what it is you have to promise never to repeat what I'm about to say to anyone. Not now or in the future. If you say no to my proposition we'll both just forget I asked. If you say yes, that will be a very different matter. What do you say, Mr Jones?'

'That I agree to your conditions, Mrs Powell. What exactly is this favour?'

'Marry my daughter, Mr Jones. And quickly.'

Elizabeth led the way upstairs. She knocked on the girls' bedroom door and opened it. Bethan was lying in semi-darkness staring at the vista of rooftops and skyline framed within the narrow confines of the sash window.

'Mr Jones wants a word with you, Bethan.' She switched on the lamp, killing the soft, pleasant, twilight glow with a cruel blast of yellow light. 'I'll be in my bedroom if you need me. All you have to do is call out.'

'Yes, Mam.'

Alun Jones hovered uneasily in the open doorway of the room.

341

He waited until Elizabeth had closed her bedroom door before speaking.

'Won't you sit down?' Bethan asked, indicating the dressing-table stool. She felt calm, flat; the tears and emotion of earlier completely spent.

'I'll just say what I've come to say, then I'll go if you don't mind.' Intimidated by Elizabeth's presence in the room next door and seeing Bethan in the intimacy of her bedroom, he shifted his weight uneasily from one foot to the other.

'Suit yourself,' Bethan said ungraciously, steeling herself.

'I've saved some money, Nurse Powell, it's not much but it's enough to put a down payment on a house and there's one going on Broadway. It's got six bedrooms and a basement flat. I intend to take in lodgers. With the pit finishing I have to think of other ways of making a living. If you'll be kind enough to marry me, we could build up a tidy business between us. I'm not saying it will be easy. There'll be a lot of cooking, cleaning, washing and so on, but as I wouldn't be working I could help out.'

'Thank you for the offer.' The inane phrase was all Bethan could manage. She might have lived under the same roof as Alun Jones for three years but she knew absolutely nothing about the man. Nor had she ever felt the urge to find out anything. Given her indifference she felt that his proposal was ludicrous. Totally and utterly ludicrous.

'I know about – about – your condition,' he stammered, pulling his earlobe and biting his lower lip in confusion. 'And. . . . ' He took the bull by the horns and blurted out what he'd really come to say. 'And I'm prepared to accept the child in return for your help in my business. Of course it will take me a week or two to sort out a mortgage for the house, perhaps longer. But if you're agreeable I could make arrangements for us to get married in the Registry Office in Courthouse Street. It wouldn't be the same as a chapel wedding of course. But I hope you'll agree that it's what comes after the ceremony that's important. And I already know of one married couple and four men who are looking for decent lodgings.'

Bethan turned away from him and stared disconsolately at one of the Rossetti prints on the wall. It had been a favourite since childhood: the wedding of St George and Princess Sabra. She couldn't even begin to count the hours she'd stared at it as a child, dreaming of the day when she'd grow up and fall in love with her very own knight. Imagining the beauty and romance of the wedding that would follow.

'May I go to the Registry Office tomorrow, Nurse Powell?'

The question intruded into her lifelong daydream, shattering it utterly. Completely and for ever. She put all thoughts of romance aside and remembered her shame, her family, and her duty in that order.

'You may.'

She couldn't even bring herself to ask him to call her Bethan.

Four weeks later Trevor pronounced Bethan fit enough to return to work. They'd argued dreadfully during her convalescence. He'd wanted to write to Andrew about her condition. By dint of lies and a fair amount of acting she'd managed to convince him that the baby was the main reason why Andrew had left Pontypridd for London. Eventually, after a great deal of soul-searching during which she'd continually reminded him that she had the full and knowing support of her mother, he'd finally agreed not to interfere.

Armed with Trevor's medical certificate and terrified of receiving a refusal she requested that she be returned to night duty. To her amazement Matron agreed. She failed to find out whether she'd been given the shift because the hospital was short of night staff, or because Trevor had balked at carrying out his threat to ask that she be transferred to days. But once she knew she was being returned to her old shift she didn't care about the reason. She was simply grateful that she was being allowed to work with a skeleton staff, away from Laura's concerned and prying eyes.

All she could think of was holding out. Keeping the child within her a secret, from everyone except her mother and Trevor, the only two people acquainted with her shame. And maintaining her distance from Laura, her father, brothers, Maud – everyone who was likely to ask questions she didn't want to answer. It was easier to do that when she worked nights and slept during the day. The evenings were the only dangerous times, and she even managed to cut down on those by staying in bed until an hour before she was due on the ward.

At the end of Bethan's first week in work, Elizabeth made breakfast, saw Evan and the boys off down the hill, but, instead of settling down to do the housework she broke with her normal routine and went straight back upstairs to wash and change. When she came down a letter was lying on the doormat, just inside the door. She picked it up and turned it over in her hand. It was addressed to Bethan and bore a London postmark. The third to come in as many weeks. Why couldn't the man leave Bethan alone! She clutched it tightly, wanting to destroy it or open it, but lacked the courage. She'd sorted Bethan's problems out beautifully without help from anyone, except perhaps poor dead Hetty. She didn't need this. A few hours from now Bethan would be Mrs Alun Jones; a respectably married housewife with a lodging house and a husband to take care of, and a nice steady income flowing in to keep the wolf from the door. That is unless . . . unless she suspected . . . .

Elizabeth stuffed the envelope into her pocket, consoling herself with the thought that she might be reading more into the letters than they contained. Perhaps the man merely wanted Bethan to return something he'd given her. Perhaps he was warning her not to press a paternity suit. Yes, that was it. His parents had heard rumours, perhaps from Trevor Lewis, and he wanted to make sure that Bethan didn't implicate him in any way. After all, he hadn't ever really cared for Bethan. If he had, he'd have stayed in Pontypridd to look after her.

'Mam, I didn't see you, did I knock you?' Bethan asked as she walked in from work, drenched to the skin by the early morning autumn rains.

'No. No you didn't.' Elizabeth hastily laid her hand over her pocket, crunching the paper. 'Letter from the bank manager,' she explained. 'No doubt he's wondering, like I am, how exactly your father intends to pay the mortgage. You look soaked,' she said to Bethan, sounding positively garrulous for once.

'It's filthy out there.' Bethan went into the kitchen, hung her dripping cloak and uniform dress on the airing rack, and tied the dressing gown that her mother had ready around herself.

'No one's home except Alun,' Elizabeth volunteered as she laid bread and jam out on the table. Bethan knew that Maud would be in school. She didn't ask where her father and brothers were.

If they hadn't planned anything, her mother would have found some pretext to send them out. And then again they never needed much persuasion to leave the house. Her mother hadn't created much of a home to linger in, she thought miserably, closing her eyes to the dingy kitchen.

'And there's no time for sleeping either,' Elizabeth said abruptly. 'The ceremony's set for ten sharp.'

'I know,' Bethan agreed wearily. 'I'll go up and change now.'

'I'll bring your washing water up.'

'Thank you.' Bethan knew why her mother was being nice and resented her for it. Nevertheless she dragged her feet and went upstairs.

As soon as she was alone Elizabeth pulled the letter out of her pocket again. She looked at it one last time then she opened the dresser drawer, and thrust it next to the others, beneath a pile of tea towels. Only then did she fill the jug and take it up to Bethan.

Bethan washed and dressed mechanically, putting on her blue serge skirt and a white blouse. She packed her spare underclothes, uniform, slippers and dressing gown into the cardboard suitcase her mother had left lying on the bed. She'd already slept her last night, or rather day, in Graig Avenue. She took one final wistful look at the double bed she'd shared with Maud for so many years and went downstairs.

Half an hour later she walked back down the hill in company with her mother and Alun. He carried her suitcase; he'd taken his own to the house on Broadway the night before. She wore her old, shabby black coat which soaked up the rain like a sponge despite the umbrella Elizabeth held over both their heads.

They sat in the damp ante-room to the Registry Office and waited. There were puddles of dirty water on the mock-mosaic floor, and the brown paint on the woodwork was cracked and peeling. Bethan felt strange, remote. As if she wasn't really in the room at all, but watching from the outside. She started to weave a pretence that she was in the White Palace, seeing a film about someone sitting in a doctor's waiting room waiting for news of their loved one. Then Alun offered to help her off with her coat, and she returned bleakly to the world of reality.

She noticed that he was wearing a black suit, shiny with age and frayed at the cuffs. Not wanting to meet his eyes she looked away and saw a huge patch of damp that had spread across the whole of one corner, staining both walls and ceiling. She wove a fantasy, imagining it was a map, and when she was in the middle of populating it with towns and villages the registrar called their names. They left their uncomfortable seats and walked into a second room, smaller than the first. There were two rows of schoolroom chairs, a large wooden desk that held a book that had already been opened out, and a vase of dusty wax flowers. The registrar murmured something to Alun then left the room for a few moments, returning with a woman Bethan had never seen before.

'We need a second witness,' Alun explained.

The ceremony, such as it was, began. Afterwards Bethan remembered little of it. Mainly the absence of what should have been. There were no flowers, no music, no choir, no relatives, no friends, no laughter, no joy and no good wishes. Only the cold, damp brown and cream room, the rain beating on the window, the long silences whenever the registrar ceased speaking, and the strange woman and her mother standing behind her, blocking her only exit.

She must have said 'yes' when the important question was asked, because Alun pushed a ring on to her finger. She recognised it: a heavy gold band, dark with age and engraved in the centre with a single cross. It had been her mother's mother's. As a child she'd never been allowed to touch it. It had lain in pride of place in Elizabeth's half-empty jewellery box. She found it peculiar that a ring she hadn't been allowed to touch then, now bound her to a man she didn't know – or love.

'You may kiss the bride.'

She stared at the registrar then at Alun and panicked. She stepped back, stumbling over her own feet. Alun put out his hand and caught her before she fell. The registrar laughed.

'All brides are shy in company, Mr Jones,' he joked. 'But don't worry, you'll soon be alone with Mrs Jones.'

'Mrs Jones.' She looked around, confused for a moment. Then the enormity of what she'd done hit home. She was Mrs Jones.

Chapter Twenty-One

After the ceremony Elizabeth led the way back into the waiting room. The registrar and the witness said goodbye, and the communicating door between office and ante-room closed behind them.

'Well . . . ' Elizabeth looked at Bethan and Alun, and gave them a tight little smile, which neither returned. She debated whether or not to break into a pound of the twenty she had left of Hetty's money and offer to buy them a meal in Ronconis' café, but on reflection she thought better of the idea. After all, it was Alun who was sitting on the lion's share of the money, not her.

'We'd better be going,' Alun said, picking up his and Bethan's coats. 'I think the house is ready to sleep in but Bethan may have other ideas.'

'I'll see you soon, Bethan.' Elizabeth walked over to Bethan, pecked her cheek and left the building. She paused in the doorway for a moment to put up her umbrella, then began the long, lonely walk back up the hill.

She'd done it! She'd bought Bethan respectability, but her elation was tempered by the knowledge that the worst was to come. She had yet to break the news to Evan.

'This is it.' Alun turned the key in the lock and pushed open the glass-panelled door. The wood, swollen by damp, scraped grudgingly over the tiled floor of the porch, and Bethan found herself facing an inner door, glass-panelled again, this time in ornate etched glass. She turned the knob and stepped into a dark, damp, musty-smelling passage.

'It needs a lot doing to it, but I've got everything in hand. A few months and you won't recognise the place, I promise you. And you're seeing the worst bit,' he gabbled, afraid that her silence meant disapproval. 'The kitchen should be nice and warm.' He walked ahead of her to the end of the passage and opened a door. 'I paid the woman next door to lay a fire ready for us and clean up the place a bit. She's been at it all week. I won't be able to afford to pay her again of course, but seeing as how you worked last night and had a week's wages coming to cover the cost I decided it would be worth it.'

'That was thoughtful of you.'

He failed to detect the irony in her voice.

'You carry on and have a good look round while I put your case in the bedroom.'

He stepped past her and she walked on into the kitchen alone. It was a large square room, built one storey up from the garden. A range was set into the centre of the wall to her right. Clean, newly blackleaded, it radiated a little warmth into the chilly atmosphere, but the air was still several degrees colder than in her mother's kitchen at home. Shivering in the draught she went to close the door just as Alun came in.

'Sink in the kitchen,' he said proudly, pointing to a stone sink complete with wooden draining-board fixed under the window with a tap high on the wall above it. 'You won't have to carry water far for cooking or washing.'

'So I see. Did you buy the furniture?'

'Most of it came with the house,' he admitted. 'I know it's old, but it's solid.' He kicked the leg of the pine Victorian table to demonstrate its strength. The six matching upright chairs, two easy chairs and dresser were of the same wood. Chipped, stained, yellowed with age – the best that could be said about them was that they were still strong. The covers on the easy chairs were threadbare but clean; obviously the 'woman next door' had done some washing as well as cleaning. The shelves of the dresser were crammed with china, but when she went to examine it she tripped over the lino. She glanced down and saw that the floor covering was torn as well as stained.

'It needs a lot doing,' he repeated. The phrase was beginning to irritate her. Like the refrain on a cracked record.

'Is this the way down to the back?' Treading carefully, she opened a door in the far wall. It led into the washhouse. Glass-roofed and half walled in cracked, dusty glass, it was built out over the back yard. Another door led to a flight of rickety wooden steps down to the garden below.

'At least the kitchen's reasonably clean,' she commented, trying

348

hard to find something complimentary to say, as she returned to the kitchen.

'Told you I paid the woman next door to give the house a good going through,' he said, brightening at her show of interest. 'I know the walls could do with a lick of paint, but we'll soon have that done.'

She looked at the peeling paint, the damp patches above the sink and around the windows and thought it needed a lot more than a 'lick of paint' but she didn't contradict him.

'Come on, I'll show you the parlour.' He led the way into the front, bay-windowed room. A deal table-desk and chair were set on the bare floorboards, which had been swept, and a fire was laid in the cast-iron grate, but there were no curtains at the window and no shade over the naked bulb. 'I bought the desk off the second-hand stall on the market. I would have got more, but as this is going to be your room as well, I thought you might like to choose something yourself. When the money comes in to pay for it, of course.'

She stared at the peeling wallpaper and scarred surfaces of the skirting boards and windowsill.

'It needs decorating first.'

'I'll give you a hand to do that.'

He shut the door and led the way into the middle room. Dark and dingy, it was lit only by a single tiny window sandwiched between the protruding kitchen wall on one side and the house next door on the other.

'I'd thought we'd sleep in here. You can't hear the traffic like you can in the front.'

She looked around. As in the front room, the wallpaper was hanging loose off the walls. But this room was fully furnished. A large double bed, gentleman's and lady's wardrobes, a tallboy, dressing table, washstand and bedside cabinets all in the same clumsily carved heavy dark wood were crammed into its narrow confines. There was barely room to stand between one item of furniture and the next. The smell of beeswax polish hung suffocatingly in the still, stale air.

'All the bedding is new,' he said proudly, patting the dark green candlewick bedspread. 'The woman next door bought it in Leslie's. The furniture was the best in the house so I brought it down here. Would you like me to light the fire?' He pointed to the grate where a fire was laid, but unlit.

'It might be an idea. The whole house seems a bit damp to me.' She shuddered as much at the sight of the bed as from the chill in the air. It was ridiculous, particularly in view of the condition that had forced her to marry Alun in the first place, but until that moment she hadn't really considered that sharing a bed with him was part of the bargain.

'That could be because your coat's soaking wet. Come on, hang it up in the kitchen next to the oven so it can dry, and then I'll show you the upstairs.'

Taking her coat off and hanging it up was the first small act that brought home to her that this was the house she was going to live in from now on. Until then she'd felt like a visitor; someone who'd been invited to look over a friend's new house.

He gave her a conducted tour of every room except those in the basement; he'd already let them for six shillings a week.

'Not as much as I hoped for,' he apologised as if she'd been expecting more. 'But then letting it go unfurnished saves me the expense of buying beds and tables, and they don't come cheap.'

He'd furnished every bedroom. Three had double beds, two had twin single beds, the rest only one. He'd even managed to squeeze a short put-you-up into the box room.

'Could come in handy,' he explained. 'Even if I only charge four shillings a week for sleeping here, I'll soon recover the price of the put-you-up.'

'It must have cost a lot?' she observed, wondering where he'd got the money from. 'All this furniture as well as the down payment to buy this place.'

'I've a mortgage of a hundred and fifty pounds,' he offered defensively. 'And until the rent starts coming in we'll have to manage on your wages and savings and the five pounds which is all I've got left from my pit money and savings. It may have to last us as long as a month, and I warn you now the mortgage is seventeen shillings and sixpence a week. I also thought I might waive the first week's rent for anyone who's prepared to decorate their own room.'

'That might be an idea. The woman next door must have worked hard, but you can't clean dirty wallpaper.'

'We are in the worst room.'

They were standing in the bay-windowed bedroom built over the parlour. Like all the other rooms, it contained beds, complete with old but clean sheets and clean blankets. No bedspreads. A chest of drawers, a washstand, toiletware and a wardrobe. Nothing else. Not even a picture or an ornament.

'The first four lodgers are moving in on Sunday. If they're not agreeable about the decorating I'll give you a hand to do it when they're out during the day.'

There it was again, the 'I'll give you a hand'. This time she couldn't let it pass. 'I've never decorated a room in my life,' she countered.

'Didn't your mother teach you? I watched her when she did out your kitchen two years ago. She's a dab hand.'

'That's my mother, not me. Besides, I may have to work for a while yet. They'll not be able to replace me on the ward that easily.'

'I thought . . . I thought with the baby coming and everything you'd have to give up working in the hospital,' he said awkwardly.

'I don't intend to tell anyone that I'm pregnant just yet,' she snapped back tartly.

'That suits me,' he agreed. 'And if you're happy to carry on working it might be just as well if you do earn a wage for a few weeks longer. Just until all the rooms are full. That way we might even stretch to paying for someone to do the wallpapering.'

'I think that would be better than expecting me to do it.'

A crushing silence fell between them, accentuated all the more by the sound of the cries of the rag and bone man passing by on his cart. Alun sensed that somehow they'd got off on the wrong foot. He'd expected her to show more pleasure in the house; to be grateful to him for allowing the child to use his name, and for the roof he was providing for both of them. After all, there weren't many men prepared to marry a woman who was carrying another man's bastard. He'd even gone out of his way to make things easy for her. He hadn't had to employ Ada Richards to set the house to rights, but he'd done it. He'd given Bethan a lot better start than most wives had. Now it was time for her to pull her weight and show willing. Every woman knew what a wife had to do. And every husband had the right to demand that a wife do everything necessary to turn a house into a home. But instead of displaying the humble appreciation he'd expected, Bethan faced him unbowed, and unrepentant. Refusing to even try her hand at wallpapering, when everyone knew that the woman, not the man of the house, saw to things like that.

'I'll have to go into work early tonight before the day shift finishes,' she informed him briskly. 'I have to make an appointment to see Matron in the morning, to tell her I'm married.'

'Yes, of course. Are you hungry?' he asked as an afterthought. 'Because if you are, there should be food in the cupboard. I asked. . . . '

'I know, you asked the woman next door to buy some.'

He looked at her with such a peculiar, hurt expression that she couldn't help but smile. 'No, I'm not hungry, Alun, but I am tired,' she admitted, suddenly realising why she was so irritable. It was a strain just to stand and face him, let alone think about the future. 'I've been up all night, and if I'm to see Matron I have to leave before six tonight.'

'That early?'

'Yes,' she said firmly, knowing full well what was on his mind.

'Bethan, we haven't really sorted anything out, but then if you're tired, now's probably not the time.'

'No it isn't. I'm going straight to bed.'

'Would you like me to come and keep you warm? Just for a bit?' he asked suggestively.

'Not now if you don't mind, Alun,' she said stiffly. 'I really am tired.'

He reached out and squeezed her left breast hard. 'You don't know what you're turning down,' he leered, trying to unbutton her blouse.

'I said I'm tired,' she repeated, pulling her blouse together and backing away from him.

'Just one quick look.'

'I said not now,' she snapped, on the verge of hysteria.

'Tomorrow morning then.' He rubbed his hands together. 'First thing.' He might have been talking about a milk delivery. 'The *ty bach* is out the back. It's a bit of a climb up and down the

352

steps. It's not right next to the house, that's the coal shed. It's along a bit.'

'I'll find it.'

Shaken and repelled by Alun's crude advances she ran downstairs, opened up her suitcase, took out her damp uniform and hung it over the airing rack next to her coat. Returning to the bedroom she sank wearily down on the bed and looked around at the signs of masculine occupancy. She should unpack, but she couldn't bear the thought of lifting her clothes out and putting them away. Not here, not in this room that she'd have to share with Alun.

Eventually she closed her case and lifted it, clothes and all, on top of the tallboy. Steeling herself to pass him, she walked through the kitchen and into the outhouse. The steps down to the back were rotten in places and slippery with rainwater. The garden, if you could call it that, was a wilderness of waist-high weeds and discarded rubbish. She made out the rusting shapes of old cooking pots, pram or 'bogey' wheels, and a hill built up of old tin cans. When she finally climbed back up the steps she saw Alun sitting at the table eating a slice of cold pork pie smothered in mustard.

'Sure you won't change your mind about the food?' he asked.

She looked at the pie, thick with congealed fat, and almost retched.

'I'm sure, thank you. Will you call me at five?'

'It's twelve now.'

'That can't be helped. I'll try to make up for lost sleep tomorrow.'

'As you like.'

She went into the bedroom. The ancient cotton curtains were so rotten they fell apart in her hands when she tried to pull them. Hooking the ragged ends over the rail in an attempt to give herself a little privacy she checked the jug on the washstand. It was empty so she returned to the kitchen to fill it. Alun was at the sink rinsing his plate. He took the jug from her hand and put it under the tap.

'I've always been fond of you, Bethan,' he said clumsily, rubbing himself against her. 'You do know that don't you? That's why I agreed to marry you when your mother asked.'

She walked to the stove, ostensibly to warm herself, glad to be out of his reach. Then she looked at him, really looked at him for the first time in her life. Not that many years separated him from her father. And like her father he was broad built, although a good deal shorter, only about the same height as herself. There was nothing obnoxious about him. In fact the worst she could have said about his looks was that they were nondescript. Instantly forgettable.

His face was plump, circular, his skin pock-marked, his features regular, even. His round, dark brown eyes had the same appeal as those of her father's lurcher. But despite his not unattractive appearance and his bungling attempts at kindness she could not bring herself to respond to his brutish attempts to caress her.

'I need time, Alun,' she emphasised, as he carried the jug towards her.

'Not too long. After all, it's not as if you're not used to it.' He lifted her skirt and she pulled it down.

'Once more and I'm going home,' she hissed.

'This is your home, bach,' he said flatly.

She backed towards the door. Catching it with her hip she inadvertently closed it. Exhausted and frightened, she fumbled for the handle. He slammed his free hand above her head, holding it shut behind her.

'I'll take the water before I go,' she said bravely, holding out her hand.

'Bethan . . . ' He tried to fondle her. Instinctively she lashed out, kicking his shin and pushing him away from her at the same time. He tipped the water, soaking the front of her skirt and blouse.

'Serves you right,' he said angrily, 'for getting me going like that.'

'Getting you going?' she shouted frenziedly. 'I told you I was tired. That I'd been up all night.'

He turned to put the empty jug on the table. Taking advantage of his movement away from her, she wrenched open the door, ran out into the passage and into the bedroom, slamming the door behind her. Fortunately it had a lock. Not a very strong one, but still a lock. She turned the key and walked to the far side of the bed. Heaving with all her might she pushed it against the door for extra security. Just as she'd finished, the doorbell rang. She heard the murmur of voices as Alun answered it. He walked back down the passage, tried the doorknob, and when it wouldn't give, called out to her.

'That was the woman downstairs. Appears there's a problem with water coming up through the basement floor. I have to go and look at it. I'll see you later, but don't worry, I won't try and touch you again. Not today,' he said acidly. 'I can wait until tomorrow morning. After all, we've our whole lives ahead of us.'

It was with that thought in mind that, still fully dressed in her soaking wet clothes, Bethan finally cried herself to sleep between the freezing, damp sheets on the bed.

'You've done *what*, woman?' Evan thundered.

Elizabeth backed away trembling. She'd made Evan angry many times before. But she'd never seen this cold, savage temper burn in his eyes before.

'I saw our Bethan married to Alun Jones this morning . . . ' She looked past his shoulder and fell silent. Evan turned and glimpsed Eddie and Haydn, white-faced and dumbstruck, standing behind him in the passage.

'I want to speak to your mother, boys. Alone!' he ordered. Eddie retreated but Haydn stood firm.

'I have as much right as you, Dad, to know why our Bethan married the lodger without saying a word to any of us about it.' He folded his arms and stood his ground.

'She left me no choice,' Elizabeth said defensively. 'I had to arrange it. She brought disgrace on all of us. Would you have rather she'd brought a bastard into this house?' she asked belligerently.

'She wouldn't have been the first Powell to roll with a man before she was married,' Evan countered aggressively.

'At least I was able to marry the father of my bastard in chapel,' she shouted. 'Which is more than your precious Bethan could have done.'

It was the first time Elizabeth had raised her voice in anger. That, as much as what she'd said, sent Haydn and Eddie scuttling back down the hall and out on to the front doorstep.

'That's always been your problem, hasn't it, Elizabeth?' Evan ranted. 'You never could truck our Bethan being more beautiful and clever than you ever were. . . . '

'What good's beauty or brains to a woman,' Elizabeth hissed, 'when men use a woman for one thing and one thing only? You weren't concerned with what I thought, or my looks, when you walked me home by Shoni's pond that night after choir practice.'

'You didn't exactly fight me off. You damn well enjoyed it every bit as much as I did.'

'If I enjoyed it, I've paid for it every day of my life since. Putting up with your groping night after night. Bearing your children. Living amongst common worthless people who insult me every time I show my face in the street. Hearing whispers about you or your low, criminal family behind my back every time I walk into a shop. One slip. Just one slip. . . . '

'I wouldn't have touched you that night if you hadn't led me on, and if I hadn't quarrelled with. . . . '

'Go on, say it,' Elizabeth taunted. 'If you hadn't quarrelled with the great love of your life.'

'You knew damn well then and you know now that I wouldn't have touched you if I hadn't been drunk. All you had to do was push me away. Tell me to stop. But not you . . . you. . . . '

'Don't go trying to blame me for that night, Evan Powell. If it hadn't been me it would have been some other girl. Any other girl. You were like a dog looking for a bitch, and any bitch would have done.'

'I found my bitch,' he thundered violently. 'A bitch on heat. On the one and only night in your life you behaved like a female of any species. I wish to God I had gone with someone else,' he uttered fervently. 'Almost anyone would have done, because I don't think any other woman would have brought as much misery to this house, my children, or me as you have.'

'How dare you! You . . . you. . . . ' Lost for words Elizabeth lashed out with her fists. Evan caught her arm before she had a chance to hit him. Instinctively, without thinking of the consequences, he slammed her full in the face with his open hand. The blow sent her reeling to the hearthrug, bleeding from a cut on her mouth. Too stunned even to cry.

'Swine!' Eddie exclaimed feelingly as he sat on the doorstep.

'Who?' Haydn asked blankly, too stunned to think coherently.

'That smarmy bloody doctor, who else?' Eddie demanded viciously. 'Well if this is what I think it is, he can look out,' he threatened. 'If he ever sets foot in Pontypridd again, he can look out.'

Evan walked out of the house just after four. He'd left Elizabeth nursing a swollen face, split lip and black eye. The knowledge that he'd hit a woman for the first time in his life left a sour, rancid taste in his mouth, but it didn't stop him from hating Elizabeth with every fibre in his body. This time she'd gone too far. He'd never forgive her for what she'd done to Bethan. He'd worked with Alun Jones for ten years, long enough to know that the man didn't do any favours for anyone unless money was involved. He couldn't begin to imagine how Elizabeth had paid him. She of course had hotly denied that she had, speaking only of Alun's regard for Bethan. Regard! Pah! He spat in the gutter. He had to see Bethan so he could hear the truth for himself. But he didn't know her address. Elizabeth had said that Alun Jones had bought a house on Broadway. She hadn't even bothered to find out the number. And that was another thing – Alun Jones had talked about opening a lodging house for years. But he was too fond of the drink to save anything like the kind of money needed to put a down payment on a house the size of the ones on Broadway. There were far too many unanswered questions in this 'marriage' for his liking.

He clenched his fists tightly at the thought of Bethan being handed over to the man like a parcel of unwanted goods. As a lodger and fellow miner Alun Jones was one of the boys. But the idea of him as a son-in-law, sleeping every night in the same bed as Bethan, incensed him. Elizabeth had said she thought he'd make a good husband. What the hell did Elizabeth know about the darker side of a man's nature? The bloody woman had never taken her nightdress off once in all the time they'd been married, and more fool him, he'd never made her. When Bethan had been conceived . . . he thrust the image swiftly from his mind and concentrated on the bitter, frigid years that they'd shared a bed-room. The years when she'd used every excuse she could think up to repulse his advances. And he'd never pushed her, or forced her once, no matter how much he'd burned and ached for a sensual touch.

He tried to recall all the rumours he'd heard about Alun. There'd been a widow in Zoar Street who'd sported a black eye that gossip attributed to Alun's doing. And he'd seen the man himself going off with tarts in the pubs in town. Drink and women – that's where Alun Jones' wages had gone. Some life in store for his favourite daughter.

Inwardly seething, he slowed down when he reached the foot of the Graig hill. He strolled over to the group of idlers standing on the Tumble, and watched the traffic. People trudged past with shopping bags full of windfall apples and potatoes. Children carried newspaper cones that the bakers had filled with a shilling's worth of stale ends. Some of the toddlers already had the white pinched look of hunger about their faces that he remembered from the strikes of the twenties. His own children along with many others from the Graig had been fed then in the soup kitchens set up by the Salvation Army. And the *Observer* had reported that the Salvationists, ever ready to help in any crisis, were reopening the Jubilee Hall kitchens on the Graig again for the children of the unemployed. Charity stuck in his craw. But at least in the twenties the miners had the option of going back to work, albeit for less money. *They* had taken that option away this time, and he trembled not only for the bleak, hungry future of his own family, but for that of every other miner in the town. He damned the government, and the system, that had brought a whole class of workers to this misery.

Slowly, gradually the stream of pedestrians and carts dwindled to a trickle. The painted ladies of the town began to leave the two foot nine and join him on the station square.

'Out of work, love?' asked one small, improbable blonde who lisped badly because her front teeth were missing.

He nodded, not wanting to get into conversation.

'Come on then, sunshine, I'll give you one for free. For luck.'

He shook his head. There was something familiar about the woman. Something. . . . 'Dottie?' he asked tentatively. 'Dottie Miles?'

'Evan Powell?'

'It's a long way from Graig infants' school, Dottie.'

'That it is.'

'I thought you married Bill Moss.'

'I did. He died four years ago. Pit accident. Got to feed the kids somehow so I'm here,' she said, clearly ashamed that he'd recognised her.

'Do you remember when me and Richie Richards fought over you in the playground and Mr Lewis caught us and gave us ten whacks each?' he laughed.

'That I do,' she smiled, holding her hand in front of her mouth so he couldn't see the full extent of the damage to her teeth.

'Here, Dottie, take this.' Evan fumbled in his pocket.

'I'll not take handouts, Evan Powell. From you or no man. I earn my corner. Now if you should want to take a walk with me, it'd be a different thing.'

'I would if I could,' Evan refused gently. 'But I'm waiting for my daughter.'

'Didn't know you had one.'

'I have two, and two sons. The one I'm waiting for is a nurse.'

'That must be nice. Well can't stay around here all night talking to you. See you, Evan.'

'Bye, Dottie.'

She walked off down the station yard. The Cardiff train had just come in and she hovered at the foot of the steps eyeing the men as they ran down them.

At last Evan saw a tall slim figure dressed in nurse's uniform striding across the road from the slaughterhouse.

'Bethan love?' He intercepted her as she stepped on to the pavement in front of the station.

'Dad, I . . . ' she faltered. The nerves that had been blissfully numbed and deadened since Elizabeth had begun to make all her decisions for her jangled agonisingly back to life when she saw the pain in her father's eyes.

'Look, can you spare a minute? I have to talk to you,' he pleaded.

She opened her cloak and glanced at her watch. It was no more than a formality; she'd left the house a whole hour and a half before she needed to, simply to get away from Alun. She'd woken up, forgone any thought of washing, rubbed herself over with cologne and dressed in the bedroom, stuck her head around the kitchen door and said goodbye. She wouldn't even eat tea with him, telling him that she always ate in the hospital.

'We could go to Ronconis' café,' Evan said persuasively.

'All right, Dad,' she agreed reluctantly.

He went to the counter and ordered two teas while she found a table.

'You look a bit peaky, love. Do you want anything to eat?' he asked solicitously.

'The pies are good today. Fresh in,' Tina shouted from behind the counter.

'Then I'll have one please.' She wasn't hungry but she suddenly realised that she hadn't eaten all day. Still refusing to think about the baby's needs, only her own, she decided that if she was to survive the night shift she ought to put something in her stomach.

'Take the teas, Mr Powell, and go and sit down, I'll bring the pie over when it's ready,' Tina said as she pushed one into the steamer.

'Mam told you?' Bethan asked as her father sat across the table from her.

'She did.' His mouth set in a grim line. 'Beth, why didn't you come to me?' he rebuked.

'You had enough on your plate. Losing your job and everything. Mam said – '

'I don't want to hear a bloody word that your mam said,' he cursed savagely, slamming his fist into the table. Heads turned as the other customers gawped in their direction.

'Dad, please.' Embarrassed, she stared down at the table.

'Just tell me one thing. Was it your idea to marry him or your mother's?'

'Does it matter?'

'Yes?'

'He asked me. It was the only offer I had, and the way things are – '

'What about your young man?' he demanded angrily. 'Your Doctor John. He seemed a nice enough fellow. Surely if he knew the circumstances he'd come running.'

'He wouldn't, Dad,' she asserted bitterly.

Tina interrupted them, bringing over the pie and a knife and fork. She smiled at Bethan.

'How are things on the night shift?' she asked cheerfully.

'Fine,' Bethan replied mechanically.

The smile died on Tina's lips as Bethan turned away. She remembered the pit closures. It must be difficult for Bethan and her father, with only Bethan's wages coming into the house now. Just enough money to stop the family getting dole. She resumed her place behind the counter without another word.

Picking up the knife and fork, Bethan prodded the pie. She couldn't see what she was doing. Tears blinded her, as she remembered the last time she'd seen Andrew. The foul, cruel words he'd flung at her: 'You've dragged me down as far as I'm prepared to go.'

'He left me, Dad,' she mumbled. 'It's the old, old story. I should have known better. I'm sorry. I was such a stupid fool.' Tears fell on the surface of her tea.

He put his hand over hers. 'I didn't come looking for you to make you cry, love.' He had to struggle to keep his voice level. 'I wanted to tell you that you can come home. You don't have to stay with Alun.'

'But Mam . . . ' she began.

'Your mam's got no say in the matter,' he snapped. 'Come home, love. Where you belong. I promise I'll look after you. . . .' His voice trailed pathetically as the same thought crossed both their minds. How could he look after her when he wasn't bringing a penny into the house?

Bethan pulled a handkerchief out of her sleeve and blew her nose, wiping her eyes at the same time in the hope that no one else in the café had seen her tears. 'Alun's bought a house on Broadway,' she prattled in a forced, bright manner. 'It's been empty for a while, so it's in a bit of a state, but he intends to do it up. Turn it into a lodging house. He needs someone to cook and clean. . . . '

'So you're his bloody skivvy?'

'I'm his wife,' she contradicted with a firmness that amazed herself. 'He's promised to give my baby his name.'

'But at what price? Oh God, I wish you'd come to me with this instead of your mother.'

'Don't be too hard on her, Dad,' she whispered, remembering how kind her mother had been when she'd found her in the

361

parlour. 'She picked up the pieces when I tried to get rid of it.' She looked up. Evan was staring at her, horrified. 'I know, it was a stupid thing to do. Particularly when you think I'm half a trained midwife. But I was desperate. And when she found me, Mam didn't say one unkind word. Whatever she did, Dad, she did because she thought it was best.'

'Then you intend to stay with him?'

'I knew what I was doing when I married him. I'm not a child any more,' she declared vigorously.

He'd never been prouder, or pitied her more than he did at that moment. 'I know you're not, darling.' He spooned sugar into his rapidly cooling tea and stirred it. 'But please, Beth love, listen to me. We all make mistakes. God alone knows I've made enough in my time. But if there's one thing I've learned in nearly fifty years, it's this. There's no mistake so bad that you can't walk away from it.'

'Auntie Megan can't walk away from hers,' she blurted out unthinkingly.

'I wasn't talking about stupidity. Megan's made her bed, she's going to have to lie on it. What I'm trying to tell you, snookems, is that you only have one life. It's no good making a mess of it and sticking with the mess simply because you think it's the right thing to do. No one's going to pat you on the back or give you a putty medal for being noble. If you can't live out your life to make yourself happy, what chance have you got of bringing happiness to anyone else?'

He sat back and stared out of the window, embarrassed by the depth of feeling he'd put into his speech. It was fine enough. Pity he hadn't thought to take some of his own advice years ago.

'I know what you're trying to tell me, Dad. And I'm grateful. I really am.' She pushed the virtually untouched pie aside. 'But I married Alun because I couldn't see any other way out. And I still can't. I work in the homes. I see what happens to the unmarrieds.'

'That would never happen to you.'

'Dad, I'm beginning to think we're all one short step away from the workhouse. Alun was kind enough to take me on, and he's found a way for both of us to make a living. I owe him for that.'

'But. . . . '

'Look, I have to go. I have to make an appointment to see Matron in the morning.' She left the table, then turned back. 'Do the boys and Maud know I'm married?'

'They know.'

'Give them my love and tell them I'll see them soon.'

'I will.'

He pushed back his chair and left the café with her. 'The next few weeks aren't going to be easy for you,' he warned. 'Another day or so and the ins and outs of your wedding will be all over the Graig.'

'The sooner the better,' she said with more bravado than conviction. 'There's no going back. But thank you for offering to stand by me, Dad.'

She turned the corner, amazed at her own resolution. Perhaps she'd needed to talk to her father to sort out things in her own mind. She owed Alun for the use of his name and the respectability he'd lent to her condition. At that moment she resolved that it was her duty to pay him back in any and every way she could. Tomorrow she'd share his bed. If she closed her eyes and gritted her teeth, it wouldn't be that bad. After all, the thought of facing unpleasantness was always worse than living through the reality.

Chapter Twenty-Two

Evan waited until it was dark before he slipped out of the back door of the Graig Hotel and up the road. He looked around as he reached Phillips Street. When he was sure no one was about he climbed the steps stealthily and turned the key in the lock.

'Oh it's you, Evan Powell.'

'Good evening, Rhiannon.' He closed the front door and stepped through into the passage. 'Phyllis around?' he asked.

'Upstairs resting,' Rhiannon said tersely.

'May I go up?'

'You most certainly may not. I'll call her. Go and wait in the front parlour. And make sure you pull the curtains before you turn the light on. I don't mind telling you, Evan Powell, you're only welcome in this house because Phyllis won't allow me to make it any different.'

'Thank you, Rhiannon.' Evan closed the curtains and switched on a small table lamp in the parlour. Then he sat on the edge of the cold, hard *chaise-longue* and waited. A large, oak-framed studio photograph of Rhiannon's husband stared down at him. Below it, on the mantelpiece, stood a smaller one of a group of people crowding in front of a charabanc. He walked over to it and picked it up. The picture had been taken outside the chapel just before an outing. He studied the faces and recognised himself, his brother William, Rhiannon's son Albert, Elizabeth, Phyllis and John Joseph amongst the revellers. He, Phyllis and Elizabeth all looked so young, no older than his children were now. It had been taken the year before he'd married. Half a lifetime ago. They'd been on their way to Roath Park in Cardiff.

'Evan.' Phyllis came in moving with the slow awkward gait of a woman who's almost at full term. 'It's lovely to see you,' she murmured shyly.

'And you.' He kissed her sleep-flushed cheek, and smoothed her tousled hair away from her face.

'Sit down, won't you?'

'If Rhiannon will let me. To be honest, every time I come here I half expect her to put me outside the door.'

'She wouldn't do that. She's only worried that someone will watch the back and front of the house at the same time to see who stays.'

'I know she worries about you. I won't stay long. But look love, I've been thinking. . . . '

'So have I.' She smiled. Completely captivated, Evan watched her. She was beautiful when she smiled. Happiness softened the lines around her mouth and eyes, and lent her face a gentle radiance that never failed to warm his heart.

'Phyllis, please listen for a minute.' He took her hands into his own. 'You know I haven't got anything.'

'No one can say I went after you for your money, boyo,' she laughed.

'Let's go away together,' he suggested recklessly.

'I can't go very far at the moment.' She patted her stomach.

'Have you still got the money I gave you from the bet I put on Eddie?'

'Evan, it's only five pounds.'

'It's enough to get us away from Pontypridd.'

'To where?' she probed gently.

'Does it matter?' Anywhere, as long as it's away from here.'

'It will matter when the five pounds runs out. And while we're running what will Elizabeth and the children do?'

'Elizabeth and the children don't need me any more. Not even Maud. She's going to work in a hospital next month. Bethan's married. . . . '

'Bethan!' Phyllis exclaimed. Then she sensed the pain within him and fell silent.

'The boys can take care of themselves,' he continued quickly, agitatedly. 'Haydn's got a steady job and will see Eddie all right.'

'And Elizabeth?' she enquired softly.

'I couldn't give a damn about Elizabeth,' he said harshly.

'Evan, I want us to be together more than anything else in the world, but not like this. Not because you're angry with Elizabeth. That would be for all the wrong reasons.'

'What about this little one – ' He curved his strong calloused

365

hands with their blackened, broken nails tenderly around her stomach. 'Isn't he reason enough for us to be together?'

'Not when you have other duties and other calls on you, Evan. I never intended to trap you or make you unhappy.'

'And you haven't.'

He left his chair and knelt at her feet.

'Phyllis, if I talk to Elizabeth. If I square it up with her, will you come away with me?'

'Please, sweetheart, don't make it harder for me than it already is. You know I'd like to say yes, but I'm not sure I can. Rhiannon's been good to me. I can't leave her.'

'We'll find someone else to look after Rhiannon.'

'Even if we did, running away from our problems won't solve them. Nor will five pounds keep us for very long,' she said practically.

He sank back on his heels. 'There has to be something I can do,' he said, raging at his own impotence.

She cupped her hands round his face. 'Keep on coming to see me from time to time. Like this.'

'And if I leave Elizabeth?'

'Please don't. Not on my account. We both have responsibilities. Me to Rhiannon. You to Elizabeth.'

'Then we'll never live together,' he said bitterly.

'I didn't say that.'

'Yes you did.'

The grandmother clock ticked deafeningly into the silence. He buried his head in her lap. She ran her fingers through his thick black hair, noticing many grey strands that hadn't been there a year ago.

'If we could sit like this, *Sion a Sian* in front of a fireplace most nights, Evan Powell, I'd be happy,' she murmured. 'Even if the whole world shunned me in the day, and I didn't have a penny to buy a lump of coal for the fire, or a slice of bread for the table.'

He lifted his head and looked at her. 'Do you mean that, Phyllis Harry?'

She kissed the tip of his nose, and smiled into his black eyes. 'I mean it, cariad.'

'Then I'll try to find a way for us to be together. I promise you I'll try.'

'The only promise I want you to make is to call in and see me whenever you can,' Phyllis replied. More realistic than Evan, she'd long since learned to be content with the cards that the fates had dealt her.

Bethan was still writing out the patients' reports when Laura walked into the office at five-thirty in the morning.

'You're early,' Bethan said, closing one of the files.

'I saw your Haydn yesterday. Beth, how could you do it? How could you marry Alun Jones without saying a word to anyone? What about Andrew?'

'He went to London.'

'Beth, did you ever look into his face when he looked at you? Even that first night when he and Trevor took us to the theatre, and I wanted him for myself. I tried every trick in the book and a few more, but he wouldn't take his eyes off you. If that wasn't love I don't know what is. The man clearly adores you.'

'It was that belief that got me into the condition I'm in,' Bethan retorted crudely.

Laura's hand flew to her mouth. 'Oh Holy Mother of God! Haydn didn't say. . . . '

'He was probably too embarrassed.' Bethan put down her pen and leaned back in her chair. She was finding it a lot easier to talk about her situation than she'd expected.

'Why didn't you tell me?' Laura demanded when she managed to speak again.

'So you could do what?' Bethan asked coolly.

'I don't know,' Laura said in exasperation. 'It's just that I thought I was your best friend.'

'You are.' Bethan smiled. A grim, wintry smile that failed to touch her eyes. 'Look on the bright side. I'm a lot better off than the Maisie Crocketts of this workhouse.'

'But what about Andrew? Does he know you've married Alun?'

'No, and I doubt that he'd care.'

'Of course he'd care. He loves you. And if he knew there was a baby. . . . '

'He'd do sweet nothing. I really don't want to talk about

367

Andrew,' Bethan said petulantly. 'He left me, not the other way round. I have to think of myself.'

'So you married Alun Jones?'

'The child needs a name, Alun was kind enough to offer. No one else came forward.'

'But you and Andrew were like Trevor and me,' Laura persisted stubbornly. 'You had something special. . . . '

'He had something special all right,' Bethan said harshly. 'He had a girl who was stupid enough to open her legs when he said he loved her.'

Laura sat down abruptly. She'd come in early to give Bethan a piece of her mind, believing that Bethan had married Alun Jones on the rebound purely to spite Andrew because they'd had a silly row. Now she didn't know what to think.

'Is there anything that I can do?' she asked finally.

'You could congratulate me,' Bethan suggested flatly.

'But Beth,' Laura ventured tentatively. 'Is this what you want?'

'Whether I want it or not, this is what I've got.'

'Oh Bethan.' Laura shook her head miserably. She felt suddenly guilty for having a wedding and Trevor to look forward to.

'Please, no pity. Not from you, I couldn't stand it. It's friendship I need. Now more than ever.'

'You've got it.' Laura crushed her in an enormous hug. 'You'll always have it. I promise you.'

'Even when you're a doctor's wife and live on the Common?' Bethan tried to smile but tears fell despite her efforts. She rubbed her eyes with her sleeve. 'I'm sorry, all I seem to do these days is cry.'

'That's all right, the starch in my uniform could do with softening. And yes, I'll be your friend even when I'm a doctor's wife. That's if you'll come to my wedding?'

'Laura, I don't know,' she answered uneasily.

'Please, you agreed to be bridesmaid.'

'Not like this.' Bethan laid her hand across her abdomen. 'I'm getting married in six days not six months.'

'In six days I will be almost six months.'

'You don't look it. Are you sure?'

'You're asking a nurse who almost made it to midwife.'

'All right, I'll let you off being my bridesmaid,' Laura compromised, 'on condition you come to the wedding as an honoured guest. I hope you realise this means that I'm going to have to put up with all five of my sisters trotting up the aisle after me in their Whitsun dresses, because if I choose one the others won't speak to me for months, if ever again.'

'Please, Laura, I'd really rather not come if you don't mind,' Bethan begged.

'I do mind.'

'I couldn't face him.' Bethan didn't have to say who 'him' was. They both knew.

'I don't think he'll come,' Laura said hesitatingly. 'I made Trevor write to him. . . . '

'To tell him what?' Bethan interrupted anxiously.

'Nothing about you, I swear,' Laura reassured quickly. 'I told Trevor I didn't want him there. Not if you two weren't speaking. After all, you're my best friend and Andrew's. . . . '

'What?' Bethan broke in quickly.

'Only a friend of Trevor's. And that puts him way down in the pecking order of importance when it comes to *my* wedding.'

'Oh Laura!' A peculiar expression, half pain, half tenderness, crossed Bethan's face.

'Then you'll come?'

'I'll see.'

It wasn't the assurance Laura wanted, but she knew that for the moment it was all she was going to get.

The pride that had sustained Bethan in her encounters with her father and Laura left her, and she felt weak, tired and sick when she finally left the hospital after seeing Matron at the end of her shift. Without thinking she turned right instead of left in High Street and began to walk up the Graig hill towards Graig Avenue. She reached Temple Chapel before she realised she was going the wrong way. Feeling extremely foolish she turned and began the walk down the hill and out along Broadway. Another two weeks . . . that's all she had left in the hospital before she'd be spending every minute of every day in Alun's company.

The interview with Matron hadn't gone as smoothly as she'd hoped. Astute, and experienced in life, particularly in Pontypridd life, Matron had taken one look at her, asked if she was pregnant, and dared her to say no. Bethan had to admit it. There was generally only one reason for marriages as quick and secretive as hers and Alun's, and when she recalled the gossip she and Andrew had generated in the hospital – gossip that Matron was undoubtedly aware of – she blanched in embarrassment.

'To be honest, I'll be sorry to lose you, Nurse Powell,' Matron announced briskly. 'Good nurses who are responsible, reliable and prepared to work nights are few and far between.' Bethan wondered if there really had been a flicker in Matron's eye when she'd said the words 'responsible and reliable', or if it had been her imagination. 'But as you no doubt appreciate, I cannot have a pregnant nurse working on the wards,' she continued practically. 'Particularly the maternity ward where there's so much heavy lifting to be done.'

'I'll be sorry to leave,' Bethan apologised.

'Well at least I know why you've neglected your studies of late.'

'I'm sorry, Matron,' Bethan repeated dully.

'I suppose it's perfectly understandable, if disappointing given the circumstances. Young girls will marry. But don't allow that brain of yours to atrophy, Nurse Powell. You're an intelligent woman. Don't forget it. And should you ever want to return to nursing, please come and see me first, before applying to any other hospital.'

'I will, Matron. Thank you.'

She'd walked away, trying not to think of her shattered career – of Alun waiting for her in the dingy house on Broadway. She shuddered at the thought of what lay ahead of her that morning. The imminent prospect of sharing Alun's bed, of his sweaty, hairy body lying next to hers, of him touching her as Andrew had. Kissing her, sharing the most intimate moments of her life.

She almost turned back when she reached the slaughterhouse at the town end of the road. Then she remembered she had nowhere else to go. She thought of Hetty, and something akin to envy stirred within her. Oblivion seemed a preferable alternative to the life that stretched before her in that damp, bleak, run-down house.

She walked on along the shining, waterlogged grey pavement,

glancing up at the other houses in the terrace. Some were bright, clean, gleaming with new paint and freshly washed lace curtains at the windows. If it had been the old Andrew of the spring and early summer who'd been waiting for her further down the road instead of Alun, she'd be running towards him, not dragging her feet. Making plans to transform the house into a comfortable and cosy haven from the world.

She had to force herself to recall that Andrew had rejected her. That he despised her. Never wanted to see her again. It was Alun not him who was waiting. . . .

'Can't go in there, Nurse,' a young constable barked officiously as he rocked on his heels in the doorway, full of self-importance at the task that had been entrusted to him.

'I live here,' Bethan protested mildly.

'Do you now?'

'She does.' Megan's brother Huw interrupted from the porch behind him. He looked down at Bethan. 'You'd better come in, love,' he said gently. 'I think we've got some news for you.'

The young constable stepped aside. She followed Huw down the passage, squeezing past two policemen who were standing outside the open bedroom door watching Alun dress. One of them stepped inside and closed the door as she passed.

'What's going on?' she demanded of Huw. The sight of so many men milling around in uniform took her back to that fateful Sunday morning in Megan's. And all the foul, disastrous repercussions of that awful day.

'Is it all right if I tell her, Sarge?' Huw asked the same sergeant who'd supervised the ransacking of the houses in Leyshon Street.

'Go ahead.' The sergeant squinted at Bethan as he left the back kitchen. 'Haven't I seen you before, Nurse?'

'Yes,' she answered briefly, not about to volunteer information as to where.

Huw guided her into the kitchen where the kettle was just beginning to boil on the stove. Without stopping to take off her cloak, she walked over to the range, lifted it off the hotplate and picked up the hook to replace the cover.

'Don't do that, love,' Huw stopped her. 'I'll make us both a cup of tea. You look as though you could do with one. It's a long cold walk from the hospital to here in the rain.'

'It is,' she agreed, taking off her cloak and sitting in one of the easy chairs.

The tea caddy, sugar basin, milk jug and cups were already laid out on the table. Huw put the kettle back on to boil while he warmed the pot and spooned in the tea.

'You got married yesterday then?' he asked.

'Yes,' she answered flatly.

'Bit sudden, wasn't it?'

'No doubt you've guessed the reason why,' she retorted sullenly, resenting his prying.

'We were afraid of that.'

'We?' She looked questioningly at him as he spooned three sugars into both of the teas without asking her what she took.

'Me and my sergeant.' He handed her a cup.

'Who I marry is none of your, or your sergeant's, concern.'

'If it's Alun Jones it could be,' he said mysteriously. 'And then again from what Megan told me I never reckoned on you marrying Alun. I thought you were going out with that doctor fellow.'

'I was.'

'Tell me,' he eased his bulk into the small rickety chair opposite her, 'do you love Alun?'

'Why do you ask?'

'It could be important.'

'No,' she answered honestly, taking a sip of the strong, bittersweet tea. 'Why? Has he done something terrible?'

'To you, love, yes. Mary Bennett came down the station last night. Know her?'

'I'm afraid I don't.'

'I thought you might at least have known the name. Alun's had his feet under her table for years, if you take my meaning.'

'Is she the widow who lives down the bottom of the Graig hill?' she asked, recalling something Megan had said.

'That's the one. She heard the gossip about you and Alun yesterday, and came to see us. Appears he told her years ago that he wanted to marry her, but couldn't because he wasn't free.' He took Bethan's cup from her fingers, and enveloped her freezing hands in his great calloused paws. 'He's already married, love. Left a wife and two children in North Wales ten years ago. Never sent them a word or a penny in all that time. Not even a present for the kiddies at Christmas or on their birthdays. We telegraphed Wrexham last night. There's no doubt that it's him. He even admitted it when we tackled him about it this morning. He thought he could get away with it. And knowing you, love, I'm not surprised he tried. You would make any man a wife to be proud of. I'm only sorry that I have to be the one to tell you.'

She stared at him, dumbfounded.

'It's not that you've done anything wrong,' Huw tried to reassure her, putting his huge tree-trunk of an arm round her shoulders. 'But you've still got to come down the station. Just to make a statement. There's nothing to worry about, I promise you. I'll stay with you all the time if you want me to. And afterwards I'll ask the sergeant if I can borrow a police car and driver to take you home.'

'Home?' She stared at him blankly.

'Graig Avenue,' he suggested gently.

'Alun's already married?' she repeated dully, trying to digest the enormity of what he was telling her.

'Yes.'

'Then the ceremony yesterday . . . ?'

'Doesn't mean anything, love.'

'The wedding certificate?'

'Isn't worth the paper it's printed on.'

She began to laugh. A high-pitched giggle that bordered on hysteria.

'Please, love, don't take on so.'

She bent her head and kissed Huw's bristly cheek. 'I'm not married?'

'No,' he replied, bewildered by her reaction.

'Uncle Huw, you're a wonderful, wonderful man. Don't look at me like that,' she commanded between gales of laughter. 'Can't you see how hilarious this all is!'

True to his word, Huw took charge of everything. He suggested that she pack all her belongings before they left the house, and carried her case out to the waiting police car. Alun, he assured her, had gone ahead in a police van. He steered her thoughtfully through the procedure at the station, oiling the formalities with several cups of sickly sweet, strong tea. He sat with her while she made her statement, explaining every detail in simple terms that could be easily understood, even by her, in her shocked state. He parried the sergeant's suggestion that she should see Alun, allowing her to make her own response.

It was swift, and decisive.

'If I never see Alun Jones again it will be too soon.'

The policemen who overheard her shook their heads knowingly. They saw a beautiful, wronged woman smarting from hurt pride. Not one of them realised she genuinely felt indifferent towards Alun and his fate. But she didn't see, care for or solicit their sympathy. All she could think of was that she was in possession of her own life again. She had her freedom. Penniless, pregnant, it danced ahead of her, a glittering spectre that brightened her future. At that moment she failed to see the other ghosts crowding in the wings. The shades of hunger, shame and destitution.

'Dad, please, do the rights and wrongs matter?' Bethan pleaded wearily. 'What's done is done. Can I or can I not come home?'

'Of course you can, Beth,' Evan said, ashamed of himself for keeping her and Huw talking in the passage when by the look of her all she needed was her bed. 'Look, I'll carry your case upstairs.'

'Will you take a cup of tea with us, Constable Griffiths?' Elizabeth asked as Evan left the room, struggling to remember her manners after suffering the trauma of having Bethan walk through the door with a policeman in tow, who told tales of Alun Jones and bigamy.

'I won't if you don't mind, Mrs Powell,' Huw refused, trying not to show too much interest in the cuts and bruises on Elizabeth's face. 'I've got to get back to the station. We'll probably need you in court, Bethan. You know that. But it won't be for a few weeks yet.'

Bethan sank wearily on to a kitchen chair and nodded. 'Thank you for bringing me home, Uncle Huw.'

'That's all right, love. Mrs Powell. Evan.' He passed Evan in the passage on his way out.

'Uncle Huw!' Bethan ran after him.

'Yes, love?'

'Have you seen Auntie Megan?'

'Yes. Last week.'

'How is she?'

'As well as can be expected,' he said uneasily, conscious of Elizabeth's disapproving eye in the background.

'She is still in Cardiff prison, isn't she? They're not going to move her?'

'Not as far as I know.'

'Next time you see her, tell her I'll be in to see her as soon as I can,' Bethan said, not even considering Elizabeth's wishes. For the first time in her life she was thinking only of herself. Of how much she wanted to talk over what had happened to her with someone who would understand. She knew of no one who would understand better than Megan.

'We'll both go and see her,' Evan echoed. 'I'll see you out, Huw.'

'Just one more thing, Uncle Huw,' Bethan smiled. 'Thank Mrs Bennett for me.'

'Who's Mrs Bennett?' Evan asked mystified.

'Perhaps you'd like to tell him, Uncle Huw,' Bethan said as she returned to the kitchen.

Elizabeth was standing in front of the tiny window staring blankly at the Richards' garden wall.

'I'm sorry, Mam,' she apologised, closing the door behind her.

'What for?' Elizabeth asked coldly. 'This has all worked out to your advantage. You never wanted to marry Alun Jones in the first place.'

'No I didn't. But if he hadn't already had a wife, you would have gained what you wanted most of all. A respectably married daughter.'

'Would that have been so terrible?' Elizabeth demanded, turning to face her. 'Tell me, what are we going to do now? No money coming into the house. You having to give up work with a bastard to keep. . . .'

'I'll tell you what we're going to do, Elizabeth,' Evan said harshly as he opened the kitchen door. 'We're going to survive. It's high time I carried the responsibilities for this family. I'm going back to work, and I'm going to bring in a living wage.'

'You –' Elizabeth began to sneer, then a gleam in Evan's eye stopped her in her tracks. Her face was still smarting from the blow he'd given her the night before; she didn't want to risk pushing him into giving her another.

'I'm going into business,' Evan announced bluntly.

'Doing what, Dad?' Bethan ventured.

'Tatting.'

'Rag and bone man!' Elizabeth's blood ran cold at the thought of her husband shouting in the streets for people's rubbish.

'It's a perfectly legal and respectable occupation.'

'I'll never be able to hold my head up again.'

'That's as may be,' Evan said unconcernedly. 'But while you're staring in the gutter you'll be looking over a full belly.'

'And that's all that matters to you?'

'At this moment, woman, I can't think of anything that matters more.' He turned his back on his wife and looked to Bethan. 'It's good to have you home, snookems,' he said feelingly.

'It's good to be home.' She hugged her father and went to her mother. Elizabeth stood grim-faced and rigid, ready to repulse any show of emotion. Bethan pecked her withered cheek, opened the door and left the room.

'Where are you going to get the money from, Dad?' Haydn asked Evan a few days later as everyone except Elizabeth sat huddled around the range, trying to siphon off some of the warmth it radiated into their chilled bodies.

'Charlie's offered to lend me a fiver,' Evan said. 'He's a good mate.'

'Will you need as much as that, Dad?' Bethan asked, afraid that her father was plunging into more debt than he could afford on her account.

'I hope not.' Evan stretched out his legs and put his pipe into his mouth. He hadn't bought any tobacco since the pit had closed, but old habits died hard, and he stilled pulled it and his empty pouch out of his pocket every time he sat in front of the fire. 'I've taken ten bob off him to start with, that should see us right for a week. It's only sixpence a day to hire a shire horse and cart down Factory Lane. So tomorrow morning bright and early, Eddie and me will be down there picking out the best they have to offer.'

'So many people have tried tatting, Dad,' Bethan ventured prudently.

'Not where Dad and I are going to try, Beth,' Eddie said enthusiastically. 'We're not going round here. We're going where the crache live. They're the ones who can afford to throw out old for new.'

'And if we can't find any saleable junk tatting, we'll offer to cart garden rubbish away,' Evan suggested.

'Or move furniture,' Eddie chipped in.

'Powell and Sons, no carting job too big,' Haydn murmured.

'Or too small,' Evan said philosophically.

'Don't forget, Beth, I'm still working on Wilf Horton's stall as well as the Town Hall.'

'And you've got a week's money to come, Beth,' her father smiled.

'And we haven't got Maud to worry about any more,' Haydn added, thinking back to the tearful scene that morning when he and William had put Maud and Diana on the Cardiff train.

'If she sticks it in the Royal Infirmary,' Bethan commented.

'She'll stick it,' Haydn said firmly. 'She's like you. Stubborn little thing.'

'Charming.'

'So you see, Miss Pessimist, there's no problem. The finances of the Powell family are all worked out, and you and my grandson are going to want for nothing,' Evan said firmly.

'We've also got money coming in from our new lodgers.' Haydn left his chair and began to stack the dirty plates on the table.

'Mam let that room out quick,' Bethan commented.

'Mam didn't. I did.' Evan leaned forward in his chair. 'Will's had to give up Megan's house. Now the pit's closed Sam's moving on, but Charlie's staying. He and Will are going to share the front room.'

'What is Mam going to say about that?' Bethan looked from Haydn to her father.

'The same she said about my tatting,' Evan said carelessly. 'Nothing. Right, it's nearly six. I'm off out.'

'To see a man about a dog?' Eddie winked at Haydn.

'Something like that. Who's going to clear up before your mother gets back from Uncle Joe's?' Evan asked.

'Not me, I have to get to work.' Haydn reached for the mug holding the toothbrushes.

'So do I.' Bethan picked up her veil from the back of her chair.

'And I have to get to the gym,' Eddie protested.

'That settles it. You can do with one less sparring match. We lose our jobs if we're late,' Haydn pointed out logically.

'That's not fair,' Eddie complained.

'I can see we're going to miss Maud more than we thought,' Evan mused. 'You did say you were giving up work at the end of next week, Beth?'

Bethan looked at her father. She was grateful for the sentiment, but miserably conscious of her forthcoming dependence on her already overburdened family. 'I'm not sure, I went to see Matron about staying on for a bit this morning.'

'I hope she said no,' Evan countered sternly. 'You're soon going to have your work cut out for you, love.' He laid his hand on her shoulder as he left his chair. 'So if I were you I'd get all the rest you can, while you can.'

'She said I could do relief work on the unmarrieds ward starting next week. It's not strenuous. . . .'

'I'd rather you didn't.'

'It'll only be for another two weeks at the most, Dad.'

He glanced at the kitchen clock. 'I've got to go. We'll talk about it tomorrow night. And you,' he pointed to Eddie, 'no staying on down that gym too late. We've got work early in the morning,' he warned.

'Work! Tatting is only a stopgap, Dad. I'll make my money boxing.'

'Not this week you won't. Table, boy. Don't forget.'

Chapter Twenty-Three

'You're not worried about money are you, Sis?' Haydn asked as they left the house. 'You heard Dad. We'll all take care of you.'

'You shouldn't have to.'

'After all the months you took care of us? Come on.'

'I've made a right pig's ear of my life, haven't I?'

'There's some who would say that.' He looked at her and they both laughed. 'Hello, Glan,' he greeted him as he walked around the vicarage corner towards them.

'Haydn,' Glan said abruptly.

'Is it my imagination or did he cut you?' Haydn demanded, temper flaring in his nostrils as he turned his head to look back at Glan.

'It doesn't matter.' Bethan hooked her arm into her brother's and pulled him around the corner.

'Beth. . . . '

'It really doesn't matter,' she repeated warmly.

'How much of that has gone on?'

'Enough for me to find out who my friends are.'

'I'll kill the bastard. . . . '

'Haydn, he's not worth bothering with. Please. You can't kill half of Pontypridd.'

'Half? Beth, I had no idea. Honestly.'

'And some of the other half aren't quite sure whether to cut me because I'm pregnant and have no husband. Or because I'm pregnant and was a party to bigamy. Or because I went around with a doctor who dumped me.'

'It's that bad?'

'I lied to Dad earlier. Matron didn't find me that job on the unmarrieds ward as an extra. She moved me there last night because the women in the ward complained about having to be nursed by me. And even with Matron's protection I'm only there now because they're desperately short-staffed. The minute they find a replacement I'll be out.'

'Is that why you won't go to the wedding on Saturday?'

'That's part of it,' she admitted reluctantly.

'And the other part is Doctor Andrew John?' He barely managed to speak Andrew's name.

'Laura doesn't think he's coming. But whether he is or he isn't, I'd really rather go to bed. I'll need the sleep after a week on nights.'

'Laura'll miss you.'

'She'll have you and Eddie to make up for it.'

They walked on down Llantrisant Road, towards Griffiths' shop. Jenny was on the pavement outside, handing a large box to the delivery boy. She turned and waved to them.

'Jenny!' The upstairs window of the shop banged open, and her mother stuck her head out of the window. 'Jenny, I want you. Inside this house now.'

'In a minute, Mam.' Refusing to look up at her mother, Jenny smiled at Haydn, mischief glowing in her pale blue eyes. 'Haydn and Bethan are walking down the hill and I want to have a word with them.'

'Jenny Griffiths, you get back here this minute,' her mother shrieked.

'I will, Mam, after I've talked to them,' she shouted defiantly, walking away from the shop and up the hill to meet them.

'Hello, Bethan,' she said quietly, as she slipped her hand into Haydn's.

'You're still going out with this brother of mine then, I see.' Bethan's voice came out sharper than she'd intended. It was a struggle to hold in check the emotion Jenny's friendly greeting elicited.

'He just can't seem to stop following me around,' Jenny answered quickly, with a possessive glance at Haydn.

Bethan saw that the Jenny standing next to Haydn had come a long way from the shy girl who'd sat on the edge of her seat in the New Inn and answered Andrew's questions in monosyllables. 'Well I've got to get down to the hospital,' she said briskly, wanting to get away from them and their obvious loving happiness. The sight of it hurt more acutely than she would have believed possible, in her present emotionally battered state.

'Hang on a minute, I'm coming, Beth.' Haydn pulled away from Jenny.

'You've still got a few moments, and I really do have to go,' Bethan insisted. 'See you in the morning,' she called over her shoulder.

'She's a big girl, Haydn,' Jenny prompted, holding him back. 'Let her have a little time to herself.'

'I don't like her walking down the hill alone.'

'She has to, sooner or later. You can't protect her for ever.'

'I can try.'

'Haydn, she's not going to want you around for the rest of her life,' Jenny said in exasperation. 'Not like me,' she murmured in a softer voice.

He read the message in her eyes. 'Will I see you tonight?' he asked, forgetting Bethan for a moment.

'I could leave the store-room door open for you after the show,' she teased.

'Does that mean you will?'

'Perhaps, if you promise to be nice to me.'

'Will it be safe?' he asked anxiously.

'Mam'll be snoring by the time you walk up the hill. And Dad sleeps soundly enough now he's taken to going to the Morning Star every night to drown his misery at losing Megan.'

'Then I'll see you about eleven.' He squeezed her hand.

'I'll hold my breath.'

'Not too hard I hope,' he smiled, winking as he left.

Bethan walked down to the hospital along Albert Road, a side street that ran parallel to and behind Llantrisant Road. She knew she was being cowardly. But she'd rather not face people until she had to, and Albert Road was never as busy as the main thoroughfare at this time of night.

She felt strange, peculiar, as though something was missing. Then it came to her. She was alone, albeit in the street, for the first time since she'd returned home. She hadn't realised until that moment just what a protective shell her father and her brothers had woven around her. Haydn escorted her down to the hospital every night, and Eddie had been waiting for her at the main gates every morning, with the excuse that he'd come down early to try to get work in the brewery and there'd been none going. She'd been suspicious, and in view of the number of people who suddenly seemed unable to see her, or hear her simple greetings, grateful. Too grateful to resent their mollycoddling.

She paused for a moment and stared at the rows of terraced houses clinging to the hillside as it swept down to the Barry sub railway station and the Maritime colliery. The chill of winter was in the air, but precious few chimneys smoked. It seemed madness: people going cold and hungry for want of coal and the food that wages could buy when the colliery buildings lay, blackened, deserted and lifeless like the husk of a plundered coconut, discarded, useless, with nothing more to give. She went on slowly, thinking about the future that waited in store for the Graig, her family and herself.

For the first time she considered the needs of the child that was growing all too rapidly within her. Her father was, in his own clumsy way, trying to make things easier for her with his frequent and proud references to his coming grandson. But in so doing he was forcing her to do the very thing she least wanted to: making her see the child as an accomplished fact, a being in its own right who in the space of a few short months would take over and totally disrupt her life.

She hadn't been so afraid since the night she'd tried to abort it. She felt as though she were losing everything she'd worked for, everything she valued and had striven so hard to gain. Her career. Her prospects of qualifying as a midwife. Andrew . . .

Andrew. She pictured him laughing next to her in the Empire Theatre. Driving in shirt-sleeves through warm, green, sun-dappled countryside. And then as he'd been that last time in the hospital. Well dressed in his blue suit, white collar and tie; smelling of cologne and soap, his chin smooth, freshly shaved. Incredibly handsome, but for a contemptuous sneer that contorted his full and sensuous lips. She was sure that at that moment he'd hated her. Everything that had passed between them, all the experiences and loving they'd shared had meant nothing to him. Nothing at all.

He'd seen her as an embarrassment. Something dirty to be washed from his life, his mind . . . and his bed. Yet even now, after everything that had happened her senses responded alarmingly to the remembrance of their lovemaking. She gripped her fingers together. If she must think of Andrew at all, she had to think of the way he'd looked when he told her that she'd dragged him down as far as he was prepared to go. If she didn't . . . if she didn't, then what?

She'd told her father and Laura the truth. Andrew and her — it was the old, old story. Probably the oldest in the world. She had to thank her lucky stars that her family were prepared to keep her. And as for Andrew — she looked back and saw cold calculation in everything he'd done. Seduction behind every kindness he'd offered her. Lust, not love, in his caresses.

She walked on as her battered emotions groped their way painfully back to awareness. Only this time it was hatred not love that bore her forward on the crest of life.

It was nearly midnight when Andrew left the illuminated platform of Pontypridd station and walked down the steps to street level. The porter who struggled behind him shouldering his trunk groaned as he finally dumped the box at the foot of the steps.

'There's no taxis, sir,' he crowed, stating the obvious.

'So I see.' Andrew looked around the dimly lit, deserted yard and wished he'd telephoned his father from Cardiff. But then he'd been wary of disturbing his mother. She could well be alone if his father'd had to go out on a night call. And no one was expecting him to arrive until tomorrow.

Not for the first time that day he cursed the impulse that had led him to take a half-day holiday from the hospital and run off to Paddington station. Impulse, or image of Bethan? Her face came vividly to mind, just as it did at least a dozen times a day. It haunted him.

'You want to put your trunk in the stationmaster's office, sir?' the porter suggested.

'Would it be possible to use the telephone?' he asked, hoping to catch Trevor in his lodgings.

'I'm not allowed to let the public near the telephone, sir,' the porter said officiously. 'Besides, it's all locked up and I haven't got the key.'

'Looks like I've no choice but to leave my trunk in the stationmaster's office,' Andrew replied resignedly.

'Righto then, sir. I'll put it away for you.'

Andrew watched as the man heaved the trunk into the ticket office on the ground floor and locked the door behind him. Afterwards he pulled the compacted steel trellis across the wide doorway and secured it with a padlock.

'Safe as houses until five-thirty tomorrow, sir.'

'And then?' Andrew enquired wryly.

'It's got your name on the label, sir, Doctor John. They're not likely to hand it over to anyone else.'

Andrew tipped him sixpence.

'Thank you, sir. If there's nothing else, I'll be off. I'm on early shift again tomorrow.'

'Thank you for your help. Goodnight.'

'Goodnight, sir.'

Andrew picked up his doctor's bag. Even that was heavy. Too heavy to lug all the way up to the Common, he thought as he took the first step forward. The Tumble, so alive with people during the day, was devoid of life. The lamps flickered over grey, vacant pavements and the shuttered façades of Ronconis' café and the New Theatre. There was nothing for it but to keep going.

The air was freezing, so he thrust his free hand into his pocket. He paused for a moment outside the station and looked up the Graig hill, wondering if Bethan was working nights. He was sorely tempted to walk up to the homes. But then what if she wasn't on the ward? How could he possibly explain his presence there when he hadn't worked in Pontypridd for weeks?

Turning his back on the Graig hill he faced downtown, and forced himself forwards.

Eddie had lingered late in the gym built behind the Ruperra Hotel. Much later than usual. Joey Rees had arranged a sparring match for him with Bolshie Drummond. Bolshie had been a first-class boxer, and unlike most of the old-timers in the gym, not that long ago. The match had gone on for hours. They'd all lost track of time. Especially him, and he should have known better, because ever since Joey had trusted him enough to clean up and lock up after everyone left he rarely got home much before twelve. Tonight it would be nearer one o'clock. And that was bound to set Mam off.

He quite enjoyed staying on in the gym by himself. He liked walking around the ring imagining himself winning bouts. He liked being able to look at the photographs of past champions without being disturbed, but most of all he liked having his gym subs waived and the five shillings a week Joey slipped into his pocket. It was worth handing it over to his mother intact to cut down on her continual nagging about money.

He ran as far as the fountain in the centre of town then, hands on knees, paused to breathe in deeply. He heard someone walking towards him. He looked up expecting to see Megan's brother Huw, or one of the other policemen. Instead . . . instead . . . his heart thundered, and his mouth went dry.

A man was walking towards him, no ordinary man. Even under the shadowy lights of the street lamps he could see that he was wearing an expensive overcoat. One he knew was made of cashmere wool. He was carrying a small case in his hand and his hat was pulled low over his forehead.

'Doctor John?' he ventured.

Andrew stopped. 'Yes.' He squinted into the darkness. 'Do I know you?'

'Too bloody royal you do.'

The first punch caught Andrew unawares and sent him reeling backwards. He dropped his case and cried out as the back of his head connected painfully with the pavement. Eddie allowed him no time to recover. He jumped on top of Andrew. Hauling him up from the pavement, Eddie smashed into Andrew's jaw with his clenched fist.

'In God's name,' Andrew mumbled through loosened teeth, as he desperately attempted to defend himself. It was useless, the attack had been too quick, too sudden. His opponent had all the advantage. A boot connected with his ribs.

'You bastard. You smarmy bastard. That's for what you did to my sister.' Eddie was sobbing and oblivious to the fact. 'She's in one hell of a state and you . . . ' Eddie thrust forward. His toe connected with the soft part of Andrew's stomach.

'I love Bethan,' Andrew protested through a haze of pain. 'I've come back to marry her,' he mumbled, lost in a red and black fog of anguish. 'Please, please . . . I want Bethan. . . . '

A whistle blew. The blows ceased. He heard the sound of feet running away. But all he was capable of doing was lying where he'd fallen on the spittle and dog-fouled pavement, curled in excruciating torment.

Chapter Twenty-Four

Elizabeth was woken by a hammering on the door. She put out her hand and touched Evan as he left the bed.

'It's all right, I'll see to it.' He reached down to the floor for his trousers. 'It's probably one of the boys. Had too much to drink.'

'They'd keep quiet, not make a racket if they were drunk,' Elizabeth said, unable to conceal her fear. Bethan could have had an accident at the hospital. Eddie could have been hurt in a fight. Haydn – oh God, not Haydn! She shivered at the thought of anything happening to her favourite.

'They wouldn't keep quiet if they were too drunk to find the key in the door,' Evan said baldly. 'Stay there, girl, I'll be back in a minute.'

He flicked on the light and checked the time on the battered alarm clock on the bedside table. The hands pointed to three-thirty. When he opened the bedroom door, the hammering began again. Haydn stepped out on to the landing.

'Do you want me to see to it, Dad?'

'No, I will. Is Eddie in his bed?' Evan asked as an afterthought as he was half-way down the stairs.

'I didn't look,' Haydn replied truthfully. 'I'll check now.'

'Who's there?' Evan demanded irately, and somewhat ridiculously considering that the door had its key protruding from the lock.

'Huw Davies.'

Evan opened the door, shivering in the blast of cold air that rushed into the passage. 'What's wrong?' he asked, staring at Huw's uniform. 'Official visit, is it?'

'I'd rather talk in your kitchen if you don't mind,' Huw said, glancing up at Haydn who stood white-faced on the stairs.

'He's not there, Dad.'

'You'd better come in, Huw.'

Huw lifted off his helmet and stroked his bald head nervously.

Pulling the edges of her dressing gown close together Elizabeth left her bedroom.

'What's wrong?' she demanded.

'In the kitchen, Elizabeth,' Evan said, leading the way. He switched on the light and walked over to the stove. Opening the door he poked life into the coals. 'Tea, Huw?'

'When I've done perhaps.'

'Well, sit yourself down, man.'

Huw took the easy chair Evan pointed to. Elizabeth and Haydn entered. Sitting quietly on the hard, wooden kitchen chairs, they turned their faces expectantly to his.

'They brought your Eddie into the station an hour ago,' Huw explained bluntly, without embellishment. 'He attacked a man.'

'Is he hurt?' Evan demanded.

'Not your Eddie. He's fine. The one he had a go at is a mess. We had to call the police doctor out to see to him. By rights he should be in hospital. But he wouldn't go. Leastways he wouldn't when I left an hour ago.'

'Who did he attack?' Haydn asked shrewdly.

'Doctor John. Doctor Andrew John.'

Evan gripped tightly at the poker in his hand.

'Your Eddie,' Huw continued, 'he could go down for a long time on this one.'

'Can we see him?' Evan demanded.

'In the morning. He's already been charged, Evan. He's going to need a solicitor.'

'We've no money for one of those,' Elizabeth retorted quickly.

'Quiet, woman,' Evan hissed, holding his head in his hands. He tried desperately to think.

'You going back to the station now, Huw?' he asked.

'Yes.'

'I'm coming with you.'

'Me too,' Haydn said, jumping up.

'You're staying,' Evan said firmly. 'Bethan will need fetching in a few hours. And someone has to stay here with your mother.'

'Why me?' Haydn replied without thinking.

'Because you're the only one here,' Evan said harshly. 'Go on, boy, back up to bed. As soon as there's any news I'll get word to you. You'd best go on up too, Elizabeth,' he said in a gentler tone, remembering that Eddie was every bit as much her son as his.

'I'll just make Huw a cup of tea while you dress, Evan,' she said stoically, adopting the role she'd had most practice in. That of martyr.

'I warn you now, they'll not let him go without setting a bail too high for you or anyone around here to pay,' Superintendent Hunt insisted dogmatically as he faced Evan from behind his desk. He'd had a bad night. Hauled out of his warm, comfortable bed just after he'd fallen into a deep sleep by a panic-stricken telephone call from the station. Dr John's son had finally had his head cracked by the brother of the pretty nurse he'd courted and abandoned to the tender mercies of a bigamist. His emotions were divided between pity for the pathetic, duped girl, admiration for Eddie for giving Andrew John what he deserved, and a desire to punish the lad at the same time for setting on the doctor in the middle of the night and disturbing his rest.

'How much will it be?' Evan pressed tentatively.

'The amount's for the magistrate to set in the morning.'

'Can I see Eddie?'

Instead of answering, the superintendent glared eagle-eyed at Huw who was hovering close to the door. 'You've had quite a lot of favours between one thing and another with your family lately,' he cautioned bluntly. 'Go — Davies,' he jerked his head towards the door. 'Take him down to the cells to see his son. But no more than five minutes. And you stay in the cell the whole time. The last thing I need is an attempted cell break. As it is, my neck's stuck out so far it's likely to drop off with the next change of wind.'

Eddie didn't look up from the floor as the door to his cell opened. He sat, stiff, immobile on the edge of the bare planks of the wooden bunk. The temperature in the basement was uncomfortably low; but seemingly oblivious to the cold, Eddie hadn't attempted to make use of the blanket folded on the boards next to him. His jacket, belt, braces and shoelaces had been taken and he was dressed only in a thin, collarless cotton shirt and summer trousers. His laceless shoes and the turn-ups of his well-worn

389

trousers were spattered with blood, his knuckles red from burgeoning bruises.

'Are you all right, son?' Evan sat down on the bunk next to him.

'They shouldn't have dragged you down here. Not at this time of night,' Eddie said truculently.

'If you're in trouble I want to help.'

'I'm not sorry for what I did.' Eddie lifted his face, clearly unbowed and unrepentant. 'If they'd let me get near the bastard, I'd do it again. I only wish I'd done it last spring when he first started messing with our Bethan.'

Huw stepped inside the cell and pulled the door to, lest anyone overhear them. 'That's not the line to take, Eddie,' he warned seriously. 'Not when you're seeing the magistrate first thing in the morning. You gave that doctor a good going over. Cracked ribs, cracked skull, he's in a right mess. And the way they'll see it is that he's crache, and you're as good as a professional boxer.'

'I couldn't give a damn what they see,' Eddie retorted defiantly.

'If you tell them about Bethan,' Huw began doubtfully, 'they might go a bit softer on you.'

'No,' Eddie interrupted quickly. 'She's been through enough.'

'You don't seem to understand. You could go to jail. For a long time,' Huw advised bluntly.

'I'd be happy to swing for the bloody swine. And I would be swinging if I'd had enough time to put him where I wanted to. In a box.'

'Eddie, please, this kind of talk isn't going to help you or Bethan.' Evan put his arm round his son's shoulders. Eddie was cold. Cold as ice.

'I mean it, Dad.' Tears rolled down Eddie's face. 'I mean it,' he repeated, raising his arm and wiping his nose and eyes on the sleeve of his shirt. 'I'm not sorry.'

'Time to go, Evan.' Huw opened the cell door.

Unlike Eddie, Evan had many regrets. But his biggest one when he left Eddie alone in the cell was that he hadn't chanced upon Andrew John before his son.

'Bethan?' Sister Thomas walked into the ward and called her into the office.

390

'You're early.' Bethan hung the patients' duty sheets back on to a nail hammered into the wall and followed her. 'I'm not quite ready for the change-over.'

'There's no time for the change-over.' She hung her cape on the back of the door. 'Matron wants to see you in her office. Now.'

'I'll come back afterwards, shall I?' Bethan asked as she lifted down her own cape.

'I think Matron has other plans for you. She told me to make sure you took everything with you. Your cape, your bag. She could be moving you back on to maternity,' Sister Thomas smiled. 'If she is, good luck, and thanks for the help.'

Bethan gathered her things together and left the building. The grey light of early dawn was just beginning to streak across the sky. It promised to be a fine, dry autumn morning, if a little cold. She hoped that the weather would hold until Sunday for Laura's wedding. Shivering, she walked quickly across the yard. The door to the office was open and Matron was already behind her desk. Bethan checked her watch. It was seven o'clock; a full half-hour before the day shift officially started.

'Come in, Nurse Powell, and close the door behind you.'

Bethan did as she was asked and sat on the same hard chair that she'd occupied when she'd last been called to see Matron. The day she found out she'd qualified as a nurse.

She looked back on the thoughts that had occupied her mind then. Ideas of advancing her career – getting enough money together to buy Haydn and Eddie suits, ways to avoid dancing with Glan at the hospital ball. So many changes. So much had happened in the space of two short seasons. She felt like an old, old woman when she recalled the girl she had been. And all the changes including the ageing process had stemmed from Andrew, who'd been waiting for Squeers to allocate him a second nurse. She wondered if her life would be any different now if she'd been working on the men's ward instead of maternity.

'I'm sorry, Nurse Powell,' Matron said briskly, facing an unpleasant situation the only way she knew how, 'but I'm going to have to let you go.'

'Let me go,' Bethan echoed in amazement. 'But I'm leaving at the end of next week.'

'You *were* leaving at the end of next week,' Matron contradicted. 'I had a telephone call last night from the chairman of the Hospital Board. They've found a replacement for you. You may go immediately. Here,' she opened her desk drawer and withdrew an envelope, 'this is for you. Payment for services rendered to date and a little extra.'

'But yesterday you said. . . . '

'I think this is for the best, Nurse Powell,' Matron said kindly. 'After all you really should be resting more at this stage.'

'And after the baby's born,' Bethan pressed. 'You said that I might be able to come back.'

'Get in touch with me by all means.' Matron evaded the question. 'But I'm not sure there'll be a vacancy. Goodbye and good luck.' She rose majestically, shook Bethan's hand and ushered her through the door, closing her out into the corridor.

Hugging the envelope to her, Bethan walked away in bewilderment. Something must have changed since she'd last talked to Matron. But what?

When she saw Haydn's tall, fair figure lounging against the gatehouse she ran to him, too wrapped up in her own affairs to notice the expression on his pale, tired face.

'Haydn, they've laid me off. I haven't a job any more. . . . '

He put his arms round her and told her as gently as he knew how to what Eddie had done to Andrew John. Bewildered no longer, she understood everything. Only too clearly. There'd been no Hospital Board appointment of a replacement nurse. Just one short quick telephone call to Matron from Dr John senior. She ripped open the envelope Matron had given her. Inside were two five-pound notes. Haydn only just stopped her from tearing them up. He was anything but proud of the way he did it.

'We may need them for our Eddie's defence,' he muttered practically.

'There you are, darling.' Isabel John removed the lunch tray that the maid had brought up earlier, and gently smoothed the satin coverlet over the guest bed that Andrew was lying in. 'You should feel a little better by tonight,' she murmured soothingly.

'For goodness' sake, Mother,' he snapped irritably. 'It's only a mild concussion.'

'And cracked ribs,' she emphasised.

'Cracked rib,' Andrew corrected bad-temperedly.

'Dreadful.' His mother shook her head briskly as she fussed with the trunk that Dr John senior had arranged to have brought up from the station. 'I don't know what the world's coming to when a man can't walk down the main street of his home town in safety.'

'I do,' Andrew said shortly. 'I had it coming to me. I didn't exactly treat his sister very well.'

'If I remember rightly you treated her extremely well,' Isabel protested indignantly, watching him carefully out of the corner of her eye. 'Took her to nice places. Introduced her to all the right people.'

'And left her high and dry, knowing that she loved me.' He couldn't look his mother in the eye. Love between a man and a woman was something they'd never discussed in a personal context.

'Loved you? Really, Andrew, you're deluding yourself. The girl barely waited for you to leave town before getting married.'

'Married? Bethan? Come on, Mother, don't try that one on me. I don't believe it.' He rejected the news contemptuously.

'Well, perhaps it wasn't quite that soon after you left. I think it happened two or three weeks ago. Mrs Llewellyn-Jones told me all about it.'

'She would,' Andrew commented scathingly. 'And who exactly is Bethan supposed to have married?'

'Apparently a man who was lodging with her family. At least that's what Mrs Llewellyn-Jones heard. A miner like her father.' She slowed her speech, conscious of saying too much, too fast. She wanted to get the revelations just right, so he wouldn't ask any questions of anyone else while he was in Pontypridd. He'd told her he only had four days' leave. Trevor was getting married tomorrow so he wouldn't see him. And really there wasn't anyone else. At least not anyone who'd talk about Bethan Powell. 'Anyway they've opened a lodging house down Broadway,' she concluded briskly. 'So please, darling, don't go upsetting yourself over a girl like that. She simply isn't worth it.' She picked up the tray from the floor. 'Will you be all right with the maids if I go out? Normally I wouldn't dream of leaving you, but the Reverend

Price has called an emergency committee meeting of the Distress Fund. . . . '

'Go ahead please, I really would like a long sleep.'

'Well, if you're sure, darling. I'll be as quick as I can. An hour or two at the most.' She stroked the hair back, away from his bandaged forehead.

'I intend to sleep longer than that.'

'I'll see you later. Arrange a nice dinner to be brought up.'

'I'll get up for dinner.'

'We'll see what your father has to say about that. Sleep well, darling.'

Andrew lay back on the pillows and stared at the whitewashed ceiling listening to his mother's footsteps as she descended the stairs. He couldn't believe it! He didn't want to believe it. And he didn't. But he found it equally difficult to believe that his mother was lying. He knew she'd never liked Bethan. He just didn't realise that the dislike ran deep enough for her to fabricate an entire story. Lowering the standards of behaviour and integrity she'd adhered to all her life.

The last thing Eddie had shouted at him before he'd lost consciousness had been that Bethan was in a hell of a state . . . 'One hell of a state'.

Confused, needing to know more, he fought his instinct to rest. He waited until the front door opened and closed. The Distress Fund committee meeting would well and truly buzz with gossip this afternoon, he reflected sourly. A few minutes later he rang the bell.

'You wanted something, sir?' Mair knocked on the door and opened it a crack as though he were a wild animal that would bite.

'Yes, Mair.' It didn't occur to him to ask Mair whether Bethan was married or not. His mother had brought him up too well to see servants as people with lives and minds of their own. 'Would you make a telephone call for me to Doctor Lewis. You do know how to use the telephone?' he added as an afterthought.

'Of course, sir,' she said, offended.

'Tell him I need to see him as soon as possible. It's very urgent. Can you remember that?'

Trevor was packing in his rooms when the call came. Another five minutes and he would have left for the house that he and Laura had rented in Graig Street, opposite St John's church. It wouldn't have a telephone for another two weeks and three days – all the honeymoon that he'd managed to squeeze out of Andrew's father.

'It's good of you to come. I know you must have things to do for the wedding tomorrow.'

'I was in the middle of moving out of my digs into the new house,' Trevor said ungraciously.

'Are you and Laura going away?'

'To London for a week. She's never been there.'

'You should have told me, I could have arranged a hotel. . . . '

'All done. I knew of a good place close to Marble Arch.'

'Hope you have a good time.' Smarting at Trevor's dismissal of his offer of help, Andrew waved a bandaged hand at the surroundings. 'I'd rather be in my own rooms,' he said, changing the subject. 'But Father insisted on putting me in here, so he and Mother could keep an eye on me.' He realised Trevor was watching him with a professional eye. For all of his efforts to appear normal, he knew his speech was slurred, like that of a drunk. And quite apart from his throbbing head, his bandaged ribcage stabbed into his chest every time he drew breath.

'I saw your father briefly in the hospital this morning. He said you've got concussion and a cracked rib. Considering Eddie's talents, you're lucky.'

'Very,' Andrew agreed drily. 'I think he was out to kill me.'

'That's hardly surprising,' Trevor commented coolly.

'Look, won't you sit down?' Andrew asked as he struggled to sit up.

'I can't stay long.'

'I know. It was good of you to come.' He fumbled on the bedside table for his cigarettes, holding out the case to Trevor. 'It hurts having to ask this, especially when it's a question that I of all people should be able to answer, but I didn't know who else to get in touch with.'

'If I were you I'd lie down. You're not making much sense.'

Trevor took two cigarettes. He lit them with a lighter Laura's father had given him and handed one back to Andrew.

'I need to know how she is. I don't need you to tell me I don't deserve to. I treated her abominably that last night.' Andrew puffed nervously at his cigarette, avoiding Trevor's eyes. 'I wrote to her. Three letters. She didn't answer one of them. I don't blame her, not really, not after what I said. . . . '

'You wrote to her and she didn't reply?'

'Not a word. That's why I came back a day early. I hoped to straighten things out between us before your wedding tomorrow. I behaved like a bloody fool.' He drew hard on the cigarette and tapped the ash out into a tray on the floor. 'I should never have left for London the way I did. But my father said — ' he looked up at Trevor — 'no!' he said vehemently. 'No, that really would be the easy way out wouldn't it? Blame him. Blame everyone except the person most at fault. Me. The simple truth of the matter is I went away thinking I'd soon get over her. But I didn't realise what I had,' he murmured softly. 'Not then. Not until weeks later. You could say I didn't really appreciate her until I'd lost her. I thought I'd find another girl to take her place.' He laughed derisively. 'I found plenty all right. But not a one to touch her. There wasn't anyone who could come anywhere near her.'

'And now, after everything you've done, you've come back to carry on where you left off?' There was incredulity as well as contempt in Trevor's voice.

'I hoped to,' Andrew said defensively. 'I thought I had a chance. She'd told me she loved me. I still love her. . . . '

'My God.' Trevor turned on his heel, opened the window and threw his cigarette outside.

'Trevor, what's wrong?' Andrew pleaded. 'I know something's happened, but no one will tell me anything. Mother gave me some cock and bull story about Bethan getting married. . . . '

'It's true.'

'It can't be!' Andrew protested. 'She loved me. She cared for me. . . . '

'Oh she cared for you all right. That was the bloody trouble.'

'She really is married?' Even Andrew's lips were white, bloodless.

'You bastard!' The vehemence in Trevor's voice hit Andrew with a greater force than Eddie's blows. 'You walked away leaving her destitute, and now you've got the gall to lie there and ask me questions about her marriage.'

'Destitute? She had her job. . . . '

'For Christ's sake, man. Do I have to spell it out for you? She tried to keep it a secret from everyone, but I found out when she fell down the stairs in the hospital . . . ' He faltered, remembering the reason for her fall. 'Afterwards she told me the truth. That you went to London to get away from her and the baby.'

'The baby?' Andrew stared at him dumbfounded.

'The baby. Your damned baby. Why else do you think she'd marry a man like Alun Jones? She wanted to give it a name.'

'My God.' Andrew felt as though the room was spinning around him. 'Do you think I'd have left her if I'd known there was a baby?'

Trevor stared at him. 'Didn't you know?'

'No.'

It was such a flat, blunt denial Trevor couldn't help but believe him. 'She said she'd told you. That you'd gone to London to get away,' he finished slowly.

Andrew lay back stiffly on the pillows. 'Do you really think so little of me?'

'You must admit you couldn't wait to go. You even asked me to take her a letter and say goodbye for you.'

'I did, didn't I?' he murmured as if he was talking about someone else not himself. 'God, how she must hate me. Not to have said a single word . . . Trevor, how is she?' he pleaded.

'As well as can be expected. I haven't seen her for two days. But I do know that she was given her cards and her pay at the hospital this morning. It's not done for a nurse to have a brother who beats up the Senior Medical Officer's son.' He couldn't resist the gibe.

'Then she's still working?'

'Until this morning.'

'What about . . . about her husband?' he asked, choking on the word.

'Alun Jones? He's in jail,' Trevor admitted sheepishly, regretting the impulse that had made him want to see Andrew squirm.

'He was arrested the morning after the wedding. Apparently he had a wife already in North Wales.'

'Then she's not married?' Andrew stared at him keenly.

'Not legally, no.'

'Did she love . . . did she. . . . '

'I've told you all I know,' Trevor said finally, as he moved restlessly towards the door. 'She doesn't confide in me. After Alun was arrested, the family closed ranks around her. You know what they're like.'

'I can imagine.' He lifted the bedclothes back. 'She's living with them now?' He sat up and swung his legs out of bed.

'You don't think for one minute she'll see you?'

'Eddie will when I go to the police station to drop the charges against him. I just hope he'll listen to me. And take her a message.'

'I doubt it,' Trevor observed realistically. 'You'd be better off lying there until you can think straight and talk coherently.'

'Do me a favour?' Andrew said grimly, wincing as he opened the wardrobe door and reached for a shirt.

'What?'

'It's nothing too dreadful.' Andrew stripped off his pyjama jacket. 'Go downstairs and call me a taxi.'

'The police station is on my way back to the Graig. If you're set on going there anyway, I suppose I could drive you down seeing as how you're incapable.' He smiled at Andrew for the first time.

'That would be good of you. Just one more thing?'

'What?'

'Do up my shoelaces, there's a good chap. My head hurts like hell when I bend down.'

'This is most irregular, sir,' the duty sergeant protested.

'Not at all,' Andrew said evenly. 'Don't you understand? There was no fight.'

'But. . . . '

'No "buts" either, Sergeant.' Andrew smiled wanly as he leaned against the high desk in the reception room. 'I fell over and hit my head. The boy was trying to help me.'

'But he ran off when our man came.'

'Very possibly to avoid the type of accusation he's facing now.'

398

'You expect me to believe this fairy story?' the sergeant demanded aggressively.

'I was there, Sergeant,' Andrew pointed out calmly. 'You weren't.'

'And this gentleman?' Sergeant Thomas looked at Trevor.

'Offered to bring me down here. I have a concussion.' Andrew pointed to the bandage on his head. 'I didn't think it safe to drive myself.'

'And you're sure you want to do this, sir?'

'How many times do I have to tell you? I'm absolutely sure that there are no charges for the man to answer to. If I'd been fully conscious last night they wouldn't have been made in the first place.'

'If you'll take a seat, sir,' the sergeant moved out from behind his high desk, 'I'll get the paperwork.'

The 'paperwork' turned out to be half a dozen forms of interminable length, each of which seemed to require at least three signatures to a page.

'He will be released straight away?' Andrew asked as he signed the last one.

'As soon as we can bring him up from the cells,' the sergeant replied suspiciously. He wondered if the doctor had some sort of private revenge lined up for young Powell once he left the security of the police station.

'I'd like to see him if I may,' Andrew said, reading the sergeant's thoughts. 'I'd like to thank him.'

'Thank him, sir?'

'For coming to my assistance.'

'I'll ask if he wants to see you. If he does I'll bring him here.'

Trevor waited until the sergeant left before speaking out. 'Wouldn't it be better to wait until you can be sure he's calmed down? Eddie's always been a hothead, from what Laura's told me.'

'I have to see Bethan, and the quickest way to her is through Eddie. Trevor. . . .'

The door opened and Eddie, jacket slung over one shoulder, stood framed in the doorway.

'Come back for more, John?' he threatened viciously, raising his fist. 'I'd like to kill you here and now. . . .'

'No fight?' Sergeant Thomas queried disbelievingly, pushing his bulk between Andrew and Eddie.

'No fight, Sergeant,' Andrew said flatly. 'Mr Powell has clearly been upset by spending a night in the cells. A natural enough reaction from an innocent man. I'd like to apologise, Eddie. For everything,' he emphasised warmly. 'If I'd known what was happening last night you wouldn't have been put in the cells.'

'You. . . .'

The sergeant pushed Eddie into a corner so Trevor and Andrew could walk past. 'You'll have to sign for your things,' he told Eddie sharply.

'Come near me again if you dare, John,' Eddie called out savagely. 'Five minutes. That's all I need. Five minutes and you're dead.'

'Now what?' Trevor asked as they walked into the car park, which was bounded by low grey walls built of the same stone as the police station.

'Drop me off at the railway station, and I'll get a taxi.'

'Home?' Trevor asked hopefully. When Andrew didn't answer, he said, 'You're going up there aren't you? To Graig Avenue?'

'I have to see her.'

'I doubt you'll manage that. The rest of her family are likely to be as friendly as Eddie.'

'I have to at least try.'

'Get in. If you're hell bent on killing yourself you'll need a doctor along with you.'

Andrew sat slumped in the front seat as Trevor drove slowly up the Graig hill. He pulled his hat down low, to hide his battered face and avoid recognition. The streets were teeming with people: women and children hauling heavy bags of vegetables and offal up from the market; boys hanging around the outside of shops, barefoot, bare-headed, hoping to earn an extra penny or two running errands for the shopkeepers; groups of men congregating around lamp-posts, hands in pockets, caps pulled down over their eyes; idlers who didn't want to be idle; miners with no money in their pockets and no prospect of earning any.

'If I park in Graig Avenue you'll have every neighbour in the street nosing at the car,' Trevor commented. 'This really isn't a good idea.'

'Drop me off at the vicarage.'

'I've a better idea. Why don't I ask Laura to go down there and see her for you?'

'Would she?'

'I don't know,' Trevor replied honestly. 'But I think Laura's a better bet than trying to get past her brothers or her father.'

He stopped the car outside Laura's house in Danycoedcae Road. Even when he was standing on the pavement he could hear feminine giggles and raised voices of excitement. 'I think there's a crowd of women in there. I'll go by myself and ask her.'

'So Laura hates me too?'

'Afraid so,' Trevor said honestly.

'Well that's understandable. I don't like myself very much at the moment either,' Andrew said philosophically, unable to keep a trace of self-pity from his voice.

Trevor closed the car door, walked up the steps to Laura's house, turned the key and stepped inside the front door.

'Mamma mia!' Laura's mother, bulk quivering, came down the passage to greet him, blocking his path with her ample figure. 'Don't you know it's unlucky for the groom to see the bride the day before the wedding?'

'That's the morning of the wedding, not the day before, Mama,' Laura walked out of the back kitchen. She looked quizzically at Trevor. 'Hello, sweetheart, you haven't come to tell me that you've changed your mind have you?'

'Nothing like that,' Trevor smiled, kissing the top of her head and wanting to kiss a whole lot more. 'Is there anywhere we can talk?'

'In this house?' She stared at him in astonishment. 'There's the *ty bach*.' Grinning at his uncomfortable look, she relented. 'I was joking.' She stuck her head round the door of the front parlour. 'Gina, Tina, out for five minutes,' she barked.

'What's the matter, Laura? Can't wait until you're alone with him tomorrow night?' Gina giggled at the blush that was spreading over Trevor's cheeks.

'Less of your cheek, madam.' She pushed them out of the room and pulled Trevor in. 'Can't close the door I'm afraid,' she apologised. 'Not even with the wedding tomorrow, Mama and Papa wouldn't stand for it.'

'I've got Andrew outside in the car,' he blurted out.

'You've got *what*?'

'Ssh, not so loud. He's just been to the police station to drop charges against Eddie.'

'Least he could do,' Laura said unforgivingly.

'He wants to see Bethan.'

'What for? So he can insult her and leave her all over again?'

'Laura, he says he didn't know about the baby, and I believe him.'

'Yes, well, that's the difference between us, Trevor. You're gullible. I'm not.'

'And if he's telling the truth?'

'Even if he is, which I don't believe for a minute, Bethan's got her head screwed on the right way. She knows when she's well off. She won't want to see him again, take my word for it.'

'Can't you persuade her?'

'Why should I try?' she demanded indignantly.

'She loved him once. He wants to marry her.'

Laura snorted sceptically.

'Won't you at least go and see her?' Trevor coaxed.

'There's no point. When I left her half an hour ago she was going to bed. And Haydn and her mother are standing guard. They'll never let me wake her.'

'Laura, it's his baby.'

'He should have thought of that when he left her.'

'I think he's really sorry.'

'I'll believe that when I see it.'

'Then you will see him?'

Caught in a snare of her own making she went to the window and looked out. 'Where is he?'

'In the car.'

'Oh no he isn't.'

Trevor joined her and looked through the bay. 'Damn him,' he muttered. 'He wouldn't bloody well wait.'

Chapter Twenty-Five

Andrew pulled the collar of his coat up until it met the brim of his hat and knocked on the Powells' front door. He had to knock three times before he heard the sound of footsteps echoing over the flagstones in the passage.

'The key's in the door,' a voice shouted in exasperation. When he didn't turn it the door was wrenched open. Haydn stared at him in total disbelief. 'You've got a bloody nerve coming here!' he exclaimed when he recovered from the shock.

'I would like to talk to Bethan,' Andrew ventured, summoning up all his courage.

'Well she doesn't want to talk to you,' Haydn retorted belligerently.

'Then your father. It's really important.'

'Who is it, Haydn?' Elizabeth called out from the kitchen.

'Nobody.'

'It's Andrew John, Mrs Powell. May I see you for a moment?'

The silence that greeted his request closed around him and Haydn, immuring them in a tense world of red shadows and threatening, imminent violence.

'Now can you see that you're not wanted here? And if you try setting foot on this doorstep again I'll finish what my brother began last night.' Not trusting himself to remain within striking distance of Andrew a moment longer, Haydn slammed the door in his face. He leaned back against it, breathing heavily.

'Haydn?' Bethan stood at the top of the stairs, her long nightgown flowing round her ankles, her hair ruffled from the pillows, her eyes puffy from crying. 'Was that who I think it was?'

'Go back to bed, Bethan.' Haydn went to the foot of the stairs.

'Was it?' she repeated.

'Yes, and he's got a bloody cheek coming round here. But don't worry, Sis, I sent him packing. He won't be round again.'

Bethan returned to her bedroom, but she didn't climb back into bed. Instead she pulled the curtains aside and looked down at the street. Andrew was standing in the middle of the unmade road in front of the house. She withdrew quickly, a host of conflicting emotions surging within her. She'd seen enough to know that Eddie'd done some damage. She'd noticed the bandage on Andrew's hand and beneath his hat; his pale face and bloodless lips. But she consoled herself with the thought that he must be all right to be walking around – better than Eddie who was still in jail.

Why did he want to see her? Why? After what he'd said to her the last time they'd spoken she had nothing to say to him. Nothing at all.

Andrew saw the curtains in the bedroom twitch and guessed that it had been Bethan who had moved them. He lowered his head and looked up and down the street, uncertain what to do next. As he was deliberating, the door in the garden wall opposite opened and Evan Powell emerged on to the street.

'Mr Powell,' he said eagerly.

Evan stared at him blankly for a moment. Then anger dawned as he recognised Andrew. 'You're the last person I expected to see standing outside my house,' he said heatedly.

Refusing to be intimidated or put off, Andrew pressed his unexpected advantage. 'I'd like to talk to you for a few moments if I may, Mr Powell.'

'Why?'

'Please, I know what you must think of me but it's important. Not to me, to Bethan.' He waited patiently for Evan's reply.

'All right, boy, I'll talk to you,' Evan relented gruffly. 'But not here. In the Graig Hotel around the corner. I'll be down in five minutes. The back bar.'

'Thank you, sir. I'm very grateful.'

Despite his thumping headache Andrew almost ran down the street. He entered the hotel through the double doors at the front, and looked down the dark central passageway that divided the building into two. Bars opened out either side of him, typical valley pub bars that gleamed with polished mahogany, shining brasswork and highly coloured, leaded light windows. He glanced into both: one was a men's bar, the other a lounge. He knew

404

there was a jug and bottle that opened from a side entrance. But he could see no sign of a back room.

'Can I help you, sir?' the landlord asked, through a serving hatch cut into the passage wall.

'I've arranged to meet someone in the back bar, but I can't seem to find it.'

'Through there.' The landlord pointed past the stairs.

'Thank you.' Andrew had been wondering if Evan had deliberately led him astray. 'Could I have two pints of beer please?'

'If you pay now, I'll bring them through.'

Andrew counted out the correct money from the loose change in his pocket, and walked on.

The room was empty as Evan knew it would be. Dark and gloomy, it was lit by one small, high window that was overshadowed by the garden wall of Danygraig House. The dark brown paintwork and the wallpaper of pinkish chintz were overlaid with a thick nicotine-stained patina from the smokers who congregated in the room most nights. Andrew sat on an uncomfortable, overstuffed horsehair chair, pulling it close to an iron-legged, marble-topped table.

It was ten minutes, not five, before Evan arrived and he came carrying his own pint.

'I bought you one, sir,' Andrew said, rising as Evan walked into the room.

'I'd rather drink my own,' Evan said bluntly. 'Well, say what you want to, and quickly. This place will be closing for the afternoon in a quarter of an hour.'

'I've dropped all the charges against Eddie. He should be home soon.'

'Do you expect me to be grateful to you for that?'

'No. Not at all,' Andrew stammered, realising what he must have sounded like. 'I just thought you'd like to know. You must be worried about him.'

When Evan didn't say anything, he stumbled on, tripping over his words, wishing he could think clearly, that his head didn't hurt quite so much. 'I know I treated Bethan badly. . . . '

'You don't have to state the obvious,' Evan said briefly.

'I was sorry as soon as I left. I wrote to her, three times. When she didn't answer my letters I didn't know what to think. I came

405

home yesterday hoping to see her before Laura and Trevor's wedding. I intended to ask her to marry me. . . . '

'Bit bloody late.'

'Mr Powell, I take full responsibility for what I did to Bethan, but I swear to you I would never have left her if I'd known about the baby. I didn't find out until this afternoon when Trevor told me. Please, Mr Powell, all I want is to see her. Explain why I left if I can – and try and straighten all this out between us.'

'You're not short of guts, Andrew John. I'll give you that,' Evan said grudgingly before he drained his pint.

'Please, Mr Powell. I know I'm not welcome in your house. But I'll be in the New Inn tonight between six o'clock and eight. I'll wait for any message she might want to send me. Would you please just tell her that?'

'Aye, I will.'

'There's just one more thing,' he said wretchedly. 'Tell her . . . tell her that I love her,' he said simply. 'That I never stopped loving her. Not for one minute.'

'He said he wrote to me?' Bethan looked at her father through dark-rimmed eyes.

'Three letters.' Evan pushed his feet out on to the hearthrug, accidentally kicking Haydn and Eddie.

'I never got any letters.' She looked at Elizabeth, who was stirring a pot on the range. 'Mam, did any letters come for me?' she asked. 'Mam?' she asked again when Elizabeth failed to answer.

'Yes. But they came too late,' Elizabeth replied without turning around. 'You'd already married Alun.'

'You could have given them to me afterwards, when I came home,' Bethan reproached.

'I could have, if I'd remembered them.'

'Can I have them now?'

Elizabeth went to the dresser drawer. Pushing aside a neat pile of clean, ironed and darned tea towels she extracted three envelopes and handed them to Bethan. Bethan stared at them for a moment, turning them over in her hand, reading the address on the other side. Then she looked at the postmarks. The first had come two weeks before she'd married Alun. The second a week later, the third had been posted the day before her wedding.

'I kept them from you because I believed it was for the best, Bethan,' Elizabeth said coolly. 'I thought you had a respectable married life ahead of you with Alun. This one's crache. And they don't marry girls like you.'

'He's offering, Elizabeth,' Evan contradicted angrily.

'Mam's right for once,' Eddie said unexpectedly. 'He's a smarmy sod.'

'Language,' Evan reprimanded strongly. 'And after the scrape you've just got out of, you'd better keep your mouth closed and your fists for the ring.'

'Yes, Dad,' Eddie said meekly, elated because it was the first time that his father had recognised boxing as an essential part of his life.

'You don't intend to take up with him again do you, Beth?' Haydn demanded warily.

'No,' she said shortly, rising from her chair. She went to her mother and kissed her withered cheek. 'I know you did what you thought best, Mam, and I'm grateful for it,' she said kindly. 'I understand. I really do. I might even have done the same thing myself if I'd had a chance to.'

She left the room, carried the letters upstairs, lay on her bed and opened the first one.

Dear Bethan,
I'm sorry. Those two pathetic words are totally inadequate. They don't express a millionth part of the remorse I'm feeling right this minute. I love you, I miss you, and I want you, here in this cold miserable room of mine right now. Then I could tell you to your face that I didn't mean any of those things I said in the hospital that last night. Please, Bethan, can you forgive me?

If you came here, to London, we could rent rooms around the corner from the hospital. You'd like London. There's so many things to do and see, parks to walk in, fine buildings to look at, so much I could show you, museums, art galleries . . . we'd have to visit those because they're free and we wouldn't have much money. It will take me a few years

*to get my career to a stage where we'd be comfortable but
I could put up with a little discomfort as long as it was with
you. I know now that the only thing that matters to me is
you. Bethan, if you want to just sneak away from Pontypridd, write to me and I'll send you a train ticket. Just say
the word . . . .*

The letters danced before her on the page, especially the final
line –

Bethan, I love you.

I love you – The words seared into her mind as she opened the
other two letters. They were in the same vein, except for questions
as to why she'd ignored the first one. She could see Andrew's
hand penning them, read the selfishness behind the sentiments.
Selfishness that she'd refused to recognise when they'd been
together. He would have liked nothing better than for her to
sneak away unnoticed from Pontypridd, and join him in London.
And if he was talking marriage now, it was only since he'd found
out about the baby. There was mention of rooms that they could
share in the letter, but no marriage. She left the papers on the
bed and went to the window, half expecting to see him still
standing in the street. But it was empty, the thickly gathering
twilight casting shadows on to the stone-strewn roadway.

Weak, selfish, pampered, spoilt, sensual, kind – loving . . . all
those adjectives and more could be applied to him. She felt she
knew him better than he knew himself. And for all his arrogance,
all his faults, she knew now that she loved him. Would always
love him.

She closed the curtains, switched on the light, opened her dressing-table drawer and took out the chocolate box. Lifting the lid
she resisted the temptation to explore the treasures it contained
and laid the letters on top. After she closed it, she pulled down
an old ribbon of Maud's that was hanging over the mirror and
tied it round the box. Taking her time, she fashioned the ends
into a neat bow before stowing it away again. Memories and a
memory box. She felt as though she were physically consigning
Andrew John to her past.

'Bethan?' Her father knocked on the bedroom door.

'Come in,' she called out as she closed the drawer.

Evan didn't enter the room. He opened the door and remained on the landing. 'I forgot to tell you. He told me to say that he'd be in the New Inn tonight between six and eight if you wanted to send a message.'

'Thank you, Dad.'

'You've no intention of seeing him?'

'No.'

'You know your own mind best.'

'He left me,' she said bitterly, 'not the other way round.' She tensed herself, forcing the tears back that hovered behind her eyes. 'He hurt me. He hurt me. . . . '

'And now you're afraid to see him in case he does it again. Is that it?'

'Something like that.'

'Bethan love.' He went up to her and put his arm round her shoulders. 'I told you the night you married Alun that you only have one life. The best advice I can give to you is live it. Do whatever you want to do without being afraid of anything or anybody. Even failure.'

'You think I should see him, don't you?'

'I think you have to make your own mind up about that.'

'You must have an opinion,' she pressed.

'He's one unhappy young man who was brave enough to face me, Eddie and Haydn today in an attempt to get a message through to you. His last words to me in the pub were "Tell Bethan that I love her. That I never stopped loving her." '

'Then I'll go.'

'Not for me, love. You don't get out of it that way. Your own decisions and your own mistakes, remember. Besides I've only met him twice. I don't know him well enough to tell when he's lying. If you go and see him, end up marrying him and make a pig's ear out of your life you could come back to me and say "I took your advice, Dad, and look at the mess I'm in." I'm not taking responsibility for a decision like that.'

'Oh Dad,' she laughed as she buried her head in his shoulder. 'What would I do without you?'

'I hope you won't have to, girl. Look, Bethan, we all love you, and we'll take care of you, never fear. Only you can know if you want this chap or not. It appears he's there for the taking, but so is what you've got here. Suit yourself, girl, and make at least one person happy. Yourself.'

He looked over her head to the lights that burned behind Rhiannon Pugh's wall. He knew then that he'd never take his own advice. Caught between two women he'd live out his life as they dictated and as he lived it now. Facing Elizabeth's daily disappointments and bitterness, and handing out crumbs of comfort to Phyllis because that was all she was prepared to accept from him. Any more would upset the safe little world she had cocooned herself and Rhiannon in.

'We all love you, snookems, but in the end you have to do what's right for you,' he murmured. 'If you don't you'll make a dog's dinner of your life like your mother has. And,' he closed his eyes to Rhiannon's light, 'and like I have,' he whispered softly. So softly she failed to hear him.

It was deserted in the New Inn at six o'clock when Trevor walked in with Andrew.

'She won't come, you know,' he said bluntly.

'I know. But anywhere's better than home. I couldn't have sat with my parents for another minute.'

'Trouble?' Trevor raised his eyebrows. 'They didn't approve of you dropping the charges against Eddie?'

'That and the few home truths I told them about getting Bethan pushed out of the Graig Hospital this morning.'

'I see. Happy families.'

'Take note. It could be you one day.'

'Not me, I'm going to be the perfect father.' He faltered as Andrew paled. 'I'll get the drinks. What do you want? Whisky?'

'With concussion?'

'Should go nicely.'

'I'll stick to a small beer.'

Trevor went to the bar and carried the beer and a whisky over to the unobtrusive corner table that Andrew had chosen.

'Some bachelor party. I'm sorry,' Andrew apologised.

'I'm meeting Laura's brothers at seven in the Vic. If you want to come you can.'

'Would I be welcome?'

'With Laura's brothers? I don't know,' Trevor replied honestly. 'Feelings run pretty high in that family, and they're all fond of Bethan. You know what Graig people are like about one of their own.'

'I'm beginning to find out.'

'I invited Evan Powell, Haydn, William, Charlie and Eddie as well. Haydn can't come until later because he's working, but it's a fair bet the others will. Can you see yourself drinking round the same table as them?'

'Not really. Well here's to you and yours.' Andrew raised his glass, and pushed a small package across the table.

'What's this?'

'Wedding present. Sorry I won't be able to make it tomorrow but I'm catching the early train to London.'

'I thought you had four days off.'

'I have. I want to spend a couple of them looking for a new place. It's time I moved on from Fe and Alec's house.'

Trevor tore open the brown paper package and stared at the notebook it contained. He looked quizzically at Andrew.

'I've booked dinners and tickets to seven shows in London. The venues, dates and times are all there. Do turn up, I've already paid for them. I telephoned a chap who works in my bank this afternoon to arrange it all.'

'I don't know what to say.'

'Laura deserves a decent honeymoon. And we all know that your idea of an evening's entertainment is a newspaper full of fish and chips and an evening's stroll.'

'Not my idea. My pocket's.'

'Enjoy yourself. On me. Time for one more?' he asked, picking up the glasses.

'Quick one.'

She walked in when he was at the bar. Her old black coat hid her figure, but she was thinner in the face, paler than he remembered.

'I'll see you, Andrew.' Trevor walked into the next room, where Ronnie and William were sitting, full pints in front of them.

'You brought bodyguards?' Andrew said caustically. 'For pity's sake what did you think I was going to do to you in here of all places?' He could have kicked himself. He hadn't meant to open on this tack.

'Ronnie brought me down, and he's taking me back. Eddie and Haydn guessed where I was going and they wouldn't let me come on my own. Not on a Saturday night, and after what happened yesterday I wouldn't let either of them come with me. This is a compromise.'

'Can I get you something?'

'No thank you,' she said politely. 'I can't stay very long. Ronnie wants to go back in a few minutes. Big night, Trevor's bachelor party.' She shrugged her shoulders. 'And I promised to spend the evening with Laura.'

'A coffee then?'

'No really, nothing thank you.'

'It appears I can't buy any Powell a drink,' he commented lightly, remembering her father and the pint he'd refused that afternoon.

Their conversation might have been one spoken by total strangers. But the quick, nervous movements of her hands and his eyes betrayed their emotions. She sat in the chair Trevor had vacated. 'You wanted to see me?' she asked.

'I'm sorry. . . . '

'I know. I read your letters. I didn't get them until today.'

'I meant what I said in them. I know it's late to ask, but will you marry me?' he said quietly, with dignity.

'Because I'm carrying your child?'

'No. Because I love you. God, when I think of what you've gone through . . . marrying Alun Jones – '

'He didn't touch me,' she snapped defensively. 'Not in the way you did.'

'Beth, you don't have to explain what happened. Not to me. I blame myself for all those dreadful things I said. Please, can't we put it behind us? Won't you come to London with me tomorrow? We'll get married there as soon as I can arrange it.'

'You think it's that simple? Do you realise you're asking me to uproot myself from everything I know? My friends. My family. . . . '

'I know I'm asking a lot.'

'You're asking for too much,' she said firmly. 'My brothers

412

hate you. My father's desperately trying to be fair, but he doesn't like you, not really. . . . '

'Beth, that's your family,' he protested. 'Not you.'

'Your family despise me. It's good of you to ask, Andrew. Particularly given my background. . . . '

'Bethan!'

'Please let me finish. It wouldn't work, Andrew. We're from different worlds.'

'We could live in the same one in London.'

'Even in London there's bread and dripping and melba toast and caviare. I'm one, you're the other.'

'You don't love me any more?'

'I don't trust you any more, and London's a long way from help and my family.'

'I'd look after you, Beth. And you could come back whenever you wanted to. It's only a day away by train.'

He wanted to change her heart and mind so much he had to restrain himself from reaching out and physically carrying her off there and then. He racked his memory, trying to remember eloquent phrases. Words with which to convince her that he was sincere.

'When you left, my family were wonderful,' she said quietly. 'I realised then how lucky I was to have them. I know them. I trust them, and my father and brothers have promised to look after me and the baby after it's born. With their support I can build a life for both of us. A good life. I hope to go back to nursing if I can. My mother will take care of the baby.'

'You're shutting me out,' he said despairingly.

'No. I'm choosing the safe option. One I know will work. One I'm familiar with.'

'You'll let me pay maintenance or whatever it is?'

'For the baby when it comes.'

'I could give you some money now.'

'I'd rather you asked your father to influence the Hospital Board to look kindly on any future job applications I make.'

'Beth, I'm sorry, I had nothing to do with that.'

'I know.' She rose from her chair. 'Goodbye, Andrew, I really do have to go.'

'You sure you won't reconsider? I'm leaving on the eight

413

o'clock train tomorrow. If I thought there was a chance that you'd change your mind. . . . '

'There's no chance.' She held out her hand. He took it, but instead of shaking it he held it tight.

'Beth, does it have to end like this?'

'Goodbye, Andrew,' she said loudly. William and Ronnie left their seats. Moving close to Bethan they stood behind her, waiting.

'Goodbye, Bethan,' he whispered forlornly, as he watched her leave.

'Drink?' Trevor held out a fresh half-pint.

'No thank you. I have packing to do.' He smiled. 'Have a good wedding tomorrow.'

'I'll try,' Trevor replied, feeling utterly helpless as he watched Andrew walk out.

'You didn't have to wait up for us, love,' Evan said as he walked into the house with the boys and Charlie.

'I couldn't sleep. Never can after a stint on nights. And judging by the state of you, it's just as well I've made some tea. You could all do with something to water it down with.'

'Water nothing down,' Haydn grumbled. 'I've only had two pints.'

'You're the only one who did,' she said, watching Charlie prop William up as he tripped over the step up to the washhouse.

'If you think we're bad,' William slurred, 'you should see Trevor.'

'Oh God, what have you done to him?'

'Nothing Laura won't be able to fix tomorrow,' William laughed maliciously.

'Quiet,' Bethan commanded, 'or you'll wake Mam up and then we'll all be for it.'

It took the combined efforts of Evan, Charlie and her to get the three boys to bed. But she didn't feel tired, not even after she cleared up the dishes they'd left.

'You saw him then?' Evan sat in his chair pulling on his empty pipe, watching Beth as she moved around the room.

'Yes.'

'And?'

414

'And nothing, Dad. After what he did I just don't trust him any more.'

'I see. Just answer me one thing, love,' he said slowly. 'Do you love him?'

'I thought I did,' she answered sharply.

'And now?'

'I don't know,' she said wearily, sitting on her mother's chair.

'You've sent him packing?' She nodded her head. 'I hope you're not making a mistake, Beth. It's just that the way you spoke to the boys just now, you put me in mind of your mother.'

Bethan knew he would never have made such a damning comparison if he'd been sober.

'Don't grow old and bitter before your time.' He tapped his empty pipe from force of habit against the range as he left his chair. 'It blights lives.'

He could have added 'like ours have been blighted by your mother', but didn't. The inference hung unspoken in the air, like smoke from damp coals smouldering on a fire.

Andrew paid the porter to carry his trunk and case up from the car to the train. The platform was cold and windswept, the rain snarling in great sheets under the overhanging roof, soaking his socks and the legs of his trousers.

'Pity about the weather,' he said as he huddled into his coat. 'Trevor and Laura deserve a better day.'

'I wish you wouldn't rush back this way,' his father fussed.

'I want to get back.'

'But you're not one hundred per cent, and there's no real hurry. You said so yourself. You can hardly work with that head of yours.'

'I'm well enough. And I want to use the next couple of days to look for an apartment. I can't live with Fe and Alec for ever.'

'You've upset your mother. She's very disappointed.'

'I'm sorry she's disappointed. But the time has come for me to make my own decisions, and run my own life.'

'So I see.'

'Dad, there's really no point in discussing this any more.'

'If all this nonsense had been about a decent girl I might have understood it. But about the daughter of a miner . . . . '

415

'Here's my train.' Andrew breathed a sigh of relief, shook his father's hand and followed the porter to the first-class carriages behind the engine.

'We'll see you soon,' his father called out as Andrew stepped on board.

'I'll write,' he replied briefly.

Goodbyes said, he settled down in a compartment that was mercifully empty. His trunk safely stowed above him, he stretched out and opened his small doctor's case, extracting the newspaper he'd bought from the boy outside the station. Underneath it he saw a book, the same book he'd tried and failed to read the night he'd gone to the hospital to tell Bethan it was over between them. He'd never read it, and he didn't want to start now. Next to it he'd packed her photograph. He picked it up and unwrapped it from the scarf he'd wound around the glass to protect it. The whistle blew. The train moved slowly out of the station. Disconsolately he stared out of the window – at the blackened brick walls that led out of the station; the dirty moss-green and bracken-spattered hillsides; the tips, slag heaps, smoking chimneys of the terraced houses . . . everything reminded him of her. He was leaving Bethan behind and he felt as though his heart was being wrenched out of his body.

The stations passed and his newspaper remained unread. Treforest . . . Taffs Well . . . .

'I only had enough money for third class so if you want to sit with me you're going to have to come down in the world, Doctor John.' Bethan stood in front of him in her shapeless black coat. A cardboard suitcase in her hand. A ridiculous cloche hat on her head. 'I'll be honest with you. I'm not at all sure that I'm doing the right thing. I've a feeling that I've just made the biggest mistake of my life. I meant every word that I said to you last night. . . .'

He rose to his feet and silenced her by placing his mouth over hers. She dropped the suitcase as he gathered her into his arms.

'I love you, Bethan Powell,' he murmured after he'd kissed her. 'More than you'll ever know.'

She clung to him, burying herself in the old familiar sensations:

416

the warmth of his body close to hers, the smell of his tobacco mixed with his cologne, the feel of his fingers stroking her neck.

'I love you too, Andrew John, but is love enough?' she asked seriously. 'We're different beings from different worlds, you and I. We've nothing in common. I'll never be a lady like your mother and you'll never be a collier like my father.'

'We could try being ourselves.' He pressed his cheek against hers.

'I mean it,' she murmured, reeling from the hunger he aroused within her. 'You should know what you're taking on. All I own in the world is in that suitcase, and the whole lot isn't worth much more than a pound. I'm six months pregnant, and practically penniless. . . . '

'Tickets!' the conductor called as he walked down the corridor towards them.

'I have to go,' she said. 'Back to third class where I belong.'

'I could pay the difference.' He swung her down on to the seat beside him.

'You could, but you still won't make a silk purse out of a sow's ear,' she smiled.

'Then how about we split the difference, my love, and move down to second class?'

She laughed softly as he swung her into his arms.

'Is this where married life begins; with you demoting me to second class?' he asked.

She looked at him with her enormous dark eyes, and held out her hand. 'Yes please, Doctor John,' she murmured quietly. 'Shall we go?'

One Blue Moon

For my cousin Marion Goodwin and all those who
have fought the illnesses associated with
the Welsh valleys armed with nothing more
than patience, courage and the
indomitable Welsh sense of humour

Acknowledgements

The 'research' (if you can grace it by that name, for I was totally unaware that I was doing anything so grand) for this book began years ago, when as a schoolgirl anxious to earn pocket money, I took a Saturday job in Pontypridd, in where else but an Italian owned and run café. I very quickly discovered that the Italian race are warm, generous (dare I say soft) hearted and, like the Welsh, ever ready to help anyone in genuine need. My employers and my co-workers taught me a great deal, and not just about the café and restaurant business.

I also owe a great debt of gratitude to Mr Romeo Basini of Treorchy, who is every bit as wonderful as his name, for his inexhaustible fund of knowledge both about the Welsh/Italian cafés, and about rural life in Bardi in the 1930s. He very kindly allowed me to monopolise many of his lunch hours when I am sure he would have been far happier taking his customary walk and breath of fresh air.

I would also like to thank my parents Glyn and Gerda Jones, for their love, and the continual help they both give me with my research.

Mid-Glamorgan County Library Service, the County Librarian Mr J. I. Davies, and all the staff of Pontypridd Library, especially Mr Adrian Burton and Mrs Penny Pughe for their constant ongoing assistance and support in ways far too numerous to mention.

My husband John and my children Ralph, Sophie and Ross, for only moaning 'a little bit' when I took this unfinished book on our annual holiday.

Jennifer Price and Margaret Bloomfield without whose friend-ship and practical help I would cease to function.

And above all my editor Jo Frank, who was always on the end of the telephone when I needed a sympathetic ear, and who kept the book firmly on course, and my agent Michael Thomas for his help and many kindnesses.

Thank you.

I have again taken the liberty of mixing real people with my fictional ones, particularly theatrical artistes, such as Willi Pantzer who actually toured South Wales in the 1930s. However, I would like to stress that all my main characters, although firmly rooted in the Welsh and Italian Welsh communities of the valleys in the thirties are entirely fictional and creations of my imagination. And while gratefully acknowledging all the help I have received with my research I would also like to say that any errors in *One Blue Moon* are entirely mine.

Catrin Collier, August 1992

Chapter One

Most people, especially men, thought of Diana Powell as pretty. She was, in a fresh, youthful, plump kind of a way. Red, rosy cheeks highlighted flawless, creamy skin, her brown eyes sparkled with vitality, and as she travelled towards Pontypridd in the train with her cousin Maud, her lips were as perfect, pouting, expressive and red as Carole Lombard's on the poster for her latest film *Lady by Choice*. A poster that had been plastered over every available inch of hoarding heading out of Cardiff station, thus giving Diana ample time to study and imitate. Even the curls that escaped from beneath Diana's market stall version of the current fashionable cloche hat bounced shining and wavy, despite the damp, heavy atmosphere.

Maud Powell didn't resent her cousin Diana's attractive looks. Envy had never been a part of Maud's nature, and her naturally sunny disposition was the one constant that remained, even now, with her body weak and devastated by sickness. But occasionally, she wished – and dreamed herself into health every bit as exuberant and vigorous as Diana's. Slumped back against the grimy upholstery of the sagging railway carriage bench seat, she closed her eyes and indulged in what had rapidly become her favourite occupation – daydreaming.

She was in danger, terrible danger, but the peril wasn't great enough to interfere with her grooming. A long, creamy satin gown clung to her figure, suddenly, miraculously transformed from scrawny to curvaceous in all the right places. Swirls of ostrich feathers swanned around her ankles in a fashion reminiscent of Ginger Rogers. White kid gloves clad her arms to the elbow, her blonde hair was immaculately waved and gleaming. Her face, no longer pale and haggard, was stunningly, heart-stoppingly beautiful. And every time she moved, the perfume of magnolia blossom wafted from her skin, scenting the atmosphere. (She didn't have a clue what magnolia blossom smelt like, but she'd liked the sound of the name when Robert Taylor had praised it in one of his films.)

1

She was running – running along an upstairs corridor in a Hollywood version of the English country manor (the only version she'd ever seen) that was filled with acrid smoke. Flames licked at her heels as she stood, alone and vulnerable at the top of a magnificent burning staircase. She cried out, and there walking towards her through the smoke and the fire, arms outstretched waiting to carry her away, was – was . . . this posed the most difficult question in any daydream. She hated having to choose between tall, elegant, aesthetic, poetic Leslie Howard, and robust, cynical, darkly handsome Clark Gable.

A coughing fit shook her thin frame, jolting her sharply back into the present. Lifting her sodden handkerchief to her stained lips, she looked around the railway carriage in bewilderment.

'Off on a fancy again? With Robert Donat instead of that porter, I hope,' Diana said caustically. 'Here, you're hopeless.' Seeing the state of Maud's handkerchief she pulled a crumpled white cotton square out of her coat pocket.

'I can't take yours. I'll stain it, and it won't wash out,' Maud gasped breathlessly.

'Then I'll just have to bleach it before I put it in the wash, won't I?' Diana thrust the handkerchief impatiently into Maud's hand. 'Here. Yours is soaking.' She rummaged in her coat pocket, found an empty triangular sweet bag and held it out.

'Thanks.' Maud dropped her bloodstained handkerchief into the bag as she turned to stare out of the rain-spattered window. All her carefully nurtured romantic images had fled. Unable to rekindle the sense of exoticism, she despised herself for her foolish fancies. Looking the way she did, a tramp wouldn't waste time on a second glance, let alone Clark Gable.

As she closed her eyes again, another, darker image came to mind. A winter's scene. Cold, dismal. Rain noisily spattering the bark and dead leaves of the skeletal trees that laced the grey skies above Glyntaff cemetery. On the ground, vibrant splashes of white and red flowers piled next to a mound of freshly dug earth – would they have to be wax flowers if it was winter? The headstone in the mason's yard close to the gate, already chiselled and embossed with shiny new black Gothic lettering

Here lies Maud Powell
Cut down in the full flush of youth
aged 16 in 193—

Nineteen thirty what? Would it be this year's date, or next? Would she live to see the New Year in? If she did there'd be Christmas to look forward to. Her father nearly always managed to get a chicken, and she could hang up her stocking . . .

'Almost there,' Diana observed briskly, shattering Maud's lachrymose thoughts as moss-green hills crowned by precarious pyramids of black slag began to roll sedately past.

'Unfortunately,' Maud snapped with unintentional harshness as she was prised from the tragic scenario of her own funeral.

'Well, it might not be the homecoming we dreamed of when we left for Cardiff, but at least it is a homecoming,' Diana commented philosophically, buttoning the old red wool coat that she'd 'turned' at the beginning of winter.

'I'm dreading telling everyone that Matron asked me to leave.'

'You won't have to say a word,' Diana reassured her bleakly. 'One look at you will be enough. You're in no fit state to be a patient in the Royal Infirmary, let alone a ward maid.'

'If I get better, they will take me back, won't they?' Maud demanded, struggling for breath.

'If you've any sense left, you won't ask,' Diana retorted. 'No one with a brain in their head would want to work as a skivvy in that place.'

'It wasn't that bad,' Maud protested. 'And they would have taken us on as trainee nurses when we were seventeen.'

'You, perhaps, Miss Goody Two-Shoes, not me.' Seeing despondency surface in Maud's face yet again, Diana reached out and touched her cousin's hand. 'A couple of months' rest at home, in the warm, in front of the fire, and you'll be right as rain,' she asserted boldly, hoping she sounded more convincing than she felt. 'Then if you really want to carry on scrubbing floors, emptying bedpans and cleaning lavatories for the rest of your life, I'm sure they'll welcome you back with open arms.'

'I didn't like that side of it, any more than you did,' Maud countered irritably. 'But it was a way into nursing, and all I've wanted since Bethan passed her exams was to be a nurse like her.'

3

'Little sister, big sister! Well thank God I've no one's footsteps to follow in except dear brother William's, and as he's an absolute waster, that leaves the coast clear for me to do as I like.' Diana deliberately chose not to mention her mother, Megan, who was in jail for handling stolen goods. 'And before you go all noble, sacrificial and Florence Nightingale on me, remember, even Bethan got out of it as soon as she could.'

'After she qualified, and only when she married,' Maud remonstrated.

'Aha! So that's it. You want to marry a doctor. Well it beats me how Bethan managed to hook one. The nearest I ever got to the almighty breed was to scrub their dirty bootmarks off the floor after they'd passed by. A long time after they'd passed by,' she qualified sourly.

'I do hope Bethan's taking care of herself,' Maud murmured absently. 'It's bad enough having to live amongst strangers in London, but being pregnant as well must be horrible.'

'She's better off than most with a doctor for a husband.' Diana rose to her feet and lifted down their shabby and threadbare gladstones from the knotted string rack above their heads. 'He'll bring home enough to keep her in the lap of luxury. Bet he even buys her roses and chocolates on pay night, which is more than you and me'll ever have if we don't pull our fingers out and start looking for something better than that porter you got mixed up with in the Infirmary,' she added practically.

'I wasn't mixed up with him!'

'No, you only held his hand every time you thought no one was looking.'

'He was so far from home, and lonely.'

'And you're a sucker for a corny line.'

'I am not!' Maud gasped indignantly.

'Jock Maitlin was a self-righteous, self-seeking, selfish clot, who wanted someone to wash his dirty socks, and you didn't even wait for him to ask.'

'Diana, everyone knows how helpless men are.'

'And helpless they'll remain while there are idiots like you willing to run after them. Look, we're here.' Diana turned away from Maud and gathered up her handbag.

Maud rose unsteadily to her feet, succumbed to yet another

4

vicious coughing fit that lent unhealthy colour to her face, and sank weakly down on the seat again. Diana flung open the door, threw out their bags and looked back at her cousin.

'Here, grab my arm!' she commanded ungraciously. 'The guard's about to blow the whistle, and I've no intention of carrying on up to Trehafod.'

'I'm sorry,' Maud whispered hoarsely, as she clutched Diana's sleeve and stumbled out on to the platform.

'Oh God, what am I going to do with you?' Diana griped as, ignoring their bags, she struggled to dump Maud on a bench set against the wall of the refreshment bar. Maud had no voice left to apologise a second time. She fell on to the grubby seat and continued to cough into Diana's now bloody handkerchief.

'Damn! There's not a soul around we know,' Diana cursed, as she scanned the crowds that were leaving the train and pushing their way past the ticket collector's booth at the top of the wide, steep stone flight of stairs that led down into the station yard. 'And it's raining cats and dogs,' she continued to moan, brushing away the raindrops that were falling on to her head from the high roof of the open platform. 'Well you'll just have to jolly well sit there while I carry the bags,' she asserted forcefully, abandoning Maud and picking up their luggage. 'I'll leave them downstairs, and come back up for you.'

'I'll take your bags, Miss.'

Diana stared coolly at the young, scrawny, ginger-haired porter.

'I haven't any money to tip you,' she said bluntly.

'I'd settle for a kiss,' he grinned cheekily.

'Chance would be a fine thing,' Diana retorted.

'Visit to the pictures tonight, then? Dutch treat.'

'I'd sooner go out with . . .' The whistle blew and the sound of the steam engine drowned out the rest of Diana's words, which was probably just as well.

'Why don't you stick to old ladies, Pugh, and leave the young ones to those experienced enough to deal with them?' A square-built, thickset porter elbowed Pugh aside and swept Diana's bags from her hands.

'Here, where do you think you're going?' she shouted furiously.

'Station yard,' he called back glibly, running smartly down the stone steps.

5

'Men!' Diana gripped her handbag firmly in her left hand, and offered her right to Maud.

'I'm sorry for being such a trouble,' Maud wheezed from behind the handkerchief she still clutched to her mouth.

'For pity's sake stop apologising,' Diana snapped.

'Diana . . . I . . .' Black mists swirled upwards from Maud's feet. The grey stone platform spotted with black coal smuts, the mass of ill-dressed women and damp, red-nosed children revolved headily around her. She slumped forward.

'She's in a bad way,' the young porter observed tactlessly as he struggled to catch Maud's head before it hit the flagstones. 'Consumption, is it?'

'Of course it's bloody consumption,' Diana raged as the anger she'd barely managed to hold in check all morning finally erupted. 'Any fool can see that.'

'She looks just like my older sister did before she went.' For all of his slender build, the boy scooped Maud high into his arms. 'She died last year,' he added forlornly.

Diana heard what he said, but her temper had risen too high for her to think of commiserating on his loss.

'Is there anyone meeting you?' he asked, as he carried Maud down the steps.

'No one,' Diana said flatly. 'Our family don't even know we're on our way home.'

'There's usually a taxi waiting in the yard.'

'Do we look as though we've money to pay for a taxi?' she demanded hotly.

'Have you far to go?'

'The top of the Graig hill.'

'I could always carry her to the Graig hospital. It's only around the corner.'

'I *do* know where the Graig hospital is. I've lived here all my life, and I'm not putting her' – she pointed at Maud – 'in any TB ward. There's only one way they come out of there, and that's feet first, in a box.'

The boy turned white; Diana's bluntness conjured up painful images of his sister's death and funeral. Images that constantly hovered too close to consciousness for peace of mind.

'She needs help,' he emphasised bitterly. Turning left at the foot

6

of the steps he walked swiftly through the rain into the shelter of the booking hall.

'What do you think you're doing, Pugh?' the porter who'd carried Diana's bags down demanded.

'Young lady passed out cold.'

'Yes well, that's as may be. But now you'd better leave her to me and get back on to the platform before you're missed. I'll call you a taxi, Miss,' he smirked at Diana.

'You most certainly won't,' Diana said fiercely. She thought quickly. If her brother William's friend Giacomo 'Ronnie' Ronconi was working in his family's café on the Tumble, his Trojan van wouldn't be far, and once he saw the state Maud was in he could hardly refuse to drive them up the hill. 'Carry her across to Ronconi's café,' she ordered Pugh, as she picked up her bags from the older porter's feet. 'Ronnie's a friend of ours. He'll see us home.'

'Pugh, you know you're not allowed to leave station yard during working hours,' the older porter lectured, ruffled by Diana's offhand dismissal of his services.

'That's all right. I'll take the lady from here.' A tall thickset man with light brown curly hair, who for all of his size, weight and athletic build had a soft feminine look about him, lifted Maud from Pugh's arms.

'Wyn Rees!' Forgetting her brother's antipathy to Rees the sweetshop's son, who was more commonly known in the town as 'Rees the queer', Diana hugged him out of sheer joy at seeing a familiar face. 'Where did you spring from?'

'Saw the commotion as I was on my way back to the shop from the post office,' Wyn explained. 'Dear God, Maud's lost weight!' he exclaimed, shifting her to a more comfortable position. 'What have you two been doing to yourselves in Cardiff?'

'Working ourselves to the bone.'

'So I see. Did I hear you say you wanted to go to Ronnie's?'

Diana nodded.

Tenting his coat over Maud's head, he walked out of station yard and crossed the road quickly, avoiding a milk cart laden with churns that came rattling down the Graig hill at full tilt. Sidestepping a couple of boys on delivery bicycles, he pushed through a gawping group of gossiping women, and into the café.

7

Struggling with the two gladstones, Diana failed to keep up with him. By the time she'd opened the café door, Tina Ronconi, Ronnie's sister, had taken Maud from Wyn, uprooted two customers, stretched Maud out across their chairs and was bathing her temples with cold water.

Hot, steamy air, and mouthwatering warm aromas of freshly ground coffee and savoury frying, blasted welcomingly into Diana's face as she dropped her bags and closed the door. The interior of the café was dark, gloomy and blessedly, marvellously, familiar. A long mahogany counter dominated the left-hand side of the room, with matching shelves behind it, backed by an enormous mirror that reflected the rear of the huge mock-marble soda foundtain, and stone lemon, lime and sarsaprilla cordial jars. A crammed conglomeration of glass sweet jars, open boxes of chocolate bars, carefully piled packets of cigarettes, cups, saucers and glass cases of iced and cream cakes filled every available inch of space on the wooden shelves.

She paused and listened for a moment, making out the distinctive voice of her old schoolfriend, Tony Ronconi, as it drifted noisily above the din of café conversation from behind the curtained doorway that led into the unseen recesses of the kitchen. All the tables she could see were taken. They were every Saturday morning, especially those around the stove that belched warmth into the 'front' room of the café. Through the arched alcove she could see a tram crew huddled round the open fire in the back area, shoes off, feet on fender drying their soaking socks.

'I see you looked after Maud all right?' Ronnie, the eldest and most cynical of the second generation of Ronconis, called from behind the counter where he was pouring six mugs of tea simultaneously.

'I'd like to see you look after anyone where we've come from, Ronnie Ronconi,' Diana scowled, moving the bags out of the doorway and closer to the chairs Maud was lying on.

'Here,' Ronnie pushed a cup of tea and the sugar shaker across the counter towards her. 'Tony?' he called out to the brother next in line to him, who was working in the kitchen. 'Take over for me.'

'Who's going to do the vegetables for the dinners if I have to work behind the counter?' Tony asked indignantly as he appeared from behind the curtain. 'Angelo can't. He's still washing

8

breakfast dishes. At half speed,' he added. Noticing Diana for the first time, he smiled and nodded to her.

'It's only ten o'clock,' Ronnie countered, quashing his brother's complaints. 'Papa and I used to get out seventy dinners in two and half hours on a Saturday in High Street with no help, and only an hour's preparation. Time you learnt to do the same, my boy.'

Maud began to cough.

'Prop her up, you stupid girls,' Ronnie shouted at his sister and Diana. 'Can't you see she's choking?' Lifting himself on the flat of his hands he swung his long, lithe body easily over the high counter. He pushed his hand beneath Maud's back and eased her into a sitting position. Startled by how light she was, he failed to stop the shock from registering on his face. He looked up. Diana was watching him. 'I've seen more meat on picked chicken bones,' he commented. 'Didn't they feed you in the Infirmary?'

'Slops and leftovers, and not enough of those,' Diana said harshly.

'You back for the weekend, Diana?' Tina asked brightly in a clumsy effort to lighten the atmosphere generated by Ronnie's insensitive questioning.

'No, back for good,' Diana said flatly.

'Job didn't work out then?' Tina asked.

'They gave us all a medical yesterday. Afterwards they told Maud she was too ill to work. Swines handed over her wages along with her cards. I could hardly let her come home on her own.'

'Language!' Ronnie reprimanded. 'If you were my sister I'd drag you into the kitchen and scrub your mouth out with washing soda.'

'Then it's just as well I'm not your sister.'

'One more word from you, young lady, and I'll put you outside the door.'

Diana fell silent. Although Ronnie was eleven years older than her, and more her brother's friend than hers, she knew him well enough. He wasn't one for making idle threats, and she was too worried about Maud to risk being parted from her now, when they were so close to home.

'They only told Maud to leave yesterday?' Ronnie demanded incredulously as he brushed Maud's fair curls away from her face with a gesture that was uncommonly tender, for him.

9

'It was as much as they could do to let us sleep in our beds in the hostel last night. New girls took over from us today.'

'Maud didn't get like this in a day or two, I know.'

'She never was very strong,' Diana insisted defensively. 'And as soon as the weather turned really cold, she got worse.'

'Stop talking about me as if I wasn't here,' Maud murmured, consciousness coinciding with yet another coughing fit.

'See what you get for trying to talk?' Ronnie unpinned the corners of the tea towel he was wearing round his waist and flung it at Tony. 'I'm going to get the Trojan out of the White Hart yard. You'll have to hurry the dishes and do the vegetables as well Angelo,' he ordered his fifteen-year-old brother, who was peeking out from behind the kitchen curtain to find out what all the commotion was about.

'I was going to the penny rush in the White Palace. Why should I do Tony's jobs as well as my own?' he complained.

'Because Tony's needed behind the counter, and because I'm telling you to,' Ronnie said forcefully.

'Well I'm not doing the cooking as well.' Angelo slammed the pile of tea plates he was holding on to the counter. 'And that's final.'

'I wouldn't trust you to,' Ronnie rejoined.

'Then who is?' Angelo demanded.

'Tina, and before you say another word, think of Tony. He'll have to manage both the counter and the tables for half an hour.'

'But Ronnie, you promised I could go to the penny rush this week. You promised.'

'Just stop your griping and get on with it, will you? It's time all three of you learned to cope on your own for five minutes.'

'Ronnie . . .'

'One more word out of you, Angelo, and you'll be working every night next week.' He looked at the girls. 'When you hear the horn, get Maud ready. I'll come in and carry her outside.'

'Thanks, Ronnie.' Diana was grateful to him for not making her beg for the lift. She finally picked up her tea from the counter and sugared it.

'There's no need to thank me. I owe Will a favour. And you,' he glared at Tina. 'Take a good look at these two and think twice before you try to nag Papa or me into letting you leave home again.'

10

'See what you've done, Diana,' Tina hissed as Ronnie went out. 'Now they'll never let any of us leave home.'

'Except to visit our grandmother in the back end of Italy,' Angelo crowed. He'd never had any desire to leave Pontypridd.

'Don't you dare go rubbing it in, Angelo Ronconi,' Tina snapped.

'Leaving home's not all it's cracked up to be. Is it kid?' Diana helped Maud to sit up while looking around for Wyn. She wanted to thank him. The first familiar face in Pontypridd had shown her that she no longer had to shoulder the problem of Maud's illness alone. But she couldn't see him anywhere.

Maud closed her eyes again, too weak even to voice agreement with Diana. At that moment she would have given every penny that she'd managed to save since September to turn the clock back two years. She wanted to be fourteen again. Curled up in her big, warm, comfortable, flannel-sheeted double bed, a stone foot-warmer at her feet, and her big sister Bethan to soothe and cuddle her.

But Bethan wasn't home, and before she'd be allowed go to bed she'd have to face her mother. One glance at the apprehension on Diana's face was enough to tell her that she wasn't the only one dreading the encounter.

Chapter Two

'You're going the wrong way,' Diana protested, struggling to prevent Maud from falling on to Ronnie as he swung the Trojan around a sharp left turn a third of the way up the Graig hill. Ronnie had insisted on sandwiching Maud on the bench seat between them, but with Maud still teetering on the point of collapse, Diana was finding the drive up the hill more of a strain than the train journey.

'I'm stopping off at Laura and Trevor's,' Ronnie announced. 'What's the point in having a sister married to a doctor if you don't make use of him occasionally?' The eldest of eleven children, he was accustomed to making decisions and assuming authority. Authority strengthened by the business responsibilities his father had thrust upon him at an early age, and his mother's habit of deferring to him almost as much as she deferred to her husband.

'I think Maud should go straight home to bed,' Diana said forcefully.

'And I think she needs to see a doctor,' Ronnie countermanded, swinging the van round to the right and pulling up outside a low terrace of stone houses that fronted directly on to the pavement. 'And if you're worrying about Trevor's bill, don't. Your uncle pays Trevor his penny a week same as all the other families on the Graig. Trevor won't charge him any more for looking at Maud now.'

'I didn't think he would.' Diana flung open the door of the van and turned to help Maud, but Ronnie had already lifted her cousin from the van. Cradling Maud in one arm, he opened the front door of one of the houses with his free hand.

'Laura!' he shouted, walking straight past the parlour, down the narrow passage and into the back kitchen.

'Ronnie?' Laura answered from the range where she was stirring a pot of stew. 'I am honoured,' she said sarcastically. 'What brings you here in the middle of the day, and a market day at that . . . Dear God!' She stepped back, dropping the spoon to the floor as

12

Ronnie carried Maud into the tiny room and set her down in an easy chair comfortably placed in front of the fire.

'She's ill,' Ronnie announced somewhat superfluously as Laura, still very much the nurse despite her new status of housewife, loosened the collar of Maud's coat and checked her temperature by laying her cool hand against Maud's flushed cheek. She looked up and nodded to Diana, who was hovering awkwardly in the passageway just outside the kitchen door. Seeing condemnation where none was intended in Laura's glance, Diana forced back the tears that were stinging the back of her eyes.

'The Infirmary didn't work out then?' Laura asked.

Diana shook her head.

'They've just come in on the Cardiff train,' Ronnie explained briefly. 'Maud fainted in the station so I thought it might be as well if Trevor took a look at her before I take her home.'

'He's in the Central Homes.' Laura glanced up at a smart black modern clock on the wall. 'I'll telephone and see if I can get hold of him. Morning ward rounds should be about finishing by now. I'm sure he'll be able to spare a few minutes.'

'I'm fine,' Maud murmured faintly.

'I can see just how fine you are my girl,' Laura said in a calm voice that reminded Maud of her sister Bethan. 'I'll telephone. Diana, get your hat and coat off and make us all some tea.'

Diana did as she was asked, while Laura went into the hall. Ronnie sat in the easy chair at the opposite end of the range to Maud's. He pulled the *Pontypridd Observer* out from behind the cushion at his back, propped his feet up on a kitchen chair, and began to read.

Diana bustled around, checking the kettle was full, lifting cups down from the dresser, all the while marvelling that Laura – the Laura she'd known ever since she could remember – had a telephone in her house, and a doctor for a husband.

'Trevor will be here in five minutes.' Laura wiped her hands on her overall and checked her reflection in the bevel-edged mirror that hung above the table. She had to lean over the table in order to do so: there wasn't much free space to move around in between the range, easy chairs, dresser, table and kitchen chairs.

'Bride primping for hubby?' Ronnie teased, peering over the top of the paper.

13

'Just checking to see I don't look as scruffy as you.' Laura kicked the chair out from under Ronnie's feet. 'And don't treat my home like a dosshouse,' she ordered.

'Tea's poured,' Diana interrupted. The fights between the Ronconis, particularly the two eldest, were legendary on the Graig.

'Is it sugared and stirred?' Ronnie extended his hand from behind his paper.

'You paralysed, or what?' Diana retorted.

'Just looking after my driving arm.'

Conscious that Ronnie had only ferried them half-way up the hill, Diana heaped three sugars into the tea, stirred it and handed it to him.

'Maud, do you want some tea?' Laura asked in the slightly loud voice that nurses on public wards usually adopt when talking to their patients.

Heaving for breath, Maud shook her head.

'Laura, I'm home.' The door banged and Trevor strode into the house. Not quite up to Ronnie's six-foot mark, he was dark and slightly built. His thin face flushed with pride as he looked briefly at his wife before turning to Diana and Maud.

'Back already from the Infirmary?'

'It didn't work out,' Diana muttered, embarrassed by the constant repetition of her and Maud's failure.

'The Infirmary's hard on junior doctors,' Trevor said kindly, 'but I've heard it's even harder on ward maids.' He glanced at Ronnie. 'It's good to see you, Ronnie, you should come down more often.'

'I would if dear sister didn't live here.' Ronnie finished his tea, stood up and stretched. 'I've been meaning to check the oil in the van for days. Give me a shout when you're ready to go, Diana. See you Trevor, Laura.' He closed the door behind him.

Trevor took Maud's pulse while Diana squeezed another cup of tea out of the pot for him.

'Looks like you've had too much work, not enough food and nowhere near enough rest.' Trevor released his hold on Maud's wrist.

'They said it was consumption,' she said flatly, taking deep breaths in an effort to stop coughing.

14

'Did they take an X-ray?' he asked.

'They X-rayed all of us twice. Once when we started in September, and again last week,' Diana answered for her.

'And they asked you to go after they had the results of last week's tests?'

'Yes,' Maud whispered.

'How long have you been coughing like this?'

'For a couple of weeks,' Maud mumbled vaguely.

He wrapped his hand around her fist, and forced her fingers open. Diana's sodden and bloody handkerchief lay in her palm.

'And how long have you been coughing up blood?' he asked quietly.

'A week, perhaps two,' she replied reluctantly.

'Home for you, young lady,' Trevor decreed. 'Warm room, warm bed, and plenty of rest. Tell your mother I'll be up as soon as I've finished in the hospital for the day.'

'I'll be fine.'

'Who's the doctor here, me or you?' He looked at Diana. 'You'll see she behaves herself?'

'I tried my best the whole time we were in the Infirmary. I'm not likely to stop now,' Diana replied. She felt as though the whole world were blaming her for the state Maud was in.

'I'll give Ronnie a shout.' Laura opened the door. 'Tell Mrs Powell I'll call in and see her when I come up to visit Mama.'

'I'll do that,' Diana said dully, picking up her coat and handbag.

'They'll all be glad to see you safely back home.' Laura smiled brightly as she helped Maud button her coat.

'I'm not too sure of that,' Diana answered as she walked down the passageway. Her Aunt Elizabeth had never attempted to hide her dislike of her, her brother Will or their widowed mother Megan, and after her mother had been arrested Aunt Elizabeth had publicly announced that none of Evan's dead brother's family would ever set foot in her house again. Diana had nearly collapsed when she'd received a letter from Will two weeks after she and Maud had started work in the Infirmary telling her that both he and their mother's Russian lodger, Charlie Raschenko, had moved in with their uncle and aunt, after he'd been forced to sell their house to pay off their mother's fines. But for all of Will's cheery determination to make the best of a bad situation, and

15

Laura's sentimental forecast of a warm welcome, she rather suspected that the atmosphere in Graig Avenue would be strained enough, without her and Maud adding to the already overcrowded household.

Elizabeth was alone in the house, dredging sugar over the pastry top of an enormous bread pudding, when Diana and Ronnie walked into the back kitchen, half carrying, half dragging an exhausted Maud between them. Ronnie took one look at the deserted room and remained only as long as it took him to exchange pleasantries with Elizabeth before returning to the van for Maud and Diana's bags. He left them in the passageway, shutting the front door behind him.

'What's this, then?' Elizabeth demanded, although a look at Maud had been sufficient for her to sum up the situation.

'They wouldn't let me stay on in the Infirmary,' Maud began to explain in a cracked whisper.

'They gave Maud her cards yesterday,' Diana interrupted. 'I couldn't let her go home by herself.'

'Then you'll be wanting a bed tonight too,' Elizabeth sighed in a martyred voice.

'Diana's come home for good. Same as me Mam,' Maud broke in quickly.

'And pray tell, what are the pair of you going to live on?'

'I'm sure I'll find something soon.' Diana knew full well that the question had been directed more at her than Maud. 'I promise I won't be any trouble, Aunt Elizabeth.'

'And I know you won't, my girl!' Elizabeth echoed harshly. 'First sign of any nonsense and you'll be out through that door quicker than you walked in. That's something I'm promising you.'

Taking Elizabeth's idea of 'nonsense' as a veiled reference to her mother's transgressions, Diana found it difficult to hold her tongue.

'Heaven only knows where I'm going to put you,' Elizabeth complained, crashing open the oven door and thrusting the bread pudding inside. 'The house is full to bursting with William and Charlie lodging here as it is.'

'Diana can share with me,' Maud said faintly from the depths of her father's easy chair, where Ronnie had left her.

16

'I think not,' Elizabeth contradicted. 'Not with that cold. If Diana shares a bed with you, like as not she'll catch it, and the last thing I need is two of you to nurse.'

'Diana and I have been sharing a room for months, and it's not a cold . . .'

'Of course it is, girl,' Elizabeth broke in too quickly. 'You obviously haven't been looking after yourself the way I taught you to. I don't expect you've been airing your clothes properly, or wearing the warm flannel underwear I stitched for you.' She shook her head briskly. 'It was the same with Bethan. She wouldn't listen, and look where that got her. And when she was ill, what did she do? Expected me to drop everything and nurse her, same as you do now.'

'I don't expect anything, Mam,' Maud croaked.

'She has been wearing her warm underwear, Aunt Elizabeth,' Diana protested, angered by her aunt's lack of sympathy.

'Seeing is believing,' Elizabeth chanted smugly. 'She wouldn't be lying there like that if she had. Neglect! Pure neglect and selfishness, that's what this is.'

'I think Maud ought to go to bed, Aunt Elizabeth,' Diana suggested. 'She fainted twice on the journey here and the doctor said . . .'

'What doctor?' Elizabeth commanded, instantly on the alert.

'Doctor Lewis. Ronnie stopped off at Laura's house on the way up the hill, so Maud could see him, and Doctor Lewis said Maud should be put to bed in a warm room right away, and he'd call in tonight after he finished in the hospital.'

'And just what did Ronnie Ronconi think he was doing, taking my daughter to a doctor when he wasn't asked?' Elizabeth ranted. 'Is his brother-in-law so short of work now that he has to tout for trade for him? And I suppose Trevor Lewis suggested that we go and buy some expensive concoction or other in the chemist's, when any fool can see all that's wrong with Maud is a common cold.'

'He didn't prescribe anything,' Diana said coldly, before Maud, who was struggling for breath, managed to speak. 'All he said was that Maud should go to bed.'

'As if I need a doctor to tell me to put my own daughter to bed when she's in that condition,' Elizabeth sneered. 'Well, doctor or not Maud, I'm afraid you're going to have to make do in your father's easy chair with a stool at your feet for an hour or two while I make up and air your bed. It will do more harm than good for you to go upstairs the way it is now. I don't think your bedroom door's been opened more than once or twice since Bethan left. And seeing as how you're here,' she turned to Diana, 'you may as well make yourself useful. You can bring up some sticks and half a bucketful of coals, and lay a fire to chase the damp out of the room. And don't go thinking that you can have a fire in there every day either,' she cautioned her daughter. 'We haven't money to waste on coal for anyone's bedroom, ill or not. We're hard pushed to keep the kitchen stove going, even in this weather, on what little your father and Eddie bring in. This will be a one-off treat because the room's not been used since the cold weather started.'

'Don't put yourself out on my account,' Maud bit back, her eyes heavy with anger and exhaustion.

'Looks like I'm going to have to, whether you want me to or not.' Elizabeth opened the washhouse door and lifted out her brushes and dusters.

'Won't take long, Maud.' Diana lifted Maud's feet on to a kitchen chair. Taking her coat off, she draped it over Maud, who was still wearing hers.

'There's spare blankets in the ottoman at the foot of my bed,' Elizabeth said. 'You can bring one down. It will be a sight more serviceable than your damp coat.'

'Yes, aunt.' Inwardly seething, Diana left the room. She brought down a thick grey blanket that smelt of moth-balls and folded it around Maud. Her cousin was already asleep. Slumped sideways in the chair, her fair hair was plastered close to her head in tendrils that had been curled into tight ringlets by the rain. Her face was flushed with illness and the heat of the fire. An overwhelming sense of guilt washed over Diana as she tucked the blanket around Maud's emaciated figure. She should have done something weeks ago: persuaded Maud to leave the Infirmary when the signs of tuberculosis had become increasingly apparent; rushed her home when she had first coughed up blood, not a couple of weeks ago as Maud had told Trevor, but months back. During the first week they'd spent in Cardiff.

It was four o'clock in the afternoon before Elizabeth had organised Maud's bedroom to her satisfaction. Spotlessly clean furniture had been dusted and polished unnecessarily. The immaculate linoleum had been scrubbed with a bucket of warm water, lye soap and a well-worn scrubbing brush. The fire had been laid, lit, and the grate cleaned and blackleaded – by Diana. As soon as she'd finished, Elizabeth propped the double mattress against the dressing-table stool in front of the flames for airing, and it was two hours to the minute before she allowed Diana to lift it back on to the bed. The sheets, blankets and pillowcases that Elizabeth had removed from her ottoman were carried downstairs and hung over the wooden airing rack and hoisted above the range for the same magical two hours before they too were allowed on the bed.

When the bed was finally made up to Elizabeth's exacting requirements, she and Diana woke Maud from her unnaturally deep sleep and helped her upstairs. Elizabeth undressed her while Diana unpacked Maud's bag. Diana's own bag still stood ostentatiously alone and abandoned in the hall.

'I suppose you'll be wanting something to eat,' Elizabeth muttered as she pulled the curtains against the light. Maud didn't reply. Worn out, she was asleep again, curled comfortably into the depths of the great bed.

'I'm not hungry,' Diana answered curtly. She would have died rather than admit she was starving.

'If you want a cup of tea, I'll make you one,' Elizabeth offered brusquely. The bread pudding was cooked, but she wouldn't have dreamed of cutting into it before the men came home.

'I'll wash and change, and go into town.' Diana glanced at the clock as they returned to the kitchen. 'I need a job and the sooner I start looking, the sooner I'll find one.'

'There's plenty of advertisements in the *Observer* for live-in kitchen and parlour maids in England,' Elizabeth suggested in a marginally lighter tone. 'There's an agency opened in Mill Street. You can find out more there.'

'One stint in the Infirmary was enough,' Diana insisted. 'I don't intend to go back into service. Besides, I really would like to stay in Pontypridd close to Will.'

'Beggars can't be choosers,' Elizabeth recited in a schoolmarm voice. 'I didn't say too much in front of Maud because I didn't want to risk upsetting her, but we've no room for you here. Your brother and your lodger Charlie are sharing the downstairs front room as it is. Haydn and Eddie are in one bedroom, your uncle and I in the other and there's no way Maud can share a room in her condition. The box room as you well know isn't even furnished, and we've no way of furnishing it. Not with the way things are at the moment.'

'In that case I'd better see if I can find somewhere else.' Diana concealed the pain of her aunt's rejection beneath the façade of belligerent abrasiveness she had adopted as both shield and defence mechanism since the day her mother had been wrenched out of her life.

'Your Uncle Huw is still living in Bonvilston Road,' Elizabeth reminded her. Huw, Megan's bachelor brother, was a policeman in the town and worked all kinds of unsocial shifts.

'Perhaps I'll go and see him. Is Will still working on Charlie's stall?'

'He was when he left this morning.'

'As soon as I've washed I'll go down and see him.'

'I've cleaned all the bedrooms I intend to for today, and I'm certainly not going to traipse up and downstairs with any more buckets. If you want to wash you can use the washhouse. There's no one to disturb you. You'll find soap in the dish, and a towel on the top shelf.'

'Thank you.' Diana didn't even attempt to keep the sarcasm from her voice.

It was a long, cold walk down the Graig hill, made all the more unbearable by a cordial greeting from the Reverend Mark Price and his pretty young wife, who assumed that Elizabeth would be ecstatic to have her daughter and niece back home again. Pulling the collar of her sodden red coat high around her ears, Diana struggled to make civil replies to their polite enquiries after her own and Maud's health, before trekking on, past the rows of dripping stone cottages. The downpour turned into a drenching torrent. Twilight became a dark and early night, but sentiment took precedence over reason, and she paused for a few moments at the junction of Llantrisant Road and Leyshon Street.

She'd known it would hurt, and it did – more than she would have believed possible – but she couldn't stop herself from looking down the narrow terraced road towards the tiny house that her parents had bought when they'd married. She and William had both been born there in the front bedroom, where, as her mother had told them with brimming eyes glittering with happy memories, they'd also been conceived. She'd never known her father. He'd died in the mud of the Western Front six months before she'd been born. Her mother had hung his photograph on the wall of the kitchen so she and William would at least know what he'd looked like, but the photograph had faded with time, until there was only a blurred face that looked remarkably like her Uncle Evan. Quiet, kind Uncle Evan who'd been led a dog's life by Aunt Elizabeth for as long as she could remember.

Tears mingled with the rain on her cheeks as she stared at the house that had once been her home. She closed her eyes, wishing with all her might that she could walk down the street, turn the key that protruded from the lock, and enter the house. But then it wouldn't be the same. She didn't even know who lived there now. William had written to say that he and Charlie had taken the best of their mother's furniture across town to their Uncle Huw's before the bailiffs had moved in, but that was all. Perhaps it was just as well. If it was an old friend or a neighbour she'd have an excuse to call, and the sight of unfamiliar objects within the familiar walls would be more than she could bear right now. Even from where she stood she could see strange curtains hanging limply at the windows. Made of green and gold artificial silk, they sagged a little lopsidedly. The front door had been given a new coat of paint as well. A grim, unwelcoming shade of dark brown so different from the vibrant sapphire blue Will had painted it at her mother's instigation.

'Lost your way, Diana?' Glan Richards, a porter in the Graig Hospital, and the next-door neighbour of her Uncle Evan and Aunt Elizabeth, stood before her.

'Glan! How are you?' she cried out eagerly, sentiment causing her to forget the antagonism that had once existed – and for all she knew, still did exist – between him and her brother.

'Better than you by the look of it.' He thumbed the lapel of the new raincoat that he'd bought in Leslie's stores on a sixpence-a-week card. 'Lost a bob and found a farthing?'

21

'I'm great,' she smiled through her tears. 'It's just this damned cold and wet.'

'Back for the weekend?'

'No, for good,' she said, forgetting for an instant that she had nowhere to sleep that night.

'Couldn't stand the pace?' he asked snidely.

'No, the wages,' she said cuttingly. 'I've had enough of hospital slave labour. I'm off to town to look for something better.'

'If you find it, let me know. I've had about enough of hospital slave labour too, but then, whenever I've looked I've never found anything better. There's a depression on, or so they tell me.'

'Could be that you're not looking in the right places, and then again could be that you haven't the talent I've got on offer,' she retorted, regaining some of her old spirit as she lifted the hem of her coat provocatively to her knees. 'See you around.'

'In the Palladium, six o'clock tonight?' he asked hopefully.

'With an old man like you?' she laughed. 'I'm kind to the elderly, but not that kind.'

'Since when has twenty-two been old?'

'Twenty-three,' she corrected. 'You're four years older than Will and that makes you *ancient*!' She stuck her tongue out cheekily. 'See you around, Grandad.'

Glan laughed in spite of the brush-off as she walked away. He'd forgotten what a Tartar Diana was. Life was certainly going to perk up with her living next door.

22

Chapter Three

'I hate Saturdays,' Tina moaned to her younger sister Gina who'd been ordered into the café by Ronnie to put in an hour's practice in the cashier's chair. 'Here, move over.' She nudged her sister from the edge of her seat, unlaced her shoes and rubbed her aching feet through her thick, cable-knit stockings. 'And I hate waitressing,' she added emphatically. She affected a whining voice: ' "Miss . . . Miss, I ordered two teas, not coffee . . . Miss there's only butter on one side of this Chelsea. It costs a penny farthing you know . . ." Never mind that the lump of butter I slapped on the other side of the bun is big enough for four. Next week I'm sitting on the till, dear sister. It's time you got blisters on your feet.'

'I'm too young to wait tables,' Gina said. 'Too much exercise stunts growing bones.'

'In that case you'll grow into a ruddy giant.'

'I'll have none of that language in here, Tina,' Ronnie reprimanded her. 'And get your shoes on – sharpish. You're putting the customers off their food.'

'Slave driver.' Her voice pitched high as her temper flared. 'I must have walked twenty miles today around these tables . . .'

'And you can walk twenty more. With your shoes on,' he added loudly, slapping the ice cream and coffee she'd ordered on to the marble-topped section of the counter. 'Serve these. After you've washed your hands.'

'He's getting far too big for his boots,' Tina hissed at her sister as she laced her shoes back on and fired mutinous glances in Ronnie's direction. 'Sometimes I think he's in training to become another Papa.'

'He's ten times worse than Papa ever was,' Gina answered, smiling as one of the market boys approached the till with a sixpence in his hand. 'Mama can always soften Papa.'

'It'll take a blue moon for a woman to want to stand close enough to Ronnie to soften him.'

23

'Tina!' Ronnie snarled.

'I'm going. I'm going,' she shouted irritably. Pushing her way around the counter she threw back the curtain and stormed into the kitchen, where she washed her hands with as much fuss and splashing of water as she could manage.

A pretty girl with unfashionably long fair hair and soft grey eyes opened the café door, folded her umbrella, shook the rain from her coat and walked up to the counter.

'Seen Haydn Powell, Ronnie?' she asked quietly as she looked shyly around the room.

'No but he'll be here in – ' Ronnie glanced at the clock ' – five minutes. Usual?'

'Yes please.' She rummaged in her handbag and pulled out a well-worn leather purse. 'And . . .' she peered through the steamed-up glass on the cases that held the cakes. 'One of those custard slices, please Ronnie, and a . . .'

'Knife and two plates. I know,' he grumbled good-naturedly. 'With customers like you and Haydn Powell I'll be in the bankruptcy court next week.'

'Better half a sale than none. Leastways, that's what's my dad always says.'

'Your father has a thriving shop and the whole of the Graig to sell to.'

'And you have an enormous café and the whole of the town to peddle to,' she smiled. She pulled a chair out from a table crammed into a corner between the counter and the till. It was the only free table in the café but precious few meals were being eaten. A couple of customers had plates in front of them that held buns, cold pancakes or sandwiches, but most were nursing tepid cups of tea or Oxo.

'Here you are. One tea, once iced custard slice, a knife and two plates.' Ronnie left the counter and laid them on her table himself. 'How's that for service?'

'Wonderful.' She smiled at Gina. 'Does he do this for all the girls?'

'Only other people's girlfriends,' Gina said mildly. 'That way he knows he can stay safely married to Papa and the business.'

'Time you started bagging some of that change in the till, Gina,' Ronnie ordered.

24

'You know I hate doing that. My fingers get filthy and my nails break . . .'

'Gina!' Ronnie warned in a voice that was used to being obeyed.

'People are saying that you're thinking of opening another café in that vacant shop opposite the fountain,' Jenny interrupted tactfully.

'Are they now?' Ronnie murmured as he returned behind the counter.

'Well are you?'

'Better go and ask whoever told you. Seems they know more about my business than I do.'

'Make way for two drowned rats,' William shouted as he and Haydn burst, dripping and cold, into the café.

'Hello sweetheart,' Haydn ruffled Jenny's curls with a damp hand.

'I've got us a custard slice,' she beamed, her face lighting up.

'Can I take your order?' Tina sidled close to William, pouted her well-formed lips, hitched her skirt up slightly, and stood in what she hoped was a fair imitation of the Jean Harlow pose.

'Two teas, is it?' Ronnie shouted from behind the counter.

'And a couple of Welsh cakes,' William replied, winking at Tina. 'I'm starving.'

'Aren't you always?' Haydn commented scathingly.

'I haven't a Jenny to take my mind off food.' William stared at Tina. 'Corner of Griffiths' shop, ten o'clock tonight,' he whispered teasingly. 'I'll walk you home if you spend the evening with Jenny. Sorry I can't make it any earlier, but you know the market on Saturday nights.'

'Tina, those back tables need clearing, and wiping down,' Ronnie directed. He was too far away to hear what William was saying but he knew William – and Tina. They'd had a soft spot for one another ever since they'd been classmates in Maesycoed primary school. A soft spot that had led his father to decree that Tina could only talk to William in the presence of himself or one of her grown-up brothers. It was a rule that Tina made a point of breaking wherever and whenever she could.

Ronnie watched as Tina reluctantly dragged herself off to the back of the café. They stared belligerently at one another through the thick, smoky atmosphere as she began to heap dirty dishes into

25

a pile. Finally her temper flared up again, to the delight of all the customers except William.

'I *am* eighteen,' she snapped.

'And when you're twenty-one you can do as you like,' Ronnie said softly. 'Until then you do as Papa and I say.'

Ronnie took his duties as older brother seriously, very seriously indeed. It had hurt when his father had blamed his lax attitude for Laura finding time to fall in love with an Irish Catholic doctor, as opposed to the nice Italian boy he'd wanted for his eldest daughter. Trevor had eventually gained acceptance, but not before Papa Ronconi had told his other five daughters, including little Theresa who was barely eight years of age, that when the time came they would be introduced to nice Italian or Italian Welsh boys who met with *his* approval. Apart from William's wholly Welsh antecedents, there were other drawbacks. His wheeler-dealing, both on and off the market, coupled with the receiving charge that had led to his mother's imprisonment, had given him a not entirely undeserved shady reputation. And Ronnie, who'd always had a discreet eye for the ladies, was beginning to see a far more reckless philanderer than himself in William, that made him all the more determined to keep William as far away from Tina as possible.

'Bad luck about your sister, Haydn, I'm sorry,' Ronnie sympathised.

'Bethan?' Haydn asked quickly, wondering what gossip had found its way to the café via the maids who worked for Doctor John senior, Andrew's father, in his house on the Common. It still grieved him that the Johns had found out about Bethan and Andrew's marriage (via the telephone) before any of her own family.

'Not Bethan, Maud,' Ronnie corrected. 'I'm sorry, I thought someone would have gone to the market to tell you. She came in this morning on the Cardiff train.'

'Maud's home?' Haydn asked in bewilderment.

'She's ill,' Tina announced thoughtlessly, relishing the importance that the imparting of the news gave her. 'She collapsed in the station. Wyn Rees carried her over here, then Ronnie had to drive her and Diana home.'

'Diana's home too?' William interrupted.

'They've left the Infirmary. Maud was told she was too ill to work . . .'

'Tina, you'd better finish clearing those tables before they're needed for another customer,' Ronnie broke in, silencing her. He poured himself a tea and looked around the café. Seeing no one clamouring for anything, he shouted to Tony, who was washing dishes in the kitchen, to take over the counter, then carried his tea to Haydn and William's table.

'I thought you would have heard,' he explained as he sat down. 'Half of Pontypridd saw Maud being carried out of the station.'

'It obviously wasn't the same half that's been hanging around Charlie's meat stall all day,' William said caustically.

'Or Horton's second-hand stall.' Haydn cupped his hands tightly around his tea. 'What's wrong with Maud?' he asked Ronnie.

'I took her to Trevor's. He had a quick look at her before I drove her and Diana up to Graig Avenue,' Ronnie murmured, wanting to delay the moment when he'd have to tell Haydn the truth. Then he looked into Haydn's eyes and saw that he already knew. 'It's TB,' he admitted bluntly, not knowing how else to phrase it. 'Your mother and Diana were putting her to bed when I left.'

Haydn didn't say anything, but his hand shook as he reached for the sugar bowl. Jenny fumbled for his other hand beneath the tablecloth. There were tears in the corners of her eyes.

'How's Diana?' William demanded.

'Diana's Diana,' Ronnie replied. 'Cheeky as ever.'

'Did she say if she's staying?'

'She said she had no intention of going back.'

'Then she's going to need a job.'

'And a place to live.' Diana closed the door behind her and shrugged her arms out of her sodden coat.

'Long time no see, sis,' William said unemotionally, moving his chair so she could fit another one in beside him.

'My gain, your loss,' she sang out as she hung her coat and scarf on the hat stand behind the till.

'Didn't expect to see you back in here today.' Tina paused in between clearing tables. 'How's Maud?'

'In bed asleep when I left.'

'Best place for her,' Ronnie said authoritatively.

Diana went to the counter. 'I'll have a tea and a hot pie, please Tony,' she said. He poured the tea and gave it to her.

'I'll bring the pie when it's ready,' he smiled.

'Surely you're going to stay with us, Diana,' Haydn said as she moved a chair between him and William.

'Your mother says there's no room.'

At the mention of Elizabeth everyone fell silent. Haydn could almost taste the air of oppression his mother carried with her whenever she walked into a room.

'If Maud is ill you can't share with her, that's for certain.' Haydn replaced his cup on his saucer. 'But there's always the box room. We can squeeze a single bed in there – just.'

'But there is no single bed,' Diana protested feebly, not wanting to tell her brother and Haydn about Elizabeth's decisive pronouncement on her presence in the house.

'You took your furniture over to your Uncle Huw's, Will. Was there a bed?' Haydn asked.

'Five.' William finished his tea. 'Three single and two doubles. I saved all of Mam's bedroom suites, bedding, rugs and china, as well as all the downstairs furniture. Uncle Huw threatened to hold an auction there when I left.'

'That's settled then.' Haydn rose from his seat and reached for his coat and muffler. 'Soon as you finish on the stall you can go over and get whatever Diana needs to furnish the box room. Dad can take it up on the horse and cart.'

'Your father and Eddie will be calling in here before they finish for the day,' Ronnie shouted above the hissing of the steamer. 'They're bringing my flour over from the canal wharf.'

'In that case nothing could be simpler. You stay and wait for them, Di,' Haydn suggested, 'then you can go over to Bonvilston Road, pick out whatever you want, and they can take it up.'

'Wouldn't it be easier if I just moved in with Uncle Huw for a bit?' Diana pleaded.

Haydn looked at her and instinctively knew where the problem lay.

'Not with Will living the other end of town. It would look funny.'

'Come on, Di, you don't need me to tell you what a tip Uncle

Huw's house is. I don't think he's cleaned it since the Great War,' William said drily.

'Open horse and cart isn't ideal in this weather,' Ronnie commented practically. 'The Trojan's empty at the moment. There's more than enough room for a bed and bedding in the back.'

Diana squirmed uncomfortably. 'Aunt Elizabeth isn't expecting me back,' she said slowly.

'Dad's got a tarpaulin,' Haydn said tactfully. 'And the yard doesn't close until late on a Saturday, so he won't be in a hurry to take the horse and cart back. Best to leave it to him.' Everyone took that to mean leaving Elizabeth to him, not the moving of the furniture.

'If he needs a hand between six and seven, come and get me,' Will offered. 'There's usually a slack time then. It picks up around eight o'clock, because people know Charlie cuts the price of any joints that are left, rather than see them get knocked down in the nine o'clock bell when the leftovers are auctioned. But if it's not between six and seven, it'll have to wait until after nine.'

'I doubt there'll be anything that Dad and Eddie won't be able to handle between them.' Haydn squeezed Jenny's hand and whispered in her ear. She smiled and clung to him.

'Walk me over to the Town Hall?' he asked her.

'It's a hard life being a callboy,' Will joked. 'Nothing but pretty chorus girls, chocolates and nips of whisky backstage.'

'I'd swap jobs with you any day!'

'Need muscles to hump meat around, not pretty-boy looks,' Will teased, flexing his biceps and wrapping his arm round his sister. 'See you later, sis.'

'Thanks, Will. Haydn.' She wiped her eyes hoping that everyone would think she was still rubbing raindrops from her face.

'One pie.' Tony laid it on the table in front of her.

'Before you go,' she called out to William, Jenny and Haydn as they opened the door. 'Any of you know of a job that's going?'

'No, but I'll keep an eye open,' Haydn shouted as he left.

'Two, even,' Will grinned as he followed Haydn.

'What about you?' Diana pressed Ronnie as he rose from his seat and cleared the dishes from the table.

'With two sisters and two brothers over fifteen out of work, I always live in hope of hearing something, but at the moment there's nothing about.' Ronnie stacked the dishes on the edge of the counter.

'Your family all work here!' Diana remonstrated.

'Work? Call that work?' Ronnie pointed to where Tina was sitting perched on the back of a chair, deep in conversation with a couple of chorus girls from the show that was currently playing in the New Theatre. 'My family visit here every day. They eat and drink the profits of the place, but they don't work. They don't know the meaning of the word.'

'It's that bad around here?' Ignoring his grumbles, Diana stared glumly at her pie.

'I'd start eating that while it's hot,' Ronnie advised. 'The situation's bad,' he modified his opinion a little, 'but it's not that bad. Not for a smart girl. Pity I can't call either of my sisters that.'

Diana cut the pie and began to chew it slowly, savouring its rich meaty taste. She made a mental list of places she could try for vacancies. If there had been anything going on the market or in the Town Hall, William or Haydn would have known about it, but then the market was only open on Wednesdays and Saturdays. A few of the food stalls, like Charlie's, opened on Fridays too, but it was hard going, trying to keep yourself on three days' pay a week. The only places that were open five and a half days were the big shops like Wien's, Rivelins, Gwilym Evans and the Co-op, the three cinemas, and the theatres. If the New Theatre had needed help, Ronnie would have known about it with half the company eating in the café. As she scraped the last of her pie from her plate she decided to start on the big shops first.

'Will you be working very late?' Jenny asked Haydn as they pushed and jostled their way through the miserable, wet crowd of evening shoppers in the glistening, black and gold lamplit market square.

'You know Saturday nights.' He shrugged his shoulders. 'One company moves out, another in. They'll want a hand to move their costumes, props and scenery into the vans.'

'And with their last-night party.' Her voice held a bitterness she couldn't have concealed, even if she'd wanted to.

'Jenny,' he pulled her into the brightly lit shelter of the Co-op Arcade. 'Don't let Will's teasing upset you. You know they never invite the likes of the callboy to the after-show party.'

'I know no such thing. I saw the way that – that – chorus girl', she almost exploded in indignation, 'ogled you when we were sitting in the café yesterday afternoon.'

'The girls do that to everyone,' he said wearily, already tired of the conversation. It was one she insisted on having at least twice a week. 'It's habit. Nothing more. They're so used to making eyes and smiling on stage, they don't know when to stop. Half the time they don't even realise they're doing it. Will you wait up for me?' he pleaded, grasping her hand.

'That depends on what time you walk past the shop.' Her voice was brittle. 'I'll be in bed by twelve.'

'As I'm not likely to be walking up the hill much before one, I'll not bother to call in.'

Devastated by the news about Maud, up at five to help set up and work on Horton's stall, cold, tired, wet through and dreading the prospect of coping with keyed-up comics and chorus girls during an exhausting, final double house of revue which would last at least another seven hours, he was too numb to rise to Jenny's bait. At that moment he decided if that was the way she wanted to play their relationship, she could play alone. Pulling down his cap, and turning up the collar of his good, partly worn overcoat that had come courtesy of Horton's stall in lieu of wages, he stepped out into the rain-soaked throng milling around the stalls. Too proud to follow, Jenny continued to wander up the arcade towards Gelliwastad Road.

Inwardly she burned with righteous indignation, but the display windows either side of her grew misty as her eyes clouded with unshed tears. She loved Haydn with all her heart, but she felt threatened by the facets of his life that took him away from her. His job as callboy swallowed every night of the week except Sunday, and that meant they could never spend an ordinary night when the cinemas or theatres were open 'courting', like every other young couple on the Graig. Even the busiest and best market mornings were out, because he helped out on Horton's second-hand clothes stall. She had to count herself lucky if he stole enough time, as he had today, to grab a quick cup of tea in

Ronnie's before going to the Town Hall to begin his shift there. She knew his family needed the money, but she only wished he could earn it somewhere alone, in isolation, not in the Town Hall which was full of half-naked, predatory chorus girls, or Horton's stall which acted like a magnet to all the would-be maneaters and vamps in the town.

Whenever she saw him standing beneath the canvas that covered Horton's trestles, he was surrounded by admiring and giggling groups of females, and whether they were twelve years old or pushing thirty, they all looked at him with blatantly plaintive and adoring eyes. 'Cow's eyes', she'd called them the last time she and Haydn had rowed. Every word he exchanged with them, every smile he sent their way, sliced agonisingly through her heart.

She'd frequently crept away from Horton's stall before he'd noticed her presence. Running home where she could assuage her wounded pride by indulging in mild flirtations with the boys who picked up their mother's groceries or bought odd cigarettes from her father's shop. But no matter how late the shop closed, Haydn was inevitably still at work, and she was left with the dreary routine of supper eaten in a grim, oppressive silence with her mentally, if not physically, estranged parents. Followed by the door closing on her father as he left for the Morning Star to drown his sorrows over the loss of his one true love, Megan.

Her mother was no comfort. She lived out her life in a sweetly smiling torpor which enabled her, outwardly at least, to ignore most of the unpleasant aspects of her life, including and especially her husband. Desperate for conversation and companionship, some nights Jenny walked up the Graig hill and called in on the Ronconi girls. The large, warm family overflowed into every corner of their double-bayed terraced house on Danycoedcae Road, but their company, pleasant and amusing as it was, only seemed to accentuate her evening loneliness; and when she'd tried to discuss her problems with Tina Ronconi, Tina had laughed, telling her frankly that if she was tired of Haydn there were plenty of others, herself included, willing to take him off her hands.

What made her present row with Haydn all the more unpalatable was that she'd seen it coming. For weeks now her jealousy had simmered dangerously close to the surface. Lying in bed at night she'd rehearsed the scene a hundred times over. Even down to the final bitter words she'd flung at Haydn. Only in her imaginings he had always apologised, reaching to her with outstretched arms and tears of contrition in his eyes. If only she'd known that he would walk away . . . Would he come back? Or was this the end?

Last night she'd dared to interrupt the Mother Riley show in an attempt to discuss her confused feelings with her mam. Her mother had merely smiled wanly as she'd strained to catch the punch line of a joke. During the subsequent laughter of the radio audience, she'd murmured that she simply couldn't understand why Jenny should want a boyfriend at all. Jenny had dropped the subject. At eight years old she'd caused great amusement in the playground of Maesycoed junior school by innocently mentioning her parents' separate bedrooms. That casual remark had made her the laughing stock of the girls' yard. Glan Richards' sister Annie had taken her to one side and told her in graphic and fearsome detail exactly what married men and women did when they went to bed together, and as if that wasn't enough, Annie had concluded by telling Jenny that her own father didn't want to do it to her mother because he did it every night to Megan Powell, William and Diana Powell's widowed mother.

She'd called Annie a liar and hit her, but Annie was bigger than her, and pushed her over. She went home that day with a bloodied nose and a torn pinafore, but when she answered her mother's probing questions, telling her precisely and truthfully what had happened, her mother slapped her legs hard and told her never to repeat such wicked stories again. And she'd learned to do just that.

Five years later she'd noticed Haydn Powell. All the girls had, with his handsome regular features, shining blond hair and piercingly blue eyes. The miracle was, he'd noticed her right back. When she knew him well enough, she told him the story and he laughed. But her mother hadn't laughed when she found out that Haydn was 'walking out' with her daughter. Instead she'd taken Jenny into her own prim, virginal bedroom, shut the door, sat with her back to it, and told her in words every bit as cold, clinical and sordidly detailed as the ones Annie Richards had used, what marriage and lovemaking really meant.

33

Only by then Jenny knew better. She'd spied on her father, peeping through her bedroom curtains as he stepped lightly along the street and in through the door late at night. She'd heard him whistling as he walked up the stairs after his evening visits to Megan Powell's house, and she'd seen Megan. A happy, plump, good-humoured woman who had a hug and a kiss for everyone. So different from her mother, who for all of her smiles, flinched from physical contact even with her own daughter, and especially with her husband.

So Jenny had watched, listened, learned how to return Haydn's kisses, and drew her own conclusions about the way relationships should progress. Most nights she stole downstairs after her parents went to their separate rooms. Slipping the latch against a piece of woollen cloth to muffle the click, she sat on the boxes of tinned sardines, cocoa and tomatoes in the back storeroom, and waited for Haydn to call in on his way home. And when the months of their courtship turned into years, she allowed him a few 'liberties' as befitting his status of long standing boyfriend. Afterwards she lay on the boxes of canned and dried goods and revelled in his whispered protestations of true, single-minded and everlasting devotion. But now . . . now had she had destroyed all that?

But while Haydn worked endless evening shifts, it was what she wanted, wasn't it? The freedom to find a real and devoted boyfriend who could be by her side all the time.

She tried to remember if she had ever been happy with the situation. In the beginning perhaps, before Haydn had begun to work in the Town Hall. Even later it hadn't been so bad, not just after he had got the job. The worm of discontent had only really begun to gnaw when Laura Ronconi had married Doctor Trevor Lewis, and Bethan, Haydn's sister, had run away to London with a posh doctor. Laura and Bethan were only two years older than her. And after Laura's wedding it hadn't been enough for Haydn to tell her that he loved her. She'd wanted him to declare it publicly, and she'd told him so. She wanted to wear his ring, to be with him all the time. By his side where she could keep him away from all the other girls who made eyes at him.

Why had he allowed a simple thing like lack of money to come between them? Why wouldn't he change his job for a daytime one and marry her? They'd find somewhere to live even if it was only a rented room. Then she'd cook and clean for him. Be there whenever he came home. Why couldn't he realise that she needed him all to herself? That every time he talked to, or smiled at another girl it hurt. Enough for her to create the scene that had driven them apart.

Chapter Four

Evan and Eddie hadn't had a bad day. Leaving home at half-past five, they'd paid their sixpence to hire a shire horse and cart for the day from the yard down Factory Lane. It had become easier since they'd been counted as regulars. They no longer had to fight their way into the stalls to get one of the better horses or sounder carts. Ianto Watkins kept back one of the best rigs for them, and Goliath, a huge shire whose ferocious appearance and rolling eyes belied his sleepy nature.

By eleven they'd unloaded and sold two cartloads of rags to the pickers' yards. Rags that they'd called in on the streets of Cilfynydd. But it had cost them. Eddie'd had to hand over every last farthing, halfpenny and penny of the three shillings' worth of change Evan had set aside to tempt the women into selling their family's worn clothes; clothes that of choice they would have kept until the cold weather had abated. But then, Saturday mornings were special. Good days for the rag and bone men with every household trying to scrape together the ten pennies they needed to buy a beef heart for Sunday's roast.

Between eleven and three they'd delivered goods to customers of Bown's second-hand furniture shop, one of the few that was surviving the recession comparatively unscathed. Evan was proud of his Bown's contract, and justifiably so. It didn't bring in much – seven shillings a week at most – but as he pointed out to an unimpressed, scornful Elizabeth, it paid for the cart rental.

It wasn't easy trying to make a living out of rags. Evan hadn't been the only unemployed miner to think of the idea, and there were far too many carts on the streets for comfort. It had taken Evan eight weeks just to pay back the pound he'd borrowed off their lodger Charlie to set up in the trade, but now he and Eddie were clearing a steady pound a week during the bad weeks, and as much as thirty shillings in the better ones. It wasn't good money by pre-pit-closure days, just enough to pay the bills and the mortgage. But as Elizabeth frequently and sourly pointed out, there wouldn't be much in the way of food on the table if it wasn't for the seven and six a week Charlie and William each paid to lodge with them, and the twelve shillings a week Haydn handed over out of the twelve and six he earned in the Town Hall, as well as the six shillings he picked up for his three short days on Horton's stall.

They were surviving. 'Getting by', as his mother used to say, Evan mused as he wearily flicked the reins in an effort to keep a tired Goliath plodding on. And surviving was more than some of their neighbours were doing. Bobby Jones, whose wife was in the same jail for the same offence as Megan, had taken his five children to the workhouse and abandoned them there. An hour later the bailiffs had moved into his house, carried out the furniture, loaded it into their van and driven off. No one knew where Bobby had gone. Rumour had it he was on the 'tramp'. And Bobby's family weren't the only ones who had ended up in the workhouse or were heading that way. The Richards next door would be out on the street if it wasn't for the eighteen shillings and sixpence their son Glan earned as a porter in the Central Homes, and the five shillings Mrs Richards made scrubbing out the Graig Hotel every morning.

What worried Evan the most was having no savings to fall back on. As soon as he managed to put a few shillings aside in the hope they'd grow into pounds, they slipped through his fingers. Either his or Elizabeth's shoes finally gave out, or a saucepan had to be replaced because it had gone too far for patching, or the price of coal went up, and rags down. There was always something. . .

'You're quiet, Dad,' Eddie commented, biting into a wrinkled winter apple the manager of the canal warehouse had thrown him when they'd picked up Ronnie's flour.

'Thinking how we can do better than we are.'

'Give me a cart of my own,' Eddie said impatiently.

'There's too many calling the streets as it is. If you go out on your own, all we'll do is double our outlay to a bob a day for two carts, instead of a tanner for one. We'll have no more rags to show for it at the end of the day.'

'Don't know unless we try,' Eddie insisted optimistically. 'I could always get up earlier and try further afield. The Rhondda, or down Cardiff way perhaps.'

'There's plenty working the trade down there without you adding to their number. There's got to be more ways to make a living around here if only we knew where to look.'

'I don't see how,' Eddie snapped. 'We're carting all the furniture and rags we can now, and since Fred Davies switched to lorries there's precious little removal work going on.'

'That's what we need,' Evan said decisively. 'A lorry.'

'Joe Craggs bought one off the Post Office last month for twenty-five pounds,' Eddie said eagerly. 'It only cost him ten pounds to get it ready for the road . . .' He fell silent. From what they made on the cart last month, thirty-five pounds might as well be three hundred and fifty.

Evan heaved on the reins, and slowed Goliath to a halt outside Ronconi's café.

'Don't pull back the tarpaulin. Ease the flour bags out from under it,' he cautioned Eddie, 'or you'll soak the whole load.' Eddie jammed his sodden cap further down on his head, leaped off the side of the cart, and pulled the first of the flour sacks from under the tarpaulin. He manoeuvred carefully, but not carefully enough. A puddle of standing water slithered off the cart and drenched his trousers. Cursing under his breath he heaved the sack on to his shoulders and pushed open the door of the café. Evan tied the reins to a lamp-post and climbed awkwardly off the cart. His joints were stiff after sitting in the cold and damp all day, but it had been worth a little discomfort. Between them he and Eddie had made eighteen shillings: a nice little cushion to set against the two bob they'd made last Monday, the quietest day they'd ever had.

He pulled out the second sack, took the weight on his bowed shoulders and staggered into the café.

'Wet enough for you, Mr Powell?' Ronnie called from behind the counter where he was sitting on a stool, watching his brothers and sisters work.

'Could be worse, Ronnie. Could be snow.' Evan carried the flour behind the counter and into the kitchen where Eddie was standing, wringing the water out of his cap into the square stone sink.

'Tea, Mr Powell?' Tony offered politely.

'Thanks, but Eddie and I'd better move on.' Evan thought of

the Cross Keys pub a few yards up the road. A dram of brandy was what he needed before they took the cart back.

'Tea's no good on its own in this weather, Tony.' Ronnie walked into the kitchen behind Evan. 'Take over the counter for me Angelo, and bring in three teas.' He pulled his watch chain out of his waistcoat pocket, picked out a key from amongst the fobs and inserted it into the lock of a cabinet the size of a wardrobe set discreetly behind the door. It swung open to reveal rows of bottles. Some fruit essence, some ice cream flavourings, a few wines and spirits and, at the bottom, half a dozen bottles of beer.

'Café stock for cooking,' Ronnie explained nonchalantly, amused by the amazement on Eddie's face. 'Diana and Maud are home,' he murmured, pouring a generous measure of brandy into two of the three-quarter-full cups of tea Angelo carried in. He handed one to Evan and took the other himself. 'Boxer indulging?' he enquired, holding the bottle poised above Eddie's cup.

Eddie shook his head. 'Hope to be fighting next week,' he explained defensively.

'The girls back for the weekend?' Evan took the cup into his freezing hands.

'No, for good. Maud's ill.'

'TB.' It was a statement, not a question. Evan had read the signs when he and Eddie had taken the cart down Cardiff way a month ago and called into the Infirmary. The only reason he hadn't dragged Maud home with him then was the hope that she'd be better off working in a hospital than anywhere else.

'I took her to see Trevor. He said he'd call in your house after he finished in the hospital for the day.'

'That's good of him.'

'It's what you pay him for,' Ronnie said casually. 'Diana went to your house with Maud, but she came back down this afternoon. She's looking for a job and – ' Ronnie took a packet of cigarettes out of his top pocket and handed them round. Evan took one but Eddie didn't ' – she said, a place to stay. Apparently the only empty room in your house is unfurnished.'

'We'll manage to put her up somehow.' Ronnie didn't have to say any more. Evan knew precisely what had gone on between his wife and his niece.

'William said he put all his mother's furniture in Huw Davies' place. Even if Huw's on duty the key'll be in the door. I offered to go over in the Trojan and get whatever Diana wanted, but Haydn thought it might be better if we waited for you. You know the size of the room, what it will take, and what it won't,' he added diplomatically.

'Is Diana here now?'

'She was until half an hour ago. Then she got edgy. She went to Rivelin's with Tina to see if there's any jobs going. Not that they've a snowball in hell's chance of finding anything.'

Evan stared down at the dregs in his cup. Just when he'd been congratulating himself on keeping his head above water, two more mouths had appeared who'd need feeding. And not only feeding. Illness meant bills for medicine and extra, invalid's food. He stubbed his cigarette out in the sink. Ronnie looked into the teacups. The tea had gone, but that didn't prevent him from pouring more brandy into his own cup, and Evan's.

'Sure you don't want a hand to shift the furniture, Mr Powell?' he offered, raising his cup to Evan's.

'Sure, thank you,' Evan echoed hollowly, downing the contents of his cup in one gulp. 'Tell Diana to go home when she gets back. I'll fetch what's needed for tonight. If she wants more it will have to wait until Monday.' He turned to Eddie. 'We'd best be off, boy, if we want to finish before midnight.'

'I'll pass that message on to Diana.' Ignoring the covetous looks that Tony and Angelo were bestowing on the brandy bottle, Ronnie corked it and returned it to the cupboard. 'But don't expect her back too early,' he warned. 'I know Tina and her idea of job hunting. She'll do all she can to inveigle Diana into the pictures. I bet you a pound to a penny they're sitting in the back row of the Palladium this very minute on the strength of a rumour, which Tina alone has heard, that an usherette is about to hand in her notice.'

'I just hope she doesn't raise Diana's expectations too high.' Evan laid his cup down on the edge of the stove. 'Sounds to me as though the poor girl has had enough knocks for one day.'

'Nothing in Rivelin's, nothing in Wien's, nothing in Leslie's,' Tina opened her umbrella and held it more over her own head than Diana's as they stepped out of Rivelin's doorway into the street.

40

'And none of the other shops are big enough to take on staff. God, what wouldn't I give to escape Ronnie's clutches and work for someone decent, and human!' she swore daringly. 'He's a swine of a brother, but he's an even worse boss. He never lifts a finger himself. Just stands behind the counter all day shouting orders. "Do this! Do that! And do it quicker while you're at it." He's ten times worse than Papa ever was. You're lucky to have William for a brother.'

'I'd be luckier still if William were able to give me paid work,' Diana snapped, irritated by Tina's grumblings. From where Diana was standing, Tina had everything a girl could possibly want: paid work; money in her pocket; a settled home, with a mother and father waiting. It was bad enough to be unemployed, but to be unemployed without a home to fall back on was infinitely worse. She would have given her eye teeth at that moment for one of her mother's cuddles, and a bowl of home-made cawl eaten in the warmth of the back kitchen of her old home.

She looked down, pretending to study her worn shoes. The soles were leaking. She could feel water, icy and damp, soaking through her woollen stockings, freezing her toes. She had to stop thinking about the past. It only made her cry. And crying made her weak when she had to be strong. The old days had gone. Her mother wouldn't be released for another nine years eight months and four days, and already the woman she visited in Cardiff prison didn't look like her mother any more. The last time she'd seen her, Megan had been pale and drawn. A painfully thin shadow of the vivacious, loving woman who'd steered her and Will through baby and childhood.

She hesitated for a moment. Glancing under the overhanging shade of the umbrella, she looked up and down Taff Street. The shop windows shone, bright golden beacons that illuminated tempting displays of the new season's flared skirts, long jumpers and shiny glass and brass jewellery. All well beyond her pocket. Away from the pools of light, a patchwork of dismal grey and black shadows blanketed the rain-burnished flag and cobble-stones. Too early for the nine o'clock market bargain rush and too late for the day shoppers, the crowds had thinned from the torrent that had flooded the street at midday, to a trickling stream. Women in cheap coats that had shrunk in the rain dumped their string and brown paper carrier bags at their feet, while they waited for trams. Men and older children, who'd escaped the discomfort of their homes by lingering in the light and warmth of the shops and cafés, were buttoning their shabby jackets in preparation for long, cold and wet walks home. The last time she was home she'd noticed that more and more people were behaving as though they didn't have homes to go to. When she'd mentioned this to Will and Charlie they told her that most families had taken to lighting their kitchen stoves only two days a week. The price of coal being what it was, they had no choice. It was either freeze and eat bread and jam, or be warm and go hungry.

Pulling her collar higher to avoid the rain that poured down her neck from a bent spoke in the umbrella, she stepped decisively forward.

'I'll try Springer's shoe shop,' she said briskly, wanting to delay the moment when she'd have to return to the café. She knew her uncle would probably be waiting for her, but she was gripped by an overwhelming sense of urgency. It was already half-past five. She had to – simply had to find a job before the shops closed at six so that when she walked back into her uncle's house she could look her aunt squarely in the eye and say, 'I won't be a burden to you. I have a job. I can pay my own way.'

'There's no point in trying there. They laid off Ginny Jones last week.' Tina dampened Diana's hopes before they'd even begun to smoulder, let alone flame. 'You'd stand a better chance in one of the pictures. Why don't we walk up to the Palladium?' she suggested artfully. 'If there's nothing going there, we could try the Park and the White Palace on the way back.'

'I'd rather work in a shop,' Diana protested, remembering Haydn's complaint that his mother never saw his evening job in the Town Hall as a 'proper job'.

'Beggars can't be choosers,' Tina said cruelly.

'I'm not a beggar.'

'Not yet, but it can be arranged,' Tina said, annoyed by Diana's refusal to go to the Palladium.

Tina was wrong, Ginny Jones hadn't been laid off in Springer's. That was Ginny's and the Springers' story, concocted so neither party would lose face. Ginny had been fired by Beatrice Springer,

42

the wife of the owner, Ben. Beatrice had visited the shop unexpectedly in the middle of the day and caught her husband looking up Ginny's skirt, while Ginny was perched on a ladder lifting down a stock of miners' boots that hadn't shifted in months, and wasn't likely to while the pits remained closed. Ginny had been sent packing with a week's wages in her pocket, but Mrs Springer's indignation at the sight of Ginny 'leading a respectable married man on' hadn't extended as far as volunteering to work in the shop herself. She had four children and an unmodernised house with a Victorian range and no indoor plumbing to look after, with only one 'skivvy' to help. Ben had been left to fend for himself in the shop all week. Not over-fond of hard work, he'd resented having to do all the humping of stock himself. With no minion to order around, he'd also had to climb the ladder and wait on the ladies of the crache, who were unbelievably finicky and thought nothing of surrounding themselves with twenty pairs of shoes only to buy the first pair he'd brought out, if any at all. So when Diana walked in with her damp clothes clinging to her well-developed figure, her cheeks and lips rosy from the cold and her brown eyes sparkling with raindrops, he saw her as something of a godsend. He looked, he stared, he coveted, licked his lips and uttered a silent, grateful prayer that his wife wasn't around to vet Diana's request for a job. Beatrice had turned down five girls in a row last Monday morning, and the news travelled. Enough to put off any other girl who'd thought of applying for the vacancy Ginny's leaving had created.

'So you're looking for work?' he said somewhat superfluously, nodding enthusiastically, more at the sight of Diana's breasts outlined beneath the tight bodice of her outgrown coat than at the prospect of having someone to order around again.

'I've good references,' Diana said eagerly, her heart pounding with excitement. He was talking to her. He hadn't sent her on her way. That had to mean something.

'Well there's no denying I need help,' he mused. 'But I'd have to see those references.'

'I have them here.' Diana opened her handbag and pulled out the envelope they'd given her when she'd handed in her notice. 'They're from the Royal Infirmary,' she said proudly, thrusting the papers into his hands. 'In Cardiff.'

'What were you doing there?' he asked as he opened the envelope.

'Working as a ward maid.'

'And before that?'

'I was in school.'

'Then you've no experience of shop work?'

'Not in an actual shop,' Diana admitted reluctantly, 'but I'm keen, and quick to learn. It says so in there.' She indicated her references.

'All ward maids do is scrubbing and cleaning. There's some of that here, but not much,' he shook his head. 'I don't know if you'll suit. I need someone who's good with customers. Particularly the crache. The wrong girl will put them off. I've found that out to my cost before now, and whoever I take on will have to be quick on their feet, and ac-cur-ate', he articulated the word slowly, mulling over each syllable, 'with figures,' he finished as he studied Diana's legs.

'I came top of my class in Maesycoed seniors in arithmetic,' she interrupted brightly.

'You'd have to dress the part.'

'I have a white blouse and black skirt.' She crossed her fingers behind her back, hoping she could squeeze herself into Maud's blouse.

'I suppose I could give you a try.' He scratched the top of his balding head doubtfully.

'I promise you won't be sorry, Mr Springer.'

He looked hard at Tina, who was standing next to the counter studying the pictures of shoes drawn on the side of the boxes.

'I only came back to Pontypridd today,' Diana explained, following his glance. 'My friend offered to help me look for a job.'

'She's not looking for work herself, then?'

'She works in Ronconi's café.' Diana didn't elaborate on Tina's family connections.

'I'll give you a trial. One week, starting Monday morning. Seven sharp,' he warned. 'I like the shop clean and tidy before it opens.'

'And the wages?' she ventured boldly.

'Six shillings a week.'

Diana swallowed hard, only just managing to contain her

44

indignation. 'That won't even pay for my board and lodging,' she said quietly.

'Then your mam will have to cut corners.'

'I don't live with my mam. I have lodgings to pay for.'

'And I have overheads. I can get any number of girls to work for that money,' he replied testily.

She hesitated.

'Tell you what,' he said airily. 'We'll leave it at that for the week's trial. If it works out, we'll talk about your wages again.'

'I was getting seven and six and my keep in the Infirmary,' Diana protested.

'I might go as high as seven shillings, if you prove to me that you're worth it.'

'It's a long way short of seven and six and my keep.'

'If you liked the Infirmary so much, why did you leave?'

'You will discuss a pay rise at the end of the week?'

'Are you going to turn up on Monday morning or not?' He was beginning to regret talking to this girl. Her outward appearance of youth and naivety had proved deceptive, and the last thing he needed was another forceful woman in his life. One Beatrice was enough.

Diana took a deep breath. She knew she wasn't going to find anything better, at least not before Monday morning.

'I'll be here,' she conceded with as good a grace as she could muster.

'Six days a week. Seven to half-past six, except Thursdays. It's half-day and we close at one, but sometimes I'll need you for stocktaking. There's no dinner break, but if you bring sandwiches you can eat them in the back when it's quiet.'

'Thank you.' She wasn't quite sure what she was thanking him for.

'Black skirt and white blouse, mind you!'

'Yes sir,' Diana replied meekly. She had a feeling that her training in the shop business had just begun.

45

Chapter Five

'You're not really going to work for him, are you?' Tina asked as they picked their way through the gritty puddles that filled the pot-holes in Taff Street. 'He's an old lech.'

'Beggars can't be choosers.' Diana tossed back Tina's own words. Not even the prospect of being closeted in Springer's shop with Ben Springer and his funny looks could dampen her spirits. Monday morning was the whole of Sunday away. And there was nothing to stop her from continuing to look for something better. It would turn up. She had succeeded in finding one job when she'd been assured there was nothing about. And everyone knew it was easier to get a position when you were already in work. She'd ask Will, Charlie, Haydn and Ronnie to keep a look-out. Between them they virtually covered the whole town. Somewhere there'd be work that paid more. There had to be. The sum total of her savings amounted to just over five pounds, and that wouldn't last long with her aunt wanting at least seven shillings and sixpence a week to cover her keep. But she had a foot in the commercial door of Pontypridd. It was a start. The only way forward was up.

'Me, Gina, Tony and Angelo are going to the pictures. It's a good one,' Tina wheedled. 'Want to come?'

'No thanks. Not tonight. I'll come to the café with you and see if my uncle's there, then I'd better get going. I want to see how Maud is.'

'Do you think her mother would mind if Gina and I called in tomorrow to see how's she's doing?'

'Maud would like to see you,' Diana answered evasively.

'What will you do, Di?' Tina asked, with her hand on the café door. 'I mean if he . . . if he . . .'

'Tries anything?' Diana supplied the words for her.

Tina nodded.

'Deal with him,' Diana said flatly. 'I've eaten his sort for breakfast before now.'

46

'Have you really?' Tina's eyes were enormous.

'A girl has to know how to take care of herself. Especially when she leaves home,' Diana said airily.

'Well I wouldn't like to be alone in that shop all day with Ben Springer.' Tina pushed the door open. 'Hey, guess what?' she shouted, stealing Diana's thunder. 'Diana's got a job.'

'Six o'clock, Ronnie.' Gina shut the till with a bang and left her chair.

'You know the rules. No leaving until the next shift comes in.' Ronnie picked up a rag and began idly to polish the steam off the tea urn.

'Come on, have a heart.'

'Off to the pictures, are we?' He looked from Gina and Tina to his brothers, who were hovering behind the curtain that covered the kitchen door.

'There's a musical on in the White Palace,' Tina bubbled, showing more enthusiasm than she had done all day. '*The Lady of the Rose*. It has a full soundtrack. Vivienne Segielle and Walter Pidgeon are in it. Vivienne plays a bride and Alma said her wedding dress is simply stunning. Gorgeous! The best she's ever seen . . .' Tina's voice trailed off as she saw a strange glint in Ronnie's eyes.

'If the main picture is so good, you won't mind missing the second feature, or the cartoon, or even the Pathé newsreel,' he said heartlessly.

'Come on, Ronnie,' Tony pleaded. 'It's quiet now, and we've all worked . . .'

'Worked! Worked!' Ronnie repeated incredulously. 'Not one of you knows the meaning of the word.'

'Ronnie, Papa said if we put in a full day we could finish at six,' Angelo interrupted.

'Don't see me finishing at six, do you?' Ronnie crossed his arms and glared at them.

'You're different.' Tina's temper flared.

'May I ask how, little sister?' Ronnie demanded. 'Pray tell me, are there new rules governing the eldest in the family now?'

'This is your business, not ours. Papa gave it to you . . .'

'Papa gave it to me? Gave it to me?' he repeated as though he

47

couldn't believe what he was hearing. 'Let me tell you something Miss Knowitall. I built this café up from nothing, by sheer hard work. By working seventeen-hour days when I was a damned sight younger than you . . .'

'And you've a lot more to show for it than the rest of us,' Tony intervened, elbowing Tina out of the way before the argument grew uglier.

'I suppose you're going to the pictures too?' Ronnie asked Tony belligerently.

'Papa said the girls could go, if Angelo and I went with them.'

'The sooner you go to the seminary the better.'

Tony was about to retort that he didn't want to go to the seminary at all, but managed to bite his tongue.

'If you and Angelo both go, who's going to work in the kitchen tonight?' Ronnie asked softly.

'You've got help coming in.' Angelo untied his apron.

'Only Alma, and she's a waitress. What happens if we get busy?'

'You were the one who told Papa that you didn't want to replace Bruno when he went to Italy.'

'Only because the fool will want a job when he comes back.'

'He said he wasn't coming back,' Tina chimed in irritatingly.

'One month in that backwater of Bardi is more than any man can stand,' Ronnie insisted feelingly.

'You left there when you were five. It could have changed since then,' Gina said.

'Places like Bardi never change,' Ronnie replied firmly. 'If you're going, you'd better move,' he shouted angrily, irked by the lot of them.

'Oh God, Ronnie, I'm awfully sorry.' Alma Moore ran in breathlessly, her red hair soaking wet, plastered to her beautifully shaped head, and her coat flapping, open to the cold wind and the rain. 'I didn't want to walk through town in this downpour, but all the trams were running late,' she explained. 'And then the one I was on was held up by a brewery cart that had pulled up all skewwhiff opposite the fountain.'

'I must remember to complain to the tram company for delaying my staff,' Ronnie snapped humourlessly. He stared at his brothers and sisters. 'Well, what are you waiting for? Off with the lot of you,' he commanded. 'There's no point in my trying to keep you here. I won't get another ounce of work out of any of you with your heads stuffed full of Hollywood nonsense.'

'Thanks, Ronnie,' Tina said heavily.

Tony hung his apron behind the door, then as he passed the counter on the way out, he reached towards a box of P.K. chewing gum. Ronnie grabbed his wrist before his fingers could close over a packet.

'Not until you give me a penny.' Ronnie held out his hand.

'Ronnie, come on. . . .'

'Come on nothing! I'll not have anyone, especially family, eating my profits.'

Tony fumbled in his pocket and handed over a penny.

'Bye, Ronnie. Hurry up, Tony.' Angelo, Tina and Gina had their coats on and were holding open the door.

'Have a good time,' Alma called after them. 'I know you'll enjoy the film.'

'They'll enjoy anything that involves sitting on their arses and doing no work,' Ronnie commented scathingly.

'Just us tonight, then.' Ignoring his griping Alma glanced around the café. Apart from a couple of market boys on tea break the place was empty.

'Just us.' Ronnie carried a tray of pies out from the kitchen and heaved them on to the shelf next to the steamer.

'What happens if it gets busy?'

'We've plenty of pies, and Tony's left some cooked dinners that can be heated up.'

'And if the customers want egg, bacon and chips?'

'You'll have to watch the front while I make them. It's never that busy when the weather's like this. We'll manage.' He pushed a cigarette between his lips and lit it with a silver lighter. She smiled at him and he gave her a scarcely perceptible wink, as he turned to one of the market traders.

'A tea, a pie and a Chelsea?'

'That's right Ronnie.'

'Seeing as how it's you, we'll call it ninepence. And cheap at half the price,' he mocked in market-style patter.

Diana had plenty of time to think over her day as she walked up the Graig hill towards Graig Avenue. Darkness had settled over

49

the mountain, black, glittering with silver raindrops caught in the glow of the street lamps. The slate roofs of the terraced houses shone, slabs of polished jet. The blank, staring front windows reminding her of the sightless eyes of the blind in the Infirmary. Occasionally an odd square of etched glass above a front door shone with a dim, subdued passage light. No one on the Graig lived in their front parlour. Even the cold, laid fires of coal and sticks traditionally set up in the grates of the front rooms against celebration or trouble times had been raided in most homes. Every stick and lump of coal was needed for the kitchen range.

Slowing her steps, she walked beneath the shadow of the high wall of the workhouse. She jumped in shock as a basket appeared from nowhere and hit her on the head as it was lowered none too gently over the wall.

'Psst! Psst!' A harsh, cracked, disembodied voice grated through the darkness. 'Psst!'

'I've got it,' she whispered. Catching the string, she pulled the basket into her hands.

'There's twopence in there, love. Get me two fags and an apple over the road,' the voice pleaded.

'OK. Hang on.'

'For pity's sake be quick, love. If the master's around he'll have my guts for garters. I'm in enough stick as it is.'

'I'll be as quick as I can,' she called back touchily. It was one thing to agree to do a favour, quite another to be told how to do it. She took the twopence and crossed the road to the corner shop, smiling, despite the cold and the rain, at the memory of an awful fight she'd had with her brother Will, when she'd found out that he and Eddie had once stood under the wall collecting the pennies and pocketing them. After half an hour the inmates had become suspicious, but not before the pair of them had collected one and a penny. They'd spent the entire haul on penny dabs, farthing sherbets, sweet tobacco and Thomas and Evans pop. And what was even worse, they'd refused to give her or her cousin Maud a single lick of their ill-gotten gains.

Burning with temper, an unassuaged sweet tooth and self-righteous indignation, she'd run home and told her mam. Megan had hurtled down the hill to replace the money from her own meagre stock, making both boys stand in the cold for a further two hours until someone found the courage to lower another basket. But they'd never been sure that the inmates who'd paid over the pennies had been the same inmates who'd got the goods. The best part about the escapade was that William had been denied sweets for an entire month afterwards. How she'd enjoyed licking all her lollies and toffees, slowly . . . very slowly . . . in front of him during that month.

Still smiling, she pushed open the door of the shop. The swollen wood grated over the uneven red quarry-tiled floor, accompanying the shrill clang of the bell with a deeper resonance.

'Diana, it's lovely to see you back home love,' Mr Rees, Wyn's father, chirped cheerfully from behind his counter.

'It's good to be back home,' Diana replied, feeling happy for the first time since her train had pulled into Pontypridd that morning. 'I'll have an apple and two cigarettes please, Mr Rees.'

'Basket across the road?' he wheezed as he took the coins.

'You guessed.'

'They're starting early tonight. The master caught them at it a couple of weeks back and threatened to put out all the casuals.'

'And himself out of a job?'

'Fat chance,' Mr Rees laughed.

'Tell you what,' Diana produced another penny from the depths of her damp handbag. 'I'll take another two Woodbines please, Mr Rees.'

'Taken up smoking have you, love?'

'Something like that,' Diana said lightly. 'Oh and by the way, will you please thank your Wyn for me? I meant to do it myself but he disappeared before I had a chance to. He carried our Maud out of station yard over to Ronnie's café this morning, when she fainted. I don't know what I would have done without him.'

'I won't forget, love,' he smiled with an odd expression on his sickly yellow face.

'Thanks.' Diana smiled as she shut the shop door behind her.

'That one's as soft as her mam ever was,' Mr Rees told his next customer fondly, as he watched Diana cross the road clutching her apple and cigarettes. 'And Megan was one in a million,' he murmured, remembering a courtship he had begun two years after his wife's death; it had come to an untimely end, with the appearance of Harry Griffiths on the scene.

51

As Diana put the apple and four cigarettes into the basket and gave it a tug, an illogical, superstitious, almost prayer-like hope crossed her mind. Perhaps the fates – and her Aunt Elizabeth – would be kinder to her for sharing what little she had with those who had even less.

'Haydn, fasten this for me, will you?' Tessie Clark, one of the more 'forward' girls, stepped out of the grubby, sweet-smelling, communal dressing room that the female chorus shared. Her silver, sequined shorts snaked over her hips like a second skin, but the back of the matching bra flapped provocatively as she held the cups loosely over her ample bosom.

'All the girls' hands full in there, are they Tess?' Haydn enquired caustically.

'You know how it is, Haydn.' She wriggled past him in the narrow corridor, brushing the front of his trousers with her buttocks and allowing the cups of the bra to slip below her nipples. 'Women simply don't have the strength to pull the edges together and button the back.' Her warm breath wafted headily over his right ear.

'Is that right now?' Dropping the *South Wales Echo* that he'd bought for the lead comic, he gripped the edges of her bra between his forefingers and thumbs. Heaving with all his might, he pulled the straps back.

'Ow, that hurt!' Tessie complained playfully, wiggling her hips and batting her eyelashes coyly.

'Women have to suffer to be beautiful, or so my girlfriend's always telling me. There, all done. Can I get on with what I was doing now?' he asked wearily.

'Sneaking a whisky with Ambrose?' she said loudly, piqued by the reference to his girlfriend.

'Not before the show.'

'Goody Two-shoes.'

'Only where maneating vampires are concerned,' he countered, remembering this was the revue's last night, and that if he were fortunate he'd never see Tessie again.

'Not queer, are you?' she taunted.

'My girlfriend doesn't seem to think so,' he replied softly as he went on his way.

52

'No luck, Tessie?' One of the girls' mocking laughter followed him along the narrow corridor.

'Boys, they're all the bloody same!' Tessie muttered savagely. 'Don't know what to do with it.'

Haydn heard the remark as he banged on Ambrose's door. It slid away like jelly from a spoon. None of it stuck, or hurt. Not any more. The manager of the Town Hall had warned him when he'd taken him on that the first six months would be the worst. They had been: crawling past in red-faced embarrassment, he'd answered cries for help from the girls' dressing room, only to walk in on crowds of half-naked, giggling girls, who had nothing better to do than torment him by drumming the tips of their fingers on his flies. More than once he'd found himself running messages along the corridors with vital buttons undone. His boss had said nothing. He'd seen it all before.

And there was more than just teasing. Offers of intimacy had come thick and fast, and not only from the girls. Naturally easygoing, he'd made an effort to remain pleasant and friendly while turning them down, but his refusals hadn't always been well received. The kinder ones gave up when they realised that they could neither embarrass nor use him; others went out of their way to humiliate him.

When he got to know variety girls better, he began to understand them. Every revue carried about four times as many girls as men. Moving to a new town every week, or at best fortnight, they spent their days bored out of their skulls, and their evenings prancing around with next to nothing on, while strange men ogled every inch of flesh that the Lord Chamberlain allowed them to bare. And no matter how they tried to live their private lives they were regarded – and treated by the locals of the towns they played – as little better than prostitutes. It wasn't a lifestyle that allowed for sanity, or morality, but he could honestly say he'd never been tempted. Not with Jenny to go back to. Jenny who – he slammed the door shut on the painful memories of that afternoon, valiantly suppressing the urge to try to leave the theatre early so he could go knocking on her door.

As Will would say, there were plenty of other fish in the sea. And not all of them were like Tessie.

For once he wouldn't rush home. He'd go to the last-night

party, that's if he was invited. Take a good look round. Watch the girls; not Tessie – perhaps one of the quiet ones like small, dark-haired Betty. If he was lucky, word would get back to Jenny. Then she'd realise he could survive without her.

Yes that was it. He'd really give her something to think about. And for once perhaps her nagging would be justified.

Diana walked the long way round to Graig Avenue. She didn't want to take the short cut up past Leyshon Street, and through Rhiannon Pugh's house. One look at her old home had been enough for one day, and she'd met too many old friends and neighbours as it was. She was tired of telling people why she and Maud had left Cardiff. She couldn't take any more sympathetic, knowing nods from women who'd soon be baking for Maud's funeral. And it would be even worse if her aunt didn't listen to the boys and her Uncle Evan, and threw her out. The disgrace of trying to explain why she'd moved away from Will, across town to Bonvilston Road to live with her bachelor uncle, would be the final, bitter straw.

The first thing she saw when she walked over the rise past the vicarage was her uncle's horse and cart. He and Eddie were struggling up the steps with the spring base of Will's old bed.

'It seems you're moving in then?' Elizabeth said acidly, as Diana walked slowly up the steps behind them.

'I told Diana she had no choice in the matter. It would look bloody funny, a girl of her age moving in with her bachelor uncle when her brother and married uncle are living here,' Evan panted as he and Eddie hauled the bedstead on to the doorstep.

'I've a job, Aunt Elizabeth,' Diana announced proudly, too excited to wait for a more propitious time to announce her news.

'You've a *what*?' Evan dropped the bedsprings on to the hall floor.

'Don't you dare scuff that lino, Evan Powell!' Elizabeth shouted angrily. 'Lino doesn't grow on trees. And with what you bring in we'll never be able to replace it.'

'It's resting on my foot, woman,' Evan snarled. 'Where are you working?' he asked Diana in a gentler tone, as he turned his back on Elizabeth.

'Ben Springer's.'

'Oh! Oh! Oh! You'd better watch that one.' Eddie forgot Elizabeth's presence for a moment. 'We may have to punch him on the nose.'

'What do you mean?' Diana asked, knowing full well what he meant.

'If you don't know, I'm not going to tell you,' Eddie mumbled, looking at the floor as his mother cast her disapproving eye on him.

'And I'll have none of that filthy double talk in my house, Edward Powell,' Elizabeth ordered.

'I can look after myself,' Diana asserted, lifting her chin defiantly.

'If you get any trouble from him, love, just tell me.' Evan picked up the bed again. 'How much is he paying you?'

'Six bob for the moment, but he said he'd review it if I suited the job.'

'That's bloody slave labour,' Eddie cursed.

'And how much do you intend paying me out of six shillings a week?' Elizabeth demanded, too concerned with the changes in the family's income to chastise Eddie for swearing.

'Whatever Will and Charlie are paying you,' Diana said boldly. 'I can afford to make it up until I get a pay rise. I've got savings,' she said boldly.

'They're paying seven and six a week. Each.' Elizabeth folded her arms and stepped aside so Evan and Eddie could move the bed on to the stairs.

'There's no way a slip of a girl like Diana will eat the same as those two great hulking men,' Evan protested. 'Four bob a week is more than fair.'

'Evan!' Elizabeth exclaimed.

'I've spoken, Elizabeth,' he said decisively. 'Right, Eddie?'

Carefully, so as not to tear the twenty-year-old jute carpet on the stairs, they manhandled the bedstead into the hall and over the banisters. It was tricky manoeuvring it through the narrow passageway and into the box room, but eventually they managed it, and laid it on its side beneath the window opposite the door.

'I don't know where you think you're going with all that furniture,' Elizabeth said as she peered through the darkness at the lumpy tarpaulin on the cart. 'That box room is full as it is.'

'Eddie and I will empty what's there into the attic,' Evan said calmly, refusing to allow himself to be rattled.

'Like as not, on top of the plasterboards, so you'll bring the ceiling down.'

'I hope tea is about ready, Elizabeth,' Evan reminded her. 'As soon as we've finished here, Eddie and I'll be wanting to eat.'

Elizabeth knew when she was beaten. Muttering under her breath, she retreated to the back kitchen.

'This room could do with a bit of a sweep out.' Evan brushed aside the dust as he handed Eddie the first of the boxes.

'I'll do it,' Diana called out from the hall, smiling in response to Eddie's wink, as he walked along the landing. Happy at the thought of making herself useful, she took off her wet coat and hung it on one of the hooks behind the front door, then rushed through to the washhouse to get a duster and a broom.

'As you're intent on staying here, you may as well know first as last that I'll have no barging around in this house,' Elizabeth shouted, stepping out of the way as Diana entered the kitchen.

'Sorry, Aunt Elizabeth,' Diana murmured. But she wasn't really downcast. She'd forgotten just how nice her Uncle Evan could be. And Eddie. She glanced at the clock. It was past seven. Another couple of hours and Will and Charlie would be home. Maud might wake up at any minute. Living in Graig Avenue wasn't going to be so bad after all.

56

Chapter Six

'We closing early tonight then, Ronnie?' Alma asked as Ronnie switched off the electric lights in the front of the café, and locked the door after the shop's last customers left.

'Hardly early, that was the last bus down from Ferndale.' He pulled a cigarette out of the top pocket of the boiled white shirt he was wearing beneath his jacket, and pushed it into his mouth. 'Rake the coals out of the fire on to the hearth and douse them, there's a good girl,' he ordered absently. 'I'll sort out the kitchen.'

Alma topped up the salt, pepper and vinegar bottles on the tables while Ronnie did what little had to be done in the kitchen. She wiped down the tables and chairs and swept the floor, as he opened the till and counted the money. It was their normal routine, and had been for two years.

Papa Ronconi had never liked any of his own girls to work the evening shifts, and as his wife was kept busy taking care of the younger children, he and Ronnie had been forced to employ part-timers in the family's two cafés. Evening hours suited Alma. Every morning she helped out in the tailor's shop lower down Taff Street. Work was slack because of the depression, so they could only afford to pay for her services two and a half days a week. The six nights a week she worked for Ronnie made all the difference. Apart from a small widow's pension her wage was all the money she and her mother had to live on.

A slim, green-eyed redhead, Alma had the kind of looks that turned men's heads, and she wasn't unaware of the fact; but she'd set her sights high – on Ronnie. She knew she was fighting fierce competition. Tall, dark, handsome, in a typically warm-blooded Latin way, with craggy, masculine rather than Hollywood good looks, Ronnie attracted women like syrup attracted flies. And most of them came to the same sticky end. It was probably true that Ronnie's attractions lay as much in his flourishing business as his looks. Security was a luxury few women had been able to aspire to since the pit closures.

But whatever good points Ronnie possessed, charm was most definitely not one of them. Lazy to the point of lethargy socially, when it came to wooing women he merely sat back and waited for them to come to him. Even when his friends or sisters dragged him to a late-night dance he never graced the floor. His forte seemed to be leaning on the bar, glass in hand, watching the world go by. Alma didn't mind. Not even when he refused to take her to the few annual dances that still went on after the café closed for the evening. When all was said and done, they saw one another six nights a week. What other couple could say that? And if he hadn't publicly acknowledged their relationship, so what? It would only be a matter of time. He simply wasn't given to gushing displays of sentimentality or affection, that was all. Besides, the words 'I love you' were the most overworked in the English language. They didn't mean anything: not when glib, flashy Romeos who fancied themselves as ladykillers used them over and over again. Men like Glan Richards, who murmured them to any girl foolish enough to go to the pictures with him, only to use the same phrase the next night, when he moved on to the next gullible female. She didn't need Ronnie to make any declarations of love to her. He showed her in so many ways other than words. Besides, what more could she ask of him? When they were alone . . .

'Ready then?'

She looked up and smiled. 'Ready for what?' she asked innocently, knowing full well what was coming.

'Upstairs, woman. Now!' He patted her behind. 'Then if you're good I just might take you home.'

'Via the mountain?' she asked hopefully.

'What for?'

'Look at the scenery?'

'It's raining. There's nothing to see.'

'It might clear up.'

'Even if it does, there'll only be slagheaps lit by the moon and the stars,' he teased, a deadpan expression on his face.

'Men!' she exclaimed disparagingly. But his lack of romance didn't prevent her from running up the back stairs to the small bedroom that he'd furnished for the nights when he told his parents he was too tired, or as they privately believed, too drunk to drive the Trojan home.

Ronnie ran his hand through his Vaselined, slicked-back hair and glanced at his profile in the huge mirror that hung on the back wall behind the counter. Smiling broadly, he studied his teeth. Satisfied with what he saw, he checked around the café one last time before stuffing the contents of the till into a cloth cash bag. He pushed it into one of the capacious pockets of the loose-cut khaki jacket he kept for work. Pulling down the door blind, he tried the lock on the front door to make sure it was fastened, switched out the back lights and followed Alma.

He knew she would be undressed, ready and waiting for him between the sheets of the small single bed. If he'd ever stopped to think about their relationship he might have realised just how much he took her for granted. Almost as much as he took every other female in his life for granted, including his mother and his sisters. Used to being one of the family's breadwinners from an early age, the responsibility had made him, if not callous, then at least indifferent to their needs and desires. Without thinking, he tended to treat those dependent on him like children. Beings to be petted when they were good, chastised when they were not, and to be kept in the dark about his private thoughts and any problems he might have, lest the need to confide in someone be misinterpreted as weakness.

Alma was undoubtedly the prettiest, brightest and longest-lasting of his many girlfriends, but he had never allowed her to be the only woman in his life. Their physical relationship, satisfying as he found it, didn't prevent him from paying regular visits to a shy little widow in Rickards Street. Not to mention Molly the flower and peg seller who had a stall on the market, Lucy the usherette who worked in the New Theatre . . . Ronnie, like all Italian men of his class, saw unblemished virtue, abstinence and chastity as an integral part of the make-up of every decent woman. A vital and essential attribute in his sisters, his mother, and the woman he would eventually marry; but something he, his father and his brothers could comfortably ignore when it came to their own affairs.

'You took your time coming upstairs,' Alma complained, wriggling between the sheets as he walked into the bedroom and shrugged his arms out of his jacket.

'Just checking around.' He felt in his shirt pocket for his cigarettes, and lit one. Throwing his coat on the only chair in the room, he sat on the bed, rested his ankle on his knee and pulled his shoe off. He glanced across at Alma. She was lying on her back, the sheet tucked demurely beneath her chin. He reached over and yanked it down.

'Ronnie!' she cried out angrily. Blushing, she grabbed the top blanket and hastily covered herself.

'Can't see any point in you doing that.' He took off his socks and tossed them on top of his shoes. 'Not when you consider what we're going to be up to in five minutes.'

'I don't like it,' she said petulantly.

'Only when I can see, and the lamp is lit.' He slid his hand beneath the sheet, and reached for her breast. 'You never object to this when I do it in the dark,' he whispered, as he fondled her.

'Come to bed,' she snapped touchily.

'Is that an order, Miss?'

She tried and failed to suppress a smile.

'That's better,' he laughed. Turning his back on her, he pulled the collar and tie from his neck and began to unbutton his shirt.

'Ronnie?' Alma asked hesitantly, wondering if she dare mention Liz Williams and Dickie Shales' engagement, or if that might be a bit obvious. She knew he reacted angrily when she talked about anything that could be remotely construed as 'pressurising', and it wasn't as if she was unhappy with their relationship. Last month he'd even asked her to stay on in the café after hours, so she could attend his parents' wedding anniversary celebrations. Granted she'd ended up by acting as waitress and helping Tina and Gina clear up, but the invitation was more than any other girl had received from him. She knew that for a fact, because Tina, fishing for gossip about her brother, had told her so.

That marvellous, wonderful evening, all the Ronconis, senior as well as junior, had been incredibly kind to her. So much so, she'd wondered if any of them other than Tina had their suspicions about her and Ronnie. She wasn't quite sure where she stood with him. From the moment she had allowed him to make love to her she had considered herself engaged, assuming that he would take their relationship as seriously as she did. That eventually it would lead somewhere, hopefully marriage. But occasionally, like now, she felt that their unspoken understanding was something that was understood only on her side.

'Yes?' he threw his shirt on to the chair.

'Are you staying here tonight?' she asked, losing courage and saying the first thing that came to mind.

'That's a strange question.' He unbuttoned his vest.

'Well, it's just that if you are, I could always walk home. It's not far.'

'It won't kill me to take the van as far as Morgan Street,' he murmured carelessly. He took the burning cigarette from his mouth and handed it to her to hold, as he heaved his vest over his head. Unbuckling his belt, and unbuttoning his braces and fly, he pulled off his trousers, took the cigarette and climbed into bed beside her.

'Ow, you're bloody freezing!' he complained as his legs met her feet between the sheets.

'It's this bed. It's not aired properly.'

'That's because it's not slept in enough.' He set his cigarette down carefully in an ashtray placed strategically at the side of the bed. 'Here,' he pulled her close. 'May as well get it over with.' He held her close, rubbing his hands over her shivering body, lingering over her breasts and thighs. She knew him too well to expect words of endearment.

'Ronnie?'

'Yes.'

'Turn down the lamp.'

'I want to see you.'

'Please, just for me.'

'Two years of this, and you're still shy?' Despite his grumbling, he leaned over and turned down the wick on the oil lamp. Some time he'd have to see about running electricity cables up here, but it would be difficult to justify the expense to his father. As he turned, she lifted her face to his so he could kiss her. He did so, thoroughly and expertly. He also knew her well. He may have been an inarticulate lover when it came to words, but he was anything but inarticulate when it came to the physical side of their relationship.

Afterwards there was no teasing, only quiet, relaxed fulfilment, and the sound of their breathing, muted, soft as Alma lay with her head on Ronnie's shoulder. Outside the street was still. The second houses in the New Theatre and the Town Hall had long since ended. Even the staff in the cinemas had gone home, and those who had the money and the inclination to spend the early hours drinking in pubs where the landlords were brave, or foolhardy enough to defy the licensing hours, were already there.

'Happy, Ronnie?' she asked, satisfaction and contentment making her bold.

'No.' He paused for a moment, watching her eyes cloud over. 'But I will be once I have a cigarette.'

'You're impossible,' she laughed, tickling his armpits.

'Here watch out, I might burn you.' He struck his lighter.

'Have you thought about the future?' she asked, wrapping her arms around his chest.

'Nothing but.' He inhaled deeply. 'How do you feel about giving up your job in the tailor's?'

'Giving up?' Her eyes glittered with dreams poised on the brink of transformation into reality. Of course, he wouldn't want his wife working. At least, not for anyone else.

'My father has just bought the lease on the empty shop in the centre of town. You know, the one by the fountain.'

'I know.' Her green eyes grew large, almost luminous in the soft glow of the lamp.

'It's huge,' he mused thoughtfully, flicking ash into the ashtray. 'You've never seen anything like the size of the basement.'

'Then it's big enough to set some rooms aside for living quarters?' Of course it wouldn't be ideal. Living in the middle of town. There'd be nowhere to hang washing. But then, if they were both working, and making enough money, they could send their linen out to the Chinese laundry in Mill Street. Her mother would be close: Morgan Street was no distance at all from the fountain. And the park would be just around the corner. Handy when they had children. She'd never spoken to him about children, but she was sure that he'd want lots. Just like his parents. When the time was right he'd put away the ghastly, thick, rubber French letter he used when they made love and . . .

'Not living quarters,' he laughed, 'a restaurant. A big one. Enormous, even. We're turning the basement into a kitchen the like of which this town has never seen before. Half of it will be used to turn out cooked meals, the other half will be a first-class

62

confectioner's kitchen. I'm going into cakes and confectionery in a big way. There's a hell of a market there, and St Catherine's café in the Arcade hasn't even scratched the surface. When you consider it, it's amazing no one's thought of it before. Everyone in this town has a birthday, and not everyone's on the breadline.'

'Only about half the population,' she interrupted bitterly.

'Exactly,' he enthused. Carried away by his grand scheme, he failed to pick up the acid tone of sarcasm in her voice. 'And we'll cater for the other half. We'll make cakes for every occasion. Weddings, christenings, to celebrate someone in the family getting a job – and the bakery will be only part of it. There's two windows at street level. We'll fill one with pastries, the other savouries. Pies, pasties, faggots, pease puddings – you know the sort of thing. We're knocking all the ground floor rooms into one. Putting counters and four tables in the front to cater for tea and snacks, and behind those there'll be an archway that will lead into the main restaurant. More upmarket than this. It'll specialise in cooked dinners and set teas. The second floor is big enough to house a function room. You wait until you see it, it's as big as the silver and blue ballroom in the New Inn. Not that we'll be anywhere near as pricey, because all our profit will be made on the food. I think we'll aim for the club dinners. The Tennis Club, the Golliwog club. The store do's like Rivelin's . . .'

'And where exactly do I fit into all this?' she asked icily, moving as far away from him as the small bed would allow.

'I'll need a head waitress.'

'What about your sisters?'

'Too young, too inexperienced. They haven't the staying power. I need to put someone who's hard-working and knows what they're about in charge, to set them a good example. It'll be worth . . .' he thought carefully for a moment, weighing up all of Alma's pluses. She certainly knew how to work, and there was no shirking of unpleasant tasks with her. The first thing she did when she started a shift was to look around and set about what needed to be done, whether it was scrubbing the floor or serving one of the town councillors. On the minus side, he realised that once he set her wages he'd have to pitch everyone else's to them, including the cook's, and that could prove expensive.

'How does twelve shillings a week plus tips sound to you?' he asked, running his fingers through her red curls.

'Sounds like more than I'm getting now.' She struggled to feign gratitude. After all, a job and a pay rise had to be worth something, even if it wasn't the engagement ring she'd hoped for.

'Then you'll give it a try.' He fumbled in the bedclothes at the bottom of the bed for the underpants he'd kicked off earlier.

'I'll give it a try.'

'Good, that's settled then. Come on girl,' he threw back the sheet. 'If you make a move, we'll go through the back door of the Horse and Groom for a quick one.'

'Looking like this?'

He jumped out of bed.

'You don't need to dress, not on my account, but your lipstick has wandered up as far as your nose, and your hair needs a good combing.'

'Why you – ' she threw the pillow at him.

'Come on, woman. It's good drinking time you're wasting,' he grumbled irritably as he pulled on his trousers.

'Here's to the next town, and the next audience.' Ambrose, the producer cum comic of the revue shouted as he held up a bottle of champagne. 'May they be as kind, welcoming and, God willing, a little more forthcoming and richer than the audiences here.' He looked around, gauging the reaction to his poor joke. 'Is everyone's glass full?' he asked abruptly.

'Not mine,' Tessie giggled.

'Yours is never full, Tessie,' he reprimanded humourlessly.

'Never,' she simpered in a voice that squeaked from too much cheap sherry.

'And here's to the best callboy in the business.' Ambrose touched his glass to Haydn's and winked. Haydn pretended not to see the wink. He'd been careful to leave Ambrose's dressing-room door open all week when he'd delivered the evening *Echo*.

'If the oldest,' Tessie sniped.

'Leave it off, Tess,' Patsy the head chorus girl muttered through clenched teeth.

'Right then, where are we going to carry on?' Ambrose slurred.

'Depends on what you mean by "carry on",' Tessie giggled archly.

'Two foot nine I think,' the manager suggested, pointedly ignoring Tessie. 'They're not too particular there about closing hours.' He had the urge to add, 'or clientele'. Some of the girls had a disconcerting habit of dressing for the stage, off it. Half a dozen looked modest enough. They could have sat in the New Inn and passed unnoticed, but a few, Tessie included, could have lost themselves amongst the ladies of the town who were touting for trade in station yard.

'Everyone game?' Ambrose downed the last of his champagne. When his glass was empty he looked around the stage. 'Everything packed here?' he demanded imperiously of the stagehands.

'Did you doubt it, sir?' one of the hands answered in a wounded voice.

'Just checking, dear boy. Just checking. It's all right for you people, you have no idea what it's like to sit on a filthy train all night, only to arrive in the back end of Aber-cwm-llan-snot with half your bloody props missing, and what's worse, no spirit gum to stick the stars and spangles on the girls. They don't look very alluring performing in their shimmys and knickers, believe you me,' he whispered conidentially, wrinkling his nose.

'Shut up, Ambrose,' Patsy snarled, pushing her status as head girl to the absolute limit.

'You sound just like a mother hen, darling,' Ambrose cooed patronisingly. 'Come on then girls and boys. Are we all ready?'

'I'm glad you're coming with us Haydn,' Betty whispered, tottering precariously on her high heels over the littered cobblestones of Market Square as she struggled to keep up with his long-legged stride.

'Why's that?' he asked vacantly, his thoughts still preoccupied with Jenny.

'Because you're sane and normal,' she murmured in a voice that sounded incredibly old and tired for one so young.

'That's a funny thing to say.' He ushered her around a pile of soggy newspapers heaped high on the spot where the china stall had stood.

'It's true. You've no idea what this life is really like.'

'It can't be any worse than life around here.'

'Don't you believe it. My mother warned me not to go on stage,' she confessed tremulously, sliding her fingers surreptitiously into his as they followed the others round the corner into Taff Street. He didn't like the touch of her skin very much. It felt damp and greasy, not at all like Jenny's cool, dry hand. 'But I wouldn't listen,' she continued. 'Thought I knew everything, didn't I? Two of my aunties were in variety, and they got me an audition. It all seemed so glamorous. Whenever I saw them they were smothered in furs and jewellery, and they spent hours telling me about the famous people they knew, and the places they'd seen. It all sounded absolutely heavenly.'

'Will I have heard of them?' Haydn asked quickly, knowing full well just how many doors one famous name could open for a beginner.

'No, of course no,' Betty answered scornfully. 'Aunt Edie is running a boarding house in Blackpool now, with a comedian who turned to drink. He's horrid, and the house is disgusting. Not even clean. I stayed there last summer. She keeps it "exclusive".' Betty adopted what she considered a 'posh voice'. 'Theatricals only darling,' she purred. 'It has to be, because no tripper would look twice at the dump. And Auntie Rita ended up in the workhouse,' she said coldly. 'She's a live-in cook.'

'That's not so bad,' Haydn smiled, seeing the irony in the story. 'At least she has enough to eat, and a captive audience to practise on.'

'Perhaps I should join her,' Betty whined.

'Come on,' Haydn said. 'Pontypridd on a Saturday night, or should I say early Sunday morning, isn't that bad.'

'It's not the place, or rather places,' she said hastily, wary of offending him. The one thing she had learned about the Welsh was that they could be touchy about Wales, especially their home towns, which were inevitably coated with a thick, filthy layer of coal-dust and crumbling around the edges from the worst effects of the depression. 'It's the other girls,' she moaned. 'They're so bitchy. I have to share a bedroom with four of them, and because I'm the youngest and last in, I've no choice as to who I share a bed with. And Tessie . . .' she hesitated for a moment.

'If you're homesick why don't you go home?' he suggested

66

brutally. Any well of sympathy he might have felt for the ego-induced traumas of theatrical life had been sucked dry by a succession of chorus girls who had sobbed out the most horrendous stories on his shoulder, only to switch to smiles and laughter when someone better heeled had come along and offered to buy them a drink or a meal.

'Pride, I suppose,' she intoned dramatically. 'Besides,' she curled her damp sweaty fingers around his, 'there's nine of us kids in a two-bedroomed house in Bermondsey. It's so bloody full. You can have no idea what it's like . . .'

'You can't tell me anything about overcrowding,' he said shortly. 'As of today there's eight of us living in our house.'

'Then you *do* know what it's like.' She fluttered her lashes in the direction of his blue eyes.

'Not really,' he dismissed her attempt to steer the conversation into intimacy. 'We all get on pretty well.'

He thought of William, Charlie, his father, Diana and now Maud. If she was as ill as Ronnie had hinted, God only knew how much longer they'd have her with them.

He already missed his older sister Bethan more than he would have thought possible. He hadn't realised just how much he'd talked to her, or relied on her judgement, until she was in London and out of everyday reach. Maud was no Bethan. She'd always been the baby of the family: the one who needed protecting and keeping safe from the harsher realities of life. He shuddered, hating himself for even thinking of a time when Maud would no longer be in the house. As though he were precipitating tragedy by giving free rein to such thoughts.

'We all get on very well,' he murmured again, superstitiously crossing his fingers and hoping that his home and house as it stood now, full of family and cousins, would remain exactly as it was that night. He wished with all his might that he could make it last for ever. But even as he formulated intense wishes into silent prayers he knew it wouldn't. Because change, whether welcome or not, was inevitable.

Chapter Seven

'Here we are,' Ambrose announced loudly, halting outside the entrance to the pub. 'In you go, girls and boys.'

'If he calls us "girls and boys" once more I'm going to thump him right where it hurts with my handbag,' Betty whispered in Haydn's ear.

They filed down the tiled passageway and into the long, narrow back room that had been named after the length of the bar. Ambrose clicked his fingers and shouted for the head barman in a voice calculated to be heard in every nook and cranny of the building. He pulled a five-pound note out of his wallet and held it upright between his thumb and forefinger.

'Drinks for the entire cast, and all the stage crew of the Town Hall,' he ordered flamboyantly. 'No doubles or trebles,' he muttered confidentially into the barman's ear. 'And just so you can't say you haven't been warned, these are coming out of the profits of the tour,' he explained to his fellow artistes. 'You'll be drinking your bonus.'

'Old fart,' Patsy griped. 'Has to hold centre stage, even when he's out of the theatre.'

'What's yours, Patsy?' Haydn asked, looking for an excuse to move away from Betty.

'Gin and T, darling,' she called out as she sank into the sagging plush upholstery of a couch pushed against the back wall. 'Treble,' she added defiantly, eyeing Ambrose.

'Seeing as how it's you darling, I'll make an exception.' Ambrose mouthed an OK to the barman.

'Same for me, Haydn,' Betty demanded, pouting because he'd left her side.

'And me,' Tessie cried out.

Before Haydn knew what was happening, he was acting as waiter, ferrying gin and tonics, whisky-and-its, and brandy and sodas between the bar and the seats. A good quarter of an hour elapsed before he was free to look for a seat for himself. Clutching a full pint he rested his heel on the brass rail, turned his back on the bar and looked around.

'Haydn!' Betty patted a stool she'd commandeered. Puckering her lips, she blew him a kiss. Seeing no other seat he reluctantly moved towards it.

'And I'm telling you now, Myra won't make it. There's a world of difference between the chorus in the London Pavilion and the real big time,' Patsy lectured a young and astonishingly pretty blonde who was sitting next to her.

'But she's got talent,' Alice protested vehemently.

'Talent on its own is never enough. Haydn?' Patsy smiled, showing two rows of large, improbably white teeth as he shifted his stool as far away from Betty as space would allow. 'Be an angel and find me a light,' she pleaded, jamming a cigarette into an extremely long, mother-of-pearl-handled holder.

'My pleasure.' He produced a box of matches and struck one.

'Of course I'm not saying you can get anywhere without talent,' Patsy qualified, 'but it's not enough. Not on its own. And a break that takes you as far as the Pavilion chorus –'

'And what would you know about the Pavilion, Patsy?' Tessie sniped bitchily.

'I've covered five seasons there, and ten in the Adelphi,' Patsy countered brusquely, 'which is more than you'll ever do. And I could have stayed in both.'

'If you were so great, what are you doing in the sticks with Ambrose now?' Tessie enquired nastily.

'If you must know, paying back a favour to an old friend.'

'Sure it wasn't because your face was beginning to look like an old prune?'

'Tessie!' Alice hissed angrily.

Haydn stared down at the table, twirling his empty glass in his hand. He was waiting for the eruption that generally splintered a group when one of the chorus took on the head girl.

'I retired five years ago,' Patsy's voice was ominously calm, 'after I'd had more than my fair share of moments of glory. Unlike you, I've realised all my ambitions. I've enough money stowed away in the bank for a rainy day or two, and a man waiting for me in Brighton when this revue finishes. And I can't wait, because when it does, it'll be "bye, bye" touring for good.'

69

'You're giving up the stage?' Haydn asked incredulously.

'I've had a good run.' Patsy flicked the ash from her cigarette delicately into the ashtray on the table. 'I lasted until, as Tessie just so tactfully pointed out, "the wrinkles came", which is a darned sight longer than most. I wouldn't have come out of retirement if it had been anyone other than Joe Carver who'd asked. The head girl for this tour took up an American offer a month before it was due to start. Joe's done a lot for me over the years. I felt I couldn't really refuse him.'

'How long have you been in retirement?' Alice asked.

'Two years.'

'I would never have thought so from your dancing, and those damned rehearsals you put us through,' Betty complained.

'I keep telling you,' Patsy finished her drink and put her glass down on the table. 'Constant rehearsing is the secret of a successful show. And then again, a dancer can never retire. That's if she wants to keep her body from seizing up like a rusty piece of old machinery. I've kept my hand in. My sister and I run a dancing school in Brighton, and that's where I'll be a week from now. For good! Joe Carver can shout till he's blue in the face next time. He's called in every favour I owe him with this one. Sixteen years on the road is long enough.'

'I wonder if I'll last as long,' Alice murmured.

'You won't.' Patsy crunched her cigarette out, and telescoped her holder to flick out the end. 'The chorus is not for you, my girl. You're headed for the big time. You listening?' She dug Haydn in the ribs. 'Watch out for this one. You'll be seeing her up on the silver screen one day. She may look quiet, but she has more talent in her little finger than the rest of this troupe put together. Not only can she dance and act, but she can sing as well. Like an angel. And she has plenty of what counts most in this rotten business. Ambition.'

'I wish Ambrose thought as highly of me as you do,' Alice said between clenched teeth.

'You won't always be working with an egotistical comic who tries to dominate the whole show.' Patsy smiled insincerely at Ambrose, who was holding forth at the bar.

'How about giving us a song now?' Haydn suggested to Alice in an attempt to dispel the clouds of last-night gloom that were gathering in the atmosphere. 'There's a piano in the corner.'

70

'I've met pub pianos before,' she replied derisively.

'So have I, and that one's not too bad. Come on, I'll play for you.'

'Can you?'

'Try me and you'll find out.' He left his stool and Betty, who was beginning to annoy him with her games of footsie under the table.

'Hey everyone!' Viv the barman shouted when he saw Haydn heading for the piano. 'Quiet! Haydn's going to sing.'

'You sing?' Alice asked as she perched on a high stool next to the piano.

'Only for pints on Saturday nights,' he laughed. 'Nothing like you, and certainly not professionally. What do you want me to play?'

'Do you know "If I Should Fall in Love Again?" '

Although Alice had danced, kicked and sung her way through the chorus routines of a matinée and two shows, she threw all she had into her performance. Haydn sensed that it wouldn't have been any different if she'd been playing centre stage at His Majesty's Theatre in London. The hubbub of conversation died in the hot, smoky bar as the customers turned their attention to the corner where Alice sat, legs demurely crossed at the ankles, singing her heart out. Soon only the clean, clear, pure notes of her music filled the air.

'That's some voice the little lady's got, Haydn. Why don't you sing alongside her?' Viv asked when the applause finally died down.

'And show myself up? Not likely. I'm not in her league.'

'Says who? Have you heard him sing?' the barman demanded of Ambrose and the Town Hall manager.

'Haven't had the pleasure, old boy,' Ambrose replied in a bored voice.

'What about you?' Viv demanded of the manager.

'Only when he's sweeping the floor of the stage,' the manager replied flippantly.

'Give the lad a chance,' Viv said sternly.

'I'm game for anything at this time of night,' Ambrose grinned superciliously.

'Go on, Haydn. This is my pub. You won't drink here again if you don't.'

71

'I can't. Not in this company, Viv,' Haydn pleaded. 'It's different when there's only the boys around.' He fumbled in his pocket for change, and asked for another half, all he had money for.

'Come on, Haydn.' Freda the barmaid took up the chorus. 'Please, just for me. "Heart and Soul". '

'An artiste never disappoints his public. First lesson a trouper has to learn.' Ambrose slapped Haydn heartily across the shoulders, splashing most of his precious beer down his shirt front. 'Besides, I've always been one for giving the hired help a chance. Come on, we'll turn this into a talent contest,' he shouted, putting himself centre stage yet again. 'Don't be shy, lad. I'll play for you myself.'

'I only sing for pints,' Haydn said firmly. 'I'm not a professional.'

'You told me when I took you on that you wanted to go on stage some day,' the manager said insensitively. 'How are you going to manage that if you won't even stand up and sing in a bar?'

'A bar full of professionals,' Haydn thought angrily. People who were used to hearing top names perform, not the dregs of raw talent like him. He held no illusions about his voice. It wasn't trained. It was reasonable, good even, for the chapel choir and Saturday nights in the pubs of Ponty, but it wasn't up to Adelphi standard.

He downed what little remained of his half-pint. Ambrose was already sitting at the piano.

'Come on, Haydn. I'll sing with you if you want,' Alice offered sympathetically, hating the way he'd been pressurised into performing.

'What's is to be then, old boy?' Ambrose shouted above the noise of the bar.

' "Heart and Soul",' Freda called out.

' "Heart and Soul" it is.' Ambrose flourished his hands over the keys and began to play. Haydn dumped his empty glass on the bar and walked over to where Alice was still sitting on her stool. He'd sung in pubs, including this one, many times but the audience of professionals totally unnerved him. He opened his mouth and the first note that issued forth fell cracked and discordant into the atmosphere. Tessie tittered. He glared at her and stiffened his back as Ambrose began to play the introduction again. Alice took his hands in hers, looked into his eyes and lent her voice as backing to his for the first line.

'Heart and Soul, I fell in love with you. Heart and Soul the way a fool would do . . . Madly . . .'

Staring into the depths of her eyes, seeing nothing else, he took his cue from her and sang. The third line went well. The fourth better. When Ambrose began to play the second verse, Alice fell silent. Haydn didn't need her any more. He was singing to the bar as he'd done so many nights before.

Freda stood, tea towel in hand, tears flowing down her withered cheeks, rapt, lost in emotion. Even the manager of the Town Hall left his drink untouched on the bar.

'Good Lord, he's good. Really good,' he uttered in amazement when Haydn had finished, and the applause had begun.

'Pretty, too.' Patsy cast a critical eye over Haydn's smooth blond hair, blue eyes and six-foot, slim frame. 'Given the right break he could do well,' she mused critically, taking another cigarette.

Ambrose looked at Haydn and mouthed, 'Another?' Haydn nodded, and went into his standard repertoire of, 'I'll take you home again Kathleen', 'Goodnight, my love', and 'Just let me look at you'. Alice joined in the last one, and it was evident that the two of them were lost in their own enjoyment, singing only for one another. Patsy fumbled for a light as she watched them, her thoughts racing. They made a very good couple. Two blonde angels together. Given the right lighting, the right costumes, the right parts . . .

'You want a job, just say the word. Three pounds a week, boy in the chorus, with a chance of solo spots whenever they can be fitted in,' Ambrose offered expansively. Haydn looked Ambrose in the eye; saw the way the comedian ran his tongue over his fat, wet lips as he looked him up and down.

'No thanks,' he said quickly. Too quickly. 'I can't tour, I've too many commitments that keep me here.'

'Good boy,' the manager enthused, thinking of all the slots he could ask Haydn to fill at minimum payment.

'Never look a gift horse in the mouth, old boy.' Ambrose laid his arm across Haydn's shoulders and pinched his cheek. 'Think about it, and while you're thinking I'll buy you and Alice another drink. Gin and T?'

'I only drink beer,' Haydn replied ungratefully. 'And Viv's just poured me one.'

'There's worse than Ambrose around in this business,' Alice commented after Ambrose had left them for the bar. 'Much worse. All you have to do is say no to the man, and he'll back off.'

'Is that the voice of experience talking?' Haydn asked, studying Ambrose's fleshy back.

'As you're asking, yes. I mentioned my steady boyfriend and he apologised, handsomely.'

'And have you a steady boyfriend?' Haydn asked, wondering why he'd never noticed Alice before.

'Oh yes.' Alice picked up her handbag and took out a packet of Du Mauriers. 'And a good-looking boy like you must have a steady girlfriend.'

'I did until this afternoon.'

There was something so comically mournful about his expression that Alice laughed out loud.

'If the spat had been serious, you wouldn't have just thrown Ambrose's offer back in his face.'

'It's not Jenny that's keeping me here,' he explained. 'It's my family. They rely on what I bring home.'

'Your parents.'

'And my kid brother. My youngest sister came home today as well, from a live-in job in a hospital. She has consumption,' he added bitterly, suddenly ashamed of himself for pouring out his troubles to her. He wondered why he was doing it. Perhaps it was the beer on top of an empty stomach.

'That's tough. Consumption, I mean. My mother died of it when I was two. Ciggie?' she offered him the packet, and he took one. 'Look Haydn, that is your name isn't it? Haydn?'

He nodded.

'If anyone makes you an offer like Ambrose's again, grab it with both hands,' she advised seriously. 'That's if you really want to go on stage.'

'I've never wanted anything else.'

'Offers like that aren't two a penny. I don't know if you've got what it takes to make it. I don't mean talent,' she added, sensitive to the hurt look in his eyes. 'Despite what Patsy said earlier, I don't think anyone can predict who's going to make it in this business. It's nothing as simple as ambition or talent. It's luck, being in the right place at the right time . . .'

'And this tour could have been that?'

'Don't knock the provinces. Word gets around, and every audience you play teaches you something.'

'Thanks for the tip.'

'Well, I'm for bed.' She knocked back the last of her gin. 'Two gins and one cigarette is enough for me after a show, and we still have to be on the early train for Swansea tomorrow.'

'I'll walk you home if you like.'

'As long as you realise that it will be just that. A walk.' She raised her enormous blue eyes until they were level with his.

'I wouldn't dream of trying to turn it into anything else.' He picked up his cap and coat from the top of the piano.

'See you, Haydn,' Viv shouted from behind the bar.

'In work bright and early Monday morning, Haydn. New scenery to set up, and calls to check,' the manager warned.

'I'll be there. Goodnight.'

'Good luck, boy,' Patsy called out. 'Look after that talent of yours.'

Ambrose turned his back as Alice and Haydn walked out of the door. He was too angry with Haydn's refusal even to say goodbye.

'Where are you staying?' Haydn asked as he and Alice left the shelter of the tiled doorway.

'Lodgings on Broadway.'

'At least it's not far to go.' He fastened the collar of his coat. The early evening rain had turned to pounding hailstones, and the street was covered with a fine layer of slippery ice. Alice put up her umbrella and held it over both their heads.

'Take my arm.' He held out his left arm. 'Or is that going too far?'

She laughed as she hooked her hand into the crook of his elbow. 'I was wrong about you, Haydn. You shouldn't take up the next offer an Ambrose makes you.'

'Why?' he demanded innocently.

'Because you're far too nice for the theatre,' she teased. 'You take a girl at her word.'

Jenny Griffiths sat on an empty, upturned pop crate and huddled into her thick, red Welsh flannel dressing gown. She was freezing. Not wanting to go upstairs for a blanket in case she missed the all-important footstep on the hill, or the hand on the latch, she looked around the storeroom for something she could use to warm herself. A couple of empty sacks lay in the corner. Shivering, she pulled them towards her. Two were potato sacks, one had held carrots. Plumping for the cleanest, she took the carrot sack. She wrapped it around her shoulders on top of her dressing gown. Both her parents had been snoring when she'd crept silently down the stairs, so she'd risked leaving the door between the storeroom and the shop open in the hope of siphoning off any warmth that remained in the shop from the paraffin heater that had burnt there all day. Crouching on the crate, she stared up at the back door. Her eyes had become accustomed to the darkness. She could see the bolt that she had drawn back earlier. Her gaze flickered from the bolt to the latch. She concentrated with all her might, willing the metal bar to lift.

Haydn had to come! He simply had to! He'd been tired that afternoon. That was all. He'd been tired, and she'd been miserable at the thought of spending one more Saturday night alone. That was why they'd had that stupid row. He, like her, would have calmed down by now. He wouldn't pass the shop, not without testing the latch to see if she'd left the door open. She wondered if it was one o'clock yet. She'd left her room at twelve. It seemed like she'd been sitting here for hours, but she'd spent enough early mornings waiting for Haydn in the storeroom to know that the passage of time could be deceptive. She'd probably only been here for half an hour, and if Haydn was loading scenery into the back of a van . . .

Steps echoed along the pavement in front of the shop. She jerked upright and ran stiffly to the shop window, hovering just behind the counter. She saw the back of a constable's broad figure, lamplight burnishing the buttons on the shoulders of his overcoat. Disconsolate, she checked the clock on the wall behind the counter. Its hands pointed to five to one. Haydn couldn't be much longer now – unless he'd gone to the last-night party with the chorus girls. Jealousy began to bubble violently inside her as she returned to the storeroom. Curling her feet beneath her, she clutched the sack across her shoulders and waited, her stomach kneading itself into tight little knots that were half fear, half anticipation. What if – what if Haydn had thought she meant what she said? What if he'd taken her seriously? What if he never spoke to her again?

She'd been such a fool. She couldn't survive without Haydn. If he came back she'd never allow her jealousy to surface so destructively again. Never speak sharply. Never . . . Even as she made heady promises to herself, and to whatever peculiar deity she believed presided over lovers blighted by misery, her eyelids grew heavy. She curled herself tightly into the corner. The walls at her back and side were cold, but just about bearable. The sacking helped to insulate her from the brick's freezing temperature.

Haydn dragged himself wearily up the hill. Every step took an enormous effort that drained his strength even further, but in spite of his exhaustion he was restless and on edge. His throat burned full of indigestible remorse. What insane impulse of self-destruction had led him to give Ambrose the wrong answer when he'd invited him to join the revue? He'd never get another offer like that. Not in a million years. He'd allowed his dislike of Ambrose and what he was to ruin his whole life.

How often had he told his sister Bethan that all he wanted was to go on stage? Now his bluff had been called. At the slightest suggestion that his lifelong ambition might be realised, he'd turned chicken and run. Flung an offer that any aspiring chorus boy in the country would have sold his soul to get, back in Ambrose's indignant face. As Alice had said, if Ambrose or anyone else for that matter had made overtures to him, he could always have said no. He'd been a fool. A stupid fool. And for what? To turn up at the Town Hall again at eight o'clock on Monday morning to begin another fourteen-hour day. Three pounds a week Ambrose had offered! He could have lived like a king on two, and sent a pound home. Eight shillings more than he paid his mother now, and he wouldn't have been eating any of her food. But it was too late. He'd seen the look on Ambrose's face after he rejected the offer. If he went crawling back now Ambrose would kick him in the teeth, and quite rightly so. He'd been too stupid to recognise a golden egg when it had been laid in front of him.

He flung the cold cigarette butt that he held clamped between his lips to the ground. He was too upset and too angry to think any more about the implications of what he'd done. He paused to get his breath. Fury had turned his walk up the Graig hill into a run, and the Graig hill wasn't built for speed. He looked around, taking his bearings. He was standing in the road in front of the fish shop. Opposite, a street lamp shed a benign yellow glow over the front of Griffiths' shop, highlighting the displays of tins of tomatoes, polish and sardines. To the left he could see the sweets: as mouthwateringly tormenting as they'd been during his childhood and, since the shop was closed, just as unattainable. Everlasting strips, Five Boys chocolate, pear drops – he remembered their sharp acidic taste and suddenly craved it. It was comforting to think of childhood. The only problems he'd had then were connected with money. Finding enough pennies to go to the Saturday morning rush in the White Palace, and to buy his liquorice sticks and 'jelly comforters'. He'd had no regrets then, made no wrong decisions to beat himself over the head with. He hadn't even really known Jenny.

He walked closer to the shop on his toes, taking care to keep his steps silent. Fumbling in his pocket he took out the last of the two cigarettes he'd bought earlier in the kiosk in the Town Hall. He struck a match and lit it before walking softly round to the back of the shop. Lifting the latch on the gate set into the wall of the yard he stepped up to the back door. Hand on the leaf of the latch he paused. What would he do if it was locked? She could be on the other side of the door, waiting, ready to laugh at him as the door failed to give. She might even wake her father, and what on earth could he say to Harry Griffiths if he were caught here, skulking like a burglar?

Turning on his heel, he walked quickly away. Retracing his steps he continued his journey up the hill.

Stil lying on the upturned crate with the sack wrapped round her, Jenny didn't hear a sound. Head slumped forward she slept on, oblivious to everything. Even Haydn's absence from her life.

78

Chapter Eight

'You feeling any better this morning?' Diana walked into Maud's bedroom, set the tray she was carrying down on the empty half of the bed, and drew the curtains.

'I feel fine,' Maud lied.

'You look better,' Diana agreed. 'But not better enough. You know what Doctor Lewis said last night. Plenty of rest and – '

'Good food, warmth and plenty of doing nothing. Come on, Di, don't put me in a box before my time,' Maud snapped, regaining, along with her strength, some of the rage against being singled out for tuberculosis.

'I'm not putting you anywhere before your time,' Diana retorted, her hackles rising at the hint of self-pity in Maud's voice. Maud had tuberculosis, but tuberculosis could be fought, especially by people who had a family to look after them and a home to call their own. 'Are you going to eat that salt fish I cooked with my own fair hand or not?'

'I am,' Maud took the cup of tea from the tray and placed it on the bedside cabinet, then picked up a slice of bread and butter and began to eat. 'What's everyone doing?' she asked.

'Seeing as how it's ten o'clock, their usual Sunday morning business. The boys have gone rabbiting over the mountain with your father, Charlie and the dog. But knowing William and Eddie they'll probably return via the coal tip in the Maritime.'

'They can get done for that.'

'They don't need you to tell them that,' Diana said crossly. Maud could be stupid at times. The boys would never risk going near the guarded dumps of the closed pits if it wasn't for Maud. There'd been quite an argument over breakfast about whether enough coal could be spared to light a fire in Maud's bedroom, or not. Elizabeth had insisted that they couldn't afford it. Evan had said they had to, and Charlie hadn't helped by offering to pay more for his board and lodging. Diana had seen William nod to Eddie across the table, and she knew precisely what that meant.

They intended to solve the problem in what was rapidly becoming a typical valley way, without any money changing hands.

'Where's Mam?' Maud asked, wondering if Diana was snapping because her mother had upset her more than usual.

'In chapel.'

'So that's how you managed to bring me breakfast in bed,' she smiled, knowing her mother would never willingly have countenanced food, especially fish, being carried upstairs.

'Don't worry, I'll air the bedroom well afterwards.' Diana walked to the narrow sash window and looked down at the street. It was quiet. The children who were used to obeying their parents were in chapel, the others were up the mountain with the men and the dogs. 'Are you coming down today?'

'You bet your life. I don't intend to lie up here all day and play the invalid.'

'I'll bring you warm water to wash.'

'Thanks Di,' Maud said fondly as her cousin opened the door.

'For what?'

'For looking after me,' she said huskily, her voice raw with the cold she'd picked up.

'If I don't, you'll never get well enough for that trip to Spain we promised ourselves. Remember!'

They both laughed. Brought up on their Spanish-born grandmother's tales of her homeland, when they were five they'd decided to go to Spain. William, Haydn and Eddie had teased them unmercifully about it at the time, telling them not to spend any of the pennies they scrounged on sweets, because they'd need them for their boat tickets.

Maud was up, washed, dressed and sitting downstairs by the time Elizabeth returned from chapel. Diana had washed the breakfast dishes, including the ones she'd taken up to the bedroom. She'd also opened Maud's bedroom window, sprinkled precious drops of essence of violets in the air to disguise the smell of fish, and made the bed. And in an effort to please Elizabeth she had the dinner well under way. The potatoes for boiling were peeled, ready in a saucepan of water. She'd cleaned out the two beef hearts and breast of lamb that William had brought home from the stall the night before, stuffed them and put them in the oven, along with a generous portion of second-quality dripping from Elizabeth's pot, and was now cleaning carrots and swedes to go with them.

'Girls,' Elizabeth nodded briefly as she came in. 'Are you well enough to be sitting up, Maud?'

'I think so, Mam,' Maud replied.

'Either you are, or you're not,' Elizabeth countered briskly.

'I don't want to stay in bed all day,' Maud retorted.

'I'll have none of that tone in this house. What you want, or don't want, is immaterial where your health is concerned.' Elizabeth sounded every inch the schoolmarm she'd once been. 'You heard Doctor Lewis last night same as I did. Rest, warmth plenty of good food . . .'

'I'm hardly running a marathon sitting here!' Maud exclaimed indignantly.

'No, but you're exposing yourself to draughts as Diana walks back and for to the pantry.' She looked suspiciously at Maud's hair, clean and fluffed out. The fair curls shone like a halo around her thin, pale face and deep blue eyes. 'You've washed your hair, haven't you?' she asked accusingly.

'It needed it.'

'Not in your condition it didn't.'

'I helped her dry it right away, Aunt Elizabeth,' Diana interrupted, forcing her aunt to acknowledge her presence for the first time since she'd entered the room. 'And I've all of the dinner under way,' she added, hoping to deflect Elizabeth's attention. 'It should be ready by half-past one. That is when you eat on a Sunday, isn't it?'

'It is. I've tried to ensure that this family keeps normal hours,' Elizabeth sniffed, debating whether to make a deprecating comment on the hours Diana was brought up to keep by her jailbird mother.

'The hearts are in and roasting . . .' Diana began defensively.

'Have you basted them well?' Elizabeth opened the oven door and lifted the lids of the two roasting pans sitting on the shelf.

'I think so, Aunt Elizabeth.'

'Think so! What's got into you girls? What have they been teaching you in that hospital? Don't either of you give straight answers to straight questions any more? *I think*', she pronounced decisively, 'that I'd better see what you've done for myself.' With a martyred sigh Elizabeth took down the rag-stuffed stocking potholders and lifted first one pan then the other on to the iron top of the stove. She removed their lids, and poked at the meat. She knew, and Diana knew, there was more than enough fat in the pan, but that didn't prevent her from lifting down her fat jar and adding another dollop to both pans. She turned the potatoes that were sizzling nicely in the molten dripping at the side of the meat. 'Don't you think you put them in a little early?' she criticized.

'They always seem to take hours to brown,' Diana protested, biting back the urge to scream at her aunt.

'They will if you don't baste them regularly.' Elizabeth took a wooden spoon from the kitchen table drawer, and began to spoon fat from the base of the pans over the contents.

'I can do that,' Diana said mutinously.

'And what are we having for dessert, young lady?' Elizabeth enquired, ignoring Diana's offer.

'Dessert?' Diana looked blankly at her aunt.

'Afters,' Maud supplied helpfully.

'You know I hate that word, Maud.'

'Diana and I are both used to hospital language, Mam.'

'Then it's as well you both left when you did.'

'I was going to make an apple crumble with some of the apples from the sack at the back of the pantry,' Diana said, wondering if her aunt would find fault with the suggestion.

'They're windfalls, so be careful to cut out all the bruised bits or the whole crumble will taste rotten, and that would be a waste of good sugar, fat and flour, not to mention apples,' Elizabeth warned.

'I do know how to cut up apples,' Diana said testily.

'You're just like your mother, Diana. She never would take telling either.'

Diana didn't trust herself to answer.

'You'll find custard powder at the back of the top shelf in the pantry,' Elizabeth continued. 'Right-hand side, next to the tins. And in this house it's made with half milk, half water.' She pulled on her gloves.

'You going out, Mam?' there was a hint of relief in Maud's voice.

'Seeing as how Diana's here to help with the cooking, I'll walk back down the hill and check your Uncle John Joseph is all right.'

'I thought he was moving to the Rhondda,' Maud said.

'He is, next week. But that's all the more reason for me to go down there now. I've been working there day and night for the past two weeks, emptying and cleaning the house out for the next minister. You've no idea how much rubbish your Aunt Hetty accumulated. God rest her soul,' Elizabeth added, remembering that it wasn't done to speak ill of the dead.

Diana fell into Elizabeth's chair as soon as Elizabeth shut the front door behind her. She looked across at Maud and smiled. 'If we were back in the hospital, I'd suggest tipping one of the porters to get us a bottle of stout.'

'Mam would die at the very thought of her daughter knocking back beer at home.'

'Chance and money would be a fine thing,' Diana said sourly. 'Never mind, how about a cup of tea?'

Maud smiled at her. 'It'll do until we can afford Champagne.'

'Roll on next week,' Diana laughed.

The front door opened and closed.

'The boys,' Diana said excitedly.

'They'd come the back way,' Maud pointed out. 'More likely Mam forgot something.'

'Hello, it's me,' a familiar drawl echoed down the passage.

'Ronnie?' Maud made a face at Diana. 'What on earth does he want?' she hissed, keeping her voice low and resenting the intrusion.

'Taxi fare for taking us home yesterday?' Diana suggested.

Ronnie opened the kitchen door and walked in.

'All alone?' he asked.

'We did invite Clark Gable and Robert Donat to call in, but they were busy. Said they had more interesting things to do on a Sunday morning than watch a girl slave over housework.' Diana picked up an enamel bowl from the kitchen table and resumed peeling carrots.

'Do you want to see the boys?' Maud asked.

'Not particularly. Is there any tea going?' Ronnie pulled a chair out from under the table, sat on it, and propped his long legs up on the rail in front of the stove. He glanced across at Maud. She

83

looked very different from the girl he had carried into his van yesterday. Her face sparkled with animation despite her emaciated appearance. Her hair shone pale yellow, the same glowing shade as the early daffodils that bloomed for St David's day, and her eyes were blue, so blue they reminded him of the eyes on his little sister Theresa's china doll. Even the vivid colour of her crimson thick-knit woollen suit went some way to disguising her deathly pallor and skeletal figure.

'You're looking a bit more human,' he said flippantly, conscious that he'd been staring at her.

'Thought I was on the way out yesterday, did you?'

'No,' he replied slowly. 'But I didn't expect to see you sitting up in a chair today.'

Diana lifted the cover on the hotplate and set the kettle, which had been warming on the hearth, to boil.

'Take sugar and milk?' she asked curtly, annoyed with herself for forgetting the manners her mother had drilled into her since childhood, and Ronnie for asking for tea before it had been offered.

'Three sugars and a quarter of an inch of milk.'

'If you're that finicky, you can measure it yourself.' She carried the milk jug out of the pantry and set it on the table. Pouring half the contents into a china bowl she picked up an egg and a cupful of flour, and tossed them in on top of the milk.

'Good heavens, don't tell me they taught you to cook in that place as well?' Ronnie laughed as she set about the mixture with a fork. 'I thought I'd never see the day.'

'There's a lot about me you don't know, Ronnie Ronconi,' Diana said brusquely.

'Apron too,' he mocked. 'I take my hat off to them, you really do look the part of the little housewife.'

'Becomes me, doesn't it?' Half flirting, half hoping to annoy, she twirled around in front of him.

'Depends on what you consider becoming,' he said cryptically.

'Did you call in for anything special?' Maud interrupted, tired of listening to their banter.

'Oh yes.' His attention was distracted by Diana, who was spooning tea into the warm teapot. 'No more than four in a pot that size, you stupid girl,' he admonished. 'Don't you know anything?'

'I know a sight more than a man who's only ever made tea in a giant café urn,' Diana bit back.

'*You* know more than *me*?' he asked incredulously. 'You're still wet behind the ears. I can see I'm going to have to give William a lesson or two in keeping little sisters under control.'

'How many sugars did you say you wanted?' Diana asked, holding the bowl just out of reach.

'You said you called in for something?' Maud reminded him tersely.

He turned away from Diana, and faced Maud again. There was something pathetic, disturbing even, in her fever-bright eyes and skeletal hands.

'Do you know Alma?' he asked, turning to Diana again. It was easier to look at Diana, with her healthy, rosy cheeks and robust, firm-breasted figure.

'Yes, we know Alma.' Diana glanced knowingly at Maud. Tina loved to gossip about her speculations on Ronnie's love life.

'She's working in the tailor's at the moment. You know, the one on top of the Express café, but we're opening another place soon. More of a restaurant than either of the places we have now. It'll be smarter, posher and as soon as it does open, Alma'll be working for us full time. I thought, as you were looking for a job, you might like to apply to the tailor's now. Get your name down first before the rush starts. I don't know what it's like in Cardiff, but it's hard here, and with Ben Springer's record of laying off girls, you might be better placed in the tailor's than the shoe shop.'

'Thanks for thinking of me.' Diana took down three cups and saucers from the dresser, picked up the teapot and poured out the tea. She was touched by his concern. Yesterday in the café he'd left her with the distinct impression that he either hadn't heard her talking about her problems, or hadn't cared.

'You know me, your friendly neighbourhood benefactor,' he sipped his tea and winked slyly at Maud. 'Not bad,' he pointed to his cup. 'A few more lessons and it might even be passable.'

'I'm grateful Ronnie, but don't push your luck.' Diana glared at him.

'As soon as the restaurant gets going, you can have Alma's old job in the café if you want it. Saturday nights, Sundays and four nights in the week. Alma has Wednesday off but I might be able to sort out another one if you prefer it.'

'Mam will never stand for anyone in this house working a Sunday,' Maud warned.

'It wouldn't be for long,' Ronnie interrupted. 'As soon as the new place gets going, we may be able to offer you full time in the day. We're going to need a lot of waitresses. I talked it over with Papa. He said someone lively like you might suit us. Full time, six days a week, eight until six pays nine shillings plus tips, but just so there's no misunderstanding, it's hard work. Tina'll confirm that. She's not only the worst waitress I've ever had to cope with, she also loathes the job more than most.'

He was talking to Diana but he couldn't get his eyes – or his mind – off Maud.

'There's nothing for me, is there Ronnie?' Maud asked somewhat poignantly.

'There might be when you're better,' he said with more diplomacy than usual.

'I'm fine now, really. It was just the shock of losing my job on Friday, and then the journey home.'

'That's not what Trevor told me this morning when I asked after you in church.'

An awkward silence fell over the room. Ronnie didn't have to say any more. Maud knew just what a liability people with tuberculosis were, especially in places that sold food.

'We're back, and we're starving.' The door to the washhouse slammed opened and shut, and William, closely followed by Haydn, walked through to the kitchen.

'Good God, look what the wind's blown in. What's up, Ronnie? Lose your way into town?' Will asked.

'He's opening a new café,' Diana explained, 'and when he does there might be a job there for me.'

'It'll beat working for that creep in the shoe shop.' William picked up the teapot and two cups and poured tea for himself and Haydn. 'Better make some more, Di. Uncle Evan, Eddie and Charlie will be in as soon as they've cleaned the rabbits and bedded the dog down.'

'How many did you get?' Maud asked.

'Would you believe four? Genius, that's what I am. Led them

straight to the burrow. Up the top, close to the glass tower.' He referred to the remains of a folly that the industrialist Crawshay had built on the summit of the Graig mountain for no good, practical or particular reason.

'Eddie got a fight arranged soon?' Ronnie asked.

'Looking to make some money to set up the new café?' William laughed.

'Not that way.'

'Eddie's always a sure thing,' Haydn asserted defensively.

'Touch wood!' Maud demanded urgently. 'You know you should never say anything like that.'

'Superstitions!' Ronnie scoffed. 'The Welsh are worse than the Italians. Well I'd be better off. Tony'll be screaming for me as it is. Father O'Kelly's been giving me a hard time lately. Tony opened up so I could go to mass. See you down the café later?'

William looked at Haydn, who seemed to be slumped deep in his own thoughts, just as he had been all morning. When Haydn didn't respond, he followed Ronnie to the door.

'I'll see you out,' he offered.

'Bye.' Ronnie smiled at everyone and took his leave, but as he walked through the door his backward glance was for Maud. She was so thin it was difficult to see where the patched cushions of the chair began and she ended. She was a child, and because of her sickness hardly a beautiful one. He told himself that it was the look of death in her eyes that disturbed him. Nothing more.

Every family in Pontypridd, no matter how poor, tried to organise themselves a Sunday dinner. Since the pits had closed it was very often the only hot meal of the week, and after the last slices of bread had mopped the final vestiges of gravy from thick earthenware plates, and the remaining crumbs of pudding had been licked from spoons slippery with watery custard, a quiet peace settled over the terraces that clung to the hillsides. Graig Avenue was no exception.

When Elizabeth rose to clear the table, Diana steeled herself for yet another rebuff, and suggested she do it for her. Before Elizabeth had the chance to either accept or reject Diana's offer, William left his chair and began to ferry the dirty plates into the washhouse. His helpfulness wasn't born out of any finer feelings for his aunt, but from a desire to get her out of the kitchen, and out of the way, as quickly as possible. He knew her Sunday routine well. As soon as the table was cleared and the plates, pots, pans and stove washed and scoured, she liked to 'retire' to the front parlour to read her Bible. Winter or summer, the temperature of the room made no difference. She sat stiffly upright on one of the slippery, Rexine-covered chairs in front of the cold, screened-off fireplace, slowly turning the pages of the heavy, leather-bound Bible that had been treasured by her family for four generations. If Evan made tea, which he sometimes did late in the afternoon, she always refused a cup with a glare that suggested it was sacrilege even to suggest carrying boiling liquid into the hallowed 'best room'.

When William had first moved into his uncle's house he found it peculiar to think that on the one traditional day of rest, his aunt actually preferred the cold, sterile atmosphere of the parlour to the warmth and companionship of the back kitchen. But then there was no accounting for tastes, especially his aunt's. His mother had never had the luxury of a front parlour, at least not within his memory. Megan had been forced to let out the room to lodgers to make ends meet. Perhaps if she'd had one, she might had sat there.

'Seems we have two skivvies to help you now, Elizabeth,' Evan commented as William returned for more dishes.

'Just as well, given the increased workload in this house.' She turned to examine the stove.

'I'll clean that for you,' Diana offered.

'Just be sure you do it properly. Any food left on the hotplates smells the whole house out.'

'I know, we had a stove exactly like it at home,' Diana said in an injured tone.

'What are you going to do, Snookems?' Evan asked Maud, in an attempt to divert his wife's attention from his niece.

'Go dancing,' she suggested mischievously.

He looked at her plate: she'd scarcely touched her meal. Elizabeth, with her customary caution and inbred loathing of waste, had only dished out small portions of meat, stuffing and vegetables on to Maud's plate, consoling herself with the thought that there was always the extra she'd allowed for Monday's fry-up

88

waiting in the pantry if Maud wanted more. But a good half of the meagre portion remained untouched, ineffectually hidden beneath the knife and fork.

'You're not going to have the energy to go dancing on what you've just eaten, love,' Evan reprimanded her mildly.

'No one in this family will go dancing on a Sunday while I have breath in my body!' Elizabeth exclaimed, taking their conversation literally.

'I was joking, Mam,' Maud protested wearily, exhaustion getting the better of her.

'Why don't you sit next to the fire for a bit?' Charlie suggested in his quaint accent. Three years in Wales had left his harsh Russian consonants untouched, while lending the thick, Slavic speech the singsong lilt of the valleys. 'Your father's promised me a game of chess, and you can help me beat him.'

'I never was a good player,' Maud said dully, watching William, Diana, Haydn and Eddie rush around. Saturday nights and Sundays were special in Pontypridd. Nearly all the girls and boys their age dressed up in whatever finery they could beg, borrow or steal, and walked in groups from one end of the town to the other. Crowds passed, the boys catcalling the girls they fancied, the girls returning the smiles of any boys they didn't want to openly discourage, and occasionally, very occasionally, the two very separate groups stopped to talk, but the real talking usually came later when everyone, even the ones without money, went to Ronconi's. The 'Bunny Run' they called it, and at that moment Maud would have given a month of whatever was left of her life to join them.

She watched William rattle the change in his pocket and wink at Haydn. Suddenly she felt angry and restless. Angry because she was going to be left behind, stuck at home while they were all going to town and the café to have a good time. And restless because she knew that even if her mother allowed her to go, she wouldn't be able to manage the walk down, let alone back up the hill. And probably couldn't for some time.

'If you're tired sis I'll help you upstairs.' Stung by the look of sheer misery on Maud's face Haydn held out his arm.

'You will not,' Elizabeth said sharply. She had never allowed the boys to enter the girls' bedroom, and had no intention of changing her notions of propriety now, just because Maud was ill.

'It's all right Elizabeth, I'll take her.' Evan rose from his chair.

'I don't want to go to bed,' Maud protested petulantly.

'If you rest now, you'll feel better later on. You can always get up for the evening,' Evan said patiently.

'Gina and Tina want to come and see you,' Diana interrupted. 'If it's all right with you, Aunt Elizabeth, I'll ask them to call in on their way back from the café this afternoon.'

'You going down the café with the boys, Diana?' Elizabeth demanded coldly.

'For a little while,' Diana murmured mildly, reining in her temper. 'Ronnie called earlier and mentioned that he and his father would be looking for more waitresses soon. They're opening a new place, and I thought I'd like to find out a bit more about what jobs they'll have on offer.'

'Ronnie called in when you two girls were alone in the house?'

'We were here,' Haydn broke in not entirely truthfully. 'He wanted to talk to Eddie about some haulage work,' he added, straying into the realms of fiction.

'Then it's a pity you didn't think to discuss whatever jobs he has on offer with him while he was here, Diana,' Elizabeth sniffed.

'Diana was busy cooking the dinner at the time. Besides, the boys commandeered most of his attention,' Maud snapped.

'Come on, Snookems, up the wooden hill.' Evan scooped her into his strong arms. 'A couple of hours' sleep now will do you the world of good. Set you up for when Diana brings the girls back.' He looked at his wife as he helped Maud out of the room, daring her to say anything more.

Chapter Nine

Charlie set up his chessboard on the side of the table closest to the stove, amusing himself by making a few practice moves while he waited patiently for Evan to return from upstairs. The boys and Diana rushed round him as they scurried between the kitchen and washhouse, spending as much time on sprucing themselves up as on clearing the dishes.

'You coming down the caff later, Charlie?' William asked, bending his knees so he could see enough of himself to Vaseline and brush back his hair in the low-hung mirror on the back wall.

'Perhaps,' Charlie replied impassively.

William knew better than to push. Charlie was always polite. Pleasant and helpful when he could be, but eighteen months of living with him, six months in the same room, had taught him that when it came to making plans, Charlie was a law unto himself.

Dishes washed in record time, Diana raced upstairs to the cell that had now become her bedroom. Her uncle had brought a bed, bedclothes, pillows and a chest of drawers from Bonvilston Road. No rug, no pictures, no toilet set and no personal knick-knacks. In the absence of a wardrobe she'd folded her clothes into the drawers. Opening them one after another she dug out a thick, navy-blue, home-knitted sweater that William had grown out of, and pulled it on over her blouse. Tiptoeing out on to the landing she stood silently and listened. She heard the creak of damp, rusting springs as Elizabeth settled on a chair in the front parlour. Picking up her handbag, she crept quietly across to Maud's bedroom and lifted the latch slowly, starting at the loud scraping click the iron bar made when it finally left its rest.

'Who's there?' Maud called out.

'Ssh, it's only me.' Diana stole in, pushing the door to behind her. 'How are you feeling?'

'Fed up and tired,' Maud said irritably.

'You might be well enough to come with us next week.'

'I doubt it.'

Diana stood in front of the bed feeling impotent and entirely useless.

'The mirror's over there.' Maud nodded at the dressing table where a shawl lay draped over the top, concealing the glass.

'How did you know what I was after?' Diana asked sheepishly as she lifted the shawl.

'Your hair looks a mess,' Maud smiled, relenting a little. After all it was hardly Diana's fault that she was ill. 'You will bring Gina and Tina back with you, won't you?' she pleaded.

'Even if I have to twist their arms. What time does your mother go to evening service in chapel?'

'It starts at six, but she generally leaves about a quarter-past five to see if she can help the deacons' wives with anything that needs doing.'

'And what time is she back?'

'Never much before half-past eight. After Aunt Hetty died she took over making my uncle's Sunday supper.'

'I'll see if I can get the girls to come about half-past five then. We'll wake you if you're not up. Promise. Sleep tight, don't let the bugs bite,' Diana whispered as she left the room.

Irritation almost abated by the thought of having something to look forward to, Maud snuggled down as she heard the latch drop. The old mattress was soft, the room comfortingly familiar and wonderfully warm from the fire Eddie had banked up with small coals that morning. She listened to the rain patter on the slates that covered the top of the downstairs bays, below her window. The light was grey, dull where it crept through the partly closed red plush curtains. Flickering firelight glowed dimly, its reflection shining in the polished mahogany panels of the wardrobe and dressing table. She plucked at the itchy, scratchy, Welsh flannel blanket with thin fingers, covering herself to the chin with the soft flannelette beneath it.

Downstairs she heard the raised voices of Haydn, Eddie and William as they walked along the passage and slammed the front door behind them. She didn't doubt Diana was with them. Closing her eyes, she allowed her body to relax. It was good to be home, even if she was ill.

The thought of her illness held sway for a moment, carrying with it a chill, icy portent of nothingness, and death. The conception of oblivion worried her more than the imminent prospect of pain. She thrashed desperately in the bed. She had to think of something else, and quickly. And not her own funeral! What about the last film she'd seen in Cardiff with Diana? *Camille*? No, that was no good. *It Happened One Night*. That was better: she would try to imagine what it would be like to share a bedroom with Clark Gable. Pleased with herself for conjuring up the diversion, she fantasised about what Clark Gable's lovemaking was *really* like!

Her imagination was strong enough to drive the spectre of death temporarily from her mind. And for that she was grateful. She didn't want to think about her own end. Not yet. Not until she was old and miserable – like her mother.

Jenny Griffiths prowled restlessly from behind the counter of the shop to the storeroom door and back. She looked out of the shop window, peering over the display of cheap farthing sweets and tins. Wanting a better view she went to the front door and pressed her nose against the dusty glass panel, staring disconsolately at the rain falling into the empty street. The hands of the clock above the counter pointed to a quarter-past three. Usually Haydn was in Ronnie's café by now, and until now he'd *always* called for her on his way down the hill. She'd eaten her Sunday dinner in record time, gulping it down so she could return to the shop. Even her mother had noticed her uncharacteristic haste, threatening her with a tablespoonful of bicarbonate of soda to counteract indigestion.

What if – what if – he was already there? She'd been behind the counter since a quarter to two so he couldn't have passed her, not if he'd stayed at home to eat his own dinner. But then he could have avoided the hill altogether by walking along Leyshon Street and down the steps at the end into Graig Street. That's if he really didn't want to see her.

'Come to take over so you can go down the café, love,' her father said as he opened the door between the shop and the stairs, knocking her into the glass. 'That's a funny place to stand,' he commented, setting down the *News of the World* he was carrying on the counter. 'Haydn late, is he?'

'He's not coming, Dad.'

93

'You two haven't had a spat, have you?'

'No,' she lied quickly.

'There's not a blue moon tonight, is there?'

'He's staying home. Maud came back yesterday.'

'So I heard.' He shook his head sadly. 'Mrs Richards came in yesterday and told me. My heart goes out to Evan Powell. You do know Maud's not expected to last long don't you?'

'Says who?' Jenny demanded, her blood running cold.

'Everyone, love. Come on, I don't have to tell you what a killer consumption is.'

Jenny lowered her head so he wouldn't see the tears, or the fear in her eyes. Five of her schoolfriends had died of it before they'd even tried their school-leaving exam.

'That doesn't mean they can't do anything for Maud,' she said defiantly.

'No, it doesn't. Look, why don't you go on up and see her? Take her a couple of bars of chocolate, and one of those fruit cakes we had in from Hopkin Morgan yesterday.'

'I don't know, Dad,' she murmured doubtfully.

'Go on, love. If you can't call there, no one can. You're practically family.'

'I'll think about it.' She opened the door between the shop and their living quarters. Harry watched her go and wisely said nothing. Lovers' spats, quick to blow up, and just as quick to blow over if his experience with Megan was anything to go by. He gritted his teeth as he visualised Megan. Her absence from his daily life had left an aching void that nothing and no one could fill. And as he couldn't count himself as family he didn't even have visiting rights to see her in prison. He had to rely on William's generosity; but the lad was good enough, allowing him every other monthly visit.

He sat and stared at the blank wall that faced the counter, reliving the past, seeing once again each and every nuance of expression flit across Megan's face. Her quiet, knowing smile, her frowns of annoyance, beams of joy, the slight puckering of the top lip that meant she was bored. She never could keep any emotion from him. What wouldn't he give for one of her hugs right now. Right this minute.

*

94

'Wet enough for you?' Tina asked Trevor as he walked into the café with an expression on his face that matched the weather.

'Just about. Is Ronnie in the back?'

'Where else on a Sunday afternoon. Laura with you?'

'No.'

'It was a bad row you had then?'

Trevor stopped dead in his tracks.

'How do you know we quarrelled?' he demanded.

'Because it's a wet Sunday afternoon and you're here, not tucked up at home with her. Take your coat off, and go and sit in front of the fire in the back,' she ordered, mothering him with the authority of her status as eldest sister-in-law. 'I'll bring you a hot Oxo.'

'I'd prefer coffee.'

'Oxo is better for you.'

'Who's the doctor here?'

'Doctors know nothing. Here, dry yourself on this.' She handed him a rough glass towel so he could dry his face. Pushing him into the back, she carried his coat into the kitchen and hung it next to the stove.

Ronnie, Haydn, William, Eddie, Tony, Angelo, Glan Richards and an assortment of boys from the Graig were sitting at two tables pulled close to the fire. They were playing brag. Small piles of farthings and halfpennies were heaped in front of them. They all knew they risked a fine or, on a magistrate's off day, a couple of weeks' imprisonment for playing cards for money in a public place, but with Tina, Gina, Alma and Diana watching the front they felt safe enough. Or at least, a whole lot more comfortable and safe than they would have done playing in the rain on a street corner, which was the only alternative to the café on a Sunday.

'Seat, brother-in-law.' Ronnie pushed a spare chair towards Trevor. Rubbing his hair with the towel, Trevor joined him. Tina breezed in carrying Trevor's Oxo and slapped it down in front of him.

'Better be kind to him,' she said in a loud voice to no one in particular. 'Laura's thrown him out.'

'Dear sister performing true to form then?' Ronnie queried as he laid out his cards. 'Well you can't say I didn't warn you what she was like before the wedding.'

Acutely embarrassed, Trevor remained silent.

95

'Anything else?' Tina demanded.

'This will do fine, thank you.' Trevor picked up the cup. It was boiling hot, just what he needed to thaw out his white and frozen fingers.

William managed to catch Tina's eye, as he scooped the winning hand. Shovelling the pile of copper from the table into his trouser pocket, he glanced around. 'Anyone want anything?' he asked as he left his chair.

'I'll have a glass of lemonade,' Glan said. William followed Tina out through the door.

'What time are you leaving tonight?' he whispered as he leant over the counter.

'Five. Gina and I are going up to see Maud with Diana.'

'And when are you going to see me?' he demanded.

'You know it's difficult.'

'Difficult? It's downright bloody impossible!'

'Ssh, Ronnie might hear.'

'What if he does?' he demanded belligerently. 'He can't lock you up for ever.'

'Only till I'm twenty-one,' she said mournfully.

'Look, how about the pictures tomorrow night? White Palace. Six o'clock.'

'Tina, the back tables need clearing and wiping down.' Ronnie appeared in the archway between the back and front rooms.

'I'll be there as soon as I've poured out Glan's lemonade,' she shouted irritably.

'Alma or Gina can do that.' He smiled at William. 'Everything all right?' he asked coldly.

'Fine, Ronnie, what more could a man want than you supply here?' William grinned cheekily. 'Good food, good drink, good surroundings, a warm stove, and – ' he winked at Tina, much to Ronnie's annoyance, ' – beautiful waitresses.'

'Just as long as you remember that the waitresses aren't what's on offer here,' Ronnie said sharply.

'As if I'd ever think that.' William picked up the lemonade that Tina had just poured for Glan. 'Cheers mate!' He raised the glass to Ronnie as he returned to the back room.

'It must be catching then,' Gina whispered to Tina as Ronnie followed William.

'What?' Tina demanded angrily.

'Rows. You told Diana about Jenny Griffiths?'

'What about Jenny Griffiths?' Diana enquired lazily from the corner next to the stove where she was studying magazine fashion plates with Alma.

'She was in her Dad's shop when Tina and I walked down the hill. We saw her through the window, so we called in and asked her to come down with us, but she wouldn't.'

'So?' Diana waited for more.

'So she must have had a row with your Haydn,' Gina crowed.

'Perhaps they just wanted to give one another a day off, for a change,' Diana suggested disinterestedly.

'You think so?' Gina pressed.

'I think it's their business,' Diana replied evenly.

The bell clanged and the café door opened again. Wyn Rees stood on the outside doormat, his coat clinging to his legs like a second, slippery skin. The torrential downpour that was flooding Taff Street had soaked it as thoroughly as if it had just been pulled out of the washtub. He eased the coat off his back, shook himself and finally stepped inside, sliming the floor with a layer of mud from his boots as he did so.

'You're well and truly dripping, and filthy with it,' Tina complained as he lifted off his hat, inadvertently pouring the water that had collected in the brim over the mud on the floor.

'I'm afraid I am.' He shrugged his well-muscled shoulders out of his damp jacket, exposing his fancy Sunday waistcoat and best trousers. 'All right if I hang my jacket and coat here?' he asked, holding them poised next to the rack.

'Don't see what else you can do with them. Just keep them as far away from the others as you can.'

'Wyn?' Diana left the back corner and the fashion plates, and walked to the counter. 'Never seen you in here on a Sunday before.'

'I don't usually come,' Wyn admitted diffidently.

'I wanted to thank you for carrying Maud out of the station yesterday, only you didn't stay around long enough.'

'It was nothing,' he said shyly.

'You want anything?' Tina asked, tired of waiting for him to order.

'Whatever it is it'll have to be warm by the look of you. Tea?' Diana asked.

'Yes please. And something to eat. Whatever's easiest for you,' he said to Tina.

'I can warm you up a dinner in the stove, or a pie in the steamer. Anything else and I'll have to roust Ronnie out of the back.'

'A dinner will do me fine. Thank you.'

'If you sit next to the stove, I'll bring your tea over.' Diana pointed to the tables next to the stove in the front area.

'Taken up waitressing, Diana?' Tina whispered as Diana remained next to the counter waiting for her to produce Wyn's tea.

'If I'm going to work for Ronnie the sooner I start learning the ropes the better.'

'You know he's . . . he's . . .' Tina glanced around furtively. When she was sure no one could overhear them, she continued. 'A queer,' she blurted out.

'That's why I suggested he sit by the stove in here and not next to the fire in the back room with the boys. Will and Haydn can't stand him, and Eddie's always moaning that he shouldn't be allowed in the gym.'

'I didn't know that.'

'Thanks for the tea. Give me a shout when the dinner's ready,' Diana said loudly, cutting Tina short as she took Wyn's tea over to him.

'You always go for long walks through mud on rainy Sundays?' Diana asked tactlessly as she dumped Wyn's tea down in front of him, slopping it in the saucer.

'Only sometimes.'

She sat in the chair next to his. Alma had left the café for the kitchen, probably to see to Wyn's dinner, and Gina had taken herself and her magazine over to the counter where she was whispering and giggling with her sister. 'Something wrong then?' she asked.

Wyn lifted his wet face to hers. 'You don't want to be burdened with my problems,' he said quietly.

'Oh I don't know. They're not my problems, so I won't really feel burdened by them, not enough to cry about them any road. And you'll feel better for talking about them, because by telling someone else your troubles you'll have halved your load.'

98

'Who says so?'

'My mam for one.'

Diana looked at Wyn and remembered a time when Will had been railing against queers in general, and Wyn in particular, and her mother had looked at him and said, 'Poor dab. You just remember, William Powell, there but for the grace of God goes you or any man. And the world would be a lot poorer place if there was no room for anyone who was a bit different.'

'It's my Dad,' Wyn admitted. 'We had a row.'

'Before you had your Sunday dinner.'

'You've got it in one.'

'That's bad luck. Before dinner I mean, but then most families row from time to time. You should have seen me and my mam.'

'Really?'

'At it hammer and tongs. Next door used to complain like anything.'

'Dad and I have always had trouble getting on, and it's grown a lot worse since Mam died.'

Diana looked at the thick mud on his shoes, and instinctively knew where he'd been.

'You've been to the cemetery, haven't you?'

'Mam's buried in Glyntaff. It's not too far to walk . . .'

'On dry days.'

'I know she's not there,' he smiled self-consciously. 'Not really there, but it helps to go and talk to her as if she could he r me. You think I'm crazy, don't you?'

'No,' Diana said seriously. 'Not in the slightest. Rhiannon Pugh used to spend a lot of time talking to her son and old man after they both got killed in a pit accident. It was only natural really, they were all she had. And it was my mam who suggested she do it. You see my dad got killed in the war before I was born. Mam used to keep two photographs of him, one in the kitchen and one next to her bed, and she used to talk to him every night before she went to sleep, and every morning before she got up. She said it was no different from when he was alive. He never used to listen to her then either. But it helped her to say what she had to say and to get it off her chest.' She looked wryly at Wyn, 'I'm sorry, I know I'm probably not making much sense. Will, that's my brother, he's always telling me off for gabbling. But what I mean is, Mam would have gone to a grave if she'd had one. But she didn't, at least not here. And it's not the same talking to a cenotaph. Although she used to go to the sunken garden in the park a lot. It helped war widows you know, having the Memorial Park dedicated to all those who were killed in the war.'

'Your mother sounds a sensible woman. I was sorry when I heard what happened.'

'Yes well, couldn't be helped I suppose. She broke the law and ended up in clink. Although I still think the sentence she got was a bit much. And I do miss her. Like hell!' she exclaimed feelingly.

'I can see why.' He tried to remember the *Pontypridd Observer* article he'd read on Megan Powell's trial, but he couldn't recall how long she'd been sent down for so he decided against reminding Diana that she was luckier than him, because at least she'd get her mother back some time, whereas he'd never see his again.

'Do you want another cup of tea with your dinner, or after?' she asked.

He looked down at the table and realised that Alma had put his meal in front of him. Two thick slices of breast of lamb, four round ice cream scoops of mashed potato, four roast potatoes, two scoops of stuffing, a pile of mashed swede and sliced carrots, the whole covered with piping hot thick gravy.

'After, please,' he said to Diana. 'Thank you,' he shouted to Alma, who'd retreated behind the counter. 'This looks great.'

'We don't usually do dinners this late in the afternoon, but it should be all right. If you want more, just give me a shout.'

'I'll be doing fine if I manage to eat all this.' He picked up his knife and fork and began.

'If you've anything better to do I won't keep you,' he said between mouthfuls to Diana as he heard a loud burst of masculine laughter coming from the back room. A girl like Diana was bound to have a boy in tow, and the last thing he wanted was to have his quiet talk with Diana Powell misconstrued by an over-protective, jealous boyfriend.

'I've nothing better to do,' Diana replied. 'And I certainly don't want to go and sit in the back with that noisy rabble,' she shouted, trying to make herself heard above another deafening roar.

'If you're sure.'

'I'm sure. My cousin Eddie says you train down the gym at the back of the Ruperra. You a boxer too?'

'No, I'm not quick enough on my feet, but I play rugby now and then on a Saturday, when my father can spare me from the shop.'

'Tell me, what's it like running a sweet shop so close to the New Theatre? Do you get to meet the stars?'

'Once in a while.'

'Bet they buy pound boxes of chocolates.'

'Two-pound sometimes,' he grinned. 'Now it's your turn. Tell me about Cardiff and the Royal Infirmary.'

Diana told him, and he listened and commiserated on the hardships she and her cousin Maud had endured at the hands of over-zealous supervisors; as they talked he reflected that he had never found a woman so easy to get on with before, except of course his beloved mother. Not even his older sister Myrtle. He finished his dinner and persuaded Diana to let him buy her a tea and a slice of apple pie, scarcely daring to hope as they ate companionably together that this could be the beginning of a real friendship. He'd never experienced anything that remotely resembled a real, unselfish, disinterested friendship outside of his family, in his entire life.

Chapter Ten

At five o'clock the rain turned to hailstones. Ronnie looked around: the café was relatively quiet, and in this weather nothing was likely to happen that Tony, Angelo and Alma couldn't handle between them.

'If you're going to see Maud I'll run you all up in the Trojan,' he said to his sisters.

'You'll never get all of us in the Trojan,' Haydn protested.

'The back's empty,' Ronnie said carelessly. He felt most peculiar. A strange excitement was curling in the pit of his stomach. He didn't want to analyse the feeling, knowing it was in some way connected with the prospect of seeing Maud, and he wondered if he was turning into a ghoul like Mrs Richards, Glan's mother, who made it her business to visit everyone on the Graig who was in the remotest danger of 'passing on', taking it upon herself to issue bulletins on the patient's progress, or lack of it, right up until the day that Fred the dead, the undertaker, was called in.

Alma touched his arm and smiled at him, breaking into his reverie. 'Are you going to be long?' she asked pleasantly.

'Not long,' he replied irritably, ignoring the touch of her hand as he reached over and took a box of best-quality chocolates from one of the shelves. She said nothing as she moved away, but his curt response hurt. She'd half hoped to be included in the small excursion. They could have driven back down the hill together after leaving everyone in Graig Avenue. Stopped off for a few moments somewhere quiet. It wouldn't have had to be anywhere special. The car park of the closed White Hart provided privacy enough on a Sunday night.

She busied herself clearing away the dishes left on the tables as Tina and Gina fussed around getting their coats and Trevor's from the kitchen. Glan ordered a meat pie, and by the time she'd heated it in the steamer, the girls were shouting goodbye. She looked up, just in time to shout, 'Give Maud my love' as Diana shut the door behind her.

'Three sugars, Ronnie?' Diana asked pointedly as she made tea for everyone in the back kitchen of Graig Avenue.

'You'll have to impress me with more than that if you want me to give you a job,' he mocked, pulling the kitchen chair he was sitting on closer to the stove and, incidentally, closer to the easy chair Maud was half lying, half sitting in. 'Ronconi waitresses have to remember all the customers' likes and dislikes, or they're out of a job, right Tina?'

The Powells' square back kitchen was furnished in old-fashioned, clumsily carved oak furniture. A huge dresser dominated the back wall opposite the oven. A large oak table and dark-stained deal kitchen chairs commandeered what little space was left, which meant that the Ronconis and Powells were squashed into close proximity whether they liked it or not, and it was fairly obvious to anyone who took the trouble to look that Tina and Gina did like it. They sat either side of William on the arms of the easy chair that he, with his innate love of comfort, had organised for himself, shrieking with laughter at his bad jokes. Eddie wasn't so fortunate. He knelt on a chair in front of the dresser, the furthest point in the room from the warmth of the fire, leaning over the table as he watched Charlie and Haydn play chess. Only Diana was moving around, stepping cautiously over William's long, outstretched legs as she set the kettle on to boil.

'Your mam and dad out?' Ronnie asked Maud, for once apparently unconcerned about his sister's flirtation with William.

'Mam's in chapel, Dad could be anywhere,' she said carelessly. 'He has a lot of friends.'

'I've noticed.'

'When do you think you'll be opening your new restaurant?' she asked.

'As soon as we get around to finishing everything that needs doing in the place. It's a tip at the moment.'

'One week? Two?'

'The impatience of youth,' he said in a grand tone more suited to a forty-seven than a twenty-seven-year-old. 'It'll be months not weeks before we open the doors, but don't worry – ' he pulled his cigarettes out of his shirt pocket and offered them to Charlie,

103

Haydn and William, ' – there'll be a job for you there when you're up to working again.'

'Do you mean that?' Her eyes glittered with excitement – and fever.

He glanced round the room to make sure no one was listening to their conversation. He knew from signs and symptoms he'd seen in others that it was extremely unlikely that Maud would ever work again, but what use was there in reinforcing her worst nightmares and telling her that? With nothing to look forward to she'd only wither and die all the sooner.

'I'm not in the habit of saying things I don't mean.' He pulled the box of chocolates out from under his coat. 'Here, if you eat all these by yourself you may put some meat on your bones. God knows you could do with some,' he murmured, ashamed of his own generosity.

'Thank you . . .' she gasped, overwhelmed by the quality and size of the box.

'Quick, hide them,' he hissed. 'Before Gina sees them. Another pound around her waist and she'll be fatter than Mama.'

Maud laughed as she pushed them beneath the blanket that covered her, and the laughter brought on a short-lived coughing fit. Ronnie watched helplessly as she spat blood into the handkerchief that had become a permanent fixture in her hand.

'You know what you should do, don't you?' he asked seriously.

'Go into the Graig Hospital?' she answered bitterly.

'No,' he contradicted flatly, disregarding the underlying hint of fear in her voice. 'When the fine weather comes, spend as much time as you can on the mountain. Fresh air is what you need.'

'So they told me in the Infirmary.'

'They were right.' He lit his cigarette and puffed it carefully, blowing the smoke away from her face.

'Trevor said I should go into hospital.'

'What does he know?' Ronnie asked laconically. 'He'll be lucky if he keeps himself out of the place, and I don't mean as a doctor. The fool got soaked earlier, walking down the hill to the café when he's got a car sitting outside his front door. You should have heard Laura shout at the state of him when I dropped him off at Graig Street.'

'I can imagine,' Maud laughed again. Her laughter triggered off

104

yet another coughing fit. Ronnie sat by, helplessly watching her shoulders shake with the effort. Haydn and Eddie looked across from the table.

'Want me to open the window, Maud?' Diana asked briskly, handing her a clean handkerchief and removing the soiled one. Taking care of Maud in an alien environment for three months had given her the confidence to tackle even the most unpleasant aspects of her illness.

'No! No thank you,' Maud gasped breathlessly, ramming the clean handkerchief into her mouth. Ronnie saw fresh blood stain the cloth. He made tight fists of his hands, butting his knuckles together. He wasn't used to sitting idly by, witnessing things he didn't like. He'd always charged at problems, bull at a gate, demolishing them whenever possible, tackling them head on when he couldn't. He found it intensely difficult to accept anything unpleasant as inevitable, especially the progression of a potentially fatal illness.

'Maud, I think it's time I took you upstairs,' Haydn said with an air of authority he only dared to assume when his father was absent from the house.

'I've been there all afternoon,' Maud snapped.

'You look tired,' he persisted.

'I'm not!' she retorted vehemently. The room fell silent, everyone assuming a sudden interest in Haydn and Charlie's chess game. Charlie brought his rook down with a flourish, displacing Haydn's queen.

'Do you play chess?' Ronnie asked Maud quietly, finally shattering the stillness.

'Check!' Haydn shouted gleefully.

'You fool,' Eddie reprimanded. 'You've walked right into his trap.'

'I'm nowhere near bright enough to play,' Maud murmured in answer to Ronnie's enquiry. 'Bethan and Haydn got all the brains in this family.'

'It doesn't take brains to play chess,' Ronnie mocked. 'At least not the sort that matter.'

'And what sort are those?' Maud asked.

'The brains that enable you to count the money you've earned.'

'And you have those?'

'In vast quantities,' he winked. 'If you're good I'll let you come and watch me bag my gold some time.'

'You're risking it, Ronnie,' Gina crowed from the corner.

'Risking what?' he demanded laconically.

'Leaving Tony and Angelo in charge of the café for so long. They've probably eaten the whole day's profits by now.'

'If they have, you two will be working for nothing next week.'

'You wouldn't dare . . .' Gina began.

'Wouldn't I just? You're only half-trained girls and everyone knows what they're worth,' Ronnie taunted mischievously.

'Papa', Tina asserted haughtily, 'would never stand for it.'

'That's just what I mean,' Ronnie continued. 'Women can never stand on their own two feet, they always have to hide behind a man's coat tails.'

'Why you . . .' Tina didn't know whether to be angrier with Ronnie for his outrageous teasing, or her sister for drawing his attention to them in the first place.

'Time for goodbyes,' Ronnie rose to his feet. 'Please accept my apologies everyone for my ill-mannered sisters. I won't let them out again until they're on their best behaviour,' he joked heavily, blanching at the sight of the high spots of unhealthy colour on Maud's cheeks.

'If you're in a hurry to go back to the café I'll walk the girls home, Ronnie,' William offered lightly.

'There's no need to put yourself out, Will,' Ronnie replied evenly. 'As it's past their bedtime I'll take them up now.'

'Ronnie!' Tina whined.

'It's Sunday night, Tina,' Ronnie smiled condescendingly. 'You know how Papa likes to have all the little ones home and tucked up in bed by seven.' Ronnie put his teacup on the table. 'See you tomorrow, Diana,' he said as he walked towards the door. 'Let me know how Springer's goes.'

'I will, and thanks.'

'For what?' He stepped aside and looked at his sisters pointedly, leaving room for them to walk past him to the door.

'For letting me know about Alma's job.'

'You're not brilliant,' he smiled, 'but there's a lot around who are even more incompetent, and if you work mornings in the tailor's it'll leave your afternoons free for when I need you.'

'Thanks a bundle Ronnie, you really know how to make a girl feel wanted,' she complained.

'Any time. You two moving or not?' he asked in exasperation.

Tina rose clumsily, falling as she tried to rise from the arm of the chair, and landing right in William's lap.

'Tina!' Ronnie snarled.

'Sorry William, sorry Ronnie.' She bit her lower lip hard, to stop herself from laughing.

'See you,' Haydn left his chair and showed them out. When he returned to the kitchen Maud was slumped against the back of the chair.

'Bed for you, my girl.' He wrapped the blanket containing the chocolates around her frail figure and lifted her high into his arms. This time Maud made no protest. Too tired to argue, she allowed him to carry her out of the room and up the stairs.

Ronnie didn't go into his house. He dropped Tina and Gina off in the street and waited only as long as it took to see them safely inside. He'd noticed the way Tina and William had looked at one another, and didn't entirely trust her, even now, believing her quite capable of sneaking back down to Graig Avenue. Once the door had closed on them and the light had dimmed in the passage, he turned the cumbersome vehicle laboriously in the narrow road, pointing it towards the end of the street and town.

He drove slowly down the hill, but he didn't go straight to the café. Instead he turned right, up Graig Street, and drew the van to a halt outside Laura and Trevor's house.

'Mama mia!' Laura exclaimed as he walked through the kitchen door. 'Twice in as many days. You out to set a record?'

Ignoring Laura, Ronnie took one look at Trevor sitting huddled in a red tartan dressing gown and striped pyjamas, his feet soaking in a bowl of hot water and mustard, and burst out laughing.

'Sure you've wrapped him up well enough, Laura?'

'You men,' she burst out angrily. 'You're all the same. Think it's clever to go out and get yourself soaked. Never give a thought to the poor women who have to stay at home and nurse you.'

'No one has to stay at home and nurse me,' Trevor protested mildly.

'And I suppose that *you*, like him, believe that brandy is

the cure for all ills,' Laura continued, this time targeting Ronnie.

'Now that you mention it, that's not a bad idea.' As Ronnie sat in the vacant easy chair he noticed the brandy bottle and glass on the table in front of Trevor. 'Got a spare glass, dear sister?'

Laura stormed across the tiny kitchen and lifted down a small, uncommonly thick glass from the dresser. She almost threw it at Ronnie. He picked it up and held it to the light.

'Wedding present from Tony,' Trevor explained. 'I think he won them on the fair.'

'I hope you make him drink out of them when he comes to visit.'

'Join us?' Trevor smiled lovingly at Laura.

'Some of us', she tossed her head as high as her five-foot-three-inch frame could reach, 'have more important things to do.'

'Like what?' Ronnie sneered, filling both glasses to the tiny brim.

'Mary Price asked if I'd take a look at her baby.'

'Don't you want to eat, woman? You're doing your own husband out of a job.' Ronnie touched his glass to Trevor's and started to drink.

'Alf Price drinks everything the dole gives him, even the penny a week Mary tries to earmark for the doctor. The children only know what breakfast is because the Salvation Army dish it up three days a week in Jubilee Hall before school.'

'I'd look at her baby for nothing,' Trevor protested in a wounded voice.

'I know that, sweetheart,' Laura said gently, ruffling his unruly mop of hair. 'And so does Mary, but like most people around here, having to beg for charity sticks in her craw. It hurts having to rely on handouts to feed and clothe your kids. And then again,' she bent to kiss Trevor's cheek as she lifted her coat down from the peg on the back of the door, 'if it's something serious you know I'll call you. See you, Ronnie.' She pulled the rug a little higher over Trevor's shoulders before she walked out of the door.

'Married bliss,' Ronnie mocked.

'You can't beat it,' Trevor replied gravely.

Ronnie fell silent. He looked around the warm, cosy kitchen. There was nothing worth more than a pound or two in the entire room. Laura, with Tina and Gina's help, had made the rag rugs that lay on the floor. The furniture was pine, second-hand, mellowed and scarred with age. The dishes and saucepans, plain and serviceable, had been donated by his parents as wedding presents. But with the aid of a few beautifully embroidered cloths that his mother and aunts had passed on to Laura for her 'bottom drawer', and a couple of cheap vases filled with dried bulrushes from Shoni's, Laura had contrived to make the room look homely and welcoming. He was suddenly very ashamed of his earlier, derisive comments. Picking up his glass he finished his brandy in one gulp and reached for the bottle.

'Tony and Angelo still minding the shop?' Trevor asked, holding out his own glass for a refill.

'Yes.'

'It's not like you to leave them in charge for so long.'

'It's high time they learned that running a business means more than emptying the till at the end of the day.' Ronnie lifted his feet on to the fender and pulled his cigarettes from his top pocket.

'Abdicating your responsibilities in the Tumble café in readiness to open the new place?'

'No, just trying to get lazy little brothers to do more.' He lit his own and Trevor's cigarette and rested his head on the back of the chair. 'This is the life. People who stay home evenings don't realise how lucky they are.'

'You could be lucky if you'd learn to walk away from work, at least one day a week.'

'Fat chance with Papa wanting the new place open in eight weeks.'

'Anything I can do to help?'

'Persuade the Hospital Board to hold their annual dinners there.'

'It's Doctor John you should be talking to about that, not a mere minion like me.' Trevor sipped his brandy, allowing its heady warmth to percolate through his veins. His body was glowing from the rub-down Laura had insisted on giving him, which had inevitably led to something even more enjoyable. The quarrel of earlier that afternoon forgotten, he felt cosseted, loved and just a little bit smug to have landed a wife as warm and passionate as Laura. He wondered why Ronnie had called, but his curiosity wasn't keen enough for him to disturb the peaceful atmosphere with extraneous talk. If Ronnie wanted anything he would get round to telling him in his own good time. Meanwhile there was his cigarette and glass of brandy to enjoy.

'That William Powell is a menace,' Ronnie said at last.

'William?' Trevor raised his eyebrows.

'He won't leave Tina alone. Encourages her to behave like a fool. Whenever he's around, all she does is gaze at him vacantly, like a stupid kewpie doll.'

Trevor recalled the interference he'd been forced to put up with from his in-laws when he'd been courting Laura, and almost said 'Perhaps they want to stare vacantly at one another', but he managed to keep his opinion to himself. The subject of his beginnings with Laura was still too raw to joke about.

'Has anything new in the way of TB treatments come out lately?' Ronnie asked casually, as he picked up the brandy bottle for the third time.

'You're thinking of Maud Powell?'

'Has she got it bad?'

Trevor looked carefully at Ronnie before he answered. 'If you're worried about Tina or Gina catching it off her, don't,' he reassured. 'Tuberculosis is rife in this town. They're as much at risk from the customers in the café as they are from Maud. The fact that they've reached the age they have without getting it says something. They're healthy girls, and in my opinion likely to remain so.'

'You didn't answer my question,' Ronnie continued impatiently. 'Has Maud Powell got it bad?'

'I've only examined her briefly,' Trevor procrastinated, then looked at Ronnie again and saw that he knew. 'If you want my opinion, very bad,' he admitted finally.

'She told me tonight that you want to put her in the Central Homes.'

'I suggested the idea to her father. It's probably the best place. She's going to need a lot of nursing, and warmth. The Respiratory wards are kept at a constant high temperature. The Powells can barely afford to heat their kitchen.'

'Supposing she did go in. Could you do anything for her once she was there?'

'Difficult to say. We'd have to do a whole lot of tests first, including X-rays. If one lung is more affected than the other it might be possible to deflate it – '

'How?' Ronnie demanded, moving to the edge of his seat.

'Cut through the ribcage, collapse it manually. It sounds much worse than it is. It's a bit like letting air out of a balloon.' Trevor refused to elaborate, or linger over the details.

'That means an operation?'

'Yes, but the technique can only be used on one lung. The idea is to render the most diseased lung useless in order to give the other a chance to work healthily and recover from any contamination it's been exposed to.'

'Does it work?'

'Not often,' Trevor replied brutally, his tongue loosened by brandy. 'But then, she hasn't much chance anyway.' There was a peculiar expression on Ronnie's face that Trevor couldn't quite fathom. 'I know Maud's the same age as Gina, and that must cut deep, but the chances of anyone surviving tuberculosis as bad as she has it aren't good,' he murmured.

'Then it's not simply a question of money?'

Trevor was touched. Most people in Pontypridd looked only as far as the well-stocked shelves in the Italian-owned and run cafés, and the food that came out of the kitchens, and assumed that all the owners were millionaires. They didn't realise just how small the profit margins were, or see the coal and electricity bills that had to be paid in order to keep the places warm and open all hours just to serve a cold bus driver and conductor a cup of tea at a thumping great loss. What little money the Ronconis had made they'd earned the hard way, and there were a lot of them to lay claim to it.

'No, Ronnie,' he said quietly, 'it's not simply a question of money, at least not the kind of money you'd find in this town.'

'Explain that.' Ronnie reached for the brandy again, pouring it out with an unsteady hand.

'If she was the daughter of a rich man, a very rich man,' Trevor qualified, 'there are clinics in Switzerland, set high in the mountains. Fresh air, good diet centred around dairy foods might do the trick, and then again it might not. You could spend hundreds if not thousands of pounds looking for a cure for Maud Powell and still not find one.'

Ronnie stared at him. 'How long do you think she's got?'

'If it doesn't get any colder, and we get a good, early spring and a warm summer, she might live through this winter and see the next,' he predicted harshly. 'But I don't believe she'll see more than one more spring in. It's a pity,' he continued, unnerved by Ronnie's silence. 'She's a pretty little thing, or she would be if she wasn't ill. Her spirit and character remind me a lot of Bethan. Not her looks, of course, they couldn't be more unalike.'

He lifted the bottle of brandy. It was empty. Ronnie took it from his hand and carried it out to the back. Trevor heard it smash as Ronnie threw it into the ash bin.

'I'll go down the café, hand over the keys to Tony, pick up another bottle and drop it in on the way back,' Ronnie said.

'How about we open that one too?' Trevor suggested.

'Developed a taste for it?'

'Sometimes, just sometimes I hate my job!' Trevor exclaimed savagely. 'Every time I come across someone in Maud's state I feel so bloody, pathetically useless,' he explained in answer to Ronnie's enquiring look.

'You and me both, mate. You and me both,' Ronnie replied as he walked unsteadily through the door.

Diana stood washed, hair pristinely waved and combed, and as neatly dressed as the combined contents of her own and Maud's wardrobes would allow, on the doorstep of Springer's shoeshop at precisely ten minutes to seven on Monday morning. Terrified of being late, she'd run the last two hundred yards down Taff Street. She felt breathless and, for all her show of bravado in front of the boys in Graig Avenue earlier that morning, apprehensive.

She tugged down the old school skirt that had been made when her figure was straighter and skinnier, removed the home-knitted, grey woollen glove from her right hand, and slipped her numb and frozen fingers beneath her coat. She pulled the edges of Maud's white cotton blouse together, hoping it had somehow miraculously stretched since she had last looked at it in Maud's dressing-table mirror. It gaped a good half-inch across her bust, straining the buttonholes to their utmost. There was no getting away from the fact: Maud was at least four inches narrower across the chest than her, if not more. Perhaps if she stitched the plackets together it wouldn't gape. On the other hand it might be better if she went to the post office and broke into the five pounds she'd saved. She'd get a good white blouse for half a crown in Leslie's, only then she wouldn't have five pounds any more, she'd have four pounds seventeen shillings and sixpence. And once she went down that road it would be easier to draw money out the next time she needed it – and the next; and before she knew it the five pounds would be four pounds, or even less.

It was simple to break into savings, and an uphill struggle to replace them when you were earning reasonable money. Impossible on the pittance that Mr Springer was paying her. The five pounds was all the cushion she had against having to take live-in domestic work. It was enough money to keep her for ten weeks or more, and it could take that, or even longer, to find another job in Pontypridd if she lost this one. A new blouse would have to wait until Ronnie found her some part-time work. She'd sew up the placket on this one tonight. That would stop Ben Springer ogling her the way he had last Saturday.

The clock struck seven and still she waited in the cold, dark, inadequate shelter of Springer's doorway. At least the rain had stopped, although a keen wind blew, freezing her ankles even through her thick lisle stockings. Heads down, coats buttoned to their chins, shop workers scurried around her. Shop doorways opened and closed, lights flickered on above counters. Gwilym Evans' display windows grew brighter as the shop lights went on behind them. A brewer's dray thundered down the street, pulling back sharply as a tram raced forward. She stamped her feet and swung her arms. Her coat still felt damp from the drenching it had got when she'd walked down the Graig hill to the café yesterday afternoon. She'd hung it in the passage overnight, but as the passage was never heated it was hardly surprising that it hadn't dried out. But then, that was where the boys had hung theirs. Aunt Elizabeth might be a great believer in 'airing' but she obviously wasn't a believer in drying wet coats, especially those belonging to lodgers.

'Glad to see you on time.' Ben Springer walked up to the door as the clock on St Catherine's church spire struck a quarter-past seven, and just as the final vestiges of feeling were leaving Diana's lips and nose.

'Good morning, Mr Springer,' she mumbled politely through chattering teeth.

'I'd prefer "sir" if you don't mind, Diana,' he corrected her curtly. Unlocking the door, he preceded her into the shop and switched on the lights. 'Hang your coat in the back, then you can

113

start by picking up and putting away any stock that's lying around. I'll tell you where. Every box has its allotted place in this shop and it has to go there. If it doesn't, we'll soon be in a pretty pickle, ordering stock when it's not needed, and running short of good selling lines. As soon as the general tidying's done, I want every surface in the shop dusted and polished until you can see your face in them. You'll find beeswax and dusters in the stockroom. When you've finished the polishing, you can do the floor. Well what are you waiting for, girl? Move!'

The stockroom door was in the centre of the back wall of the shop.

'Light to the left of the door,' he shouted as she went in.

She found the switch without any trouble. The room was really a narrow cupboard, running the entire length of the shop. It was about fourteen feet wide, but no more than five feet deep. Shoe boxes were stacked on foot-wide shelves from floor to ceiling. Bewildered by the vast array of boxes, she blinked dully, then after a few moments realised that the narrow wall on her far right sported a few hooks and two shelves that held cleaning materials and shoe polish. There was also a stiff broom, propped head upright in the corner.

'What are you doing, girl?' Ben appeared alongside her in the cramped doorway. 'Come on, we haven't got all day. Coat off, make a start.' She took her coat off reluctantly, walked deep into the cupboard and hung it on one of the pegs.

'Turn round,' he barked. 'Let's see if you'll do.' She did as he asked. 'Your shoes could be cleaner,' he commented, studying the shabby navy lace-ups that she'd cleaned that morning.

'I'm afraid there were a lot of puddles on the hill this morning after the rain, Mr Springer.'

'I would have thought it might have been possible for you to avoid at least some of them. There's a rag, brushes and shoe cream behind the furniture polish, you'd better use it. But in future you'll have to bring clean shoes with you. The one thing I will not abide in this shop is an assistant wearing dirty, shabby shoes.'

'I only have the one pair,' Diana confessed.

'In that case I'll have to give you a pair,' he said irritably, rummaging through the boxes. 'But I won't allow you to take them out of the shop until they're paid for.'

'I don't have the money – '

'And I just told you that I can't have an assistant in this shop with shabby shoes. Wear those in here and there'll be no point in you cleaning the place. You'll be tramping mud all over everything. Leave them with your coat.'

She slipped her shoes off obediently and stood them neatly beneath her coat. When she turned, Ben was watching her. He held out a pair of sturdy black lace-ups. Strong, unattractive walking shoes of the ilk that Diana instinctively knew Elizabeth would approve of, and Ben would have trouble selling.

'Try these,' he barked. Facing him, she crouched down so she wouldn't expose any length of leg, slipped them on, and tied the laces. Unfortunately they fitted perfectly.

'They'll do.' He peered at the side of the box. 'Twenty-one shillings . . .'

'I haven't any money, Mr Springer.'

'Seeing as how you need them to work here, I'll sell them to you for eighteen.'

'I can't afford that,' she protested.

'Course you can, girl. Sixpence a week.'

Diana's heart sank to her boots. With her wages knocked down to five shillings and sixpence a week, she'd only have one and sixpence for herself. And knowing her aunt, she'd have to buy all her own soap, for washing her clothes as well as herself. By the time she bought bread for her lunch out of what was left over she wouldn't be able to afford a Sunday cup of tea in Ronnie's, let alone a weekly visit to the pictures.

'Now let me see,' Ben pondered slow-wittedly. 'That's sixpence a week for thirty-six weeks. I'll just make out a card.' He reached past her to where a stack of 'tally' cards was piled up and as he did so his hand brushed against her breast. She moved back quickly, unsure whether his touch was calculated or inadvertent.

'Well now that I've provided you with shoes, you've no excuse to dally,' he said, apparently unaware of her unease. 'Come on, get a move on. There's an apron next to the polish, you'd better make sure you keep your skirt clean.'

'Yes, Mr Springer.'

'I told you "sir" once. I'll not remind you again.'

'Yes, sir.' She picked up the polish and a rag and left the

stockroom for the front of the shop. She wasn't sorry to move. She'd felt extremely uneasy, confined in such a small space with Ben Springer.

By half-past seven she'd polished every inch of dark oak wood that was on view. Her arm ached, and her fingers were bright red from the effort it had taken to keep a grip on the slimy rag. She paused for a moment, standing back to admire the long run of gleaming counter and dust-free edges of the shelves. Ben had even made her polish the two wooden shoe-fitting stands.

'The carpet now,' he barked from the stool where he was counting change into the till, 'and tomorrow you'd better work a lot faster. The till should be Brassoed every morning, but there's no time for you to do it now.'

She was sweeping the last of the dust into a cracked and warped metal pan when the door opened and the first customer of the day walked in.

'So this is what you've hired, Ben Springer?' An extremely large lady dressed in a navy cape coat, which lay unflatteringly tight over her thick arms and wide shoulders, towered above Diana. Diana's eyes were on a level with the woman's ankles. Wreathed in rolls of flabby fat, they spilled over the top of her elaborately decorated, expensive leather court shoes. 'Well stand up girl, let's take a look at you!'

Diana rose slowly to her feet. The woman's face was puffy, swollen by layers of fat that matched those on her ankles. Her small, greedy eyes darted unnervingly in deep sockets set beneath a low forehead, crowned by a navy felt Tyrolean hat held in place with two enormous, pearl-headed pins.

'Do you think she'll do, Beatrice?' To Diana's amazement her employer was suddenly transformed from shop owner, manager and bully to servile lackey.

'I hope you ascertained that before you took her on.'

'It's not easy to find good help these days.'

'As we've found out to our cost,' Mrs Springer pronounced heavily. It was obvious from the curl of Beatrice Springer's lower lip that Diana did not meet with her approval, but she was totally unprepared for her next question.

'Is that rouge I see on your lips and cheeks, girl?'

'No, Mrs Springer,' Diana faltered, wondering if she should

116

address her as ma'am, as she'd been taught to address the senior female staff in the Infirmary.

'Hmm. Naturally florid complexion then.' Beatrice Springer made it sound like a disease. 'Turn around, girl.'

Feeling intimidated and humiliated, Diana did as Beatrice commanded.

'Your blouse is tight.'

'I've put on weight lately,' Diana lied.

'Comes of being unemployed and idle. Tell me – the truth, mind – when was the last full day of work that you put in?'

'Last Friday,' Diana protested spiritedly. 'I've only just left the Infirmary in Cardiff. I was working as a ward maid – '

'You don't have to tell me any more,' Mrs Springer cut her short. 'When my husband told me that he'd taken on a new girl, I made it my business to find out all I could about you. Diana Powell, isn't it? From Leyshon Street?'

'I live with my uncle and aunt now in Graig Avenue.'

'And I know why.' She glared at Diana. 'Take after your mother?'

Diana felt silent. Experience had taught her that it was the best thing to do whenever anyone brought up the subject of her mother.

'Just as long as you know that I'll be watching you.' Mrs Springer crossed her stubby arms across her ample bosom. 'And to let you know that we – that's both me and Mr Springer – will be a great deal more fussy about someone who works for us than a supervisor in an Infirmary who hasn't got their own place and their own trade to worry about. So before you do anything else, I suggest you sweep out the shop again. There's dust in the corners. Mr Springer, being a man, may not always notice sloppy, half-hearted cleaning, but I warn you I always do.'

'Yes, Mrs Springer. Diana sank to her knees again, wondering if there was a chance that Ronnie would open his restaurant before she answered either of the Springers back. Or if she'd soon find herself unemployed again.

Chapter Eleven

'Hey listen to this, Haydn, Maud,' Eddie held up the copy of the *Pontypridd Observer* that he had found folded behind the cushion of Evan's chair and read out:

' "Do the general public realise the skill, patience and practice necessary to perfect an act like that presented by Mr Willi Pantzer and his wonderful troupe of performing midgets at the New Town Hall, Pontypridd next week? We think not. Willi Pantzer is a lifelong vaudeville artist, he and his little men have been together many years, and his search for midgets is never ending." What do you think, Haydn? Worth shrinking for, eh? He may even offer you a contract,' Eddie mocked.

Haydn had burned in a fever of ambition ever since he had turned down Ambrose's offer to join his revue, and Jenny's absence from his life hadn't helped one bit. He'd bored William, Eddie, Maud and Diana to screaming pitch with extrapolations of 'might have beens' until Eddie was ready to seize any opportunity to get his own back.

'Don't be cruel, Eddie,' Maud said primly from the depths of her mother's chair. Her bedroom and the easy chairs in the kitchen still encompassed her entire world. But like wishful children, her family clung to the entirely irrational hope that the excitement of Christmas, followed by a warm spring, would bring a visible improvement to her health.

'I'm not being cruel,' Eddie insisted, a mischievous glint in his eyes. 'Who knows where an opportunity like this could lead?' He rustled the paper ostentatiously and continued to read. ' "His present company includes midgets of all nationalities," ' – there's your big chance now, Haydn,' he suggested gravely. 'He may not have a Welsh one.'

Haydn picked up the cat that was sleeping peacefully on one of the wooden chairs and threw it at him.

'Haydn, you'll hurt it!' Maud protested, as the cat sank its claws into Eddie's trouser legs and scrammed him.

118

'Ow!' Eddie screeched, as the cat fled. Undeterred, he carried on reading. ' "A great little artiste is Willi Pantzer. He creates most of the comedy and enacts the role of Jack Dempsey in the boxing ring" – Hey do you think you could put a word in for me? This could be the start of a whole new career.'

'Only if you allow me to chop your legs off,' Haydn said viciously, furious with Eddie for daring to joke about feelings that were painfully tender.

'I'm sorry for getting your hopes up, Haydn, they wouldn't want you after all. Listen to this: "Willi Pantzer's troupe are all modest, genial little fellows." That leaves all bad-tempered growly bears like you out. "Mr Willi Pantzer is an athlete, boxer and wrestler and in addition he models in papier mâché, wonderful little dolls he uses in the Pantzer Trot." What do you say Will? Worth going to see, just for the dolls?'

'Eddie if you don't shut up, I'll shut you up,' Maud threatened as a thunderous look crossed Haydn's face.

They all fell silent. None of the boys smiled at her ridiculous outburst. Maud's ill-health hung, a dark and gloomy portent of the inevitability of death, over the entire household.

'You walking down the hill, Haydn?' William asked, breaking into the oppressive atmosphere. It was late on a foul and filthy Thursday afternoon. So foul that Eddie and Evan, having nothing to do except call the streets, had packed in their carting at midday. Charlie and William had finished early in the slaughterhouse. Setting up their stall for the Friday trade in record time, they had returned home early, much to Elizabeth's delight. She had tea on the table before five o'clock, and put Diana's meal on top of a saucepan of water on the shelf above the stove so it could be heated up later. Then she'd rushed down the hill to catch the six o'clock bus for her Uncle John Joseph's house in Ton Pentre. She'd organised his move from the Graig; now she was busy organising his furniture in the new house.

Evan and Charlie had left straight after tea for the Institute for the Unemployed in Mill Street. Although neither of them were unemployed in the strict sense of the word, like dozens of others they used the centre as a meeting place, especially on nights when Evan couldn't scrape together the money for a half of mild in any of the pubs.

'As I'm working in half an hour I suppose I'd better make a move,' Haydn said miserably.

'Nothing like it, boyo,' William grinned. 'You may have Willi Pantzer and his performing midgets next week, but this week you have some cracking chorus girls. Saw one going through the stage door yesterday that brought tears to my eyes.'

'A red head, wearing a blue, fur-trimmed coat?'

'That's the little beauty.'

'Stuck-up madam, more like it.'

'Enjoyed that, did you?'

'What?' Haydn asked in bewilderment.

'Shattering my dreams.' William pulled a comb out of his pocket and ran it through hair so heavily Vaselined it barely moved. 'You ready or not?' He winked at Maud. 'Tell that sister of mine to catch up on some rest. Shops close on Thursday afternoons for the staff to enjoy time off, not scrub the place out.'

'She's still trying to make a good impression.'

'Nothing would make a good impression on Ben Springer.'

'You be all right if I walk down with them, Maud?' Eddie asked.

'Of course I will,' she retorted. 'I'll enjoy the peace and quiet.'

'That's a nice thing to say to your brother.'

'Fight coming up soon?' William asked.

'Not until the Easter Rattle Fair.'

'Don't expect to clean up this year like you did last,' Haydn warned. 'They know your face now, boy.'

'Just practise for the big time. Joey says that if I do well enough at Easter he'll take me up to Blackpool this summer.'

Maud had to force herself to hold her tongue. She'd never liked Eddie's boxing any more than her mother or sister had. In their opinion the dangers far outweighed any rewards.

'Right, if we're going, we'd better go.' Haydn picked up his cap from the back of the chair where he'd left it to dry, and patted Maud on the head.

'I'm not a dog.'

'No, but you're too big to kiss goodbye.'

William finished lacing on his boots, then with Eddie trailing in the rear the boys left.

The house was remarkably still. Maud lay back in her chair, listening to the quiet sounds she'd associated with home since childhood. The dull tick of the kitchen clock that had been a wedding present to her mother from her Uncle John Joseph. A soft hiss, as a damp piece of coal crumbled into the flames in the stove, probably one of the pieces that Eddie or Will had risked prosecution over on one of their scavenging trips to the Maritime tip. She'd seen their blackened hands and faces when they'd sneaked in over the back wall after adding their ill-gotten spoils to the meagre stock in the coalhouse when her mother wasn't looking.

'Hello, anyone in?' The front door slammed and footsteps echoed on the lino in the passage.

'Ronnie?' Half asleep, Maud peered through the gloom as Ronnie's tall figure emerged from the shadows that lay thickly in the corner by the door.

'Just passing, so I thought I'd call in and see how the boys are doing. Haydn must be about ready to walk down the hill.'

'They've already gone to town,' Maud said, expecting him to walk straight back out again. Instead he came closer to the fire and pulled his hat off.

'Leaving you all alone?'

She bristled at the hint of criticism. 'It's nice to be alone sometimes,' she replied tartly.

'I know what you mean.' He took off his rain-spattered coat and hung it over the back of one of the kitchen chairs. Walking over to the range, he placed his hand against the side of the teapot.

'No one will be back for ages.' She resented him intruding into her peace and quiet and wanted him to go so she could sit back and dream. Of Jock Maitlin, the porter in the Infirmary who'd shown more than a passing interest in her. Of the career in nursing that she'd wanted so badly, and now realised she'd never have.

'Not even Diana and your parents?'

'My father and Charlie have gone to a meeting in the Unemployed Club.'

'The anti-Mosley meeting?'

'I really don't know, I don't pay much attention. My mother's gone to Uncle Joe's and won't be back until late. And Diana's – '

'As soon as Diana finishes work she's meeting Tina to go to the pictures,' Ronnie told her. 'When Tina saw Ben Springer walk into the bank this morning, she ran to the shoe shop and persuaded her. I sometimes wonder if those two have anything on their minds other than what they read in Hollywood star magazines. Where's William?' he asked suspiciously.

'You know Will?' she answered carelessly.

'Yes I do,' he frowned, thinking how often Tina had gone to the pictures with Diana lately. 'Want some tea?' He held up the cold teapot.

'No thank you,' Maud refused primly, suddenly conscious of being totally alone in the house with him. Her mother's warnings about placing herself in a vulnerable position with a man, any man, rang clearly through her mind. Then she remembered how long Ronnie had been a friend to her family, and the vast difference in their ages. Sickness was making her paranoid. The problem was she'd never really had a boyfriend, only dreams. She couldn't even count Jock Maitlin, they'd never actually gone anywhere together. Diana was right: doing a man's washing and darning his socks was no substitute for romance.

She allowed herself to drift into a cold, comfortless tide of self-pity. Looking the way she did now, she'd never experience love first-hand. And unless she made a remarkable recovery she wouldn't even be seeing it on a cinema screen again.

The sound of Ronnie replacing the teapot on the shelf above the range jolted her back to the present. She watched him as he settled into the easy chair opposite her own.

'Don't you ever get fed up of the same four walls?' he asked, tapping a cigarette out of a packet he'd removed from his shirt pocket.

'A little,' she admitted reluctantly.

'The Trojan's outside. It's not the most comfortable of rides, but I could take you down to the café for an hour or two. Gina and Angelo are there, and Alma,' he added as an afterthought.

'I don't know,' she murmured hesitantly. The prospect excited her, but she knew her mother, and probably her father, would quite rightly be furious when they found out what she'd done. As they undoubtedly would. Pontypridd was no place for secrets.

'Come on,' Ronnie coaxed, 'I'll have you down and back before half-past seven. No one will be any the wiser,' he smiled.

The smile decided the matter for her. 'All right,' she said resolutely.

122

'You'll have to dress up warm,' he commanded in the tone of voice he usually reserved for his eight-year-old sister and six-year-old brother.

'You can't get much warmer than what I've got on,' she protested strongly.

'That's just the problem. You've been sitting in thick clothes in a warm room for weeks. A strong dose of real, fresh air is likely to . . . knock you for six,' he said quickly, almost kicking himself. He'd almost said 'finish you off'.

She threw back the grey rug that covered her legs. He was right about her clothes. She was dressed for a trip to town on a freezing, damp and miserable market day. Thick flannel skirt more serviceable than attractive. Winceyette blouse, topped by the red cable-knit jumper from her suit, and cable-knit lisle stockings.

'I'm not taking you out of here without a cardigan. Where can I find one?' he demanded.

'On top of this, you must be joking. I'd feel like a bundle of laundry.'

'You don't put one on, I don't take you.'

She glared at him, but it had no effect. Used to dealing with the tantrums and vagaries of ten younger brothers and sisters, Ronnie shrugged off her display of temperament without a second thought.

'I'll get one from my room,' she said, suddenly thinking of her hair – her face – she didn't even have a dab of powder on her nose, and if she was going out she really ought to put some scent on. Her spirits suddenly soared at the prospect of sitting in the café. Talking to the girls. Seeing people . . .

'Are you allowed to walk upstairs?' he asked sharply.

'Of course, how do you think I get to bed?' she retorted.

'There's a difference between walking up and down once a day and running up and down for no good reason in between. And before you say another word,' he flicked his lighter on and lit his cigarette, 'I know what's on your mind. You don't want to go upstairs to get a cardigan, you just want to primp in front of the mirror.'

'I do not!' Her voice rose high in indignation.

'Tell me what you want and I'll bring it down,' he interrupted just as she was about to burst into full flow.

123

Gripping the sides of her armchair she levered herself upwards. Ronnie wavered alarmingly within her sight. The room began to sway, and black spots swam before her eyes as they always did whenever she tried to rise.

'You're as weak as a kitten.' He pushed her gently down into the chair and she fell back, grateful for the feel of its solid support beneath her. 'Which is your room?'

'Right at the top of the stairs.' She felt a draught of cold air as he opened the kitchen door. 'The grey cardigan,' she called after him. 'It's on the stool in front of the dressing table.' She blessed her mother's rigid housekeeping. Her bedroom would be immaculate, just as it always was when she returned upstairs after a day in the kitchen. 'And bring my handbag as well,' she shouted, hearing his step on the stairs. 'It's next to the bed.'

'Women!' he moaned when he returned a few moments later with her handbag and the cardigan. 'They've always got to primp themselves up, even for a trip out the back.'

He watched her as she squinted into the mirror. She'd washed her hands and face after tea, so comforting herself with the thought that she was at least clean, and very conscious of him watching her, she ran a comb through her hair, holding the mirror up in an effort to get a better view.

'Your hair's fine,' he reassured her. It was, she noted with relief. Diana had helped her wash it yesterday evening when her mother had left to go to a chapel committee meeting. It had always been her best feature, and since she'd been ill she'd tried to make the most of what her father called her 'crowning glory', torturing her sleeping hours by wearing metal grippers in an effort to tame the unruly curls into fashionable waves. The only problem was, since her illness the contrast between the rich golden colour of her hair and the deathly pallor of her skin had become even more noticeable. Putting away her comb, she pushed up her lipstick with her thumbnail and spread it over her mouth. It was bright red, a colour Diana had assured her, suited her when she'd first gone to the Infirmary. Now it made her mouth look like an ugly red wound against the unnatural whiteness of her face. She lifted the stick, intending to dab some on her cheeks.

Stung by the pathos of what she was doing to herself, Ronnie turned away. Maud painting her thin, sickly face for her first outing in weeks reminded him of an incident he'd witnessed as a child. The curtains had been drawn in the house next door to theirs. He'd asked his heavily pregnant mother if he should go next door and tell Mrs Brown that it was daytime. She'd warned him tersely not to go near the house. It was the lack of explanation that intrigued him: he'd sensed that something secret, something forbidden, was going on behind those closed drapes. When his mother had called him for dinner he'd scoffed it in record time. Then sneaking out into the deserted street, he'd crept up the short flight of steps to next door's front door. The curtains were still drawn, but there was a crack at the side where they didn't quite cover the edge of the bay. He'd crouched down and looked through the small gap. Mr Brown was lying on the table in the parlour. Mrs Brown was bending over him, tenderly washing a thick layer of coal dust from his grey, dead face.

He rubbed his eyes. Why had he thought of that incident now? He hadn't called it to mind for years.

'I'm ready.'

Maud had put away her lipstick and powder and closed her handbag. She was sitting forward on the edge of her chair, the grey cardigan round her shoulders. The air was sweet, redolent with essence of violets, but he noticed, thankfully, she'd decided against reddening her cheeks.

'Your hat and coat by the front door?'

'They are.'

'Green coat, isn't it?'

'Yes,' she was surprised he'd remembered. 'And the black tam's mine.'

He fetched them. She rose somewhat unsteadily from the chair. He caught her shoulder as she staggered. Slipping her arms quickly into the sleeves of her coat, he lowered her back into her chair.

'Stay there for a minute,' he ordered, unnerved by her fragility. She looked down at her feet and saw the old slippers she'd inherited from Bethan. Tartan with red pom-poms, their ugliness hurt.

'Shoes?' Ronnie asked abruptly.

'They're in the washhouse on the shelf. Plain black with a bar.'

He found them and brought them out. She kicked off the

slippers, but when she bent to do up the buckles, she almost fell head first on to the floor. Ronnie knelt and fastened the buckles for her. Embarrassed, she made a bad joke.

'Does your girlfriend know you play Prince Charming with other girls?' She didn't dare mention Alma's name.

'You're not a girl, you're a baby,' he contradicted her. 'Right, blanket around your shoulders.'

'Ronnie . . .'

'It's not up for discussion. Either you do it or you don't go. I've left an umbrella by the door. It'll keep off the worst of the rain, but not all of it. Right, can you walk by yourself or do I carry you?' he asked, looking at her critically.

'I can walk,' she asserted forcefully, swaying precariously.

He put his arm round her waist and pulled her close to him, steadying her. 'One slip and I'm carrying you.'

He helped her as far as the door, then opened his umbrella and gave it to her to hold. Stepping outside, he swung her up into his arms. 'Don't argue,' he ordered, silencing her protests. 'It's too damned wet to hang around here quarrelling.' He carried her down the steps and set her on her feet by the side of the van. Pulling open the door, he lifted her on to the bench seat inside. He ran around to his side of the van, took the starting handle from beneath his seat and swung the engine into life, before climbing in. 'Right, first stop the café.' He looked across at her and smiled. The smile froze on his lips. She was lying back against the seat, her thin face grey in the watery lamplight. Perhaps this had been a crazy idea after all. What right did he have to come in and sweep her off to the café for some social life just because her family had left her alone for the evening? Then he remembered what Trevor had said: this was her last year. She deserved every minute of animation and life he, or anyone else, could give her.

'I would much rather have gone to the pictures,' Diana moaned to Tina as they queued outside the Town Hall.

'I would have gone with you if the boys hadn't hogged the only decent talkie in town.'

'It's the pictures, for pity's sake. Half the town would have been there, as well as my brother and Glan Richards. Just what are you afraid of?'

126

'Being seen sitting too close to Will by someone who'd carry tales back to Papa or Ronnie.'

'It's not as if you don't like my brother . . .'

'That's just it. I like him, and Ronnie and Papa know it.'

'And just what could they do to you if they did find out that you were going out with Will?' Diana demanded testily, convinced that Tina was making a melodrama out of absolutely nothing.

'Send me to Italy,' Tina said flatly.

Diana stared at her incredulously. 'They wouldn't.'

'They would,' Tina assured her.

'But you've never been there, it'd be . . .' The queue shuffled forward and Tina grabbed her arm and pulled her up the line. 'You're serious, aren't you?'

'I'm serious,' Tina whispered. 'Didn't Bethan ever tell you what Laura had to put up with when Papa found out about her and Trevor Lewis? My father wants – no, *expects* – all of us to marry Italians, or at the very least, Welsh Italians. I think secretly he still regards Laura's marriage as a disgrace to the name of Ronconi, and he certainly doesn't intend to stand by and do nothing while any of the rest of us dishonour it any more than Laura already has.'

'But he seems to get on all right with Trevor Lewis,' Diana protested, trying to recall the few times she'd seen Mr Ronconi senior and Doctor Lewis together.

'Get on with has nothing to do with it. He *gets on* with Trevor, likes him even for being a doctor, and a Catholic. What he doesn't like is Trevor being Irish/Welsh instead of Italian.'

'But isn't Ronnie keen on Alma Moore?' Diana persisted.

'Perhaps,' Tina said darkly. 'And then again perhaps not. Ronnie's made sure that no one really knows, not even Alma. But believe you me, even if he is keen on Alma, "keen on" is nowhere near marrying.' The queue surged forward again, and this time Diana pulled Tina on. 'Ronnie'll never marry a Welsh girl,' Tina pronounced decisively. 'Take my word for it, even if he loves Alma Moore, he'll walk up the aisle with Papa's choice. For the last four Mondays Mama's invited Maria Pauli to tea. She was born in Wales, but Papa's prepared to overlook that, as both her parents are from Bardi and like us they speak Italian at home. Her father has a café in Ferndale,' she informed Diana matter-of-factly. 'And I think both Papa and Mama are expecting Ronnie to succumb to her charms any day now. I overheard Papa tell Ronnie three times last week that a man should be married before his twenty-fifth birthday. Ronnie was twenty-seven last month.'

'Does Alma know any of this?' Diana demanded.

'If she doesn't she's a fool,' Tina said. 'She's been mooning around after Ronnie for years. If she can't read the writing on the wall by now, she never will.'

Diana remembered the blatant adoration on Alma's face every time she looked at Ronnie. 'Knowing someone and being in love with them are two different things,' she sighed theatrically, recalling the plot of a Claudette Colbert film she and Maud had seen in Cardiff. 'I think when you love someone you can forgive them anything, and overlook everything.'

'If Ronnie was anywhere near serious about her, he would have married her years ago,' Tina said impatiently. 'If you want my opinion, I think she's just someone he's passing the time of day with,' she continued airily with all the worldliness of her sixteen years.

'Well I'm sorry, but I think that's a foul way for Ronnie to behave towards any girl, let alone one as nice as Alma.'

'He wouldn't go out with Alma if she wasn't nice.'

'I don't think I like your brother very much!' Diana pronounced resolutely, already half-way into weaving a tragic romance in which Alma was the wronged, doomed heroine.

'All the years you've known him, and you've never come to that conclusion before? I'll let you into a secret. I've never liked him,' Tina grinned. 'Two sixpences please,' she said to the girl in the cashier's kiosk, as they reached the box office.

'I would have rather had fourpenny seats.' Diana rummaged in her handbag for her purse. Tonight was a real extravagance. Tina had caught her at a low ebb when she'd come into the shop mid-morning. After four stern dressing-downs from Ben Springer, and three from his wife, she hadn't needed much persuading to agree to an outing, although she knew perfectly well there was no way she could really afford it. Despite Ben Springer's assertion that he'd review her pay at the end of the week, she knew now that she wouldn't dare bring up the subject of her wages again. Not after seeing so many girls her age walking the shops in Taff Street every day in a last-ditch attempt to find local work before resorting to the domestic agencies that trained women for service in England.

'This one's on me,' Tina insisted, pushing the change she'd received from half a crown into her handbag. 'I'm rich. Ronnie actually paid me this week.'

'Don't be silly,' Diana scolded. 'You can't afford to treat me.'

'Tell you what, you buy ice-cream wafers in the interval and we'll call it quits.'

'They're only twopence . . .'

'And cornets are a penny. Look, we can swap over next time if it makes you feel any better. Give us a good excuse to go out together again.' She ran up the steep flight of steps into the hall.

'I don't like owing money.' Diana reluctantly returned her purse to her handbag. Like all people living close to the bone, she resented taking 'charity' from anyone.

Tina led the way down the long corridor to the usherette, who guided them to the rear of the stalls.

'At least they're right at the back,' she said cheerfully. 'We can put our seats up if we have to, and sit on them. Chewing gum?' she flipped open a packet of P.K. and flicked one into Diana's hand.

'Did you pay for these?' Diana asked.

'They fell on the floor when I was opening a new box. Can't sell spoiled goods to the customers,' she grinned.

The orchestra began to tune up, scratchily and noisily. Diana settled back in her seat. The manager walked out in front of the curtain and held up his hand.

'Oh, oh, here comes a programme change,' Tina moaned. 'What's the betting that the leading lady and all the chorus girls are sick and they're bringing on the Dan-y-Lan Coons instead.'

'Ssh!' Diana hissed as heads turned towards them.

'Ladies and Gentlemen,' the words fell unheard into the auditorium. He lifted the microphone stand towards him and tapped it. A hollow boom echoed around the theatre.

'Something you ate, Dai,' a wag shouted from the front row. A gale of laughter drowned out the manager's words.

'Ladies and Gentlemen . . . Ladies and Gentlemen . . .' It took a full minute of stammering repetition for him to regain the attention of the restless audience. When hush finally descended he continued, 'I regret to inform you . . .'

'Told you,' Tina crowed.

'Ssh!' Diana commanded as she tried to listen.

'. . . is ill. To take his place we have a local boy, who works here, and I want all of you to give him a chance,' he shouted above the cat-calls and jeers. Someone offstage pushed Haydn in front of the curtain. He bowed quickly and dashed off, but not before the audience had dissolved into mirth at the costume he was wearing. A ruffled matador shirt strained tightly across his broad shoulders and gaped across his chest where the buttons refused to meet the buttonholes. A short cloak hung half-way up his back and a ridiculously small tricorn was perched on the crown of his head.

'The hat looks like a pimple on a haystack,' Tina giggled helplessly. 'And I would have loved to see him in the trousers that went with that outfit. He looks like Gulliver dressed by the Lilliputians.'

Diana alone out of all the people packed into the auditorium kept a straight face.

'I wonder what he's going to do?' Tina wiped tears of laughter from the corners of her eyes with the back of her hand.

'Something good, I hope,' Diana murmured, crossing her fingers and hoping against hope that Haydn wasn't about to make a fool of himself.

Chapter Twelve

When Haydn was told that the head chorus boy was sick, and was asked to stand in for him, his spirits soared. The head chorus boy had two duets with the head chorus girl, one of which contained three precious solo verses. He felt that the gods had smiled on him – forgiving him for rejecting Ambrose's offer after all. Who knows, when the revue moved on he might be taken with it. To big cities – exotic places he'd only read about and heard of, never visited – Birmingham, Manchester, Bristol. Perhaps the biggest prize of all – London. But even as he built his towering, glittering castles of success in the air, the bombshell struck.

The manager had handed him the head boy's costume, which was at least five inches too narrow and a good six inches too short for him, with the news that he was going to fill in for the newest and least important chorus boy in the line-up. His presence was only needed to even numbers up in the dance routines, and provide another male voice in the background. All of the boys in the chorus had been understudying the head boy and praying for this moment. He watched them practise the solo verses and fight over the role while he struggled into the matador's shirt (he failed even to pull the satin trousers over his thighs). In vain he protested to the show's director and the manager that he couldn't dance.

'You don't have to dance, boy, just be there,' the director boomed in his best Shakespearean voice.

'You've seen the routine often enough, Haydn. It's not much to ask,' the manager snapped. Ice cold and paralysed with fear, Haydn watched while Dolly, a charming little teaser on stage and an absolute bitch off, executed a complicated tap step in the corridor.

'Got it now?' she asked briskly.

Haydn tried to copy her fancy footwork but his feet simply failed to respond to the directives he sent them. Tripping over his ankle, he fell flat on his face.

'He'll never do,' Dolly complained loudly, making Haydn feel about two inches high. 'He's got two left feet.'

'It's only for tonight, darling,' the director said soothingly. 'Right, everybody ready?'

'Just one more thing, hot shot,' one of the boys whispered to Haydn as he followed them up the steps to the wings. 'Don't try to drown us out with your singing. We've all heard you backstage. You haven't got a bad voice, for an amateur,' he added deprecatingly. 'But like all amateurs you obviously think the louder you sing, the better it is.'

'Mime, sweetheart.' Dolly pinched his arm viciously as she walked past him on her way to the stage. 'Just open and shut your mouth like a goldfish, stand still and you can't go wrong.'

'I hope so,' Haydn muttered fervently as he followed the others out on to the darkened, curtained stage. 'I really hope so.'

'You tired yet?' Ronnie asked Maud solicitously as she sat in front of the fire in the back room of the café with Gina on one side, Angelo on the other and him opposite her.

'A little,' she admitted reluctantly.

'How about I make you one of Papa's special ice creams to perk you up?' Angelo offered. Tony had only just taught him how to make the raspberry delights, banana splits and knickerbocker glories that formed the backbone of Ronconi's dessert menus, but so few customers could afford to order fancy ice creams that he grasped every opportunity to air his new-found skills.

'No thank you,' Maud smiled. Ronnie had whisked her off in such a rush she hadn't even thought to bring her purse with her, and even if she had, she doubted she had enough to cover the sixpence that a knickerbocker glory cost. Besides, Gina had already given her a hot chocolate on the house.

'Angelo will be so upset if you don't let him make one of his ice creams,' Ronnie coaxed. 'Go on, be reckless for once. There's nothing in this world like the taste of Ronconi's ice cream smothered in raspberry sauce.'

'I know, I've eaten it,' Maud laughed.

'Well then, you can eat one again.' Ronnie nodded to Angelo. 'Go and make her one,' he ordered.

'A very small one,' Maud pleaded. 'I really couldn't eat a lot.'

'And one for me, Angelo,' Gina shouted. 'An extremely large one. With nuts, and a cherry on top,' she added as an afterthought.

'No work, no eating,' Ronnie said briskly. 'Clear and clean down those tables.' He pointed to four tables covered in cigarette ash and sandwich crumbs that the evening tram crews had just vacated. 'When that's done, you can finish for the day. I'll take you home when I take Maud back.'

'No peace for the wicked,' Gina sighed as she rose reluctantly from the table.

'Or the idle,' Ronnie emphasised. 'Alma, I'll have a coffee,' he shouted, clicking his fingers to gain her attention.

Alma was accustomed to Ronnie's imperious ways, but familiarity with his behaviour didn't make it any easier to bear. She marched furiously to the metal coffee jug which was kept on a low oil burner behind the counter. She poured out Ronnie's coffee just the way he liked it, thick and strong, with no extra water. Adding three sugars and a dash of milk she stirred it, then carried it over to the table where he was sitting with Maud.

Gina was busy clearing the tables, and Angelo hadn't yet returned from the kitchen with the ice creams, so Ronnie and Maud were alone. A warm wave of sympathy washed over Alma as she looked at Maud. The young girl was sitting, head in hands, slumped over the table, her face pale with exhaustion, her lips bloodless. The thin veneer of cheap lipstick had worn off on the warm rim of her cup of chocolate. She seemed to be listening intently to something Ronnie was saying. Alma looked instinctively from Maud to Ronnie, and all her feelings of sympathy were washed away on a floodtide of acutely painful suspicion.

For the first time since she'd known him, Ronnie had lowered the defensive shield of cynicism he habitually used to camouflage his finer feelings. His eyes were naked, mirroring his thoughts. And she didn't like what she saw in them. Not one little bit.

A benign expression softened his features as he gazed at Maud. He was speaking too low for Alma to catch his words, but judging from the lack of response from Maud he wasn't telling her anything of vital importance. Only his eyes betrayed his feelings: speaking with an eloquence she had never suspected him of possessing.

'Your coffee, Ronnie,' she said spikily, slamming the cup on to the table and slopping the hot liquid into the saucer.

'Remind me to give you a refresher course in waitressing some time, Alma,' he reprimanded her icily.

She glared at him as she walked away.

'Two knickerbocker glories,' Angelo announced grandly, bearing his creations proudly into the back room of the café. Pink and white scoops of ice cream were piled high in silver fluted goblets, the whole creation topped with whirls of whipped cream, glazed with rivulets of raspberry sauce and sprinkled with fine layers of crumbs of toasted nuts.

'Not bad,' Gina said condescendingly as she walked over to the table. 'Not bad at all. Not as perfectly symmetrical as Ronnie's or Tony's, of course. But passable.'

'What do you mean not as symmetrical as Ronnie's or Tony's?' Angelo demanded touchily.

'Well there's more nuts on this side than the other,' she teased. 'And the sauce?' she raised her eyebrows. 'You really should have put on more sauce.'

Ronnie stared at the creations critically. 'Did you put sauce in the bottom of the dish?' he demanded.

'Yes,' Angelo answered belligerently.

'And half-way up?'

Angelo stuttered, then faltered.

'You left it out!' Ronnie exclaimed. 'What on earth do you expect it to taste like with no sauce running through the lower scoops of ice cream and chopped tinned fruit? Really, Angelo . . .'

'I put a double helping on the top,' Angelo protested strongly.

'It should have gone under the cream, Angelo, not on top,' Ronnie said heavily. 'You sour the taste of the cream by putting it on top – '

'It's delicious,' Maud interrupted, scooping a spoonful into her mouth. 'Absolutely delicious,' she smiled at Angelo.

'Thank you for saying so,' Angelo replied sullenly, glaring at Ronnie.

'Each to their own,' Alma interposed from the front of the café. 'Just because you and your father have done it one way for years, Ronnie, it doesn't mean that it's the right way.'

Ronnie stared at the counter, ignoring her comments. 'Couldn't that do with a wipe-down, Alma?' he said curtly.

She picked up a cloth and did as he asked, burning with indignation and damning him for trying to keep her out of his public life. But despite her anger she sensed he was slipping through her fingers: she felt as though she were trying with her bare hands to stem water that was pouring from a fall. Ronnie was leaving her, and she didn't know how to hold him.

She only knew that she couldn't imagine living any kind of a life without him.

'Well, boyo.' The director of the show, a fat, cigar-smoking lecher who dived into the chorus girls' dressing room on each and every pretext, eyed Haydn over the top of his rimless spectacles. 'That was a bloody disaster, wasn't it?'

Haydn stared down at his feet, encased like bursting chrysalides in a pair of varnished leather tap shoes that he had borrowed from the show's dresser. They were two sizes too small for him, and he could already feel the raw skin and blisters that had formed on his heels and toes after only an hour of wear.

'It was,' he acknowledged miserably. Pressing the front of one shoe against the back of the other, he kicked it off. A blissful, soothing feeling of ease and comfort seeped up through his body, to be superseded moments later by intense, mind-blowing, agonising pain as his battered feet stung alarmingly back to life.

'Well?' the director urged. 'Do you mind telling me why you didn't do as you were told? Hell's bells, man, you only had to stand at the back of the stage and let the girls dance around you. A tailor's dummy could have done as much. What are you? An imbecile?'

Too mortified to attempt an explanation, Haydn remained silent while the director's face turned purple with rage. He could have protested that the other members of the chorus had, for reasons of their own, resented his presence on stage and set out to deliberately make things difficult for him, but the director wasn't in a listening mood.

He'd begun the routine well enough, standing on the chalk marks that the director had drawn for him at the very back of stage left, only to be sent flying by Tom, the youngest and greenest of the chorus boys, who was ecstatic at his elevation to the third row. Mesmerised by the lights, the colour, the music, the movement, but most of all by the dark void that hid the audience, he hadn't even seen Tom coming. It was as if the boy had materialised out of

135

nowhere. Unable to prevent himself from stumbling forward, Haydn found himself centre stage, blocking everyone's path. His size hadn't helped. He'd felt like a huge, clumsy giant in a light, flitting fairyland. Stepping back quickly he'd knocked Dolly flying. Totally disorientated, he then committed the cardinal sin of continuing to move forwards not backwards, fouling the movements of the newly elevated head chorus boy Sean, an Irish lad, who had, as the director put it, 'a beautiful turn of step'. His step was anything but beautiful after Haydn had lumbered in front of him. It had been up to Dolly to rescue what was left of the number. Pushing Sean forward and Haydn backwards, she'd managed to retrieve centre stage for herself and Sean, earning herself a cheer from the restless first-house audience, whose gales of laughter at Haydn's antics had unnerved him all the more.

Mortified, Haydn had remained glued to the backdrop until the time came for the chorus to sing. Feeling that this at least was something he could do well, he ignored Sean's advice to mime the words, and added his deep, rich baritone to the chorus's efforts. Riding high on a crest of emotion and music, a good minute passed before he became aware of his fellow performers.

Dolly and Sean were both firing furious glares his way, interspersing them with the bright, brittle, artificial stage smiles they reserved for the audience. He paused, faltered, listened for the first time to the others and in a single, tingling moment of utter embarrassment and mortification, realised he'd been singing in the wrong key.

'Ah manager, there you are.' The director waylaid the manager as he walked towards them in his boiled shirt, black bow tie and evening suit. 'I was just telling this boy that we'll have to drop one and a half couples from the chorus for the next house,' he said bitterly. 'Needs must,' he boomed as he flicked a disparaging glance at Haydn. 'After all we can't really call *this* – ' he jabbed his forefinger painfully into Haydn's arm, '– half of any couple.'

'The others might be safer without his presence on stage,' the manager agreed drily.

'A whole lot safer,' the director concurred sharply.

'Do you really need to drop one and a half couples?' the manager ventured. 'Why not put Dolly and her partner centre stage and allow the others to dance around them?'

136

'Good idea, old man! Good idea, I'll get the boys and girls together to talk about it.' He immediately banged on the door of the girls' dressing room. 'Girlies!' he shouted in a sickly voice, his small piggy eyes gleaming at the thought of catching a glimpse of one of them in a state of semi-undress.

'We'll be out in a minute,' Dolly's nasal voice echoed through the door.

The manager was fond of Haydn. He'd watched him grow in confidence and competence during the months that he'd worked in the Town Hall, and he'd already marked him down for promotion to assistant manager when George Bassett, the old man who held the post at present, retired. But he was also aware of what a fiasco like this could do to the Town Hall's and his reputation when the story got back to the booking agents in London. With the coal pits closed and money a scarce commodity in the valleys, it had become almost impossible to induce good-quality acts to visit South Wales. And the few people who still had money in Pontypridd wouldn't patronise shows that weren't top drawer. Every week he and the manager of the New Theatre fought for better shows and a bigger share of diminishing audiences. And it wasn't just the New Theatre. Since the talkies had hit town, they'd had the cinemas to contend with as well.

He felt sorry for Haydn, read the misery of shattered dreams in the boy's face, but with the director's furious gaze upon both of them he didn't feel disposed to openly sympathise with him.

'The sooner you get out of that ridiculous outfit and back to work, the better,' he said frostily. 'There's a mess waiting to be cleared up in the boys' dressing room. Once you've changed, deal with it. Then come to the office. I've a list of errands for you to run between houses. Well, what are you waiting for?' he demanded. 'Get on with it. There's still the calling to be done, you know. You can't expect Judy to do your job for you just because you went out on stage for five minutes. She has her tray to set up and take out in the interval.'

'Yes sir,' Haydn mumbled. He was having a hard time grappling with mixed emotions that were half shame, half mutinous. He didn't know what he wanted to do most urgently: sock the manager and the director on the nose, or break down and cry.

'Oh, and Haydn?'

'Sir?' Haydn paused with his hand on the door of the boys' changing room.

'After tonight's little fiasco I don't want to hear any more from you about going on stage. That offer Ambrose made to you when he was drunk seems to have gone to your head. You've been fit for nothing since. Even if you hadn't refused, he would have retracted it in the morning. You *do* know that, don't you?'

'I never said I was a dancer, sir . . .'

'If you ask me you're not much of anything. Not even a callboy. Perhaps now that you've finally been given the "break" you've been whining for, you'll understand that it takes good all-round talent to get anywhere in variety. It's a tough world, and there's any amount of idiots around who can sing a few notes. Most of them even manage the right key,' the manager added sadistically, convinced he was doing the right thing in trying to keep Haydn's feet firmly on the ground. 'Believe me, boy, you need a lot more than just a pleasant voice. Talent, looks, ability to dance . . .'

Haydn couldn't listen any more. 'Sir,' he muttered dejectedly as he opened the dressing-room door and stepped inside. Feeling sick and faint he breathed in the oppressive stench of stale male sweat and greasepaint. Clothes were strewn from one end of the bench that traversed the centre of the room to the other. He nodded to the boys. They stared at him before continuing to change in silence. He knew they'd heard every word the manager had said to him. And revelled in it.

Steeling himself, he entered the room and closed the door behind him. With his back to the door he unfastened the only button of the shirt he had managed to do up, the last one, closest to the tails.

'Careful you don't rip it, callboy,' one of the boys jeered in a derisory tone. 'It's worth more than your week's wages.' Haydn stripped it off in silence, folding it meticulously, collar up, sleeves neatly tucked in behind the front. He looked around for somewhere to put it.

'You're not going to give it back to us like that, are you?' Tom, the youngest of the chorus boys and the butt of all their jokes was only too delighted to give a little of what he had to take. 'Phew!' he moved near the shirt and staggered around with his fingers over his nose in a parody of a man fainting. 'Phew! Phew!'

'Knock it off, Tom,' Sean shouted irritably, succumbing to a sudden empathy for Haydn. He'd had a rotten break on his first job too. It had been so bad his career had almost ended before it had begun, and he knew exactly what Haydn was feeling right now.

'I'll take it home and wash it,' Haydn murmured, looking around for his own shirt. He saw it, lying on the floor in the corner of the room. It was only when his fingers closed over the cloth that he realised it had been used to mop up the mess that the manager had told him about.

'What's the matter, Taffy?' Tom laughed. 'Something on your shirt?'

Dropping the shirt, Haydn looked around the room.

'Which one of you jokers did this?' he asked quietly. Only Tom, who was as insensitive as he was naive, continued to laugh.

'Can't the Welsh take a joke?' he sneered. 'Do you think that's lemonade on your shirt, Taffy?' He looked to the others for support. 'We all know different, don't we boys? That's – ' he pointed to the floor where Haydn's soiled and sodden shirt lay, a limp, discarded rag ' – that's what you get for trying to climb into boots that are too big for you, or,' he grinned as he saw the shoes that Haydn was carrying, 'in your case, too small.'

'Shut your mouth before I shut it for you,' Haydn hissed, focusing all his embarrassment, disappointment and anger on Tom.

'Ooh, masterful,' Tom pranced around in front of Haydn. Once Haydn saw Tom move he realised that he was a queer, like Wyn Rees. His emotions clarified, converging into cold, murderous rage. No one in the mining community liked queers. They were strange, unnatural . . . his hand closed into a hard, tight ball of a fist. Lashing out, he hit Tom squarely on the jaw. The boy flew backwards. The last thing Haydn saw before Tom lay, a crumpled heap on the floor, was the startled expression as Tom's eyes blinked open when the back of his head connected with the painted brickwork on the wall.

'You've killed him,' one of the boys wailed.

'Don't be so bloody soft,' Sean exclaimed, hiding his own fear behind a thin veneer of irritation. He moved before anyone else. Kneeling at Tom's side, he laid his hand over where he thought Tom's heart should be. 'He's just out cold.'

Haydn's knees gave way as a surge of relief rushed through his veins. He almost fell to the floor. Sitting there with his head resting on his knees and his back to the cold brick wall, he trembled uselessly while Sean assumed absolute control.

'We need a doctor. Haydn?' He turned and saw that Haydn was on the point of passing out himself.

'I'll get one,' Haydn breathed faintly, hoping his legs would carry him as far as Trevor's house.

'Now listen, all of you.' The note of authority in Sean's voice was unmistakable. 'Tom slipped on the metal tap of his shoe while he was trying to take it off. Does everyone understand what I'm saying here?'

The entire chorus nodded dully and in unison, as though practising a routine.

'You don't have to do that,' Haydn whispered hoarsely, finally finding his own voice.

'We're not doing it for you, but for Tom,' Sean said scornfully, looking pointedly at Haydn's shirt. 'If half of what happens in this dressing room ever got out, the gossip could kill the show dead, not to mention our careers. Particularly in one or two of the towns we've been playing in lately.'

Chapter Thirteen

It was closer to eleven than ten o'clock when Ronnie drove back down the Graig hill. He and Gina had gone into the Powells' house to sit with Maud until someone came home. They had a long wait. William and Diana didn't walk in until nearly ten o'clock, and meanwhile Maud's face grew paler, and her thin frame slumped further and further in the chair until she looked on the point of collapse.

Ronnie hadn't seen the animation in her face, or the glow in her eyes as she'd talked to Gina. Only the gaunt, grey sickness that was eating her alive. He'd wanted to kick himself for his stupidity. Only an idiot would have taken a girl as frail and ill as Maud out on a cold, rainy winter's night.

He'd sat in silence, drinking the weak tea Gina had made for them, without tasting it. He hadn't even heard a word they'd said. For once the cynicism he habitually adopted to buoy him through life had deserted him. Instead he'd visualised Maud, dead. He found himself picturing the misery of her funeral, the gap her death would create in the lives of his sisters . . . and perhaps not only his sisters. He could actually hear the awed whispers in which they would speak her name. See the babies that would be named after her.

Distraught at his own imaginings, the moment William and Diana walked into the back kitchen he'd dragged a protesting Gina out. Left to her own devices she would have gossiped with Maud and Diana all night. He drove up to Danycoedcae Road and dropped Gina off, stopping only as long as it took him to shout a quick hello and goodbye to his parents.

A pang of conscience niggled at the back of his mind. He should never have left Alma to cope for so long alone. He comforted himself with the thought that she'd had Angelo in the kitchen, but then he remembered just how useless Angelo was as soon as he was put under any pressure. But perhaps Angelo was entitled to be useless. After all he was only fifteen, no more than a kid. He

141

scrutinised his thoughts and wondered if he was going soft in the head. He'd done as much work as Angelo – and a great deal more – when he'd been only twelve.

He drove his Trojan under the archway that led into the back yard of the White Hart, and pulled into the car park. He nodded to, but didn't dare stop to pass the time of night with the landlord who was putting out a crate of empties. Hurrying around the corner it only took a few steps for him to realise his worst fears. The windows of the café were misted up, but inside he could make out the dark, shadowy shapes of blurred figures at virtually every table.

He thrust open the door. Alma glanced up from an order she was taking, and he thought he saw a fleeting look of annoyance cross her face as she pushed her hair back from her forehead. She picked up a tray from the table behind her; it was loaded with dirty dishes. Turning her back on him, she carried them out to the kitchen. He smiled thinly, acknowledging the customers he knew and checking the dirty plates to see what had been ordered. He recognised the swirls of grease and thin vestiges of egg yolk which meant the bus crews had been in, in force. They always mopped up the last traces of egg, beans and chips with double orders of bread and butter. An endless array of empty cups covered with a fine sprinkling of sugar and cigarette ash lay strewn across the tables in the back. He didn't have to ask Alma anything. He could see that she'd coped. Just!

Without waiting to don his khaki work jacket, he stacked a pile of dirty cups and saucers and carried them into the kitchen.

'Boy, did this place turn into a madhouse after you left,' Angelo grumbled loudly as soon as he caught sight of him. 'Sixteen orders of egg and chips, seven of beans and chips. Five pie and chips. The fat hasn't been off the gas ring in the last hour, and my hands are covered with spit burns . . .'

'Well, I'm here now.' Ronnie dumped his load into a sink that was already overflowing with dirty dishes, before taking his jacket down from the hook behind the door.

'What took you so long?'

'I stayed with Maud. She wasn't well, certainly not well enough to be left alone,' he explained abruptly.

'Gina could have stayed with her.'

'By herself?' Ronnie retorted derisively.

'You could have got Mama,' Angelo suggested in exasperation as he lifted yet another load of chips out of the fry basket.

'I could have, but I didn't,' Ronnie snapped, wondering why he hadn't thought of getting his mother. Angelo was right: it would have made more sense for her to have sat with Maud, than him and Gina.

'Two toasts, two boiled eggs and a pie, Angelo,' Alma shouted through the counter door.

'Damn,' Angelo swore. 'Just when I thought I could go home.'

'Finish that order and you can,' Ronnie conceded.

'Ronnie?'

'Yes?' Ronnie thrust his arms into the sleeves of his khaki coat. He could see a queue waiting to pay at the till. And the first rule of business that his father had hammered home to him was: *never* keep a man waiting when he wants to pay his dues.

'You will get a replacement cook as soon as you can, won't you?' Angelo pleaded. 'I don't mind helping out – '

'I'll start looking tomorrow,' Ronnie shouted testily as he went to the till.

Alma called off the orders of the customers as they reached him. 'One egg and chips – two eggs, beans and chips and extra bread and butter' – that one had to be a bachelor, but then who was complaining – 'one tea and a pie – one Oxo and a ham sandwich . . .' He found difficulty in adding up the money. Maud's face kept intruding into his mind: drained of all colour, like the clear lard they used for frying. He remembered her racking cough, wondered if she was coughing up shreds of her lungs along with the blood he had seen her spit into her handkerchief . . .'

'Ronnie!' Alma stared angrily at him, her temper rising precariously at his lack of response. 'Ronnie!' She repeated furiously.

He looked up blankly. The last man in the queue had gone. He glanced around the café: there were only a few late stragglers finishing their teas and Oxos. Without acknowledging that she'd spoken he picked up a damp rag and wiped down the counter, paying special attention to the area around the coffee machine. When he'd finished he lifted down a tin of coffee beans from a high

143

shelf, tipped half a handful into a small wooden grinder, and turned the handle. He refilled the coffee jug, setting it on the small oil burner to warm, making it as much for himself as for any customer. Then he took his rag and went to the tables to give Alma a hand. She'd piled a tray high with dishes and was carrying them into the kitchen. He wiped down the tables and chairs, setting them all back carefully into their allotted positions. No sooner had he finished than a dozen people walked in from the New Theatre across the road. Five minutes later they were joined by a small crowd who'd been to the Town Hall. Unlike the bus crews, they didn't buy much in the way of food. They wanted to linger in the warmth and light of the café, delaying for as long as possible the moment when they'd have to leave town for their homes, using the time they should have spent sleeping to relive the magic they had seen on stage.

Ronnie and Alma were kept busy making and serving coffee, teas, chocolates, Oxos, but mercifully few time-consuming titbits like toast. Just after the clock struck half-past eleven the door closed on the last customer.

'I think it's over,' Alma breathed heavily.

'Did you say something?'

'I was talking about the rush.' She dropped a tray piled high with cups and saucers noisily on to the counter.

'Yes, I suppose you're right,' he agreed absently. He took the dishes into the back. Angelo had tidied up before he left, but hadn't pulled the plug on the washing-up water. Ronnie tossed the cups and saucers into the sink and left them there to soak. Gina and Tina could do them in the morning. By the time he returned to the café Alma had upturned the chairs on to the tables and was sweeping the floor. He blew out the light beneath the coffee burner, and took down two cups from the shelf.

'Want a coffee?'

She shook her head. 'It'll keep me awake.'

'Chocolate, then?' he asked pleasantly, trying to make amends for his absence.

'Nothing. Thank you,' she snapped.

'Damn it all, Alma, I've said I'm sorry, what more do you want me to do?' he demanded, concealing the guilt he felt at leaving her and Angelo alone at the busiest time of the evening, behind a screen of anger.

144

'You know what more you can do!'

'No I bloody well don't. I've never seen you like this before. You're behaving like . . . like . . .'

'Like what?'

'Like a typical bloody woman,' he answered hotly. 'Like one of my sisters, if you must know,' he shouted. He felt betrayed by her mood. Other women threw tantrums or fell into black sulks, but not Alma. Never Alma. Good old reliable Alma. He propped his elbows on the counter, and sipped his coffee slowly in a determined effort to calm himself.

Keeping her back to him, Alma swept the dirt from the floor into a neat little pile.

'You still haven't told me what's the matter,' he ventured, struggling to keep his voice even.

Alma didn't reply. Picking up a tin dustpan, she swept the mess of crumbs and dirt into it. Holding it carefully aloft, she made her way through the kitchen and out to the dustbin in the back yard.

'Hello Alma,' Ronnie shouted sarcastically. 'Can you hear me? Can you see me? Am I invisible?'

She slammed the back door behind her, locking it ostentatiously, then glared at him, eyes blazing. 'You disappear for the busiest part of the evening leaving me and Angelo to work our fingers to the bone. Then you swan in two and a half hours later and casually ask me what's the matter?'

'I wasn't away for two and a half hours,' he protested mildly, picking on the one thing he could contest. He abandoned his coffee and walked over to her, settling his arm around her waist.

'You're quite right, it wasn't two and a half,' she retorted, stepping out of his reach. 'It was nearer three,' she said caustically, borrowing his habitual attitude.

'Alma, I'm sorry,' he repeated abjectly. 'I didn't realise the time . . .'

'You're so damned besotted with that . . . that girl,' she spat out the last word as though it left a foul taste in her mouth, 'you don't even know what time of year it is, let alone what time of day.'

'What girl?' he asked in genuine bewilderment.

'Ronnie Ronconi, you're the dumbest, stupidest man I've ever come across . . .'

145

'What girl?' he repeated, grabbing her wrist across the counter as she tried to pass in front of him.

'What girl?' she mocked, temper making her bold. For once she didn't care about security, or her job. 'What girl?' she asked incredulously. She attempted to pull her wrist away but he hung on to it, holding it tight. 'There is only one girl. The one you drive up and down the Graig hill every half-hour in your van for. The one you give all the best-quality chocolates and cream cakes in the café to, the one you wrap up in a blanket and bring down here "for a change of scenery",' she sneered.

He released her arm in disgust. 'You're being totally ridiculous. Maud's a child. She's Gina's age . . .'

'She may be a child, and she may be the same age as Gina, but neither of those facts have stopped you from falling head over heels in love with her,' Alma countered.

'You're crazy. She's ill. She's . . . she's . . .'

'Dying!' Alma supplied the word he couldn't bring himself to say. 'She's dying, it's eating you alive, and you can't even see it. Well I'm not going to stay around doing your dirty work and watching you cry for the moon. I've a life of my own to live . . .'

'Alma you're insane!' he cried out in exasperation.

'Have you fallen in love with her because she's dying, Ronnie? Is that it?' she taunted. 'Don't you trust yourself with a healthy girl because she might actually demand something of you, and stay around long enough to see that you give it to her? It's useful to fall in love with a girl who has one foot in the grave, isn't it? You can martyr yourself while she's alive, and mourn her forever more when she's dead, effectively keeping me and the rest of the world at bay.'

'I don't know what brought this on . . .' Ronnie began in disgust.

'Perhaps I just don't like the way you make me feel,' Alma interrupted. 'I look at Maud, and I look at you mooning over her like a lovesick dog, and I find myself wishing her dead. As if she won't be dead soon enough . . .' she burst into tears. 'Damn and blast you, Ronnie Ronconi!' She fumbled her way into the kitchen and grabbed her hat and coat. 'Damn you to hell!'

'Wait, Alma, you can't go out like that. I'll take you home.'

She ran headlong out of the café. By the time Ronnie reached the door she was half-way up Taff Street. He called her name just once, feeling foolish when Constable Huw Griffiths answered his cry from the doorway of the New Theatre, asking if there was anything wrong. Shaking his head, he retreated into the café and locked the door. Feeling restless, he went into the kitchen and heated fresh water to wash the cups and saucers he had dumped in the sink earlier. Alma had wound him up too much to sleep, so he decided he might as well work off his mood. There was certainly more than enough to do. When he finished the dishes, he scoured the pots and pans; afterwards he set about the gas stove, and the kitchen floor. Then it was the turn of the café. First the floor. He noticed a few spots on the walls, so he scrubbed those. When he couldn't find any more work to do he looked at the clock: its hands pointed to a quarter to three. He could hardly go home now. It simply wasn't worth it. Besides, he didn't want to go home. He wanted peace and quiet, one commodity that was always in short supply in Danycoedcae Road.

Freeing the key from his watch chain, he opened the cupboard at the back of the kitchen, took out a bottle of brandy, and relocked the cupboard. Picking up a glass, he struck a match and lit a stub of candle that swam in a saucer of congealed wax on the windowsill above the sink. Candle in one hand, bottle and glass in the other, he ascended the creaking staircase. The room he used as a bedroom was freezing cold and smelt of damp. He laid the saucer down next to the oil lamp. There was no oil in the reservoir, it must have burnt out the last time he and Alma had used the room.

Stripping off to his underpants, he flung back the sheets. They too felt cold and damp to the touch. He would have given a great deal to have had . . . have had who? Alma next to him? In her present mood?

For the first time he thought, really thought about what she had said. The woman was truly mad. It simply wasn't possible. He couldn't love Maud. Little skinny Maud, the baby he had warmed milk for when Bethan Powell had carried her into their High Street café after school. Bethan and his sister Laura, and Maud and Gina, two little girls playing with babies instead of real dolls. There had to be eleven years between him and Maud. Almost half his lifetime. He'd never thought of Maud as anything other than a kid. Sick as she was, she was still annoying and irritating, like . . . Gina and Tina. Surely he couldn't be in *love* with her?

Love was something else he'd hardly ever thought about. On the few occasions circumstances had forced him to consider it, he'd decided it was faintly ridiculous, and embarrassing. Something that affected others. Fools like Trevor Lewis and his half-baked sister Laura, who'd fussed and fretted for months before they finally managed to organise themselves a wedding. A wedding . . . was that what Alma wanted? Was that what all this fuss and emotion had really been about?

He shook a packet of cigarettes out of his shirt pocket and lit one on the flame of the candle. If she was unhappy with their 'arrangement' as it stood, all she had to do was say. He'd assumed that she was as content as he was. But for her to be jealous of Maud . . .

He puffed a smoke ring and watched it rise gently in the candlelight. The problem undoubtedly lay between him and Alma. The question was, did he want to marry her? Now marriage was something he *had* thought about. Even if he'd wanted to, he couldn't have avoided it, when his father brought up the subject every time they spent more than ten consecutive minutes together. And he only had to hint that he'd be home at a mealtime for his mother to invite one of the daughters of a fellow café owner. Italian, of course. Not that they'd ever made Alma feel less than welcome on the rare occasions she had attended any of their family gatherings. But then perhaps they'd never realised that Alma meant more to him than any other waitress they'd employed. Why should they, when he hadn't taken the time or trouble to explain his relationship with Alma to them? Possibly because both parents, Papa especially, had said enough to Laura when she'd brought home a non-Italian boy. Poor Trevor.

He wondered if he wanted Alma enough to go through what Laura had gone through to marry Trevor. Then he thought beyond the ceremony. Marrying Alma would mean settling down with her; living in a small house like Laura's; being with her all the time, in and out of the café; having no time to himself. And with his luck there'd soon be a parade of squalling babies who would grow into kids every bit as obnoxious and demanding as his younger brothers and sisters. If that's what marriage to Alma meant, he definitely preferred his present life.

But then, what was his present life? Work, more work, followed by the occasional foray into this bed with Alma, or a sneaky visit to one of his other 'ladies'. He had a sudden, incredibly vivid and real image of Maud. They were sitting side by side next to the fireplace in her back kitchen. She was smiling at him, and he could feel the weight of her hand in his. Only something was wrong. He sat up, almost dropping the cigarette when he realised what it was. The Maud in his vision had been plump, well; her cheeks bright with the warm glow of health, not the sickly spots of tuberculosis. The concept of Maud well elated him. Then it hit him. Alma was right. He did love her.

He was in love with a girl eleven years younger than him who had terminal tuberculosis. The thought wasn't a pleasant one. He'd always assumed that love would be something he'd be able to control, subjugate to his will. Maud was hardly the robust beauty he pictured whenever he'd thought of his future wife.

In a sudden, inspirational flash of self-knowledge, he realised why he'd never asked Alma to marry him. He didn't love her. Had never loved her. Instead he was in love with a scrawny kid who was going to die. He stubbed out his cigarette and lit another, staring up at the ceiling until the light from the candle flickered out.

He continued staring and smoking all through the night, watching the shadows move on the ceiling as Huw Griffiths paced at hourly intervals past the lamppost outside the window. He listened to the creaks and groans of the building, and heard the thunder of the milk train as it rattled noisily over the rails and out of the station. He didn't close his eyes once. And in the morning when the first customer tried the door of the café, he left the bed and dressed next to the untouched bottle of brandy.

He'd decided one thing and one thing only during his long vigil. He couldn't let Maud die. Not without putting up a damned good fight.

Chapter Fourteen

'Were you very late last night?' Laura asked as she lifted two pieces of bacon and an egg out of the frying pan on to Trevor's plate

'Not very.' Struggling to push his collar studs through both his collar and his shirt, he leant across the table and kissed her. 'I was back in bed by twelve.'

'Sorry I wasn't awake.'

'I didn't want you awake. Just warm. And you were exactly what a poor fellow needed after an hour spent in a freezing dressing room.'

'Dressing room?' Laura's eyes shone as she nosed out potential gossip. 'Anyone exciting?' she asked, taking the last piece of bacon for herself and sitting across the table from him.

'One of the chorus boys,' Trevor answered, through a mouthful of bacon and bread. 'The others insisted that he knocked himself out. Slipped while changing.'

'But you don't believe that?'

'Good God, woman, I can't keep anything from you, can I?'

'Don't blaspheme,' Laura lectured. 'And no, you can't. I know you too well. Tea?' she asked, picking up the pot.

He nodded, his mouth still full.

'What happened then?' she persisted, ferreting out the story with the dogged determination of a terrier in a rabbit burrow.

'Put it this way, he had one hell of a bruise on his chin. It almost matched the one I noticed on Haydn's fist.'

'Not Haydn Powell?'

'I don't know of any other Haydn who works in the Town Hall, do you?'

'You've got to be wrong on that score,' Laura remonstrated. 'Haydn wouldn't hurt a fly.'

'A fly maybe. After last night, I'm not so sure about chorus boys. The whole time I was there, he hung back in a corner, looking incredibly sheepish. And that's not Haydn.'

'Well?' She stared at him, an uneaten bacon sandwich in her hand.

'Well what?' he asked blankly.

'What did the chorus boy do to deserve it?' she demanded in exasperation.

'How should I know?'

'You were there,' she grumbled. 'If it had been me, I'd have found out a whole lot more.'

'I don't doubt that you would have,' he murmured drily.

A frown marred Laura's smooth forehead as a loud banging at the front door interrupted them. 'Oh heavens above, not again!' she said peevishly.

'Now who's blaspheming?' Trevor cut an enormous piece of bacon. Holding it poised only as long as it took him to shout, 'Come in', he shovelled it into his mouth.

'I hardly ever get to see you. We can't even eat a meal in peace . . .'

'You should have thought of that before you married me,' he broke in, taken aback by the vehement tone in Laura's voice.

'I did, I just assumed people would have the common courtesy to get taken ill outside of mealtimes, especially breakfast. And you're going to get indigestion eating like that. *Do* come in,' she shouted with exaggerated politeness, just as Charlie burst through the door.

'Sorry Doctor Lewis, Mrs Lewis,' Charlie apologised in his heavy Slavic accent. Not even an emergency could make inroads into Charlie's formal, courteous way of speaking.

'It's Maud.' Trevor rose from the table without waiting for Charlie to confirm his suspicions. 'My bag's in the front room,' he said as he picked up his coat from the back of the chair and disappeared into the passage.

'I'm sorry for disturbing your breakfast, Mrs Lewis,' Charlie apologised again as Laura made another sandwich of the remaining bacon on Trevor's plate.

'Can't be helped.' She gave him a tight little smile. 'How are they all coping?'

Charlie shrugged his massive, heavily muscled shoulders.

'They're coping,' he repeated unconvincingly.

'I know, they're coping because there's nothing else for them to do,' she murmured sympathetically.

'Charlie, if you're going back up, I'll give you a lift,' Trevor shouted from the hall. Charlie hung back as Laura preceded him. She thrust the sandwich she'd made into Trevor's hand.

'Give them all my love, especially Diana,' she said quietly. 'And tell Mrs Powell I'll be up to see her later.'

Trevor kissed her cheek as he opened the front door. Charlie followed him out on to the pavement.

'Jump in,' Trevor said to Charlie as he removed the starting handle from beneath the front seat. Charlie needed no second bidding.

'Don't forget to tell Mrs Powell I'll be up just as soon as I've washed the breakfast things,' Laura shouted to Trevor above the noise of the firing engine. He nodded to show he'd understood.

'How bad is it?' he asked Charlie as he steered the car up the Graig hill.

Charlie turned away from Trevor and stared out of the car window. As far as Trevor could see there was little except early morning workers and shoppers to hold Charlie's interest, but he seemed to find them fascinating.

'I'm sorry, did you say something?' Trevor asked. Between the noise of the engine, the accent and the distance, Trevor wasn't certain whether Charlie had answered or not.

'I didn't say anything,' Charlie replied flatly.

'She's haemorrhaging, isn't she?' Trevor said, hoping for a contradiction.

'It started when Diana took her breakfast up.' Charlie finally turned his head and faced Trevor. 'Diana has taken her breakfast up every morning since they've come back from Cardiff.'

'It's what I've been afraid of all along,' Trevor muttered.

Charlie was out of the car before Trevor parked it. He ran up the steps and opened the front door, slamming it straight into Evan who was sitting, head in hands, on the bottom stair.

Haydn and William, not knowing what else to do, were hovering in the passageway, effectively blocking the way into the kitchen. Eddie, anxious to be of help, had valiantly fought back his tears, and made tea in Elizabeth's chipped and cracked everyday cups. Because everyone had congregated at the foot of the stairs he'd carried a tray into the front parlour, laying it out on top of the dustcloth that covered Elizabeth's treasured mahogany octagonal table. He'd filled the teacups so much they'd slopped over into the spoons and saucers. The messy parody of a formal tea party was the first thing Trevor saw when he pushed his way into the house. He couldn't help thinking that it looked totally incongruous. Like a miner sitting in working clothes in the lounge bar of a pub.

He avoided meeting Evan's eyes as he asked, 'Upstairs?'

Evan rose silently and made room for him to pass. Trevor ran up the stairs two at a time. Diana was waiting for him in the doorway of Maud's bedroom. He felt as though he were walking into a hothouse. The atmosphere was stuffy, unpleasantly warm after the sharp freshness of the winter morning. He looked from Diana to the fire-grate, where lumps of coke still smouldered among the ashes. The Powells had evidently taken to heart his advice about keeping Maud warm. He recalled Elizabeth's moans about the cost and wondered if Evan had swallowed his pride and gone to the parish for help. Then he remembered the boys. They wouldn't have allowed Evan to succumb to the final indignity of the unemployed. There'd be no means test conducted on the Powell household while there was coal on the Maritime tip free for the thieving.

Elizabeth moved back, away from the bed, allowing Trevor his first glimpse of the unconscious Maud. She lay pale and still, like one of the waxwork effigies of murder victims in Louis Tussaud's in Porthcawl fair.

'There's nothing you can help with here, Diana,' Elizabeth voiced a harsh practicality Diana didn't want to hear. 'The best thing you can do is go to work. You don't want to lose your job now, do you?'

'I thought . . . I thought . . .'

Trevor sensed Diana's reluctance to leave Maud while her cousin's immediate future was so uncertain. 'I'll get Laura to call in the shoe shop and let you know how she gets on,' he promised quietly.

'Just go, Diana,' Elizabeth said brutally. 'You're holding up the doctor.'

Diana finally did as Elizabeth asked, closing the door behind her. But she didn't go downstairs. Instead she sat on the step outside Maud's bedroom, shivering, cold and clammy from the fear that crawled insidiously over her skin and invaded her mouth. She heard Trevor's footsteps echoing across the linoleum. There was a faint murmur of voices, but the thunder of her own heartbeat drowned out any intelligible sounds. One phrase kept repeating itself over and over again in her head. She mouthed the words, whispering them, not really knowing what she was saying: 'Please God, don't let her die. Please God, don't let her die. Please God . . .'

Trevor folded back the bedclothes; they were clean and fresh. He glanced around the room hoping to catch a glimpse of the soiled linen. He couldn't see anything.

'You changed the sheets?' he asked Elizabeth.

'I could hardly leave her lying in a pool of blood,' she retorted defensively. 'It was all over the sheets, the bedcover and the blankets,' she explained.

'Was it dark or bright blood?' He picked up Maud's wrist and checked her pulse. It was barely perceptible.

'Bright, I think,' Elizabeth faltered, suddenly unsure of her facts and wondering how much depended on the accuracy of her answer.

Trevor saw her uncertainty and didn't press her. Most of the mothers he'd seen in similar circumstances had succcumbed to hysteria when they'd faced what Elizabeth had faced that morning.

'How long has she been like this?' He replaced Maud's wrist gently on the bed.

'Since she stopped haemorrhaging,' Elizabeth's voice was brittle with emotion. He looked at her, wondering how much more she could take before she broke down. Removing his stethoscope from his bag, he unbuttoned the top of Maud's nightdress. She didn't even move when he examined her.

'I'm sorry, Mrs Powell,' he said as he finished. 'There's nothing more I can do for her here. She'll have to go into the hospital.'

'The Graig?'

The mixture of fear and condemnation in her voice struck a chord, making him effusive, almost garrulous in his defence of the hospital cum workhouse.

154

'The isolation ward is quite separate from the workhouse,' he explained, with all the emphasis on the word 'separate'. 'It's on the top floor, there's a fine view over the Maritime pit . . .' he hesitated as he realised what he'd said. An abandoned pit was hardly the view to cheer a sick young girl. 'You can see as far as the fields in Maesycoed,' he added with a forced heartiness. The fields of the farm above Maesycoed were the closest thing to countryside that could be seen from the windows of the hospital. He looked at Elizabeth. She was staring at him. He sensed that she could see beyond his pathetic attempts at bluster, read the damning, tragic diagnosis that he was struggling so hard to soften, if not conceal.

'How long has she got left, Doctor Lewis?' Elizabeth asked. She might have been enquiring about a train timetable. Unused to such direct questioning from the relatives of his patients, Trevor remained silent.

'How long?' she repeated flatly.

'I don't know,' he said slowly. 'I'm not lying,' he protested in the face of her obvious scepticism. 'I really don't know,' he insisted. 'It depends on how much damage has been done by the haemorrhage. On whether or not both lungs are affected . . . we might be able to collapse one if the other's healthy . . .' his voice trailed miserably. 'The sooner we get into the Graig and do some tests, the sooner I'll be able to give you a fuller diagnosis,' he finished on a more decisive note.

'I'll pack her things.'

'I'll go downstairs and send one of the boys for an ambulance. You do pay your extra penny a week for the use of one?'

'We do,' Elizabeth affirmed as she lifted Maud's suitcase down from the top of the wardrobe.

Diana was still sitting on the top step of the landing when Trevor emerged from Maud's bedroom. She looked up at him.

'How about you go downstairs and make a pot of tea for Mrs Powell,' he said kindly, recognising the girl's need to do something. 'I think she could do with one.'

'Maud?' she asked.

Trevor turned away from her. 'She's going into hospital,' he murmured. He could see Evan waiting for him at the foot of the stairs. He gritted his teeth, preparing to repeat the whole heart-rending, unpleasant process he'd just gone through with Elizabeth.

'There really isn't anything else left for us to do except go to work.' Charlie wrapped his arm round Diana's shoulders as they watched the ambulance bump its way over the rough, unmade road, down the incline, past the vicarage, and around the corner into Llantrisant Road.

'Come on, Di, cheer up,' William ordered, putting on a brave face.

'I'll get my coat.' Diana turned and walked back into the passage. She could hear Elizabeth already filling the wash boiler. Her aunt was obviously of the same opinion as Charlie. But then perhaps they were right, work might be the best antidote. Anything had to be better than moping around here thinking of Maud, and what she was going through right now.

'It's too late for me and Eddie to take out a cart now, Elizabeth,' Evan called into the washhouse from the back kitchen. 'I think I'll go to town and get a bucket of whitewash to do out the *ty bach*. Can you think of anything else that wants doing while I'm at it?'

'The front door could do with a coat of paint,' Elizabeth said sharply.

'Same green as before?'

'Of course. There's half a tin going to waste in the shed.'

'In that case I'll make a start and Eddie can get the whitewash.'

Eddie picked up his working and only coat from the row of pegs behind the door. Shiny with age and wear, it was a hand-me-down from Haydn, and as he was now outstripping Haydn in height, if not width, it was far too short for him. He stood next to Diana in the open doorway of the passage as he put it on.

'Beats me how they can think of things like that at a time like this,' he said sullenly.

'What else are they going to think about?' Charlie reprimanded gently. 'No one can even visit Maud until Sunday.'

'Well, they can still think of something other than the walls of the bloody *ty bach*!' he exclaimed savagely.

'Why don't you come down the market with Will and me today?' Charlie put on his own rough tweed jacket.

'And I don't want no bloody charity either,' Eddie retorted moodily.

'Not charity,' Charlie said evenly, making Diana wonder if

anything ever rattled him. 'It's gone nine o'clock. I'll be way behind with cutting up the small joints that the old people are always after. You can help Will serve, while I see to the butchery side. All right?' His ice-blue eyes focused confidently on Eddie.

'All right,' Eddie agreed, all belligerence and fight subsiding at the thought of spending what was left of the day on the market. His sister had been rushed to hospital. Was probably dying, if not already dead. And life was going on as though nothing had happened. Nothing at all.

The hands on St Catherine's church clock were pointing to a little after nine-thirty when Diana walked into Ben Springer's. She looked around, and her heart sank into her boots. She'd been so busy thinking of Maud that she'd forgotten about work, and Friday was the busiest day of the week next to Saturday. When the pits had been open, Thursday night was pay night, and the wives had got used to going into town to buy their dry goods and any bits and pieces they needed for the week, saving Saturday for fresh vegetable and Sunday joint shopping. There were no longer any pay packets given out in the closed and derelict pits on Thursday nights, neither was there enough money to stretch to buying all the necessities a family needed, but old habits died hard, and people still came into town in droves. And some of them even ended up in Ben Springer's. Not many: most children in the town went barefoot, even in winter. A few of the lucky ones – whose parents had succumbed to the demands of the parish and sold off everything they had that was worth selling in order to claim parish relief – were wearing boots that had been provided by the 'Miners Children's Boot Fund', a charity Ben had campaigned vigorously against, until he had been awarded the contract to supply them.

But that Friday morning Ben's shop looked as though the depression had ended. The tiny area that served as both shop and fitting room was packed. Ben Springer was bending over the shapely, elegant foot of Anthea Llewellyn Jones. He was crouched at just the right angle to look up her skirt, Diana noticed cynically as she surveyed the array of expensive gold leather spangled sandals laid out on the floor around them.

'You're late,' he barked as soon as he caught sight of her.

157

'I'm sorry, Mr Springer,' she apologised quickly. 'My cousin was rushed into hospital. She . . .'

'I'm sure no one here is the slightest bit interested in the comings and goings of your family,' he sneered, still smiling up at Anthea Llewellyn Jones. 'Get your coat off and start work.'

'Yes, sir.' Diana ran out to the back and tore off her coat. Hanging it and her handbag on a hook in the storeroom, she tucked in her blouse, pulled down her skirt and tried her best to smile. After all, she had something to smile about. She still had a job, and that job meant she could stay in the same town as Maud – and William. Anything had to be better than going into service. Even working for Ben Springer.

The first thing Maud saw when she opened her eyes was a shaft of brilliant sunlight cutting diagonally across the room. It illuminated a fairy world of gently swirling dust particles. Baby fairies waiting to be born, her sister Bethan had once called them. Overhead was a high, high ceiling. Far higher than anything she had ever slept under before. Green-painted metal rods stretched across it, locked into place three or more feet below the cracked plaster. She moved her chin down and saw dark green painted walls, the iron headboards of the bed opposite. Then, she realised where she was.

Tears escaped from beneath her eyelids as she closed her eyes and stretched out her body. She moved cautiously, feeling stiff, strange and awkward. But for all of that she was warm and reasonably comfortable. Crisp cotton sheets brushed against her skin, so different from the warm fleecy flannelette sheets that her mother insisted on using until the end of May. She could almost hear her lecturing, hectoring voice . . .

'Don't cast a clout until May's out.'

A rough, hollow coughing shook her back into harsh reality. She opened her eyes again and looked at the bed next to her own, where a painfully thin, dark-haired girl was sitting up, spitting into a jar that she held cradled in her hands. Seeing Maud, she smiled weakly in embarrassment as she closed the lid on the jar and returned it to the top of her locker.

'I hate doing it, but they make you,' she explained as she plucked at her bedcover with a clawlike hand and fell back on to her pillows.

'No one can make you do anything,' Maud retorted, unthinkingly voicing one of Eddie's favourite opinions.

'They can here. You'll see.'

'Our new arrival is awake, I see.' A sister, resplendent in dark blue uniform, the long sleeves finished with a set of immaculate stiffly starched cuffs, walked over to Maud's bed, a trainee nurse trailing in her wake. Maud categorised her as a trainee from the uniform. She knew it well: her sister Bethan had worn it, and not that long ago.

She had often wished for her sister's presence since Bethan had gone to London, but never more so than at that moment. If only Bethan could walk into the ward right now. Down the central aisle, pause at the foot of her bed . . .

'Turn back the sheets, Jones,' the sister demanded. The trainee speedily did as the sister asked. The sister retrieved Maud's wrist and proceeded to take her pulse.

'Am I in the Graig Hospital?' Maud asked, already knowing the answer, although she'd never been inside the place before.

'You are.'

'How soon can I go home?' Maud ventured timorously, remembering all the times she'd heard people say, 'It's easy enough to go into the Graig, plenty do it. But precious few ever come out other than feet first.'

'You've only just been admitted, my girl,' the sister said curtly. 'We'll have no talk of going home from you. Not yet.' She dropped Maud's hand abruptly, and went to the bottom of the bed where she picked up a clipboard that hung from the foot-rail. She scribbled something on it then peered at Maud over the top of her thick-lensed, metal-rimmed spectacles.

'You ever been in hospital before?' she demanded.

'No,' Maud faltered, debating whether to tell her that her sister Bethan had nursed on the maternity ward. Then she remembered all the gossip generated by Bethan's elopement and pregnancy, and decided against it.

'Well the rules here are simple and few,' the sister lectured in a voice that boomed down the long ward and back. 'If you need anything, anything vital like a bedpan that is, you call out loud and clear for a nurse. Understand?'

'Yes sister,' Maud squirmed in embarrassment.

159

'And give yourself, and us, plenty of time. My nurses and ward maids have more than enough to do without clearing up unnecessary messes. Understand?' she repeated.

'Yes sister,' Maud whispered, thoroughly humiliated.

'Just as long as you realise that you're only to call us when it's really essential. If you do that we'll come running when you shout. If you start calling us for any trivial reason we'll soon slow our pace. It's as simple as that. And you'll be the loser, because you, young lady, on doctor's orders are not allowed out of bed at all. Not to wash, not to toilet, not to anything. Your foot is not to touch the floor, under any circumstances. Am I making myself clear?'

'For how long?' Maud asked, horrified by the thought of doing absolutely everything – washing, eating, sleeping, even 'toileting' as the sister put it – within the confines of this one narrow bed.

'Until the doctor says otherwise. Are you comfortable now or do you want a bedpan?' the sister asked insensitively.

'I'm fine,' Maud lied wretchedly, fighting back the tears that were pricking at the backs of her eyes.

'When you cough, spit out whatever you bring up into the sputum jar on your locker. And mind you do just that. Don't try to swallow it. It will only contaminate your stomach. And then you'll have a sick stomach as well as sick lungs.'

'My father and mother?' Maud ventured.

'Your family know where you are.' The sister tucked in the sheet the trainee had wrenched out in order for her to take Maud's pulse, effectively sealing Maud back into her bed again. 'Visiting is for one hour every Sunday afternoon from two to three, and on Wednesdays from six to seven at doctor's discretion. If you get over-excited, you risk what little health you have, and that could result in doctor being forced to cancel your visiting.'

When Maud didn't reply to this standard conclusion to her pep talk, the sister actually wondered if she'd been too hard on the poor girl. She brushed aside the thought almost as soon as it entered her head. With only two qualified nurses, three trainees and two ward maids to see to the needs of thirty-five female patients in the various, but invariably messy, terminal stages of tuberculosis, it was probably just as well that the girl knew the full facts of her position from the outset.

160

Chapter Fifteen

Jenny knew that Maud had been taken into the Graig Hospital less than ten minutes after the ambulance had left the street. Glan's mother had waited only as long as it took her to check with Haydn (the politest and therefore the least likely of the Powell clan to tell her to mind her own business) that it was the Graig that Maud was being taken to, before walking into her back kitchen to take off her apron and put on her coat. As an afterthought she tied a scarf over her metal wavers, and picked up the worn and string-mended wicker basket that had held her shopping for the entire thirty-two years of her married life. Then she hurried down the Avenue (she hadn't used the short cut through Rhiannon Pugh's house since Rhiannon's lodger, Phyllis Harry, had given birth to an illegitimate child a few months before) and headed for Griffiths' shop, confident in the knowledge that *she'd* be the first one to impart the news to whoever was gathered there.

Jenny was serving old Mrs Evans who lived above the fish and chip shop opposite, with her daily ration of four Woodbines, two ounces of cheese and half a loaf of bread when Mrs Richards bustled in. Without pausing for breath, Mrs Richards interrupted the story that Mrs Evans was telling Jenny, about the boys that had taken to knocking her door after tying jam jars of unmentionable substances to her doorknob.

'You can just imagine,' Mrs Evans wailed dolefully, wringing her hands. 'It flew all over me. Soaking and sticking to my skirt and jumper, and the stink . . . you wouldn't believe the stink!'

'I would,' Jenny enthused, before she realised what she'd said. Hopefully Mrs Evans had changed her clothes and washed, but the odour of the *ty bach* still clung to her frail and aged frame.

'Maud Powell's in hospital!' Arms folded across her inadequate bosom, Mrs Richards stood back, waiting smugly for the impact of her news to hit her audience, but Mrs Evans continued to witter on about 'filthy boys' and 'foul stinks', oblivious to Mrs Richards' presence, let alone her gossip. 'Maud Powell's been rushed into hospital. The Graig,' Mrs Richards embellished her first revelation, but still failed to gain Jenny or Mrs Evans' attention. 'Maud Powell's in hospital,' she shouted at the top of her voice, yet she had to repeat herself twice before Jenny, odd cigarettes and triangular sweet bag in hand, turned to face her.

'She haemorrhaged,' she said proudly, airing her knowledge of the word. 'Haydn told me all about it,' she announced, heavily embroidering the truth. At the mention of Haydn, Jenny turned pale.

'Mind you,' Mrs Richards slammed a red, work-roughened hand down on the counter, 'I said when that one came home from Cardiff – I said to my Viv and my Glan – she's done for. They've worked her to death, that's what they've done. You could see it in her eyes. And her mouth. It always goes to the eyes and mouth first,' she asserted knowledgeably. 'The eyes go sort of dead looking, and the teeth – well they suddenly seem too big for the mouth, if you know what I mean.'

'The . . . the Powells. How are they?' Jenny stammered, concern for Haydn's family giving her the courage to interrupt Mrs Richards in full flow.

'They're how you'd expect them to be,' Mrs Richards sidestepped the question. 'Haydn's the one I talked to.' She gave Jenny a knowing look that set the girl's teeth on edge. 'But then, he stays calm no matter what. A born gentleman, that's what he is. Like his grandfather before him,' she asserted fondly, referring to Evan's father, not Elizabeth's. The Baptist clergy might command her respect, but never her regard.

'But what about the others?' Jenny persisted. 'Diana – '

'Now there's a baggage for you,' Mrs Richards pursed her lips, as though she'd just tasted a sour apple. 'She paints her cheeks and lips bright red. Curls her hair, even to go to work. After all the men. Just like her mother. And everyone knows what became of *that* one.'

'What's that you said, Mrs Richards?' Harry Griffiths appeared from the musty depths of the storeroom. Mrs Richards had grace enough to blush to the roots of her tightly pulled hair.

'Nothing, Mr Griffiths,' she said loudly. 'Nothing at all. Just called in to pick up a tin of tomatoes and a half-ounce of baccy for Viv's pipe.'

Harry reached down to one of the bottom shelves and picked up a small tin of tomatoes. He didn't have to ask what size she wanted; Mrs Richards never bought large tins. The Richards family always had toast for supper. The only one who ever had anything on it was her husband. He pushed the tin across the counter as he passed behind Jenny, who was engrossed in marking out a small portion of cheese to Mrs Evans' exacting requirements.

'The usual?' he asked Mrs Richards, as he rested his hand on the shelf where he kept cigarettes and tobacco.

'Please.' Mrs Richards' colour hadn't subsided at all.

'On the slate, I take it?' Harry demanded coldly.

'Only until Friday.' Mrs Richards tossed her head and turned her back on them. 'Good-day,' she murmured almost inaudibly as she went out through the door.

Jenny finished serving Mrs Evans. She felt sick and dizzy, and it wasn't just the smell of Mrs Evans. As soon as the door clanged behind the old woman she went into the storeroom and sank down on a pile of empy Corona crates.

'Shouldn't you go up there, love?' Harry asked solicitously.

'They won't be wanting me there, Dad. Not now. Not at a time like this.'

'You've got every right. You're practically family. You and Haydn . . .' he looked at her closely. 'There's nothing wrong, is there love?' he probed gently. 'You and Haydn have patched up that silly row, haven't you?'

'Oh Dad,' the single tear turned into a damburst. All the emotion she had pent up since their quarrel erupted into a paroxysm of hysterical weeping.

He knelt beside her. Wrapping his arms awkwardly around her, he tried to comfort her as he had done when she'd been a small child. Only this time, his hugs and murmurs of 'It'll be all right, love. You'll see, it'll all come right in the end' rang false, even to his own ears.

'We had such a stupid, stupid argument,' she sobbed. 'I haven't even seen him to talk to. And I don't know what to do. I love him Dad,' she pulled away from her father and wiped her eyes with the back of her hand. 'I love so much, it hurts,' she cried poignantly.

'I know,' he stroked the back of her head with his hand. 'I know,' he repeated softly, his heart twelve miles away in Cardiff prison.

163

'I didn't want you hearing it from anyone else.' Trevor heaped two sugars into the tea Ronnie had brought him and stirred it. 'Not after last night.'

'Last night?' Ronnie looked up warily from the stone-cold cup of tea he was hunched over.

'Gina stopped off to see Laura on her way down to town this morning,' Trevor said baldly. 'I saw her when I called back to finish my breakfast after I'd settled Maud in the ward. She told us that you'd taken Maud to the café last night.'

'The girl was all alone in the house,' Ronnie protested.

'And the girl should have been left all alone in the house!' Trevor exclaimed furiously. 'For heaven's sake, she has terminal tuberculosis. Do you know what that means? It means she can die at any moment. She could have died here, in the café last night,' he stressed, trying to bring home to Ronnie the enormity of what he'd done. 'And when her family find out that she haemorrhaged the morning after you took her out on a cold, miserable night . . .'

'I made her worse?' Ronnie looked so grief-stricken that Trevor relented, but only slightly.

'It's impossible to say what brought it on,' he conceded irritably. 'But it's fair to say that last night didn't help. What on earth possessed you to behave like an irresponsible lunatic? You of all people . . .'

'I love her.'

Trevor was so taken aback by the calm, matter-of-fact declaration that he dropped his cup. Tea spilled over the table and dripped down on to his trousers.

'Gina, cloth!' Ronnie shouted in an unnaturally flat voice for a man who had just made an earth-shattering announcement.

'But she's a child, she's a . . .' Lost for words, Trevor's splutterings ceased as Gina wiped his tea-stained trousers, and then the table.

'And I suppose you want me to bring you more tea,' she grumbled, picking up Ronnie's cold cup as well as Trevor's empty one.

'There's no hurry,' Ronnie said sharply. Gina knew when to leave her eldest brother alone. She retreated quickly to the front counter.

'I didn't exactly go looking for this,' Ronnie muttered as soon as Gina was out of earshot. 'It just – well it just happened,' he finished shortly, daring Trevor to reproach him.

'Does Maud know how you feel?' Trevor ventured.

'I don't think so.'

'You mean, you haven't said anything to her?' Trevor breathed a sigh of relief.

'Hardly. I only realised myself last night.' Ronnie looked around the café. It was half-past ten. Too early for the 'elevenses' rush of the market traders and bus conductors, and too late for the breakfasts of the council labourers. He and Trevor were sitting at a table for two, placed in the darkest corner of the back room. Too far away from the stove to be popular, its only advantage lay in the privacy it commanded.

'Alma and I had a row last night,' he explained briefly. After his sleepless, solitary night it was an incredible relief to talk to someone. And while he felt that Trevor might not understand him, he sensed that, being a doctor, Trevor was used to being entrusted with confidences and, unlike some people, would know how to keep them. 'The last thing Alma accused me of, before she flounced out of here in a foul temper, was being in love with Maud. I told her she was being ridiculous. That I couldn't possibly love Maud. I listed all the reasons why I couldn't. Her age, her illness. Then I thought about it . . .'

'All night, judging by the bags under your eyes,' Trevor commented cuttingly. He couldn't resist adding, 'Tina told Laura you didn't go home last night.'

'I slept – ' Ronnie grinned ruefully as he ran his hands through his hair, which for once wasn't smoothly slicked back. 'Or should I say, stayed here last night.'

'You do know she's going to die, don't you?' Trevor said brutally. 'The only question is when.'

'Can you get me in to see her?'

'Are you mad?'

'Come on, Trevor, you're a doctor in the Graig. That position must be good for something.'

'Visiting on the TB ward is strictly limited to Sunday afternoons and sometimes, at ward sister's discretion, Wednesday evenings. No more than two visitors to a patient, and anyone young, or deemed at risk, has to stay in the visitors' room behind a glass screen. Even if I managed to get you into the ward I doubt that her family would look kindly enough on you to allow you to take one of their precious places.'

'Then get me in outside of visiting,' he pleaded.

'It would be easier to get you into the vaults of the Bank of England. She's on an isolation ward, Ronnie. That means she's highly infectious – '

'There has to be a way. If I took a porter's job . . .'

'Now you're being ridiculous,' Trevor said in exasperation. 'Have you any idea of the number of applications we get for every job that comes up in the hospital?'

'Then at least take a letter to her for me?'

'Ronnie.' Trevor slowed his voice as though he were explaining complicated surgical techniques to a two-year-old child. 'She's seriously ill. When I saw her this morning she was in a coma. God knows what a letter out of the blue from you, telling her that you love her, could do to her at this point in her illness.'

'If you won't help me, then I'll find someone who will.' Ronnie turned away from him and pulled a loose cigarette from the top pocket of his jacket.

'Ronnie, be realistic,' Trevor pleaded, slightly alarmed by this strange, passionate man who had sprung from his usually laconic, always sarcastic, and generally easygoing brother-in-law.

'I am,' Ronnie stared intently at Trevor. 'Totally and utterly realistic. For the first time in my life I'm facing facts as they are, not as I'd like them to be. I'm in love. I know what I want. I want Maud. And if she hasn't got long to live, then the sooner we get together to spend whatever time she's got left with one another the better.' He rose from the table.

'I'll try to talk to her,' Trevor conceded at last. 'I can't do any more.'

'You'll find out how she is? Come back and tell me?'

There was such a look of anguish on Ronnie's face, all Trevor could do was nod.

Diana was still in Ben Springer's at eight o'clock that night. He had her humping boxes from the back of the shop to the front; stacking the shelves, rotating stock that wasn't selling to the top

166

shelves and filling the prime positions with new stock. And while she lifted, strained and struggled to carry heavy boxes of boots up and down ladders, he delicately arranged men's patent evening shoes next to gold and silver leather dancing slippers on the display stands in the window.

Hot, sweaty, tired, and worried because so little had been said about her late arrival that morning, Diana was too afraid to utter a single word of protest. What if he decided to dock her a day's pay? She'd already borrowed money off William against this week's wages. Money she knew he wouldn't ask for, but money she also knew he could ill afford to spare.

'Did you hear what I said?'

'Pardon, sir?' Jerking out of her reverie, she almost fell off the top rung of the ladder.

'I was talking to you, girl.' Ben had the till open, and was holding out his hand. 'Four shillings and sixpence. A week's wages less your shoe club money, and less tomorrow's shilling. Not that you deserve that much.'

'I'm happy to wait until tomorrow as usual, Mr Springer,' Diana protested mildly, her arms strained and aching as she descended the ladder with a full load of boxes. She tried, and failed, to stop herself from shaking. The last time she'd been offered money before the end of the week had been in the Infirmary. He couldn't be thinking of giving her notice. He simply couldn't be!

'Take it, girl,' he commanded tersely. She piled the boxes on a fitting stool and reached out nervously, delicately removing a sticky two-shilling piece and a half-crown from the sweaty palm of his hand.

'Thank you,' her voice dulled to a cracked whisper.

'And don't bother to come in tomorrow.'

'Don't . . .' her heart beat unnaturally quickly, and her throat went tight.

'I get girls in here every day looking for a job. The likes of you are ten a penny. This afternoon on my way to the bank, I called into the Labour Exchange.' He smiled maliciously, savouring the power he wielded over her. 'There was a girl there,' he continued gloatingly, 'just sitting, waiting for something to come along. Sharp young thing. Prepared to work five and half days a week for five shillings. And turn up on time every morning,' he finished pointedly.

'Mr Springer, I'm sorry,' Diana was too panic-stricken to cry. If she lost her job she wouldn't be able to pay Aunt Elizabeth her lodging money for more than a few weeks. And she wouldn't get any help from the parish. All they'd see was a young, single girl without ties who could take a domestic job anywhere in the country. They wouldn't take into account her need to be near Will, or Cardiff prison. 'Please Mr Springer. Please, it won't happen again I promise you,' she begged abjectly. 'Please. I'll make the hours up I missed. Give the shop a good going through on Sunday . . .' Her voice faded to a whisper as she tried to think of other ways – any ways – to make him change his mind and keep her on. He studied her for a moment. There was a peculiar smile hovering at the corners of the mouth, and she smiled weakly too, hoping against hope that the smile meant he was considering her offer. That she'd touched his pocket and instinct for a bargain, if not his heart.

'I'll work for five shillings a week, Mr Springer,' she begged swiftly, all sense of pride evaporating as the spectre of unemployment, real and terrifying, hovered at her elbow.

Ben continued to smile. He was wondering just how far she would go to keep her job. He eyed her up and down, noticing how the buttons of her tight cotton blouse strained over her bust. She was what he termed a 'ripe piece'. Plump in all the right places, a nice change from most of the scrawny, scarecrow women around town. And a lot more attractive than his wife, who had left plumpness behind for obesity more years ago than he cared to remember.

Diana realised he was eyeing her, and swallowed hard. She knew exactly what that look meant. When she'd left Pontypridd for Cardiff she'd hoped to put her mother's tarnished reputation, and the kind of advances it encouraged from men and boys, behind her. But events had soon led her to the conclusion that it must be something within herself that attracted the wrong sort of attentions, and made men see her as a loose woman, who was good for one thing, and one thing only.

Ben took a step towards her. Lifting his hand, he reached out, slowly, deliberately, and squeezed her left breast hard. She backed away, knocking over the pile of boxes that she'd heaped on the stool.

'I'll just pick these up.' Taking care to keep him within her sight, she crouched down and began to pick up the boxes. He squatted beside her. Sliding his hand up her skirt, he rested his damp fingers on the welt of her stocking top. His touch burnt through the lisle to her leg. She could smell his sweat, feel the unhealthy sexual excitement rising within him.

'Just a little touch . . .' His hand slid higher.

'No.' The voice was so resolute, so loud, Diana barely recognised it as her own.

'You *do* want to keep your job, don't you?' he leered as he moved his hand higher. Pushing up the elastic on the legs of her bloomers he stroked her naked thigh. 'Have you ever had it?' he murmured, lifting her skirt to her waist with his free hand.

'Mr Springer, please!' She jerked awkwardly to her feet, dropping the boot box she was holding on to his toe.

'That hurt,' he protested, rubbing his foot.

'It was meant to.'

She tugged down her skirt. Forgetting about her job, forgetting everything except the need to get out of the shop and away from Ben Springer as soon as possible, she ran into the stockroom to get her coat and bag.

'That's clever of you, Diana.' He followed her into the long, thin, windowless cupboard, and slammed the door hard behind him. She heard a dull thud as he leant heavily against it. 'It *was* too public out there. Where are you?' He clicked on the electric light. She was holding on to her coat and bag, gripping them as though they were lifelines. 'Don't stay all the way over there,' he murmured. 'Come closer.'

'No!' Panic set in as she realised she'd boxed herself in with no avenue of escape. He was leaning against the only exit. There was nowhere for her to run.

'Still pouting,' he laughed, displaying two rows of chipped, yellow and brown stained teeth. 'I'm not going to hurt you, only give you what you want. What you've been after ever since you walked through that door.'

'I'm leaving!' she announced, fear lending her false courage, but her bravado didn't extend to walking as far as the door. After what had happened in the shop she was afraid to move close to him.

'You do want to hang on to your job, don't you Diana?' he cooed softly. 'The six shillings a week that keeps body and soul together.'

'Not any more!' Terror heightened her voice to a screech.

'Such temper.' He stepped away from the door and swung round in front of her, trapping her in a blind cul-de-sac. The coat hooks were at her back, and shelves ranged either side of her. They lined the entire storeroom, even running above the door, narrowing the free space to a corridor of little more than two feet. Diana backed away, still holding her coat and handbag like a shield in front of her. He stepped closer and she cracked her back painfully aginst a hook.

'All I want is a good look,' he murmured thickly.

'Please Mr Springer, let me out,' she pleaded, more terrified than she'd ever been in her life before.

'Please Mr Springer,' he mocked cruelly. 'That's all you've said for the past ten minutes, girl. Please Mr Springer,' he repeated in a strained, high-pitched voice. 'Well now it's my turn to *please* you. Come on, you want it, you know you do. If you didn't you wouldn't have worn that tight skirt and blouse every day, or looked at me as coyly as you did, every chance you got. You would have sewn that button on tighter.' His hand darted across the front of her blouse, flicking open a button, exposing the valley of her breasts above her bust shaper. She lashed out and hit him, but her arms were hampered by her coat and handbag. He responded, slapping her soundly and squarely across the face and sending her reeling sideways into the shelves. The sharp edges bit into her forehead and cheekbones, she crumpled. Sliding down towards the floor, she fought frantically to remain upright. She opened her mouth, tried to scream, but terror muted her voice to a pathetic whimper. He laughed.

'If you find your voice, go ahead, scream,' he taunted. 'There's no one out there to hear you. You wouldn't be heard in the shop, let alone the street.' Releasing her hold on her coat and bag, she summoned all the strength she possessed. Heaving herself to her full height, she grabbed the bottom box of a pile, and tugged at it, meaning to throw it at him. But so little stock had moved out of the shop since the closure of the pits that the boxes were jammed tight against the ceiling. She screamed again, loudly this time, but her

170

voice echoed hollowly around her, muffled by the layers of boxes. He laughed, and she went beserk, fighting and spitting like a cornered alleycat.

'Let me out, let me out of here you . . .' she lashed out with her nails, ripping the skin off his right cheek. He lifted his hand, saw blood on his fingers, and his smile dropped as fury burnt in his eyes.

'Why you little bitch.' He clamped his hand over her mouth and, using his body as a weight, pressed her down on to her back. Her abdomen and limbs were crushed by the weight of him, her nostrils full of the rancid smell of his unwashed body. She tugged his hair, twisting the thin, greasy strands around her fingers in an attempt to get a tight grip. He heaved himself upwards, she took a deep breath as the pressure on her chest relaxed slightly, but the respite didn't last long.

He made a fist with his right hand, and using all the momentum he could gain in such a confined space, slammed it hard into the side of her head.

She was aware only of a wavering black smoke that blotted out most of the glow from the naked light bulb. Then the blackness was superseded by a crimson mist that carried with it an agonising awareness of pain. Bile rose on a turgid tide out of her stomach, but as she hadn't eaten anything that day, not even breakfast, there was nothing for her to bring up.

She lay back, stunned and sickened, her head and face burning with pain, utterly helpless as he plundered her body. The sharp sound of tearing cloth resounded in her ears as he caught the neck of her blouse and ripped it downwards, exposing her underclothes.

'Don't,' she mumbled weakly, through bruised and battered lips, as she felt his fingers clawing at her bust shaper. 'Don't!'

'You little slut, you're enjoying every minute of this. Girls like you enjoy it day and night. You can't get enough of it, you fuck because . . .'

She tried to close her ears to the string of obscenities that poured from his mouth. He was kneeling astride her, pinning her arms down with his massive calves. She struggled, succeeded in lifting her legs – a little. He used the opportunity to pull her skirt to her waist. Gripping the elasticated waist of her bloomers he

171

heaved on them until she screamed from the force of the elastic cutting into her back. Finally it snapped. He thrust his hand between her legs, making her squirm.

'That's it, go on,' he slavered, saliva drooling from his mouth on to her naked breasts as he played with them. 'Struggle, fight, go on girl, move . . .' Tears fell from her eyes as she realised he had her trapped. She wasn't going to escape. And her pitiful attempts to defend herself were only exciting him further. Crying at her own feebleness, vulnerability and impotence, she finally closed her eyes and fell still.

His hands sought and gripped hers. Pulling them above her head, he pinned them down together using only his left hand. He stretched out on top of her. Sliding his right hand between them he undid the buttons on his fly. She screamed as he thrust himself into her. Continued to scream the whole time he violated her. Until in the end she almost believed that she only existed as an extension of the pain, degradation and misery that he was inflicting on her.

Chapter Sixteen

Diana lay on the floor of the stockroom and cried. Her tears weren't slight or silent ones, but great racking sobs that threatened to tear her lungs apart. Even Ben, who had retreated to the far side of the stockroom to button his fly and tuck in his shirt, was unnerved by the primitive, bestial sounds she was making. He combed his hair back from his face with his fingers, staring in horror when he saw blood on them. He touched his cheek tentatively. It was wet. Was the blood his or hers? He yelped as he found a scratch she'd given him.

He looked at her, disgusted with what he saw. A weak, sordid, crumpled heap of flesh. There were great rents in her blouse, blood on the bloomers that lay, torn and discarded, beneath her.

'Stop whining, you stupid cow,' he demanded, using the adjective he applied to his wife when they had one of their frequent rows. 'Pull yourself together. You know you wanted it.'

Diana felt too used, too broken and too dirty to contradict him. She even began to wonder if she had wanted 'it', as he called the eternity of rough, banging, bruising and degrading violation. She'd wondered and dreamed about love and marriage for so long. Well now she knew exactly where all the sweet songs, tender words and poetry led.

Laying her head down on the musty-smelling floor, she closed her eyes. How could any woman want to do anything like that willingly? How did married women cope? Did they have to put up with it night after night or only sometimes?

'Cover yourself, girl,' Ben commanded abruptly as he opened the door into the shop. She heard him leave the cupboard. The noise diminished; she didn't even realise she'd been making it. Tugging down her skirt, and clutching the tattered remnants of her blouse in her fist, she curled into a ball, faced the floor, and wished herself dead.

The pain between her legs was agonising. His sweat, now cold and damp, clung to her bare skin. The stench and the brutality of him permeated every inch of her. She heard the stockroom door open again, but she kept her face turned to the floor. It didn't matter whether he was there or not. Nothing mattered any more. She just wanted to die where she lay. It would be bliss to sink into nothingness, not to feel anything, not ever again.

'Here.' He leant over her and she screamed. It did matter after all! She might not die quickly, and she couldn't bear to repeat what he'd put her through. She wouldn't be able to stand it . . .

'It's your coat,' he announced irritably, dropping it on top of her. 'For God's sake girl, you can't lie around naked. Put it on.' She struggled to her knees. Careful to keep her face averted from his, she did as he asked. He caught her roughly by the elbow and yanked her to her feet. She stared down at the floor. Her bloomers lay there, torn and stained. He picked them up and tried to ram them into the pocket of her coat, but she screamed again when he stepped near her. Only this time she didn't stop. She just kept on screaming and screaming, until the noise in her head blotted out everything else. Even his presence beside her.

He slapped her across the face. Hard. Her cheek stung. The imprint of his hand stood proud and crimson on her skin, but he failed to silence her. He lashed out repeatedly. She went crashing into the shelves again, hitting her head where she'd hit it earlier. He grabbed her arm and propelled her out through the door before she had time to fall to the floor.

She was aware of a cold draught. Looking down, she realised that the front of her coat was open, exposing her breasts. Her thighs were cold, wet and naked beneath her skirt. Her stockings were damp, stained with sweat and blood. Turning her back to the window, she hit away his hand. Trembling like a leaf she began to fasten her coat buttons, slowly, one at a time. Her fingers were huge and swollen; stiff and suddenly arthritic, they refused to obey her commands.

The huge brass till clanged open. Ben walked towards her. 'Here – ' he held out a five-pound note – 'Here, take it,' he commanded impatiently, thrusting it at her. 'After all, you earned it,' he jeered.

'You . . . you . . .' finding her voice at last, Diana could not find adjectives foul enough to express her opinion of him.

'See you, same time tomorrow?' he asked calmly.

174

'I'll never set foot over this doorstep again as long as I live,' she hissed. 'But you'll see me in court. I'm going to the police. I'll tell your wife. I'll tell – '

He threw back his head and roared with laughter. Diana hadn't been the first assistant he'd had in the stockroom, and in his, granted somewhat limited, experience, he'd learned that they were generally all right when they got to the threatening stage. And experience had also taught him how to handle the threats.

'Tell them what, dear?' he taunted. 'That you stole five pounds out of the till, and when I asked you about it you tore your clothes and threatened to cry rape? Your word against mine, and we all know whose word everyone will believe.'

'You hurt me,' she whispered hoarsely. 'I'm bleeding.' She looked down at her stained stockings.

'Everyone knows that a girl like you has a different boy every night. I've seen you myself in the café talking to the Italian boys. Not to mention Wyn Rees from the sweet shop. Now there's an odd one for you to make a beeline for,' he taunted. 'More woman than man. One word about him will be enough to set the magistrate thinking about your tastes in the bedroom department. And then there's that fair boy you wave to whenever he passes.'

'He's my cousin!'

'There's cousins and cousins. And things are not always what they seem.'

'You swine. You bastard . . .' the words she couldn't think of earlier tumbled out one after another.

He caught hold of her wrists and twisted them painfully.

'One more sound out of you and I'll spread it from the Graig end of town to the Common that you're nothing but a common prostitute. Only being your mother's daughter, you fancy yourself. Set your price higher than the vulgar herd who pick up their customers in station yard. A fiver as opposed to the bob they charge for a quickie in a shop doorway.'

'I suppose that's why I work here for six bob a week . . .'

'A girl without visible means of support soon gets picked up by the police. Your mother would tell you that if she was around,' he sneered. 'But then she didn't get it right either, did she? It wasn't enough that she was Harry Griffiths' whore. She had to steal as well. Like mother, like daughter. Thief and whore, just like Mam.

175

That's what you are, a thief and a whore,' he spat the words at her. 'And there's no one who'll see you otherwise, Diana Powell. Not when I've finished talking to them. No one.'

His laughter and his threats followed her as she ran sobbing out of the shop and down Taff Street clutching her coat over her naked bosom. A couple walking towards her stopped and stared. She ducked into the doorway of an empty shop. There were no lights there, so she felt safe, hidden by the darkness. She took a deep breath, made an effort to still the tremblings of her body, and smoothed back her hair.

As soon as she was able, she walked on, checking her reflection in the shop windows as she passed. She couldn't catch a bus or a tram. Not looking like this. If she walked up the Graig hill slowly, sticking to the shadows and the side-streets, it would give her time to calm down. Maud wouldn't be needing her blouse for a while. She could dump it together with the rest of her clothes over the mountain. If she was quick and careful she could run into the house and straight up the stairs. Change into her nightie before her aunt had a chance to see her. Whatever happened, she daren't let any one, especially Will, find out about this. He was hot-headed at the best of times. He'd give Ben a good hiding, and then Ben would see him put in jail too. Better she go into service and away from Pontypridd than that. Better anything than that.

'I didn't know you came down here.' Eddie rolled around to the side of the rink where Jenny was sitting talking to Tina, Gina and Will – who had mysteriously disappeared ten minutes after inveigling him into spending sixpence of the money Charlie had paid him for working on his meat stall – in the roller-skating rink in Mill Street.

'First time I've been here,' Jenny smiled, taking the opportunity to move away from the others. Will and Tina were getting on her nerves these days. Always flirting with one another every opportunity they got.

'Haydn picking you up?' Eddie asked.

'No,' she said quickly. Too quickly.

'No, of course not,' Eddie murmured. 'This place must close a lot earlier than the Town Hall.'

'I thought you went training every night,' she said, changing the subject.

'I do. I'll probably go down the gym later. I just came with Will after we'd finished on the market.'

'You working on the market now, then?'

'No. Only today. After . . . after . . . well it was too late to take the cart out,' he finished tersely.

'I heard about Maud. I'm sorry Eddie,' she said softly. 'But as my mother said over tea tonight, you can never tell with lung disease. The doctor told my Aunt Phoebe she wouldn't live to see her eighteenth birthday,' she smiled impishly, and Eddie noticed, not for the first time, what a beautiful smile she had. 'Well Dad says that he's sure my Uncle Arthur wishes Aunt Phoebe never proved the doctor wrong. According to Dad, he only married her because his family was nagging him to find a wife, and he finally settled on Aunt Phoebe because he didn't think she was long for this world. They've been married thirty years this year, and now she's twenty stone, and – ' she lowered her voice and put her mouth close to Eddie's ear, '– a right old nag,' she confided secretively.

'I hope Maud lives to see herself married for thirty years,' Eddie said sombrely. 'You're not having me on, are you?' he demanded suspiciously, always on the lookout for people making fun of him.

'I wouldn't, Eddie,' Jenny protested seriously. 'Not about something like that.'

'Want an orange juice?' he asked, looking longingly at the wooden trestle table set out against the back wall where a woman was dispensing drinks into small glasses, and selling bars of Five Boys chocolate from a cardboard box.

'I've used my free ticket,' she said shyly, referring to the one that was handed over for the sixpence that also bought entrance and boot hire.

'So have I, but Charlie paid me today. I'll treat you,' he offered generously.

'All right, if you let me buy the chocolate.' They sat side by side on the fringe of the area set aside for roller-skating, and took off the skates they'd hired.

'My feet feel wonderful,' Jenny beamed as they walked over to the counter. 'Like I'm walking on air.'

'I know just what you mean.' He pulled two pennies out of his pocket. 'Two glasses of orange juice please, Mrs Williams.'

'And two bars of Five Boys,' Jenny added, digging into her own purse.

Eddie dumped his skates under one of the small card tables dotted around the room and went back for the orange juices. He'd expected Jenny to sit opposite, but she sat beside him. Resting her elbows on the rickety table, she wrapped her long, thin fingers round the glass. Her perfume was the same one Maud and Diana used. He found himself staring at her hair. It was blonde, lighter than Maud's, almost white in colour.

'So?' Jenny questioned tremulously. 'What's big brother doing these days?'

'Haydn?' Eddie looked at her in surprise. 'You'd be better placed than me to answer that question.'

'Not any more.' She unwrapped first the paper, then the silver paper from her bar. Staring at the faces stamped on the squares, she concentrated on the boy who was crying. He looked as miserable as she felt.

'You saying, you and our Haydn aren't courting any more?' Eddie stared at her, dumbfounded.

'Haven't seen him in a week,' she said with a studied carelessness that she hoped concealed her pain.

'Oh I know you two,' Eddie coloured in embarrassment. 'You'll soon get back together again.'

'Not this time.' She snapped the miserable boy off the chocolate bar and ate him. It was most peculiar: she felt happier as soon as she'd swallowed the last trace of chocolate in her mouth. 'But then,' she gave Eddie a totally artificial smile, 'there's plenty of other fish in the sea.'

'So they say,' he muttered, thinking of the chorus girl Daisy, and the romp they'd enjoyed in Pontypridd Park. Pity there weren't more around like her, but then, he didn't often have the kind of money in his pocket that he'd spent on her, and he had the feeling that the likes of Daisy wouldn't be interested in a man with only two bob. He looked at Jenny's empty glass, remembered the orange juices and amended two bob to one shilling and ten pence. What the hell, may as well make it one and nine. 'Want another drink?' he asked, nursing his remaining half-glass of juice.

178

'Only if you take me home afterwards. I promised my mother I'd be in by nine.' She hadn't realised just how handsome Haydn's brother was until now. He was still young, a whole year younger than her, but he'd lost the scrawny boyish look that a lot of boys carried, even into their twenties. She noticed his muscles rippling under the patched jacket he was wearing. And in contrast to Haydn he was so dark. At that moment she felt his deep brown eyes and black hair would outshine the looks of any number of blonde Adonises.

'Are you sure I should?' Eddie asked earnestly. 'It's not that I don't want to,' he added quickly as an odd expression crossed her face. 'It's just that if Haydn should find out . . .'

'Even if he did find out, it's nothing to do with him any more. I told you. Haydn and I are finished. He doesn't want me.' Jenny fumbled in her pocket for a handkerchief, and dabbed her eyes with it. 'He doesn't even talk to me any more. If he sees me he crosses the street. And I swear he walks down the hill along Leyshon Street and the steps into Graig Street rather than pass the shop.'

'I can't see our Haydn doing that,' Eddie protested half-heartedly, suddenly remembering his brother's recent sullen moods.

'Look, the last thing I want to do is come between brothers, Eddie,' Jenny said quietly. 'It's just that . . . that . . .'

'What?' he demanded curiously.

'Oh nothing.' She put away her handkerchief and broke off another piece of chocolate.

'Go on, tell me.'

'No you'll laugh.'

'I promise I won't.'

'You'll think I'm silly, but,' she looked at him and he felt himself drowning in the clear liquid blue of her eyes, 'I've always liked you, Eddie. But then, what girl wouldn't? You're good-looking, and so strong.' She fingered the muscles on his arm playfully, taking care that William should see her. What she was doing was awful, but then she had to get Haydn to talk to her somehow. Even if she only succeeded in making him shout at her for playing around with his brother.

*

179

Diana kept to the shadows as she made her way through the town. Shoulders hunched, shivering as the cold artificial silk lining of her coat brushed against her naked skin, she walked quickly and purposefully. Like a wounded animal returning to its lair, she headed towards the Graig, and subconsciously to a home in Leyshon Street that no longer existed. At painful, spasmodic intervals the enormity of what Ben Springer had done to her hit her anew, and she choked back a sob.

Occasionally she heard footsteps ringing on the pavement. Whenever that happened, she slowed her step and lowered her head, staring down at her feet until the sound died away, either ahead of or behind her.

She couldn't help feeling that people were hiding behind the windows and in the shadows, watching her, laughing, knowing that she was practically naked underneath her coat. That they'd heard and approved of the names Ben Springer had called her. Hating herself, loathing what Ben had turned her into, she felt that she deserved to be stared at contemptuously, just as the old couple had done earlier. That the unspeakable things Ben Springer had done to her in that back room somehow made her less than human, that she really was the whore he'd have her believe she was.

'Diana?'

She heard someone call her name, but she kept her head down. When the cry was repeated she quickened her step, put her collar up and hid her face from view. She couldn't bear to look at or talk to anyone she knew. Not now. All she wanted was to get home . . . home! That was a joke! Home was her mam's warm, cosy, comfortable back kitchen. Her tears flowed faster as she realised the only place she had to go to was her Aunt Elizabeth's house. What if her aunt came out of the kitchen and walked into the passage before she managed to reach the safety of her box room? Aunt Elizabeth never missed the slightest thing. It was too much to hope that she wouldn't notice her filthy, bloodstained stockings, or her torn blouse.

Her fingers closed reluctantly around the ragged and damp bloomers that Ben had stuffed into her pocket. They were the most damning piece of evidence. Even if she threw them away, Elizabeth would miss them in the wash. After all, she only had three pairs. . .

180

'Diana! Diana!' The voice grew louder. She heard the light patter of footsteps running after her. 'Diana, what have I done?' Wyn's soft feminine drawl wafted towards her through an all-enveloping mist of misery and shame. 'Diana?' He grabbed her shoulder, and she broke away from his grasp. 'My God!' He was staring at her, horror at what he was looking at etched into his shocked and startled face.

Tears were streaming down her cheeks, mingling with the rainwater and blood that oozed persistently from a cut on her temple.

'Dear God, what happened to you?' he demanded. Gripping her hand tightly he pulled her into the shelter of the entrance to Woolworth's store. She tried to slip away from him, but his fingers banded like an iron cuff on her wrist. The light from the windows cast a yellow glow over her strained and terrified face. She turned aside so he couldn't look at her.

'Leave me alone.' She struggled to escape his hold on her. 'Please just leave me alone,' she repeated dully.

'That's just what I'm not going to do,' he said determinedly. 'You can't walk around the streets looking like this. God alone knows what could happen to you.'

'Nothing worse than what already has!' The tears started again. Hot, scalding and bitter.

'Come on.' Still holding her wrist, he put his arm round her shoulders.

'Don't touch me!' she screamed as hysteria threatened to take over once again. 'Don't you *dare* touch me. Don't you dare . . .'

'I'll let you go if you promise to come home with me,' he said in a voice full of concern. It didn't take a genius to look at the state of her, put it together with her insistence on not being touched and guess what had happened. 'Come on, you'll be safe enough,' he coaxed gently. 'My sister will be at home.'

She looked at him, and he shivered. Her eyes were cold, dead. He felt as though she were looking right through him. Then suddenly, without warning, she uttered a dry, choking cry and stretched out her arms. He gathered her close to him. Caressing the back of her head with his fingertips, he pulled her head down on to his shoulder.

'Come on, Diana.' He wrapped his arm round her waist, as

much to support as comfort her. 'Someone's coming,' he murmured. 'Let's go before they get here.'

The silence between them was terrible. The only sounds in the street were her occasional, quiet choking sobs and the patter of the rain falling into the dark, slimy pools of water that had gathered in the cracks of the broken slabs in the pavement. 'My father forgot to take his pills to work with him tonight,' he explained matter-of-factly as he turned left, guiding her into Market Square. He felt he had to talk about something – anything to break the harsh, rasping monotony of her sobs. 'He always calls into the shop I run next to the New Theatre on his way home from his High Street shop,' he continued conversationally. 'He insisted he couldn't walk another step without them, so he's looking after my shop for me while I go to the house to get them. But there's no hurry for me to rush back. I can always get little George next door to run down with them. It'll take half an hour for them to work, and George can stay with him just in case there's a surge of unexpected customers. We can have a cup of tea together . . .'

'I don't want to be any trouble.' She fought, and failed, to keep her voice steady.

'Dad really will be all right for a while. The rush rarely starts in the shop until the end of the second house in the theatre, and that's not for another hour and a half. You've given me a good excuse to skive off.' He smiled at her, and she felt safe. It was ironical. The very reason that made most men, including William, Haydn and Eddie, dislike Wyn so much was at that moment Wyn's main and only attraction. If he preferred men to women, he was about the only man in Pontypridd who wouldn't want to do the disgusting things to her that Ben had done. And the one thing she was sure of at that moment was that she didn't want another man to touch her in that way again – ever.

Chapter Seventeen

Wyn hesitated at the entrance to the Co-op Arcade. It was the way he usually walked home from the New Theatre, but the display lamps that blazed brightly in the windows illuminated the covered walkway with a light as bright and harsh as daylight. And he didn't want to risk Diana catching sight of her reflection. She couldn't possibly realise just how filthy and dishevelled she looked. He glanced sideways at her, hoping to avoid catching her eye. She looked sad, lost and incredibly pathetic. Embarrassed by his indecision, he walked on briskly, leading her up Penuel Lane. It was in darkness. He held her elbow as they crossed Gelliwastad Road, and began the climb up the hill to Tyfica Road.

Diana allowed him to drag her on. Her earlier hysteria had given way to a cold, anaesthetising numbness. It was easier to walk alongside Wyn than think of reasons why she shouldn't. To protest would have meant expending effort and energy, and she had neither. Supporting her lightly, he helped her up a short, steep flight of steps to the front door of a huge semi-detached house. A light shone through the stained-glass panel that decorated the front door, puddling the black and white tiles on the porch floor with pools of brilliant blue and crimson.

'I'm sorry,' he apologised as he turned the key that was protruding from the front-door lock. 'It looks like my sister is out. She always leaves the hall light on when she goes to chapel meetings.'

'It's probably as well.' Diana had just caught sight of herself in the hall mirror as she stepped aside. 'I look like something dead that the cat dragged in.'

'Let me take your coat.'

'No!' her voice rose precariously again.

'Look, you're in such a state, why don't you have a bath,' he offered tactfully. 'You don't have to worry about clothes. I'll get some of Myrtle's.'

'Myrtle's?' She looked at him with large, frightened eyes.

183

'My sister,' he explained patiently. 'There's plenty of-hot water,' he added persuasively. 'We never let the kitchen range go out, and it heats the water in the boiler upstairs.'

The thought of washing away the taint of what had happened to her – the smell of Ben, her blood, his sweat – of soaking her bruised and battered body in a bath was like being shown a glimpse of heaven.

'The bathroom's the first door opposite the top of the stairs.'

She halted indecisively. 'Are you sure your father and sister won't mind? I'm in such a mess.' The tears began to fall again. Quietly this time, Wyn noted gratefully.

'No one is here to mind,' he reassured her. 'And even if they were they'd be saying the same as me. There's no way you can go home as you are. I'll get Dad's pills and give them to George. Then I'll dig out some clothes for you.' He walked down the passage towards the back of the house. She panicked.

'Don't leave me,' she shouted.

He stopped and looked back at her. 'Come with me if you like.' He tried to keep his voice calm, neither insistent nor offhand. He went into the kitchen and switched on the light. There was a bottle of pills on the windowsill in front of the sink. Large blue and red ones. He picked them up and put them in his pocket. 'Here, sit down,' he suggested. She took one look at the highly polished wooden chairs and shook her head.

'I'm too dirty,' she murmured shamefacedly.

He filled the kettle and put it on the range to boil. 'You'd like a cup of tea wouldn't you?' he asked.

She studied the shining, polished brass rail on the range, the ironwork newly blackleaded, the copper saucepans polished and set out on the rack to dry, the huge dresser filled with gleaming china. It all looked so affluent, so calm, so sane, and so ordinary. She broke down again. A single glimpse of normality was too much for her after the madness of the storeroom.

'Do you want to talk about it, Diana?' Wyn asked quietly. She shook her head mutely.

'Then I'll show you where everything is upstairs.' He walked ahead of her, and she followed. Gripping the smooth, dark, mahogany banister rail, she ascended the stairs slowly. It was strange. She'd never thought of Wyn as being either 'crache' or rich, yet living in a house like this, he was obviously both. The hall was tiled to a point half-way up the wall, with beautifully designed squares in a multicoloured dark flower pattern, topped by a shining dado of deep-blue and brown tiles. She touched the dado with her fingertips. It felt cold. She looked down: her feet were sinking into the deep pile of the carpet. It was wool, not jute, brown like the tiles.

The bathroom door was open. Wyn sat on the edge of the bath, put the plug in and turned on both taps. A cloud of steam wafted into the air.

'You don't even have to carry water!' she exclaimed.

'Carry water?' he looked at her uncomprehendingly for a moment, then he coloured, ashamed of his insensitivity. 'Sorry, I suppose I'm so used to this I tend to forget that not many people have plumbed-in baths. Check the temperature's all right for you.' He brushed past her, embarrassed by the intimacy of their situation. 'I'll get you clean towels and some clothes.'

He returned with a large, thick, white fluffy towel, and a smaller one. 'For your hair,' he explained as he handed it to her. 'These were Myrtle's, she's put on a lot of weight lately. Middle-age spread,' he grinned wryly as he held out a neat pile of beautifully pressed and folded clothes. 'She put them into the rag-bag last week. Lucky for you the ragman hasn't called.'

'My uncle's a ragman.'

'Here, take them,' he thrust them at her. 'Myrtle will be happy to know they've been put to good use.' She flicked through the pile. There was a good blue serge skirt, a pair of long, thick woollen socks, a white starched cotton petticoat and a pair of pink silk bloomers.

'I can't take these, they're all brand new,' she protested.

'You can't go home as you are,' he said practically. 'I couldn't find a white blouse so this is one of my shirts.'

'I can't possibly . . .'

He was staring at her. She looked down and saw that although the top buttons of her coat were firmly fastened, the bottom ones weren't. For the first time she noticed that her skirt was as heavily bloodstained as her stockings.

'I'm sure young George next door will be only too happy to give Dad a hand in the shop until I get back. So I'll wait for you to finish. Lock the door behind me. I'll have the tea brewed by the time you've finished and dressed. And if you hear the back door opening and closing, don't worry. It'll only be me going next door. I promise I won't be gone for more than a minute or two.' He patted the pocket he'd slipped the pills into. 'Help yourself to soap, eau-de-Cologne and talcum powder. It's on the washstand.' He closed the door behind him.

She listened. When she heard the creak of the stairs, she turned the key. Safely locked in, she walked over to the bath and turned the taps off. She pulled her bloomers out of her coat pocket and threw them on to a wooden drip tray. Then she stripped off her skirt, stockings and petticoat. She tossed the rags – all that was left of her blouse, bust shaper and liberty bodice – on top of the pile.

She looked around for soap. The washstand was crammed with bottles and tins. In the centre of the display that reminded her of Boots the chemist's window, was a straw basket, packed with small, heavily perfumed bars. She'd never seen such small soaps before. Taking one, she lowered herself into the water. A wooden scrubbing brush lay in the steel bath-rack. She picked it up and began to scrub, and scrub. And scrub!

For a Friday night, the café was relatively quiet. Alma had clearly thought better of her outburst. She had walked in at her usual time, murmured a barely audible 'good-evening' to the café in general and nobody in particular, put on her apron, and began work on clearing the tables. Ronnie nodded to her absently, as he paced uneasily between the kitchen, where Tony was heating pies and frying chips, and the café, where Angelo was serving. He was barely aware of Alma's presence. All he could think of was Maud. He'd been such a fool. Wasted so much time. He could have told her last night – any night – that he loved her. But like an idiot he'd waited until she was incarcerated in the Central Homes, totally beyond his, or anyone except a doctor's reach. If only he was Trevor . . .

He racked his brains coming up with plans, each more ridiculous and outrageous than the last. If he tried to climb the ten-foot-high walls, he'd be seen. Not to mention hurt. There were precious few toeholds in the well constructed stonework. If he went through the main gate the porter would challenge him.

The side gate in Albert Street was only used for delivery vans. He could try taking the Trojan through, but he didn't have anything to deliver; besides, it was locked at night.

Thoughts writhed and slithered through his mind until he felt as though he would go mad from too much thinking. As soon as he conjured up one idea that he felt might work, he lost it, forgetting half of it before it was even conceived. Eventually his restlessness got the better of him. Putting on his street coat, he announced he was slipping out for a while.

He stood on the pavement outside the café, breathing in the damp, cold night air. He had to do something positive about Maud. He simply had to.

He debated whether or not to go and see Evan Powell and announce that he was in love with his daughter. But then what if Evan should talk to Maud, and Maud deny all knowledge of his affection? It would be better to break into the Graig Hospital and see her first. If only – if – a smile brought a strange animated light into his eyes.

He turned on his heel and returned to the café. Heading straight for the kitchen, he opened the pantry door.

'Forgotten something?' Tony asked as he lowered a full basket of newly chipped potatoes into the overflowing fat fryer.

'Yes,' Ronnie snapped enigmatically. He studied the trays of eggs ranged on the slate shelves. There were close on two dozen there. He could always go to the market early and buy some more. Taking one of the small cardboard boxes they used to put cakes in, he carefully lowered all the eggs into it. Then he looked at the cake shelf. There was only a fruit cake left; there wouldn't be fresh cream cakes until the morning. He lifted it gently into another box, then as an afterthought he pulled out his watch chain and opened the cupboard where he kept the alcohol. Looking along the shelves he found what he was looking for: a bottle of sweet Spanish sherry. He closed and locked the door, picked up the boxes and hurried out. Tony heard the clang of the front door banging behind him. It crashed even above the sizzling hiss of the fryer.

Alma walked into the kitchen with a tray of dirty dishes. 'Where's he off to?' Tony asked, pointing to the door.

'How in hell should I know?' she bit back furiously. She crashed

187

the tray down on the wooden table next to the sink. 'And even if I did know I wouldn't give a single, sweet, damn,' she shouted as she stormed out. Tony shrugged as he ladled chips out of the fat with a slatted spoon. Perhaps his father was right, he mused. The priesthood was a good life. If nothing else it would at least be quiet.

Ronnie crossed the road, walked under the railway bridge and up the Graig hill towards the Central Homes. He'd thought of taking the Trojan, but someone might see it parked close to the hospital and wonder what it was doing there. This way, all he had to worry about was getting through the gate, and what he was going to say once he was inside the building, always assuming he got that far.

The porter eyed him suspiciously as he walked along Court-house Street and up to the lodge gate. Pretending he hadn't noticed the man, he went directly to the gate and banged hard on it before the porter had an opportunity to confront him.

'Eggs for the TB ward,' he announced in a loud voice.

'At this time of night?' the porter peered at him suspiciously. 'It's after eight o'clock.'

'Donation from the Catholic Mothers' Union,' Ronnie explained. 'My mother promised to deliver them this afternoon but her rhematism played up. This is the first chance I've had to leave the café all day.'

The man squinted through the gloom, eyeing Ronnie sus-piciously. 'Oh, it's you, Mr Ronconi.' He shuffled forward to open the gate. 'You should have said so in the first place.'

'Sorry, haven't deliverd anything for the Mother's Union before,' he replied brusquely.

'And God bless them, that's what I say,' the porter mumbled. 'Even if they are Catholics. Want to leave the boxes with me?' he asked, wondering just how many eggs were inside and if one or two would be missed.

'Better not,' Ronnie said easily. 'There's something else here that my mother promised the ward sister yesterday. She made me swear that I'd take it to the ward office myself.'

'Know your way to the TB ward?'

Ronnie shook his head.

The porter leant against the gate as Ronnie walked through.

'Turn left here, and walk across the female exercise yard. Left is the female side of the Homes,' he explained laboriously. 'Men are on the right, away from the main road, less chance of them escaping that way. The first blocks you come to are the casual wards and the workhouse wards. Then you come to the un-marrieds ward. TB patients are in the end block against the wall, you can't miss it, it's the last block opposite the boiler house. The only blocks ahead of you are maternity, male acute, and J wards and they're not against the wall,' he rambled. 'TB's on the top floor,' he shouted as Ronnie walked away.

Securing the bottle of sherry in the crook of his elbow and balancing the boxes in one hand, Ronnie touched his cap as he continued on his way. The yard was an incredibly depressing place. Hemmed in on one side by a ten-foot-high stone wall, and on the other by a massive stone block that housed the dining room and kitchens, it gave Ronnie the impression that he was travelling through a long, dark, roofless tunnel. If it wasn't for the rain that dripped down on to his hat he could have sworn it had a ceiling. The towering walls and the feeling of claustrophobia fostered the effect of being trapped in a massive, damp cellar.

Lights glimmered faintly, illuminating the cross-bars of ward windows, but they did nothing to brighten his path. He stepped ankle deep into a puddle of freezing rainwater. Shaking his foot irritably in an effort to get rid of the worst of the water, he kept going. At the end of the dining-room block he passed the kitchens. He recognised them by the smell: an overwhelming stench of rotting vegetables and cabbage water assailed his nostrils. Then he heard the hum of the boiler house. He looked around: to his left was the block he'd been looking for. Balancing the boxes on one arm, he turned the doorknob and stole inside. He found himself in a white-tiled vestibule. A naked light bulb hung from the ceiling, its low wattage tingeing the atmosphere with a gloomy, dark gold light. Everything around him was tiled – the floor, half the walls, even the stairs. The distant sounds of hospital-trolleys rattling over hard floors, and clashings of china against metal echoed towards him. He tiptoed quietly towards the stairs. Holding the boxes out carefully in front of him he climbed up the steps, taking them two at a time. At the top was a closed door, adorned with a large red and white sign.

DANGER INFECTIOUS DISEASES!
ABSOLUTELY NO ADMITTANCE WITHOUT PERMISSION

He knocked softly at the door. He waited a few moments, then pushed it open.

'Do you mind telling me what you think you're doing, sir?'

Ronnie was not normally of a nervous disposition, but because the voice came from behind him, and not in front as he'd expected, he jumped, almost dropping the eggs.

'I'm looking for the sister in charge of the TB ward,' he explained briefly.

'Looks like you found her,' the middle-aged woman said stiffly.

Ronnie had learned enough from Laura to tell the difference between a staff nurse's uniform and a sister's. 'God bless the shortage of nurses,' he thought irreverently, hoping it would be easier to get round the junior hospital hierarchy.

'I've come to deliver eggs, from the Catholic Mothers' Union.'

The stern expression on her face lifted, as what might have been the beginnings of a smile played at the corners of her mouth.

'How thoughtful. I'll take them off you.'

That wasn't what he'd intended at all.

'Let me carry them into the ward kitchen for you.' He gave her his most winning smile, a smile that had melted hearts even harder than hers. 'I've put a little something for the staff in there as well,' he winked. 'Something that will probably be a bit rich for the patients' taste.' He flipped open the top of the box, so she could see and smell the fruit cake, then he removed the bottle of sherry that he had tucked under his arm and waved it under her nose.

'That's very good of you Mr . . .'

'Ronconi,' he said quickly.

'Ronconi,' the smile finally broke through her frosty interior. 'But you still can't go through that door. Can't you read?' She pointed to the sign. 'Do you want to risk getting tuberculosis?'

'I rather think I already have,' he said shortly. 'You see my – my – my – ' he almost said sister, but no one would believe that he and Maud were brother and sister, particularly now he had been idiotic enough to tell the woman his real name. But then again, what was the point in lying? He was too well known in the town as a Ronconi.

190

'My fiancée is in here,' he blurted out in desperation. 'I was hoping to have a word,' he pleaded, reading suspicion all over her face. 'You see we had the most awful row the night before she came in here – '

'What's her name?' the nurse demanded coldly.

'Maud. Maud Powell. We were to have been married next month.'

'This is the first I've heard of it.'

'There's problems.' This time he wasn't lying. If he was ever lucky enough to get as far as making the kind of plans with Maud that he dreamed about, there would be problems. Serious ones! 'You see my family are Catholics and – '

'And she's Chapel,' the sister finished for him. 'You really are a Ronconi, aren't you?' she said, studying his dark, foreign appearance. 'I've seen you in your café. You have lovely cream cakes . . .'

'I'll bring you a box of them tomorrow,' he promised rashly. 'Please,' he begged. 'There's so much I want to say to her.'

'This isn't the time or place.' Her voice wasn't as firm as it had been.

'Doctor Trevor Lewis is my brother-in-law.' He played his last card desperately. Now he'd got this far he wasn't going to be put off. 'He promised to get me in to see her tomorrow, but I just couldn't wait.'

'Then your sister is Laura – '

'Lewis, who was Ronconi,' he broke in eagerly. 'Please,' he implored. 'No one will ever find out. I promise. Please . . .'

'Everyone on the ward is sleeping.'

'I'll be as quiet as a mouse. Just a minute.'

'She's very ill, you know.'

'I know she haemorrhaged this morning, and that she was brought in, in a coma. Her father told me,' he lied, struggling to contain his irritation with the woman.

'The kitchen's along there.' The nurse finally pushed open the door. 'You can drop your eggs and cake off there. I'll go and see if she's awake. *If*,' she stressed the 'if', 'If she's awake, you can see her for a second. Just a quick peek through the door and a smile. No more, mark you.'

Ronnie felt as though he were floating on air as he watched her broad back disappear through the door marked 'ward'. He rushed down the corridor to the kitchen. The atmosphere was close and unpleasantly warm. Foul and heavy with the mixed odours of stale urine, cheap disinfectant and the strange sour-sweet smell peculiar to all hospitals. But as he left the bottle and the boxes on the kitchen sideboard the only perfume he was aware of was that of blooming roses. Outside was miserable wet winter and he was lost in the wonders of a beautiful summer that he was confident was heading his way.

Chapter Eighteen

It was a long, long time before Diana felt clean enough to stop scrubbing herself. When she finally, reluctantly returned the brush to the bath-rack she noticed her naked body. It wasn't a sight she was accustomed to, simply because she either washed in a bowl in her bedroom or the sink in the washhouse when the boys were out. And neither room had a mirror.

She shuddered, disgusted and revolted by the sight of her own nudity. She closed her eyes against the image of her full, round breasts topped by the soft, pink aureoles of her nipples. But even with her eyes closed she could still see the flat, white plain of her stomach leading down to the triangle of dark hair that lay between her scrubbed red thighs. Feeling nauseous she screwed up her face in self-loathing. She was in pain. Hurting! Not from the tingling left by the vigorous pounding she had subjected her skin to, but something more, something deeper.

Keeping her eyes closed, she ducked her head beneath the water, washing off the soap lather she'd massaged into her hair. When it was clean, she pulled the bath plug with her toe. Crouching forward, she turned on the cold tap and held her head under its steady flow, rinsing away the last vestiges of bath water from her hair. Afterwards she splashed cold water over the rest of her body. Freezing cold and shivering, she finally stood up and wrapped the larger of the two towels Wyn had left around herself. She dried her skin thoroughly, wiping all the scratched areas first with swabs of cotton wool that she found on the washstand, lest she stain the towel with blood.

Tucking the top of the towel in, she decided to clean the bathroom thoroughly, leaving it exactly as she'd found it. She was more than a little overawed by its magnificence, but then it was the first plumbed-in bathroom she'd seen in a private house. The nearest she'd ever got to an indoor bathroom before now were the spartan utility ones she'd cleaned on the wards in the Royal Infirmary, and the bleak communal wash areas she'd been allowed to use in the hostel for ward maids.

She found a cleaning cloth on the side of the slop bucket beneath the washstand. Filling the bucket with warm water and, in the absence of anything better, the remains of the soap she'd washed herself with, she wiped down the huge clawfoot bath, inside and out. Then she washed the floor, taking care to mop up every single drop of water that she'd dripped outside the bath.

She hadn't touched the massive stone sink in the corner, or its ornate, wrought-iron supports, but she cleaned them all the same. The last thing she turned her attention to was the toilet. When she lifted the dark wooden seat, she stared in disbelief. The inside was decorated with circles of beautifully painted daisies. She washed out the bucket and the cloth last of all. Lingering next to the washstand, she admired and envied the range of toiletries. The last time she'd seen a display as lavish was in Norma Shearer's bedroom in a film.

She reached out hesitantly and picked up a bowl of pearl talcum powder. The bowl was beautiful, porcelain china, decorated with a finely drawn design of white, lily-like flowers. She climbed into the bath and gingerly lifted the lid lest she spill a drop, reasoning that it would be easier to wash the powder down the plughole than wipe it off the floor. A circle of white swansdown floated on top of the deliciously perfumed fine dusting powder. She sprinkled a little sparingly over her neck and shoulders. Glancing down at the bath, she noticed with satisfaction that she hadn't wasted a single speck.

She replaced the bowl on the exact spot where it had rested before. She studied the rows of boxes, bowls and bottles, breathing in the mixture of heady perfumes and allowing them to assail her senses. Lavender water, Pears and Kay's soaps. Men's mint Cologne, bottles of Evening in Paris, 4711 eau-de-Cologne and Essence of Violets. Shaving soaps and antiseptic shaving blades. Tubes of cherry toothpaste and small tins of Erasmus tooth-powder, and at the practical end of the table, a massive jar of petroleum jelly and a large bottle of liniment rub.

Feeling like a thief despite Wyn's generous directive that she help herself, she closed her fingers around the beautiful green and gold bottle of eau-de-Cologne. Unscrewing the top, she dabbed a little sparingly behind her ears. She knew what bottles like this cost. Her mother had sold them for a few pence a year ago, but in the shops they were priced at more than she could hope to earn in a month.

At the thought of earnings she shuddered. She tried to marshal her thoughts and concentrate on replacing everything exactly as she'd found it. Even the bucket and cloth.

A man's hairbrush stood on the washstand. Judging by the strands of hair caught up in its bristles, it was Wyn's. She picked it up, automatically pulling out the hairs and preparing to use it. Then she remembered that she'd carried her handbag into the room. She found it, opened it, extracted her own comb and flicked her hair straight back, like a boy's, pushing it behind her ears. Straight hair was unfashionable, unalluring. She made a mental resolution never to wave or curl her hair again.

Using her fingers to wipe away the steam from a mirror that hung on the wall above the sink, she stared at her reflection. Her eyes seemed disproportionately large in comparison with the rest of her face. Her cheeks and lips were white, devoid of even a hint of colour. Only her right temple gleamed red. Angry and swollen where Ben had slammed her into the shelves.

She returned the comb to her handbag. Turning her back on the mirror she removed the towel and dressed quickly. The clothes hung stiff and strange on her, especially Wyn's shirt, which felt peculiar against her bare skin, but he'd been so generous already she felt she could hardly ask him to look for a bust shaper or chemise.

She glanced round the room one last time after she opened the window a crack to let out the steam. She had no more excuse to linger. Gathering up her clothes from the wooden slatted mat, she tied them into a tight little bundle and wrapped the remains of her white blouse round the outside. Only her coat remained. She picked it up, unlocked the door and descended the staircase.

Wyn had made tea. He was sitting at the kitchen table drinking a cup and reading the *South Wales Echo*.

'You look better,' he smiled as she walked through the door. 'Sit down. I'll pour you some tea.'

'I'd like to burn these first.' She dropped her coat on to a chair and held out the bundle of clothes.

'Couldn't they be washed and mended?'

195

'Even if they could, I'd never wear them again.' Her voice escalated alarmingly. 'Not as long as I live.'

He opened the door to the range. Taking the bundle from her fastidiously with the tongs, he stuffed it on top of the coals, banking it down with a log and a shovelful of small coal.

'That'll soon burn.' He replaced the tongs in the hearth set, and picked up the teapot.

'Shouldn't you be getting back to the shop?' It was warm in the kitchen, and comfortable. She felt like an outsider and, despite the bath, a dirty outsider – a tramp who had no right to sit there.

'I have another ten minutes or so.' He poured out her tea. 'Here, give me your coat.' He took it and carried it over to the sink where he proceeded to brush it down fussily with a damp cloth.

She sat on the edge of the chair, hunched over the table sipping at her tea. 'I don't know how to begin to say thank you,' she murmured in a small voice. 'I'll return the clothes after I've washed them.'

'There's no need. I told you, they don't fit my sister any more.' He dabbed some cold water on to a spot on her coat and rubbed it. 'Do you want to talk about it?' he asked quietly. She stared into her cup. 'You don't have to,' he continued. 'I just thought it might help.'

'You've probably guessed most of it,' she snapped.

'Ben Springer?'

At the mention of Ben's name, it all poured out. The rape, the humiliation, the feeling of complete and utter degradation and worthlessness . . .

He simply stood there, next to the sink, and listened. When she finally ran out of words and into tears, he walked to her and handed over her coat. She delved into the pocket, looking for a handkerchief. When she removed and opened her hand, the five-pound note Ben Springer had thrust upon her fluttered to the floor. Wyn picked it up.

'What do want to do?' he asked quietly, returning the money to her.

She took a deep breath and raised her eyes to meet his steady gaze.

'I don't know,' she admitted brokenly. 'If I tell Will or my cousins or my uncle what Ben did to me, they'd kill him for sure.'

Wyn remembered the beating Eddie Powell had given Bethan Powell's seducer for less, and nodded.

'They'd swing for Ben, that's for certain,' he agreed flatly.

'So what can I do?' she demanded, hysterically.

'You can't be thinking of going back to work there tomorrow?' he asked, genuinely alarmed by the thought.

'No!' her reply was sharp and vehement.

'Then it's obvious, you've got to find a job elsewhere.'

'And what do I tell my aunt, uncle and Will when they ask why I left?'

'Tell them he laid you off. They're hardly likely to go and challenge him about it, are they?'

She realised he was glancing at the clock, and jumped up, upsetting her full cup of tea on the scrubbed wooden table top.

'I'm sorry,' she cried, tears rising to her eyes again.

'For God's sake stop apologising every five minutes. None of this is your fault,' he said curtly, angered by his own inadequacy to deal with the situation. He threw a dishcloth over the mess, deftly mopped it up, put the cup and saucer in the sink, then picked up her coat again and helped her on with it.

'You've been great, Wyn,' she murmured, striving to contain her emotions. 'Really great. I don't know what I would have done without you. Aunt Elizabeth would have killed me if I'd gone home as I was.'

'I doubt she'd have done that.' He took the five pounds from her hand and thrust it deep into her pocket. She immediately pulled it out and walked towards the stove.

'Don't,' he ordered sharply. 'If you don't want the money you can send it back to him any time.'

She pushed it back into her pocket.

'Look,' he conceded, 'you know I work every night, except Sunday. How about I meet you Sunday afternoon? We could go to Ronconi's.'

'I don't know,' she murmured doubtfully.

'You can't let what Ben did to you spoil your life.'

At the mention of Ben's name, she lowered her head and rushed out. He heard her sobbing again, and felt entirely helpless. This was one case where tea and sympathy really weren't enough, and he had nothing else to offer – unless. He remembered something he'd seen and heard when he left the Ruperra after his training sessions. Sunday – all he had to do was wait until Sunday. It would be quiet then. He looked around the kitchen, checked that he'd left it tidy and followed Diana out of the door.

Ronnie hovered impatiently in the corridor outside the isolation area. The night nurse had disappeared what seemed like hours ago. He paced uneasily up and down, diving straight back into the ward kitchen when he heard footsteps echoing towards him from behind the closed doors of the ward, petrified in case it was someone other than the staff nurse that he'd spoken to. Someone with enough authority and acumen to throw him out. He was so close . . . so close . . .

'What are you doing here?'

He whirled around. The nurse was small, plump, dark and, he noticed thankfully, as he whispered a prayer of gratitude to the Virgin Mother – a trainee.

'It's all right, Jones,' the staff nurse he'd spoken to reprimanded sharply. 'He has my permission to wait here.'

'Sorry, staff,' the nurse apologised.

'Now go down to the porters' station as I asked you to five minutes ago,' the staff nurse ordered sharply. 'I want two of them up here with a stretcher in the next five minutes, if not sooner,' she added illogically, knowing full well that the porters' station was a brisk five-minute walk away from the ward for a nurse, and ten for a porter who knew he was wanted to ferry dead, as opposed to live, patients. 'And while you're downstairs you may as well walk across the yard and alert the mortuary that there's a body on its way.'

'Right away, staff.' Looking down at the floor to conceal her red face, the trainee scurried off.

'One of the patients died five minutes ago,' the staff nurse explained briefly to Ronnie. 'The younger nurses often have trouble dealing with the inevitable, especially when the patient is young. It upsets the other inmates too,' she commented drily. 'But then again Jones is hardly the most competent of trainees,' she finished unsympathetically.

Ronnie paled, 'It's not . . . not . . .'

'No, it wasn't your fiancée. But she was only fifteen, and, as it happens, in the next bed. She coughed up an entire lung before she went. Very messy.' She shook her head as though trying to obliterate the image from her mind. 'We had to wheel screens round her bed so none of the others could see what was happening. We've moved the body out now to the treatment room, but the screens are still up. If you promise to be quiet you can have a minute behind them with your fiancée. A minute, mind you. No longer,' she warned.

'Thank you.' Ronnie had to restrain himself from dancing past her and into the ward.

'Oh and by the way,' she gave him a tight little smile as she held the ward door open for him, 'you weren't joking when you said you had problems with her family. It took some time for her even to admit she knew you, let alone was engaged to you.'

He shrugged his shoulders and returned her smile. 'As I said, there's a lot I need to say to her.'

He crept through the door into the silent ward. The nurse didn't follow, merely pointed to the bed immediately behind the door to the left. Because it was next to the wall, the iron and canvas screening that isolated the bed next to it effectively screened it also. Craving privacy, he glanced behind him and saw a tousled, and he sincerely hoped sleeping, head in the bed opposite. The nurse closed the door of the ward softly behind her. She had been kinder than he'd expected: this was as alone as he could reasonably expect to get with Maud while she remained in hospital.

Stepping on tiptoe, lest the rubber soles of his shoes squeak on the highly polished linoleum, he stole behind the screen. For the first time since he'd left school, headmasters and canings behind him, he tasted the cold, metallic tang of fear in his mouth. Wiping his clammy hands on his coat, he swallowed hard.

'Don't forget, one minute,' the nurse warned through the closed doors of the ward, as she made her way back from the kitchen to the treatment room. 'No more.'

The reminder gave him the courage he needed to look at Maud. She was lying, propped up on three pillows, her face as white as the cotton slips behind her head. The gold of her hair and the vivid gem-like blue of her eyes were the only hints of colour in a sea of white sheeting and bedcovers.

'Ronnie?'

Her voice was faint, barely audible. The room faded, until he focused only on her. A pale golden figure shimmering in a fog of grey, wavering darkness. 'The nurse told me that you were here, and you'd asked to see me,' she whispered.

He crept close to the bed and knelt beside it. 'I couldn't rest or settle to anything, not without knowing how you were.' Locking his fingers together he rested his hands on the edge of the bed.

She laid her hand on top of his. It was pale, so white and translucent he could see the pattern of veins beneath the skin, mute evidence of her fragility and mortality. He shuddered, noticing for the first time the mixed odours of decay, disinfectant and death in the atmosphere around him.

'You don't think my being here is your fault, do you?' she asked, giving him a small smile.

'No! Yes . . . I don't know . . .' he stammered like a nervous schoolboy. 'If I hadn't taken you down the café last night . . .'

'I wouldn't have had a good time,' she finished for him. The effort it cost her to talk brought on a coughing fit. He sat helplessly as she clutched the inevitable stained, sodden handkerchief to her mouth. He heard a sound in the corridor, and remembered the nurse's injunction: 'One minute. No more.'

'Maud there's no easy way to say this,' he blurted out uneasily, worried that the nurse would return and throw him out before he had a chance to tell Maud anything important. 'Perhaps if I had more time . . . oh, what the hell. I love you and I want to marry you,' he confessed impatiently, and with a strange lack of eloquence considering the time he'd had to prepare for this momentous occasion in his life. Unnerved by the silence that greeted his outburst, a full minute passed before he dared to raise his eyes to her.

She was staring at him, dumbfounded.

'I love you,' he repeated in a softer tone. 'I've been such a fool. I should have realised sooner. I didn't even think about it until last night. Now I know I want to be with you. Always. I want to marry you . . .'

'Ronnie, I'm ill. The doctor said I'm – '

'I know what the doctor said,' he dismissed scornfully. 'I've spoken to Trevor. He's my brother-in-law, remember. But that doesn't make him any different from the rest of the pack. All he can talk about is cutting ribs, deflating lungs, and operations.'

'He said there's a chance that an operation might work . . .'

'And there's a chance that it might not.'

Maud looked through a small tear in the screen and saw the stripped and empty bed next to her own, and fell silent.

'Trevor's probably right,' Ronnie conceded grudgingly. 'An operation would be the best option if you stayed here. But you don't have to. Everyone knows that people with consumption improve if they're taken to a healthier climate with clean air. Mountain air,' he finished triumphantly.

'There's nothing but mountains around here,' she pointed out logically.

'Mountains but no clean air, the dust on the slagheaps sees to that. Coal isn't healthy, but there's no coal mining in Italy,' he began enthusiastically.

'Italy!' she exclaimed incredulously, feeling that he might as well have suggested the moon.

'Why not? I have grandparents there.' He omitted to tell her that he hadn't seen them since he was five and wasn't at all sure of the reception they'd give him if he turned up on their doorstep, let alone with a consumptive wife. 'Marry me and we'll go to Italy. I'll see to it that we're on a train before the end of the week. I'll find your father and ask him for his permission tonight . . .'

Maud knew he was talking to her because she could see his lips moving, but she could neither hear nor comprehend a word he was saying. She was too busy thinking of the pale, dark girl in the next bed. The cures she'd tried and told her about. The plans she'd been making, even up until that afternoon. Ronnie – she looked at him, seeing him in the light of a potential lover for the first time. It was the pictures come to life. True romance. Better, much better than *It Happened One Night*. His dark, rugged, brooding good looks. Italy, with a husband! For the first time since Diana had brought her back from the Infirmary she had something to think about, something to plan for other than her own funeral. She tried to sit up, then began to cough again. Her body racked by spasms, she reached out unsteadily, picked up the sputum jar and spat in it.

She sensed Ronnie looking at her, and remembered her disgust

201

when her now dead neighbour had done the selfsame thing. Had it really only been that morning? Ashamed of her disease-ridden body, she closed her eyes, afraid to look at him lest she see something of the revulsion she felt for herself mirrored in his eyes.

'This isn't a romantic disease,' she said cuttingly. 'I'm no Greta Garbo, you're not Robert Taylor. And this,' – she lifted her pathetically thin hand and waved it close to the sickly green walls of the ward – 'isn't Camille,' she said brutally. 'People with TB die horribly, messily . . .' she fought for breath, suddenly terrified – of him – of reaching out to take what he offered in case he saw her for what she was, changed his mind and rejected her. 'They cough up shreds of lungs.' She opened out her stinking handkerchief to illustrate her words, painting the blackest possible picture of the disease, so he would hold no illusions about what she was trying to tell him.

'You're not saying anything I don't already know,' he informed her smoothly.

'How can you possibly love me – '

'I've no idea, especially when you're in this mood,' he joked.

'I don't think I love you,' she said slowly, choosing her words with care. 'To be honest, Ronnie, I've never thought of you as anything other than one of Haydn's and Will's friends. And Laura's brother, of course,' she murmured as an afterthought. 'You're so old . . .'

'Not too old for anything that matters,' he said earnestly. 'Which I hope you'll soon find out. And when you marry me – ' he refused even to think of the possibility of 'if', '– you'll learn to love me. Until that happens I have more than enough love for both of us. Besides, my parents have always told me that love comes after marriage,' he grinned wryly, wrapping his huge, thick fingers round her thin, reed-like ones. 'It must be true. Just look at them, they only saw one another twice before the wedding, and that was in front of both of their entire families. At least we've seen more of each other than that, and much more than I've seen of any of the Italian girls that Mama and Papa have been trying to marry me off to for the past few years.'

'Your parents may want you to get married, but I don't think either of them will be all that happy with the thought of you marrying a girl as sick as me.'

202

'What they want isn't important. Not this time. You're what I want. All you have to do is say the word. I'll speak to your father, get you out of here, marry you and take you to Italy . . .'

'You're mad.' The idea of marrying anyone, especially Ronnie Ronconi, suddenly seemed so preposterous she wondered if she were dreaming or hallucinating.

'Very possibly,' he agreed infuriatingly.

'Well I'm not mad,' she stated positively, 'and neither will I lie to you. I don't think I love you,' she said emphatically.

'I thought we'd already dealt with that point.'

'But you're offering me so much. Italy. The girls here were talking about rich people's cures in Switzerland this afternoon, and – '

'Italy and Switzerland are next door to each other, they share the same air,' he urged persuasively.

'I want to live so much,' she said fervently.

'Then live with me.'

Tears welled in the corners of her eyes. He'd seen her cry before. Stood by helplessly while she'd swallowed silent, bitter tears of pain, watched as she'd struggled with hot, fierce tears of anger. This was different. He couldn't help feeling that she was shedding her first tears of sorrow. He instinctively knew what she was thinking. He was offering her a chance to live, and all she could think of was – how long?

'We'll marry, and take whatever time we're given,' he declared practically. 'Anything has to be better than nothing, and if our marriage lasts for years instead of months, I'll just have to take my chances that you don't turn into a nagging wife like Laura, and make my life a misery.'

'That's another thing,' she fought to keep her tears in check. 'Trevor and Laura went out together for ages. They knew all there was to know about one another before they married. You don't know the first thing about me.'

'I know everything that's important.' Sensing her exhaustion, he rose from his knees and kissed her gently on the forehead. 'Right, now that's over and done with, I may as well warn you, you'll never get me on my knees again. I'll speak to your father, see about getting you out of here. Then I have to buy some train tickets.'

'My father – '

'Don't worry about a thing. I'll see to everything. You lie there, conserve your strength and concentrate on falling in love with me. If you can manage it, I'd like it to happen before next Tuesday. I aim to be away by then.'

'You still here, Mr Ronconi?' the staff nurse hissed furiously. 'I said a minute, and you've taken ten. Quick, out,' she ordered, panicking; she'd already had word that the senior night sister was on her rounds.

Ronnie smiled at Maud, and winked at the nurse.

'Do you have a day off coming to you before Tuesday? Because if you do, you can be bridesmaid,' he grinned wickedly.

'Out,' she pushed him through the door and watched him descend the stairs. She didn't return to the ward until she heard the click of the door closing behind him.

'You look happy,' she commented to Maud as she wheeled the screens away from her bed.

'I think I am.' Maud admitted as she wriggled down between the sheets.

'I can understand that. He's very good-looking, isn't he? Funny, his sister said he'd never fall for anyone. "Heart as hard as the brass in the till," that's what she said. "Might marry another café, but never a girl." But then,' the nurse couldn't help herself; for all her professional training she responded to Maud's smile with one of her own, 'what does a sister ever know about a brother? They say the harder they are, the harder they fall. You're a lucky girl,' she said quickly, glossing over Maud's illness. 'At least he owns one café, even if you're not bringing him another. And with a café, you'll never go hungry.'

'He's taking me to Italy,' Maud murmured sleepily. Excited by the prospect, she didn't give a thought to the café or the business, or what Ronnie would be giving up to take her away from the valleys. For the first time in months she was looking forward to sleeping. Tonight she wouldn't dream of wreaths, funerals and headstones in Glyntaff cemetery, but of weddings. Of floating into chapel in the centre of a cloud of white tulle, flowers in her hair, a scented bouquet in her hand, a lace veil covering her head. The only thing that had been a little misty until now was the face of her bridegroom. She thought of Ronnie's dark, handsome features, the way he'd looked at her when he told her he loved her, and she fitted him into the grey suit with the white buttonhole. She was still smiling in her sleep when the duty sister checked the ward on her rounds an hour later.

Chapter Nineteen

'You didn't have to walk me all the way home,' Jenny said as she led the way around the corner of Llantrisant Road into Factory Lane. She halted outside the six-foot-high wooden door that fitted flushly into the eight-foot wall round the back yard of the shop. 'You'll be late now for your training session in the Ruperra, and it means making a double trip. You'll have to walk down the hill and back up again later, won't you?' she asked.

'If you're serious about boxing you can't afford to give training a miss. Ever,' Eddie said gravely.

She turned her umbrella, and was preparing to lower it when she caught sight of him staring at her. She smiled, elated. Haydn might be impervious to her charms, but his brother wasn't, and that meant she wasn't wholly unattractive after all. Perhaps given time Haydn might even change his mind about her.

Eddie was aware only of the darkness – and Jenny. The light from the lamps on the main road didn't reach as far as the shadows of Factory Lane. Their beams shafted short, over streaks of navy blue, rain-filled night air, lending a faint glow to the back of Jenny's head. Her blonde hair shone like a strip of gold between her high forehead and her umbrella. If it hadn't been for the long belted mac she was wearing, she could have taken her place amongst the angels in the illustrated Life of Jesus that Maud had won as a school prize. The book he would never have willingly opened if his Uncle John Joseph hadn't thrown it contemptuously across the room, deploring it as 'Popish'. He figured that anything that annoyed his uncle had to be worth looking at.

'Do you know, you're really pretty,' he said impulsively.

'Thank you.' It wasn't up to Clark Gable standard, but she knew it was the nearest Eddie would get to uttering poetry, and the most she could expect. He couldn't stop looking at her. Her eyes were round, enormous, like those of a frightened rabbit. He fought the urge to put his arms around her, forcing himself to remember, not for the first time that evening, that she had been, and might be again, his brother's girlfriend. But even as he reminded himself, he continued to stare at her, admiring the way her nose tilted up at the end, the rounded softness of her cheeks, the inviting pout of her lips, soft, luscious – just begging to be kissed.

Something of his thoughts must have transmitted themselves to her, because before he realised she'd moved, she was standing on tiptoe before him. Lifting her chin, she kissed him gently on the spot where his mouth ended and his cheek began. The smell of her scent wafted into his nostrils. The proximity of her smooth-skinned, curvaceous body was too much – too tempting. He didn't even wait to glance behind him to ensure no one was watching, before sweeping her into his muscular arms.

Pulling her close, he kissed her hard and brutally on the lips. His bruising, insensitive touch took her breath away. Eddie had none of Haydn's finesse, or gentleness. His tongue invaded her mouth, exploring, probing, as he clamped his hand on the nape of her neck. Alarmed as much by her own feelings as by what Eddie was doing to her, she struggled to draw back. All she'd intended when she'd met Eddie in Mill Street was to be seen with him in the hope of making Haydn jealous. Perhaps exchange a highly public, flirtatious giggle with him, or a little light banter. She'd never intended things to go this far! But then she hadn't bargained on Eddie. He'd always been so quiet in the presence of girls, she'd put it down to shyness and inexperience, never suspecting such a passive exterior could conceal so much inner passion. Or how she'd feel if such a passion was unleashed on her.

She shifted position slightly, creating a small gap between them. It was just wide enough for him to manoeuvre his other hand inside her coat. Drunk with kisses, she failed to notice what he was doing until she shivered involuntarily at the cold touch of his fingers against the bare skin of her breast. She clamped her hand firmly over his.

'You mustn't!' she commanded weakly.

'Sorry,' he murmured huskily. 'Got a bit carried away there.'

'So I see.' Too embarrassed to meet his eyes she straightened her blouse and buttoned her coat. 'I always thought you spent all your time in the gym, Eddie Powell,' she said primly, striving to regain her composure. 'Wherever did you learn to kiss like that?'

He smiled, remembering one golden, drunken afternoon spent

in the bushes of Pontypridd Park with a willing, if expensive, chorus girl.

'Just because I don't wear my girlfriends on my arm like a badge, it doesn't mean I've never had any,' he said archly.

'I'd better be going.' She reached for the latch on the high wooden door.

He laid his fingers over hers and pressed down hard. The door opened inwards, and he followed her into the small back yard. It was even darker than in the lane. Black as pitch. The only relief was the faint jet gleam of glass outlining the position of the storeroom window.

'Just one more kiss,' he begged, pushing her until she was pinned against the house door and could retreat no further. His mouth closed over hers again. She felt as though he was sucking the breath from her body. His hand once more gravitated to the contours of her breast beneath her coat. He squeezed it once, before lifting her skirt and invading her bloomers. The door opened inwards into the stockroom; she didn't know how, only that she reeled blindly backwards through it, gasping for air, her nerve ends tingling, too stunned and shocked to take in the enormity of what Eddie was doing to her.

Her coat joined his on the floor. He lifted her pullover and with it her blouse and underclothes. She lay back on the boxes, where she had lain so many nights with Haydn, digging her fingernails into Eddie's back as he caressed her breasts and nipples. His fingers were replaced by his lips as his hands delved into the soft, sensitive area between her thighs.

He removed her bloomers and pulled her skirt to her waist but she was too far gone down the road of hunger and desire that he had aroused within her to protest. If they had been lying on the bandstand in Pontypridd Park, on view to the whole world, she wouldn't have cared less. She was aware only of the sensations he engendered. The thrill, the excitement, of his lovemaking. The desires he had kindled. Of wanting him to touch her naked body. Again and again and again!

He ran his hands up her sides from her thighs to her breasts and she tore her clothes off, over her head. She lay back on the boxes, stark naked before him, arms uplifted, legs spread wide, gratefully receiving the caresses and thrusts he bestowed on her, electric touches that obliterated everything, even thoughts of Haydn, from her mind.

When it was over he did not linger long. She was aware of him moving swiftly away from her in the blackness, heard the whispers of cloth rustling, and knew that he was dressing. A cold draught blew across her exposed body, the latch slipped. She opened her eyes just in time to see his shadow disappearing out into the night. He didn't even turn back to look at her. Didn't say one single word – of endearment – of anything.

An eternity passed during which she recalled Haydn's tenderness, his gentle, sensuous touch, his sweet, lingering kisses. He had always left her craving for more – much, much more. She'd always assumed that the 'more' would come with marriage.

Eddie had left her feeling weak, battered and wasted, but to her horror she realised that Eddie had given her what her body had craved for, and never got from Haydn. Pure physical passion.

But she loved Haydn. Didn't she? Of course she did. She was sure of that much. But one thing was certain now: he wouldn't want her. Not after this. She loved Haydn and had only wanted Eddie. Had wanted him enough to forget everything that Haydn had ever been to her.

Only her ridiculous pride had prevented her from going to Haydn after that stupid quarrel. She had wanted to tell him she was sorry for precipitating the argument. She had longed for a chance to make it up to him. To make him forget that she could behave childishly, jealously, over nothing. Now she realised she would never do that. What had happened between her and Eddie would prevent her; would estrange her from Haydn once and for all.

She began to pick up her clothes slowly, all the while shedding silent tears for what she had lost. A sweet first love that was now, irrevocably, consigned to her past.

There were many rooms in the Unemployment Institute in Mill Street. Large workshops where unemployed boys and men could learn carpentry and cobbling. Smaller rooms which had been handed over to the more intellectual contingent, who used them as meeting places, to talk, play chess, and remodel the world – especially Wales – along fairer, more equal, and socialist if not communist-inspired lines.

209

Unused to comfort in their homes, the members scarcely noticed the cold or discomfort in the rooms of the Institute. The furniture, if it could be graced with that name, was a motley collection of old chairs, sofas and scarred and broken tables that had been donated by those in the town rich enough to replace their belongings when they wore out. A few pieces showed signs of clumsy, ineffectual attempts at renovation by the boys who frequented the carpentry workshops. Those with whole, unbroken springs tended to gravitate towards what was grandly referred to as the 'Reading Room', where most of the books read were borrowed from the Pontypridd Lending Library. All the Institute had on offer was a meagre, donated store of well-thumbed magazines, dog-eared copies of Dickens and a bound edition of the complete works of Karl Marx, presented courtesy of the Miners' Union.

As Ronnie walked purposefully through the front door in the hope of finding Evan, he heard the deep, melodious tones of a choir practising somewhere at the back of the building. The sweet sounds blended uneasily with the strident barkings of a retired sergeant-major who was putting the younger element through their exercises in the gym, in the hope that the Institute team would win their next rugby match.

'Seen Evan Powell?' he asked a wizened old man whose arms were crammed with political pamphlets.

'Chess room.' The man pointed down a narrow passageway lit by a single, weak, unadorned light bulb. There was only one door at the end; once green, its paint was now dry and flaking. Half glazed with grimy, bubbled glass, it shed a brighter light into the corridor but no images of what lay within. Ronnie pushed it, and it juddered alarmingly over swollen floorboards.

A foul-smelling pall of cheap tobacco smoke hung thickly in a foggy atmosphere redolent with the unhealthy warmth of unwashed bodies packed into a confined space.

'Shut that bleeding door.' Ronnie recognised Viv Richards' voice, but he couldn't see him. He did as Viv asked, scanning the packed room for Evan Powell. He spotted him at last, at the far end of the room. If he'd been a fly he could have walked across the ceiling to get to Evan, but as it was, he stood little chance of reaching him without disturbing the entire room. So much for discretion! Every available inch of space was filled with broken chairs, men's legs and bodies.

Evan didn't see Ronnie standing by the door. His attention was fixed on a chess set laid out on an upturned packing case between him and Charlie, but he was playing in a half-hearted, desultory fashion, preoccupied with thoughts of Maud.

'And I tell you we can't allow this man to hold a meeting in our Town Hall!' A fist crashed noisily on a rickety table.

'What do you want us to do then, Dai?' Viv sniped. 'Take over the Town Hall from the Council to keep him out?'

'You're worrying over nothing, Dai. Mosley won't come to Ponty,' a skeletally thin man shouted. 'The councillors might be crache, but they know what's what. I've heard tell if he wants the place, he's going to have to pay ten times the going rate. That'll be too much, even for the likes of him.'

'Four times,' a disembodied voice corrected. 'Our May works in the council offices, and she's had it from the horse's mouth.'

'If the man wants to hold his meeting badly enough, he'll pay the asking price whatever it is,' Evan commented as he moved his rook forward two places to threaten Charlie's queen.

'I agree with Evan,' Dai shouted angrily. 'And what I'm saying is, when he comes we've got to do something about it.'

'Like what?' Viv demanded truculently. 'What the hell do you expect the likes of us to do about a man like that?'

'Infiltrate his meeting,' Dai said darkly.

'Be reasonable, man,' Evan snapped. 'You can't infiltrate a public meeting.'

'You can when you're a marked man,' Dai crowed, proud of the outlaw status that his active, paid-up membership of the Communist party conferred on him.

'Here we go again,' Viv moaned. 'Communist goodies against Fascist baddies.'

'The Communists are the only ones with the ideology, dedication and strength of purpose to oppose the Fascists. And Oswald Mosley,' Dai lectured in soapbox mode, 'is Mussolini and Hitler's henchman. You heard the lady in the last meeting same as me. Mosley will heap the same indignities on British Jews as Hitler is heaping right now on the Jews in Germany.'

'Since when have you worried about the Jews, Dai?' Viv sneered.

'They're our brothers . . .' Dai began heavily.

'They're our rich bloody brothers if you ask me,' Viv spat a gob of phlegm to the floor. 'And they only help their own, never them that needs it like us. When did you last see a Jew with the arse hanging out of his pants like it hangs out of mine?'

'That's it, Viv, bring everything down to crude basics,' Dai jeered. 'People like you have sold the working classes down the river for years. As long as you're comfortable, with enough in your pocket to put food on the table, a dress on your wife's back, coal on the fire and a pint in your belly, you're all right Jack and to hell with the rest of the world. If Hitler marched into Ponty right now and gave you a job, you'd shout "Sieg Heil" along with the rest of the poor deluded sods, wouldn't you?'

'Too bloody right. And it's not just jobs that Hitler's giving out. I've heard he's building houses, proper houses with electric light upstairs, and bathrooms for his workers. And that he intends for every man to have a car – '

'Give over, Viv,' Evan said calmly, trying to defuse the argument. 'You sound like a Mosley pamphlet.'

'It could happen here,' Viv asserted defiantly. 'It could. If enough men go to Mosley's meetings, not to scoff but to listen, it could – '

'But at what cost?'

The voice was soft-spoken and quiet, but every man in the room fell silent. It wasn't often Charlie made his opinions known, but when he did, everyone listened.

'Well I for one don't care what it bloody costs to put a wage packet in my pocket,' Viv shouted furiously.

'The Jews . . .' Dai began fervently.

'To hell with the bloody Jews,' Viv screamed.

'They're people,' Dai yelled, rising to his feet. 'Same as you and me.'

'Let the buggers suffer.'

'Jews this week, miners next, Welshmen the week after?' Charlie looked steadily at Viv. 'You've been lucky in this valley. So far you've only lost your jobs.'

Charlie returned to his chessboard and made another move.

212

He'd never spoken about his past. Not once, although plenty had tried to worm more out of him. He'd never volunteered anything other than the information that he came from Russia. And few apart from the well-read miners like Evan realised just how vast that country was.

Taking advantage of the silence that followed Charlie's speech, Ronnie steamrollered his way past Viv's and Dai's abandoned chairs towards Evan.

'Mr Powell.' He extended his hand first to Evan, then Charlie.

'I've never seen you in here before, Ronnie.' Evan pushed his chair away from the chest. 'Your father sacked you?'

'Not yet,' Ronnie said gravely. 'But then, although it says unemployed over the door there's a fair few like you here Mr Powell, and Charlie, who work.'

'Not nights in our own café.' Charlie lifted his feet off the rungs of a stool, and thrust the stool at Ronnie. 'Seat?'

'Thanks.' Ronnie moved the stool between Evan and Charlie's chairs. Evan looked drawn, preoccupied, and Ronnie put it down to concern over Maud. 'I've been looking for you, Mr Powell,' he began awkwardly.

'Well now you've found me, boy, what do you intend to do with me?' Evan asked, irked by the interruption of his game. Ronnie said the one thing guaranteed to gain Evan's attention.

'I've just seen Maud.'

'You've seen her!' The sun rose on the dour landscape of Evan's face. 'How is she? Was she conscious? Did she say anything? Could she talk? Is she better than she was this morning?' The questions tumbled out faster than Ronnie could answer them.

'She was conscious, she said she felt better, we talked for a little while, but she seemed tired. Very tired,' Ronnie explained hesitantly.

'Only tired?' There was a look in Evan's eye that said he was still hoping for a miracle.

'Well, she's obviously very ill.' Ronnie pulled a packet of cigarettes out of his coat pocket and offered them round.

'They told us there was no visiting on the TB ward until Sunday. How did you manage to get in when you're not even family?' Evan asked suspiciously.

'I had to deliver some eggs to the ward. A present from the

Catholic Mothers' Union.' He'd told the lie so often he was beginning to believe it himself.

'It was good of them to think of the girls,' Evan commented sincerely, 'and it was good of you to come looking for me.'

'I really need to talk to you.' Ronnie held his cigarette in the flame of the match Charlie had produced. 'It's to do with Maud and it's important. Could we go somewhere private, Mr Powell? Perhaps the back bar of the Criterion, or the Hart?'

'All right.' Evan was intrigued, but he was not the kind of man to let his curiosity show. He pushed the wooden box that held the chess figures towards Charlie. 'Coming, mate?'

Charlie correctly read the uneasy expression on Ronnie's face. 'I promised Dai a game.'

'Come over later and have a pint?'

Charlie nodded as he began to reset the figures.

It was still raining, but the fine drizzle had given way to a sudden torrential downpour.

'Do you want to wait until it eases off?' Ronnie asked, turning up the collar of his coat.

'The one thing I've learned about Ponty is that you can wait for ever for that, boy. Tell me where you're going and I'll follow.'

'The New Inn is the nearest.'

'I'd be happier with the Criterion.'

'Criterion it is. Come on, let's make a dash for it.'

Ronnie knew he'd been stupid when he saw the expression on Evan's face as he carried the tray with two full pints and two whisky chasers over to their table. The beer would have been enough. Evan would have bought him another back and that would have been the end of it. Evan could probably just about afford to buy two beers. As it was, he had set a precedent Evan couldn't afford to follow.

'Barman owes me for a dinner he never paid for,' Ronnie lied glibly, 'so these are on the house.'

'Cheers.' Evan raised his glass to the bewildered barman.

Ronnie picked up his whisky glass, swirled it briskly in his hand and downed it in one. He sensed Evan's attention fixed on him as he turned to his beer.

'I've never seen you drink like that before,' Evan commented as he sipped his own beer slowly.

'I never have, but then I've never said anything like what I'm about to say before.'

'About Maud?'

'I love her, Mr Powell, and I want to marry her,' he announced with devastating simplicity.

Maud had been shocked, but Evan was doubly so. He stared at Ronnie, his face showing absolute disbelief. 'You what?' he said incredulously.

'I want to – '

'Yes I heard you, boy,' Evan said impatiently. 'I just wasn't sure I understood you. Maud's practically on her deathbed and you come to me . . .'

'Please, Mr Powell. All I'm asking is that you hear me out.'

'I've got one question before you say another word,' Evan said sharply. 'She's barely sixteen, you're twenty-seven. Exactly how long has this been going on?'

Ronnie almost blurted out 'since last night', then realised how that could be misconstrued.

'Nothing's been going on, Mr Powell,' he stated firmly. 'And without your permission, nothing will.'

'I'm relieved to hear it.'

'When I heard that Maud had been rushed into hospital this morning, I realised how much I loved her. I couldn't bear the thought that I'd left it too late to tell her how I felt. So I talked to Trevor – '

'Trevor Lewis, the doctor. About my daughter?'

'Yes – no . . . not about her,' Ronnie explained hastily, realising the more he said, the more he was putting his foot in it. 'I asked him about the treatments for lung disease. Her name was never mentioned between us,' he lied. 'Trevor told me about operations, cutting ribcages, deflating lungs – that sort of thing. I've lived in this town all my life, Mr Powell . . .'

'So have I,' Evan pointed out drily. 'And I think you'll grant that my life's been a little longer than yours.'

'I know how many young girls die of TB,' Ronnie continued unabashed. 'Trevor admitted that the treatments don't offer a lot of hope.'

'You don't have to spell out Maud's mortality to me,' Evan said fiercely, reaching for his whisky.

'Then Trevor said something else. He said that sometimes the rich send their children to clinics in Switzerland, where they receive special treatment, breathe clean, fresh air and eat nothing but wholesome dairy food.'

'Are you suggesting that if I had enough money to send Maud to Switzerland I would hold back? Do you think for one minute that Maud would be lying in the Central Homes if I had the money to keep her out of the place?' Evan demanded heatedly. 'Do you think the thought of sending her somewhere warm and healthy hasn't crossed my mind?'

'If it has, then you know there's a chance for Maud in what I'm suggesting,' Ronnie pleaded. 'Neither I, nor my family, have the kind of money you need to send Maud to a Swiss clinic, but I could raise enough to pay for Maud's and my own fare to my grandparents' farm in Italy. The air is just as pure in northern Italy as it is in Switzerland. Probably better,' he enthused with unintentional irony, 'because there's not so many consumptives breathing it. If you give Maud and me permission to marry, I'll take her there straight after the ceremony.'

'She can barely stand being carried downstairs and you want to drag her all the way to Italy!'

'I've thought about it. She won't be any worse off than she is lying in a hospital bed. I'll ask Aldo – he has the café by the bridge – ' he explained superfluously: Evan had known Aldo since before Ronnie was born, '– to drive us to Cardiff in his car. That way we can get a through train to London. I'll book a sleeper so Maud can lie down, then I'll get a taxi to take us from the train to Tilbury docks. If I book a cabin on the boat, all Maud will have to do is rest and sleep until we reach Calais. There's plenty of trains with sleepers on crossing the continent . . .'

'Have you thought what that little lot is going to cost?'

'Not as much as I have put away in the bank,' Ronnie said with as much dignity as he could muster. 'And once we're there, there'll be no problems. My grandmother and my aunt will take care of Maud, and I'll be around to do any heavy work like lifting . . .'

'Have you discussed any of this with Maud?' Evan questioned him bluntly.

216

Ronnie nodded. 'Yes.'

'And what did she say?'

'What you'd expect someone as unselfish as her to say. She pointed out that if I married her, I might not have a wife for very long.' Ronnie had weighed his words carefully before speaking. He knew he'd hit home when Evan didn't come back with an immediate reply.

'What about your life here?' Evan asked finally. 'Your family, your business. You're in the middle of opening up another café, aren't you?'

'A restaurant.' Even now Ronnie couldn't allow the slip to pass. 'But there's nothing here that means as much to me as Maud's life,' he said gravely.

'Does she love you?' Evan asked shrewdly.

'At the moment she's too ill to know what she wants.'

Evan finished his pint and picked up his and Ronnie's empty glasses. He went to the bar and brought back refills. He was too preoccupied to think of whisky chasers, Ronnie noticed thankfully.

'Let's see if I've got this straight,' Evan murmured as he sat down again. 'You're telling me that you've never courted, and if I'm guessing correctly, never even kissed my daughter.'

'That's right.'

Evan held up his hand to silence Ronnie. 'Yet you say you love her enough to give up everything you have, even your family, to take her half-way round the world in the hope of finding a cure for her.'

'That's right.'

'What does your father think of all this?'

'He doesn't know about it. Yet,' Ronnie stressed. 'But he will before the night's out,' he finished confidently. He shook two cigarettes out of his packet and handed one to Evan. He looked at the older man, seeking either approbation or blunt dismissal, but Evan's face remained composed, impassive. It was impossible to read what he was thinking in the set of his features, or the expression in his eyes.

'To get down to practicalities, what are you going to live on? You've said you have money, but however much you've got put away, I'll warrant you'll run out sooner rather than later, and you can't expect your family here to keep you when you no longer work in the cafés.'

'My grandfather has a farm. It supported my father and his brothers while they were growing up. It's still supporting him, my grandmother and my aunt, and once I start working there, I'm sure I'll be able to bring in enough extra to support Maud, and me.'

'I suppose your father left Italy to get away from the good living that the farm brought in,' Evan murmured caustically.

'It'll be enough,' Ronnie said calmly, refusing to allow Evan to rile him. 'As I said, there's only my grandparents and my father's sister living there. There's no able-bodied man around the place, I'm sure they'll welcome me with open arms.'

'You're sure? You don't really know?' Evan guessed.

'They're my family. They'll welcome me.'

'And Maud?'

'She'll be my wife, and that will make her family too.'

'You've already more or less admitted she doesn't love you.'

'Maud has agreed to go with me,' Ronnie pleaded. 'All we need is your permission to marry.'

'In a Catholic church?'

Ronnie looked Evan squarely in the eye. 'No. Maud's not a Catholic and there isn't time enough for a conversion.'

'But if she lives you'll want her to convert?'

'I couldn't give a hang what she is!' Ronnie exclaimed in exasperation. 'She can be a Hindu, Muslim or Buddhist, anything as long as she's alive. All I want for Maud is what she wants for herself. And a quick wedding,' he added firmly, 'so we can leave early next week. I don't think Maud should be left in that ward a minute longer than necessary.'

'Banns have to be called wherever you get married. Even a Registry Office. And that takes three weeks . . .'

'An exception can be made if the bride is ill. I talked to the Reverend Price about it this evening, after I saw Maud.'

'You're Catholic, Maud's Chapel and you went to an Anglican priest?' Evan smiled for the first time that evening.

'I wanted advice and I could hardly go to Father O'Kelly or John Joseph Bull. Both of them would have come up with a million obstacles to put in the way of things.'

218

'I suppose they would have. To you it's all so simple, isn't it? You totally disregard Maud's illness, marry her and carry her off to the hills of Italy where you hope, against all medical advice, for a miraculous recovery.'

'Isn't that all Maud's got left?' Ronnie said earnestly. 'Hope? Please Mr Powell, I'm begging you, let me marry her. This could be Maud's only chance of living . . .'

'That just what I am thinking of, Ronnie. Maud's life, or rather, what she's got left of it. Let's not mince words,' he said bleakly, looking at Ronnie over the rim of his glass. 'Maud's dying.' It hurt him almost as much to say those two words as it hurt Ronnie to hear them. 'She's dying and you want me to allow you to drag her across Europe on a wild-goose chase, that will inevitably end the same way it would if she stayed here. The difference being that if she died here she'd have her family and friends around her, while if she died in Italy . . .'

'You just said it Mr Powell. "If".'

'I said if, because she's just as likely to die on the boat or the train, and then what will you do, Ronnie? Tell me, what will you do?'

'I'd bring her body home to you, Mr Powell. I'd be devastated, but at least I'd know that I'd tried everything humanly possible to save her. Could you honestly say that, if you refuse me permission to even try?'

Even stared down into his half-empty glass.

'Please, Mr Powell,' Ronnie begged. 'Please, let me at least try to save her. I love her.'

Evan looked up into Ronnie's dark, brooding eyes. 'So do I,' he said slowly. 'So do I,' he repeated thoughtfully. 'Far too much to allow her to die amongst strangers.'

Chapter Twenty

'You're going to get me shot, Will Powell,' Tina complained as they sneaked around the corner of Danycoedcae Road, creeping close to the damp garden walls of the houses.

'No one is going to shoot you for going roller skating with Gina, you silly girl,' he murmured, squeezing her hand.

'When I come home without her?'

'For pity's sake,' he grumbled. 'You spent long enough plotting your story. You wanted a cup of chocolate in Jenny's house, and Gina didn't. Now what could be simpler than that?'

'Nothing as long as Gina remembers the story, and Papa doesn't interrogate her until she breaks.'

'You're not living in a gangster film, Tina.'

'You don't know Papa,' she retorted briskly. 'He asks more questions than the Spanish Inquisition. And generally gets better results,' she added gloomily.

'And you worry too much.' He pulled her into the shadows. 'Any chance of seeing you after work tomorrow?'

'You don't finish on the market until ten o'clock on a Saturday night.'

'More like eleven, but a fellow can live in hope.'

'Not that much.'

'Shoni's, three o'clock Sunday?'

'What if it's raining?'

'I'll bring an umbrella.'

'Fat lot of good that will do in Shoni's.'

'All you ever do is meef,' he complained playfully. 'Meef, meef, meef.'

'What on earth is meefing?'

'You should know, you do enough of it.' He was wondering whether he dare risk a kiss, when her eyes grew alarmingly round and large.

'Holy Mother of God,' she exclaimed. 'Here comes Ronnie!

220

See you.' She ran round the corner, just as Ronnie thundered his Trojan to a halt outside their front door.

'Close the café early?' she asked, trying desperately to look as though she hadn't a care in the world. He gazed straight past her, completely ignoring her, then ran up the short flight of steps to their front door.

'Serve him right if he tripped over his big flat feet,' she muttered under her breath, reaching the front door just in time for him to slam it in her face.

'Hey, what about me?' she shouted irritably, turning the key and walking in behind him. He was half-way down the passage. He didn't bother to glance back and look at her, let alone apologise. She shook her umbrella outside the door, propped it in the corner on the old tin tray that her mother put there for the purpose, threw her coat over the multitude balancing on the rack, and followed Ronnie down the long flagstoned passage that led from the front to the back of the house.

The radio was blaring into the hot, steamy kitchen. Friday had been her mother's day for making Saturday's fish soup out of the heads and tails of Friday's dinner for as long as she could remember, and the smell of herrings lingered tartly in the air.

'Hello everyone,' she shouted, going to the biscuit barrel and helping herself to a home-made oatmeal crunch. Gina looked up from where she was teaching thirteen-year-old Maria and ten-year-old Stephania how to apply lipstick, and raised her eyebrows. She was dying to ask Tina if William Powell had kissed her, but knew her questions would have to wait until their sisters slept. Nine-year-old Alfredo and six-year-old Robert swept past, sword-fighting with a pair of ill-matched wooden kitchen spoons. Her mother, oblivious to the noise and chatter, smiled absently, continuing to mend a great, long tear in eight-year-old Theresa's school skirt.

'Where's Papa?' Ronnie demanded as he emerged from the washhouse. They all turned towards him, Tina and her mother both noticing a keener edge to his voice than usual.

'He's next door. He and Mr Morris are drilling a hole so they can pass a wire through the wall to set up a wireless speaker for them,' Maria explained. 'Papa thought it would be nice for them to listen to ours. After all, it's on all day.'

'Is everything all right in the café?' Mrs Ronconi shouted above the laughter that greeted Arthur Askey's latest joke. Something in the expression on Ronnie's face made her uneasy.

'Everything's fine, Mama.' He glared at the milling children. 'Everyone under sixteen to bed,' he ordered brusquely.

'Aw Ronnie!' Maria, Stephania, Theresa, Robert and Alfredo chorused in protest.

'This finishes at nine, Ronnie, that's only five minutes. Can't we hear the end of it?' Alfredo begged, knowing that where Ronnie was concerned, his pleading would hold far more weight than that of the girls.

'None of you can hear it above the din you're making,' Ronnie observed unrelentingly. 'Come on, bed. Now!' He stood over them as they trooped mutinously to the washhouse in single file. When he heard the tap running and the sounds of teeth being brushed, he left. A moment later the front door banged shut.

'The minute the show ends,' their mother warned as Alfredo poked his head around the washhouse door, letting in an ice-cold draught of air.

'Promise, Mama. Cross my heart,' Alfredo beamed.

Ronnie opened the Morris' door and walked through to their kitchen.

'It's only me Mr Morris,' he called out as he stepped into the room, which was considerably colder and less cosy than the kitchen in his house. 'Is Papa here?'

'Papa is here,' his father answered from the depths of the cupboard that filled the alcove next to the range, where he was crouched, trying to bore a hole. 'And you're just the man we want. Come here and hold this bit steady while I drill. You wouldn't believe how solid this wall is.'

'Yes I would.' Ronnie went to the cupboard and extracted the drill from his father's hand. 'You've picked the wrong place, Papa,' he smiled. 'You won't do it there, you can't see what you're doing. Here, let me. Near the ceiling will be easier.' He picked up a scarred wooden chair, positioned it on the lino near the communal wall, climbed on it and, holding the bit steady in the crack between wall and ceiling, proceeded to drill steadily. 'Get a cloth please, Papa,' he shouted, as a stream of black mortar poured out of the hole he was making. Mr Morris rushed out the back and returned with a ragged pair of pants.

'I always keep the old clothes, especially the cotton underwear,' Mrs Morris wheezed from her easy chair next to the range. 'They make such good dusters.'

'Yes they do, Mrs Morris. Absorbent too,' Ronnie the knowledgeable café owner called out cheerfully. He persevered, working at a steady pace. 'Have you a drill with a longer bit?' he asked.

'I don't think so.' Mr Morris raked over the few odds and ends of tools that he kept proudly in a wooden box that his eldest son had made in woodwork class before he'd gone off to join the army.

Ronnie balanced the drill in one hand, wiped his eyes with the other, pushed forward, and almost fell off the chair.

'Steady,' his father shouted.

'We're through.'

'There, what did I tell you?' His father rubbed his hands and beamed at the old couple. 'Now all you have to do is put that speaker on top of the dresser. We'll poke the wire from it through the wall, and our Angelo can connect it when he gets back from the café.'

'It's very good of you to go to all this trouble, Mr Ronconi,' Mrs Morris gushed. 'We never thought we'd have radio in our own kitchen, did we Joe?' she smiled up at her husband.

'Never . . .'

'What are you doing out of the café?' Mr Ronconi demanded of his son, suddenly realising that he was home at a peculiar hour. 'No trouble, is there?'

'No trouble,' Ronnie replied evenly. 'Here, you don't have to wait until our Angelo gets home, Mr Morris. Pass me that wire, I'll push it through, go into our kitchen and connect it there.'

'Just in time for the evening theatre show,' Mr Ronconi smiled. 'Some of them are really good. Last week's was about a haunted room in an old house.'

'Ooh,' Mrs Morris squealed. 'Just think of it, Joe, theatre in our own back kitchen.'

Mr Ronconi looked around. Ronnie had already gone. 'I'll just go and see if Ronnie needs a hand,' he said as he backed out of the door. He could stand almost anything except being thanked for his kindness. 'When that speaker starts working, just knock on the

223

wall. Then we'll know to leave the wires alone.' Following his son out of the door, he returned to his own kitchen where Ronnie was putting the finishing touches to a Heath Robinson conglomeration of wires at the back of the radio.

'There, that should do it,' Ronnie announced. 'Do you want to go and check?'

'I told them to knock if they could hear it.' As if to confirm his words a loud bang came from the other side of the wall.

The younger children, hands and faces washed, teeth cleaned and hair brushed, trooped out of the washhouse and stood in a line waiting for their father and mother to kiss them goodnight. Much to Robert's disgust, Ronnie patted him on the head. He adored his big brother, but he hated being patronised. Ronnie, however, was too lost in his own thoughts to notice Robert's squirmings. He was preoccupied with his parents' frequent hints that he should marry. If he'd been about to tell them that he wanted to marry one of the daughters of the Italian community he knew that his parents would have greeted the news ecstatically. He also knew that given time, and conversion to the faith, he could possibly have talked them into accepting Alma as a daughter-in-law. But not Maud. At Gina's age, she was too young. Her religion – her illness – the hint of scandal that still clung to her sister for all of Bethan's marriage to a doctor – taken separately he might have overcome one of the obstacles. Put together, they were simply too much.

When the last of the younger children had raced down the cold passage and up the stairs, he turned to Tina and Gina.

'You two going to sit there all night?'

'It's too early to go to bed,' Tina pouted. 'I'm nineteen . . .'

'And I want to talk to Papa and Mama in private,' Ronnie countered stiffly.

Tina went white. 'If you want to talk to Papa and Mama I have every right to be here,' she began haughtily.

'You, Madam, have no right to listen in . . .'

'If it's about me, I have every right to hear.'

'And what makes you think Ronnie is about to say anything concerning you?' her father enquired suspiciously.

Caught in a trap of her own making, Tina turned on her father and brother like a cornered wildcat. 'You think I'm stupid?' she asked furiously.

'Must we answer that?' Ronnie sighed wearily.

'You think I haven't seen you,' she rounded on her brother, 'sneaking around after me. You followed me tonight, didn't you? Didn't you?' she screamed. 'That's why you want to talk to Papa and Mama. Well I'm a grown woman, not a naughty little girl. I'm old enough to make up my own mind as to who I see, where I go, what I do . . .'

Terrified by the inevitable consequences of Tina's outburst, and the thunderous expression on her father's face, Gina would have sidled out of the door if she could have. But Ronnie blocked her path. She stepped back, and stood alongside her mother, who sat rooted to her chair.

'And what do you think Ronnie saw that was so terrible?' her father shouted, pushing his face very close to Tina's. 'What? Come on, tell me. What have you been doing that you don't want your own father and mother to know about?' He folded his hands inside his arms as if he couldn't trust himself to keep them off her. 'Did you, or did you not go roller skating in Mill Street with Gina?' he asked coldly. 'Or were you lying?'

'She was in Mill Street with me,' Gina dared to interrupt, gabbling hastily. 'She stopped off to have à drink of chocolate with Jenny on the way home, I didn't want to go in with them.' Gina's explanation sounded like a well-rehearsed speech at a children's school concert.

'She was home before nine, so what's the problem?'

Tina's mouth dropped open. She couldn't believe her brother Ronnie had said that.

'If roller skating with Gina and a chocolate with Jenny Griffiths was all she'd done she wouldn't have screamed at you, or be blushing the way she is. She's been out with a boy. That's it, isn't it Tina?' her father shrieked. 'You've been sneaking around with someone behind my back. The same way your sister Laura sneaked around with that, that – '

'Husband,' Ronnie broke in quietly. 'Papa – '

'Papa nothing,' Mr Ronconi raged. 'Tina, what's been going on?'

'Nothing.' Whiter than Ronnie had ever seen her before, Tina swayed on her feet.

'You've been seeing that William Powell, haven't you?' her father raged.

225

'No!' Tina lied defiantly.

'I don't believe you.'

'Papa, you're calling your own daughter a liar,' his wife remonstrated.

Tina's bottom lip trembled and she began to cry.

'There! There, I knew it!' Papa Ronconi began a swift ascent into one of his notorious, and amongst the younger members of his family, much feared, rages.

'All I did was walk home with him,' Tina sobbed tearfully. 'It was the first time ever. We didn't do anything wrong . . .'

'You did something wrong by speaking to him. Just look at you, just look . . .' he babbled, his voice breaking into incoherence.

'Papa I . . . I . . .'

'I forbid you. I absolutely forbid you,' Papa Ronconi's face turned purple. 'I forbid you to see that boy, and what do you do? You go sneaking behind my back, you . . . you slut!'

'Papa!' Ronnie exclaimed angrily.

'Tomorrow you pack your bags and you go to your grandmother in Bardi. She'll see you married off to a decent Italian boy within the month. I'll have no daughter of mine . . .'

Ronnie looked at Tina and jerked his head sharply towards the door.

'. . . Don't you dare leave this room!' his father screamed, beside himself with rage.

'Let her go, Papa,' Ronnie said quietly, with what seemed to Tina amazing courage. 'In a minute I'm going to give you a lot more to shout about than Tina has.'

Evan pushed his way through the crowded passage of the Graig Hotel until he reached the hatch that served as bar to the back rooms. He pulled all the money he had out of his pocket, spread it on his palm and stared at it. He had just enough for two pints, with sixpence left over for the hire of a cart tomorrow, no more. And he knew there was nothing left in the old, cracked Doulton teapot that Elizabeth kept on the top shelf in the kitchen. Throwing all sense of caution to the wind, he handed over everything except the precious sixpence to the barman.

'Bitter please, Albert.'

'Your usual?' the barman asked.

'Two pints.' Evan carried them through to the half-empty back room where Charlie was sitting staring into the fire.

'Cheers, mate.' Charlie picked up his pint and supped it slowly. He'd bought the first pint they'd drunk in the Graig, and he knew Evan had drunk a pint or two earlier, with Ronnie. One was usually Evan's limit on a weekday, so he was obviously troubled by something. But Charlie knew that if Evan wanted to talk about it, he would do so in his own good time.

Will glanced in through the door. Seeing his uncle and Charlie, he walked over to them.

'Pint?' Charlie asked, putting his hand in his pocket.

'No thanks,' Will shook his head. 'I only came in to see if anyone was about. I'm going down the gym to meet Eddie. We'll probably wait until it's time for Haydn to finish, then pick up some chips on the way home.'

'Overtime burning a hole in your pocket?' Charlie smiled.

'No.' The truth of the matter was, Will couldn't wait to tell someone he'd finally walked Tina home. And he was hoping that three heads would be better than one when it came to finding a solution to the obstacles that stood in their way: principally Papa Ronconi and Ronnie. 'Tell Di I'll see her in the shop tomorrow, Uncle Evan,' he said as he went out.

'I'll do that.' Evan went back to his pint. Charlie continued to sup his and study the flames that played between the glowing embers in the fire.

'Ronnie went into the Central Homes and saw Maud tonight,' Evan volunteered eventually.

'So he said in the club,' Charlie murmured.

'So he did.' Evan put down his pint. He screwed up his face thoughtfully. 'Damned fool!' he swore absently.

'Did he say how Maud was?' Charlie asked, wondering if Evan's black mood had been caused by a worsening in her condition.

'Conscious but no better, from what I can work out. Ronnie wants to marry her,' Evan said suddenly. He looked suspiciously at Charlie. 'You don't seem surprised.'

'I thought it might have been something like that when he came into the club looking for you.'

'She's dying,' Evan said bitterly.

'We're all dying.'

227

'Some sooner than others.'

'Ronnie's an intelligent man. I'm sure he knows that.'

Something in the tone of Charlie's voice made Evan look him squarely in the eye. 'You think I should let him marry her?' he demanded incredulously.

'Provided Maud wants to marry him, I can't see any objection,' Charlie said evenly. 'He's a hard worker, he has a share in two cafés, and he's busy building up a third. I would have thought that any father in the town would be proud to have him for a son-in-law.'

'The idiot wants to give up all he owns to take her to Italy.'

'Italy!' This time Charlie had the grace to look surprised.

'He thinks the air in the mountains will cure her.'

'It might,' Charlie agreed cautiously.

'Do you really think there's a chance? Trevor Lewis more or less told me that she's pretty far gone.'

'All I know is doctors aren't God. My sister had lung disease. My mother took her to live with our uncle in the Ural Mountains. She died in the end, but at least she had ten years of life she wouldn't have had if she'd stayed with us.'

Evan knew better than to question the veracity of Charlie's story.

'So you think I should let him take her?'

'That's your decision to make, not mine. All I'm saying is that sometimes it works, and sometimes it doesn't.' He shrugged his massive shoulders and finished his pint. 'And then again he must think a lot of her to want to give up his share in the cafés. Last one for the road?' Charlie held out his hand for Evan's glass. Normally Evan would have protested about the uneven rounds, but this time he handed over his glass.

'What would you do if you were Maud's father?' he asked seriously.

'If I was Maud's father,' Charlie said gravely, 'I think I'd begin by talking to Maud.'

'Giacomo please,' Ronnie's mother begged, calling him by the baptismal name that was hardly ever heard, even in his own family. She was standing in the kitchen as far as she could get from the two men. She had seen her husband angry many times, but had

228

never been unduly perturbed. His type of anger was typical of many Italians: quick to rise, and quick to blow over – until now. This anger was different. He'd never quarrelled so vehemently with any of the children before, and for the first time since she'd met him, twenty-eight years before, she could see real and bitter pain beneath his anger.

Their eldest son was special – to both of them: the only one of their children born in Italy, in her father-in-law's farmhouse in the tiny, primitive, backwater hamlet outside Bardi. Her husband had stayed with her until the birth, then he'd left her for five long years, while he went to Wales to work in his brother's café. He'd promised to send for her the minute he made enough money to provide a comfortable home for her, and his son. But when she waved him off on the bus that left the square in Bardi, neither of them had imagined that it would take so long for him to get established.

While she'd sat and waited in her father's small spartan farmhouse, all she'd had to remind her of her young, passionate husband was her baby, and the monthly money orders he sent, which, no matter how carefully she counted them, never quite reached the figure needed to pay for her and their child's fare to Wales.

She'd cashed the orders in Bardi, spent sparingly and saved prodigiously, and in the meantime her son grew into a fine boy, and as his grandfather had said, 'old beyond his years'.

Giacomo had been born old. When the tickets to Wales finally came, it had been five-year-old Giacomo who'd helped her pack, deciding what was to go and what was to be left behind. Giacomo who'd dried her eyes when the grandparents and maiden aunt had wailed at their leaving. Giacomo who'd taken charge of their tickets, checking the train times, and pronouncing the strange place names that he'd made one of their neighbours (who'd been to Wales and returned) repeat time and again to make sure that he'd got it right. And even after they'd arrived in the two tiny rooms that were their first home, it had been Giacomo who'd helped his father mix the ice cream and stock up the handcart every morning. Giacomo who'd rushed home from school every day to wash dishes in their first café in High Street. Giacomo who'd helped her husband to make his first serious decision to borrow from their uncle to buy the second cafe on the Tumble. Giacomo who was, even now, steering the plans through for their first restaurant . . . Giacomo – always Giacomo.

She couldn't bear to see her husband and much beloved eldest son at loggerheads. The pain was vicious, cruel, almost physical.

'You want to throw up your whole life, everything we've built here,' her husband raged and ranted at Ronnie, 'for a sick girl. A dying girl!'

'I love her,' Ronnie said directly, as though those three words were enough to explain everything.

'You can't remember Bardi . . .' his father began earnestly.

'I remember Bardi,' Ronnie replied. 'Probably better than you. After all, I left it later,' he pointed out drily.

'But this girl. She's not Italian,' his mother said reasonably, as though she were afraid of her words hurting him. 'She's not even healthy, Giacomo. Listen to me, please. I had a brother who died of the lung disease, but he died after he gave it to my sister, and then she died . . .'

'Mama, please don't cry.' Ronnie wrapped his arm around his plump, diminutive mother. 'I want to get married, not die,' he smiled.

'What makes you think that Bardi is such a healthy place?' his father shouted scornfully. 'There's less money there than here. There's no work, except back-breaking farm work. The most you can make is enough food to eat. No coins to jingle in your pocket. It's poverty-stricken. In summer there's nothing but flies . . .'

'At least you can be sure of having a summer in Bardi,' Ronnie retorted.

'Surer than you can be of having food on the table,' his father taunted. 'There were times when we didn't have enough to eat. Why do you think your uncle and I left home?'

'There were a lot more of you in those days, Papa. There's only your father, mother and Aunt Theresa there now. With a young able-bodied fellow like me around the place, we'll soon produce more than enough,' Ronnie asserted forcefully.

'You?' his father ridiculed. 'You? What do you know about farming?'

'About as much as you did about the café business when you came to Wales.' He waited for his father's explosive temper to cool to the point where he could make himself heard again. 'From what I remember of farming in Bardi, the main qualities needed are hard work, brute strength, and the ability to stand foul smells.'

His father's features hardened to a stern, intractable mask. 'You go, and I cut you off with a penny. You will no longer be my son. You will not be welcome in this house. You will not darken my door again. I will give you nothing. Do you understand me? Nothing!' He spat into the fire. 'You leave this house with this girl, and to me you are dead.'

'I am sorry, Papa. I have no choice to make. I am going to marry her, and take her to Bardi.'

His mother burst into tears.

'Go ahead. Go,' his father sneered. 'What will the pair of you do for money? I know that the Powells have none . . .'

'I've worked in the business for thirteen years.'

'You've been fed and clothed. You won't see a penny more than you've already had.'

'The Trojan's in my name. I'll sell it,' Ronnie threatened. 'Even a quick sale will bring in enough for two tickets to Bardi.'

'The van belongs to the business,' his father shrieked.

'It doesn't. I bought it in my name. And I hold the logbook.' Ronnie matched his father's antagonistic glare. 'And I wasn't so dull as not to put a little aside,' he lied, wondering just how much today's takings would be. He'd have to get down to the café quick. The minute he left here.

'You, you dared to rob me? Your own father – '

'No, just took some wages.'

His father knew when he was beaten. Terrified of losing Ronnie, and having got nowhere with his bullying tactics, he tried a different approach.

'Please Ronnie, I'm asking you, begging you, please don't give up. Not now, not when everything is going so well. The new restaurant . . .'

Ronnie found this approach much harder to deal with. 'Tony knows as much as me,' he said simply.

'Tony is destined to be a priest.'

'Not the Tony I know. Ask him what he thinks of girls.'

'Girls!'

'Papa, it doesn't matter,' Ronnie said wearily. 'I didn't come

231

here to fight. I came to tell you that I will be working this weekend, after that no more. I intend to marry Maud as soon as I can. And if we can get tickets we'll be gone by Monday.'

'Then go and be damned for it!' His father turned his back on him.

'Giacomo!' His mother flung herself at him. He kissed her and helped her back into her chair, then opened the kitchen door.

'Where are you going?' his father screeched.

'To pack my clothes,' Ronnie replied. 'I presume that I can take them. They won't fit anyone else.'

'Five minutes. That's all you have, then I call the police and have you thrown out.'

Chapter Twenty-One

Tina and Gina were sitting on the edge of the double bed they shared. The three younger girls were huddled together in the other bed in the room, their eyes wide, fearful at the sounds of the argument coming from the kitchen below. Tina'd left the door open so she could listen to every word that was being said. And never in her life had she felt so much sympathy for her eldest brother.

She watched Ronnie walk upstairs. He passed the door to the girls' room as he went into the box room. It was the smallest room in the house, but until that night he'd been able to call it all his own. As the oldest child by nearly six years, his parents felt he was entitled to a room of his own, even if it was only six foot six inches by five foot.

'Ronnie.' Tina dried her eyes before she crept to the door of his room. She watched as he went to the narrow old wardrobe that scraped alongside the bottom of his small bed and lifted down the same battered cardboard suitcase he had struggled with when he had left Bardi at the age of five. He opened the wardrobe door and began packing his shirts, pants and vests, cramming them into the case anyhow, just as they fell.

'Ronnie, where are you going?' she whispered, as he picked up his one good linen skirt.

'For tonight, the café, afterwards, we'll see.'

'Ronnie, will you and Papa make up?'

'Not this time,' he smiled grimly.

'Is it true?' she ventured. 'Do you really love Maud Powell?'

'Yes,' he answered shortly. Strange, he hadn't minded talking about his feelings to Maud, Mr Powell or Trevor, but Tina was different. She was his kid sister, and he very much minded talking about his personal feelings to her.

'If you love Maud,' she swallowed hard in an effort to gain courage, 'then you must understand what I feel for Will.'

'I'm not sure I can approve of Will Powell,' he said without a

233

trace of humour. 'He's not steady enough to marry a sister of mine.'

'And Maud's too sick and too young to marry anyone,' Tina countered smartly.

'Snap.' He pushed the last of his clothes into the case and looked around. There was his alarm clock: he picked that up and dumped it on top of the clothes. Three books on the windowsill. He looked at them: there was a Bible his aunt had given him on his confirmation, a prayer book his mother had bought him one Christmas, and a western Tony had lent him.

'Give this back to Tony.' He handed Tina the western, and packed the other two books.

She clung to the book, pressing it hard against her chest. 'You're really going Ronnie, aren't you?' she asked, the enormity of what was happening just beginning to sink in.

'Oh yes.' He picked up the case and buttoned his jacket. Then he looked at her. 'I'm really going,' he said slowly.

She clung to him and began to cry again.

'Come on, no tears. Pull yourself together and help Tony, he'll be the one to make all the decisions from now on.'

'But he's going to be a priest!'

'When Papa begins to talk to you again, suggest that he tries to keep that one for Robert. He'd better not try Angelo or Alfredo. I'm afraid they're too hot-blooded. Like him.'

She heard him walk along the landing and whisper goodbyes at both the girls' and the boys' bedroom doors. Then the front door slammed. The Trojan started up. She was still standing there in the empty bedroom when her mother came up moments later. They sank on to his bed together and cried. More for themselves than for Ronnie.

Since his one brief, disastrous appearance on stage, Haydn had found his work at the Town Hall unbearable. The title 'callboy' meant a lot more than simply calling the acts to go on stage. Most of his time was spent clearing the dressing rooms of accumulated rubbish, buying evening papers, and running errands for the 'stars', collecting discarded props and making sure they were put back where they could be found for the next performance. And then, when the show was over and the performers and manager were relaxing, he and the rest of the staff under the direction of the under-manager had to comb through the rows of seats, checking them for cleanliness and things left behind.

The routine he'd so found exciting when he first worked in the Town Hall now became dull, boring and tedious in the extreme. The smell of greasepaint palled until the merest hint of it in the atmosphere made him nauseous. The sounds of the orchestra that had once set his pulse racing and foot tapping, now clattered, deafening and discordant, in his ears. Each and every day he came to loathe his work more and more, the loathing born of the realisation that there was no prospect of ever climbing as high as even the lowly ranks of the chorus. This was it! His life! All he had. All he was ever likely to have, unless he lost his job and sank into the mass of unemployed.

Dreams shattered, there were days when he could barely summon energy enough to drag himself out of bed. Ambition, aspirations, strength – all dissipated into a mood of sullen moroseness. There were no light spots, no highlights left to brighten his days. Not even Jenny. Whenever he walked past the shop he was tempted to linger, go in and find out if she'd talk to him, but fear of rejection always made him cross the road. He knew his family were beginning to look at him sideways. Not his parents – they were both too wrapped up in Maud's illness to notice anyone, or anything – but the others had observed and remarked on what William termed 'his departure from the land of the living'.

He had never found the curtailment of his social life by work so irksome. But even on those nights when he could have gone into any one of the half a dozen pubs in Pontypridd that dared to breach the strict code of licensing hours, he didn't. Occasionally he met the landlords or barmaids of the pubs he'd frequented, and they pleaded with him to return to sing, insisting that everyone was missing him. He suspected their motives, steeped in the belief that after his last fiasco people only wanted to hear him to have a good laugh at his poor performance and failed ambitions. He invariably smiled and told them he might call in later, but never did. It was easier than announcing that he'd decided to give up singing – permanently.

The first Friday night that Maud spent in hospital dragged, worse than any other. He looked around the Town Hall and tried desperately to think of a way out, both for her and himself. He was convinced that money could buy anything – even a cure for his sister – but short of robbing a bank he didn't know where to begin. If he'd studied harder in school he might have got a scholarship out of the boys' grammar school to go to university – then he remembered his father on short time and realised that even if he'd won a scholarship that had paid his fees, he wouldn't have been able to manage his living expenses. And as he was only twenty he wouldn't even be qualified yet, which meant he'd still be poverty-stricken, and of no real use to Maud at all.

'Move it, Haydn,' one of the stagehands shouted, pushing a scenery float towards him. He caught it just before it toppled on its side. Shuffling round the back curtain, they pushed it out of the way. 'Only the floor check to do and we can go home,' Fred the stagehand mumbled through his toothless gums.

Haydn stared dully at Fred's coarse, whiskery face that rarely saw a razor, noticed his broad back, curved and bowed from lifting too many heavy weights over too many years, studied his clothes, old, stained and musty smelling from lack of washing. Would this be him forty years from now? There was no one around now who could say what Fred had looked like when he'd started in the Town Hall. Perhaps he'd even wanted to go on stage, like him.

'Did you ever think about the stage, Fred?' he asked suddenly.

'You say something, Haydn?' Fred cocked his head to one side, turning his good ear towards Haydn.

'Did you ever want to go on stage, Fred?' Haydn shouted.

'Oh ay,' Fred's face split into a large, gummy grin. 'When I was a nipper, like, that's why I took a job here.'

Haydn picked up a torch from the box where they were kept between houses, slammed open the door into the auditorium, and stepped down, ready for the search. That did it. He'd have to leave. He didn't know how, or where, he only knew he had to go.

The search seemed to take three times as long as usual. By the end of it he was hot, sweaty and his hands were sticky from the discarded chewing gum, toffee wrappers and other unmentionables he'd picked up. He washed in the grimy staff toilet that never received more than a quick, cursory wipe-over; the cleaners always left it until last, knowing that the manager would never deign to enter it to check their handiwork.

He hung away his uniform jacket, bell-boy cap, collar and bow tie in the cubicle that held staff uniforms. Tying a muffler over his collarless shirt, he shrugged his arms into his own jacket and rammed his well-worn cap on his head. The night air was cold and damp, the street wet underfoot, but for the first time in days it had stopped raining.

'Haydn?'

He looked up. William and Eddie were waiting for him.

'How about a drink in the Horse and Groom?' Will grinned.

'I don't much feel like a drink.' Head down, Haydn walked on. Eddie and Will had to run to keep up with him.

'We called in Ronconi's, and Ronnie told us he'd seen Maud tonight,' Eddie burst out.

'Ronnie Ronconi?' Haydn paused in amazement.

'Apparently he delivered some eggs to the ward for the Catholic Mothers' Union,' William explained. 'He said Maud was awake, and not feeling too bad at all.'

'So you see we have got something to celebrate after all,' Eddie chirped.

'I'll celebrate the day she comes out of that place,' Haydn growled.

'Bad night?' Eddie ventured sympathetically.

'No worse than any other.'

Eddie and Will exchanged glances behind Haydn's back.

'Come on, a pint will do us all good, and it's on me,' Eddie chivvied.

'You come into money?' Haydn asked.

'In a way. I worked on Charlie's stall today.'

'And he has the makings of a fine butcher,' William added generously. 'Come on Haydn, don't be a stick-in-the-mud,' Will added his powers of persuasion to Eddie's. 'We thought if we went to the Horse and Groom we might see one of the porters, or even a nurse finishing the late shift. And you never know, they might have something to add to what Ronnie told us.'

Ashamed of his rage, Haydn nodded agreement. He'd been so wrapped up in what he saw as his own problems, he'd forgotten that Eddie and William were fond of Maud too.

The Horse and Groom, situated at the foot of the Graig hill in

High Street, was the sort of pub that only really came to life after hours. It was packed out, and Eddie had to fight his way to the bar. A chorus of voices greeted their arrival, demanding a song from Haydn. After his fifth curt refusal, he heard someone whisper that his sister was lying seriously ill in the Central Homes; after that he was left alone. He went to a quiet corner and leant his elbow on one of the standing-height marble and iron tables, the only one that was free. William looked around, searching for a familiar face. Eventually he found one.

'Glan?' he shouted. 'Just the man we want to see. Spare us a minute?' he asked, conveniently forgetting all the time he could quite cheerfully have punched Glan's head off his shoulders.

'I'll be there now.' Smelling a free pint in the air, Glan picked up his half-empty glass and pushed his way through the throng to join them.

'Have you heard how Maud is?' Will asked quietly as soon as Glan was within earshot.

'Heard she's bad,' Glan said bluntly.

'Nothing else?' Will asked hopefully.

'Just that. We brought a body down from her ward tonight. But it wasn't her. About the same age, though, and from what the nurse said, next bed.'

There was a supercilious smirk on Glan's face that Will longed to wipe off.

'Is there anyone here who works on her ward?' Haydn asked.

'Don't know of any nurses who come into this bar. A few go into the Ladies only room, but not after hours.' Glan downed most of his pint, still hoping for a free one. 'And not many porters go up to the TB ward. There's not much call for us unless there's a body that needs shifting like tonight, or a patient needs an operation. And because they operate off the wards we don't always go up for that. I'll try to find out more for you tomorrow, if you like,' he offered, pointedly twiddling his empty glass.

'I'd be grateful if you would,' Haydn replied.

'You're looking a bit down tonight,' Glan commented tactlessly.

'Anyone would, the length of time Eddie's taking to get our beer,' Will broke in quickly.

'You drinking with your brother?'

'Any reason why I shouldn't?' Haydn asked warily.

'Well, all I can say is you're more forgiving than I would be in your shoes,' Glan said airily. 'But then there's no accounting for people, and as my father says, you Powells are a strange lot.'

'What are you gabbling about?' William demanded irritably, sensing one of Glan's infamous 'stirs' coming.

'Haydn's girlfriend, of course.'

'I haven't got a girlfriend,' Haydn countered angrily, ignoring the hard look that William was giving him.

'Well you and Jenny Griffiths did go on for a long time and we all supposed – '

'Then you all supposed wrong, Glan Richards.' Haydn looked around for Eddie. All he wanted was his pint so he could drink it and get out of the pub.

'So I see. Or at least I did after I saw her wrapping herself around Eddie tonight at the top of Factory Lane. Honest to God, I thought he was going to eat her. It's just as well she took him into her back yard when she did. If she hadn't they might have both been arrested. Old Mrs Evans' eyes were nearly popping out of her head as it was. What's the betting she'll start a rumour on the Graig tomorrow that we'll see a shotgun wedding before too many months have passed?' he finished maliciously.

'Whose shotgun wedding?' Eddie lined three full pints up on the table.

'You and Jenny Griffiths.' Haydn's voice was low. Soft. 'Glan was just telling us how he'd seen the pair of you wrapped around each other at the top of Factory Lane tonight.'

Eddie looked up guiltily, and that look told Haydn everything he hadn't known, and a great deal more besides. Picking up one of the pint glasses Eddie had just placed on the table, he threw its contents full in Eddie's face.

'Haydn!' Eddie ran out of the door after him. William was half-way out of the room behind them when he remembered the beer – and Glan. He picked up both remaining glasses and drank them, one straight after the other in quick succession. Wiping his mouth with the back of his hand, he turned to Glan.

'I'll not forget this in a hurry, Glan Richards,' he said furiously, then followed his cousins.

Eddie was shouting Haydn's name as he ran up the Graig hill, beer trickling through his hair, down his face and into his clothes. He caught up with his brother outside the Temple Chapel.

'I didn't mean for it to happen,' he pleaded. 'Neither of us did. It's just that she was by herself, and I took her home – '

'She was my girlfriend.' Until that moment Haydn hadn't admitted even to himself just how much he wanted her back.

'That's just it, Haydn,' Eddie protested. 'She *was* your girlfriend. I wouldn't have taken her home if you'd still been going out with her.'

An upstairs window banged open in the terrace across the road and an irate male voice yelled, 'For Christ's sake keep it down out there! Some people have to get up in the morning.'

'She said you were through,' Eddie whispered miserably. 'I didn't go looking for her. We just bumped into one another in the roller hall in Mill Street. It was getting late and she asked me to take her home . . .'

'And you muscled in,' Haydn said furiously.

'It wasn't like that,' Eddie protested.

'Glan said you kissed her . . . and more. Did you?' he demanded savagely. 'Did you?' he repeated wildly.

Shamefaced, Eddie looked down at his boots. Haydn lashed out, catching him off guard. As Eddie fell on to the soaking wet pavement it was as much as he could do to remember that Haydn was his brother. Anyone else and he would have been up on his feet and after them before they'd gone six yards.

Ronnie moved restlessly around the café until closing time, superficially busy but in fact accomplishing very little. Customers spoke to him, told him what they wanted, paid their bills, and he managed to misunderstand at least two out of every three orders. Alma, uncertain what was going on in Ronnie's mind but fearing the worst, flounced round the tables in a foul mood. Tony and Angelo, who were working behind the counter and in the kitchen, gave both her and Ronnie as wide a berth as possible in between checking the clock. Despite the brisk trade, the evening dragged slowly for both of them until eleven-thirty, when Ronnie finally locked the door.

Turning his back on Alma, who'd already begun to pile chairs on tables and sweep the floor, he shut himself in the kitchen with an apprehensive Tony and Angelo, and told them as much about the quarrel he'd had with his father as he reasonably could without mentioning Maud's name; finally he announced that if all went well he'd be leaving Pontypridd for Bardi within the week. Ignoring their shell-shocked faces, he handed them their coats and told them to leave.

Wondering if something had happened between Ronnie and Alma, Tony tried to talk to her on his way out. But all he got for his trouble was a brusque, 'How the hell should I know what's going on with your brother?'

Ronnie saw his brothers out and pulled down the shutters. Alma finished the floor, and went to get her coat. Ronnie waylaid her on her way out.

'I'd like to talk to you,' he said quietly. She saw that he'd taken the chairs down from the table closest to the stove, and laid out two cups of coffee on it. A lump came to her throat. It was the sort of thing he'd done when they were getting to know one another, before she'd begun to go upstairs with him.

'I have to go,' she said tersely, biting her lower lip in an effort to stop herself from crying.

'Please? Just for a few minutes,' he pleaded. 'I'll drive you home afterwards.'

The spectacle of sardonic, capable and confident Ronnie, her boss and lover, quietly and softly begging her to stay and talk to him was too much. She sank down on one of the chairs and opened her handbag, rummaging blindly for a handkerchief.

'I wanted to tell you – '

'You don't have to tell me anything!' she snapped bitterly.

'But I want to, Alma. I owe you a great deal. And I know I've treated you very badly.'

'If you know, then there's no point in talking about it.'

He laid his hand gently on her arm. 'I'm sorry, Alma.' His voice was soft, sincere. 'Very, very sorry. If I'd known that I was going to fall in love with Maud Powell . . .'

'Then you do love her?'

'You were the one who told me, remember?' he murmured wryly. 'Alma, if I'd known that we were going to end up like this I wouldn't have . . . have . . .' he searched in vain for the word he wanted.

'Wouldn't have what, Ronnie?' she demanded furiously. 'Slept with me? Made me fall in love with you?'

He looked at her silently, recollecting the depth of his feelings for Maud. Knowing how devastated and broken he'd feel if it was Maud who was walking away from him.

'I wanted you to know that the last thing I intended was for you to get hurt; that I'm grateful to you. I respect you. That if there's anything you need, anything at all that I can do to help you, you only have to say the word, and I'll – '

'You'll what, Ronnie?' she cried acidly. 'Wave your magic wand and transform me into unsoiled goods? Or would it soothe your conscience to give me money, and make me feel even more like a whore than I do already?'

'What I also wanted to tell you, before you found out from someone else, is that Maud and I are to be married as soon as the ceremony can be arranged,' he said quickly, glossing over Evan Powell's refusal to give his permission. 'I spoke to Maud tonight, asked her to marry me, and she said yes.'

Alma sat white-faced and very still, but said nothing.

'As soon as we're married, we'll be leaving – '

'Leaving Pontypridd?'

'I'm taking her to Italy.'

'In God's name, why?'

When she'd screamed, 'you love Maud Powell' at Ronnie, she'd hoped against hope for a denial that she could believe. For twenty-four hours she'd lived on tenterhooks, hating herself for thinking that it could be worse. That Ronnie could have fallen in love with a girl who wasn't out of reach in the TB ward of the Graig Hospital. She'd been prepared for Ronnie to ignore her, and moon around after his sick love, but the thought that he'd leave Pontypridd had never once crossed her mind. To lose him to a girl as young and as ill as Maud Powell was torture, but the realisation that she might never see him again was purgatory.

'You'll be back,' she whispered, needing to believe it.

'No.' He looked her in the eye so there could be no misunderstanding between them. 'I'm taking Maud to Italy in the hope that she'll get well . . .'

'But she might not,' Alma blurted out thoughtlessly, loathing herself afterwards.

'And she might,' he countered sternly. 'Maud's the reason I'm going, but I won't be returning because I've burned my boats with my father. He won't have me back here.'

'But where will you go? What will you do?'

'My grandfather has a farm. We'll live on it.'

'Ronnie, think about what you're doing,' she pleaded, forgetting her fury with him for an instant, knowing just how much the business and the cafés meant to him. 'You only saw Maud Powell a few weeks ago. Your falling in love with her is like Tina falling in love with Clark Gable.'

'No,' he said abruptly, dismissing the thought: it was one he'd already considered – and rejected. 'I've known Maud Powell all my life. It just took you to make me see her in a different light, sooner rather than later. I'm sorry, Alma – ' he reached out and took her hand in his, '– I've made my choice. And my only regret is that I've caused you pain. But I promise, I'll talk to Tony, make sure you always have a job here, and in the new place. That if you want or need anything he'll help you out. I'd like to think that you and I could still be friends – '

'Friends!' She snatched her hand away, and stood up. 'Friends! Ronnie, you want it all don't you? A sweet, virginal, dying wife – and my blessing. Well you damned well can't have it. You're nothing but a selfish swine, Ronnie Ronconi. You used me . . .'

'I never meant to,' he protested.

'And you think, because you didn't mean to it will all come right. Well, it won't. I hate you! Hate you!' She swept her hand across the table, sending the coffee cups flying. They shattered against the wall and sent rivulets of coffee shooting over the floor and clean tables. 'I wish you and her dead! I wish . . . I wish I'd never set eyes on you or your bloody café.' She ran to the door and wrestled with the lock. Ronnie wisely decided against following her. Eventually she managed to wrench the door open. He watched her go with mixed feelings of shame, weariness, and relief that it was finally all over between them.

Chapter Twenty-Two

For the second night running Ronnie didn't sleep. He worked vigorously until two in the morning. The place had never been so clean. Relishing the peace and quiet, he scrubbed the kitchen tables, sink, walls and floor. The mindless labour left him free to take stock and think. He'd accomplished a great deal in one day. He'd proposed to Maud, and been accepted. He'd broken the news to his father and Alma, and suffered the worst of their rages. All that remained was to see Evan Powell again and persuade him to let Maud go. Then he could take her out of the Central Homes, marry her – and leave. It was simple. All he had to do was concentrate his energies on convincing Evan that it was the only thing to do – for Maud's sake.

When the entire café was spotless and fragrant with the smell of bleach and polish he put on his coat. He was half-way out of the door when he realised that the early hours of the morning was not the best time to make a social call.

He took off his coat and went to the big cupboard in the kitchen. Ignoring the bottles, he pulled out the ledgers and account books from the top shelf, set a kettle of water on the range to boil and made a jug of coffee. Taking the jug and the books over to the table in front of the door, he sat down and began to study. Unlike his father, he'd always been meticulous about figures: he knew to the last penny what had to be spent setting up the new restaurant, and what amount would be needed to keep it going through the first lean months when he doubted they'd cover costs. He pored over the bank books and ledgers, working out his figures carefully, checking and double-checking every balance.

He couldn't have picked a worse time to leave the business. Investing in any new venture was inevitably expensive; in a smart new restaurant, doubly so. After his father's lifetime of hard work and the thirteen years that he'd put into the business, they had a surplus of just two hundred pounds that wasn't earmarked for the new place. Deciding he couldn't take it all, he settled on half.

Picking up the chequebook he wrote out a cheque to cash. By the time he'd paid for the tickets to Bardi there wouldn't be a great deal left to begin a new life, but whatever there was would have to do. He tore the cheque out of the book, and penned a note detailing all his calculations for Tony's benefit. He smiled as he wrote. He wasn't the only one in the family who'd be getting his own way. Tony wouldn't be going into the priesthood after all. He felt sorry for Angelo, Alfredo and Robert. One of them would now undoubtedly be earmarked to bear the brunt of their father's religious ambitions.

The hands on the clock pointed to five-thirty as he locked the cupboard door on the books. He walked into the café and looked around. He'd been fifteen, Angelo's age now, when his father had borrowed money from his uncle and bought the place. Papa would never have done it if he hadn't persuaded him.

He'd spent his first full year out of school in their café in High Street, and twelve years here. He'd never known any other working life. What if his father was right? What if he couldn't adapt to farming? Pushing the unpleasant thought from his mind he opened the front door and pulled up the shutters. The sky was just beginning to lighten, there were no clouds. Perhaps it wouldn't rain today. He hoped so. Somehow it seemed like a good omen.

'You can't be serious?' Elizabeth questioned Evan sharply as he heaved himself out of bed before her for the first time in years, and pulled his trousers on over the long johns he'd slept in.

'You got any better ideas, woman?' he countered angrily.

'But Maud's sick. She's . . .'

'Dying!' Evan supplied succinctly. 'I'm going down Trevor Lewis's straight after breakfast, and I'm going to ask him to let me see Maud. If she loves Ronnie as much as he seems to love her, we'll get her out of that place today. Then we'll see about arranging a wedding.'

'But she's a child!' Elizabeth protested strongly. 'She can't possibly know what she wants, not at her age . . .'

'She's going to be a dead child very soon if something isn't done,' Evan stated bluntly. 'Ronnie's offered her a chance. Not much of one, but a chance, and if it's what Maud wants I'm not going to stand in her way.'

'Have you thought to ask what the Ronconis have to say about all this?'

'Knowing the Ronconis, they'll have enough to say, and all of it loud,' Evan replied sternly. 'I've told you what I'm going to do, Elizabeth. It's not up for discussion. If Maud wants to marry Ronnie Ronconi, then the sooner it's done and they're on their way to Italy the better.'

Diana heard her uncle leave his bedroom and go downstairs. She glanced at the hands on the battered, painted tin alarm clock on her chest of drawers. They pointed to twenty-past five; usually only her aunt was up at this hour. She pulled the bedclothes over her shoulder and explored her wakening body. Every bit of her was sore and aching, as though she'd been pushed through a crushing mill. She lay there, reliving last night's nightmare, watching the minutes tick slowly, inexorably past.

She heard her aunt leave her bed, pour water into her basin and wash. There were creaks and groans as Elizabeth walked over the bedroom floor. The wardrobe door opened and closed. Water ran as her aunt emptied her basin into the slop jar. The protest of bedsprings as the bedclothes were pulled back. She listened, but failed to hear Haydn's and Eddie's voices. They must have been out late, or had a pint too many, to sleep in until now.

The hands crept round to a quarter to six. Normally she would have been out of bed and dressed. Time to make a move. She sat up stiffly, thrusting her legs out from under the bedclothes. The last thing she wanted to do was excite her aunt's, or anyone else's, suspicions by doing anything out of the ordinary. Her handbag was on the chest of drawers, propped up against the toilet set Will had brought from their Uncle Huw's house. She looked at it in disgust. She had stuffed the five pounds Ben had given her into it last night. Five pounds! Ten weeks' rent and subsistence money. Would she be able to find a job in that time? Would she be able to walk around the town, holding her head up, after what Ben had done to her? What if anyone besides Wyn found out, or guessed . . .

Elizabeth's heavy step crossed the landing. She rapped her knuckles hard on the boys' door. 'Six o'clock,' she called briskly. 'Time you were up.' A muffled reply came from the room.

'Diana!' she shouted coldly without troubling herself to take another step along the landing.

'I'm dressing, aunt,' Diana lied, struggling to her feet. Needles of pain pierced her entire body, bringing with them a tidal wave of shame. She bent double and buried her head in her hands. When the spasm passed, she clung to the chest and peered into the small mirror that her brother had brought along with the toilet set. Her eyes were red-rimmed and puffy. There were enormous black shadows beneath them, and a plethora of red marks around her neck. Bruises were turning from red to black on her cheeks. There were bound to be questions. She'd just have to dream up some lie as an explanation.

She washed dully, mechanically, trying not to look down at her body, but as she rubbed her flannel over the flat of her stomach a ghastly thought crossed her mind. What if Ben had made her pregnant? What if his child was already forming inside her?

Revolted by the idea, she fell back on the bed. That would really be the ultimate horror. Just the thought of being pregnant disgusted her – but Ben . . .

'Diana!' her aunt called irritably up the stairs. Gulping in a great draught of air, she pulled herself together, finished washing, dressed and made her way unsteadily down the stairs, clinging to the banisters for support. Charlie, Eddie and William were sitting at the table. She thought it strange that she hadn't heard Eddie go downstairs, but she was in no mood to question him. They, like her, all seemed subdued.

She went out the back. The morning air was cold and fresh, even in the shelter of the small back yard. She used the *ty bach*, and washed her hands and cleaned her teeth in the washhouse.

'No breakfast today?' her aunt asked suspiciously as Diana laid her hand on the knob of the door between kitchen and passage.

'Not this morning, thank you aunt,' Diana mumbled meekly.

'Christ, what happened to you?' Will demanded, looking at his sister for the first time that morning, and seeing her bruises.

'A pile of boxes fell on top of me in the stockroom yesterday,' Diana lied quickly.

'Then I'll go down that shop and give Ben Springer a piece of my mind. He's obviously working you too hard. You look terrible,' Will said solicitously.

247

'Don't bother,' Diana insisted hastily. 'It was my fault, really. I tripped as I came down off the ladder. I'm going to call in and see Laura on the way into town. Just to check I haven't broken anything.'

'If you're not well you can't work, sis,' Will said firmly.

'I'm all right.'

'You don't look all right to me.'

'I told you, I'll check with Laura before I go in.'

'Promise?'

'I promise,' she agreed irritably.

'You turn up late again today and you're likely to lose your job,' Elizabeth carped.

'I'll walk down with you, sis.' Will gave his aunt a telling look as he rose from the table, leaving his breakfast half-eaten in front of him.

'If you're going now, you can open up, Will,' Charlie threw the keys of the stall at him. 'I'll go to the slaughterhouse and pick up another lamb.'

'And I've business to attend to this morning, as well,' Evan announced, walking in through the door in his best suit.

'I thought you left half an hour ago,' Elizabeth commented.

'I went upstairs to change after I washed.'

'So I see,' Elizabeth frowned disapprovingly.

'Do you want to come with me? If you do you might be able to talk to Maud yourself.'

'You going to see Maud?' Eddie asked eagerly.

'No he's not,' Elizabeth dismissed coldly. 'He's only going to try. And unlike him I haven't a morning to waste on a fool's errand.' Picking up the coal bucket, she walked out to the coalhouse.

'I'll walk down as far as Laura and Trevor's with you, Diana,' Evan said flatly, ignoring Elizabeth's comments. He looked at Eddie. 'Get the horse and cart out of the yard.' He tossed him his last sixpence. 'Can you do Cilfynydd on your own?'

'Of course. Have you got any pennies for the rags?'

'I forgot.'

'But it's Saturday.'

Evan brushed an imaginary speck of dust from his coat. 'You're going to have to make do with the sweets and bits and pieces we've got,' he asserted brusquely.

248

'Here.' Knowing how important pennies were on Saturdays, Charlie dug into his pocket and studied his change. 'There's two bob's worth of coppers there.'

'I'll pay you back tonight, Charlie,' Evan said stiffly.

'Fine.' Charlie pushed a whole round of black pudding into his mouth.

'Has anyone called Haydn?' Elizabeth asked as she walked back in with the bucket full of small coals.

'I'll call him on the way out. Ready Diana?'

Elizabeth washed her hands and began to clear the table. She heard Evan shout up to Haydn, and Haydn call back. She relaid a place at the table and pulled the letter that had come for him that morning out of her apron pocket. It was postmarked Brighton. She wondered just who Haydn knew in that town.

'You got time for a cuppa?' Laura asked Diana, as Evan and Trevor left the house.

'Yes.' Diana sat in Trevor's easy chair next to the stove. It faced the small window that overlooked the tiny paved back yard. Hemmed in by the washhouse wall on one side and the five-foot wall that separated Laura's yard from next door's on the other, the window did little to brighten the atmosphere of the gloomy kitchen, but like an imaginatively painted scene it lent an impression of what nature could do if it was given half a chance. At the end of the short, dark tunnel of walls there was a square of brilliant sunshine filled with a shiny-leaved, evergreen bush.

'Been busy gardening?' Diana asked.

'Got to do something to hide Trevor's rows of vegetables.' Laura glanced at the clock. It was a quarter-past seven. If Diana intended to go to work, she was late. An unheard-of phenomenon when there were forty girls for every job. Something was obviously very wrong, but Laura bided her time, carrying dishes to the washhouse, making a fresh pot of tea, all the while sneaking surreptitious glances at the bruises that Diana had insisted she'd picked up when stock had fallen on her in the shoe shop.

She might have fooled the men, but not Laura, who'd done a stint on the casualty ward of the Royal Infirmary. She'd seen too many women and children who'd been battered by their drunken menfolk. There was only one way that Diana could have acquired the long marks on her neck, and it wasn't by falling stock. They were very obviously finger pressure marks, and by the width and length of them, they'd been caused by large hands. The huge, spreading bruise that was on the point of turning from deep purple to black on her chin looked as though it was the result of a blow from a fist. It must have been a heavy blow to have caused such damage, but Laura suspected that for every mark she could see there were probably ten more that she couldn't.

'Two sugars?' Laura asked, deciding that if Diana hadn't said anything by the time they were both sitting down, she would forget the training that had taught her to be tactful first and curious last, and bring the subject up herself.

'Please.'

Laura spooned sugar into both cups, stirred them, handed one to Diana and sat in the chair opposite her.

'Skiving off today, are we?' she questioned lightly.

Diana was trembling too much to carry her cup to her mouth.

'Trouble with Ben Springer?' Laura asked intuitively. Diana put her head down and nodded dumbly. 'If the stories I've heard are true, you're not the first, love, and unfortunately you probably won't be the last.'

Laura laid her cup safely on the table, and reached across to take Diana's from her shaking hands. 'Did he do this?' She put Diana's cup down, before gently touching the cut on Diana's forehead. Dissolving into sobs, Diana was incapable of answering. 'Come on, love, did he hit you?' Laura continued to probe. Alarmed by Diana's silence, she laid her fingers under Diana's chin and lifted her head so she could look into Diana's eyes. 'Did he rape you?' she asked quietly.

'Yes!' Diana's confession was harsh, guttural.

'You poor, poor love.' Laura took her into her arms.

'Laura, I didn't know where to go, who to turn to,' Diana sobbed, her hair falling over her face and getting in the way of her eyes and mouth. 'He said, he said . . . terrible things about me,' she whimpered. 'He said if I told anyone what had happened, they wouldn't believe me. And now . . . now I could have a baby. Couldn't I?' she demanded, willing Laura to say otherwise.

'Not if Trevor and I have any say in the matter.' Laura smoothed Diana's hair back, away from her forehead. 'It'll be all right. You'll see, we'll sort it out, love. Don't worry. You'll be fine, there's pills you can take – '

'You don't understand,' Diana cried hysterically. 'It can't be sorted out. Not now. Not ever. What he did to me . . . what he . . . I'll never be the same again. Never!'

'Of course you will. You're still the same person.'

'No I'm not. You don't know what it was like. You weren't there. He . . . he . . .' The horror flooded over her again with renewed vigour, sparing her none of the degrading, miserable details. 'I just wish I was dead!' she moaned with a fervour that sent a chill down Laura's spine.

'We'll wait for Trevor,' Laura said insistently, struggling to conceal her panic. 'Don't worry. He'll help you. He'll know what to do.' Laura was never more grateful that she had a husband to turn to. One look at Diana made her ralise that any husband who was prepared to act as a buffer between the world and his wife would do, but in finding one as kind, gentle, loving and understanding as Trevor, she'd struck gold.

'Your breakfast is on the table,' Elizabeth said coldly to Haydn as he walked into the kitchen from the washhouse.

'I'm late,' Haydn said shortly, stating the obvious. 'I haven't time to eat.'

'You might be late, but you'll soon be ill as well if you go working all day on that stall, and all night in that . . . that place' – Elizabeth never could bring herself to say the name of the Town Hall. In the chapel's and her opinion the theatre was synonymous with all the evils of Sodom and Gomorrah – '. . . with nothing inside you. Come on now, be sensible.' She pushed towards him a bowl of thick, lumpy porridge surrounded by a moat of watery milk and topped by a gleaming cap of brown sugar.

'I told you, I don't want it,' Haydn snapped with uncommon discourtesy, for him.

'You'll be passing out half-way through the morning,' Elizabeth warned.

'More like if I eat it I'll be throwing up half-way down the Graig Hill,' he retorted vehemently.

'There's no need to be vulgar.'

'Throwing up is not vulgar.'

Elizabeth didn't know what to make of Haydn. She'd never seen him in such an aggressive mood. Deciding that it might be as well to divert his attention than argue any further about what was vulgar and what was not, she nodded towards the table.

'A letter came for you,' she said briefly.

Haydn looked at it. He could count on one hand the number of letters he'd received in his life. Sitting down in his chair he picked it up, turning it over so he could read the postmark.

'I didn't know you were acquainted with anyone in Brighton,' Elizabeth commented indifferently.

'Neither did I.'

She poured and set a cup of tea at his elbow. Hesitating for a moment, she debated whether or not to have one herself. Haydn rarely had more than one cup and there were at least three in the pot. Deciding it would be a shame to waste it, she eventually poured the second one of the morning for herself.

Forgetting his earlier assertions, Haydn absently spooned a mouthful of porridge into his mouth before attacking the envelope with his thumbnail. He ripped it open awkwardly, tearing a corner off the letter in his eagerness to read the contents.

'You should have used a knife,' Elizabeth admonished. It was not in her nature to allow an opportunity for criticism to pass unnoticed.

'Didn't see one handy.' Haydn picked up the corner and held it next to the torn sheet of paper.

'Violet notepaper,' his mother clucked disapprovingly. 'A sign of poor taste.'

Haydn didn't hear her. He was already reading the letter.

Dear Haydn.

I don't know if you remember me. I certainly remember you and the night we spent in the two-foot-nine after the show, when you and Alice entertained us all by singing 'Heart and Soul'. I'm getting together a cast for a pantomime to be performed in one of the smaller Brighton theatres. A friend of mine is putting up the money and he's given me carte blanche on the artistic side. I've already managed to book Alice Moore to play Cinderella, and when we talked about Buttons, she suggested contacting you.

If – and it is an 'if' – the show's a hit, we may tour the North with it in the New Year. I say 'if' because I don't want to mislead you. All I'm offering is twelve weeks' work initially, and that isn't much to give up a steady job like yours for.

I didn't want to write to you care of the Town Hall in case the letter got lost, so Alice rang the pub and wheedled your address out of the barmaid. If you're cross about it, be cross with us, not the barmaid. Alice can be very persuasive when she wants to be.

Please give the offer some thought before turning it down as you did with Ambrose. It's a break, as they say in this business. Not a grand break, but if you work at it, it could lead to something better. We start rehearsals Monday next. They last for four weeks, and we're offering one pound ten shillings a week during rehearsals, rising to two pounds when we open. It's not the three pounds a week Ambrose offered you but there's no strings attached, of the kind that Ambrose dangled, I promise. You can live with my sister who lets out good theatrical digs at the above address. It'll be ten shillings a week all found, and I promise you won't find better or cheaper in Brighton. Not during the season, and if you're careful you'll still be able to help out at home. (Alice mentioned you had problems there.)

Should your answer be no, would you please reply as I'll have to cast around for someone to replace you. If you agree, please send a telegram, or better still turn up yourself, as soon as you can.

yours, and best wishes,
Patsy Duval

P.S. Alice sends her special love, and wants me to say she hopes you'll come.

Haydn read the letter over slowly twice again, studying the enormous flourishing 'D' that dwarfed the remainder of Patsy's signature. Irritated by his silence, Elizabeth left the table and began to fuss and fidget with the stove.

'You're now very late,' she pointed out sourly.

'The letter is from one of the head girls.' Haydn smiled for the first time in days as he looked up at her.

'A head girl, from a school?' Elizabeth stared at him uncomprehendingly.

253

'Not a school, a chorus,' Haydn laughed.

'I didn't know they had such things.' Elizabeth frowned, tight-lipped.

'She's offered me a job for the Christmas season. In panto-mime, in Brighton.' He was unable to conceal his glee.

'Where did you say?' she demanded coldly.

'Brighton. She says I can lodge with her sister . . .'

'In what kind of a house? That's what I'd like to know. Chorus girls,' Elizabeth said scornfully, tossing her head as she picked up her cup and saucer.

'Good theatrical digs, she says.' Haydn was too excited to see or care about his mother's disapproval. All he could think of was that he'd been offered a heaven-sent opportunity to leave all his problems behind him. His job! Jenny . . . and her defection to Eddie. Thrusting the letter into his pocket, he left the table.

'I'm going to Brighton,' he announced decisively, forgetting his resolution to give up all stage and singing ambitions.

'And how long exactly is this "job" of yours going to last?' Elizabeth enquired icily. 'You said Christmas pantomime. Are you going to give up steady work here on the promise of a pantomime?'

'You don't understand, Mam.' Nothing could dampen Haydn's spirits at that moment. Not even his mother. 'It's a break. It'll lead to more work, and more. Two years and I'll be on stage in the West End, three and I'll be on the radio.' He laced on his boots. 'You'll see.'

'Stuff and nonsense,' Elizabeth dismissed the idea in annoy-ance. 'I just wonder what kind of a family I've brought up. Your father wasn't reared decently or properly, so I suppose I should excuse his rag and boning on that basis, even if it does mean I can't hold my head up straight in this town any more, but I reared you and Eddie differently. And look at the pair of you now, despite all my efforts. Eddie with all his insane ideas of making money from getting beaten to death in the boxing ring, and you wanting to go on stage. Why can't either of you concentrate on something sensible? Something that will bring in a good living – '

'It *will* bring in a good living,' Haydn snapped, hating his mother for destroying his moment of excitement. 'I'll be able to send money home, at least as much as I'm contributing now. And you won't have to feed me,' he added sourly.

254

'Well, all I can say is I hope that you've got enough money to get to Brighton, boy,' Elizabeth retorted coolly. 'Because if you haven't, I haven't any to give you. And that's for sure.'

Chapter Twenty-Three

'She's looking better, don't you think?' Evan ventured apprehensively, seeking confirmation from Trevor as they stood on the steps of the isolation block in the Graig Hospital.

'It's called hope,' Trevor smiled. 'Ronnie's given her something to look forward to. To be honest, I'm amazed. I never thought of him as the type to sweep a girl off her feet. Figuratively, that is,' he added as he saw the irony in the idea of sweeping a consumptive off her feet when she was already lying in a hospital bed. 'And then again, knowing Ronnie, I never imagined he'd fall in love with anyone. Like Laura I always assumed that any marriage he made would be a café merger.'

'I think Maud's still reeling from the shock.' If Evan could have afforded to send Maud to a kinder climate in the hope of effecting a cure without Ronnie coming into the equation, he would have. He had no doubts whatsoever about the depth or sincerity of Ronnie's love for Maud: the man's actions spoke volumes on that score. But Maud's feelings for Ronnie were something else. She was so bound up in the hope of finding a cure and the excitement at actually travelling to a foreign country that she hadn't given a single thought to marriage, or what it entailed, let alone what marriage to a man like Ronnie might mean.

Trevor cleared his throat uneasily. 'I'm sorry about what happened back there with Doctor John,' he apologised. 'I know you think he was being a bit hard on you.'

'I think it's a bit hard to tell a father he's going to kill his daughter if he takes her out of a hospital's care,' Evan agreed drily.

'He advised you as he thought best,' Trevor murmured, torn between the loyalty due to his immediate superior, and his personal feelings.

'Yes, well, it makes no difference in the long run,' Evan asserted philosophically. 'When it comes down to it, what Maud wants and what's best for her are the only things that matter.'

'Then you are going to take her out tomorrow.' It wasn't a question.

'I'll see Ronnie, and check if that suits him. He's the one who seems to think there's no problem with arranging weddings and journeys at short notice.'

'Knowing what Ronnie's like once he's made up his mind to do something, he'll make sure there're no problems.'

Trevor walked alongside Evan as he crossed the female exercise yard. Evan had been kicking his heels in the hospital for two long hours, barely ten minutes of which he'd actually spent with Maud. Trevor had warned him before they'd got there that Doctor John never came in before nine in the morning. It was probably just as well, because Trevor had had to draw on every ounce of influence to which his status as junior doctor entitled him, to get Evan a brief interview with Maud. Doctor John's disapproval of any break in the routine of visiting hours would have been all that the sister needed to turf Evan out.

Mind already made up about what he intended to do, Evan had then sat outside the sister's office for over an hour and a half, rehearsing again and again what he intended to say to Doctor John. In the event, he didn't have an opportunity to say half of it: his interview with the senior doctor lasted less than five minutes. Evan had never met Bethan's father-in-law before, but from a few hints that Bethan had dropped he'd had a shrewd suspicion that he wouldn't like the man. Now that the meeting had finally taken place, his suspicions had hardened into certainty.

Evan paused to allow a crocodile of pregnant girls and women to pass. Dressed in identical drab, grey-flannel work dresses, each carried a bucket of soapy water and a scrubbing brush as they walked in single file towards the door that led into the main kitchens and dining room.

'You know, I've lived on the Graig all my life, and this is the first time I've been within these walls. I suppose I just never had reason to come before, not even when Bethan worked here.'

'Count yourself fortunate,' Trevor said feelingly. 'My grandfather died in the workhouse in Cardiff. My mother took me to see him there just before he died. She really felt the disgrace of it all, but she had to put him there. My father had just been killed, and she was hard pressed to keep a roof over our heads, let alone his.'

257

'Then you understand why I've tried to steer clear of the place. Why I tried to keep Maud out of here.'

'Only too well.'

The last of the girls disappeared through the high, green-painted wooden doors, and they walked on. As they turned the corner Evan caught sight of a group of men in the yard behind the kitchens. They all had axes, and were chopping logs into fire-sized sticks under the supervision of a white-coated overseer.

'Don't believe in leaving anyone idle, do you?' Evan murmured.

'They're casuals who've opted to stay in another day. No work, no food,' Trevor explained uneasily, as he saw the supervisor berate a man for tardiness. The man was moving so slowly, the chances were that he was ill, but Trevor didn't dare interfere with the running of the workhouse. As Doctor John frequently said to him, 'If the man's ill, we'll find out soon enough. They'll bring him before us, tomorrow, or the day after.' Valuing his job, Trevor hadn't replied that tomorrow or the next day might exacerbate the man's condition – if he lived that long.

'I know why your boss is so set against me moving Maud out of here, but you haven't given me your opinion,' Evan said suddenly.

'I'm only a junior doctor . . .' Trevor began apologetically.

'You're qualified, and some would say a new degree is better than an old one.'

'And there's those who say experience counts for everything. Have you asked Andrew to come down and take a look at her?'

'I've thought of it,' Evan admitted. 'But with Bethan expecting, it didn't seem right to drag them all that way. Come on, tell me Doctor Lewis, what do you think? I promise I won't hold you to anything afterwards. Do you agree with Doctor John? Should Maud stay here until you've completed all your tests?'

'The tests will take time,' Trevor admitted reluctantly. 'There's a waiting list for the X-ray machine, not to mention the ambulance we'd need to book to ferry her to the Cottage Hospital to carry out some procedures. It could take as long as two weeks, and really all we'd have in the end is a better picture of the parts of her lungs that are diseased. We know what's wrong at the moment, we simply don't know the extent. Two weeks can be a long time in the progression of a disease, and it's more time than Ronnie needs to get her to Italy. The weather is better over there, even in winter. The mountain air might do the trick.'

'You really believe that?'

'After a few years in this place I've learned not to build up hope where there may be none,' Trevor cautioned, 'but I do know one thing.'

'What's that?'

'I've worked here six years, and in all that time I've never known anyone to walk out of that TB ward. If you want my opinion, Mr Powell, I'll give it to you, but I warn you, it's not based on scientific knowledge or study. Occasionally miracles do happen, and if strength and determination can overcome illness, Ronnie has enough for the whole ward, let alone one slip of a girl like Maud. We haven't anything better to offer her. Not really. Perhaps she'll die more slowly in here than she would at home. But that's all. She seems happy enough to go with Ronnie, and after what he's told me, I have no doubt he'll be ecstatic at the prospect of taking her. Let her go, Mr Powell. The worst that can happen is what would inevitably happen here.'

'That's more or less what I've been thinking.' Evan drew his empty pipe out of his pocket and put it in his mouth. 'I suppose I'd better go down the café and see if I can find your brother-in-law, and hope that something hasn't happened to change his mind now that Maud's set on going with him.'

'He won't have changed his mind, Mr Powell. And something tells me you won't have to look very hard for him either,' he grinned as he recognised Ronnie's van waiting outside the gates in Courthouse Street. 'Either Laura or Mrs Powell must have told him where you were.'

'Thanks for everything you've done for us, Doctor Lewis,' Evan said as he held out his calloused hand.

'Don't you think after all this you could bring yourself to call me Trevor?'

'It wouldn't be right,' Evan said gravely. 'Not a ragman and a doctor on first-name terms.'

'Sorry, Mr Horton,' Haydn apologised as he rushed up to the stall in the second-hand clothes market. The dealer had only recently moved there after a lifetime of trading out in the open.

'I thought I could rely on you, boy,' his boss complained in a hurt, petulant tone from behind an enormous bundle of woollen pullovers, clean, pressed and mended, that he was heaving out of a lock-up chest on to the stall. 'You know I'm getting on, and can't do things as quickly as I used to, yet you – '

'Mr Horton I'm sorry, but I've had an offer,' Haydn explained enigmatically, unable to contain his excitement.

'Well I've made you an offer. To work,' he grumbled testily. 'You'd think you'd show some gratitude after all the years I've helped you.'

'The offer is to play in a pantomime, in Brighton. I've a chance to work with professionals, in a real theatre. This could be the big break I've been looking for.'

'Ay, ay boy.' Mr Horton began to arrange the pullovers in piles on the trestles. 'I suppose it's what you've been after for a while.' He didn't even try to hide his disappointment at the prospect of losing his assistant. 'When will you be off?'

'By Monday, if I can make it.'

'That's fine. Go ahead, leave me high and dry.'

'No one's leaving you high and dry, Mr Horton,' Haydn countered. 'There's loads of boys would kill for a chance to work on this stall. My brother for one.' He might never want to see or speak to Eddie again, but family finances were family finances, after all. And he couldn't bear the thought of his parents going short when he could have done something to alleviate the situation.

'Eddie, the boxer?'

'I've only got one brother, and you know it,' Haydn smiled.

'Thought he was helping your father on the rag round.'

'The round's not going as well as it might. He could spare Wednesday, Friday and Saturday to work for you.' Haydn kept his fingers crossed behind his back. The Wednesday and Friday wouldn't be a problem, but he wasn't too sure about the Saturday, traditionally the ragman's busy day.

'He is a good strong boy,' the dealer mused thoughtfully, 'and with him around the stall, there'd be no problems with anyone trying to lift anything either. When did you say you were off?' he asked Haydn sharply.

'Monday, if I can make it.'

'Right then, he can take over on Wednesday. Tell him to be here, quarter to seven. On the dot.'

'He'll be here,' Haydn said, thinking that if his father couldn't spare Eddie, there was always Diana. Three days a week at two bob a day – always supposing that Mr Horton would pay a mere girl the same as he now paid him – was as much as she was getting in the shoe shop, and he knew she was looking for a chance to leave Ben Springer.

'That's settled then,' Mr Horton said resolutely. He hated any uncertainty especially where business was concerned. 'Your brother will take over.'

'He'll be delighted to, Mr Horton.'

'Come on then, boy, get busy. You're late, remember. Tell you what, because you've been so good to me until today, how about you take your pick of whatever you fancy at the end of the day? Three-piece suit, with waistcoat, watch pocket, the works, sports jacket, trousers and a couple of shirts. Sort of bonus.'

'That's very good of you, Mr Horton.'

'We can't let a Welsh boy go up to the English in rags, can we? It'd be like letting down Wales. And then again, you've got to look smart on stage.'

Haydn didn't have the heart to tell him that he would be wearing stage costumes. 'Thanks very much, Mr Horton,' he beamed. He would have a decent suit to travel in, and wear between shows. He still needed a suitcase, and the means to get him to Brighton, but he had two bob coming to him at the end of the day and a week's extra wages due from the Town Hall, the week in hand he'd worked when he started there. Even after handing over his lodge to his mother, he'd still be left with fourteen and six. Not enough for the fare, but something would turn up. Perhaps Charlie knew of a meat lorry going that way.

He went to the chest and lifted out the pressed and folded trousers that Mr Horton always laid out at the bottom. When he carried them over to the stall he was whistling for the first time since he'd last spoken to Jenny.

'I gave her two spoonfuls of laudanum.'

'You what?' Trevor stared in horror at his wife. 'That's a proscribed drug, it was locked in my cabinet.'

'So? I know where you keep the key, and I unlocked it,' Laura said defiantly. 'Don't be such a dyed-in-the-wool doctor, Trevor. I know as much about treating shock as you, and after a stint on the maternity ward I've probably had more experience of dealing with it. The girl was in a dreadful state. I wouldn't have dosed her if there was any other option. She needed help and she couldn't go to her aunt. Not with a story like that. You know what Bethan's mother can be like.'

'I know she was very good when Bethan was ill,' Trevor affirmed euphemistically, careful not to say too much. Not even Laura knew the full extent of Bethan's attempts to rid herself of an unwanted pregnancy.

'Look, the girl's ill. We've a spare bedroom. Can't she stay here for a night or two until she sorts herself out?'

'What about her family, Laura?' Trevor demurred, wary of treading on anyone's toes, especially the Powells with all that they had to contend with at the moment.

'I sent little Gwynfor next door up to Graig Avenue with a note, telling Elizabeth that Diana has delayed shock and that she shouldn't be moved for a day or two.'

'I don't know why you bother to consult me about anything,' he said testily. 'Seems to me you covered everything before even telling me about it.'

'I didn't cover everything,' she said furiously. 'I didn't make allowances for a dense, unsympathetic, heartless fool of a husband.' She wiped over a soup bowl with a clean tea towel and ladled out a bowlful of lamb stew, slamming it down on the table in front of him. Then she went to the breadboard that Angelo had shaped for her from a thick wedge of fresh pine, and sliced a chunk of coarse brown bread, practically throwing it at him.

'Before you rant and rave at me, Laura, just remember that rape is a criminal offence,' Trevor said in what Laura took to be a pompous tone. 'Diana is the principal witness to a criminal act, and as a doctor I should report it.'

'Do you think I don't know that?' Laura demanded hotly.

'If you knew it, why didn't you call the police?'

'I'll tell you why I didn't call the police,' Laura rounded on him like a cornered wildcat. 'I didn't call them because Ben Springer would deny the whole thing. He'd call Diana a whore. Say she'd wanted him to do all those despicable things that he did to her. That she enjoyed it.'

'Laura . . .'

'Don't you Laura me. You know this town as well as I do. You tell me, what chance would a young girl like Diana have against one of the commercial fathers of this town? For God's sake Trevor, her mother's in jail, she lives on the Graig, people talk. And what's the betting that when they do, all that business with Bethan will get dragged up all over again? And for what? For Ben Springer to get off scot-free and Diana to have what little remains of her reputation ruined.'

'Her uncle's a policeman – '

'A nice enough constable who has absolutely no clout when faced with the Ben Springers of this world, and you know it.'

A few months of marriage had accustomed Trevor to being on the receiving end of the rough edge of Laura's tongue, but this was somehow different. Here was an anger and emotion he hadn't seen in Laura before.

'I'm sorry Laura, I suppose I didn't think it through, and then again I didn't realise you'd taken this so hard,' he murmured, leaving the table and reaching out to her.

'You'd have taken it just as hard if you'd heard her.' Laura didn't try to stem the tears that were pouring down her cheeks. 'He did disgusting, revolting things to her, Trevor. You, thank God, probably aren't capable of imagining what. And then, when he'd finished, he wrapped her, half-naked, in her coat and put her out on the street. After pushing a five-pound note into her pocket,' she seethed. 'Wyn Rees stopped her from tearing it up.'

'Wyn . . .'

'Yes, queer Wyn,' Laura said shortly. 'He found her, and took her home with him. Made her some tea, let her have a bath in his house, and gave her his sister's clothes to wear home.'

'Good for Wyn,' Trevor said in amazement.

'You will let her stay here a couple of days?'

'If you think it will help,' he said resignedly.

'And you won't go to the police?'

'No,' he murmured. 'Though pity help me if any of this gets as far as Doctor John's ears.'

'It won't,' she assured him. 'Thank you. I do love you, you know. I don't mean to fly off the handle.'

'I know.' Sitting on a chair, he pulled her down on to his lap and kissed her. Diana's story still fresh in her mind, she shook her head and moved away.

'Not now, love. I'm still too angry.'

'With me?'

'Not you. Never with you. Well not seriously,' she qualified. 'Just all the Ben Springers of this world who think that women are there to be used, at their convenience.'

'Where the hell have you been?' Tony confronted Ronnie as he walked into the café at six o'clock on Saturday night. 'We've been rushed off our feet all day. Angelo couldn't manage the cooking. I had to take Gina off the till and put her out back, and that meant I had to cover the till as well as the counter. Tina didn't have any help with the waitressing, and we got behind . . .'

'If I were you I'd think about taking Maria out of school,' Ronnie said placidly. 'She's not doing anything constructive there, and with the new place opening in a couple of months, the sooner she starts learning the trade the better.'

'But she's only thirteen. You know Papa likes us all to stay on in school until we're fourteen. He says – '

'Papa more or less yanked me out of school when I was twelve, and I didn't visit the place very often before that.'

'That's not what Papa told me. He said you wouldn't stay in school even when he sent you.'

'I wouldn't go because I knew Papa needed me in the business. You lot ate more than the profits of the High Street place every week,' Ronnie informed him drily. 'And don't go thinking that it's easier now because we've got two places and another one opening soon. The overheads will be higher, as well as the profits, and there'll still be eleven Ronconi mouths to feed, even with me and Laura gone.'

Tony stared in amazement as, instead of going into the kitchen and changing out of his smart street jacket, Ronnie walked behind the counter, helped himself to a cup, and filled it with coffee. He looked around the cafe as he picked it up. 'Despite all your moaning you must have managed to keep everything under control, little brother,' he commented lightly. 'The place is still standing, and it seems quiet enough now.'

'Just when I'm due to finish for the day,' Tony griped.

'Shutting up shop early?' Ronnie enquired airily.

'Now you're back, I'm off to the pictures.'

'I'm not back.' Ronnie finished his coffee, and poured himself another.

'But you're here,' Tony protested.

'For the coffee, and to say goodbye. I told you last night, I've left the business. By the way, I've written out some notes for you on the new place. And I've balanced the accounts.'

'You're not coming in tomorrow?' Tony stared at his brother in disbelief.

'I most definitely am not coming in tomorrow,' Ronnie smiled. He pulled his watch chain out of his pocket and flicked through the fobs. 'This is now yours.' He extracted the key to the cupboard. 'There you are: official boss badge. You're in charge now, boy. Supremo! This is what you've been waiting for all your life.'

'Ronnie, I can't take over,' Tony remonstrated. 'I don't know enough.'

'If you don't, you've no one to blame but yourself. You've been under my feet for eighteen years. Is it my fault that you didn't keep your eyes and ears open?'

'But there's the new restaurant!'

'I've left you a challenge. If I were you I'd try to enlist Laura's help. For a woman, she's smart,' he teased. 'If you're pushed, I suggest you put Papa in here with Angelo, and let Tina manage High Street. That'll leave you free to run the new restaurant.'

'Ronnie!' Tony was talking to the counter. His brother had picked up his cup and taken it into the back room where Tina and Gina were clearing tables. Although it was after six o'clock on a Saturday neither of them had even attempted to leave. Tony felt that not only the fabric of his family but the routine of the café was falling apart.

'Is Alma coming in?' Tony interrupted Ronnie, as his brother hugged the girls, wrapping his arms around their shoulders.

'How should I know? It's up to the man in charge to know what shifts his waitresses are working.'

'Ronnie, please . . .'

Thrusting his fingers into his top pocket, Ronnie pulled out a packet of cigarettes and extended it to Tony. Tony nearly fell over: it was the first time Ronnie had recognised that he smoked, let alone offered him a cigarette.

'Now look,' Ronnie smiled patiently, 'it's really very simple. Give the customers what they want, keep them happy, treat Alma well, and mind you enter up the takings in the ledger every night. You leave it even one night and you're in dire trouble. You always think you'll remember the figures, but you don't. And that's the voice of experience talking.'

Tony tried to take in what Ronnie was saying, but he couldn't. He found it impossible to believe that Ronnie was really leaving. Ronnie who'd always been there when he'd needed him. Whenever there'd been trouble in school, or with friends, it had always been Ronnie who'd sorted it out for him. Ronnie, never Papa or Mama, because unlike their parents, Ronnie understood the Welsh systems and way of life, and he'd been the first Ronconi to cut the path and smooth the way for the others in the family.

'You'll remember to do all that?' Ronnie asked, sensing that Tony's attention had wandered.

'I think so,' Tony mumbled.

'You do know, don't you, that Papa doesn't understand the first thing about book-keeping?' Only his imminent departure from Wales could have wrested such a disloyal statement from Ronnie. 'If you get stuck, you could always write to me in Italy, but the Italian post isn't that reliable, or so Mama's always said.'

'Mama said you're marrying Maud Powell and taking her to Bardi. Is that right?' Tony finally ventured.

'That's right.' Ronnie winked at Tina and Gina, who were still hovering close. 'At four o'clock tomorrow afternoon.'

'On a Sunday? But Father O'Kelly – '

'We're marrying in St John's.'

'St John's! Ronnie, that's Church of Wales!'

'The Reverend Price did mention it,' Ronnie said flatly.

'But why?' Tony demanded urgently.

'Because I didn't want Father O'Kelly to make a lot of fuss.'

'Not the church,' Tony dismissed irritably. 'Why marry Maud Powell and all? Papa said – '

'Please don't tell me. I've a feeling that the saying "Least said soonest mended" should be applied to Papa and me at the moment. He made his views clear last night, and I don't blame him for them. If any of you want to come to the wedding, you'll be very welcome. Just don't expect any more than a short ceremony, that's all. And if you don't turn up, I'll understand why. And as Maud and I are leaving Ponty at six o'clock on Monday morning, if you're not coming, I'll say my goodbyes now.'

'Ronnie . . .'

'Look, I have to go and see Laura and Trevor. I'm taking my things.' He left the table and walked towards the staircase. 'If I were you I'd look at the accounts. Check them. And if you come up with any questions, call in Laura's on the way home. I'd appreciate a word about some promises I've made to Alma.'

Ronnie retrieved his case from the upstairs bedroom and left quickly, hugging his brothers, and kissing his sisters on their cheeks as he backed out through the door. He went to the White Hart car park to get the Trojan. As he pulled the starting handle out from under the seat, he made a mental note to hand the keys over to Tony later. There was so much to do, and so little time left to think of everything.

Chapter Twenty-Four

Laura and Trevor were eating tea when Ronnie walked in. Meat and potato pie, bread, cheese, fruit cake, and a very prettily iced sponge cake.

'Sit down.' Laura went to the dresser and lifted down another plate and a knife and fork.

Trevor looked at him inquisitively. 'Everything arranged?' he asked.

'We're marrying in St John's tomorrow at four, and leaving first thing Monday morning. Half-past seven train from Cardiff.'

'I'll take you to Cardiff in the car,' Trevor offered.

'I asked Aldo because I thought you'd be working.'

'Not so you'd notice at that time in the morning. I'll get the new junior doctor to cover for me.'

'You don't have to.'

'I know I don't have to,' Trevor said calmly. 'But you're going to be changing boats and trains enough with Maud as it is. Take a brotherly hand when it's offered. If not for your sake, then for Maud's.'

'In that case, thank you,' Ronnie said gratefully. 'There is one thing I was going to ask you.'

'Ask away.' Trevor helped himself to another spoonful of pie.

'Not you, Laura. You always were good with the café books,' he complimented his sister.

'If I remember rightly, I had no choice to be anything but. They drove me mad, particularly when I had to translate your figures into legible numbers. They're the sole reason I went into nursing,' she assured Trevor.

'Please, give Tony a hand with them if he gets stuck. And if you have time, keep an eye on him. It's not that he isn't up to taking over, it's just that he's going to need all the help he can get.'

'Even that of a mere woman like me?' Laura raised her eyebrows.

'I suggested to Tony that he puts Tina in charge of the High

Street café,' Ronnie went on, ignoring his sister's sarcasm. 'That will free Papa to take care of the Tumble and leave Tony to run the new place, but it would be better if everything stayed as it was and you took over the restaurant Laura, at least for a while,' he qualified, in deference to her status as newly married woman.

'To what do I owe this praise?' she demanded. 'You never told me I was any good when I worked in the cafés. All you ever did was whinge every time I dropped a plate, or burnt an egg.'

'Big brother's prerogative,' he grinned. 'You were good, but I wanted to make you even better. If you run the restaurant for Tony, there should be enough money left for you to get someone to help you with your housework. You'd let her work outside the house, wouldn't you?' he turned to Trevor.

'Let her?' Trevor shook his head. 'The first thing I learned as a married man is that you don't "let" your wife do, or not do anything. All capacity for choice is taken away the day you walk down the aisle. As you'll soon find out for yourself.'

'I'd like you both to be there, but I wouldn't want you to come if it means a quarrel between you and Papa, Laura. I know how unforgiving he can be.'

'Just try and stop me,' she smiled maliciously. 'I wouldn't miss the sight of you tying the knot for all the world. I only hope that Maud finds enough gumption to keep that ego of yours well and truly under control.'

'Thank you so very much, dear sister. Maud told her father that she wants Diana as a bridesmaid . . .'

'I'll ask her,' Laura said unthinkingly.

'Would you? I don't intend to go back up the Graig tonight. And I'll need a best man.' He looked hopefully at Trevor.

'What about Tony?' Trevor asked, failing to conceal his pleasure at being asked.

'I don't want to make Tony choose between me and Papa,' Ronnie said.

'In that case I'd be delighted.'

'Good, that's the wedding settled.'

'Got your tickets?'

'I went to Thomas Cook's in Cardiff this afternoon. I booked first-class seats to London. Hopefully, as it's coming from Wales,

269

the carriage will be empty and Maud will be able to lie down. I'll get a taxi from Paddington to Tilbury . . .'

'Bethan will be annoyed if you don't give her a chance to see the blushing bride, and Andrew will be only too happy to drive you across London,' Trevor interrupted.

'Do you really think so?'

'He'll be your brother-in-law as of tomorrow. I'll telephone him.'

'It would be a help to have a car waiting,' Ronnie agreed. 'I've booked a cabin to Calais, and from there a first-class sleeper to Genoa.'

Trevor let out a long, low whistle. 'That must have cost a pretty penny for the both of you.'

'It did,' Ronnie agreed.

'And what about tomorrow night?' Laura asked.

'As Papa's thrown me out, and I presume that means the café as well as the house, I was going to ask if I could sleep here for a couple of nights.' It was more than just his father. Ronnie had developed a sudden aversion to the bedroom in the café. It held too many memories that he'd rather forget.

'Diana's in the spare room,' Trevor blurted out tactlessly.

'Diana . . .'

'Don't ask, it's a long story,' Laura interrupted. 'But if you don't mind sleeping on the parlour couch, we can put you up.'

'I'd appreciate that very much.'

'You really are going through with this, aren't you?' Laura asked abruptly as Ronnie began to eat.

'Yes,' he mumbled, his mouth full. He was hungry. Apart from his usual endless cups of coffee, he'd hardly eaten in two days.

'I find it difficult to believe. You and Maud Powell!'

'Are you going to see Mama tonight?'

'You know I always go to see Mama on a Saturday,' she said, irritated because he obviously wasn't going to entertain her by talking about him and Maud.

'Tell her and the kids the time of the wedding, and tell them when I'm leaving. But don't forget to say that I don't want them there if it will put anyone in Papa's bad books.'

'I'll explain, and better than you just did,' Laura retorted.

'I've left the accounts books and the plans for the new place with Tony.'

'I'll call in the café on Monday.'

'Thanks Laura,' he said sincerely. 'I'd hate to see all Papa's and my hard work go down the drain.'

'Don't worry, it won't. You and Papa aren't the only Ronconis blessed with brains, you know,' she said harshly, annoyed with the thick feeling that was creeping into her throat.

'I always knew that, but boy, have the rest of you given me a hard time trying to prove it.' Ronnie smiled as he reached for another piece of pie.

'Here she is!' Diana, who'd been pressganged by Laura into putting on her best face for Maud's wedding, had gone up to Graig Avenue to help Maud dress. Laura had walked up with her, taking the entire contents of the 'best' side of her wardrobe, together with her boxed wedding dress and veil just in case Maud fancied being married in white. Elizabeth had turned out her hatbox and spread the contents on Maud's bed. Gina and Tina had sneaked away from Danycoedcae Road, and turned up with a small case that nine-year-old Alfredo had smuggled out the back and over the mountain for them. It was crammed with perfumes, powders, lipsticks, and their best dresses wrapped in tissue paper.

'Look, quick, Trevor's stopping the car!' Forgetting her misery for the first time in two days, Diana called the Ronconi girls to the window. Gina and Tina leant heavily on the sash, watching as Trevor opened the door of his car. Evan stepped out of the back, then leant over and picked Maud up from the front seat. Maud protested loud enough to be heard in the bedroom, but all to no avail. Evan carried her up the steps and in through the front door, pushing past Haydn and Eddie, who were observing an uneasy, silent truce in honour of the occasion.

Diana rushed to the landing, just in time to see William plant a kiss on Maud's cheek. Without pausing for breath, Evan continued to carry Maud straight up the stairs. He deposited her, still protesting that she could walk, on to the bed.

'And you're not to walk down the stairs,' he said firmly. 'When you're ready, give me a shout and I'll carry you down.'

271

'She won't be ready for ages yet, Mr Powell,' Laura asserted. 'We've got to turn her into a bride.'

Maud smiled at the girls. Her mother, sensing that she wasn't wanted, muttered something about 'pressing her black brocade', and left the room. The first question Maud asked when the door was shut was, 'Where's Ronnie?'

'You told Trevor you didn't want to see him before the wedding,' Laura reminded her.

'I don't, but I still want to know where he is.'

Gina and Tina laughed, and even Diana managed a smile.

'You just keep that up Maud Powell, and you'll be all right,' Laura said seriously. 'There isn't a man born who doesn't need tabs kept on him.'

Ronnie was dressing in the bedroom that Diana had thoughtfully vacated for his use, when Trevor returned from taking Maud up to Graig Avenue.

'She's looking good,' he reported. 'Evan Powell insisted on carrying her in and out of the car, but she could have walked.'

'You really think she'll be all right?' Ronnie asked anxiously.

'For a while,' Trevor assured him, not daring to voice an opinion as to how long 'a while' could be. 'Here, do you want a hand with that collar stud?' he asked as Ronnie struggled to fasten a new starched collar to his best boiled shirt.

'No, I think I've got it. There, that's done.'

'Brandy?' Trevor asked. 'I bought a new bottle.'

'I think I could manage one.' Ronnie slipped his arms through his waistcoat sleeves without bothering to do up the buttons. Picking up his tie and jacket he checked around the room to make sure he hadn't left anything, before following Trevor downstairs.

'I've got a couple of things for you.' Trevor poured out two glasses of brandy and handed one to Ronnie as they sat either side of the kitchen stove. 'First, there's a room booked in the New Inn for you and Maud tonight. You can take her there straight after the ceremony. Everything's paid for, including dinner,' he added. 'I told them you'd want it in your room.'

'Trevor, I wasn't expecting anything like this . . .'

'It's a wedding present from Laura and me,' Trevor said quickly. 'And then, you'll be needing these.' He handed Ronnie an enormous package wrapped in brown paper. 'French letters,' he explained briefly. 'I don't know whether you'll be able to get any in Italy so I scrounged a hundred for you. Write and let me know when you're running low, but be sure to give me plenty of time to send more. The one thing you can't afford to risk with Maud is pregnancy. On top of everything else it would kill her,' he warned bluntly.

'I have no intention of . . . of sleeping with Maud,' Ronnie stammered. 'At least not in that sense,' he asserted, colouring in embarrassment.

'You might not have any intention of sleeping with her in that sense now,' Trevor said matter-of-factly, 'but now is not tonight, and Maud may have other ideas on the subject.'

'She's ill,' Ronnie said quickly.

'Not that ill. She's spent the last couple of days in hospital resting, remember. She told me only this morning she was looking forward to married life, and if at the end of the day you don't take her to bed, she'll quite rightly wonder why you bothered to go to all this trouble.'

'Then it'll be all right for me to sleep with her?' Remembering Trevor's medical qualifications, Ronnie finally subdued the qualms he had about discussing such an intimate subject with his brother-in-law.

'I've never heard of it doing anyone in Maud's condition any harm,' Trevor smiled broadly. 'And if the rumours that some of your ex-girlfriends have spread around town are to be believed, it may do her some good.'

'You shouldn't believe everything you hear.' Ronnie took the package from Trevor. 'I'll put it in my case.'

'Oh, and there's this.' Trevor held out a couple of bottles. 'Cough mixture,' he grinned. 'I've given Maud six bottles. I thought you might need a couple more for the journey. Keep them to hand.'

'Anything else?'

'I don't think so.' Trevor smiled, the devil in him enjoying Ronnie's embarrassment. 'That is, unless you'd like another brandy.'

'Life is so simple for men,' Laura grumbled. 'All they have to do is

273

put on a clean shirt and collar, a tie and their best suits and they look fine, whereas we . . .'

'I had no decisions to make before you brought this lot,' Maud complained playfully. 'It would have been my blue satin dress, or my blue satin dress.'

'You can't get married in a dance dress,' Diana protested.

'You can if that's all you've got,' Maud contradicted.

'How about going traditional?' Laura opened the box she'd brought and pulled out the wedding dress and veil that the best dressmaker on the Graig had made for her wedding.

'Laura, I couldn't! Could I?' Maud asked, her eyes shining in delight at the thought.

'Yes you could,' Laura asserted. 'The only problem is it's going to be too big for you, which is why I went down the market and bought this off Mrs Jones last night.' She pulled out yards and yards of wide, gleaming white satin ribbon. 'I thought we could always tie the dress in at the waist, hiding the gathers under a big bow at the back. I just hope it's not going to be too uncomfortable.'

'We got you some new underclothes.' Tina and Gina thrust a paper carrier bag towards her. 'It's from all of us, even the boys,' Gina said, remembering that as they'd run out of money, Tony and Angelo, not to mention the till, had contributed more to the fund than they had.

They watched Maud open the bag. A fine, white silk petticoat and a beautiful, coffee-coloured, lace-trimmed satin nightdress spilled out.

'There's some other things in there too. Another petticoat, bloomers, silk stockings . . .' Gina blushed as she remembered all the silk stockings that Diana's mother had sold them.

'And this is for you.' Not to be outdone, Diana thrust an envelope containing five pounds at Maud. It was the five pounds Ben Springer had given her, but no one had to know that. Every time Diana touched it, she felt dirty, and used. At least Maud wouldn't know where it had come from.

'Diana, I can't take this,' Maud protested as she looked inside. 'This is all the money you've got.'

'There's bound to be things that you want that no one has thought of. Please take it,' Diana said curtly.

Touched by everyone's generosity Maud didn't even notice her mother standing in the doorway, a strange expression on her face.

Gina, Tina, Diana and Laura worked hard on Maud for two solid hours. They waved her hair, puffed perfumed talcum powder over her body, lightly rouged her cheeks and powdered her face, adding as the final touch before the dress went on, a lavish sprinkling of 'dabs' of Evening in Paris.

'You'd better pack Maud's things, Diana,' Laura said suddenly.

'There's no need, I'm coming back tonight.'

'No you're not,' Laura smiled. 'Ronnie has a surprise for you.'

'We're not leaving today, are we?'

'No,' Laura said mysteriously.

'Then if they're not leaving until tomorrow I think Maud should spend tonight in her own bed,' Elizabeth said quickly, as she carried a tray of biscuits and home-made lemonade into the room.

'You'll still be able to wave her off tomorrow morning.' Laura fingered a wave on Maud's forehead, sharpening its edge.

'But with the journey and everything she's going to need her rest,' Elizabeth said sharply.

'Don't worry, she'll get plenty of that.' Laura's hackles rose at the shadow Elizabeth was casting over her and Trevor's surprise, and that was without taking into account the inference that Ronnie wouldn't allow to Maud to rest.

'I would like to know where my own daughter is going . . .'

'If you come downstairs with me Mrs Powell, I'll tell you.' Laura propelled Maud's mother out of the room, leaving Diana to pack in peace. There wasn't much to stow away. The contents of two drawers and the wardrobe still left plenty of room on top of the Gladstone for the new underclothes and nightdress that the Ronconi girls had given Maud, together with her well-used sponge bag and bottles of Evening in Paris perfume and Essence of Violets.

At a quarter-past three Laura returned and helped Maud on with the dress. It was the right length but about six inches too wide everywhere. It took the combined efforts of all four girls to tie the sash to their communal satisfaction, but once the bow was finally pulled out as wide as it would go, the veil secured with combs to Maud's head, and the lace allowed to fall gently over her shoulders, the general consensus was that she was the most stunning bride that the Graig had seen since Laura had walked down the aisle with Trevor.

'Now remember,' Laura ordered as she walked around the chair that Maud was sitting on. 'Rest until it's time to go, let Diana do everything.'

'If we're going we'd better go,' Elizabeth said firmly from outside the door. Thinking that Elizabeth would want some time alone with her daughter, Laura swept everyone out of the room.

'I have something for you too.' Elizabeth took Maud's hand and folded something into it.

'Not your mother's locket, Mam, I know what it means to you.'

'It's all I have left to give you, so I'd appreciate you taking it with good grace, Maud,' Elizabeth said briskly. She kissed her daughter, grazing her cheek with chapped, dry lips.

'This wedding, and Italy. It is what you want, isn't it Maud?'

Maud looked up at her with her enormous blue eyes. 'More than anything else in the world,' she affirmed.

'That's all right then,' Elizabeth said as she walked out through the door.

Ronnie sat impatiently in the front pew of St John's church and waited. The church was strange, peculiar, unlike any he'd sat in before. It not only looked different – chilly, barren and spartan in contrast to the glitteringly gilded, image-strewn interior of the Catholic church in Treforest. It even smelt different. The sweet, lingering perfume of incense that he'd associated with prayer and God, ever since he had first been carried into a church in his mother's arms, was absent. In its place was a rank, musty odour of damp, mixed with beeswax polish and decaying flowers.

He glanced behind at the empty pews, hoping to see Trevor, not only because he felt he needed a sympathetic being next to him to lend moral support, the advent of Trevor also meant the advent of Maud in Trevor's car, and he wanted the ceremony to be over and done with as quickly as possible. He wouldn't be able to relax until the brand new gold ring he'd bought in a Cardiff jeweller's yesterday afternoon was firmly fixed on Maud Powell's finger, signalling the irrevocable change of her name to Ronconi. Once that was done, it would be too late for Evan Powell to change his mind about giving his consent to the marriage. Too late for his father to make a scene, and even too late for Maud herself to have second thoughts – a prospect that had concerned him ever since he walked away from the Graig Hospital, too worried by the ease with which she'd acceded to his proposal to be elated by his success in wooing and winning her.

He'd had so little time with her, and what he'd had, he felt he'd wasted. He hadn't told her any of the things he'd wanted to. Nothing that would make her want to be with him as urgently as he needed to be with her.

In an effort to suppress the image of Maud shaking her head and hesitating that insisted on intruding into his mind, he studied his surroundings. The plain, bare, whitewashed walls. The severe lines of the rather utility pulpit, and the unadorned wooden crucifix above it. The altar, covered by a white, gold-embroidered cloth, that looked positively empty spread with its meagre furniture of brass candlesticks and matching cross.

The Reverend Price, who unknown to Ronnie had incurred a great deal of wrath from his parishioners for agreeing to perform a marriage ceremony for an avowed Catholic and a Chapel girl, came out of the vestry, bowing and smiling at the people who'd begun to shuffle into the pews behind Ronnie. His young and astonishingly pretty wife struck up the organ – and Ronnie continued to wait. He stared at the wooden plaque that hung above the vestry door, displaying the hymn numbers for evensong. He contemplated the Reverend Price's receding hairline and attempted to divine at what point in time he would go bald; he abandoned the diversion when he realised that he might never know, as he wouldn't be there to witness the transformation.

Bardi! Did he really want to go to Bardi? He ransacked hazy, obscure, half-forgotten corners of his memory. From somewhere came an image of a farmhouse. A long, low-built, greystone building that blended into a rock-strewn, barren hillside. He remembered a stone passage running right through the house, which was cold – ice-cold on even the warmest days. People – his black-garbed, cuddly grandmother, and sharp-featured, angular grandfather – lived on one side; cows on the other. A stone pigsty in the corner of the field next to the house, a huge, fat old sow grunting and snuffling in and around the soiled straw. Vines growing against the south-facing back wall of the house, blocking the light from the few tiny windows that punctured the ancient stonework.

And inside – inside, the house was cool. He saw again his spinster aunt sweeping the dirt from the flagstoned floors out through the open door into the yard. There were rough wooden chairs and tables, so rough that if you weren't careful you picked up splinters in your hands. And everywhere the smell of garlic and strong purple onions that wafted down from the racks hoisted close to the ceiling, out of reach of the mice. The air, dark and heavy with smoke from the wood-burning stove, and the aroma of his grandfather's wine fermenting in its wooden barrels. A wine so coarse and sour that even his grandfather cut it with water from the well before he drank it.

Aunt Theresa, his father's sister, who had never married because of some great tragedy, often hinted at but never openly spoken of, spinning wool in the evening after he and his grandfather had brought the sheep down from the top fields for the night – or had it been for the summer? He simply couldn't remember any more, except the warmth. The sun, and the clean, clear air. Sun and air that Maud needed. But at what cost? Could he go back to Bardi? Live there again? Fit in? Work as a farmer?

The music changed. Red-faced, Trevor rushed up, taking his place breathlessly beside him. He turned, and saw Maud walking slowly, unsteadily down the aisle towards him. She was leaning heavily on Evan Powell's arm, her dress a fairytale princess's gleaming gown of satin, that he didn't even recognise as his sister's. Her pale, thin face was radiant beneath the lace veil. She saw him looking at her, and smiled. That smile stilled every doubt: if Bardi would give Maud a chance of life, then Bardi was what he wanted.

Chapter Twenty-Five

'Giacomo!'

'Mama, you came!' Ronnie put down the pen he'd used to sign the register in the vestry and clasped his mother's bulk in his arms. Tears poured down her cheeks on to the sleeve of his best suit.

'We all came. Even little Robert and Theresa. But not Papa.' She dabbed her eyes with a preposterously tiny square of lace-edged linen. 'He wouldn't listen to me,' she wailed. 'But then, when would he ever listen to anyone except you, Giacomo? The rest of us, we told him, we told him straight,' the borrowed Welsh colloquialism sounded strange couched in her Italian accent. 'We said we were coming, and that was an end to it. He couldn't stop us. He didn't even try,' she sobbed. 'But he wouldn't come with us, and you our eldest son . . .'

'Mama . . . Mama!' Smiling, he drew her gently round the table and put her hand in Maud's. 'Please Mama, say hello to my wife.' Mrs Ronconi wiped her eyes, clasped Maud to her ample bosom, and succumbed to another outburst. Laura looked at Trevor and rolled her eyes heavenwards.

'Everyone in our house,' she said firmly. 'For tea. You're invited too, Reverend Price, and your wife.'

'Most kind, most kind,' the Reverend Price mumbled, frantically trying to think of an excuse as to why he couldn't go. But as it was too late to walk up the hill to the vicarage and back before evensong, he didn't really have one.

'Come on, Ronnie.' Laura prodded her brother in the ribs. 'If you've finished signing your life away to Maud, you may as well get on with whatever is left to you. Lead the way.' She watched critically while Ronnie helped Maud out of the chair that the Reverend Price had thoughtfully placed in the vestry for her. 'Mr Powell, I believe you lead Mama out,' she said, briskly taking charge. 'Trevor gets the bridesmaid. Diana, where are you?' She looked around impatiently until she saw her leaning against the wall next to the outside door. 'Mrs Powell, if you don't mind walking with another woman, you can have me.' She extended her arm to Elizabeth.

'I don't mind,' Elizabeth said stiffly, in a tone that clearly said she did. But then, Laura's suggestion was just one more insult in a day that had been filled with insults and peculiarities. She dreaded having to walk into chapel that night. When the new minister and her Uncle John Joseph got to hear of this, they'd have something to say about it. Of that she was sure.

Maud clung to Ronnie's arm as the vicar opened the door for them. She gasped in amazement. She'd seen people when she'd walked down the aisle, but with eyes only for Ronnie, she hadn't realised just how many were there. She couldn't even begin to imagine how they'd all heard, when the date had only been fixed the day before. The Graig grapevine must have gone into overtime. Mr Griffiths and Jenny were there, but not his wife. Mrs Richards and Glan from next door, some of her Aunt Megan's old neighbours from Leyshon Street, their neighbours from the Avenue, the Ronconis' neighbours from Danycoedcae Road, and all the tram crews who were off duty, presumably to represent the cafe's customers.

'Just smile sweetly at everyone, and get into Trevor's car as quickly as you can,' Ronnie said quietly as he slipped his arm from Maud's and supported her round the waist.

'But Laura's only across the road,' she protested.

'I thought I just heard you promise to obey me.' He glared at her in mock anger. 'Let's start as we mean to go on. In Trevor's car, woman,' he ordered.

Ensconced in Laura's front parlour with a plate heaped high with Mrs Richards' egg sandwiches, Jenny Griffiths' sausage rolls, Tony's cream cakes, and Laura's ham and egg pie balanced in one hand, and a glass of home-made blackcurrant wine that Laura had poured her in the other, Maud watched in bewilderment as Ronnie thanked everyone for the envelope that had been presented to him by Harry Griffiths.

'It's not much,' Harry said gravely, 'but as most of us didn't know about the wedding until this morning, there wasn't time to get you anything. And then again, seeing as how you're off to Italy first thing in the morning, it's probably just as well that we didn't get you anything bulky to carry.'

Used to dealing out largesse, not receiving it, for the first time in his life Ronnie was at a loss for words. Unable to mutter more than an inadequate 'thank you', he shook the hand of everyone who'd managed to cram into Laura's tiny parlour, before his mother called them out into the kitchen for a slice of the cake she'd baked that morning in defiance of her husband's disapproving glares.

'We'll be going in five minutes, Maud.' Ronnie crouched before the chair Maud was sitting in as soon as they were alone. 'Trevor's taking us to town in his car,' he said.

'Wherever we're going, I should change.' She looked around for her case, forgetting that Trevor had left it in his car.

'No you most definitely should not, young lady,' Laura contradicted as she bustled into the room and closed the door behind her. 'Go as you are and there'll be no argument from the desk in the New Inn about wanting to see your marriage lines. Damn, I shouldn't have said. Now I've spoilt the surprise. Your boys are all hovering outside wanting to say goodbye to you Maud; you can have as long as it takes me to find Trevor.'

Eddie, William and Haydn trooped in awkwardly together. They held out a parcel.

'Charlie knocked up a fellow he knew this morning and made him open his stall,' Eddie explained, emotion making him suddenly garrulous. 'We wanted to give you something to remember us by.'

'As if I'd forget any of you!' Biting her lower lip to stop it from trembling, Maud unwrapped the brown paper parcel.

'A clock!' she exclaimed. 'It's beautiful. Really beautiful. We'll treasure it always, won't we Ronnie?' She fumbled for his hand, and he squeezed her fingers gently.

'Brass bedside clock. Real brass,' Eddie said proudly. 'And it's got a second hand. There's an alarm button on the back. That small clockface at the bottom, that's where you set the time for the bell to ring.'

Maud reached up and wrapped her arms around Eddie's neck. 'You look after yourself,' she begged. 'If you must box, please be careful. And you will write, won't you?'

'I'll try,' he murmured, screwing his cap in his hands. 'You know I've never been very good at putting things down on paper.'

'Diana and I will make him write at least once a week.' William pushed his way past Eddie, and kissed her on the cheek. 'And don't worry, I'll be behind him every fight he has,' he joked.

Haydn was the last to kiss her, and by that time her soft blue eyes were brimming with unshed tears.

'Hey,' he smiled, lifting her chin with his fingers. 'We all have to grow up and move away, that's life.' He sat on the arm of her chair and embraced her warmly. 'Tell you what, I'll give you a secret to go with,' he whispered. 'I'm leaving tomorrow morning too, for Brighton. I've finally got a job where I'll be singing on a stage, not sweeping one.'

'Haydn, are you serious?' Maud stared wide-eyed at her brother.

'I wanted you to be the first to know,' he lied, blessing Elizabeth's tight-lipped silence and forgetting the long talk he'd had with his father about the move earlier that morning.

'You're really leaving tomorrow?' Eddie and William chorused.

'Yes, and I've got you a job with Mr Horton, that's if you want it,' he said briefly to his brother. 'Sorry I couldn't get you into the Town Hall as well, but the manager knew someone. Might even have been family.'

'Your mother and father are waiting, Maud,' Laura prompted from the doorway, concerned that the boys were tiring her.

Ronnie ushered the boys out of the room, so Elizabeth and Evan could get into the parlour. It was a tight squeeze in the passageway, and some people had already spilled up the stairs and out on to the pavement.

'I've got a couple of bottles of beer in the kitchen if you fancy some, boys,' Trevor shouted from the back of the house. William followed the call like a dog to his dinner, but Eddie and Haydn hung back. Haydn held out his hand to his brother-in-law, but Eddie looked him squarely in the eye before offering his.

'Just don't ever forget one thing, Ronnie Ronconi,' he said flatly. 'That's my sister you've got there.'

'She's not just your sister any more, Eddie,' Ronnie said with a wry smile. 'She's also my wife, and you'd better be careful in the ring. I don't want anyone, not even you, upsetting her.'

*

Elizabeth kissed Maud briefly on the cheek then left the room, sensing, yet resenting, Maud's desire to be alone with her father. Evan hugged Maud, kissed her, then delved deep into the pocket of the trousers of the suit he'd had made for his own wedding.

'The Italians set great store by valuables, or so they tell me. So I want you to have this.' He pressed his father's gold pocket watch and chain into her hand. 'Keep it safe love, both the watch and the chain are real gold. I was going to knock up Arthur Faller this morning and swap them for a piece of jewellery, but then I thought, no. They're solid, safe pieces. You'll be able to sell them anywhere in the world if you need to.'

'Dad, Grandad left them to you. I can't take them off you.'

'Yes you can. It'll please me to think of you looking at them, so you must take them or you'll upset me. Take care of yourself love, and don't forget to write. Keep well.'

Ronnie, hovering in the passage, saw Maud bite her lip again, and nodded to Trevor. Two minutes later she and Ronnie were sitting in the back seat of Trevor's car, their luggage safely stowed away in the boot as they sped down the hill towards the centre of town, and the New Inn.

The house remained crowded, even after Maud and Ronnie left. Haydn stood in a corner of the kitchen, drinking a small glass of Trevor's beer and surreptitiously watching Jenny Griffiths out of the corner of his eye. Charlie had arranged a lift for him with the driver of a meat lorry who was taking a load of lambs to London. The load was leaving the slaughterhouse at five in the morning, and for all he knew, if everything worked out the way he hoped, he'd never be back in Ponty again.

Finishing his beer and leaving his glass on the table, he took his courage in both hands and walked over to where Jenny was talking to Laura and Diana.

'Hello,' he said quietly, so quietly she didn't hear him. But Laura did. Pulling Diana's sleeve, she dragged her off to the front parlour. Puzzled, Jenny looked after them, then turned and saw Haydn.

'Could I talk to you? It won't take a moment,' he murmured. Jenny glanced around the packed room. 'We could go out the back,' Haydn suggested.

She followed him through the washhouse where the Ronconi girls were clearing and stacking plates, sorting Laura's from those that had been lent by the neighbours. Haydn walked ahead of her; he didn't see the winks and nudges that Tina and Gina were giving each other, but Jenny did. He stopped at the end of the small garden, and leant on the wall.

'I can't stay long,' she said awkwardly, conscious of all the attention that was being bestowed on them from the washhouse.

'Neither can I,' he said quickly. 'I just wanted to say sorry for that stupid row we had . . .'

'Oh so do I,' the words poured out in relief. She turned to him, an emotional, intense expression on her face that made his blood run cold. Did she think he didn't know about her and Eddie?

'Please let me finish what I want to say.' He looked away from her over the scrubby clumps of brown and moss-green grass towards the top of the mountain. 'I wanted to tell you,' he was talking quickly. Too quickly. 'I wanted to tell you that I'm leaving,' he said finally.

'Leaving?' she stared at him in bewilderment.

'Early tomorrow morning.' He was determined to keep speaking so there would be no awkward silences between them. 'I've been offered a job in Brighton.'

'In Brighton,' she echoed uncomprehendingly.

'Yes.' Her repetition of his words was beginning to irritate him. She sounded like a bad chorus echoing a lead singer. 'I'll be there until the end of the pantomime season, and with luck, the job might lead to another. It's what I've always wanted.'

'But you'll be back, home I mean, for weekends?' she asserted wretchedly.

'No,' he said briefly, still refusing to look at her. 'I won't be back.' He finally turned to face her. 'Hopefully, not ever. I just wanted to tell you myself before one of the others did. And of course I want to say goodbye.' He extended his hand to her intending her to shake it, but she clung to his fingers as though they were a lifeline. 'And I wanted to wish you and Eddie luck,' he added cruelly. He pulled his hand from hers and walked quickly away, leaving her feeling totally bereft.

'Well Signora Ronconi, what do you think?' Ronnie laid Maud

down gently on the huge double bed and looked around the room. It appeared vast, and incredibily beautiful to Maud's eyes, just like a Hollywood bedroom. The walls were hung in gold brocade paper, the windows and bed draped in rich blue satin, edged with deep, crunchy ruffles of thick lace. The furniture was old, Victorian, and dark oak, but she could forgive the old-fashioned look of the bedroom suite because the room was large enough to take the pieces and still leave enough space to walk around in.

'Bathroom's out in the corridor, first door on the left,' Ronnie smiled. 'So you can have a bath whenever you like. There's electric light' – he switched on the two bedside lights as though to prove it – 'and there's even a radio.'

'It's wonderful. Ronnie you shouldn't have,' she said, suddenly remembering practicalities like money. Ronnie had never discussed finances with her, and she wondered if he knew that all she had in the world was her bank book with three pounds in it, and the five pounds Diana had given her.

'This room is a wedding present from Trevor and Laura. They said they didn't want to give us anything we'd have to carry to Italy.' He began to empty his pockets on the dressing table as the bellboy came upstairs with his suitcase and Maud's Gladstone. Picking out sixpence from his loose change, he threw it to the boy, who caught it with a grin on his face.

'Thank you, sir. I hope you'll both be very happy, sir.' He gave Maud, who was lying on the bed in her wedding dress and veil, a quick, shy look, before Ronnie closed and locked the door behind him.

'Tell me, Mrs Ronconi,' Ronnie sat on the bed next to her, 'are we going to be very happy?'

'Yes,' she said decisively. 'Most definitely yes.' She lifted her hands to her head and began to fiddle with the veil.

'Here, I'll help you with that.' He gently disentangled the lace and head-dress from her hair.

'I hate to sound like a spoilsport, but I think you should get into bed. We've got a busy few days ahead of us. I don't know why it should, but travelling wears you out. Particularly a journey as far as Italy.'

'I don't know about bed, but I think I would like to get out of this dress before I crease it any more than it is now.'

285

'Do you want some help, or can you manage?'

'I can manage,' she said quickly, blushing at the implication of what he'd said. There were some aspects of marriage she was going to have difficulty growing accustomed to.

'In that case I'll go downstairs and get the dinner menus so we can order well in advance,' he said tactfully, pulling his pocket watch out of his waistcoat. The chain felt strange, too light without the keys to the café and van that he'd handed over to Tony.

'We're eating dinner here?'

'Evening dinner. Trevor and Laura paid for that too, and asked if we could have it in our room. Here – ' he carried her Gladstone over to the corner, 'I'll put your sponge-bag next to the sink.'

'There's a sink?' she looked around blankly.

'Behind the dressing screen.' He pointed to a large silk-covered Edwardian screen in the corner. 'Promise you won't faint if I leave you alone.'

'Promise.'

As soon as Ronnie left, Maud unbuttoned the row of mother-of-pearl buttons that fastened the front of the dress. Standing rather unsteadily next to the bed, she stepped out of the dress, found a clothes hanger in the wardrobe and hung the dress away, before going to the sink to clean her teeth and wash her face. Clinging to the sink for support, she reapplied her lipstick and powdered her nose. Then she looked in her Gladstone: the nightdress and jacket that Tina and Gina had given her was on top. She slipped them on over her underclothes, dabbed a generous amount of Evening in Paris on her throat and wrists, combed her hair, and checked her reflection in the mirror. Her face was ashen, but she knew that rouge would only make it look worse. Pinching her cheeks in an effort to impart some colour, she made her way back to the bed. She stared at it for a moment, smoothing the creases from where she'd lain. Then she looked around. There was a chair beneath the window that looked out over Taff Street. She sat in it, arranging the folds of the nightdress skirt gracefully round her thin legs. There was a knock at the door, and she shouted, 'Come in', expecting Ronnie, but it was the bellboy again.

'Champagne, Madam, with Doctor and Mrs Lewis's compliments. Where shall I put it?'

'Where do you usually put it?' Maud asked, trying to look as though this wasn't the first time she'd been in a hotel room.

'On the table, Madam.' He carried the silver bucket over to a small table that stood in a corner close to her. Pulling the bottle from the bucket, he proceeded to open it.

'Please don't.' Maud sat back in the chair and smiled. She had never been so happy. 'I'd like to wait for my husband.' The word had never sounded so sweet to her ears before.

'Jenny, if you're going home I'll walk you,' Eddie offered.

'Haydn talked to me,' she said miserably.

'I know,' Eddie replied abruptly. 'He talked to me too,' he almost added for the first time in three days, but thought better of it. 'Look, it's a fine, dry afternoon. If you don't want to walk through the house and face everyone again, we could go over the back wall and across the Graig mountain.' He made the suggestion as much for his own sake as hers. The idea of avoiding everyone, especially the Ronconi girls and Glan Richards, was extremely appealing in the light of the row between him and Haydn, which had now become far too public for comfort.

'Would you help me over the wall?' she asked, thinking of her best heeled shoes, and silk stockings.

'Yes,' he agreed flatly.

He lifted her unceremoniously on top of the wall, scrambled over it himself, then lifted her down the other side.

'I'm sorry,' she murmured. 'I realise that you and Haydn must have had a row . . .'

'We did,' he said shortly, not wanting to talk about it. 'But it doesn't matter. Not now.'

'Yes it does,' she insisted, wallowing in self-pity. 'I shouldn't have asked you to take me home that night, and I shouldn't have . . . shouldn't have . . .' she ceased her stammerings when she realised exactly what she had allowed Eddie to do to her, and only two nights ago. She lowered her crimson face and stared disconsolately at the ground.

'If I remember right it wasn't only you that made the moves.' He was walking along the mountainside aimlessly, not really knowing, or caring, what direction he was heading in.

'Do you think Haydn is going away because of me?' she ventured.

'Don't kid or flatter yourself. Haydn's going away because that's what Haydn wants to do. You don't come into it. He's been mooning after a career on stage for years, you should know that.'

'Then you think he'd go, even if we were still going strong?'

'I don't doubt it,' he said with more conviction than he felt.

'But to do it now this way, with no warning . . .'

'Now is when he had the offer,' Eddie pointed out logically. But Jenny didn't want logic. She wanted Haydn to suffer, just as she was suffering. 'It's probably all for the best,' Eddie continued practically. 'If you and he had still been together, he might have felt that he shouldn't go, but he probably would have just the same. This way he can start off on the stage without feeling guilty about anything.'

'I suppose you're right,' she conceded reluctantly. 'It's just that . . . that . . .'

'Look, Jenny,' Eddie said brusquely. 'I know you feel bad at the moment, but you're not the only one. I feel terrible too, and we can't undo what's done. Perhaps we could go out together one night. A walk maybe, or to the park.' He deliberately steered clear of anything that cost money. It would be a while before he paid Charlie back for his share of the clock.

'I don't know,' she murmured. All she knew was she wanted Haydn. And she'd never have him again.

'You know I like you,' Eddie persisted.

'I know,' she said miserably. 'The problem is, at the moment I don't like myself very much. I wouldn't be fit company for anyone.'

'As you please,' he said gruffly. He wasn't one to beg or chase a girl. 'Let me know if you change your mind.'

It was quiet in the New Inn. Quiet and peaceful. Maud had drunk a glass of Champagne before her dinner, one with it, and one afterwards. And that, along with the potent cough mixture Trevor had prescribed for her, had made her ridiculously happy, light-headed, and pleased with herself. The remains of the meal had been cleared away, and she'd had her bath. Dressed in her brand new nightdress (this time without her underclothes) she was half lying, half sitting in bed sipping the fourth glass of Champagne that Ronnie had poured for her.

He was sitting in a chair that he'd pulled against the bed so he could be close to her. His jacket was in the wardrobe. He'd unbuttoned his waistcoat, and taken off his starched collar. His tie was hanging loosely around his neck and she could see the paisley pattern on his braces. She'd never seen Ronnie without a collar and tie on before, and the state of his undress carried with it an air of intimacy and excitement. Although as she'd seen her father and brothers without their collars on often enough, she couldn't have explained the peculiar feeling.

'Eight o'clock,' he murmured, putting the tickets he'd been studying back into his wallet. 'I asked them to give us a call at five so it's probably a good idea for you to get to sleep.'

'Not you?'

'I thought I might go for a walk.'

'To the café?' she enquired intuitively. 'On your honeymoon night? Don't you think everyone will think it a little strange, or worse still, me boring?'

'You boring? Never.' He picked up her hand from the bedcover and kissed her palm. 'I just feel restless.' He rose from the chair and stretched theatrically.

'I've got a cure for restlessness. Come here,' she demanded, patting the bed beside her.

'I will later. There's a couple of things I ought to talk over with Tony . . .'

'You did nothing but talk things over with Tony in Laura's,' she insisted. 'Come here!'

'I can see you're going to be a bully.' He sat beside her on the bed and cradled her in his arms.

'Laura said I should start as I mean to go on.'

'Laura! My God, you haven't been taking advice from my sister, have you?' he exclaimed in mock horror.

'How long did you say it's going to take us to get to Bardi?' Maud asked, wrapping her arms round his waist. Now she had him, she had no intention of letting him go.

'Tomorrow night, we'll be in London. Tuesday morning in France, then we have two days and nights on the train . . .'

'Then shouldn't we make the most of the time we have now?'

'Maud, you're ill.'

'Not that ill. Please, come to bed.' He could feel her trembling. Not just her hands, but her whole body.

'I'll have a bath, then I'll be back.' He opened his case and took out his sponge-bag, a bundle of clothes, and the packet Trevor had given him.

'Promise you won't go to the café?'

With his collar hanging over the back of his chair and his coat in the wardrobe, the question was faintly ridiculous. 'What café?' he asked blankly.

It had been years since Ronnie had worn anything in bed. As a child he had worn woollen nightshirts that his mother had stitched from the back and front of his grandfather's worn-out working shirts, but worried about Maud's sensitivity he had bought a brand new pair of pyjamas for himself in Cardiff along with the wedding ring.

When he returned to the bedroom, all the lights were out except the electric lights either side of the bed.

'I'll set the alarm clock that the boys gave us.'

'You've asked them to call us,' she reminded.

'So I did.' He dumped his sponge-bag and clothes on the chair, then closed the door and turned the key. 'Just in case someone mixes up our room with theirs in the dark,' he murmured.

It was ridiculous. He was behaving as if he was the in-experienced virgin, not Maud. All the women he'd known, all the evenings he and Alma had spent upstairs in the café, and he was the nervous one. He laughed suddenly, without warning.

'What's funny?' she asked.

'I was just wondering why I feel nervous, then I realised it's because I've never gone to bed with my wife before.'

Remembering Alma, and all the rumours Tina had spread about Ronnie's love life, Maud remained tactfully silent. He climbed into the bed, moving between the sheets until he lay alongside her. Sliding his arm beneath her shoulders, he pulled her head down on to his chest.

'I love you, Mrs Ronconi,' he murmured softly, ruffling her hair as he wrapped his other arm around her. She crept as close to him as she could. He could feel her skin scorching his beneath the thin layer of silk that she was wearing. He fought to keep control of himself, but innocently, apparently oblivious to the havoc she was creating within him, she snuggled close, clinging to him like a limpet.

'I never did like sleeping alone,' she murmured. 'It's good to know I won't have to again.'

'Oh yes? And how many other men have you slept with?' he teased.

'No men, silly. Only Bethan. I missed her when she went away.'

'You'll see her tomorrow,' he said without thinking, unintentionally spoiling the surprise he'd meant to give her.

'See her?' Maud asked excitedly.

'Trevor telephoned Andrew and arranged for him to pick us up from the train.'

'Did I ever tell you you're wonderful?'

'I already know, thank you. Tell me again and I might get big-headed.'

'I'm sorry,' she murmured.

'For what?'

'For dragging you away from your family and your cafés. I don't think your mother will ever forgive me.'

'Mama's forgiven you already.'

'Be honest, you would never even have thought of returning to Italy if it wasn't for me.'

'Yes I would,' he lied stoutly.

'Tony told me about your plans for the new restaurant, and the cafés, and how they'll find it impossible to manage without you.'

'No one's indispensable. And it's just as well we're leaving, because if we stayed you'd find out what a dreadful whiner and complainer Tony is.' He hugged her tight. There didn't seem to be any flesh on her bones at all.

'Ronnie I'm sorry . . .'

'Will you stop apologising?,' He kissed her forehead.

'I know I'm not very beautiful . . .'

'What are you on about?'

'I'm skinny and white, and ill, but I promise you, it won't always be this way. Would it help if I took my nightdress off?' she blurted out shyly, finally finding the courage to say what was uppermost in her mind.

'We've got a long journey tomorrow.' She was so frail he was truly terrified of hurting her, despite Trevor's approval.

'You married me,' she protested. 'I think I'm entitled to find out what being married really means. Laura said – '

'Laura always has said rather too much.'

She kissed him on the cheek, mindful of what Trevor had told her about passing tuberculosis on by mouth contact. Then she moved away from him and took off her jacket. He pulled her gently back down beside him.

'How about we take time to get to know one another first?' he murmured. Slowly, ever so slowly, he ran his fingers lightly down her arms. He was able to circle even her upper arms with his thumb and forefinger. Her bones felt so thin, so fragile, he was afraid that if he grasped her too firmly, he'd snap them.

Just as slowly, but more timidly, she responded. Somehow the buttons on his pyjama jacket came undone, and he rolled on to his side, pulling her down beside him, carefully keeping his weight on the bed, lest he crush her.

She kissed his bare chest, running her fingers through the thick mat of black curly hair on his chest and arms.

'You don't know what you're doing to me,' he whispered hoarsely. Sliding his hands down, he ran them upwards from her knees to her thighs, lifting her nightdress to her waist. Shifting slightly, he slipped his fingers between her legs, gently, tenderly, caressing and arousing her.

Despite Bethan's talks to her while she'd been growing up, the first touch brought hot flushes of embarrassment and shame to Maud's cheeks, but they lingered only as long as it took for new and wonderful sensations to erupt into life. Lifting her with one hand, Ronnie gently peeled off her nightdress with the other.

She heard the whisper of silk as it fell to the floor. Moments later, it was joined by the soft thud of cotton as his pyjama jacket fell close to it.

All feelings of naivety, shyness and inexperience dissipated as Ronnie continued to kiss and caress every inch of her. He kicked off his trousers, and she shuddered as the full length of his naked body came into contact with hers. He eased her on top of him.

'Ronnie, please,' she begged. There was a fire between her thighs that she had never experienced before. He rose to meet her until the fire was quenched by pain. She cried out, and he held her gently, while withdrawing quietly away from her.

'No, please. Don't move,' she panted breathlessly. 'Please . . .'

Still entwined, they rolled over until he was above her, resting his weight on his elbows. She moved beneath him, and for the first time he forgot her fragility, her sickness, losing himself wholeheartedly in her pleasure as well as his own.

It wasn't until afterwards, a long while afterwards when she was sleeping beside him, that he realised his face was wet with tears. The first tears he could remember shedding, and they were of sheer joy and happiness.

Chapter Twenty-Six

The customary Sunday night card game in the back room of Ronconi's café had a strangely funereal air about it. Eddie was conspicuous by his absence, and when Alma, during one of her rare moments of conversation, dared to enquire after him, Haydn almost bit her head off before William muttered something about him going down to clean up the gym.

Outwardly it seemed much the same as any other Sunday night, but as none of the Ronconi girls or Diana had come down, Alma was very conscious that it was different, because it was Ronnie's wedding day. And that consciousness burnt into her heart and mind with all the destructive force of a branding iron.

Haydn, William, Tony, Angelo and Charlie took turns to shuffle and deal the playing cards, but they did it in a mechanical, desultory fashion as though they had no interest in the outcome. And after witnessing some of the physical altercations that had taken place following the more disputed results on other evenings, Alma found the whole situation strained, and unreal. Even Tony's rather hit-and-miss attempts to play mine host in the way Ronnie had, grated on her delicate nerves. She'd already made up her mind that no one could take Ronnie's place: not in the café, not in the town, not with his family – and especially not in her heart.

She was very glad when the hands on the clock finally turned to eleven and Tony gave the order to clear up.

'Pity we can't have a drink to celebrate your good fortune,' William said mournfully to Haydn. 'That is, unless we manage to knock up the Horse and Groom.'

'They won't open up on a Sunday,' Charlie commented as he left the table. 'If they tried the magistrates would throw the book at them.'

'I suppose they would. Damned shame a man can't do what he wants in his own town because of the licensing laws. Harry Griffiths once told me that he could get a drink any time he wanted in France.'

'That's because he was there when there was a war on.' Tony picked up the chairs and began to stack them on the tables.

'No, you can drink in Europe any time you want to,' Charlie contradicted.

'Right, we'll all go to Europe,' William said gleefully.

'I didn't say they were giving it away for nothing, Will,' Charlie said seriously. 'You still have to pay.'

'Then we won't all go to Europe. Not this week anyway.'

'Nex week then?' Haydn smiled as he picked up a heavy tray loaded with their dirty cups and carried it out to the kitchen. Alma was there, dumping crockery into the overflowing bowl of warm, soapy water that Angelo had mixed to do the dishes.

'Off tomorrow then?' she asked.

'Yes.'

'You coming, Haydn?' William and Charlie shouted from the front.

'Thought I'd walk up to the gym and meet Eddie.'

William made a thumbs-up sign to Charlie. The estrangement between the brothers had upset both of them.

'In that case, we'll see you back in Graig Avenue,' Charlie replied diplomatically.

Alma untied her apron and hung it on the back of the door.

'Your brother trains at the Ruperra, doesn't he?' she asked.

'Yes. Why?'

'Can I walk along with you? I live in Morgan Street and it's on the way,' she explained awkwardly. 'I don't like walking through town on my own at this hour. Ronnie used to run me home in the Trojan, but Tony's not used to driving it, and anyway I don't like to ask him. Not after . . . after . . .'

'I'd be delighted to have your company,' he said, rescuing her from her embarrassment.

'As long as it's not taking you out of your way.'

'As you just said, Morgan Street's on a direct line to the Ruperra, or almost direct,' he qualified. He went into the café, picked up his new jacket from the back of a chair and followed her out.

'Nice night for a honeymoon,' he said unthinkingly, gazing up at the star-studded sky, which for once was cold, clear and dry.

'Yes it is,' she answered abruptly.

'I'm sorry,' he apologised. 'That was a stupid thing to say after you and Ronnie – '

'We weren't anything special to one another,' she interrupted.

'Yes, well, there's plenty of other fish in the sea, or so everyone's been telling me since Jenny and I split up.'

'I don't think I want to meet any other fish,' she replied sourly. 'Not for quite a while.'

'I know how you feel.'

By tacit agreement they kept to the right-hand side of the road, not crossing over until they'd passed the New Inn, but as they headed towards Gwilym Evans' shop, Alma couldn't resist looking back to see if there was a light on in any of the hotel bedrooms that faced Taff Street or Market Square. All were dark, and she had a sudden, heart-stopping, very real image of Ronnie and Maud lying side by side in a comfortable, luxurious bed. At that moment all she wanted to do was hurt him. As deeply and as irrevocably as he had hurt her.

'The quickest way to Morgan Street is to go past the YMCA isn't it?' Haydn asked, interrupting her illogical, vengeful thoughts as they drew close to the empty Fairfield.

'Yes.' She looked at his fair hair and finely chiselled features. 'Happy to be leaving tomorrow?' she asked.

'Hopefully it will turn into the break I've always wanted,' he replied carefully.

'I wish you well.' She couldn't help wondering what he'd do if it didn't work out for him in Brighton, now that his jobs in the Town Hall and on Horton's stall were filled.

'Thank you.' They entered the network of small streets and alleyways behind the town.

'This is it.' She paused outside a tiny two-up two-down. 'Would you like to come in for a cup of tea? I don't know why I do it after working in a café all evening, but I always make myself a fresh pot when I get home.'

'I'd like to, but I might miss Eddie. Thanks for the offer, Alma, and I hope all goes well with you too.'

He extended his hand, she took it, and lunged close to him. Her lips, warm and wet, were on his, her hands around his neck. 'My mother always goes to bed early,' she whispered in his ear. 'There won't be anyone downstairs, and I always find this time of night so

296

lonely, don't you?' She opened the door. Taking his hand she led him unprotestingly down a dark passage into the back kitchen. 'Stay there,' she ordered.

He stood in the doorway while she fumbled with a box of safety matches close to the stove. Moments later the soft glow of an oil lamp filled the room. 'We can't afford to put electricity in,' she apologised. 'Or lino on the floor.'

He looked down involuntarily. The floor was bare flagstones, scrubbed almost white. A brightly coloured rag rug had been laid down in front of the stone sink, and there were multicoloured patchwork curtains at the window, but the furniture was old and rickety: the kind of stuff that Bown's sold off for three pennies a piece in their junk pile.

'It's not much, but it's home,' she said defiantly. 'My dad was killed in the pit when I was five, and my mam had a hard job bringing me up. When she went blind four years ago, it was almost the last straw.'

'I'm sorry. I had no idea . . .'

'It doesn't matter. Not now.' She regretted telling him as much as she had. The last thing she needed – or wanted – was charity. 'Ronnie promised me the head waitress job in the new restaurant,' she said proudly, 'and Tony said tonight it's still mine if I want it. And until it opens I've enough work to keep me going.'

They were standing close to one another, so close that when she reached out to pick up the kettle from the range her fingers brushed across his arm. The effect was electrifying, and not only on him. Alma had always recognised that her relationship with Ronnie had been primarily a physical one. At the outset she'd acquiesced to his demands because she'd believed submission to be the way to hold him. Later, when he'd aroused passions she'd only dreamt existed, she'd enjoyed and looked forward to their lovemaking much more than she'd ever hinted to Ronnie. And since the night she'd quarrelled with Ronnie over Maud, no man had touched her – until now.

Dropping the kettle on to the table, she laid her hand on the back of Haydn's neck, pulled him close and kissed him again. After the kiss outside, Haydn had been waiting for her to make another move. But it all felt strange – wrong, somehow. The cooking smells in her hair from the café. Her body more angular, and thinner than Jenny's. Even her kisses – soft, experienced, passionate – were different from Jenny's. But once her small breasts pushed against his chest, and her thighs pressed against his, he lost all thoughts of Jenny.

He didn't come to his senses until she moved away from him. 'We shouldn't be doing this,' he murmured huskily, looking into her eyes. 'I'm not Ronnie . . .'

'You wouldn't be here if you were,' she said caustically.

'Alma, this isn't fair on you . . .' He looked around for his hat, forgetting that he hadn't even taken it from his head.

'It's perfectly fair,' she said clearly. 'You're not Ronnie, and I'm not Jenny. But there's no law that says two lonely people can't share just one night.'

'It might be different if I wasn't going away tomorrow.'

'I asked you to take me home because you are leaving. No ties, no apologies. No regrets.'

She unbuttoned the front of her dress and let it fall to the floor, baring herself to him as she had never done for Ronnie, not even stopping to think why. Her clothes fell in a heap at her feet. She kicked them aside and walked to him, wrapping her arms around him. He ran his hands over her body, caressing her, kissing her.

Slowly they sank to the rug on the floor. She reached up behind her and pulled down a cushion from the only easy chair. Putting it beneath her head, she drew him on top of her, easing his arms out of his coat as she did so.

As their lovemaking progressed from tentative caresses to rougher, more urgent movements, he forgot about the strange scent and the unaccustomed feel of Alma's body beneath his. He was back in Harry Griffiths' storeroom in the shop on the Graig, and it was Jenny's face, not Alma's, that floated in his mind's eye as he thrust himself satisfyingly inside her. Just as it was Ronnie's face that occupied her thoughts as she surrendered herself to her physical needs.

Ben Springer drank in the Ruperra for many reasons: it was within easy walking distance of both his shop and his house at the 'smart' end of Berw Road; it had a rough, masculine atmosphere generated by the boxers who frequented the gym at the back of the pub and who very occasionally drank a glass of orange juice in the bar; and finally because the landlord, like him, enjoyed a game of cards and a glass of whisky. A common liking that had led to the setting up of a Sunday night private card school for the exclusive use of the landlord's favoured cronies, Ben amongst them. He was a popular member, not least because he was in business and solvent and never grumbled about putting in the ten-shilling stake that the landlord insisted on.

The boys who frequented the gym had often seen him leaving on a Saturday night, followed by the landlord's directive, 'Seven tomorrow all right for you Ben?' They cast envious glances at his made-to-measure clothes, his staggering gait, the result of at least five beers and whisky chasers, and whispered stories to one another in which the ten-shilling stake multiplied in magnificence until it reached as many pounds.

The gym, like the pub, was closed on a Sunday. Eddie generally cleaned it on a Sunday afternoon, but that Sunday he didn't even begin until early evening because of Maud's wedding. When Ben left at midnight, Eddie was still there, shadow boxing in the ring, lost in glorious fantasies of cheering crowds and Lonsdale belts, the door of the gym bolted and barred behind him.

Ben was always the last to leave the pub, even on a Sunday. As he paused to light a cigarette outside the door, the landlord dimmed the lights behind him. He set his face away from town towards the White Bridge on a route that he'd walked more times than he could remember. Half-way along the road was a pretty clearing of grass sprinkled with trees, where children played and old people sat in summer. On a cold winter's night it was dark and shadowy, and one of the street lamps had failed, plunging a fair proportion of his path into blinding blackness. He quickened his step, and as he did so someone tapped him on the shoulder.

The last thing on his mind was the 'bit of fun' he'd had with his erstwhile assistant. He wasn't sure what to expect. Someone who owed him money from the shoe club who was looking for more time to pay? Or, more hopefully, someone who wanted to order a special pair of shoes? He turned, straight into a closed fist.

Before he had time to shout, or defend himself, a second punch jerked his false teeth out of his mouth and on to the pavement. They fell on to the dry stone with a dull clink, then smashed into five pieces. A third punch knocked him off his feet, then a well

299

aimed kick between his legs sent agonising, torturous pains shooting through his body. He vomited once, twice. The pains came again. Then mercifully the blackness intensified, numbing and finally blotting out the pain.

Wyn Rees walked quickly across Berw Road. He glanced over his shoulder: the street was empty. Standing close to the wall that overlooked the river he tossed a bundle as far as he could. The throw was well aimed: the bundle sank in the centre of the flowing water. He had no fears that it would rise again. He'd weighted it too well. His dead grandfather's overcoat that no one would miss was firmly wrapped round the same grandfather's steel toe-capped boots, and the stone that he'd used to put out the streetlight. He stopped just once, close to the chapel opposite the Ruperra. He had to rub his feet. The boots had been a size too small, and they'd pinched his feet.

He breathed a sigh of relief when he saw the light still on in the gym, but he had trouble getting Eddie to answer the door.

'Saw the light on,' he said, flinching as an expression of distaste curled Eddie's top lip when he saw who'd knocked him up. 'I left my wallet here last night.'

'Black one. There's nothing in it,' Eddie said flatly.

'Yes there is.' He followed Eddie into the office, took it off the desk and flipped open the secret pocket folded cleverly into the back panel. 'If you were a pickpocket you would have missed ten bob there.'

'Good job I'm not a pickpocket then.' Uneasy in Wyn's company and anxious to be shot of him, Eddie led the way to the door.

'By the way,' Wyn said casually. 'Your cousin Diana lives with you doesn't she?'

'She does,' Eddie answered shortly.

'Tell her there's a job going in one of our shops if she wants it. Starting tomorrow morning at seven. Twelve and six a week.'

'How do you know she's looking for a job?' Eddie asked suspiciously.

'She came in and asked.'

Eddie remembered Diana's job hunting. It was like her to leave no stone unturned. Even with a queer.

'You'd better warn her though, she'll be on her own. My sister will only be able to give her a hand for the first day or so. My Dad's had a funny turn, and the neighbours will help out for a while, but Myrtle really wants to take care of him herself. Doctor says his working days are over, so the job's permanent.'

'I'm sorry to hear that about your Dad.' Eddie was. Rees the sweets was a part of every Graig kid's heritage. 'But thanks for thinking of our Di. She'll be chuffed to beans. She wasn't very happy in Springer's.'

'I know. That's why I thought of her. But warn her it's until eight at night. Six days a week.'

Eddie opened the front door. Wyn Rees might be a queer, but there were plenty of others besides Di looking for work. He'd have the pick of the crop at those wages. Perhaps Di had reformed him. Perhaps he fancied her. He decided to have a word with William on the subject; after all, Diana was his sister.

'Bye Wyn,' Eddie said as he saw him out. 'And thanks again for thinking of Diana. She'll be there. Seven tomorrow?'

'High Street shop.'

Huw Griffiths ran past them as they stood talking on the doorstep. 'Seen anything, boys?' he panted, his face ruddy with exertion.

'No, why?' Wyn asked innocently.

'Man beaten up, on Berw Road. Bad by the sound of it. See you.'

'See you,' Wyn shouted. Things had worked out better than he'd hoped. He knew the way a copper's mind worked. No criminal waited around to be spotted near the scene of crime.

'Tired?' Trevor asked Laura as he folded back the sheets on his side of their bed.

'Depends on what you mean by tired.' She turned to face him, her head resting on the pillow.

'I'm whacked. Today seems to have lasted forever. Particularly the last two hours. I never thought I'd get your mother out of the car. She just wanted to talk . . .'

'And cry. She's just lost her eldest son, remember.'

'To marriage and Italy, not the scaffold.' He walked to the door and switched off the light. Using what little light percolated through the thick curtains from the street lamp outside their

301

window to manoeuvre by, he struggled to the bed. 'Damn,' he cursed loudly.

'Stub your toe on the bed leg again?' Laura asked with irritating superiority.

'Your flaming fault for buying a bed with splayed legs.'

'It looks nice.'

'It bloody well hurts.' He sat on the bed and rubbed his stinging foot.

'I'd kiss it better if it was any other part of you.'

'Promises, promises.' He lay beside her and wrapped his arms round her shoulders.

'Trevor?'

'Mmm,' he murmured as he nuzzled her neck.

'Would you mind if I took over the setting up of the new restaurant, as Ronnie suggested?'

'No, of course not.'

'There's no "of course" about it,' she insisted peevishly.

'Why not?' he enquired innocently, still kissing her neck.

'Because every husband wants his wife at home, looking after him and his children . . .'

'Laura, please . . .'

'Not Laura please!' she exclaimed irritably. 'Every other man I know would object to his wife going out to work.'

'Do you, or do you not want to run the restaurant?' He moved away from her, sat up and crossed his arms.

'Yes,' she snapped defiantly.

'Well there you are then,' he said in a patient, long-suffering tone of voice. 'I don't see what this stupid argument is about.'

'This "stupid argument", as you put it, is about you minding.'

'But I don't,' he protested helplessly.

He reached out to her and she turned her back on him. He wrapped himself around her. Burying his head in the nape of her neck beneath her hair, he whispered, 'What's the matter, sweetheart? You afraid of failing if Ronnie's ideas and figures don't add up to success?'

Furious with him for being able to read her so clearly, she retorted, 'That and – ' She bit her lip and clammed her mouth shut.

'And what?' he pressed.

'And because I want a baby.'

'Laura, we've only been married a couple of months. There's plenty of time. Believe me, one day we'll have so many babies you'll be cursing me,' he said lightly.

'You don't understand.' She turned and clung to him. 'Sometimes I'm just so afraid of everything. Of having children. Of not having children. Of making a pig's ear out of the restaurant without Ronnie around to tell me to do things differently.'

'You poor, poor darling.' He kissed her on the mouth.

'I hate you doing that when I want to be angry,' she murmured.

'Then don't be.' He pulled at her nightdress and she sat up, lifting it over her head.

Slowly, tenderly, sure of her love and her response, he caressed her body with his own.

'Is the phone going to start ringing?' she muttered.

'Not tonight. I've told everyone in Pontypridd they're not allowed to be ill.'

'Then take off your pyjama bottoms, the knot's digging an extra navel in me.'

'Can't you be a little more romantic?' he grumbled playfully, as he kicked them off, and out from the bedclothes.

'Give me Clark Gable and a mansion and I'll show you romance.'

'I've been thinking . . .'

'Don't, not now,' she pleaded.

Trevor had been more than thinking; he'd been making serious plans, and wasn't about to be put off now that he'd begun to tell her about them.

'Speaking of mansions, you know that money we've put away to buy a house?'

'You've found a mansion on offer for a hundred and twenty pounds?'

'We did have a hundred and twenty pounds,' he cautioned.

'You've spent it?'

He could feel her temper kindling.

'The hotel and the dinner for Maud and Ronnie cost me five.'

'That's all right.'

'And Maud's medicine and some other things I got, like the beer, the sherry and a few odds and ends for Ronnie came to another five.'

303

'I've got five brothers. Make a habit of this and we'll never get a house.'

'I thought, as you're intent on spending the next couple of months working towards the opening of the new restaurant, you won't have much time to think of moving house.'

'I'll have all the time that's needed,' she began hotly. 'You needn't worry, you won't suffer . . .'

'I know I won't, sweetheart,' he said evenly, irritating her simply by refusing to allow his temper to rise to meet hers. 'It's just that in a year or two we'll have all the time in the world to think of buying a house, and if I'm lucky enough to get that senior's position – '

'You don't get it, and the hospital board will have to deal with me.'

'I'm sure they're all trembling in their beds this very minute at the thought,' he said, not entirely flippantly. 'Soon you'll have an income from the restaurant, I'll be earning more money, but in the meantime there's now. We have just over a hundred pounds in the bank. How about after you set the new place up, and it's running smoothly, we go on holiday?'

'You mean take a chalet in Porthcawl or somewhere like that?' she said doubtfully.

'I mean let's take a boat and train to Italy,' he said quickly. 'I've always wanted to see Rome, Venice and Florence, and I thought you'd like to see the village your parents came from.'

'And you'd like to see Maud?' she suggested shrewdly.

'She may need a doctor in six months.'

'Is that all you give her?' she demanded, fear crawling down her spine.

'How about it, Laura?' he asked, ignoring her question. 'This may be our last chance to travel. Once you start running the café, and the babies start coming, which they will, I promise you, we won't have time to even think of ourselves, let alone go away together. Just consider it for a moment. Only the two of us – no patients, no family, no neighbours to bother us for a whole month. I know it will put back the house, but we'd see a new country, or two,' he added thoughtfully. 'We'd have to travel through France, and we could either do the Italian cities first and then go to Bardi, or go to Bardi first. Wouldn't you like to meet your grandparents?'

'Yes, yes I would.' She kissed the tip of his nose. 'It's funny, I've never really thought about them much, not even when Ronnie used to talk about them. He said Papa's father is short. I can't imagine that. And my grandmother is immensely fat.' She suddenly burst out laughing. 'You know what they say? You should always look at a woman's mother before you marry her. Be warned. Hearing about my grandmother and looking at my mother you could end up with a mountain for a wife.'

'I'd still love you.'

She closed her eyes and imagined the warm, bright yellow Italian sun, and deep blue summer skies that her father and Ronnie had described so often on cold, wet, Welsh winter nights. The old, low-built farmhouse. The fields dotted with sheep and cows. The spire of the church in the village. But as she dwelt on happy thoughts of what was to come, Trevor was thinking darker thoughts. His mind's eye was preoccupied with an Italian cemetery, and a British Christian name preceding an Italian surname carved on a foreign marble headstone.

Chapter Twenty-Seven

The call came at quarter-past one. Laura swore, wriggled down under the blankets and pulled the pillow over her head. Trevor took his clothes downstairs and dressed in front of the kitchen stove. He drove quickly to the Cottage Hospital, waving to the policemen he passed. They all knew him and his car. Which was more than Ben Springer did. He'd come round in a white antiseptic room to see a young, tall, thin doctor bending over him. All he knew was that he felt blissfully numb from the waist down.

'Soon have you right as rain, Mr Springer,' Trevor reassured him as he dripped chloroform on to a gauze mask.

Ben Springer didn't find out until after the operation exactly what the young doctor had meant by 'right as rain'. He screamed, shouted, ranted, raved, and threatened legal action, but all to no avail. Everyone who'd seen him that night, including the policemen and nurses, said that the course of action taken by young Doctor Lewis was the only one possible under the circumstances. Doctor Lewis had undoubtedly saved Mr Springer's life. If Mr Springer thought that the loss of his manhood was too great a price to pay, then that was unfortunate.

Trevor didn't mind putting up with Ben Springer's screams and insults – not when he saw the smile dawn on Laura's face when he woke her to tell her about Ben's misfortune. And as she said, 'Terrible place, Ponty, after dark. But who'd have thought something like that could happen at the Berw Road end of town?'

Diana was up at half-past four to see Haydn off. She kissed him goodbye as he went out through the front door with his father, who'd offered to walk down the hill with him. Just as she turned to make her way back up the stairs, Eddie thundered out of Charlie's room and down the passage, muffler flying, boots in hand.

'They gone?' he demanded.

'Two minutes ago,' she said in astonishment. 'Why?'

'Want to catch him up.' Knees bent, Eddie pulled on his boots as he ran but didn't stop to tie the laces. He raced out of the door, and she heard him shouting down the street.

'What's all that din?' Elizabeth stood at the top of the stairs, a thick, ugly knitted shawl thrown round her nightdress. 'We'll have the neighbours complaining.'

'Eddie wanted to say goodbye to Haydn,' Diana explained as she returned to her room.

'I thought we'd dispensed with all that nonsense last night,' Elizabeth muttered tersely. 'Well now I'm up, I suppose I'd better stay up.'

Diana heard her aunt pouring out her washing water as she returned to her own, now cold bed. She lay there in the semi-darkness, creating images to fit the shadows cast on her walls by the street light, her mind preoccupied with her worthlessness. Where could she go, and what could she do? She had no job. No family other than William, and he could do very well without her. Maud had needed her, but now she had Ronnie. Even her place in this house was dependent on her uncle's charity, and he wouldn't be in a position to keep her once her savings ran out, no matter how much he might want to. That left the agency in Mill Street and another skivvy's job which would barely bring in enough to keep her, let alone put anything aside towards the time when her mother would come out of prison. And she didn't even have the prospect of marriage to look forward to. No man would ever look at her the way Ronnie Ronconi had looked at Maud yesterday. She would never be able to wear white, never . . . but then, did it matter? After what Ben Springer had done to her, she wouldn't be able to face marriage – to anyone.

Wrapping her head in her arms, she cried. Hot burning tears of shame, misery and despondency. Later – she'd get up later and pack. She may as well give in and leave for service today, while she still had her five pounds in the Post Office.

'Haydn?' Eddie caught up with his brother and father as they reached the Graig Hotel.

'Where's the fire, boy?' his father demanded.

'No fire, just wanted to say goodbye to Haydn.' Eddie held out his hand. Haydn looked at it for a moment, then he gripped it.

'Good luck, Haydn. All the best. I mean it.'

'I know you do.' Haydn shook his brother's hand firmly.

'I'm sorry for everything.' His father stood back mystified, not understanding what Eddie was talking about.

'If it hadn't been you it would have been someone else.' Haydn clasped his brother's neck. 'Take care in that boxing ring.'

'And you take care living with the English.'

'Nothing but goodbyes lately,' their father muttered miserably. 'First Bethan, then Maud, now you . . .'

'Just think of all the places you'll be able to visit,' Haydn said on a cheerful note as he released Eddie.

Eddie bent down to tie his shoelaces. When he straightened up Evan and Haydn had been swallowed up by the darkness. But at least he and Haydn hadn't parted with bad blood between them. He was glad of that. And he smiled as he remembered the good thing he'd almost forgotten in his rush to see Haydn. He had something to tell Diana.

His mother was raking the hot ashes from the stove when he went back into the house.

'Eddie Powell, just look at the state of your bootlaces,' she grumbled as he walked into the kitchen. 'You've been running down the road with them undone. You could have broken your neck. As it is they're frayed to ribbons, good for nothing . . .'

'Diana up yet?' he asked, helping himself to a cold leftover pikelet from a plate in the pantry.

'No.' Elizabeth looked at the clock. 'And seeing as how it's only a quarter to five she doesn't need to be up. That's if she's still got a job in Springer's to get up for.'

Eddie kept his secret to himself. It didn't seem right somehow for his mother to know about Diana's good fortune before she did. He went into Charlie and William's room to collect the clothes he'd carried downstairs the night he and Haydn had quarrelled. William would be pleased to see him move back upstairs. It had been a tight squeeze, two of them in a single bed.

Elizabeth had breakfast waiting on the table when Evan returned from town. Charlie, William and Eddie were eating, but there was no sign of Diana.

'He got off all right then?' Elizabeth asked.

'Ay, he did,' Evan assured her.

'I'd be happier if I knew more about where he was going.'

'He knows the people, and he seems to think he'll be all right.'

'He's only a boy.'

'A sensible one,' Evan said firmly.

'I'm going to call Diana again.' Eddie left his seat.

'Sit down and finish the food on your plate,' Elizabeth ordered. 'I don't know what's wrong with you this morning. You're like a cat on hot bricks.'

'I've a message for her.' He pulled the door open and bumped into Diana, who happened to walk in just as he tried to walk out. She was wearing her best dark green costume, and cream blouse.

'And may I ask where you're off to, young lady?' Elizabeth asked.

'New job,' Eddie smiled.

'New job?' Diana looked at him blankly.

'Wyn Rees called round the gym late last night. His father's been taken bad, and he asked if you could take over the High Street shop for him. His sister'll help you today and tomorrow, but then you'll be on your own. Twelve and six a week because it'll be long hours. Seven until eight at night, and you'll be responsible for everything.' Diana sat down rather suddenly. 'He said you'd know all about it, because he told you what was expected when you went round asking him if he had anything going in the shops.'

'He did?'

'That's a darned sight better than Springer's any day, love,' Evan said. 'I never was very happy with you working there.'

'No.' She looked at her aunt. 'I'll be able to pay my way now, Aunt Elizabeth,' she said proudly. 'Seven and six. The same as William and Charlie.'

'Well, seeing as how Bethan and Maud have both gone, and you know how to make yourself useful around the house, supposing we keep it to four shillings on the understanding you help out. Especially on Sundays. Now that Uncle John Joseph's on his own, he needs all the help I can give him.' Evan stared at his wife in amazement as Diana stammered her thanks. 'And you may as well move your things into Maud's room. No sense in leaving a big room like that empty. You can have the box room, William, and that means you can have a room to yourself, Mr Raschenko.'

'Thank you, Mrs Powell,' he said, winking at Diana.

'Mrs Powell, Diana?' Laura walked into the kitchen. 'I'm sorry for calling so early,' she apologised.

'Not at all. Sit down. I'll pour you a cup of tea,' Elizabeth offered stiffly, smoothing over her apron.

'Please don't put yourself out, Mrs Powell. I can't stop. I'm on my way up to Mama's. I want to see Tony before he starts in the café, and I rather hoped to have a word with Diana beforehand if I could.' Laura was bubbling with suppressed excitement. 'If you'd like to walk me to the door, Diana. It won't take a minute.'

Completely bewildered, Diana followed Laura out through the door and into the freezing cold passage. The door slammed behind them. Two minutes later there was a huge shriek.

'What on earth . . .' Eddie was half-way out of his chair when William pulled him down. 'I've no idea what it's all about, but they won't want you there,' he pronounced knowledgeably, used to Diana's ways. 'Probably some stupid girl rubbish or other,' he added, hurt that Laura hadn't let him in on the secret.

'Seems to me that's the first time I've heard that girl laugh since she's come home,' Evan commented, looking sideways at his wife as he bit into his toast and dripping.

'It's five to six, I'd better see if Trevor's arrived.' Ronnie took one more look around at the room he'd begun his married life in, before kissing Maud.

'Not on the lips,' she admonished, sinking back against the cushions of her chair.

'As I'm sleeping with you, woman, it's time I got used to your germs.' Maud had insisted on getting up at four to have another bath and wash her hair. He'd helped her dry it, and it now framed her face, soft, fluffy and curly.

'Promise me something?' he asked as he picked up their bags.

'What?' she smiled.

'Don't wave your hair again. I like it just the way it is.'

'Frizzy?'

'Soft, like an angel's.' He dropped her Gladstone so he could run his fingers through it again. 'I also think it would look better long.'

'Long hair isn't fashionable.'

'It is in Italy,' he hazarded a guess.

'Then seeing as how you asked nicely, I might let it grow.'

He picked up the case again. Laura's wedding dress and veil were on the bed, where he'd laid them earlier. 'I'll bring Trevor up to take down the dress,' he said, 'and you – ' he pointed a warning finger at her, '– will not move from that chair until I lift you out.'

Maud smiled impishly.

'I mean it.'

'I'm terrified.'

'So you should be.'

He left the room, whistling happily as he ran down the magnificent wide staircase.

'Bridegroom looks happy,' Trevor grinned from the foyer.

'Bridegroom is happy. Very happy,' Ronnie beamed.

'Your chariot awaits, and someone who wants to talk to you. I picked him up half-way down the Graig hill.'

Ronnie looked behind Trevor and saw his father hovering in the doorway holding his mother's fox fur coat.

'I'll put the cases in the car,' Trevor said as he took them from Ronnie.

Ronnie walked warily towards his father and extended his hand. He'd feared a rebuff, but his father took it.

'Twenty years I've been wanting to send this to your grandfather, but there's always been something. Another café to open, or worries about it getting lost in the post, or one of you needing something . . .' He folded a fifty-pound note into Ronnie's palm. 'It's for your grandfather,' he repeated sternly as though Ronnie was likely to misunderstand him. 'To buy a white suit and a good horse. All his life he's wanted a white suit and a good horse. And I promised when I left home that I would buy them for him. And this', he gave Ronnie another twenty pounds, 'is for your grandmother and Aunt Theresa to buy new Sunday clothes. You mind you tell them what it's for.'

'I will, Papa, but the business won't stand this money being taken out . . .'

'You're not the only one who knows how to put a little by,' his father admonished. 'And this is for you.' He gave him one more fifty-pound note. 'There won't be enough food put away on the farm to feed two extra mouths until the crops come in. And I won't have your grandparents and aunt giving you their rations.'

311

'Papa – '

'Maud!'

Ronnie heard the shock in Trevor's voice and looked behind him. Maud was clinging to the elegantly carved mahogany banisters as she walked slowly down the stairs.

'Please don't be angry,' she laughed as Ronnie rushed to her side. 'I wanted to see if I could do it. And I have!' she announced triumphantly, allowing him to help her as she reached the last step.

'I told you . . .'

'I know.'

'This is your wife?' his father asked, although he'd known Maud since the day she was born.

'Yes Papa.'

'This is for you.' He thrust the fur coat at her. 'Don't thank me, it's none of my doing, it's Ronnie's mother's, and I wouldn't let her come this morning to give it to you herself. Couldn't stand any more of her fussing and crying. She won't wear it, not here where it rains all the time. And it can get cold in Italy in winter.'

'Mr Ronconi, I can't take this,' Maud gasped.

'None of my doing. Just you see that she wears it, Ronnie. Looks like she needs something to keep her bones warm. There's no flesh on them to do the job.'

'Yes Papa,' he choked back his laughter as he helped Maud into the coat.

'I've got the wedding dress and veil.' Trevor ran down the stairs with them in his arms. 'If there's nothing else we should be on our way.'

'There's nothing else.' Weighing up the austere expression on Mr Ronconi's face, and balancing it against the twinkle in his eye, Maud stepped towards him and ventured a hug. He kissed the top of her head, then propelled her gently back to Ronnie.

'I've an idea. Why don't you come to Cardiff with us, Mr Ronconi?' Trevor asked. 'You can keep me awake on the way back. I had a night call,' he explained.

'As if I can spare the time to stand on railway platforms, when this good-for-nothing son of mine leaves me to run the business on my own. Who's going to open the cafés in the morning now? That's what I'd like to know.'

312

'Goodbye Papa,' Ronnie lifted his hand again, but his father clasped him by the shoulders and kissed him on both cheeks.

'You think you could have found a healthy one,' he grumbled as Trevor helped Maud to the car.

'She's the one I want, Papa.'

'Then you'd better make her healthy.'

'I'll try.'

Ronnie stood on the steps of the New Inn and watched as his father walked away without a backward glance.

'Laura put a rug and a pillow there for you, Maud,' Trevor called from the driving seat as Ronnie finally climbed into the back of the car with her. 'She wants you to take them on the train with you.' He had to repeat himself twice before Maud and Ronnie answered. They were engrossed in watching the bowed, solitary figure of his father as he made his way through the litter-strewn streets towards the Tumble.

Andrew John stood, arms folded loosely over the barrier in Paddington Station, watching the tides of people as they flowed from the Swansea train. He kept a close eye on those leaving the third- and second-class carriages, searching for a glimpse of Ronnie's dark, slicked-back hair, or Maud's blonde curls.

'Doctor John?' Ronnie stood before him, dressed in a good winter-weight overcoat and expensive trilby.

'Ronnie?' Andrew shook his hand enthusiastically.

'It's very good of you to meet us.'

'Not at all. After all, we are brothers-in-law now.'

'So everyone in Pontypridd keeps reminding me.'

'Where's Maud?' Andrew looked over Ronnie's shoulder for the pert, pretty blonde who'd teased him in Graig Avenue when he'd gone there with Bethan.

'She's still in the carriage, I thought it best for her to stay there until I knew where your car was.'

'It's over there,' Andrew waved his hand to the left. 'When I showed them my bag and told them I was waiting to pick up a semi-invalid they let me park it by the taxi ranks.'

'I'll get the porter.' Ronnie disappeared into the crowd, re-emerging moments later with Maud in his arms and a porter in tow. Andrew rushed to open the car doors. Ronnie deposited

Maud tenderly on the back seat before walking around to help Andrew stack the cases in the boot.

'The boat sails at eleven tonight,' he murmured, heaving his suitcase next to Maud's Gladstone.

'So Trevor told me.' Andrew slammed the boot shut. 'Bethan has a meal waiting. She wanted to come, but I wouldn't let her. Not in her condition in this crush, but she's desperate to see you.'

'Me or Maud?' Ronnie smiled.

'Both.' Andrew delved under the front seat for the starting handle. As soon as the car purred into life he removed it quickly and dived into the front seat.

'Nice car,' Ronnie commented from the back seat where he'd sat next to Maud before Andrew'd had a chance to greet Bethan's sister.

'Nice of you to say so, but it's not mine,' Andrew replied as he pushed the car into gear. 'I borrowed it off my brother-in-law.'

'Sorry.'

'So am I,' Andrew replied drily as he pulled slowly out of the station and up into the light of the street. 'If it was mine, it would mean that I was doing better than I am.'

'This is London!' Maud cried out excitedly, staring round-eyed in wonder at the façades of terraces that were even longer, larger and grander than the ones she'd seen in Cardiff.

'This is London!' Andrew steered carefully around a taxi and a bus; as he pulled up at a junction he looked in the mirror and smiled at his sister-in-law. The smile died on his lips. Maud had pulled back the thick blanket and fur coat that Ronnie had wrapped round her when he had carried her from the train to the car, and was sitting forward, poised on the edge of her seat, holding Ronnie's hand. The sight of her thin, almost skeletal figure reminded him of the line, 'The skull beneath the skin', and it took no imagination on his part to place Maud amongst the cadavers that the first-year students in the hospital practised on. Realising that Ronnie was watching him, he pulled the wheel sharply to the left, and concentrated on his driving.

'Bethan's so looking forward to seeing you, and getting all the gossip from home.'

'There's lots,' Maud pronounced with an air of bright animation that belied her outward appearance of wan, sickly fragility. 'But I've no intention of telling you any of it in advance.'

'Same old Maud,' Andrew gave a rather forced laugh. 'Tell me Ronnie, do you think you'll succeed in turning her into a subservient wife?'

'A wife, yes,' Ronnie caught Maud's hand and pressed it to his lips. 'Subservient, never.'

'Beth, this is lovely. Really lovely.' Maud lay back on Bethan and Andrew's bed, watching as Bethan sat on her dressing-table stool and combed her hair.

'You like the flat then?' Bethan was horror-struck by Maud's appearance, but well schooled by her mother in the art of concealing her feelings, she kept her shock hidden. They heard the sound of male laughter coming from the living room, accompanied by the clinking of ice dropping into whisky glasses. Maud laid her hand on Bethan's.

'You're really happy, aren't you?'

'Ecstatic!' Bethan smiled, patting her enormous stomach proudly.

'I do envy you. I hope Ronnie and I have a dozen.'

'I suggest you get well first.'

'I intend to. So does Ronnie, and he always seems to get his own way.'

'With you around, he won't be doing that for long.'

She washed her hands in the bathroom, and went into the kitchen. Maud followed her and sat on one of the up-to-the-minute, art deco beechwood chairs that Andrew had bought in Barker's in Kensington.

'And you,' Bethan asked, looking her sister in the eye. 'Are you happy with Ronnie?'

'Yes. He's wonderful. I never thought of marrying him before he asked me. Well, he always seemed so much older than me. But he's terribly good-looking, and . . . and . . .'

'He swept you off your feet?'

'Something like that,' Maud answered shyly. Bethan gave her sister a hug before she began to dish out the food. It was obvious to anyone who looked that Maud was in the first flush of love – or infatuation. For both Ronnie's and Maud's sake she hoped it was the former, and of the kind that would last. With what lay ahead, they'd both need it.

'I've found you a porter, he'll take your cases to your cabin, and I had a word with a customs officer. He's promised to see you and Maud through as quickly as he can. I've also managed to get a chair. God knows how old it is, but it should hold Maud's weight until you've wheeled her to the cabin. You've got your tickets and everything?'

'Everything being our marriage certificate and my original Italian passport. There wasn't time to see to anything else. But it should be enough. Thank you for a lovely evening and for driving us here.' Ronnie shook Andrew's hand. 'Shall we see if we can prise those two apart?' He nodded to the car where Bethan and Maud were still locked in conversation.

Andrew and Bethan watched as Ronnie, porter in his wake, wheeled Maud into the customs hall.

'She's dying, isn't she?' Bethan asked, clinging to her husband.

'She has advanced tuberculosis, yes,' he admitted, 'but Ronnie is doing all he can. And if she doesn't live, it won't be for the want of him trying. He's taking her to the best place. Italy has a wonderful climate. Not too hot, not too cold. Dry, warm, clean air. It just might work.'

'And it might not.' She lifted the collar of her coat around her neck and shivered. The air was chill, with a hint of snow in it. He put his arm tenderly round her shoulders.

'If sheer bloody-mindedness counts for anything in effecting a cure, then Ronnie will have Maud fit, well and working in the fields by the end of the summer,' he pronounced resolutely. He slipped his fingers beneath her chin and lifted her face to his. 'How about we go home to bed?' he murmured huskily, suddenly very grateful for all his blessings.

Chapter Twenty-Eight

The crossing was a nightmare. The steward gleefully told Ronnie as he emptied Maud's sick bowls down the toilet that he hadn't seen a rougher one in thirty years. And the whole time Maud tossed and turned uncomplainingly in her narrow bunk, Ronnie crouched on his knees beside her, spongeing her feverish face with tepid water and holding empty bowls to her mouth. He had to take the coats that he'd hung on the door and fold them on to the bunk he didn't have time to sleep in, as their alarming swaying from side to side began to affect him too.

He had cause to remember his glib words to Evan many times over during the course of that interminable crossing: 'I'll get a cabin with a berth, then all Maud has to do is sleep until Calais.' No one slept. Not Maud. Not him, and none of the other passengers if the noises coming from the corridors were anything to go by. And the nightmare didn't end with the docking of the ship.

Calais was still shrouded in grey misty night when he wheeled Maud off the ship. He peered in the direction that a blue-coated official pointed him in, and just about managed to make out the wavering lights of the customs sheds that punctuated the darkness ahead. The French excise officers were neither as sympathetic nor as understanding as the ones Andrew had spoken to in Tilbury. They shouted at him in harsh guttural French, which they repeated loudly, syllable for syllable, even when he shrugged his shoulders and spoke to them in English and Italian. They made no allowances for Maud's weakness, insisting that she leave the wheelchair so they could search the folds of the fur coat and blankets, and when Ronnie tried to help her back into the chair when they'd completed their search, he discovered to his fury that someone had taken it. He supported Maud as best he could, while the officers rummaged through her Gladstone and fingered her clothes. All he could do was stand by incensed, watching helplessly as they heaped the silk underwear his sisters had bought

Maud on to their rough wooden tables, and opened the packet of contraceptives Trevor had given him. Long before the search was finished Maud fainted, the dead weight of her head lolling weakly against his shoulder.

Eventually the officials moved on to their next victim, leaving him, and an unconscious Maud, to repack their own bags. Fortunately an elderly British couple came to his assistance, the husband going in search of porters while the wife packed for him.

Even then it seemed to take an eternity of shouting, arguing and bad-tempered exchanges before he managed to leave the customs shed. Tipping the porter with an English ten-shilling note, the lowest coinage he had, he persuaded the fellow to follow him to the trains. There, only after ten harassed minutes, they managed to locate the carriage that was to take them to Genoa. The Italian steward helped him get Maud aboard, stowed away their suitcases in the stateroom he had booked, pulled down their beds, and offered to heat up some soup for Maud who had still not recovered from her faint.

Pathetically grateful for the steward's kindness, help and blessedly familiar language, Ronnie gave him a pound, promising the man more if he would help him care for Maud on the journey. As soon as they were alone, Ronnie undressed her and put her between the stiff, starched sheets on the makeshift bed. She lay there like a wax doll, white, silent and just as lifeless.

She came round as dawn was breaking over the horizon of the French countryside. Pushing aside the chicken soup Ronnie tried to feed her, she insisted on sitting up and looking at everything; exclaiming at the red-roofed, greystone French farmhouses, similar yet different from the ones in Wales. The flat country, the level patchwork of fields, the towns, so strange, peculiar and foreign after Pontypridd. Afraid of missing anything, her eyes darted in their sockets as she tried to assimilate all that could be seen from the window. She found something to wonder over with every mile they passed: a windmill, a French peasant woman driving a donkey, a man wearing a beret . . . When she began to cough Ronnie fed her three spoonfuls instead of the usual single spoonful of mixture in the hope that it would induce her to rest, but if anything it had the opposite effect. Bright-eyed, feverish, she point-blank refused to lie down.

The steward brought them a meal when Ronnie declined to visit the dining car. Ronnie laid the trays over their knees on the bed. Sitting next to Maud, he tried to force her to eat, slipping morsels of chicken and potato into her mouth as she continued to stare in wonder at her first foreign country. He stayed with her even after the steward removed the trays, propping her against him, holding her while her skin grew first warm, then uncomfortably hot, until it burned his chest through the thick linen of his shirt.

He tried to listen to her enthusiastic cries and make suitable comments, but his mind was elsewhere. Evan had posed the question of what he would do if Maud died on the journey. Had Evan had a premonition of sorts? Had his own stubborn streak set Maud on a course that was going to end here, in this carriage?

By nightfall she was delirious. Mindful of Ronnie's large tip and the promise of extra money, the steward produced iced water, soup, and more pillows at regular intervals. Ronnie did what little he could, and sat holding Maud's hand as her colour heightened and her eyes grew wild.

That night they stopped to take on coal. The steward disappeared, reappearing an hour later with a doctor, who shook his head and gave Ronnie a bottle of laudanum in exchange for an English pound note. Ronnie had no compunction about using it, hoping that the drug would finally compel Maud to rest.

When the train began to move, he lay beside her. As the next dawn broke the steward looked into their room, but he did not raise their blinds, figuring that sleep was better medicine than chicken soup for both the sick young signora and her exhausted husband.

When Maud finally woke again the sun was high, and Ronnie's eyes were open as he lay, fully dressed, beside her. She smiled, and he breathed again: the smile was one of recognition, not delirium.

Somewhere on that interminable train journey, Maud's infatuation with Ronnie died. She found it impossible to remain infatuated with a man who sat beside her in shirt-sleeves, braces and no collar, with two days' growth of black stubble covering his cheeks, feeding her while she lay in bed as weak and helpless as a baby. He washed her, changed her, dressed her in clean clothes, and while he cared for her generously, selflessly, and more tenderly than any nurse the image of the tall, dark, sardonically handsome Ronnie, always dressed immaculately in clean jacket, boiled shirt and stiff white collar as he cracked acidic jokes in the café was replaced by a weary, grey-faced exhausted Ronnie who winced every time she coughed. And as infatuation died, so it was supplanted by a sounder emotion, rooted firmly in his caring, obsessive passion for her.

She forced herself to eat when he spooned food into her mouth, even though she felt food would choke her. She smiled at him, and held his hand, because they were the only ways open to her in which to show her gratitude. But he was too busy nurturing the flame of life that flickered weakly inside her to notice the change. All he knew was that she was mercifully quieter.

'Genoa, Signor!'

Although he had dressed Maud and repacked their suitcases in preparation for reaching the town, Ronnie had been dreading the end of the rail journey. It meant having to leave the steward's care and the security of the bedded stateroom that had enabled him to care for Maud with at least the rudiments of comfort to hand.

'I'll find you a porter, Signor,' The steward offered.

'And a taxi,' Ronnie pleaded, slipping him two more pounds. 'I need to get to the Bardi bus. But first I need to change my English money for Italian lire . . .'

'Signor, all the buses leave outside the station. May I make a suggestion? My cousin's wife runs a small *pensione* here. You can leave your wife with her while you change your money and find your bus.'

'I'll do that.' Ronnie grasped eagerly at the idea of finding another bed for Maud to lie in.

The steward returned with a porter and handed Ronnie a small heap of coins.

'You paid me much too much, Signor,' he said gravely. 'I have already tipped the porter and told him where to take you. Good luck to you and your wife.'

Ronnie shook the man's hand appreciatively. Picking up Maud, he stepped off the train into an icy blast.

320

'Italian winds are just as bloody freezing as Welsh ones,' he muttered as he gritted his teeth and followed the porter.

'Did you say something?' Maud mumbled sleepily. After the excitement of the the journey through France and the attack it had precipitated, Ronnie was taking no chances. There'd been more than a spoonful of laudanum in the coffee he'd fed her after their last meal.

It was six o'clock in the evening. The square was full of people hurrying home from work. A sprinkling of travellers lingered in the cafés waiting for their buses and trains. A few steps and he found himself in the small lodging house. The room the proprietress showed him to actually overlooked the square. It was clean, and the woman friendly. If Maud's condition was bringing them sympathy and good service, he certainly wasn't too proud to accept it. He put Maud to bed, and left after asking the woman to keep an eye on her. He had no choice. They needed Italian money, and he hᵗ to find out about buses to Bardi.

'The day after tomorrow!'

'They only go once a week, Signor. Bardi is not a popular place. Every market day, one bus comes in and one goes out. It will leave at noon.'

The market bus. He had a sudden memory of that bus. Packed with gnarled old countrywomen laden with chickens and geese, the whole shrieking every time the ancient, battered vehicle jerked over pot-holes that speckled the unmade roads, like currants in Welsh cakes.

'There's no other way? A car, perhaps?'

'A car! To Bardi? No, Signor.' The driver laughed at his naivety.

There was nothing for it. He returned to the *pensione*, lay next to Maud on the bed and waited. Perhaps it was just as well she could rest before the worst part of their journey began. And their landlady proved as kind as she was friendly, doing their washing for them and bringing rich minestrone soups and omelettes to their room to tempt Maud's non-existent appetite.

The Signora had a cousin who knew the driver. At her injunction

321

he kept seats for Ronnie and Maud close to the front of the bus, where they could receive some benefit from the warmth of the engine. They needed it. The Signora's husband carried their cases on board, and Ronnie carried Maud.

The journey from Genoa to Bardi was every bit as hellish as Ronnie had feared. They bumped and rocked their way painfully over dirt roads, stopping at every out of the way hamlet and farmstead, and all he could do was hold Maud suspended on his lap and hope that the cheeses and live chickens stowed overhead on the string racks next to their suitcases wouldn't fall on to their heads.

They eventually reached the square in Bardi at five in the afternoon, and even Ronnie was cold, tired and exhausted. He left Maud slumped in her seat and carried the suitcases off first, then he went back for her. He stood feeling totally lost and bewildered in the darkening square, holding a sick and barely conscious Maud in his arms.

He couldn't remember anything. Not even the road out of the town to his grandfather's farm.

'You look as though you need help, Signor.' The man was old, bent and grey. A busybody. A blessed busybody who might know everyone in the village – and outside.

'I need to get to Signor Ronconi's house,' Ronnie blurted out urgently, worried about the darkness and the rapidly dropping temperature. 'My wife is sick.'

The man studied him thoughtfully in the lamplight.

'You are related to Signor Ronconi, perhaps?'

'His grandson.'

'Ah, now I see, you are Giacomo's son?'

'I am Giacomo too.'

'Come, we will go to Mama Conti. She will look after you, please follow me.' The man led the way to a large house on the edge of the square. Trusting to fate to look after their cases, Ronnie followed him. Mama Conti, a large and warm-hearted Italian housewife, asked no questions – at first. She opened her door, took them in, sat Maud by the fire and spoonfed her minestrone soup – which Ronnie was beginning to think was the Italian cure for all ills.

Bit by bit he told his story, and a boy was dispatched to the square to pick up their cases. An ox was found which would draw a wheel-less sled to his grandparent's farm, both to carry their luggage and bring news of their arrival, and later, much later, when they were both fed and rested and after much discussion as to the best way of conveying Maud there, they were allowed to leave with a guide who promised to show Ronnie the way to their new home. He carried Maud. It seemed the easiest solution to the problem. Too weak to sit on a horse, even if one could be found, and far too delicate to withstand the bumping of the local sleds, the only solution seemed to lie in Ronnie's strong arms.

He had been warned it was eight kilometres. He had remembered it as five, but when he finally saw the oil lamp flickering in his grandfather's kitchen window he would have believed anyone who had told him it was twelve.

Maud was taken from him, and carried upstairs by his aunt and a neighbour who had been summoned to help. His grandparents embraced him, sat him by the fire in the only chair that boasted both a cushioned seat and back and fed him minestrone soup and wine that was so raw it hurt his throat. They asked only one question: 'Are you here to stay?'

When he said yes, they nodded and smiled so broadly he felt that he really had come home.

Maud was sunk deeply into a fluffy feather bed that had enveloped itself around her. She felt warm, cosy, sheltered and very, very comfortable. She opened her eyes. The first thing she saw was her own arm, encased in the sleeve of an unfamiliar linen nightdress, the wrist ornamented by thick, crunchy cotton lace. She looked up. A candle flickered on a pine chest next to the bed she was lying in. Two brown faces looked down at her, both smiling, one old and wrinkled, the other impossibly ancient. There was a single moment of blind, urgent panic.

'Ronnie?' she called out weakly.

'I'm here.' His hand grasped hers, strong and reassuring.

'Ronnie, don't leave me,' she pleaded.

'Not now darling,' he murmured. 'Not ever.'

Epilogue

It had been a glorious summer, and the weather showed no sign of abating even in late September. The harvest had been a rich and golden one. The vines had never been as full, nor the grapes as sweet. Ronnie had even suggested to his grandfather that for once the wine might not need watering down. The sheep grazed, bald and contented, on dried grass that was already hay on the lower slopes of the valley. The cattle chewed on a sweeter cud nearer the stream and the farmhouse. The sow suckled her thirteen piglets, and even the runt that Aunt Theresa had taken to feeding wrapped in a shawl in the farmhouse kitchen was doing well enough to warrant a prognosis of continued life rather than a sticky end as a glazed suckling pig for Sunday dinner.

The animals lazed in the sties and the fields, Aunt Theresa and grandmother spun wool as they sat on the wooden kitchen chairs that grandfather had carried outside for them, and held their noses as they watched Ronnie carry buckets in and out of the stone tank beneath the farmhouse.

There'd been so many things he had forgotten about Bardi, he reflected, choking on raw sewage fumes as he lowered himself and his buckets into the murky depths of the cesspit. Not least the ritual, twice-yearly emptying out of the huge stone waste pit beneath the house.

The animals in the barn rested their hooves on a slatted stone floor. The slats were carefully spaced, close enough to allow the hoofs a firm grip, but not too close to obstruct the animal waste from falling into the tank. It didn't help that the waste from the farmhouse drained into the same pit from chutes that led out of the kitchen sink and outhouse.

He carried his buckets to another tank, two fields away, built conveniently close to the vegetable plot. Stopping to breathe in clean air for a moment, he doused his hands in a horse trough before picking up his wooden buckets again. The walk back and forward across the fields he enjoyed; it was the short descent into the pit that was unpleasant. Only this time, he noted with satisfaction, the job was done. He was hard pushed to fill both buckets.

'Dear God, I never expected to see Ronnie Ronconi, the immaculate Ronnie, dressed in work dungarees and up to his eyes in . . .'

'You don't have to say the word.' Ronnie struggled out of the pit. Putting down his buckets, he extended his hand.

'I'd rather not, if you don't mind,' Trevor shook his head.

'Coward,' Ronnie smiled. They walked together across the fields. Trevor watched while Ronnie emptied the buckets and washed them in the wooden trough, before tipping it out on its side.

'Shouldn't you have stepped in there?' Trevor asked gravely.

'I've a better place lined up,' Ronnie grinned. A set of perfect white teeth gleamed through the grime on his face. He walked on down to the stream. Trevor followed. Ronnie stepped straight into the cold water, still wearing his grandfather's old working dungarees. He scrubbed the worst of the filth from them with sand, then, taking them off, he scrubbed himself with a crude wooden brush and bar of strong carbolic soap that he'd had the foresight to place on the bank before he began his job.

'Looks like you've done this before,' Trevor commented, squatting on his heels.

'Second time this summer. Did you and Laura have a good journey?'

'No. And as you've done it yourself, how can you even ask?' Ronnie lay down, full length in the stream, and allowed the water to rinse off the soapsuds.

'By the time we reached Bardi – '

'You were tired, hot and hungry. And as the last straw, you found you had no other choice but to walk here.' Ronnie left the water and pulled a pair of rough black cotton trousers over his slim, soaking flanks.

'Aren't you going to dry yourself?'

'No need to in this heat.' He picked up an unevenly woven linen shirt, and a leather belt.

'How on earth did you manage with Maud, when you reached here?' Trevor asked.

'That was difficult.' Ronnie's face fell serious. 'She was so done in by the time we got to Bardi, she was barely conscious. I met one of my grandfather's friends. He had a sled – '

'Don't tell me,' Trevor groaned. 'One of those wonderful contraptions pulled by an ox, with no wheels, that bumps over every lump in the road.'

'Good God, man, don't tell me you and Laura tried to sit on it?'

'For about five minutes.' He watched Ronnie tuck his shirt into his trousers and pull the leather belt tightly around his waist. 'You've lost weight,' he said critically.

'I could afford to,' Ronnie said carelessly. 'Those sleds are all right for luggage.'

'That's what we ended up using it for.'

Ronnie picked up his filthy overalls. Wrapping them in a bundle and grabbing the soap and brush, he began to walk up the hill, back towards the farmhouse. 'I carried Maud here,' he said quietly.

'She must have been exhausted.'

'Half dead might be a better description,' Ronnie told him. They reached the top of the hill. Trevor was panting from the heat and the unaccustomed exertion, but Ronnie was as fresh as if he'd just left his bed.

'As I said, I carried Maud here. It's only about four miles.'

'Dear God, Ronnie, weren't you tired yourself? I could barely drag myself up the hills to here. The thought of carrying Laura as well . . .'

'Maud's lighter than Laura,' Ronnie pointed out. 'And by that time I'd seen enough to jog my memory. I remembered enough of my grandmother and my aunt to be sure of our welcome. I wasn't disappointed. My grandmother had already stripped, cleaned and made up the biggest bed, in the best bedroom, for Maud. Not that they wanted me to share it with her,' he complained drily. 'Between them, Aunt Theresa and my grandmother elbowed me very nicely out of the way. They must have been bored out of their minds before we turned up, because judging by the amount of time they spent nursing Maud they couldn't have had anything to do before. They spoonfed her the best spaghetti, the freshest vegetables, the richest cream. They stayed with her day and night, pouring weird concoctions of herbal teas down her throat. They talked to her, sang to her – not that poor Maud understood a single word they were saying – and I couldn't swear to it, but in my opinion I think they even resorted to casting a spell or two.'

Ronnie looked to the back of the house where his grandfather had carried out three more chairs and a small table. The older women had put away their spinning, and a bottle of his aunt's strawberry wine stood on the table together with four glasses. Maud, still thin, but more robust than she had been in Wales, was sitting engrossed in conversation with Laura.

'You had a chance to examine her before you came looking for me?' Ronnie asked Trevor.

'Only a third of her right lung is functioning, and her left is badly scarred, you do know that?'

'The local doctor told me she'll never be strong.'

'He's right,' Trevor agreed flatly. 'And if you're asking for my opinion I think a return to Wales would be as good as a death sentence for her.'

'Who wants to go back to Wales?'

'You're happy here?' Trevor asked incredulously, staring at the primitive farmhouse, and Ronnie's rough clothes.

'Blissfully,' Ronnie laughed. Maud looked up, saw Ronnie and smiled. He smiled back, and Trevor saw everything.

'Good God, she's now as besotted with you as you were with her!' he exclaimed.

'Of course. Did you doubt my ability to make her fall in love with me?' Ronnie slapped his brother-in-law soundly on the back. 'Come on, I'm still waiting for you to tell me what you think of Maud's progress.'

'Considering she's only been here a few months, it's incredible. She might not be strong, might never be strong, but the disease is no longer active. Provided she takes things quietly – '

'As if my aunt will allow her to do anything else,' Ronnie interrupted.

'It's a complete and utter miracle.'

'No, not a miracle.'

'Then what?' Trevor asked.

'Just my wife.' Ronnie went to the well and pulled up a rope. Attached to the end of it was a bottle of his grandfather's rough wine.

'It's not best brandy, but I guarantee you won't have tasted anything like it before,' he warned, handing the cool bottle to Trevor after pulling the cork with his teeth and taking a deep and satisfying draught himself.

'What are we drinking to?' Trevor asked.

'Life, health and happiness.'

Trevor looked across at Laura, remembered the secret she had told him that morning, and saw the bloom it had already brought to her cheeks.

'I must be the luckiest man alive,' he murmured as he put the bottle to his lips.

Ronnie walked towards his wife, smiling, thinking of what they had to look forward to that night once they were closeted in the privacy of their bedroom.

'You're wrong,' he said firmly, taking the bottle from a coughing, spluttering Trevor. 'If there's such a thing as a luckiest man alive, I'm it.'

ALSO BY CATRIN COLLIER

Swansea Girls

'Lily deliberately held back for a few moments as the other three walked into the ballroom. She loved everything about Saturday night at the Pier, where she could listen to snatches of other girls' conversations and share in their hopes and expectations, if only for a second or two . . .'

On a Saturday night the Pier Ballroom in Swansea is the place to be: for Lily, an evacuee unclaimed by her family at the end of the war; for Judy, taught independence by her war widow mother; for Katie, the product of a marriage between a drunken, violent father and a cowed, beaten mother; and for spoiled, wilful Helen. It is an evening that fuels jealousies and sows the seeds for friendship and romance.

From post-war austerity to the 'never had it so good' era, Swansea Girls is a wonderfully nostalgic story of friendships, hopes and dreams.

ALSO BY CATRIN COLLIER

Swansea Summer

In the Swansea of the fifties, there is only one thing for a boy to do when he gets a girl 'into trouble' and that is to marry her – and quickly.

Blighted by an unhappy childhood, passionately in love for the first time in his life, Jack can't wait to do the right thing. A happy family of his own is all he ever wanted but not even in his wildest dreams did he envisage a wife like Helen.

Beautiful, intelligent and loving, Helen is headstrong enough to defy both her family and convention for jack and, when her father gives them his blessing, their future beckons assured and glittering – until tragedy strikes and tears them apart . . .

ALSO BY CATRIN COLLIER

A Silver Lining

In strictly chapel Pontypridd in 1938, tongues are quick to wag when Alma Moore, abandoned by her lover, is rushed to hospital with stomach pains. The doctor may call it appendicitis, but the scandalmongers think they know better. And then Bethan John, who's too good for the rest of them since she married a doctor, comes back to her mining family's house with her new baby – but without her husband, or any word of explanation.

Ostracised by most – even their own mothers – Alma and Bethan face a lonely struggle to survive. Then taciturn Russian Charlie, an outsider haunted by his own past, reaches out the hand of friendship to them both, and in so doing begins to thaw his own heart . . .

Spoils of War

The war is over, and every survivor can come home. But home – and the survivors – are not what they were.

The new independence of the women, and the changes that mark so many of the men, take some adjusting to for everyone – and the Ronconis must also reconsider how to run the café business, no longer enough to support them all. Then US Colonel David Ford reappears, putting further strains on Bethan and Andrew's marriage, and Tony Ronconi brings home Gabrielle, a German refugee, as his fiancée, to the horror of many townspeople, including Tony's own mother.

Alma and Charlie Raschenko face an impossible decision when he discovers his first wife, Masha, was not killed in a Stalinist purge as he thought but has been found alive in a German concentration camp . . .

Tiger Ragtime

In the colourful 1930s community of Tiger Bay the docks are home to people from all walks of life. Destitute and homeless, Judy Hamilton finds work and lodging with Edyth Slater, but her dreams are of a career in show business.

David Ellis has left his isolated Breconshire farm to make his fortune. But in a depression-ridden world where both work and money are scarce the enterprising natives flout the law, and open illegal casinos and drinking dens for those who can still afford a 'good time'. None is more ruthless than handsome, mysterious Aled James who owns the glamorous Tiger Ragtime.

With Aled's help, Judy breaks into the glittering paste and cardboard world of the city's nightclubs and theatres, and David becomes a bookie's runner. But Aled demands a high price for his assistance and David and Judy soon discover that money is no compensation for tarnished or broken dreams.